Library of America, a nonprofit organization,
champions our nation's cultural heritage
by publishing America's greatest writing in
authoritative new editions and providing resources
for readers to explore this rich, living legacy.

AMERICAN SCIENCE FICTION

FOUR CLASSIC NOVELS 1960–1966

AMERICAN
SCIENCE FICTION
FOUR CLASSIC NOVELS 1960–1966

The High Crusade • Poul Anderson
Way Station • Clifford D. Simak
Flowers for Algernon • Daniel Keyes
. . . *And Call Me Conrad* [*This Immortal*] •
Roger Zelazny

Gary K. Wolfe, *editor*

THE LIBRARY OF AMERICA

Published in the United States by Library of America.
Visit our website at www.loa.org.

This paper exceeds the requirements of
ANSI/NISO z39.48–1992 (Permanence of Paper).

Distributed to the trade in the United States
by Penguin Random House Inc.
and in Canada by Penguin Random House Canada Ltd.

Library of Congress Control Number: 2019939871
ISBN 978-1-59853-501-3

First Printing
The Library of America—321

Manufactured in the United States of America

Contents

Introduction

BY GARY K. WOLFE

The emergence of the American science fiction novel at midcentury as a sophisticated, culturally significant, and ultimately enduring genre is amply demonstrated in the two-volume predecessor of the present collection, *American Science Fiction: Nine Classic Novels of the 1950s.* The rise of the paperback book, together with the almost paradoxical convergence of postwar technological optimism with the dual fears of nuclear doom and totalitarianism, provided science fiction writers with a new and wider stage than the magazines of the pulp era had offered, new themes, and a new kind of market as well. Novels conceived *as* novels, not as "fix-ups" assembled from magazine stories, were suddenly welcomed by mainstream publishers, after having long been viewed as the province of specialist fan imprints, as oddball offshoots of mystery or thriller fiction, or as suitable mainly for young adult readers. Even by the early 1950s, reviewers in *The New York Times* were speculating that science fiction might soon rival mysteries, Westerns, historical novels, and romances in popularity—a benchmark the newly prominent genre never quite achieved. Over the course of the 1950s, however, writers like Alfred Bester, Leigh Brackett, Robert A. Heinlein, Fritz Leiber, and James Blish left a body of work that continues to find new audiences and to influence American literature.

From a specifically literary viewpoint, the 1960s proved to be even more significant than what had come before. The beginning of the decade can be characterized as a moment when writers who had started their careers in the 1930s or 1940s produced some of their finest mature work, such as Theodore Sturgeon with *Venus Plus X* (1960), Poul Anderson with *The High Crusade* (1960), Heinlein with *Stranger in a Strange Land* (1961), and Clifford D. Simak with *Way Station* (1963). But distinctive new voices also gained prominence. The Hugo Award for best novel in 1961 went to Walter M. Miller, Jr.'s somber and ambitious postnuclear fable *A Canticle for Leibowitz*, while the 1963 award went to Philip K. Dick's complex alternate history *The Man in the High Castle*. In England, the more cerebral and experimental fictions of the so-called New Wave found inspiration in sources as diverse as the French *nouveau roman*, the work of William S. Burroughs, and even the French protosurrealist Alfred Jarry. In America, editors such as Frederik Pohl, Cele Goldsmith, and Judith Merril also promoted more stylistically adventurous, genre-bending fiction. Goldsmith's editorship in the early 1960s of the traditionally pulpish magazines *Amazing* and *Fantastic* helped introduce U.S. readers not only to New Wave authors from across the Atlantic, but to early work by Ursula K. Le Guin, Roger Zelazny, Piers Anthony, David R. Bunch, and many others. Merril sought to extend the literary range of science fiction in a series of popular "year's best" anthologies from 1956 to 1968, and her 1968 New Wave anthology rather unfortunately titled *England Swings SF* included such American authors as Pamela Zoline and Thomas M. Disch. Pohl, editing the magazines *Galaxy* and *If*, promoted brilliantly idiosyncratic writers like R. A. Lafferty and Cordwainer Smith (the latter eventually revealed as a pseudonym of political scientist Paul Linebarger), and encouraged more experimental work from prolific younger writers such as Robert Silverberg and Harlan Ellison, whose dystopian parable "'Repent, Harlequin!' Said the Ticktockman"— published by Pohl in 1965—was widely recognized as one of the seminal stories defining the American version of the New Wave. (Ellison himself edited two highly influential anthologies of the "new" science fiction, *Dangerous Visions* in 1967 and *Again, Dangerous Visions* in 1972.)

Book editors as well were seeking new voices that could reflect an increasingly sophisticated aesthetic for the genre. Terry Carr's "Science Fiction Specials," an influential paperback series edited for Ace Books beginning in 1968, included Le Guin's *The Left Hand of Darkness*, Lafferty's *Past Master*, Joanna Russ's *Picnic on Paradise*, Alexei Panshin's *Rite of Passage*, Zelazny's *Isle of the Dead*, and John Sladek's *Mechasm*. In 1965, Chilton, a publisher known mostly for automotive repair manuals, branched into fiction with a novel already rejected by most major publishers, Frank Herbert's *Dune*, which became a popular classic and the source of one of science fiction's more enduring franchises. A year later the traditionally literary publisher Harcourt, Brace & World issued Daniel Keyes's *Flowers for Algernon*, which provided the basis for the 1968 film *Charly*, the first science fiction film to receive an Academy Award for Best Actor (for Cliff Robertson). By the end of the decade, Kurt Vonnegut, Jr., who had begun his career in the 1950s with science fiction novels *Player Piano* and *The Sirens of Titan*, earned his most substantial literary accolades to date with the bestseller *Slaughterhouse-Five, or The Children's Crusade* (1969).

Thus, if the 1960s began with science fiction that looked largely like the mature-stage growth of the 1940s and 1950s, the decade ended with a dramatically more diverse and more mainstream genre. *Star Trek* debuted on TV in 1966, featuring a few well-known science fiction figures among its scriptwriters, and, though lasting only three seasons, gave birth to a multimedia franchise still going strong a half-century later. Science fiction film, largely the domain of low-budget monster movies, drew the attention of the great director Stanley Kubrick, first with his doomsday comedy *Dr. Strangelove, or How I Learned to Stop Worrying and Love the Bomb* (1964), and later with the visionary but meticulous *2001: A Space Odyssey* (1968), one of a handful of science fiction films to engage seriously with major genre themes such as commercial space travel, artificial intelligence, evolution, and alien contact. And, of course, the Apollo 11 moon landing on July 20, 1969, gave science fiction writers a public platform and media prominence not seen since the advent of the atomic bomb back in 1945.

In approaching the selection of novels to represent this varied decade in the two-volume *American Science Fiction: Eight Classic Novels of the 1960s*, length was a necessary consideration. During much of the 1950s and the early 1960s, science fiction novels tended to be relatively short, sometimes due to constraints as mundane as the ways paperback books were manufactured and distributed. This began to change dramatically in the 1960s, with lengthy and ambitious epics such as Herbert's *Dune* or Heinlein's *Stranger in a Strange Land* (either of which might have precluded two or three other novels from being printed here). Heinlein, almost certainly the most influential science fiction writer of the middle decades of the century, is represented in *American Science Fiction: Nine Classic Novels of the 1950s*, and no authors from that collection are included in the present one. Nor does this collection include novels available in their authors' own Library of America editions, such as Dick, Vonnegut, Le Guin, and Madeleine L'Engle. Finally, an effort was made to balance the halves of the decade, though it would certainly be possible to fill two volumes with excellent work from the final two years of the decade alone. One of science fiction's occasional banner years, 1968 saw the publication of Samuel R. Delany's *Nova*, Russ's *Picnic on Paradise*, and Lafferty's *Past Master* (all included here), as well as Dick's *Do Androids Dream of Electric Sheep?*, Disch's *Camp Concentration*, Panshin's *Rite of Passage*, Simak's *Goblin Reservation*, and Silverberg's *Hawksbill Station* and *The Masks of Time*.

Of the authors included here, three can be said to represent that mature-stage growth of earlier traditions: Anderson and Jack Vance, whose first stories appeared in the 1940s, and Simak, who began publishing as early as 1931 but attained his greatest significance in the 1940s and 1950s. (Lafferty, who was actually older than Vance or Anderson, did not begin publishing science fiction until he was in his forties, in 1960, and thus is regarded among the "new" writers of the 1960s.) Zelazny and Delany, along with Le Guin and Disch, were part of science fiction's remarkable "class of 1962," each publishing their first genre work in that year. Both Russ and Keyes had published some short fiction in the 1950s, but emerged as major figures in the new decade, Keyes almost entirely on the strength of his classic 1959 short story "Flowers for Algernon" and the 1966 novel developed from it. Russ gained recognition not only as one of SF's most trenchant and groundbreaking feminist voices, but as a critic and reviewer in scholarly journals and popular science fiction magazines. Delany also emerged as a major critic and theorist of the field by the end of the decade.

As might be expected from such a transitional period, science fiction of the 1960s was characterized by a broad range of styles and themes, and representing that variety was another consideration in assembling this collection. The earliest novel, Anderson's *The High Crusade*, reflects the genre's long-standing fascination with historical fiction, dating back at least to L. Sprague de Camp's 1939 *Lest Darkness Fall* and arguably even to Mark Twain's 1889 *A Connecticut Yankee in*

King Arthur's Court. But while such novels usually dealt with time travel, and efforts to introduce modern technologies to an earlier era, Anderson's ingenious inversion has an alien space-ship landing in fourteenth-century England, with results that make up in comic invention what they may lack in credibility. Anderson's fascination with history was evident in his 1953 fantasy novella "Three Hearts and Three Lions" (expanded into a novel in 1961) and in short stories of the Time Patrol, charged with visiting different eras to preserve the historical timeline from renegade time travelers. *The High Crusade* also permitted Anderson to celebrate another of science fiction's most popular traditions, the large-scale space opera, with its multiple alien societies and fearsome galactic empires. The novel proved to be one of his most popular, providing the basis of a 1983 role-playing game and a much altered 1994 film, and earning admiration from leading science fiction writers Silverberg, Greg Bear, Eric Flint, and Jo Walton.

Simak's *Way Station* reflects a gentler, more pastoral tradition that Simak himself pioneered, although it is also evident in the work of Ray Bradbury, Sturgeon, Zenna Henderson, and Brackett. Set in the same remote southwestern Wisconsin farm country where Simak was born, the novel's central character is a Civil War veteran who mysteriously never ages. Yet his isolated homestead proves a nexus for the sort of vast galactic civilization that Simak celebrated in his own earlier space opera tales. The implicit anti-urban theme of the novel, not uncommon in midwestern fiction, was even more explicit in Simak's 1940s stories, which were eventually collected in 1952, with connective material, as *City*. The title is ironic, since the stories depict the abandonment of cities because of improved transportation, leading to a more distributed and bucolic economy, and eventually to a dispersal of humanity, leaving much of the earth to intelligent dogs and evolved ants. *Way Station*, a more unified novel, celebrates the classic American values of small communities and isolated individuals who may unassumingly hold a key to humanity's future.

Vance, who also began publishing in the 1940s and whose career extended to within a few years of his death in 2013, was a transitional figure of another sort. Like Simak, his early work reflected the space operas and planetary romances of the pulp era, but the tales that would eventually be collected in several volumes beginning with *The Dying Earth* (1952) made him one of the most influential writers of the modern genre, with authors as diverse as Gene Wolfe, Neil Gaiman, and George R. R. Martin acknowledging their debts to him. The reasons for Vance's continuing influence are twofold. Unlike many pulp-era authors, Vance cultivated an evocative and poetic style; his world-building has a sustained lyrical precision rare in the earlier genre. His settings also influenced a tradition of extreme far-future "dying Earth" tales in which the imagery and language of magical fantasy merge with those of science fiction in a manner sometimes referred to as "science-fantasy" —a blurring of genre boundaries arguably more relevant today than when Vance first began inventing such worlds. *Emphyrio* is perhaps the strongest of Vance's "stand-alone" novels not connected to a series, and it reflects not only his mature style but his interest, then comparatively uncommon in science fiction, in problems of art and culture.

Keyes's *Flowers for Algernon*, after selling millions of copies in dozens of languages, becoming a widely used text in college, secondary, and even middle school classes, and inspiring films, TV shows, and stage plays, is certainly the most widely familiar novel here. That very familiarity, however, is part of what qualifies it as another transitional work of the 1960s. Few of its readers are aware of Keyes's origins in the science fiction community, and some are surprised to learn that the novel is science fiction at all, despite its central conceit of artificially increased intelligence. Keyes focuses not on the medical procedure, but on the character and narrative voice of Charly Gordon, whose tonal and stylistic shifts reflect the narrative arc as clearly as Charly's own pattern of alienation and self-discovery. In other words, the science fictional core of the story is subordinated to its literary ambition, presaging a tradition of humanistic, character-driven science fiction that remains vital today. Yet Keyes began his career editing pulp magazines and comic books; his early mentors included the influential science fiction writers Lester del Rey and Philip Klass (whose satirical science fiction appeared under the name William Tenn); and the original short story "Flowers for Algernon" was workshopped at the well-known Milford Writers Conference by

such science fiction luminaries as Merril, Damon Knight, Kate
Wilhelm, Avram Davidson, and Blish. It later won the Hugo
Award for best short story; a few years after that, the novel
earned a Nebula Award from the Science Fiction Writers of
America. Despite the story's clear links to its genre origins, it
became one of the first science fiction tales to be celebrated
almost entirely for its characters and literary technique rather
than its speculative inventions.

With Zelazny, Russ, Delany, and Lafferty, however, the sense
is less one of transition than of revolution. Zelazny seemed to
burst upon the science fiction scene fully formed in 1962, with a
series of pyrotechnic stories that appeared determined to rede-
fine the genre both stylistically and thematically. The most well
received of these early stories, "A Rose for Ecclesiastes" (1963),
concerned a poet and linguist who, studying the dying ancient
Martian civilization, finds parallels between their doom-laden
fatalism and the book of Ecclesiastes. While the story echoes
the "dying Earth" theme as transplanted to another civilization, it also is notable for its exploration of religious impulses
and its focus on a troubled and eventually disillusioned protagonist, a sharp contrast with the heroic space adventurers of
an earlier era. In these and other stories, Zelazny sought con-
nections between science fiction and the roots of storytelling
in ancient myths and legends. His first novel, *This Immortal*
—printed here under the title Zelazny preferred, . . . *And
Call Me Conrad*—opens with pointed allusions to the classical
past. The narrator's girlfriend, significantly named Cassandra,
describes him as a *kallikanzaros*, from the destructive underground goblins of Greek legend. Other classical and literary in-
fluences appear throughout the novel—Zelazny held a master's
degree from Columbia in Elizabethan and Jacobean drama—
and Conrad himself can be viewed as a kind of Promethean
figure. While the novel retains several recognizable elements
from the science fiction of the 1950s and earlier—an Earth population diminished by nuclear war, ruined cities, outer space
colonies on Mars and Titan, alien overlords, a central figure of
ambiguous origins but potentially godlike power—it becomes
clear that Zelazny is using such materials to explore ancient
myths and rituals of identity, rather than for technological
speculation or simple adventure. Some reviewers at the time

worried that this newfound literariness was too inward looking and constituted a regressive turn away from the concerns that had made science fiction great in the first place. Nevertheless, on the basis of its abridged initial appearance in *The Magazine of Fantasy and Science Fiction*, the novel went on to tie with Herbert's more traditional science fiction epic *Dune* for the 1966 Hugo Award. In both *. . . And Call Me Conrad* [*This Immortal*] and such later novels as *Lord of Light* (1967), Zelazny took pains to construct narratives that could support being read as either science fiction or fantasy—a distinct step beyond the "science-fantasy" of Vance's "dying Earth" tradition and one that further blurred traditional notions of genre. Zelazny's fascination with myth and ritual eventually led to his most commercially successful novels, the long-running Amber series, which began with *Nine Princes in Amber* in 1970, continued over the following two decades, and is now viewed as among the first multivolume fantasy series of the sort that became almost ubiquitous in the following decades.

Another member of the class of 1962, Delany, five years Zelazny's junior, was only twenty when *The Jewels of Aptor* appeared as part of an Ace Double paperback in 1962 (a publishing gimmick in which two short novels were printed back-to-back). As with Zelazny, the novel combined a familiar postnuclear setting—virtually a genre convention by then—with a plot drawn from older quest-fantasies, involving an effort to retrieve a jewel with special powers. A similarly conventional setting and structure governed his next three novels, a trilogy collectively titled *The Fall of the Towers* (1963–65). Increasingly, however, significant themes of language, poetry, and mythmaking became dominant in later novels such as *The Ballad of Beta-2* (1966), which received the Nebula Award, the first in a remarkable string of four such awards for short fiction over the next three years. With *The Einstein Intersection* (1967), *Nova* (1968), and short stories such as "Aye, and Gomorrah . . ." (1967) and "Time Considered as a Helix of Semi-Precious Stones" (1968), it was clear that Delany was emerging as the leading exemplar of the New Wave in the U.S. *Nova* in particular is interesting for its pointedly revisionist relationship to pulp-era space opera, combining large-scale outer space spectacle with themes drawn from Prometheus and Grail legends, and an outlaw protagonist hitherto rare in science fiction—a black trickster musician and poet echoing the tradition of many such transgressive outsider figures. In one of the more famous contemporary reviews, the critic and novelist Algis Budrys proclaimed in *Galaxy* that "Samuel R. Delany, right now, as of this book, *Nova*, not as of some future book or some accumulated body of work, is the best science fiction writer in the world, at a time when competition for that status is intense."

Except for one story published in 1959, Russ might also have been counted among 1962 debuts, with her accomplished vampire tale "My Dear Emily." A graduate of Cornell and the Yale School of Drama, Russ shared some of Zelazny's academic sophistication, and later became an influential reviewer and one of the formative figures of feminist science fiction criticism with essays for academic journals and in books like *How to Suppress Women's Writing* (1983) and *To Write Like a Woman: Essays in Feminism and Science Fiction* (1995). In 1967, she began publishing short stories about a shrewd, acerbic time-traveling mercenary named Alyx—unusually, two of these stories first appeared in the same volume of Damon Knight's important series of *Orbit* anthologies—and in 1968 Alyx became the central figure of Russ's first novel, *Picnic on Paradise*. While not as polemical as her groundbreaking feminist novel *The Female Man*, written in 1970 but not published until 1975, its taut style, knowledgeable deployment of familiar science fiction tropes, and sharply satirical voice were striking; as the critic John Clute later wrote, "The liberating effect of the Alyx/Trans Temp tales has been pervasive, and the ease with which later writers now use active female protagonists in adventure roles, without having to argue the case, owes much to this example."

As individual and innovative as the fiction of Russ, Zelazny, and Delany might have been, possibly the most brilliantly idiosyncratic author to enter the field in the 1960s—in fact, one of the most idiosyncratic authors in midcentury American literature—was born more than two decades before any of them, in Iowa in 1914. From early childhood, Lafferty lived in Oklahoma, serving in the U.S. Army in World War II, but he did not begin publishing fiction until 1959, with his first science fiction story in 1960. While he earned a considerable following in the 1960s, largely among fellow writers, his debut as a novelist was as striking as any of the decade; three novels—*Past Master*, *The Reefs of Earth*, and *Space Chantey*—appeared within a few months of each other in 1968, with *Past Master* bearing endorsements from Delany, Zelazny, and Ellison. Lafferty's unique approach to fiction seemed to owe little to any earlier science fiction at all, or to any coherent sense of genre; his work combined deeply conservative Catholicism with quirky readings of history and philosophy and an energetic, headlong style that often echoed the American tall tale tradition. Despite admiration from later writers such as Wolfe and Gaiman, much of his work fell out of print; at one point, only his 1972 historical novel *Okla Hannali*, tracing the history of the Choctaw Indians, remained available. Many of Lafferty's manuscripts remained unpublished even years after his death in 2002, despite his acknowledged influence on the genre.

American Science Fiction: Eight Classic Novels of the 1960s presents a necessarily incomplete but varied portrait of a genre in rapid transition and with a newfound sense of literary ambition, yet with a clear sense of traditions that had evolved over the preceding decades. The authors, born as early as 1904 and as late as 1942, have in the last half-century proved to be as influential on the genre's development as their forebears, but in the 1960s the nature of that influence began to shift noticeably from matters of plot and theme to matters of style and structure, and that shift, in its various iterations, is a large part of what this collection attempts to represent.

THE HIGH CRUSADE

Poul Anderson

To JENS CHRISTIAN and NANCY HOSTRUP—
as well as PER and JANNE—
gratefully and hopefully

As the Captain looked up, the hooded desk lamp threw his face into ridges of darkness and craggy highlights. A port stood open to alien summer night.

"Well?" he said.

"I've got it translated, sir," answered the sociotechnician. "Had to extrapolate backward from modern languages, which is what took me so long. In the course of the work, though, I've learned enough so I can talk to these . . . creatures."

"Good," grunted the captain. "Now maybe we can discover what this is all about. Thunder and blowup! I expected to come across almost anything out here, but this—–!"

"I know how you feel, sir. Even with all the physical evidence right before my eyes, I found it hard to believe the original account."

"Very well, I'll read it at once. No rest for the wicked." The captain nodded dismissal, and the sociotech departed the cabin.

For a moment the captain sat motionless, looking at the document but not really seeing it. The book itself had been impressively ancient, uncials on vellum between massive covers. This translation was a prosaic typescript. Yet he was nearly afraid to turn the pages, afraid of what he might find out. There had been some stupendous catastrophe, more than a thousand years ago; its consequences were still echoing. The captain felt very small and alone. Home was a long ways off.

However . . .

He began to read.

Chapter I

ARCHBISHOP WILLIAM, a most learned and holy prelate, having commanded me to put into English writing those great events to which I was a humble witness, I take up my quill in the name of the Lord and my patron saint: trusting that they will aid my feeble powers of narrative for the sake of future generations who may with profit study the account of Sir Roger de Tourneville's campaign and learn thereby fervently to reverence the great God by whom all things are brought to pass.

I shall write of these happenings exactly as I remember them, without fear or favor, the more so since most who were concerned are now dead. I myself was quite insignificant, but since it is well to make known the chronicler that men may judge his trustworthiness, let me first say a few words about him.

I was born some forty years before my story begins, a younger son of Wat Brown. He was blacksmith in the little town of Ansby, which lay in northeastern Lincolnshire. The lands were enfeoffed to the Baron de Tourneville, whose ancient castle stood on a hill just above the town. There was also a small abbey of the Franciscan order, which I entered as a boy. Having gained some skill (my only skill, I fear) in reading and writing, I was often made instructor in these arts to novices and the children of lay people. My boyhood nickname I put into Latin and made my religious one, as a lesson in humility, so I am Brother Parvus. For I am of low size, and ill-favored, though fortunate to have the trust of children.

In the year of grace 1345, Sir Roger, then baron, was gathering an army of free companions to join our puissant King Edward III and his son in the French war. Ansby was the meeting place. By May Day, the army was all there. It camped on the common, but turned our quiet town into one huge brawl. Archers, crossbowmen, pikemen, and cavalry swarmed through the muddy streets, drinking, gaming, wenching, jesting, and quarreling, to the peril of their souls and our thatch-roofed cottages. Indeed, we lost two houses to fire. Yet they brought an unwonted ardor, a sense of glory, such that the very serfs thought wistfully about going along, were it but possible. Even I entertained such notions. For me it might well have come true, for I had been tutoring Sir Roger's son and had also brought his accounts in order. The baron talked of making me his amanuensis; but my abbot was doubtful.

Thus it stood when the Wersgor ship arrived.

Well I remember the day. I was out on an errand. The weather had turned sunny after rain, the town street was ankle-deep in mud. I picked my way through the aimless crowds of soldiery, nodding to such as I knew. All at once a great cry arose. I lifted my head like the others.

Lo! It was as a miracle! Down through the sky, seeming to swell monstrously with the speed of its descent, came a ship all of metal. So dazzling was the sunlight off its polished sides that I could not see its form clearly. A huge cylinder, I thought, easily two thousand feet long. Save for the whistle of wind, it moved noiseless.

Someone screamed. A woman knelt in a puddle and began to rattle off prayers. A man cried that his sins had found him out, and joined her. Worthy though these actions were, I realized that in such a mass of people, folk would be trampled to death if panic smote. That was surely not what God, if He had sent this visitant, intended.

Hardly knowing what I did, I sprang up on a great iron bombard whose wagon was sunk to the axles in our street. "Hold fast!" I cried. "Be not afraid! Have faith and hold fast!"

My feeble pipings went unheard. Then Red John Hameward, the captain of the longbowmen, leaped up beside me. A merry giant, with hair like spun copper and fierce blue eyes, he had been my friend since he arrived here.

"I know not what yon thing is," he bellowed. His voice rolled over the general babble, which died away. "Mayhap some French trick. Or it may be friendly, which would make our fear look all the sillier. Follow me, every soldier, to meet it when it lands!"

"Magic!" cried an old man. "'Tis sorcery, and we are undone!"

"Not so," I told him. "Sorcery cannot harm good Christians."

"But I am a miserable sinner," he wailed.

"St. George and King Edward!" Red John sprang off the tube and dashed down the street. I tucked up my robe and panted after him, trying to remember the formulas of exorcism.

Looking back over my shoulder, I was surprised to see most of the company follow us. They had not so much taken heart from the bowman's example, as they were afraid to be left leaderless. But they followed—into their own camp to snatch weapons, then out onto the common. I saw that cavalrymen had flung themselves to horse and were thundering downhill from the castle.

Sir Roger de Tourneville, unarmored but wearing sword at hip, led the riders. He shouted and flailed about with his lance. Between them, he and Red John got the rabble whipped into some kind of fighting order. They had scarcely finished when the great ship landed.

It sank deep into pasture earth; its weight was tremendous, and I knew not what had borne it so lightly through the air. I saw that it was all enclosed, a smooth shell without poop deck or forecastle. I did not really expect oars, but part of me wondered (through the hammering of my heart) why there were no sails. However, I did spy turrets, from which poked muzzles like those of bombards.

There fell a shuddering silence. Sir Roger edged his horse up to me where I stood with teeth clapping in my head. "You're a learned cleric, Brother Parvus," he said quietly, though his nostrils were white and his hair dank with sweat. "What d'you make of this?"

"In truth I know not, sire," I stammered. "Ancient stories tell of wizards like Merlin who could fly through the air."

"Could it be . . . divine?" He crossed himself.

"'Tis not for me to say." I looked timidly skyward. "Yet I see no choir of angels."

A muted clank came from the vessel, drowned in one groan of fear as a circular door began to open. But all stood their ground, being Englishmen, if not simply too terrified to run.

I glimpsed that the door was double, with a chamber between. A metallic ramp slid forth like a tongue, three yards downward until it touched the earth. I raised my crucifix while Aves pattered from my lips like hail.

One of the crew came forth. Great God, how shall I describe the horror of that first sight? Surely, my mind shrieked, this was a demon from the lowest pits of hell.

He stood about five feet tall, very broad and powerful, clad in a tunic of silvery sheen. His skin was hairless and deep blue. He had a short thick tail. The ears were long and pointed on either side of his round head; narrow amber eyes glared from a blunt-snouted face; but his brow was high.

Someone began to scream. Red John brandished his bow. "Quiet, there!" he roared. "'Steeth, I'll kill the first man who moves!"

I hardly thought this a time for profanity. Raising the cross still higher, I forced limp legs to carry me a few steps forward, while I quavered some chant of exorcism. I was certain it would do no good; the end of the world was upon us.

Had the demon only remained standing there, we would soon have broken and bolted. But he raised a tube held in one hand. From it shot flame, blinding white. I heard it crackle in the air and saw a man near me smitten. Fire burst over him. He fell dead, his breast charred open.

Three other demons emerged.

Soldiers were trained to react when such things happened, not to think. The bow of Red John sang. The foremost demon lurched off the ramp with a cloth-yard arrow through him. I saw him cough blood and die. As if the one shot had touched off a hundred, the air was suddenly gray with whistling shafts. The three other demons toppled, so thickly studded with arrows they might have been popinjays at a contest.

"They can be slain!" bawled Sir Roger. "Haro! St. George for merry England!" And he spurred his horse straight up the gangway.

They say fear breeds unnatural courage. With one crazed whoop the whole army charged after him. Be it confessed, I, too, howled and ran into the ship.

Of that combat which ramped and raged through all the rooms and corridors, I have little memory. Somewhere, from someone, I got a battle-ax. There is in me a confused impression of smiting away at vile blue faces which rose up to snarl at me, of slipping in blood and rising to smite again. Sir Roger had no way to direct the battle. His men simply ran wild.

Knowing the demons could be killed, their one thought was to kill and have done.

The crew of the ship numbered about a hundred, but few carried weapons. We later found all manner of devices stored in the holds, but the invaders had relied on creating a panic. Not knowing Englishmen, they had not expected trouble. The ship's artillery was ready to use, but of no value once we were inside.

In less than an hour, we had hunted them all down.

Wading out through the carnage, I wept with joy to feel the blessed sunlight again. Sir Roger was checking with his captains to find our losses, which were only fifteen all told. As I stood there, atremble with exhaustion, Red John Hameward emerged. He had a demon slung over his shoulder.

He threw the creature at Sir Roger's feet. "This one I knocked out with my fist, sire," he panted. "I thought might be you'd want one kept alive awhile, to put him to the question. Or should I not take chances, and slice off his ugly head now?"

Sir Roger considered. Calm had descended upon him; none of us had yet grasped the enormity of this event. A grim smile crossed his lips. He replied in English as fluent as the nobleman's French he more commonly used.

"If these be demons," he said, "they're a poor breed, for they were slain as easily as men. Easier, in sooth. They didn't know more about infighting than my little daughter. Less, for she's given my nose many hefty tweaks. I think chains will hold this fellow safe, eh, Brother Parvus?"

"Yes, my lord," I opined, "though it were best to put some saints' relics and the Host near by."

"Well, then, take him to the abbey and see what you can get out of him. I'll send a guard along. Come up to dinner this evening."

"Sire," I reproved, "we should hold a great Mass of thanksgiving ere we do anything else."

"Yes, yes," he said impatiently. "Talk to your abbot about it. Do what seems best. But come to dinner and tell me what you've learned."

His eyes grew thoughtful as he stared at the ship.

Chapter II

I CAME AS ordered, with the approval of my abbot, who saw
that here the ghostly and secular arms must be one. The
town was strangely quiet as I picked my way through sunset
streets. Folk were in church or huddled within doors. From
the soldiers' camp I could hear yet another Mass. The ship
brooded mountainous over all our tiny works.

But we felt heartened, I believe, a little drunk with our
success over powers not of this earth. The smug conclusion
seemed inescapable, that God approved of us.

I passed the bailey through a trebled watch and went directly to the great hall. Ansby Castle was old Norman work:
gaunt to look on, cold to inhabit. The hall was already dark, lit
by candles and a great leaping fire which picked weapons and
tapestries out of unrestful shadow. Gentlefolk and the more
important commoners of town and army were at table, a buzz
of talk, servants scurrying about, dogs lolling on the rushes.
It was a comfortingly familiar scene, however much tension
underlay it. Sir Roger beckoned me to come sit with him and
his lady, a signal honor.

Let me here describe Roger de Tourneville, knight and
baron. He was a big, strongly thewed man of thirty years, with
gray eyes and bony curve-nosed features. He wore his yellow
hair in the usual style of a warrior peer, thick on the crown
and shaven below—which somewhat marred an otherwise not
unhandsome appearance, for he had ears like jug handles. This,
his home district, was poor and backward, and most of his time
elsewhere had been spent in war. So he lacked courtly graces,
though shrewd and kindly in his fashion. His wife, Lady Catherine, was a daughter of the Viscount de Mornay; most people felt she had married beneath her style of living as well as
her station, for she had been brought up at Winchester amidst
every elegance and modern refinement. She was very beautiful, with great blue eyes and auburn hair, but somewhat of a
virago. They had only two children: Robert, a fine boy of six,
who was my pupil, and a three-year-old girl named Matilda.

"Well, Brother Parvus," boomed my lord. "Sit down. Have a stoup of wine—'sblood, this occasion calls for more than ale!" Lady Catherine's delicate nose wrinkled a bit; in her old home, ale was only for commoners. When I was seated, Sir Roger leaned forward and said intently, "What have you found out? Is it a demon we've captured?"

A hush fell over the table. Even the dogs were quiet. I could hear the hearth fire crackle and ancient banners stir dustily where they hung from the beams overhead. "I think so, my lord," I answered with care, "for he grew very angry when we sprinkled holy water on him."

"Yet he did not vanish in a puff of smoke? Hah! If demons, these are not kin to any I ever heard of. They're mortal as men."

"More so, sire," declared one of his captains, "for they cannot have souls."

"I'm not interested in their blithering souls," snorted Sir Roger. "I want to know about their ship. I've walked through it since the fight. What a by-our-lady whale of a ship! We could put all Ansby aboard, with room to spare. Did you ask the demon why a mere hundred of 'em needed that much space?"

"He does not speak any known language, my lord," I said.

"Nonsense! All demons know Latin, at least. He's just being stubborn."

"Mayhap a little session with your executioner?" asked the knight Sir Owain Montbelle slyly.

"No," I said. "If it please you, best not. He seems very quick at learning. Already he repeats many words after me, so I do not believe he is merely pretending ignorance. Give me a few days and I may be able to talk with him."

"A few days may be too much," grumbled Sir Roger. He threw the beef bone he had been gnawing to the dogs and licked his fingers noisily. Lady Catherine frowned and pointed to the water bowl and napkin before him. "I'm sorry, my sweet," he muttered. "I never can remember about these new-fangled things."

Sir Owain delivered him from his embarrassment by inquiring: "Why say you a few days may be too long? Surely you are not expecting another ship?"

"No. But the men will be more restless than ever. We were almost ready to depart, and now *this* happens!"

"So? Can we not leave anyhow on the date planned?"

"No, you blockhead!" Sir Roger's fist landed on the table. A goblet jumped. "Cannot you see what a chance this is? It must have been given us by the saints themselves!"

As we sat awestruck, he went on rapidly: "We can take the whole company aboard that thing. Horses, cows, pigs, fowls —we'll not be deviled by supply problems. Women, too, all the comforts of home! Aye, why not even the children? Never mind the crops hereabouts, they can stand neglect for a while and 'tis safer to keep everyone together lest there should be another visitation.

"I know not what powers the ship owns besides flying, but her very appearance will strike such terror we'll scarce need to fight. So we'll take her across the Channel and end the French war inside a month, d' you see? Then we go on and liberate the Holy Land, and get back here in time for hay harvest!"

A long silence ended abruptly in such a storm of cheers that my own weak protests were drowned out. I thought the scheme altogether mad. So, I could see, did Lady Catherine and a few others. But the rest were laughing and shouting till the hall roared.

Sir Roger turned a flushed face to me. "It depends on you, Brother Parvus," he said. "You're the best of us all in matters of language. You must make the demon talk, or teach him how, whichever it is. He's got to show us how to sail that ship!"

"My noble lord—" I quavered.

"Good!" Sir Roger slapped my back so I choked and nearly fell off my seat. "I knew you could do it. Your reward will be the privilege of coming with us!"

Indeed, it was as if the town and the army were alike possessed. Surely the one wise course was to send messages posthaste to the bishop, perhaps to Rome itself, begging counsel. But no, they must all go, at once. Wives would not leave their husbands, or parents their children, or girls their lovers. The lowliest serf looked up from his acre and dreamed of freeing the Holy Land and picking up a coffer of gold on the way.

What else can be expected of a folk bred from Saxon, Dane, and Norman?

I returned to the abbey and spent the night on my knees, praying for a sign. But the saints remained noncommittal. After matins I went with a heavy heart to my abbot and told him what the baron had commanded. He was wroth at not being allowed immediate communication with the Church authorities but decided it was best we obey for the nonce. I was released from other duties that I might study how to converse with the demon.

I girded myself and went down to the cell where he was confined. It was a narrow room, half underground, used for penances. Brother Thomas, our smith, had stapled fetters to the walls and chained the creature up. He lay on a straw pallet, a frightful sight in the gloom. His links clashed as he rose at my entry. Our relics in their chests were placed near by, just out of his impious reach, so that the thighbone of St. Osbert and the sixth-year molar of St. Willibald might keep him from bursting his bonds and escaping back to hell.

Though I would not have been at all sorry had he done so.

I crossed myself and squatted down. His yellow eyes glared at me. I had brought paper, ink, and quills, to exercise what small talent I have for drawing. I sketched a man and said, "*Homo*," for it seemed wiser to teach him Latin than any language confined to a single nation. Then I drew another man and showed him that the two were called *homines*. Thus it went, and he was quick to learn.

Presently he signaled for the paper, and I gave it to him. He himself drew skillfully. He told me that his name was *Branithar* and that his race was called *Wersgorix*. I was unable to find these terms in any demonology. But thereafter I let him guide our studies, for his race had made the learning of new languages into a science, and our task went apace.

I worked long hours with him and saw little of the outside world in the next few days. Sir Roger kept his domain incommunicado. I think his greatest fear was that some earl or duke might seize the ship for himself. With his bolder men, the baron spent much time aboard it, trying to fathom all the wonders he encountered.

Erelong Branithar was able to complain about the bread-and-water diet and threaten revenge. I was still afraid of him but kept up a bold front. Of course, our conversation was much slower than I here render it, with many pauses while we searched for words.

"You brought this on yourself," I told him. "You should have known better than to make an unprovoked attack on Christians."

"What are Christians?" he asked.

Dumfounded, I thought he must be feigning ignorance. As a test, I led him through the Paternoster. He did not go up in smoke, which puzzled me.

"I think I understand," he said. "You refer to some primitive tribal pantheon."

"It is no such heathen thing!" I said indignantly. I started to explain the Trinity to him, but had scarcely gotten to transubstantiation when he waved an impatient blue hand. It was much like a human hand otherwise, save for the thick, sharp nails.

"No matter," he said. "Are all Christians as ferocious as your people?"

"You would have had better luck with the French," I admitted. "Your misfortune was landing among Englishmen."

"A stubborn breed," he nodded. "It will cost you dearly. But if you release me at once, I will try to mitigate the vengeance which is going to fall on you."

My tongue clove to the roof of my mouth, but I unstuck it and asked him coolly enough to elucidate. Whence came he, and what were his intentions?

That took a long time for him to make clear, because the very concepts were strange. I thought surely he was lying, but at least he acquired more Latin in the process.

It was about two weeks after the landing when Sir Owain Montbelle appeared at the abbey and demanded audience with me. I met him in the cloister garden; we found a bench and sat down.

This Owain was the younger son, by a second marriage with a Welsh woman, of a petty baron on the Marches. I daresay the ancient conflict of two nations smoldered strangely in his breast; but the Cymric charm was also there. Made page and later esquire to a great knight in the royal court, young Owain had captured his master's heart and been brought up with all the privilege of far higher ranks. He had traveled widely abroad, become a troubadour of some note, received the accolade—and then suddenly, there he was, penniless. In hopes of winning his fortune, he had wandered to Ansby to join the free companions. Though valiant enough, he was too darkly handsome for most men's taste, and they said no husband felt safe when he was about. This was not quite true, for Sir Roger had taken a fancy to the youth, admired his judgment as well as his education, and was happy that at last Lady Catherine had someone to talk to about the things that most interested her.

"I come from my lord, Brother Parvus," Sir Owain began. "He wishes to know how much longer you will need to tame this beast of ours."

"Oh . . . he speaks glibly enough now," I answered. "But he holds so firmly to out-and-out falsehoods that I have not yet thought it worth while to report."

"Sir Roger grows most impatient, and the men can scarcely be held any longer. They devour his substance, and not a night passes without a brawl or a murder. We must start soon or not at all."

"Then I beg you not to go," I said. "Not in yon ship out of hell." I could see that dizzyingly tall spire, its nose wreathed with low clouds, rearing beyond the abbey walls. It terrified me.

"Well," snapped Sir Owain, "what has the monster told you?"

"He has the impudence to claim he comes not from below, but from above. From heaven itself!"

"He . . . an angel?"

"No. He says he is neither angel nor demon, but a member of another mortal race than mankind."

Sir Owain caressed his smooth-shaven chin with one hand. "It could be," he mused. "After all, if Unipeds and Centaurs and other monstrous beings exist, why not those squatty blueskins?"

"I know. 'Twould be reasonable enough, save that he claims to live in the sky."

"Tell me just what he did say."

"As you will, Sir Owain, but remember that these impieties are not mine. This Branithar insists that the earth is not flat but is a sphere hanging in space. Nay, he goes further and says the earth moves about the sun! Some of the learned ancients held similar notions, but I cannot understand what would keep the oceans from pouring off into space or—"

"Pray continue the story, Brother Parvus."

"Well, Branithar says that the stars are other suns than ours, only very far off, and have worlds going about them even as our own does. Not even the Greeks could have swallowed such an absurdity. What kind of ignorant yokels does the creature take us for? But be this as it may, Branithar says that his people, the Wersgorix, come from one of these other worlds, one which is much like our earth. He boasts of their powers of sorcery—"

"That much is no lie," said Sir Owain. "We've been trying out some of those hand weapons. We burned down three houses, a pig, and a serf ere we learned how to control them."

I gulped, but went on: "These Wersgorix have ships which can fly between the stars. They have conquered many worlds. Their method is to subdue or wipe out any backward natives there may be. Then they settle the entire world, each Wersgor taking hundreds of thousands of acres. Their numbers are growing so fast, and they so dislike being crowded, that they must ever be seeking new worlds.

"This ship we captured was a scout, exploring in search of another place to conquer. Having observed our earth from above, they decided it was suitable for their use and descended. Their plan was the usual one, which had never failed them hitherto. They would terrorize us, use our home as a base, and range about gathering specimens of plants, animals, and minerals. That is the reason their ship is so big, with so much empty space. 'Twas to be a veritable Noah's ark. When they returned home and reported their findings, a fleet would come to attack all mankind."

"Hm," said Sir Owain. "We stopped that much, at least."

We were both cushioned against the frightful vision of our poor folk being harried by unhumans, destroyed or enslaved, because neither of us really believed it. I had decided that Branithar came from a distant part of the world, perhaps beyond Cathay, and only told these lies in the hope of frightening us into letting him go. Sir Owain agreed with my theory.

"Nonetheless," added the knight, "we must certainly learn to use the ship, lest more of them arrive. And what better way to learn, than by taking it to France and Jerusalem? As my lord said, 'twould in that case be prudent as well as comfortable to have women, children, yeomen, and townsfolk along. Have you asked the beast how to cast the spells for working the ship?"

"Yes," I answered reluctantly. "He says the rudder is very simple."

"And have you told him what will happen to him if he does not pilot us faithfully?"

"I have intimated. He says he will obey."

"Good! Then we can start in another day or two!" Sir Owain leaned back, eyes dreamily half closed. "We must eventually see about getting word back to his own people. One could buy much wine and amuse many fair women with his ransom."

Chapter III

Aɴᴅ ꜱᴏ we departed.

Stranger even than the ship and its advent was that embarkation. There the thing towered, like a steel cliff forged by a wizard for a hideous use. On the other side of the common huddled little Ansby, thatched cots and rutted streets, fields green beneath our wan English sky. The very castle, once so dominant in the scene, looked shrunken and gray.

But up the ramps we had let down from many levels, into the gleaming pillar, thronged our homely, red-faced, sweating, laughing people. Here John Hameward roared along with his bow across one shoulder and a tavern wench giggling on the other. There a yeoman armed with a rusty ax that might have been swung at Hastings, clad in patched wadmal, preceded a scolding wife burdened with their bedding and cooking pot, and half a dozen children clinging to her skirts. Here a cross-bowman tried to make a stubborn mule climb the gangway, his oaths laying many years in purgatory to his account. There a lad chased a pig which had gotten loose. Here a richly clad knight jested with a fine lady who bore a hooded falcon on her wrist. There a priest told his beads as he went doubtfully into the iron maw. Here a cow lowed, there a sheep bleated, here a goat shook its horns, there a hen cackled. All told, some two thousand souls went aboard.

The ship held them easily. Each important man could have a cabin for himself and his lady—for several had brought wives, lemans, or both as far as Ansby Castle, to make a more social occasion of the departure for France. The commoners spread pallets in empty holds. Poor Ansby was left almost deserted, and I often wonder if it still exists.

Sir Roger had made Branithar operate the ship on some trial flights. It had risen smoothly and silently as he worked the wheels and levers and knobs in the control turret. Steering was childishly simple, though we could make neither head nor tail of certain discs with heathenish inscriptions, across which quivered needles. Through me, Branithar told Sir Roger that the ship derived its motive power from the destruction of matter, a horrid idea indeed, and that its engines raised and propelled it by nullifying the pull of the earth along chosen directions. This was senseless—Aristotle has explained very clearly how things fall to the ground because it is their nature to fall, and I have no truck with illogical ideas to which flighty heads so easily succumb.

Despite his own reservations, the abbot joined Father Simon in blessing the ship. We named her *Crusader*. Though we only had two chaplains along, we had also borrowed a lock of St. Benedict's hair, and all who embarked had confessed and received absolution. So it was thought we were safe enough from ghostly peril, though I had my doubts.

I was given a small cabin adjoining the suite in which Sir Roger lived with his lady and their children. Branithar was kept under guard in a near-by room. My duty was to interpret, to continue the prisoner's instruction in Latin and the education of young Robert, and to act as my lord's amanuensis.

At departure, however, the control turret was occupied by Sir Roger, Sir Owain, Branithar, and myself. It was windowless, like the entire ship, but held glassy screens in which appeared images of the earth below and all the sky around. I shivered and told my beads, for it is not lawful for Christian men to gaze into the crystal globes of Indic sorcerers.

"Now, then," said Sir Roger, and his hooked face laughed at me, "let's away! We'll be in France within the hour!"

He sat down before the panel of levers and wheels. Branithar said quickly to me: "The trial flights were only a few miles. Tell your master that for a trip of this length certain special preparations must be made."

Sir Roger nodded when I had passed this on. "Very well, let him do so." His sword slithered from the sheath. "But I'll be watching our course in the screens. At the first sign of treachery—"

Sir Owain scowled. "Is this wise, my lord?" he asked. "The beast—"

"Is our prisoner. You're too full of Celtic superstitions, Owain. Let him begin."

Branithar seated himself. The furnishings of the ship, chairs and tables and beds and cabinets, were somewhat small for us humans—and badly designed, without so much as a carven dragon for ornament. But we could make do with them. I watched the captive intently as his blue hands moved over the panel.

A deep humming trembled in the ship. I felt nothing, but the ground in the lower screens suddenly dwindled. That was sorcerous; I would much rather the usual backward thrust of a vehicle when it starts were not annulled. Fighting down my stomach, I stared into the screen-reflected vault of heaven. Erelong we were among the clouds, which proved to be high-floating mists. Clearly this shows the wondrous power of God, for it is known that the angels often sit about on the clouds, and do not get wet.

"Now, southward," ordered Sir Roger.

Branithar grunted, set a dial, and snapped down a bar. I heard a clicking as of a lock. The bar stayed down.

Hellish triumph flared in the yellow eyes. Branithar sprang from his seat and snarled at me: "*Consummati estis!*" His Latin was very bad. "You are finished! I have just sent you to death!"

"What?" I cried.

Sir Roger cursed, half understanding, and lunged at the Wersgor. But the sight of what was in the screens checked him. The sword clattered from his hand, and sweat leaped out on his face.

Truly it was terrible. The earth dwindled beneath us as if it were falling down a great well. About us, the blue sky darkened, and stars glittered forth. Yet it was not nightfall, for the sun still shone in one screen, more brightly than ever!

Sir Owain screamed something in Welsh. I fell to my knees.

Branithar darted for the door. Sir Roger whirled and grasped him by his robe. They went over in a raging tangle.

Sir Owain was paralyzed by terror, and I could not pull my eyes from the horrible beauty of the spectacle about us. Earth shrank so small that it only filled one screen. It was blue, banded, with dark splotches, and round. *Round!*

A new and deeper note entered the low drone in the air. New needles on the control panel quivered to life. Suddenly we were moving, gaining speed, with impossible swiftness. An altogether different set of engines, acting on a wholly unknown principle, had unwound their ropes.

I saw the moon swell before us. Even as I stared, we passed so near that I could see mountains and pockmarks upon it, edged with their own shadows. But this was inconceivable! All knew the moon to be a perfect circle. Sobbing, I tried to break that liar of a vision screen, but could not.

Sir Roger overcame Branithar and stretched him half-conscious on the deck. The knight got up, breathing heavily. "Where are we?" he gasped. "What's happened?"

"We're going up," I groaned. "Up and out." I put my fingers in my ears so as not to be deafened when we crashed into the first of the crystal spheres.

After a while, when nothing had occurred, I opened my eyes and looked again. Earth and moon were both receding, little more than a doubled star of blue and gold. The real stars flamed hard, unwinking, against an infinite blackness. It seemed to me that we were still picking up speed.

Sir Roger cut off my prayers with an oath. "We've this traitor to handle first!" He kicked Branithar in the ribs. The Wersgor sat up and glared defiance.

I collected my wits and said to him in Latin, "What have you done? You will die by torture unless you take us back at once."

He rose, folded his arms, and regarded us with bitter pride. "Did you think that you barbarians were any match for a civilized mind?" he answered. "Do what you will with me. There will be revenge enough when you come to this journey's end."

"But what *have* you done?"

His bruised mouth grinned. "I set the ship under control of its automaton-pilot. It is now steering itself. Everything is automatic—the departure from atmosphere, the switch-over into translight quasi-velocity, the compensation for optical effects, the preservation of artificial gravity and other environmental factors."

"Well, turn off the engines!"

"No one can. I could not do so myself, now that the lock-bar is down. It will remain down until we get to Tharixan. And that is the nearest world settled by my people!"

I tried the controls, gingerly. They could not be moved. When I told the knights, Sir Owain moaned aloud.

But Sir Roger said grimly: "We'll find whether that is the truth or not. The questioning will at least punish his betrayal!"

Through me, Branithar replied with scorn: "Vent your spite if you must. I am not afraid of you. But I say that even if you broke my will, it would be useless. The rudder settings cannot be changed now, nor the ship halted. The lock-bar is meant for situations when a vessel must be sent somewhere with no one aboard." After a moment he added earnestly: "You must understand, though, I bear you no malice. You are foolhardy, but I could almost regret the fact that we need your world for ourselves. If you will spare me, I shall intercede for you when we get to Tharixan. Your own lives may be given you, at least."

Sir Roger rubbed his chin thoughtfully. I heard the bristles scratch under his palm, though he had shaved only last Thursday. "I gather the ship will become manageable again when we reach this destination," he said. I was amazed how coolly he took it after the first shock. "Could we not turn about then and go home?"

"I will never guide you!" said Branithar to that. "And alone, unable to read our navigational books, you would never find the way. We will be farther from your world than light can travel in a thousand of your years."

"You might have the courtesy not to insult our intelligence," I huffed. "I know as well as you do that light has an infinite velocity."

He shrugged.

A gleam lit Sir Roger's eye. "When will we arrive?" he asked.

"In ten days," Branithar informed us. "It is not the distances between stars, great though they are, that has made us so slow to reach your world. We have been expanding for three centuries. It is the sheer number of suns."

"Hm. When we arrive, we have this fine ship to use, with its bombards and the hand weapons. The Wersgorix may regret our visit!"

I translated for Branithar, who answered, "I sincerely advise you to surrender at once. True, these fire-beams of ours can slay a man, or reduce a city to slag. But you will find them useless, because we have screens of pure force which will stop any such beam. The ship is not so protected, since the generators of a force shield are too bulky for it. Thus the guns of the fortress can shoot upward and destroy you."

When Sir Roger heard this, he said only: "Well, we've ten days to think it over. Let this remain a secret. No one can see out of the ship, save from this place. I'll think of some tale that won't alarm the folk too much."

He went out, his cloak swirling behind him like great wings.

Chapter IV

I WAS THE least of our troop, and much happened in which
I had no part. Yet I shall set it down as fully as may be, using conjecture to fill in the gaps of knowledge. The chaplains
heard much in confession, and without violating confidence
they were ever quick to correct false impressions.

I believe, therefore, that Sir Roger took Catherine his lady
aside and told her how matters stood. He had hoped for calm
and courage from her, but she flew into the bitterest of rages.

"Ill was the day I wed you!" she cried. Her lovely face turned
red and then white, and she stamped a small foot on the steel
deck. "Bad enough that your oafishness should disgrace me
before king and court, and doom me to yawn my life away in
that bear's den you call a castle. Now you set the lives and the
very souls of my children at hazard!"

"But, dearest," he stammered. "I could not know—"

"No, you were too stupid! 'Twas not enough to go robbing
and whoring off into France, you must needs do it in this aerial
coffin. Your arrogance told you the demon was so afraid of you
he would be your obedient slave. Mary, pity women!"

She whirled, sobbing, and hurried from him.

Sir Roger stared after her till she had vanished down the
long corridor. Then, heavyhearted, he betook himself to see
his troopers.

He found them in the afterhold, cooking their supper. The
air remained sweet in spite of all the fires we lit; Branithar told
me the ship embodied a system for renewing the vital spirits of
the atmosphere. I found it somewhat unnerving always to have
the walls luminous and not know day from night. But the common soldiers sat around, hoisting ale crocks, bragging, dicing,
cracking fleas, a wild, godless crew who nonetheless cheered
their lord with real affection.

Sir Roger signaled to Red John Hameward, whose huge
form lumbered to join him in a small side chamber. "Well,
sire," he remarked, "it seems a longish ways to France after all."

"Plans have been, um, changed," Sir Roger told him carefully. "It seems there may be a rare booty in the homeland of

this ship. With that, we could equip an army large enough not only to take, but to hold and settle all our conquests."

Red John belched and scratched under his doublet. "If we don't run into more nor we can handle, sire."

"I think not. But you must prepare your men for this change of plan and soothe whatever fears they have."

"That'll not be easy, sire."

"Why not? I told you the plunder would be good."

"Well, my lord, if you want the honest truth, 'tis in this wise. You see, though we've most of the Ansby women along, and many of 'em are unwed and, um, friendly disposed . . . even so, my lord, the fact remains, d' you see, we've twice as many men as women. Now the French girls are fair, and belike the Saracen wenches would do in a pinch—indeed, they're said to be very pinchable—but judging from those blueskins we over-mastered, well, their females aren't so handsome."

"How do you know they don't hold beautiful princesses in captivity that yearn for an honest English face?"

"That's so, my lord. It could well be."

"Then see you have the bowmen ready to fight when we arrive." Sir Roger clapped the giant on the shoulder and went out to speak similarly with his other captains.

He mentioned this question of women to me somewhat later, and I was horrified. "God be praised, that He made the Wersgorix so unattractive, if they are of another species!" I exclaimed. "Great is His forethought!"

"Ill-favored though they be," asked the baron, "are you sure they're not human?"

"Would God I knew, sire," I answered after thinking about it. "They look like naught on earth. Yet they do go on two legs, have hands, speech, the power of reason."

"It matters little," he decided.

"Oh, but it matters greatly, sire!" I told him. "For see you, if they have souls, then it is our plain duty to win them to the Faith. But if they have not, it were blasphemous to give them the sacraments."

"I'll let you find out which," he said indifferently.

I hurried forthwith to Branithar's cabin, which was guarded by a couple of spearmen. "What would you?" he asked when I sat down.

"Have you a soul?" I inquired.

"A what?"

I explained what *spiritus* meant. He was still puzzled. "Do you really think a miniature of yourself lives in your head?" he asked.

"Oh, no. The soul is not material. It is what gives life—well, not exactly that, since animals are alive—will, the self—"

"I see. The brain."

"No, no, no! The soul is, well, that which lives on after the body is dead, and faces judgment for its actions during life."

"Ah. You believe, then, that the personality survives after death. An interesting problem. If personality is a pattern rather than a material object, as seems reasonable, then it is theoretically possible that this pattern may be transferred to something else, the same system of relationships but in another physical matrix."

"Stop maundering!" I snapped impatiently. "You are worse than an Albigensian. Tell me in plain words, do you or do you not have a soul?"

"Our scientists have investigated the problems involved in a pattern concept of personality, but, so far as I know, data are still lacking on which to base a conclusion."

"There you go again." I sighed. "Can you not give me a simple answer? Just tell me whether or not you have a soul."

"I don't know."

"You're no help at all," I scolded him, and left.

My colleagues and I debated the problem at length, but except for the obvious fact that provisional baptism could be given any nonhumans willing to receive it, no solution was reached. It was a matter for Rome, perhaps for an ecumenical council.

While all this went on, Lady Catherine had mastered her tears and swept haughtily on down a passageway, seeking to ease her inner turmoil by motion. In the long room where the captains dined, she found Sir Owain tuning his harp. He leaped to his feet and bowed. "My lady! This is a pleasant . . . I might say dazzling . . . surprise."

She sat down on a bench. "Where are we now?" she asked in sudden surrender to her weariness.

Perceiving that she knew the truth, he replied, "I don't know. Already the sun itself has shrunk till we have lost view of it among the stars." A slow smile kindled in his dark face. "Yet there is sun enough in this chamber."

Catherine felt a blush go up her cheeks. She looked down at her shoes. Her own lips stirred upward, unwilled by herself.

"We are on the loneliest voyage men ever undertook," said Sir Owain. "If my lady will permit, I'll seek to while away an hour of it with a song cycle dedicated to her charms."

She did not refuse more than once. His voice rose until it filled the room.

Chapter V

THERE IS little to tell of the outward journey. The tedium of it soon bulked larger than the perils. Knights exchanged harsh words, and John Hameward had to crack more than one pair of heads together to keep order among his bowmen. The serfs took it best; when not caring for livestock, or eating, they merely slept.

I noticed that Lady Catherine was often at converse with Sir Owain, and that her husband was no longer overjoyed about it. However, he was always caught up in some plan or preparation, and the younger knight did give her hours of distraction, even of merriment.

Sir Roger and I spent much time with Branithar, who was willing enough to tell us about his race and its empire. I was reluctantly coming to believe his claims. Strange that so ugly a breed should dwell in what I judged to be the Third Heaven, but the fact could not be denied. Belike, I thought, when Scripture mentioned the four corners of the world, it did not mean our planet Terra at all, but referred to a cubical universe. Beyond this must lie the abode of the blessed; while Branithar's remark about the molten interior of the earth was certainly consonant with prophetic visions of hell.

Branithar told us that there were about a hundred worlds like our own in the Wersgor empire. They circled as many separate stars, for no sun was likely to have more than one habitable planet. Each of these worlds was the dwelling place of a few million Wersgorix, who liked plenty of room. Except for the capital planet, Wersgorixan, they bore no cities. But those on the frontiers of the empire, like Tharixan whither we were bound, had fortresses which were also space-navy bases. Branithar stressed the firepower and impregnability of these castles.

If a usable planet had intelligent natives, these were either exterminated or enslaved. The Wersgorix did no menial work, leaving this to such helots, or to automata. Themselves they were soldiers, managers of their vast estates, traders, owners of manufactories, politicians, courtiers. Being unarmed, the enslaved natives had no hope of revolting against the relatively small number of alien masters. Sir Roger muttered something about distributing weapons to these oppressed beings when we arrived and telling them about the Jacquerie. But Branithar guessed his intent, laughed, and said Tharixan had never been inhabited, so there were only a few hundred slaves on the entire planet.

This empire filled a rough sphere in space, about two thousand light-years across. (A light-year being the incredible distance that light covers in one standard Wersgor year, which Branithar said was about 10 per cent longer than the Terrestrial period.) It included millions of suns with their worlds. But most of these, because of poisonous air or poisonous life forms or other things, were useless to the Wersgorix and ignored.

Sir Roger asked if they were the only nation which had learned to fly between the stars. Branithar shrugged contemptuously. "We have encountered three others, who developed the art independently," he said. "They live within the sphere of our empire, but so far we have not subdued them. It was not worth while, when primitive planets are such easier game. We allow these three races to traffic, and to keep the small number of colonies they had already established in other planetary systems. But we have not allowed them to continue expanding. A couple of minor wars settled that. They have no love for us; they know we will destroy them someday when it is convenient for us to do so, but they are helpless in the face of overwhelming power."

"I see," nodded the baron.

He instructed me to start learning the Wersgor language. Branithar found it amusing to teach me, and I could smother my own fears by hard work, so it went quite fast. Their tongue was barbarous, lacking the noble inflections of Latin, but on that account not hard to master.

In the control turret I found drawers full of charts and numerical tables. All the writing was beautifully exact; I thought they must have such scribes it was a pity they had not gone on to illuminate the pages. Puzzling over these, and using what I had learned of the Wersgor speech and alphabet, I decided this was a set of navigational directions.

A regular map of the planet Tharixan was included, since this had been the home base of the expedition. I translated the symbols for land, sea, river, fortress, and so on. Sir Roger pored long hours over it. Even the Saracen chart his grandfather had brought back from the Holy Land was crude compared to this; though on the other hand the Wersgorix showed lack of culture by omitting pictures of mermaids, the four winds, hippogriffs, and similar ornamentation.

I also deciphered the legends on some of the control-panel instruments. Such dials as those for altitude and speed could readily be mastered. But what did "fuel flow" mean? What was the difference between "sub-light drive" and "super-light drive"? Truly these were potent, though pagan, charms.

And so the sameness of days passed, and after a time which felt like a century we observed that one star was waxing in the screens. It swelled until it flamed big and bright as our own sun. And then we saw a planet, similar to ours save that it had two small moons. Downward we plunged, till the scene was not a ball in the sky but a great rugged sweep of landscape under our footsoles. When I saw heaven again turned blue, I threw myself to the deck in thanksgiving.

The lock-bar snapped upward. The ship came to a halt and hung where it was, a mile in the air. We had reached Tharixan.

Chapter VI

S IR ROGER had summoned me to the control turret, with Sir Owain and Red John, who led Branithar on a leash. The bowman gaped at the screens and muttered horrid oaths.

Word had gone through the ship that all fighting men must arm themselves. The two knights here were in plate, their esquires waiting outside with shields and helmets. Horses stamped in the holds and along the corridors. Women and children huddled back with bright fearful eyes.

"Here we are!" Sir Roger grinned. It was eldritch to see him so boyishly gay, when everyone else was swallowing hard and sweating till the air reeked. But a fight, even against the powers of hell, was something he could understand. "Brother Parvus, ask the prisoner where we are on the planet."

I put the question to Branithar, who touched a control button. A hitherto blank screen glowed to life, showing a map. "We are where the cross hairs center," he told us. "The map will unroll as we fly about."

I compared the screen with the chart in my hand. "The fortress called Ganturath seems to lie about a hundred miles north by northeast, my lord," I said.

Branithar, who had been picking up a little English, nodded. "Ganturath is only a minor base." He must put his boasts into Latin still. "Yet numerous spaceships are stationed there, and swarms of aircraft. The fire-weapons on the ground can blast this vessel out of existence, and force screens will stop any beams from your own guns. Best you surrender."

When I had translated, Sir Owain said slowly: "It may be the wisest thing, my lord."

"What?" cried Sir Roger. "An Englishman yield without a fight?"

"But the women, sire, and the poor little children!"

"I am not a rich man," said Sir Roger. "I cannot afford to pay ransom." He clumped in his armor to the pilot's chair, sat down, and tapped the manual controls.

Through the downward vision screens, I saw the land slide swiftly away beneath us. Its rivers and mountains were of home-like shape, but the vegetation's green hues were over-laid with a weird bluish tint. The country seemed wild. Now and again we saw a few rounded buildings, amidst enormous grainfields cultivated by machines, but otherwise it was bare of man as the New Forest. I wondered if this, too, were some king's hunting preserve, then remembered Branithar's account of sparse habitation everywhere in the Wersgor Empire.

A voice broke our silence, chattering away in the harsh blue-face language. We started, crossed ourselves, and glared about. The sounds came from a small black instrument affixed to the main panel.

"So!" Red John drew his dagger. "All this time there's been a stowaway! Give me a crowbar, sire, and I'll pry him out."

Branithar divined his meaning. Laughter barked in the thick blue throat. "The voice is borne from afar, by waves like those of light but longer," he said.

"Talk sense!" I demanded.

"Well, we are being hailed by an observer at Ganturath fortress."

Sir Roger nodded curtly when I translated. "Voices out of thin air are little compared to what we've already seen," he said. "What does the fellow want?"

I could catch only a few words of the challenge, but got the drift of it. Who were we? This was not the regular land-ing place for scout craft. Why did we enter a forbidden area? "Calm them," I instructed Branithar, "and remember I will understand if you betray us."

He shrugged, as if amused, though his own brow was also filmed with sweat. "Scoutship 587-*Zin* returning," he said. "Urgent message. Will halt above the base."

The voice gave assent, but warned that if we came lower than a *stanthax* (about half a mile), we would be destroyed. We were to hover until the crews of patrol aircraft could board us.

By now, Ganturath was visible: a compact mass of domes and half-cylinders, masonry over steel skeletons as we later found out. It made a circle about a thousand feet in diameter. Half a mile or so northward lay a smaller set of buildings. Through a magnifying view screen, we saw that out of the latter jutted the muzzles of huge fire-bombards.

Even as we came to a halt, a pale shimmering sprang up

around both parts of the fortress. Branithar pointed. "The defensive screens. Your own shots would spatter harmlessly off. It would be a lucky hit that melted one of those gun muzzles, where they thrust out beyond the shield. But you are an easy target."

Several egg-shaped metallic craft, like midges against the huge bulk of our *Crusader*, approached. We saw others lift from the ground, the main part of the fortress. Sir Roger's fair head nodded. "'Tis as I thought," he said. "Those screens stop a fire-beam, mayhap, but not a material object, since the boats pass through."

"True," said Branithar by way of me. "You might manage to drop an explosive missile or two, but the outlying section, where the guns are, would destroy you."

"Aha." Sir Roger studied the Wersgor with eyes gone pale. "So you possess explosive shells, eh? Doubtless aboard this very craft. And you never told me. We'll see about that later." He jerked a thumb at Red John and Sir Owain. "Well, you two have seen how the ground lies. Go back to the men, now, and be ready to emerge fighting when we land."

They departed, nervously eying the screens, where the aircraft were very near us. Sir Roger put his own hands on the wheels that controlled the bombards. We had learned, with some experimentation, that those great weapons almost aimed and fired themselves. As the patrol boats closed in, Sir Roger cut loose.

Blinding hell-beams stabbed forth. They wrapped the aircraft in flame. I saw the nearest one cut in two by that fiery sword. Another tumbled red-hot, a third exploded. Thunder boomed. Then all I saw was falling metal scrap.

Sir Roger tested Branithar's claims, but they were true: his beams splashed off that pale, translucent screen. He grunted. "I looked for that. Best we get down now before they send up a real warship to deal with us, or open fire from the outlying emplacement." While he spoke, he sent us hurtling groundward. A flame touched our hull, but then we were too low. I saw Ganturath's buildings rush up to meet me and braced myself for death.

A ripping and crunching went through our ship. This very turret burst open as it brushed a low lookout tower. But the battlements of that were snapped off. Two thousand feet long, incalculably heavy, the *Crusader* squashed half Ganturath beneath itself.

Sir Roger was on his feet even before the engines went dead. "Haro!" he bellowed. "God send the right!" And off he went, across the canted, buckled deck. He snatched his helmet from the terrified esquire and put it on as he strode. The boy followed, teeth chattering but nonetheless in charge of the de Tourneville shield.

Branithar sat speechless. I gathered up my robe and hurried off to find a sergeant who would lock up the valuable captive for me. This being done, I was able to witness the battle.

We had come down lengthwise rather than on our tail, protected by the artificial weight generators from tumbling around inside. Havoc encompassed us, smashed buildings and sharded walls. A chaos of blue Wersgorix boiled from the rest of the fortress.

By the time I got to the exit myself, Sir Roger was out with all his cavalry. He didn't stop to gather them, but charged into the thick of the nearest enemies. His horse neighed, mane flying, armor flashing; the long lance spitted three bodies at once. When at length the spear was broken, my lord drew his sword and hewed lustily. Most of his followers had no scruples about unknightly weapons; they eked out blade, mace, and morningstar with handguns from the ship.

Now archers and men-at-arms poured forth, yelling. Belike it was their own terror that made them so savage. They closed with the Wersgorix ere our foe could unleash many lightning bolts. The battle became hand-to-hand, a leaderless riot, where ax or dagger or quarterstaff was more useful than fire-beam or pellet gun.

When the space about him was cleared, Sir Roger reared on his black stallion. He clashed back his visor and set bugle to lips. It shrieked through the din, summoning the mounted force. These, better disciplined than the foot soldiers, disengaged themselves from the immediate fray and joined the baron. A mass of great horses, men like steel towers, blazoned shields and flying plumes and lances aloft, formed behind my lord.

His gauntleted hand pointed to the outlying fort, where the skyward bombards had ceased their futile shooting. "That we must seize, ere they rally!" he cried. "After me, Englishmen, for God and St. George!"

He took a fresh shaft from his esquire, spurred his charger, and began to pick up speed. The earthquake roll of hoofs deepened behind him.

Those Wersgorix stationed in the lesser fort poured out to resist the attack. They had guns of several kinds, plus small explosive missiles to be thrown by hand. They picked off a couple of riders. But in that short distance there was no time for more long-range shooting. And they were unnerved in any event. There is no sight more terrifying than a charge of heavy cavalry.

The trouble of the Wersgorix was that they had gone too far. They had made combat on the ground obsolete, and were ill trained, ill equipped, when it happened. True, they possessed fire-beams, as well as force shields to stop those same fire-beams. But they had never thought to lay down caltrops.

As it was, the frightful blow struck their line, rolled over it, stamped it into mud, and continued without even being slowed.

One of the buildings beyond gaped open. A small spaceship —though big as any seagoing vessel on Earth—had been trundled forth. It stood on its tail, engine growling, ready to take off and flame us from above. Sir Roger directed his cavalry thither. The lancers hit it in a single line. Shafts splintered; men were hurled from the saddle. But consider: a charging cavalryman may bear his own weight of armor, and have fifteen hundred pounds of horse beneath him. The whole travels at several miles per hour. The impact is awesome.

The ship was bowled over. It fell on its side and lay crippled.

Through and through the lesser fort, Sir Roger's horsemen ramped, sword, mace, spurred boot, and shod hoof. The Wersgorix died like swatted flies. Or say rather, the flies were the small patrol boats, buzzing overhead, unable to shoot into that melee without killing their own folk. To be sure, Sir Roger was killing their own folk anyway; but by the time the Wersgorix realized that, they were too late.

Back in the main section where the *Crusader* lay, the fight sputtered down into a question of slaying bluefaces or taking them prisoner or chasing them into the near-by forest. It was still one vast confusion, though, and Red John Hameward felt he was wasting the skill of his longbowmen. He formed them into a detachment and quick-stepped across open ground to aid Sir Roger.

The patrol boats swooped low, hungrily. Here was prey they might get. Their thin beams were intended for short ranges. On the first pass, two archers died. Then Red John yelled an order.

Suddenly the sky was full of arrows. A cloth-yard shaft with a six-foot yew bow behind it will go through an armored man and the horse beneath him. These little boats made matters worse by flying directly into the gray goose flock. Not one of them escaped. Riddled, their pilots quilled as hedgehogs, they crashed. The archers roared and ran to join the fray ahead.

The spaceship which the lancers had knocked over was still manned. Its crew must have recovered their wits. Suddenly its gun turrets spurted flame, no mere hand-weapon beam but thunderbolts that knocked down walls. A horseman and his steed, caught in that fire, were instantly gone. Vengefully, the lightnings raked around.

Red John picked up one end of a great steel beam, part of the dome shattered by those bombards. Fifty men aided him. They ran toward the entry port of the ship. Once, twice, crash! Down came the door, and the English yeomen stormed within.

The Battle of Ganturath lasted for some hours, but most of that time went merely to ferret out hidden remnants of the garrison. When the alien sun smoldered westward, there were about a score of English dead. None were badly wounded, for the flame guns usually killed if they hit the mark at all. Some three hundred Wersgorix were slain, roughly an equal number captured; many of these latter were minus a limb or an ear. I would guess that perhaps a hundred more escaped on foot. They would carry word of us to the nearest estates—which, however, were not very close by. Evidently the speed and destructiveness of our initial attack had put Ganturath's far-speakers out of action before the alarm could go abroad.

Our true disaster was not revealed till later. We were not dismayed at having wrecked the ship we came in, for we now had several other vessels whose aggregate volume would hold us all. Their crews had never gotten a chance to man them.

However, in her atrocious landing, the *Crusader* had burst open her control turret. And the Wersgor navigational notes therein were now lost.

At the moment, all was triumph. Red-splashed, panting, in scorched and dinted armor, Sir Roger de Tourneville rode a weary horse back to the main fortress. After him came the lancers, archers, yeomen—ragged, battered, shoulders slumped with exhaustion. But the Te Deum was on their lips, rising beneath the strange constellations that twinkled forth, and their banners flew bravely against the sky.

It was wonderful to be an Englishman.

Chapter VII

WE MADE camp at the nearly intact lesser fort. Our people chopped wood from the forest, and as the two moons rose, their blazes leaped up. Men sat close, faces picked out of darkness by the homely unrestful light, waiting for the stew-pots to be ready. Horses cropped the native grass without enjoying its taste. The captured Wersgorix huddled together under guard of pikemen. They were stunned; this did not seem possible. I felt almost sorry for them, godless and cruel though their dominion was.

Sir Roger summoned me to join his captains, who were camped near one of the gun turrets. We manned what defenses were available, against expected counterattack, and tried not to wonder what new frightfulness the foe might have in their armory.

Tents had been erected for the more wellborn ladies. Most were abed, but Lady Catherine sat on a stool at the edge of the firelight. She listened to our talk, and her mouth was drawn into bleak lines.

The captains sprawled, weary, on the ground. I saw Sir Owain Montbelle, idly thrumming his harp; scarred, fierce old Sir Brian Fitz-William, the third of the three knighted men on this voyage; big Alfred Edgarson, the purest of Saxon franklins; gloomy Thomas Bullard, fingering the naked sword on his lap; Red John Hameward, shy because he was the lowest born of them all. A couple of pages poured wine.

My lord Sir Roger, the unbendable, was on his feet, hands clasped behind his back. Having removed his armor like the others, while leaving his clothes of pride in their chest, he might have been the humblest of his own sergeants. But then one saw the sinewy jut-nosed face and heard him talk. And spurs jingled on his boots.

He nodded as I came into view. "Ah, there, Brother Parvus. Sit down and have a stoup. You've a head on your chine, and we need all good redes tonight."

A while longer he paced, brooding. I dared not interrupt with my dreadful news. A medley of noises in the dark deepened

38

its twin-mooned otherness. These were not frogs and crickets and nightjars of England: here was a buzz, a saw-toothed hum, an inhumanly sweet singing like a lute of steel. And the odors were alien, too, which disturbed me even more.

"Well," said my lord. "By God's grace, we've won this first encounter. Now we must decide what to do next."

"I think—" Sir Owain cleared his throat, then spoke hurriedly: "No, gentles, I am sure. God aided us against unforeseeable treachery. He will not be with us if we show undue pride. We've won a rare booty of weapons, with which we can accomplish great things at home. Let us therefore start back at once."

Sir Roger tugged his chin. "I'd liefer stay here," he answered, "yet there's much in what you say, my friend. We can always come back, after the Holy Land is freed, and do a proper job on this fiend's nest."

"Aye," nodded Sir Brian. "We're too alone now, and encumbered with women and children and aged and livestock. So few fighting men against a whole empire, that were madness."

"Yet I could like to break another spear against these Wersgorix," said Alfred Edgarson. "I haven't won any gold here yet."

"Gold is no use unless we bring it home," Captain Bullard reminded him. "Bad enough campaigning in the heat and thirst of the Holy Land. Here, we know not even what plants may be poisonous, or what the winter season is like. Best we depart tomorrow."

A rumble of assent went up among them.

I cleared my throat miserably. Branithar and I had just spent a most unpleasant hour. "My lords—" I began.

"Yes? What is it?" Sir Roger glared at me.

"My lords, I do not think we can find the way home!"

"What?" They roared it out. Several leaped to their feet. I heard Lady Catherine suck a horrified breath in between her teeth.

Then I explained that the Wersgor notes on the route to our sun were missing from the shattered control turret. I had led a search party, scratching about everywhere in the attempt to find them, but had no success. The interior of the turret was blackened, melted in places. I could only conclude that a stray fire-beam had come through the hole, played across a drawer burst open by the violence of our landing, and cindered the papers.

"But Branithar knows the way!" protested Red John. "He sailed it himself! I'll wring it out of him, my lord."

"Be not so hasty," I counseled. "'Tis not like sailing along a coastline, where every landmark is known. There are un-counted millions of stars. This scouting expedition zigagged among them looking for a suitable planet. Without figures which the captain wrote down as they sailed, one might spend a lifetime in search and not happen on our own sun."

"But doesn't Branithar remember?" yelped Sir Owain.

"Remember a hundred pages of numbers?" I responded. "Nay, none could do that, and this is the more true since Branithar was not the captain of the ship nor the one who kept track of her wanderings and heaved the log and performed other navigational duties, rather our captive was a lesser noble whose task was more among the crewmen and in working with the demonic engines than—"

"Enough." Sir Roger gnawed his lip and stared at the ground. "This changes things. Yes. . . . Was not the *Crusader*'s route known in advance? Say by the duke who sent her out?"

"No, my lord," I said. "Wersgor scoutships merely go off in any direction the captain likes and look at any star he deems promising. Not till they come back and report does their duke know where they have been."

A groan went up. Those were hardy men, but this was enough to daunt the Nine Worthies. Sir Roger walked stiffly over to his wife and laid a hand on her arm.

"I'm sorry, my dear," he mumbled.

She turned her face from him.

Sir Owain arose. The knuckles stood forth pale on the hand that clutched his harp. "This have you led us to!" he shrilled. "To death and damnation beyond the sky! Are you satisfied?"

Sir Roger clapped hand on hilt. "Be still!" he roared. "All of you agreed with my plan. Not a one of you demurred. None were forced to come. We must all share the burden now, or God pity us!"

The younger knight muttered rebelliously but sat down again.

It was awesome how swiftly my lord rebounded from dismay to boldness. Of course it was a mask he put on for the others' benefit; but how many men could have done that much? Truly he was a peerless leader. I attribute it to the blood of King William the Conqueror, a bastard grandson of whom wed an illegitimate daughter of that Earl Godfrey who was later outlawed for piracy, and so founded the noble de Tourneville house.

"Come, now," said the baron with a degree of cheerfulness. "'Tis not so bad. We've but to act with steadfast hearts, and the day shall yet be ours. Remember, we hold a good number of captives, whom we can use as a bargaining point. If we must fight again, we've already proven they cannot withstand us under anything like equal conditions. I admit there are more of them, and that they have more skill with these craven hellweapons. But what of that? 'Twill not be the first time brave men properly led have driven a seemingly stronger army from the field.

"At the very worst, we can retreat. We have sky-ships enough, and can evade pursuit in the trackless deeps of space. But I'm fain to stay here, bargain shrewdly, fight where needful, and put my trust in God. Surely He, who stopped the sun for Joshua, can swat a million Wersgorix if it pleases Him: for His mercy endureth forever. After we've wrung terms from the foe, we'll make them find our home for us and stuff our ships with gold. I say to you, hold fast! For the glory of God, the honor of England, and the enrichment of us all!"

He caught them up, bore them on the wave of his own spirit, and had them cheering him at the end. They crowded close, hands on his hands above his great shining sword, and swore to remain true till the danger was past. Thereafter an hour went in eager planning—most of it, alas, wasted, for God seldom brings that to pass which man expects. Finally all went to their rest.

I saw my lord take his wife's arm to lead her into his pavilion. She spoke to him, a harsh whisper, she would not hear his protests but stood there denouncing him in the enemy night. The larger moon, already sinking, touched them with cold fire.

Sir Roger's shoulders slumped. He turned and went slowly from her, wrapped himself in a saddle blanket, and slept in the dews of the field.

It was strange that a man among men was so helpless against a woman. He had something beaten and pitiful about him as he lay there. I thought it boded ill for us.

Chapter VIII

WE HAD been too excited at first to pay attention, and afterward we slept too long. But when I woke again, finding it still dark, I checked the movement of stars against trees. Ah, how slowly! The night here was many times as long as on Earth.

This unnerved our folk badly enough in itself. The fact that we did not flee (by now, it could no longer be concealed that treason, rather than desire, had brought us hither) puzzled many. But at least they expected weeks to carry out whatever the baron decided.

The shock, when enemy ships appeared even before dawn, was great.

"Be of good heart," I counseled Red John, as he shivered with his bowman in the gray mists. "'Tis not that they have powers magical. You were warned of this at the captains' council. 'Tis only that they can talk across hundreds of miles and fly such distances in minutes. So as soon as one of the fugitives reached another estate, the word of us went abroad."

"Well," said Red John, not unreasonably, "if that's not magic, I'd like to know what is."

"If magic, you need have no fear," I answered, "for the black arts do not prevail against good Christian men. However, I tell you again, this is mere skill in the mechanic and warlike arts."

"And those do prevail against g-g-good Christian men!" blubbered an archer. John cuffed him to silence, while I cursed my own clumsy tongue.

In that wan, tricky light, we could see many ships hovering, some of them as big as our broken *Crusader*. My knees drummed under my cassock. Of course, we were all inside the force screen of the smaller fort, which had never been turned off. Our gunners had already discovered that the fire-bombards placed here had controls as simple as any in the spaceship, and stood prepared to shoot. However, I knew we had no true defense. One of those very powerful explosive shells whereof I had heard hints could be fired. Or the Wersgorix might attack on foot, overwhelming us with sheer numbers.

42

Yet those ships did only hover, in utter silence under the unknown stars. When at length the first pale dawnlight streamed off their flanks, I left the bowmen and fumbled through dew-wet grass to the cavalry. Sir Roger sat peering heavenward from his saddle. He was armed cap-a-pie, helmet in the crook of an arm, and none could tell from his face how little sleep had been granted him.

"Good morning, Brother Parvus," he said. "That was a long darkness."

Sir Owain, mounted close by, wet his lips. He was pale, his large long-lashed eyes sunken in dark rims. "No midwinter night in England ever wore away so slowly," he said, and crossed himself.

"The more daylight, then," said Sir Roger. He seemed almost cheerful, now when he dealt with foemen rather than unruly womenfolk.

Sir Owain's voice cracked across like a dry twig. "Why don't they attack?" he yelled. "Why do they just wait up there?"

"It should be obvious. I never thought 'twould need mentioning," said Sir Roger. "Have they not good reason to be afraid of us?"

"What?" I said. "Well, sire, of course we *are* Englishmen. However—" My glance traveled back, over the pitiful few tents pitched around the fortress walls; over ragged, sooty soldiers; over huddled women and grandsires, wailing children; over cattle, pigs, sheep, fowl, tended by cursing serfs; over pots where breakfast porridge bubbled—"However, my lord," I finished, "at the moment we look more French."

The baron grinned. "What do they know about French and English? For that matter, my father was at Bannockburn, where a handful of tattered Scottish pikemen broke the chivalry of King Edward II. Now all the Wersgorix know about us is that we have suddenly come from nowhere and—if Branithar's boasts be true—done what no other host has ever achieved: taken one of their strongholds! Would you not move warily, were you their constable?"

The guffaw that went up among the horse troopers spread down to the foot, until our whole camp rocked with it. I saw how the enemy prisoners shuddered and shrank close together when that wolfish noise smote them.

As the sun rose, a few Wersgor boats landed very slowly and carefully, a mile or so away. We held our fire, so they took heart and sent out people who began to erect machinery on the field.

"Are you going to let them build a castle under our very noses?" cried Thomas Bullard.

"'Tis less likely they'll attack us, if they feel a little more secure," the baron answered. "I want it made plain that we'll parley." His smile turned wry. "Remember, friends, our best weapon now is our tongues."

Soon the Wersgorix landed many ships in a circular formation —like those stonehenges which giants raised in England before the Flood—to form a camp walled by the eerie faint shimmer of a force screen, picketed by mobile bombards, and roofed by hovering warcraft. Only when this was done did they send a herald.

The squat shape strode boldly enough across the meadows, though well aware that we could shoot him down. His metallic garments were dazzling in the morning sun, but we discerned his empty hands held open. Sir Roger himself rode forth, accompanied by myself gulping Our Fathers on a palfrey.

The Wersgor shied a trifle, as the huge black stallion and the iron tower astride it loomed above him. Then he gathered a shaky breath and said, "If you behave yourselves, I will not destroy you for the space of this discussion."

Sir Roger laughed when I had fumblingly translated. "Tell him," he ordered me, "that I in turn will hold my private lightnings in check, though they are so powerful I can't swear they may not trickle forth and blast his camp to ruin if he moves too swiftly."

"But you haven't any such lightnings at your command, sire," I protested. "It wouldn't be honest to claim you do."

"You will render my words faithfully and with a straight face, Brother Parvus," he said, "or discover something about thunderbolts."

I obeyed. In what follows I shall as usual make no note of the difficulties of translation. My Wersgor vocabulary was limited, and I daresay my grammar was ludicrous. In all events, I was only the parchment on which these puissant ones wrote, erased, and wrote again. Aye, in truth I felt like a palimpsest ere that hour was done.

Oh, the things I was forced to say! Above all men do I reverence that valiant and gentle knight Sir Roger de Tourneville. Yet when he blandly spoke of his English estate—the small one, which only took up three planets—and of his personal defense of Roncesvaux against four million paynim, and his singlehanded capture of Constantinople on a wager, and the time guesting in France when he accepted his host's invitation to exercise the *droit de seigneur* for two hundred peasant weddings on the same day—and more and more—his words nigh choked me, though I am accounted well versed both in courtly romances and the lives of the saints. My sole consolation was that little of this shameless mendacity got through the language difficulties, the Wersgor herald understanding merely (after a few attempts to impress us) that here was a person who could outbluster him any day in the week.

Therefore he agreed on behalf of his lord that there would be a truce while matters were discussed in a shelter to be erected midway between the two camps. Each side might send a score of people thither at high noon, unarmed. While the truce lasted, no ships were to be flown within sight of either camp.

"So!" exclaimed Sir Roger gaily, as we cantered back. "I've not done so ill, have I?"

"K-k-k-k," I answered. He slowed to a smoother pace, and I tried again: "Indeed, sire, St. George—or more likely, I fear, St. Dismas, patron of thieves—must have watched over you. And yet—"

"Yes?" he prompted me. "Be not afraid to speak your mind, Brother Parvus." With a kindness wholly unmerited: "Ofttimes I think you've more head on those skinny shoulders than all my captains lumped together."

"Well, my lord," I blurted, "you've wrung concessions from them for a while. As you foretold, they are being cautious whilst they study us. And yet, how long can we hope to fool them? They have been an imperial race for centuries. They must have experience of many strange peoples living under many different conditions. From our small numbers, our antiquated weapons, our lack of home-built spaceships, will they not soon deduce the truth and attack us with overwhelming force?"

His lips thinned. He looked toward the pavilion which housed his lady and children.

"Of course," he said. "I hope but to stay their hand a short while."

"And what then?" I pursued him.

"I don't know." Whirling on me, fierce as a stooping hawk, he added: "But 'tis my secret, d' you understand? I tell it to you as if in confession. Let it come out, let our folk know how troubled and planless I truly am . . . and we're all done."

I nodded. Sir Roger struck spurs to his horse and galloped into camp, shouting like a boy.

Chapter IX

URING THE long wait before Tharixan reached its noon-tide, my master summoned his captains to a council. A trestle table was erected before the central building, and there we all sat.

"By God's grace," he said, "we're spared awhile. You'll note that I've even made them land all their ships. I'll wrangle to win us as much more respite as may be. That time must be put to use. We must strengthen our defenses. Also, we'll ransack this fort, seeking especially maps, books, and other sources of information. Those of our men who're at all gifted in the mechanic arts must study and test every machine we find, so that we can learn how to erect force screens and fly and otherwise match our foes. But all this has to be done secretly, in places hidden from enemy eyes. For if ever they learn we don't already know all about such implements—" He smiled and drew a finger across his throat.

Good Father Simon, his chaplain, turned a little green. "Must you?" he said faintly.

Sir Roger nodded at him. "I've work for you, too. I shall need Brother Parvus to interpret Wersgor for me. But we have one prisoner, Branithar, who speaks Latin—"

"I would not say that, sire," I interrupted. "His declensions are atrocious, and what he does to irregular verbs may not be described in gentle company."

"Nevertheless, until he's mastered enough English, a cleric is needed to talk to him. You see, he must explain whatever our students of the captured engines do not understand, and must interpret for any other Wersgor prisoners whom we may question."

"Ah, but will he do so?" said Father Simon. "He is a most recalcitrant heathen, my son, if indeed he has any soul at all. Why, only a few days ago on the ship, in hopes of softening his hard heart, I stood in his cell reading aloud the generations from Adam to Noah, and had scarcely gotten past Jared when I saw that he had fallen asleep!"

"Have him brought hither," commanded my lord. "Also, find One-Eyed Hubert and tell him to come in full regalia."

While we waited, talking in hushed voices, Alfred Edgarson noticed how I sat quiet. "Well, now, Brother Parvus," he boomed, "what ails you? Methinks you've little to fear, being a godly fellow. Even the rest of us, if we conduct ourselves well, have naught to fear but a sweating time in purgatory. And then we'll join St. Michael at sentry-go on heaven's walls. Not so?"

I was loath to dishearten them by voicing what had occurred to me, but when they insisted, I said, "Alas, good men, worse may already have befallen us."

"Well?" barked Sir Brian Fitz-William. "What is it? Don't just sit there sniveling!"

"We had no sure way to tell time on the voyage hither," I whispered. "Hourglasses are too inaccurate, and since reaching this devil-made place we've neglected even to turn them. How long is the day here? What time is it on our earth?"

Sir Brian looked a trifle blank. "Indeed, I know not. What of it?"

"I presume you had a haunch of beef to break your fast," I said. "Are you sure it is not Friday?"

They gasped and regarded each other with round eyes.

"When is it Sunday?" I cried. "Will you tell me the date of Advent? How shall we observe Lent and Easter, with two moons morris-dancing about to confuse the issue?"

Thomas Bullard buried his face in his hands. "We're ruined!"

Sir Roger stood up. "No!" he shouted into the strickenness. "I'm no priest, nor even very godly. But did not Our Lord himself say the Sabbath was made for man and not man for the Sabbath?"

Father Simon looked doubtful. "I can grant special dispensations under extraordinary circumstances," he said, "but I am really not sure how far I can strain such powers."

"I like it not," mumbled Bullard. "I take this to be a sign that God has turned his face from us, withdrawing the due times of the fasts and sacraments."

Sir Roger grew red. He stood a moment more, watching the courage drain from his men like wine from a broken cup. Then he calmed himself, laughed aloud, and cried:

"Did not our Lord command his followers to go forth as far as they were able, bringing His word, and He would be with them always? But let's not bandy texts. Perhaps we are venially sinning in this matter. Well, if that be so, a man should not grovel but should make amends. We'll make costly offerings in atonement. To get the means for such offerings . . . have we not the entire Wersgor Empire at hand, to squeeze for ransom till its yellow eyes pop? This proves that God himself has commanded us to this war!" He drew his sword, blinding in the daylight, and held it before him hilt uppermost. "By this, my knightly sigil and arm, which is also the sign of the Cross, I vow to do battle for God's glory!"

He tossed the weapon so it swung glittering in the hot air, caught it again and swung it so it shrieked. "With this blade will I fight!"

The men gave him a rather feeble cheer. Only glum Bullard hung back. Sir Roger leaned down to that captain, and I heard him hiss: "The clinching proof of my reasoning is, that I'll cut anyone who argues further into dogmeat."

Actually, I felt that in his crude way my master had grasped truth. In my spare time I would recast his logic into proper syllogistic form, to make sure; but meanwhile I was much encouraged, and the others were at least not demoralized.

Now a man-at-arms fetched Branithar, who stood glaring at us. "Good day," said Sir Roger mildly, through me. "We shall want you to help interrogate prisoners and instruct us in our studies of captured engines."

The Wersgor drew himself up with a warrior's pride. "Save your breath," he spat. "Behead me and be done with it. I misjudged your capabilities once, and it has cost many lives of my people. I shall not betray them further."

Sir Roger nodded. "I looked for such an answer," he said. "What became of One-Eyed Hubert?"

"Here I am, sire, here I am, here's good old Hubert," and the baron's executioner hobbled up, adjusting his hood. The ax was tucked under one scrawny arm, and the noosed rope laid around his hump. "I was only wandering about, sire, picking flowers for me youngest grandchild, sire. You know her, the little girl with long gold curls and she's so honey-sweet fond

o' daisies. I hoped I could find one or other o' these paynim
blooms might remind her o' our dear Lincolnshire daisies, and
we could weave a daisy chain together—"

"I've work for you," said Sir Roger.

"Ah, yes, sire, yes, yes, indeed." The old man's single rheumy
eye blinked about, he rubbed his hands and chuckled. "Ah,
thank you, sire! 'Tis not that I mean to criticize, that ain't old
Hubert's place, and he knows his humble place, him who has
served man and boy, and his father and grandsire afore him,
executioners to the noble de Tournevilles. No, sire, I knows
me place and I keeps it as Holy Writ commands. But God's
truth, you've kept poor old Hubert very idle all these years.
Now your father, sire, Sir Raymond, him we called Raymond
Red-Hand, there was a man what appreciated art! Though I
remember his father, your grandsire, me lord, old Nevil Rip-
Talon, and his justice was the talk o' three shires. In his day,
sire, the commons knew their place and gentlefolk could get
a decent servant at a decent wage, not like now when you let
'em off with a fine or maybe a day in the stocks. Why, 'tis a
scandal—"

"Enough," said Sir Roger. "The blueface here is stubborn.
Can you persuade him?"

"Well, sire! Well, well, well!" Hubert sucked toothless gums
with a pure and simple delight. He walked around our rigid
captive, studying him from all angles. "Well, sire, now this is
another matter, 'tis like the good old days come back, 'tis, yes,
yes, yes, Heaven bless my good kind master! Now o' course I
took little equipment with me, only a few thumbscrews and
pincers and such-like, but it won't take me no time, sire, to
knock together a rack. And maybe we can get a nice kettle of
oil. I always says, sire, on a cold gray day there ain't nothing so
cozy as a glowing brazier and a nice hot kettle of oil. I think o'
my dear old daddy and I gets tears in this old eye, yes, sire, that
I do. Let me see, let me see, tum-te-tum-te-tum." He began
measuring Branithar with his rope.

The Wersgor flinched away. His smattering of English was
enough to give him the drift of conversation. "You won't!" he
yelled. "No civilized folk would ever—"

"Now let's just see your hand, if you please." Hubert took
a thumbscrew from his pouch and held it against the blue

fingers. "Yes, yes, 'twill fit snug and proper." He unpacked an array of little knives. "*Sumer is icumen in,*" he hummed, "*lhude sing cucu.*"

Branithar gulped. "But you're not civilized," he said weakly. Choking and snarling: "Very well. I will do it. Curse you for a pack of beasts! When my people have smashed you, it will be my turn!"

"I can wait," I assured him.

Sir Roger beamed. But suddenly his face fell again. The deaf old executioner was still counting over his apparatus. "Brother Parvus," said my lord, "would you . . . could you . . . break the news to Hubert? I confess I've not the heart to tell him."

I consoled the old fellow with the thought that if Branithar were caught lying, or otherwise failing to give us honest help, there would be punishment. This sent him hobbling happily off to construct a rack. I told Branithar's guard to make sure the Wersgor saw that work.

Chapter X

At last it came time for the conference. Since most of his important followers were occupied with the study of enemy materials, Sir Roger made out a full score for his party by taking their ladies along in their finest clothes. Otherwise only a few unarmed troopers, in borrowed court panoply, accompanied him and me.

As they rode across the field toward that pergolalike structure which a Wersgor machine had erected in an hour between the two camps, of some shimmering pearly material, Sir Roger said to his wife: "I would not take you into peril like this if I had any choice. 'Tis only that we must impress them with our power and wealth."

Her face remained stony, turned from him toward the vast, sinister columns of grounded ships. "I will be no more endangered there, my lord, than are my children back in the pavilion."

"God's name!" he groaned. "I was wrong. I should have left that cursed vessel alone and sent word to the King. But will you hold my mistake against me all our lives?"

"They will not be long lives, thanks to your mistake," she said.

He bridled. "You swore at the wedding—"

"Oh, yes. Have I not kept my oath? I have refused you no obedience." Her cheeks flamed. "But God alone may command my feelings."

"I won't trouble you any more," he said thickly.

This I did not hear myself. They rode ahead of us all, the wind tossing their scarlet cloaks, his plumed bonnet and the veils on her conical headdress, like a picture of the perfect knight and his love. But I set it down here, conjecturally, in light of the evil luck which followed.

Being of gentle blood, Lady Catherine controlled her manner. When we drew up at the meeting place, her delicate features showed only a cold scorn, directed at the common foe. She took Sir Roger's hand and dismounted cat-graceful. He led the way more clumsily, with stormy brows.

Inside the curtained pergola was a round table, encircled by a kind of cushioned pew. The Wersgor chiefs filled one half, their snouted blue faces unreadable to us but their eyes flickering nervously. They wore metal-mesh tunics with bronze insignia of rank. In silk and vair, golden chains, ostrich plumes, cordovan hose, slashed and puffed sleeves, curl-toed shoes, the English showed like peacocks in a hen yard. I could see that the aliens were taken aback. The contrasting plainness of my friar's habit jarred them all the worse.

I folded my hands, standing, and said in the Wersgor tongue, "For the success of this parley, as well as to seal the truce, let me offer a Paternoster."

"A what?" asked the chief of the foe. He was somewhat fat, but dignified and with a strong visage.

"Silence, please." I would have explained, but their abominable language did not seem to have any word for prayer; I had asked Branithar. "*Pater noster, qui est in coelis*," I began, while the other English knelt with me.

I heard one of the Wersgorix mutter: "See, I told you they are barbarians. It's some superstitious ritual."

"I'm not so sure," answered the chief dubiously. "The Jairs of Boda, now, have certain formulas for psychological integration. I've seen them temporarily double their strength, or stop a wound from bleeding, or go days without sleep. Control of inner organs via the nervous system. . . . And in spite of all our own propaganda against them, you know the Jairs are as scientific as we."

I heard these clandestine exchanges readily enough, yet they did not seem aware of my awareness. I remembered now that Branithar had seemed a little deaf, too. Evidently all Wersgorix had ears less acute than men. This, I learned subsequently, was because their home planet had denser air than Terra, which made them wont to hear sounds more loudly. Here on Tharixan, with air about like England, they must raise their voices to be heard. At the time, I accepted God's gift thankfully, without stopping to wonder why nor to warn the foe.

"*Amen*," I finished. We all sat down at the table.

Sir Roger stabbed the chief with bleak gray eyes. "Am I dealing with a person of suitable rank?" he asked.

I translated. "What does he mean by 'rank'?" the head Wersgor wondered. "I am the governor of this planet, and these are the primary officers of its security forces."

"He means," I said, "are you sufficiently wellborn that he will not demean himself by treating with you?"

They looked still more bewildered. I explained the concept of gentle birth as well as I could: which, with my limited vocabulary, was not well at all. We must thresh it over for quite some time before one of the aliens said to his lord:

"I believe I understand, *Grath* Huruga. If they know more than we do about the art of breeding for certain traits—" I must interpret many words new to me from context—"then they may have applied it to themselves. Perhaps their entire civilization is organized as a military force, with these carefully bred superbeings in command." He shuddered at the thought. "Of course, they wouldn't waste time talking to any creature of less intelligence."

Another officer exclaimed, "No, that's fantastic! In all our explorations, we've never found—"

"We have touched only the smallest fragment of the Via Galactica so far," Lord Huruga answered. "We dare not assume they are less than they claim to be, until we have more information."

I, who had sat listening to what they believed were whispers, favored them with my most enigmatic smile.

The governor said to me: "Our empire has no fixed ranks, but stations each person according to merit. I, Huruga, am the highest authority on Tharixan."

"Then I can treat with you until word has reached your emperor," said Sir Roger through me.

I had trouble with the word "emperor." Actually, the Wersgor domain was like nothing at home. Most wealthy, important persons dwelt on their vast estates with a retinue of blueface hirelings. They communicated on the far-speaker and visited in swift aircraft or spaceships. Then there were the other classes I have mentioned elsewhere, such as warriors, merchants, and politicians. But no one was born to his place in life. Under the law, all were equal, all free to strive as best they might for money or position. Indeed, they had even abandoned the idea of families. Each Wersgor lacked a surname, being identified by a number instead in a central registry. Male and female seldom lived together more than a few years. Children were sent at an early age to schools, where they dwelt until mature, for their parents oftener thought them an encumbrance than a blessing.

Yet this realm, in theory a republic of freemen, was in practice a worse tyranny than mankind has known, even in Nero's infamous day.

The Wersgorix had no special affection for their birthplace; they acknowledged no immediate ties of kinship or duty. As a result, each individual had no one to stand between him and the all-powerful central government. In England, when King John grew overweening, he clashed both with ancient law and with vested local interests; so the barons curbed him and thereby wrote another word or two of liberty for all Englishmen. The Wersgor were a lickspittle race, unable to protest any arbitrary decree of a superior. "Promotion according to merit" meant only "promotion according to one's usefulness to the imperial ministers."

But I digress, a bad habit for which my archbishop has often been forced to reprove me. I return, then, to that day in the place of nacre, when Huruga turned his terrible eyes on us and said: "It appears there are two varieties of you. Two species?"

"No," said one of his officers. "Two sexes, I'm sure. They are clearly mammals."

"Ah, yes." Huruga stared at the gowns across the table, cut low in shameless modern modes. "So I see."

When I had rendered this for Sir Roger, he said, "Tell them, in case they are curious, that our womenfolk wield swords side by side with the men."

"Ah." Huruga pounced on me. "That word *sword*. Do you mean a cutting weapon?"

I had no time to ask my master's advice. I prayed inwardly for steadiness and answered, "Yes. You have observed them on our persons in camp. We find them the best tool for hand-to-hand combat. Ask any survivor of the Ganturath garrison."

"Mmm . . . yes." One of the Wersgorix looked grim. "We have neglected the tactics of infighting for centuries, *Grath* Huruga. There seemed no need for them. But I do remember one of our unofficial border clashes with the Jairs. It was out on Uloz IV, and they used long knives to wicked effect."

"For special purposes . . . yes, yes." Huruga scowled. "However, the fact remains that these invaders prance around on live animals—"

"Which need not be fueled, *Grath*, save by vegetation."

"But which could not endure a heat beam or a pellet. They wave weapons out of the prehistoric past. They come not in their own ships, but in one of ours—" He broke off his murmur and barked at me:

"See here! I've delayed long enough. Yield to our judgment, or we shall destroy you."

I interpreted. "The force screen protects us from your flame weapons," said Sir Roger. "If you wish to attack on foot, we shall make you welcome."

Huruga turned purple. "Do you imagine a force screen will stop an explosive shell?" he roared. "Why, we could lob just one, let it burst inside your screen, and wipe out every last creature of you!"

Sir Roger was less taken aback than I. "We've already heard rumors of such bursting weapons," he said to me. "Of course, he's trying to frighten us with that talk of a single shot being enough. No ship could lift so great a mass of gunpowder. Does he take me for a yokel who'll believe any tinker's yarn? However, I grant he could fire many explosive barrels into our camp."

"So what shall I tell him?" I asked fearfully.

The baron's eyes gleamed. "Render this very exactly, Brother Parvus: 'We are holding back our own artillery of this sort because we wish to talk with you, not merely kill you. If you insist on bombarding us, though, please commence. Our defenses will thwart you. Remember, however, that we are not going to keep our Wersgor prisoners inside those defenses!'"

I saw that this threat shook them. Even these hard hearts would not willingly kill some hundreds of their own people. Not that the hostages we held would stop them forever; but it was a bargaining point, which might gain us time. I wondered how we could possibly use that time, though, save to prepare our souls for death.

"Well, now," huffed Huruga, "I didn't imply I was not ready to hear you out. You have not yet told us why you have come in this unseemly, unprovoked manner."

"It was you who attacked us first, who had never harmed you," answered Sir Roger. "In England we give no dog more than one bite. My king dispatched me to teach you a lesson."

Huruga: "In one ship? Not even your own ship?"

Sir Roger: "I do not believe in bringing more than is necessary."

Huruga: "For the sake of argument, what are your demands?"

Sir Roger: "Your empire must make submission to my most puissant lord of England, Ireland, Wales, and France."

Huruga: "Let us be serious, now."

Sir Roger: "I am serious to the point of solemnity. But in order to spare further bloodshed, I'll meet any champion you name, with any weapons, to settle the issue by single combat. And may God defend the right!"

Huruga: "Are you all escaped from some mental hospital?"

Sir Roger: "Consider our position. We've suddenly discovered you, a heathen power, with arts and arms akin to ours though inferior. You could do a certain amount of harm to us, harassing our shipping or raiding our less firmly held planets. This would necessitate your extermination, and we're too merciful to enjoy that. The only sensible thing is to accept your homage."

Huruga: "And you honestly expect to— A hatful of beings, mounted on animals and swinging swords—bub-bub-bub-bub—"

He went into colloquy with his officers. "This confounded translation problem!" he complained. "I'm never sure if I've understood them aright. They *could* be a punitive expedition, I suppose. For reasons of military secrecy, they *could* have used one of our own ships and kept their most potent weapons in reserve. It doesn't make sense. But neither does it make sense that barbarians would blandly tell the most powerful realm in the known universe to surrender its autonomy. Unless it's mere bluster. But we may be completely misunderstanding their demands . . . and thereby misjudging them, perhaps to our own serious loss. Hasn't anyone got any ideas?"

Meanwhile I said to Sir Roger, "You aren't serious about this, my lord?"

Lady Catherine could not resist saying: "He would be."

"Nay." The baron shook his head. "Of course not. What

would King Edward do with a lot of unruly bluefaces? The
Irish are bad enough. Nay, I hope only to let myself be bar-
gained down. If we can wring from them some guarantee to let
Terra alone—and perhaps a few coffers of gold for ourselves—"

"And guidance home," I said gloomily.

"That's a riddle we must think on later," he snapped. "No
time now. Certainly we dare not admit to the enemy that we're
waifs."

Huruga turned back to us. "You must realize your demand
is preposterous," he said. "However, if you can demonstrate
that your realm is worth the trouble, our emperor will be glad
to receive an ambassador from it."

Sir Roger yawned and said languidly, through me: "Spare
your insults. My monarch will receive your emissary, perhaps,
if that person adopts the true Faith."

"What is this *Faith*?" asked Huruga, for again I must use an
English word.

"The true belief, of course," I said. "The facts about Him
who is the source of all wisdom and righteousness, and to
whom we humbly pray for guidance."

"What's he babbling about now, *Grath*?" muttered an officer.

"I don't know," Huruga whispered back. "Perhaps these,
uh, English maintain some kind of giant computing engine to
which they submit the important questions for decision. . . .
I don't know. Confounded translation problem! Best we delay awhile. Watch them, their behavior; mull over what we've
heard."

"And dispatch a message to Wersgorixan?"

"No, you fool! Not yet, not till we know more. Do you want
the main office to think we can't handle our own problems? If
these really are mere barbarian pirates, can you imagine what
would happen to all our careers if we called in the whole navy?"

Huruga turned to me and said aloud: "We have ample time
for discussion. Let us adjourn until tomorrow, and think well
in the meantime on every implication."

Sir Roger was glad of that. "Let's make certain of the truce
terms, though," he added.

I was getting more facility in the Wersgor language with every hour, so I was soon able to elucidate that their concept of

a truce was not ours. Their insatiable hunger for land made them the enemy of all other races, so they could not imagine a binding oath exchanged with anyone not blue and tailed.

The armistice was no formal agreement at all, but a statement of temporary mutual convenience. They declared that they did not at present find it expedient to fire on us, even when we grazed our kine beyond the force screen. This condition would prevail as long as we refrained from attacking any of them who moved about in the open. For fear of espionage and missile dropping, neither side wished the other to fly within view of the camps, and would shoot at any vessel which lifted. That was all. They would surely violate this if they decided it was to their interest; they would work us harm if they saw any method of doing so; and they expected us to feel likewise.

"They have the better of it, sire," I mourned. "All our flying craft are here. Now we can't even jump into our spaceships and flee; they'd pounce ere we could elude pursuit. Whereas they have many other ships, elsewhere on the planet, which may hover freely beyond the horizon and be ready to assail us when the time comes."

"Nevertheless," said Sir Roger, "I perceive certain advantages. This business of neither giving nor expecting pledges —aye—"

"It suits you," murmured Lady Catherine.

He whitened, leaped to his feet, bowed at Huruga, and led us out.

Chapter XI

THE LONG afternoon allowed our people to make considerable progress. With Branithar to instruct them, or to interpret for those prisoners who understood the art in question, the English soon mastered the controls of many devices. They practiced with spaceships and small flying vessels, being careful to raise these only a few inches off the ground, lest the foe observe it and shoot. They also drove about in horseless wagons; they learned to use far-speakers, magnifying optical devices, and other esoterica; they handled weapons that threw fire, or metal, or invisible stunning beams. Of course we English had, as yet, learned to use far-speakers, magnifying optical devices, and no inkling of the occult knowledge which had gone into making such things. But we found them childishly simple to use. At home, we harnessed animals, wound intricate crossbows and catapults, rigged sailing ships, erected machines by which human muscles might raise heavy stones. This business of twisting a wheel or pulling a lever was naught in comparison. The only real difficulty was for unlettered yeomen to remember what the symbols on the gauges stood for —and this, indeed, was no more complicated a science than heraldry, which any hero-worshiping lad could rattle off in detail.

Being the only person with pretensions to reading the Wersgor alphabet, I busied myself with papers seized in the fortress offices. Meanwhile Sir Roger conferred with his captains and directed the most oafish serfs, who could not learn the new weapons, in certain construction work. The slow sunset was burning, turning half the sky gold, when he summoned me to his council board.

I seated myself and looked at those gaunt hard faces. They were animated with fresh hope. My tongue clove to my mouth. Well I knew these captains. Most of all did I know how Sir Roger's eyes danced—when hell was being hatched!

"Have you learned what and where the principal castles of this planet are, Brother Parvus?" he asked me.

"Yes, sire," I told him. "There are but three, of which Ganturath was one."

"I can't believe that!" exclaimed Sir Owain Montbelle. "Why, pirates alone would—"

"You forget there are no separate kingdoms here, or even separate fiefs," I answered. "All persons are directly subservient to the imperial government. The fortresses are only lodging for the sheriffs, who keep order among the populace and collect the taxes. True, these fortresses are also supposed to be defensive bases. They include docks for the great star ships, and warriors are stationed there. But the Wersgorix have fought no true war for a long time. They've merely bullied helpless savages. None of the other star-traveling races dare declare open war on them; only now and then does a skirmish occur on some remote planet. In short, three fortresses are ample for this whole world."

"How strong are they?" snapped Sir Roger.

"There is one hight Stularax, on the other side of the globe, which is about like Ganturath. Then there is the main fortress, Darova, where this proconsul Huruga dwells. That one is by far the largest and strongest. I daresay it supplied most of the ships and warriors we see facing us."

"Where is the next world inhabited by bluefaces?"

"According to a book I studied, about twenty light-years hence. Wersgorixan itself, the capital planet, is much further off than that—farther away than Terra, even."

"But the far-speaker would inform their emperor at once of what's happened, would it not?" asked Captain Bullard.

"No," I said. "The far-speaker acts only as fast as light. Messages between the stars must go by spaceship, which means that it would take a brace of weeks to inform Wersgorixan. Not that Huruga has done so. I overheard him speak to one of his court, to say they would keep this affair secret awhile."

"Aye," said Sir Brian Fitz-William. "The duke will seek to redeem himself for what we have done, by crushing us unaided ere he reports anything whatsoever. 'Tis a common enough way of thinking."

"If we hurt him badly enough, though, he'll scream for help," prophesied Sir Owain.

"Just so," agreed Sir Roger. "And I've thought of a way to hurt him!"

I realized gloomily that when my tongue had cloven to my mouth it knew what it was doing.

"How can we fight?" asked Bullard. "We've no amount of devil-weapons to compare with what sits out on yon field. If need be, they could ram us, boat for boat, and count it no great loss."

"For which reason," Sir Roger told him, "I propose a raid on the smaller fort, Stularax, to gain more weapons. 'Twill also jar Huruga out of his confidence."

"Or jar him into attacking us."

"'Tis a chance we must take. Come worst to worst, I'm not altogether terrified of another fight. See you not, our *only* chance is to act with boldness."

There was no great demurral. Sir Roger had had hours in which to jolly his folk. They were ready enough to accept his leadership again. But Sir Brian objected sensibly: "How can we effect any such raid? Yon castle lies thousands of miles hence. We cannot flit thither from our camp without being fired upon."

Sir Owain raised mocking brows. "Mayhap you've a magic horse?" He smiled at Sir Roger.

"No. Another sort of beast. Hearken to me. . . ."

That was a long night's work for the yeomen. They put skids under one of the smaller spaceboats, hitched oxen to it, and dragged it forth as quietly as might be. Its passage across open fields was disguised by driving cattle around it, as if grazing them. Under cover of darkness, and by God's grace, the ruse was sufficient. Once beneath the tall thick-crowned trees, with a screen of scouts who moved like shadows to warn of any blue soldiers—"They had the practice for it, poaching at home," said Red John—the work was safer but also more hard. Not until nearly dawn was the boat several miles from camp, so far off that it could lift without being seen from Huruga's field headquarters.

Though the largest vessel which could possibly be moved thus, it was still too small to carry the most formidable weapons. However, Sir Roger had during the day examined the explosive shells fired by certain types of gun. He had had it explained to him by a terrified Wersgor engineer, how to arm the fuse thereon, so that it would go off on impact. The boat carried several of these—also a disassembled trebuchet which his artisans had constructed.

Meanwhile, everyone not toiling with this was set to work strengthening our camp defenses. Even women and children were given shovels. Axes rang in the near-by forest. Long as the night was, it seemed even longer when we labored thus exhaustingly, stopping only to snatch a piece of bread or a wink of sleep. The Wersgorix observed that we were busy—it could not be avoided—but we tried to conceal from them what we actually did, lest they see we were merely ringing the lesser half of Ganturath with stakes, pits, caltrops, and chevaux-de-frise. When morning came, with full daylight, our installations were hidden from view by the long grass.

I myself welcomed such backbreaking labor as a surcease from my fears. Yet my mind must worry them, like a dog with a bone. Was Sir Roger mad? There seemed to be so many things he had done awry. Yet, to each successive question, I found only the same answer as himself.

Why had we not fled the moment we possessed Ganturath, instead of waiting till Huruga arrived and pinned us down? Because we had lost the way home and had no chance whatsoever of finding it without the help of skilled space sailors. (If it could be found at all.) Death was better than a blind blundering among the stars—where our ignorance would soon kill us anyway.

Having gained a truce, why did Sir Roger run the gravest risk of its immediate breach by this attack on Stularax? Because it was plain the truce could not last very long. Given time to ponder what he had observed, Huruga must see through our pretensions and destroy us. Thrown off balance by our boldness, he might well continue to believe us more powerful than was the truth. Or if he elected to fight, we should have our hands strengthened by whatever arms were seized in the forthcoming raid.

But did Sir Roger seriously expect so mad a plan to succeed? Only God and himself could answer that. I knew he was improvising as he went along. He was like a runner who stumbles and must all at once run even faster so as not to fall.

But how splendidly he ran!

That reflection soothed me. I committed my fate to Heaven and shoveled with a more peaceful heart.

Just before dawn, as mist streamed among buildings and tents and long-snouted fire-bombards, under the first thin light creeping up the sky, Sir Roger saw his raiders off. They were twenty: Red John with the best of our yeomen, and Sir Owain Montbelle as chief. It was curious how that knight's often faint heart always revived at the prospect of action. He was almost gay as a boy when he stood there wrapped in a long scarlet cloak, listening to his orders.

"Go through the woods, keeping well under cover, to where the boat lies," my lord told him. "Wait till noon, then fly off. You know how to use those unrolling maps for guide, eh? Well, then, when you come to this Stularax place—'twill take an hour or so if you fly at what seems a reasonable speed hereabouts —land where you have cover. Give it a few shells from the trebuchet to reduce the outer defenses. Dash in afoot, while they're still confused; seize what you can from the arsenals, and return. If all is still peaceful hereabouts, lie quietly. If fighting has broken out, well, do what seems best."

"Indeed, sire." Sir Owain clasped his hand. That gesture was not fated to occur between them again.

As they stood there under darkling skies, a voice called: "Wait." All the men turned their faces toward the inner buildings, where mist smoked thickly. Out of it came the Lady Catherine.

"I have only now heard you were going," she said to Sir Owain. "Must you—twenty men against a fortress?"

"Twenty men—" He bowed, with a smile that lit his face like the sun—"and myself, and the memory of you, my lady!"

The color crept up her pale countenance. She walked past a stone-stiff Sir Roger, to the younger knight, till she stood gazing up at him. All saw that her hands bled. She held a cord in them.

"After I could no more lift a spade this night," she whispered, "I helped twine bowstrings. I can give you no other token."

Sir Owain accepted it in a great silence. Having laid it within his shirt of chain mail, he kissed her scarred small fingers.

Straightening, his cloak aswirl about him, he led his yeomen into the forest.

Sir Roger had not moved. Lady Catherine nodded a little. "And you are going to sit at table today with the Wersgorix?" she asked him.

She slipped away in the fog, back toward the pavilion which he no longer shared. He waited until she was quite out of sight before following.

Chapter XII

OUR PEOPLE made good use of the long morning to rest themselves. By now I could read Wersgor clocks, though not precisely sure how their units of time compared to Terrestrial hours. At high noon I mounted my palfrey and met Sir Roger to go to the conference. He was alone. "Methought we were to be a score," I faltered.

His countenance was wooden. "No more reason for that," he said. "It may go ill for us in yon rendezvous, when Huruga learns of the raid. I'm sorry I must hazard you."

I was sorry, too, but wished not to spend time in self-pity which could be more usefully devoted to telling my beads.

The same Wersgor officers awaited us within the pearly curtains. Huruga looked his surprise as we trod in. "Where are your other negotiators?" he asked sharply.

"At their prayers," I replied, which was belike true enough.

"There goes that word again," grumbled one of the blueskins. "What does it *mean*?"

"Thus." I illustrated by saying an Ave and marking it off on my rosary.

"Some kind of calculating machine, I think," said another Wersgor. "It may not be as primitive as it looks on the outside, either."

"But what does it calculate?" whispered a third one, his ears raised straight up with uneasiness.

Huruga glared. "This has gone far enough," he snapped. "All night you were at work over there. If you plan some trick—"

"Don't you wish you had a plan?" I interrupted in my most Christianly sweet voice.

As I hoped, this insolence rocked him back. We sat down.

After chewing on it a moment, Huruga exclaimed: "About your prisoners. I am responsible for the safety of residents of this planet. I cannot possibly treat with creatures who hold Wersgorix captive. The first condition of any further negotiations must be their immediate release."

"'Tis a shame we cannot negotiate, then," said Sir Roger via myself. "I don't really want to destroy you."

"You shall not leave this place until those captives are delivered to me," said Huruga. I gasped. He smiled coldly. "I have soldiers on call, in case you, too, brought something like this." He reached in his tunic and pulled out a pellet-throwing handgun. I stared down the muzzle and gulped.

Sir Roger yawned. He buffed his nails on a silken sleeve. "What did he say?" he asked me.

I told him. "Treachery," I groaned. "We were all supposed to be unarmed."

"Nay, remember no oaths were sworn. But tell his disgrace Duke Huruga that I foresaw this chance, and carry my own protection." The baron pressed the ornate seal ring on his finger, and clenched his fist. "I have cocked it now. If my hand unclasps for any reason before 'tis uncocked again, the stone will burst with enough force to send us all flying past St. Peter."

Through clattering teeth, I got this mendacious message out. Huruga sprang to his feet. "Is this true?" he roared.

"I-i-indeed it is," I said. "B-b-by Mahomet I swear it."

The blue officers huddled together. From their frantic whispers I gathered that a bombshell as tiny as that sealstone was possible in theory; though no race known to the Wersgorix were skillful enough to make one.

Calm prevailed at last. "Well," said Huruga, "it looks like an impasse. I myself think you're lying, but do not care to risk my life." He slipped the little gun back in his tunic. "However, you must realize this is an impossible situation. If I can't obtain the release of those prisoners myself, I shall be forced to refer this whole matter to the Imperium on Wersgorixan."

"You need not be so hasty," Sir Roger told him. "We'll keep our hostages carefully. You may send chirurgeons to look after their health. To be sure, we must ask you to sequestrate all your armament, as a guarantee of good faith. But in return, we'll mount guard against the Saracens."

"The what?" Huruga wrinkled his bony forehead.

"The Saracens. Heathen pirates. You've not encountered them? I find that hard to believe, for they range widely. Why, at this very minute a Saracen ship could be descending on your own planet, to pillage and burn—"

Huruga jerked. He pulled an officer aside and whispered to

him. This time I could not follow what was said. The officer hurried out.

"Tell me more," said Huruga.

"With pleasure." The baron leaned back in his seat, at cross-legged ease. I could never have achieved his calm. As nearly as I could gauge, Sir Owain's boat must now be at Stularax; for recall how much slower this conversation was than I have written it, with all the translation, the pauses to explain some uncomprehended word, the search for a telling phrase.

Yet Sir Roger spun out his yarn as if he had eternity. He explained that we English had fallen so savagely upon the Wersgorix because their unprovoked attack led us to think they must be new allies of the Saracens. Now that we understood otherwise, it was possible that in time England and Wersgorixan could reach agreement, alliance against this common menace. . . .

The blue officer dashed back inside. Through the door flap I saw soldiery in the alien camp hurrying to their posts; a roar of awakening machines came to my ears.

"Well?" Huruga barked at his underling.

"Reports—the far-speaker—outlying homes saw bright flash —Stularax gone—must have been a shell of the superpowered type—" The fellow blurted it out between his pantings.

Sir Roger exchanged a look with me as I translated. Stularax gone? Utterly destroyed?

Our aim had only been to reave some more weapons, especially light portable ones for our men-at-arms. But if everything had vanished in smoke . . .

Sir Roger licked dry lips. "Tell him the Saracens must have landed, Brother Parvus," he said.

Huruga gave me no chance. Breast heaving with wrath, amber eyes turned blood-red, he stood shaking, pulled out his handgun again and screamed: "No more of this farce! Who else was with you? How many more spaceships have you?"

Sir Roger uncoiled himself, till he loomed above the stumpy Wersgorix like an oak on a heath. He grinned, touched his signet ring meaningfully, and said: "Well, now, you can't expect me to reveal that. Perhaps I'd best return to my own camp, till your temper has cooled."

I could not phrase it so smoothly in my halting words. Huruga snarled: "Oh, no! Here you stay!"

"I go." Sir Roger shook his close-cropped head. "Incidentally, if for any reason I don't return, my men have orders to kill all the prisoners."

Huruga heard me out. With a self-mastery I admired, he replied: "Go, then. But when you are back, we shall attack you. I do not propose to be caught between your camp on the ground and your friends in the sky."

"The hostages," Sir Roger reminded him.

"We shall attack," repeated Huruga doggedly. "It will be entirely with ground forces—partly to spare those same prisoners, and partly, of course, because every spaceship and aircraft must get aloft and search for those attackers of Stularax. We will also refrain from using high-explosive weapons, lest we destroy the captives. *But*—" He stabbed a finger down upon the table. "Unless your weapons are far superior to what I think, we will overwhelm you with sheer numbers, if nothing else. I don't believe you even have any armored wagons, only a few light ground cars captured at Ganturath. Remember, after the battle, such of your folk as survive will be our prisoners. If you have harmed a single one of those Wersgorix you hold, your people will die, very slowly. If you yourself are caught alive, Sir Roger de Tourneville, you will watch all of them die before you do yourself."

The baron heard me render this for him. The lips were very pale in his sunburned face. "Well, Brother Parvus," he said in rather a small voice, "it's not worked out as well as I hoped —though perhaps not quite as badly as I feared. Tell him that if he will indeed let us two return safely, and confine his attack to ground forces, and avoid high-explosive shells, our hostages shall be safe from anything but his own fire."

He added wryly: "I don't think I could have made myself butcher helpless captives anyhow. But you need not tell him that."

Huruga merely jerked his head, an icy gesture, when I gave him the message. We two humans left, swung into the saddle and turned back. We held our horses to a walk, to prolong the truce and the feel of sunlight on our faces.

"What happened at that Stularax castle, sire?" I whispered.

"I know not," said Sir Roger. "But I'll hazard that the blue-faces spoke truly—and I didn't believe it!—when they said one of their more powerful shells could wipe out an encampment. So the weapons we hoped to steal are gone. I can only pray that our poor raiders were not also caught in the blast. Now we can but defend ourselves."

He raised his plumed head. "Yet Englishmen have ever fought best with their backs to the wall."

Chapter XIII

So we rode into camp, and my lord shouted haro as if this battle had been his dearest wish. In a great iron clangor, our folk went to their stations.

Let me describe our situation more fully. As a minor base, Ganturath was not built to withstand the most powerful forces of war. The lesser portion, which we occupied, consisted of several low masonry buildings arranged in a circle. Outside that circle were the armored emplacements of the fire-bombards; but these, being meant only to shoot upward at skycraft, were useless to us now. Underground was a warren of rooms and passages. There we put our children, aged, prisoners, and cattle, in charge of a few armed serfs. Such older people, or others not fit for combat, as were spry enough, waited near the middle of the buildings, prepared to carry off the wounded, fetch beer, and otherwise aid the fighting line.

This line stood on the side facing the Wersgor camp, just within the low earthen wall erected during the night. Their pikes, bills, and axes were reinforced at intervals by squads of bowmen. The cavalry poised at either wing. Behind them were the younger women and certain untrained men, who shared out our all too few pellet weapons; the force screen made fire guns useless.

Around us shimmered the pale heat-lightning of that shield. Behind us rose the ancient forest. Before us, bluish grass rippled down the valley, isolated trees soughed, and clouds walked above the distant hills. It all had the eerie loveliness of a landscape in Faerie. Preparing bandages with the aboveground noncombatants, I wondered why there must be hatred and killing in so sweet a realm.

Flying craft thundered skyward and out of sight from the Wersgor camp. Our gunners dropped a few ere they were all gone. A number remained on the ground, held in reserve. They included some of the very largest transport ships. At the moment, however, my chief interest was the ground.

Wersgorix streamed forth, armed with long-barreled pellet weapons and in well-ordered squads. They did not advance in close ranks but scattered as much as possible. Some of our folk let out a cheer at this, but I knew it must be their ordinary ground-fighting tactics. When one has deadly rapid-fire guns, one does not attack in solid masses. Rather, one employs devices to take the enemy's guns out of action.

Such engines were in fact present. Doubtless they had been flown hither from the central bastion of Darova. There were two kinds of these horseless war-wagons. The most numerous sort was light and open, made of thin steel, holding four soldiers and a couple of rapid-fire weapons. They ran immensely fast and agile, like water beetles on four wheels. As I saw them whip and scream about, bouncing at a hundred miles an hour over broken terrain, I understood their purpose: to be so difficult to hit that most of them could work up to the very bombards of the foe.

However, these small cars hung back, covering the Wersgor infantry. The first line of actual attack was the heavy-armored vehicles. These moved but slowly for a powered machine, no faster than a horse could gallop. This was because of their size —big as a peasant's cottage—and the thick steel plating which could withstand all but a direct shellburst. With bombards projecting from their turrets, with their roaring and dust, they were like unto dragons. I counted more than twenty: massive, impervious, grinding forward on treads in a wide line. Where they had passed, grass and earth were smashed into stone-hard ruts.

I am told that one of our gunners, who had learned how to use the wheeled cannon which threw explosive shells, broke ranks and dashed for such a weapon. Sir Roger himself, now armed cap-a-pie, rode up and knocked him asprawl with his lance. "Hold on, there!" rapped the baron. "What're you about?"

"To shoot, sire," gasped the soldier. "Let's fire at 'em ere they break over our wall and—"

"If I didn't think our good yew bows could deal with such overgrown snails, I'd have you priming yon tube," said my lord. "But as it is, back to your pike!"

It had a salutary effect on the badly shaken spearmen, who stood with weapons grounded to receive that frightful charge. Sir Roger saw no reason to explain that (judging from what had happened at Stularax) he dared not use explosives at such short range, lest he destroy us, too. Of course, he should have realized that the Wersgorix would have many kinds of shell of graded potency. But who can think of everything at once?

As it was, the drivers of those moving fortresses must have been sorely puzzled that we did not fire on them, and wondered what we held in reserve. They found out when the first war-wagon toppled into one of our covered pits.

Two more were similarly trapped ere it was understood that these were no ordinary obstacles. Surely the good saints had aided us. In our ignorance, we had dug holes broad and deep, which by themselves would not have been escape-proof for such powerful vehicles. But then we added great wooden stakes, almost by sheer habit, as if we expected to impale outsize horses. Some of these caught in the treads which girdled the wheels, and erelong those wheels were jammed tight with wood pulp.

Another wagon evaded the pits, which were not continuous. It approached the breastworks. A rapid-fire gun spat from it, seeking the range, and stitched small craters along our earth wall. "God send the right!" roared Sir Brian Fitz-William. His horse spurted from our lines, closely followed by half a dozen of the nearer cavalrymen. They galloped in a semicircle, just beyond reach of the gun. The vehicle lumbered in pursuit, seeking to bring its smallest-bore cannon to bear. Sir Brian got it headed the way he desired, winded his war-horn, and galloped back to shelter as the wagon plunged into a hole.

The war-turtles drew back. In that long grass, and with our cunning camouflage, they had no way of knowing where the other traps were. And these were the only such machines on all Tharixan, not to be lightly hazarded. We English had trembled lest they continue. Only one would have had to get through to wipe us out.

Even though his information about us, our powers, and our possible spaceborne reinforcements was scanty, I think Huruga should have ordered the heavy wagons onward. Indeed, the Wersgor tactics were deplorable in all respects. But remember that for a long time they had not fought seriously on the ground. Their conquest of backward planets was a mere battue; their skirmishes with rival starfaring nations were mostly aerial.

Thus Huruga, discouraged by our pits but heartened by our failure to use low-power shellfire, withdrew the great cars. Instead, he sent the infantry and the light vehicles against us. His idea was plainly for them to find a path between our traps and mark it for the giant machines to follow.

The blue soldiers came at a run, scarcely visible through the tall grass, divided into little squads. I myself, being placed far back, saw only the occasional flash of a helmet and the poles which they stuck up here and there to mark a safe channel for the heavy wagons. Yet I knew they numbered many thousands. My heart thudded within me, and my mouth longed for a beaker of ale.

Ahead of the soldiers came racing the light cars. A few of them went into pits and at such speeds were horribly wrecked. But most sped in a straight line—straight into the stakes we had planted in the grass near our breastworks, in case of a cavalry charge.

So fast were they traveling, the cars were almost as vulnerable to such a defense as horses would be. I saw one rise in the air, turn over, smash back to earth, and bounce twice ere it broke apart. I saw another impale itself, spout liquid fuel, and burst into flame. I saw a third swerve, skid, and crash into a fourth.

Several more, escaping the abatis, ran over the caltrops we had scattered around. The iron spikes entered the soft rings encircling their wheels and were not to be gotten out. A car so injured could at best limp feebly from the battle.

Commands in the harsh Wersgor tongue must have rattled over the far-speaker. The majority of the open cars, still unscathed, ceased to mill about. They drew into a loose but orderly formation, and advanced at a walking pace.

Snap! went our catapults and *crash!* went our ballistae. Bolts, stones, and pots of burning oil hailed atrociously among the advancing vehicles. Not many were thus disabled, but their line wavered and slowed.

Then our cavalry charged.

A few of our horsemen died, caught in a storm of lead. But they had not far to gallop to reach the enemy. Also, the grass fires started by our oil pots confused Wersgor vision with their heavy smoke. I heard a clang and boom as lances burst against iron sides, then had no more chance to watch that struggle. I know only that the lancers failed to disable any car with their shafts. However, it startled the drivers so much that these often failed completely to defend themselves against what followed. Rearing horses brought down hoofs, to crumple the thin steel plates; a few quick swipes of ax, mace, or sword emptied a vehicle of its crew. Some of Sir Roger's men used handguns to good effect, or small round shells which burst and scattered jagged fragments when thrown after a pin was released. The Wersgorix had similar weapons, of course, but less determination to use them.

The last cars fled in terror, hotly pursued by the English riders. "Come back, there!" bellowed Sir Roger at them. He shook the fresh lance given him by his esquire. "Come back, you caitiff rogues! Stand and deliver, you base-born heathen!" He must have been a splendid sight, gleaming metal and fluttering plumage and blazoned shield upon the restless coal-black stallion. But the Wersgorix were not a knightly folk. They were more prudent and forethoughtful than we. It cost them dearly.

Our horsemen must quickly retreat, for now the blue foot was close, firing their guns as they pulled into larger masses for the assault on our breastworks. Armor was no protection, only a bright target. Sir Roger bugled his men to follow him, and they scattered out onto the plain.

The Wersgorix set up a defiant cheer and rushed. Across the seething confusion of our camp, I heard the archer captains howl their command. Then the gray goose flock went skyward with a noise as of mighty winds.

It came down, gruesomely, among the Wersgorix. While the first arrow flight was still rising, the second was on its way. A shaft with so much force behind it pierces the body and comes out on the other side with its broad cutting head all bloody. And now the crossbows, slower but still more powerful, began to mow down the nearest attackers. I think that during those last few moments of their charge, the Wersgorix must have lost half their folk.

Nonetheless, dogged almost as Englishmen, they ran on to our very wall. And here our common men-at-arms stood to receive them. The women fired and fired, pinning down a goodly part of the foe. Those who came so close that guns were useless, must face ax, spear, billhook, mace, morningstar, dagger, and broadsword.

Despite their awesome losses, the Wersgorix still outnumbered our folk two or three to one. Yet it was scarcely fair. They had no body armor. Their only weapon for such close-in fighting was a knife attached to the muzzle of the handgun, to make a most awkward spear . . . or the gun itself, clubbed. A few did carry pellet-firing sidearms, which caused us some casualties. But as a rule, when John Blueface fired at Harry Englishman, he missed even at pointblank range, in all that turmoil. Before John could fire again, Harry had laid him open with a halberd.

When our cavalry returned, striking the Wersgor infantry from the rear and hewing away, it was the end. The enemy broke and ran, trampling his own comrades in blind horror. The riders chased them, with merry hunting calls. When they were far enough away, our longbows cut loose once more.

Still, many escaped who must otherwise have been spitted on a lance, for Sir Roger saw the heavy wagons trundling vengefully back and retreated with his folk. By God's mercy, I was so occupied caring for the wounded fetched to me that I knew nothing of that moment when our leaders thought we were undone after all. For the Wersgor charge had not gone for naught. It had succeeded in showing the turtle-cars how to avoid our pits. And now the iron giants came across a field turned into red mud, and naught we knew could stop them.

Thomas Bullard's shoulders slumped where he sat mounted near the baronial pennon. "Well," he sighed, "we gave what was ours to give. Now who will ride out with me to show them how Englishmen can die?"

Sir Roger's weary face drew into grave lines. "We've a harder task than that, friends," he said. "We were right to hazard our lives on a chance of victory. Now that we see defeat upon us, we've no right to throw those lives away. We must live—as slaves, if need be—so that our women and babes are not altogether alone on this hell-world."

"God's bones!" shouted Sir Brian Fitz-William. "Are you gone craven?"

The baron's nostrils flared. "You heard me," he said. "We stay here."

And then—lo! It was as if God Himself had come to deliver His poor sinful partisans. Brighter than lightning, a blue-white flash burst, several miles off in the forest. So lurid was the radiance that those few who chanced to be looking in that direction were blind for hours afterward. No doubt a great many Wersgorix were thus incapacitated, since their army faced it. The roar that followed knocked riders from their saddles and men from their feet. A wind swept us all, furnace hot, and carried tents before it like blown rags. Then, as that shattering wrath departed, we saw a cloud of dust and smoke arise. Shaped like an evil mushroom, it towered almost to heaven. Minutes passed before it began to dissipate; its upper clouds lingered for hours.

The charging war-cars ground to a halt. They knew, as we did not, what that burst signified. It was a shell of the ultimate potency, that destruction of matter which I cannot but feel to this day is an impious tampering with God's work, though my archbishop has cited me Scriptural texts to prove that any art is lawful if it be used for good purposes.

This was not a very strong shell, as such weapons go. It was meant to annihilate a half-mile circle, and produced comparatively little of those subtle poisons which accompany such explosions. And it had been fired distantly enough from the scene of action to harm no one.

Yet it put the Wersgorix in a cruel dilemma. If they used a similar weapon to wipe out our camp—if they overran us by any means—they might expect a hail of death. For the hidden bombard would have no further reason to spare the area of Ganturath. Thus they must suspend their assault upon us, until they had found and dealt with this new enemy.

Their war-wagons lumbered back. Most of the aircraft they had in reserve lifted and scattered widely, searching for whoever had fired that shell. The chief implement of this search was (as we knew from our own studies) a device embodying the same forces as are found in lodestone. Through powers which I do not understand, and have no desire to understand since the knowledge is unessential to salvation if not smacking of the black arts, this device could smell out large metallic masses. A gun big enough to fire a shell of the known potency should have been discovered by any aircraft flitting within a mile of its hiding place.

Yet no such gun could be located. After a tense hour, while we English watched and prayed on our walls, Sir Roger gusted a deep breath.

"I don't want to seem ungrateful," he said, "but I do believe God's helped us through Sir Owain, rather than directly. We ought to find his party somewhere out in the woods, even if those enemy flyers don't seem able to. Father Simon, you must know who the best poachers are in your parish—"

"Oh, my son!" exclaimed the chaplain.

Sir Roger grinned. "I ask for no secrets of the confessional. I'm only telling you to appoint a few . . . shall we say, skilled woodsmen? . . . to sneak their way through the grass into yon forest. Have them locate Sir Owain, wherever he is, and order him to hold his fire till I send word. You needn't tell me who you appoint, Father."

"In that case, my son, it shall be as you command." The priest drew me aside and asked me to give spiritual comfort to the injured and frightened as his *locum tenens*, while he led a small scout party into the forest.

But my lord found another task for me. He and I and an esquire rode out under a white banner toward the Wersgor camp. We assumed the foe would have wit enough to understand our meaning, even if they did not use the same truce signal. And thus it was. Huruga himself drove out in an open car to meet us. His blue jowls looked shrunken, and his hands trembled.

"I call upon you to yield," said the baron. "Stop forcing me to destroy your poor benighted commoners. I pledge you'll all be treated fairly and allowed to write home for ransom money."

"I, yield to a barbarian like you?" croaked the Wersgor. "Just because you have some . . . some confounded detection-proof cannon—no!" He paused. "But to get rid of you, I'll allow you to leave in the spaceships you've seized."

"Sire," I gasped when I had translated this, "have we indeed won escape?"

"Hardly," Sir Roger answered. "We can't find our way back,

remember; and as yet, we dare not ask for a skilled navigator to help us, or we'd reveal our weakness and be attacked again. Even if we did somehow win home, 'twould still leave this nest of devils free to plot a renewed assault on England. Nay, I fear that he who mounts a bear cannot soon dismount."

So with a heavy heart, I told the blue noble that we had come for more than some of his shoddy, old-fashioned space-ships, and if he did not surrender we would be forced to devastate his land. Huruga snarled for reply and drove back.

We also returned. Presently Red John Hameward came from the forest with Father Simon's party, which he had encountered on his way to our camp.

"We flew to that Stularax castle openly, sire," he related. "We saw other sky-boats, but none challenged us, taking us for a simple ship o' their own. Still, we knew no fortress sentries'd let us land without some questions. So we put down in some woods, a few miles from the keep. We set up our terbuchet and put one o' those bursting shells in't. Sir Owain's idea was to lob a few to shake up their outer defenses. Then we'd slip closer afoot, leaving a crew to fire some more shells when we was near and break down their walls. We expected the garrison'd be scurrying about in search of our engine, so we could slip in, kill whatever guards were left behind, lift what we could carry from their arsenal, and return to our boat."

At this point, since it is no longer used, I had best explain the trebuchet. It was the simplest but in many ways the most effective siege engine. In principle it was only a great lever, freely swinging on some fulcrum. A very long arm ended in a bucket for the missile, while the short arm bore a stone weight, often of several tons. This latter was raised by pulleys or a winch, while the bucket was loaded. Then the weight was released, and in falling it swung the long arm through a mighty arc.

"I didn't think much o' those shells we had," Red John went on. "Why, the things didn't weigh no more'n five pounds. We'd trouble rigging the terbuchet to cast 'em only those few miles. And what could they do, I wondered, but burst with a pop? I've seen terbuchets used proper, laying siege to French cities. We'd throw boulders of a ton or two, or sometimes dead horses, over the walls. But, well, orders was orders. So I m'self cocked the little shell like I'd been told how to, and we let fly. Whoom! The world blew up, like. I had to admit this was even better to throw nor a dead horse.

"Well, through the magnifying screens we could see the castle was pretty much flattened. No use raiding it now. We lobbed a few more shells to make sure it were reduced proper. Nothing there now but a big glassy pit. Sir Owain reckoned as we was carrying a weapon more useful nor any which we could o' lifted, and I'd say he were right. So we landed in the woods some miles hence and dragged the terbuchet forth and set it up again. That's what took us so long, m' lord. When Sir Owain had seen from the air what was happening about that time, we fired a shell just to scare the enemy a bit. Now we're ready to pound 'em as much as you wish, sire."

"But the boat?" asked Sir Roger. "The foe have metal-sniffers. That's why they haven't found your trebuchet in the forest: it's made of wood. But surely they could discover your flying boat, wherever you've hid it."

"Oh, that, sire." Red John grinned. "Sir Owain's got our boat flitting up there 'mongst t'others. Who's to tell the difference in yon swarm?"

Sir Roger whooped laughter. "You missed a glorious fight," he said, "but you can light the balefire. Go back and tell your men to start shelling the enemy camp."

We withdrew underground at the agreed-on moment, as shown on captured Wersgor timepieces. Even so, we felt the earth shudder, and heard the dull roaring, as their ground in-stallations and most of their ground machines were destroyed. A single shot was enough. The survivors thereof stormed in blind terror aboard one of the transport ships, abandoning much perfectly unharmed equipment. The lesser sky-craft were even quicker to vanish, like blown sea scud. As the slow sunset began to burn in that direction we had wistfully named the west, England's leopards flew above England's victory.

Chapter XIV

SIR OWAIN landed like some hero of a chanson come to earth. His exploits had not required much effort of him. While buzzing around in the middle of the Wersgor air fleet, he had even heated water over a brazier and shaved. Lithely now he walked, head erect, mailcoat shining, red cloak aflutter in the wind. Sir Roger met him near the knightly tents, battered, filthy, reeking, clotted with blood. His voice was hoarse from shouting. "My compliments, Sir Owain, on a most gallant action."

The younger man swept him a bow—and changed it most subtly to Lady Catherine's, as she emerged from our cheering throng. "I could have done no less," murmured Sir Owain, "with a bowstring about my heart."

The color mounted to her face. Sir Roger's eyes flickered from one to another. Indeed, they made a fair couple. I saw his hands clench on the haft of his nicked and blunted sword.

"Go to your tent, madame," he told his wife.

"There is still work to do among the wounded, sire," she answered.

"You'll work for anyone but your own husband and children, eh?" Sir Roger made an effort to sneer, but his lip was puffy where a pellet had glanced off the visor of his helmet. "Go to your tent, I say."

Sir Owain looked shocked. "Those are not words to address a gentlewoman with, sire," he protested.

"One of your plinking roundels were better?" grunted Sir Roger. "Or a whisper, to arrange an assignation?"

Lady Catherine grew quite pale. She took a long breath before words came. Silence fell upon those persons who stood within earshot. "I call God to witness that I am maligned," she said. Her gown streamed with the haste of her stride. As she vanished into her pavilion, I heard the first sob.

Sir Owain stared at the baron with a kind of horror. "Have you lost your senses?" he breathed at last.

Sir Roger hunched thick shoulders, as if to raise a burden. "Not yet. Let my captains of battle meet with me when they've washed and supped. But it might be wisest, Sir Owain, if you would take charge of the camp guard."

The knight bowed again. It was not an insulting gesture, but it reminded us all how Sir Roger had transgressed good manners. He departed and took up his duties briskly. A watch was soon set. Thereafter Sir Owain took Branithar on a walk around the blasted Wersgor camp, to examine that equipment which had been far enough away to remain usable. The blue-face had—even during the past few busy days—picked up more English. He talked, lamely but with great earnestness, and Sir Owain listened. I glimpsed this in the last dim twilight, as I hurried to the conference, but could not hear what was being said.

A fire burned high, and torches were stuck in the ground. The English chieftains sat around the trestle table with alien constellations winking to life overhead. I heard night sough in the forest. All the men were deathly tired, they slumped on the benches, but their eyes never left the baron.

Sir Roger stood up. Bathed, clad in fresh though plain garments, a sapphire ring arrogant on one finger, he betrayed himself only by the dullness of his tone. Though the words were brisk enough, his soul was not in them. I glanced toward the tent where Lady Catherine and his children lay, but darkness hid it.

"Once again," said my lord, "God's grace has aided us to win. In spite of all the destruction we wrought, we've more booty of cars and weapons than we can use. The army that came against us is broken, and only one fortress remains on this entire world!"

Sir Brian scratched his white-bristled chin. "Two can play that game of tossing explosives about," he said. "Dare we remain here? As soon as they recover their wits, they'll find means to fire on us."

"True." Sir Roger's blond head nodded. "That's one reason we must not linger. Another being that it's an uncomfortable dwelling place at best. By all accounts, the castle at Darova is far larger, stronger, and better fitted. Once we've seized it, we need not fear shellfire. And even if Duke Huruga has no means left him whereby to bombard us here, we can be sure he's now swallowed his pride and sent spaceships off to other stars for

help. We can look for a Wersgor armada to come against us."
He affected not to notice the shudder that went among them,
but finished, "For all these reasons, we want Darova for our
own, intact."

"To stand off the fleets of a hundred worlds?" cried Captain
Bullard. "Nay, now, sire, your pride has curdled and turned to
madness. I say, let's get aloft ourselves while we can, and pray
God that He will guide us back to Terra."

Sir Roger struck the table with his fist. The noise cracked
across all forest rustlings. "God's wounds!" he roared. "On the
day of a victory such as hasn't been known since Richard the
Lion Heart, you'd tuck tail between legs and run! I thought
you a man!"

Bullard growled deep in his throat, "What did Richard gain
in the end, save a ransom payment that ruined his country?"
But Sir Brian Fitz-William heard him and muttered low, "I'll
hear no treason." Bullard realized what he had said, bit his lip
and fell silent. Meanwhile Sir Roger hastened on:

"The arsenals of Darova must have been stripped for the
assault on us. Now we have nearly all which remains of their
weapons, and we've killed off most of its garrison. Give them
time, and they'll rally. They'll summon franklins and yeomen
from all over the planet, and march against us. But at this moment, they must be in one hurly-burly. The best they'll be able
to do is man the ramparts against us. Counterattack is out of
the question."

"So shall we sit outside Darova's walls till their reinforcements come?" gibed a voice in the shadows.

"Better that than sit here, think you not?" Sir Roger's laugh
was forced, but a grim chuckle or two responded. And so it
was decided.

Our worn-out folk got no sleep. At once they must start
their toil, by the brilliant double moonlight. We found several of the great transport aircraft which had been only slightly
damaged, being on the fringes of the blast. The artisans among
our captives repaired them at spearpoint. Into these we rolled
all the weapons and vehicles and other equipment we could.
People, prisoners, and cattle followed. Well before midnight,
our ships had lumbered into the sky, guarded by a cloud of
other vessels with one or two men aboard each. We were none

too soon. Hardly an hour after our departure—as we learned later—unmanned flyers loaded with the strongest explosives rained down upon the site of Ganturath.

A cautious pace, through heavens empty of hostile craft, brought us over an inland sea. Miles beyond it, in the middle of a rugged and thickly forested region, we raised Darova. Having been summoned to the control turret to interpret, I saw it in the vision screens, far ahead and far below but magnified to our sight.

We had flown to meet the sun, and dawn glowed pink behind the buildings. These were only ten, low, rounded structures of fused stone, their walls thick enough to withstand almost any blow. They were knitted together with reinforced tunnels. Indeed, nearly all that castle was deep underground, as self-contained as a spaceship. I saw an outer ring of gigantic bombards and missile launchers poke their snouts from sunken emplacements, and the force screen was up, like Satan's parody of a halo. But this seemed mere trimming on the strength of the fortress itself. No aircraft were visible, save our own.

By now I, like most of us, had had some instruction in the use of the far-speaker. I tuned it until the image of a Wersgor officer appeared in its screen. He had obviously been trying to tune in on me, so we had lost several minutes. His face was pale, almost cerulean, and he gulped several times before he could ask: "What do you want?"

Sir Roger scowled. Bloodshot, dark-rimmed eyes, in a face whose flesh seemed melted away by care, gave him a frightful appearance. I having translated, he snapped: "Huruga."

"We . . . we shall not surrender our *grath*. He told us so himself."

"Brother Parvus, tell that idiot I only want to talk to the duke! A parley. Haven't they any idea at all of civilized custom?"

The Wersgor gave us a hurt look, since I told him my lord's exact words, but spoke into a little box and touched a series of buttons. His image was replaced with that of Huruga. The governor rubbed sleep from his eyes and said with forlorn courage, "Don't expect to destroy this place as you did the others. Darova was built to be an ultimate strong point. The heaviest bombardment could only remove the aboveground works. If you attempt a direct assault, we can fill the air and the land with blasts and metal."

Sir Roger nodded. "But how long can you maintain such a barrage?" he asked mildly.

Huruga bared his sharp teeth. "Longer than you can mount the assault, you animal!"

"Nonetheless," Sir Roger murmured, "I doubt if you're equipped for a siege." I could find no Wersgor term in my limited vocabulary for that last word, and Huruga seemed to have trouble understanding the circumlocutions by which I rendered it. When I explained why it took me so long to translate, Sir Roger nodded shrewdly.

"I suspected as much," he said. "Look you, Brother Parvus. These starfaring nations have weapons nigh as powerful as St. Michael's sword. They can blow up a city with one shell, and lay waste a shire with ten. But this being so, how could their battles ever be prolonged? Eh? Yon castle is built to take hammer blows. But a siege? Hardly!"

To the screen: "I shall establish myself near by, keeping watch on you. At the first sign of life from your castle, I'll open fire. So 'twere best that your men stay underground all whiles. At any time you wish to surrender, call me on the far-speaker, and I'll be pleased to extend the courtesies of war."

Huruga grinned. I could almost read the thoughts behind that snout. The English were more than welcome to squat outside, till the avenging armada came! He blanked the screen.

We found a good camp site well beyond the horizon. It lay in a deep, sheltered valley, through which a river ran clean and cold and full of fish. Meadows were dotted throughout the forest; game was abundant, and off duty our men were free to hunt. For a few of those long days, I watched cheer blossom fresh among our people.

Sir Roger gave himself no rest. I think he dared not; for Lady Catherine left her children with their nurse and walked among bowers with Sir Owain. Not untended—they were careful of the proprieties—but her husband would glimpse them and turn to snarl a command at the nearest person.

Hidden away in these woods, our camp was safe enough from shellfire or missiles. Its tents and lean-tos, our weapons and tools, were not a large enough concentration of metal to be sniffed out by one of the Wersgor magnetic devices. Such of our aircraft as maintained watch on Darova, always landed elsewhere. We kept trebuchets loaded, in case any activity were revealed about the fortress; but Huruga was content to wait passive. Sometimes a daring enemy vessel passed overhead, having come from some other spot on the planet. But it never found any target for its explosives, and our own patrol soon forced it away.

Most of our strength—the great ships and guns and war-wagons—were elsewhere all this time. I myself did not see the hunting Sir Roger undertook. I stayed in camp, busying myself with such problems as teaching myself more Wersgor and Branithar more English. I also started classes in the Wersgor language for some of our more intelligent boys. Nor would I have wished to go on the baron's expedition.

He had spacecraft and aircraft. He had bombards to fire both flame and shell. He had a few ponderous turtle-cars. He had hundreds of light open battle-cars, which he hung with shields and pennons and manned with a cavalryman and four men-at-arms each. He went out across the continent and harried.

No isolated estate could withstand his attack. Looting and burning, he left desolation behind him. He killed many Wersgorix, but no more than necessary. The rest he stuffed captive into the huge transport ships. A few times, the franklins and yeomen tried to make a stand. They had hand weapons only; his host scattered them like chaff and chivvied them across their own fields. It took him only a few days and nights to devastate the entire land mass. Then he made a quick foray across an ocean, bombed and flamed whatever he chanced upon, and returned.

To me it seemed a cruel butchery, albeit no worse than this empire had done on many worlds. However, I own I have not always understood the logic of such things. Certainly what Sir Roger did was ordinary European practice in a rebellious province or a hostile foreign country. Yet when he landed in camp again, and his men swaggered forth loaded with jewels and rich fabrics, silver and gold, drunk on stolen liquor and boasting of what they had done, I went to Branithar.

"These new prisoners are beyond my power," I said, "but tell your brothers of Ganturath that before the baron can destroy them, he must take off my own poor head."

The Wersgor gave me a curious look. "What do you care for our sort?" he asked.

"God help me," I replied, "I do not know, save that He must also have made you."

Word of this reached my lord. He summoned me to the tent he now used instead of his pavilion. I saw forest glades choked with captives, milling about like sheep, mumbling and terrified under the English guns. True, their presence was a shield to us. Though the ships' descent must now have revealed our location closely enough to Huruga's magnifiers, Sir Roger had taken care that the governor knew what had happened. But I saw blueskin mothers holding little wailing blue cubs, and it was like a hand about my heart.

The baron sat on a stool, gnawing a haunch of beef. Light and shadow, filtered through leaves, checkered his face. "What's this?" he cried. "Are you so fond of yon pigfaces you'll not let me have those we caught at Ganturath?"

I squared my skinny shoulders. "If nothing else, sire," I told him, "think how such a deed must harm your own soul."

"What?" He raised his thick brows. "When was it ever forbidden to set free the captive?"

My turn came to gape. Sir Roger slapped one thigh, guffawing. "We'll keep some few, like Branithar and the artisans, who're useful to us. All the rest we'll herd to Darova. Thousands and thousands. Don't you imagine Huruga's heart will melt with gratitude?"

I stood there in sunlight and tall grass, while "Haw, haw, haw!" bellowed about me.

So under the jeers and spear-prods of our men, that uncounted throng stumbled through beck and brake, until they emerged on cleared land and saw the distant mass of Darova. A few stepped out of the crowd, timorous. The English leaned grinning on their weapons. One Wersgor began to run. No one fired at him. Another broke away, and another. Then the entire swarm of them pelted toward the fortress.

That evening Huruga yielded.

"'Twas easy enough." Sir Roger chuckled. "I had him bot-
tled up in there. I doubted he had more than just enough
supplies, for siegecraft must be a lost art in this country. So,
first, I showed him I could lay his whole planet waste—which
he'd have to answer for even if we were conquered in the end.
Then I gave him all those extra mouths to feed." He slapped
my back. When I had been picked up and dusted off, he said,
"Well, Brother Parvus, now that we own this world, would you
like to head its first abbey?"

Chapter XV

O F COURSE I could not accept any such offer. Quite apart from difficult questions of consecration, I hope I know my humble place in life. Anyhow, at this stage it was mere talk. We had too much else to do, to offer God more than a Mass of thanksgiving.

We let nearly all the recaptured Wersgorix go. On a powerful far-speaker, Sir Roger broadcast a proclamation to Tharixan. He bade every large landholder, in those areas not yet ravaged, to come make submission and take several of the homeless ones back with him. The lesson he had taught was so sharp that for the next few days it swarmed with blue visitors. I must needs deal with them, and forgot what sleep was like. But for the most part they were very meek. Indeed, this race had been supreme among the stars so long that only their soldiers now had occasion to develop a manly contempt for death. Once these had submitted, the burgesses and franklins quickly did likewise—and were so used to having an all-powerful government above them that they never dreamed it might be possible to revolt.

Most of Sir Roger's attention in that period went to training his folk in garrison duty. The castle machines being as simple to operate as most Wersgor equipment, he soon had women, children, serfs, and aged manning Darova. They should be able to hold it against attack for at least a while. Those who seemed hopelessly incapable in the diabolic arts of meter-reading, button-pushing, and knob-twisting, he put on a safely distant island to care for our livestock.

When transplanted Ansby was thus able to defend itself, the baron gathered his free companions for yet another expedition into the sky. He explained his idea to me beforehand: as yet, I alone had any fluency in the Wersgor tongue, though Branithar (with Father Simon's assistance) was instructing others apace.

"We've done well so far, Brother Parvus," Sir Roger declared. "But alone, we'd never hurl back the Wersgor hosts being raised against us. I hope by now you've mastered their writing and numerology. At least well enough to keep watch on a native navigator and see that he doesn't steer us where we would not go."

"I have studied the principles of their star maps a little, sire," I answered, "though in truth they do not employ charts, but mere columns of figures. Nor do they have mortal steersmen on the spaceships. Rather, they instruct an artificial pilot at the start of the journey, and thereafter the homunculus operates the entire craft."

"How well I know that!" grunted Sir Roger. "'Twas how Branithar tricked us hither in the first instance. A dangerous wight, that, but too useful to kill. Glad I am not to have him aboard on this voyage; and yet I'm not easy in my heart at leaving him in Darova. . . ."

"But where are you bound, sire?" I interrupted.

"Oh. Aye. That." He knuckled eyes sandy with weariness. "There are other kings than Wersgor. Lesser star-traveling nations, who dread the day when these snout-face fiends will decide to make an end of them. I shall seek allies."

It was an obvious enough move, but I hesitated. "Well?" demanded Sir Roger. "What ails you now?"

"If they have not yet gone to war," I said weakly, "why should the advent of a few backward savages like us make them do so?"

"Hearken, Brother Parvus," said Sir Roger. "I'm weary of this whining about our own ignorance and feebleness. We're not ignorant of the true Faith, are we? Somewhat more to the point, maybe, while the engines of war may change through the centuries, rivalry and intrigue look no subtler out here than at home. Just because we use a different sort of weapons, we aren't savages."

I could scarcely refute his argument, since it was our only hope except for a random flight in search of lost Terra.

The best spaceships were those which had lain in the vaults of Darova. We were outfitting these, when the sun was darkened by a still greater vessel. As it hung up there like a thundercloud, it threw dismay among our folk. But Sir Owain Montbelle came running with a Wersgor engineer in tow, snatched up myself to interpret, and led us to the far-speaker. Standing out of sight of the screen, with sword drawn, Sir Owain made the captive speak with the master of the ship.

It proved to be a merchant craft, paying a regular call at this planet. The sight of Ganturath and Stularax turned into holes horrified its crew. We could easily enough have blasted the ship down, but Sir Owain used his Wersgor puppet to tell the captain there had been a raid from space, beaten off by the Darova garrison, and that he should land here. He obeyed. As the ship's outer portals opened, Sir Owain led a swarm of men aboard and captured it without trouble.

For this, they cheered him night and day. And he made a brave, colorful figure, always prepared to fling a jest or a gallantry. Sir Roger, toiling without pause, grew ever more uncouth. Men stood in awe of him, and some little hatred, since he drove them to such exertions. Sir Owain contrasted, like Oberon versus a bear. Half the women must have been in love with him, though he had songs only for Lady Catherine.

The booty from the giant ship was rich. Best of all, however, were many tons of grain. We tried some of this on our livestock on the island, which was growing thin on the detested blue grass. They accepted the feed as eagerly as if it were English oats. When he heard this, Sir Roger exclaimed, "Whatever planet that comes from is the one we must capture next."

I crossed myself and hurried elsewhere.

But we had little time to lose. It was no secret that Huruga had dispatched spaceships to Wersgorixan immediately after the second battle of Ganturath. They would take a while to reach that distant planet, and the emperor would need a while more to raise a fleet among his widely scattered domains, and thereafter it would take time for the fleet to get back here. But already days had fled from us.

To head the Darova garrison of women, children, aged, and serfs, Sir Roger appointed his wife. I am told that our chroniclers' practice of inventing speeches for the great persons whose lives they write is unscholarly. Yet I knew those two, not just the haughty exterior but (in glimpses, for it was shy) the soul. I can all but see them, in a buried room of the alien castle.

Lady Catherine has hung it with her tapestries, spread rushes on the floor, and left the walls darkened in favor of sconced

candles, that this place might seem less eerie to her. She waits
in garments of pride, while her husband bids their children
farewell. Little Matilda weeps openly. Robert withholds the
tears, more or less, until he has closed the door on his father;
for he is a de Tourneville.

Slowly, Sir Roger straightens. He has stopped shaving, for
lack of time, and the beard curls like wire on his scarred hook-
nosed face. The gray eyes look burnt out, and a muscle in his
cheek will not stop twitching. Since hot water runs freely here
from pipes, he has bathed; but he wears his usual rough old
jerkin and patched hose. The baldric of his great sword creaks
as he advances toward his wife.

"Well," he says awkwardly, "I must begone."

"Yes." Her back is slender and very straight.

"I believe—" He clears his throat. "I believe you've learned
everything needful." When she does not answer: "Remember,
'tis most important to keep those students of the Wersgor
tongue hard at their lessons. Otherwise we'll be deaf-mutes
among our foes. But never trust our prisoners. Two armed
men must always be with each one of them."

"Indeed." She nods. She is uncoifed, and candlelight slides
along the coiled auburn hair. "I shall also remember that the
pigs don't require that new grain we give the other animals."

"Most important! And be certain to stock this stronghold
well. Those of our folk who have eaten native food are still in
health, so you can requisition from Wersgor granaries."

Silence thickens about them.

"Well," he says, "I must begone."

"God be with you, my lord."

He stands a moment, studying each smallest tone in her
voice. "Catherine—"

"Yes, my lord?"

"I've wronged you," he forces out. "And I've neglected you,
what's worse."

Her hands reach out, as if of their own accord. His coarse
palms close about them.

"Any man could be mistaken, now and then," she breathes.

He dares look into the blue eyes. "Will you give me a token?" he asks.

"For your safe return—"

He drops hands to her waist, draws her close and cries joyous: "And my final victory! Give me your token, and I'll lay this empire at your feet!"

She pulls herself free. Horror bestrides her lips. "When are you going to start looking for our Earth?"

"What honor is there in slinking home, when we leave the very stars our enemies?" Pride clashes in his words.

"God help me," she whispers, and flees him. He stands a long while, until the sound of her feet has vanished down the cold corridors. Then he turns and walks out to his men.

We could have crowded into one of the big ships but thought it best to disperse ourselves in a score. These had been repainted, using Wersgor supplies, by a lad who possessed some heraldic skill. Now they were scarlet and gold and purple, with the de Tourneville arms and the English leopards emblazoned on the flagship.

Tharixan fell behind us. We went into that strange condition, ducking in and out of more dimensions than Euclid's orderly three, which the Wersgorix called "super-light drive." Again the stars flamed on every hand, and we amused ourselves with naming the new constellations—the Knight, the Plowman, the Arbalest, and more, including some which are not fit to put in this record.

The voyage was not long: a few Earth-days only, as near as we could estimate from the clocks. It rested us, and we were keen as hounds when we coursed into the planetary system of Bodavant.

By now we understood that there are many colors and sizes of suns, all intermingled. The Wersgorix, like humans, favored small yellow ones. Bodavant was redder and cooler. Only one of its planets was habitable (the usual case); and while this Boda could have been settled by men or Wersgorix, they would find it dim and chilly. Thus our enemies had not troubled to conquer the native Jairs but merely prevented them from acquiring more colonies than they had when discovered, and forced them into grossly unfavorable trade agreements.

The planet hung like a huge shield, mottled and rusty, against the stars, when the native warships hailed us. We brought our flotilla to an obedient halt. Rather, we ceased to accelerate, and simply plunged through space in a hyperbolic sub-light orbit which the Jair craft matched. But these problems of heavenly navigation make my poor head ache; I am content to leave them to the astrologers and the angels.

Sir Roger invited the Jair admiral aboard our flagship. We used the Wersgor language, of course, with myself as interpreter. But I shall only render the gist of the conversation, not the tedious byplay which actually took place.

A reception had been prepared, with an eye to impressing the visitors. The corridor from the portal to the refectory was lined with warriors. The longbowmen had patched their green doublets and hose, made their caps gay with feathers, and rested their dreadful weapons before them. The common men-at-arms had polished what mail and flat helmets they owned, and formed an arch of pikes. Beyond, where the passage grew high and broad enough to allow, twenty cavalrymen gleamed in full armor of plate, banner and scutcheon, plume and lance, astride our biggest chargers. At the final door, Sir Roger's huntmaster stood with hawk on wrist and a pack of mastiffs at his feet. Trumpets blared, drums rolled, horses reared, dogs gave tongue, and as one we made the ship roar with the deep-throated cry: "God and St. George for merry England! Haro!"

The Jairs looked rather daunted but continued to the refectory. It was hung with the most gorgeous of our looted fabrics. At the end of the long table, Sir Roger, in broidered garments, surrounded by halberdiers and crossbowmen, sat on a throne hastily knocked together by our carpenters. As the Jairs entered, he raised a golden Wersgor beaker and drank their health in English ale. He had wanted to use wine, but Father Simon had decided to reserve it for Holy Communion, pointing out that foreign devils wouldn't know the difference.

"*Wâes hâeil!*" declaimed Sir Roger, an English phrase he loved even when speaking his more usual French.

The Jairs hesitated until page boys showed them to their places with as much ceremony as the royal court. Thereafter I said a rosary and asked a blessing upon the conference. This was not, I confess, done for purely religious reasons. We had already gathered that the Jairs employed certain verbal formulas to invoke hidden powers of body and brain. If they were benighted enough to take my sonorous Latin for a still more impressive version of the same thing, the sin was not ours, was it?

"Welcome, my lord," said Sir Roger. He, too, looked much rested. There was even a sparkle of deviltry about him. Only those who knew him well could have guessed what emptiness housed within. "I pray pardon for my unceremonious entrance into your domain, but the news I bear will scarcely wait."

The Jair admiral leaned tensely forward. He was a little taller than a man, though more slender and graceful, with soft gray fur over his body and a white ruff around his head. The face was cat-whiskered and had enormous purple eyes, but otherwise looked human. That is to say, it looked as human as the faces in a triptych painted by a not very skillful artist. He wore close-fitting garments of brown stuff, with insignia of rank. But drab indeed they looked, he and his eight associates, next to the splendor we had scraped up. His name, we found later, was Beljad sor Van. Our expectation that the one in charge of interplanetary defenses would stand high in the government proved well founded.

"We had no idea the Wersgorix would trust any other folk enough to arm them as allies," he said.

Sir Roger laughed. "Hardly, gentle sir! I am come from Tharixan, which I've just taken over. We're using captured Wersgor ships to eke out our own."

Beljad sat bolt upright. His fur bristled with excitement. "Are you another star-traveling race, then?" he cried.

"We hight Englishmen," Sir Roger evaded. He did not wish to lie to potential allies more than he must, for their indignation on discovering it might prove troublesome. "Our lords have extensive foreign possessions, such as Ulster, Leinster, Normandy—but I'll not weary you with a catalogue of planets." I alone noticed he had not actually said those counties and duchies *were* planets. "To put it briefly, ours is a very old civilization. Our records go back for more than five thousand years." He used the Wersgor equivalent, as nearly as possible. And who shall deny that Holy Writ runs with absolute accuracy from the time of Adam?

Beljad was less impressed than we had expected. "The Wersgorix boast a mere two thousand years of clearly established history, since their civilization rebuilt itself after its final internecine war," he said. "But we Jairs possess a reliable chronology for the past eight millennia."

"How long have you practiced space flight?" Sir Roger asked.

"For about two centuries."

"Ah. Our earliest experiments of that sort were—how long ago, would you say, Brother Parvus?"

"About thirty-five hundred years, at a place called Babel," I told them.

Beljad gulped. Sir Roger continued smoothly, "This universe is so large that the expanding English kingdom did not run into the expanding Wersgor domain until very recently. They didn't realize our true powers but attacked us unprovoked. You know their viciousness. We're a very peaceful race ourselves." We had learned from contemptuous prisoners that the Jair Republic deplored warfare and had never colonized a planet which already had inhabitants. Sir Roger folded his hands and rolled his eyes upward. "Indeed," he said, "one of our most basic commandments is, 'Thou shalt not kill.' Yet it seemed a greater sin, to let so cruel and dangerous a power as Wersgorixan continue to ravage helpless folk."

"Hm." Beljad rubbed his furry brow. "Where does this England of yours lie?"

"Now, now," purred Sir Roger. "You can't expect us to tell even the most honored strangers that, until a better understanding has been reached. The Wersgorix themselves don't know, for we captured their scoutship. This expedition of mine has come hither to punish them and gather information. As I told you, we captured Tharixan with small loss to ourselves. But 'tis not our monarch's way to intervene in affairs that concern other intelligent species, without consulting their wishes. I swear King Edward III has never dreamed of doing so. I'd much prefer to have you Jairs, and others who've suffered at Wersgor hands, join me in a crusade to humble them. And thus you'll earn the right to divide up their empire fairly and squarely with us."

"Are you—the head of a single military force—empowered to undertake such negotiations?" Beljad asked doubtfully.

"Sir, I am no petty noble," the baron answered with great stiffness. "My descent is as lofty as any in your realm. An ancestor of mine, by the name of Noah, was once admiral of the combined fleets of my planet."

"This is so sudden," Beljad faltered. "Unheard of. We cannot —I cannot—it has to be discussed, and—"

"Certes." My lord raised his voice till the chamber rang. "But don't dawdle overly long, gentles. I offer you a chance to help destroy the Wersgor barbarism, whose existence England can no longer suffer. If you'll share the burden of war, you'll share the fruits of conquest. Otherwise we English will be forced to occupy the entire Wersgor domain: for someone must keep order in it. So I say, join the crusade under my leadership, and haro for victory!"

Chapter XVI

T**HE JAIRS**, like the other free nations, were no simpletons. They invited us to land and be guests on their planet. Strange was that stay, as if we spent it in timeless Elf Hill. I remember slim towers, bridges looped airily between, cities where buildings mingled with park to make one gigantic pleasance, boats on bright lakes, scholars in robe and veil who would discourse with me of English learning, enormous alchemical laboratories, music that still haunts my dreams. But this is no geographical book. And even the soberest account of ancient non-human civilizations would sound wilder to a common English ear than the fantasies of that notorious Venetian, Marco Polo.

While Jair war leaders, wise men, and politicians sought to probe us for information, however courteously, an expedition hastened to Tharixan to see for itself what had happened. Lady Catherine received them with much pomp and allowed them to interview any Wersgorix they chose. She hid away only Branithar, who would have given too much truth. The rest, even Huruga, had nothing but a confused impression of irresistible onslaught.

Being unfamiliar with the variations in human appearance, they did not realize that the Darova garrison was composed of our weakest. But they counted it and could hardly believe that so small a force as ours had accomplished all this. Surely we must have unknown powers in reserve! When they saw our neatherds, riders on horseback, women cooking over wood fires, they swallowed easily enough an explanation that we English preferred as much open-air simplicity of life as possible; it was an ideal of their own.

Fortunate we were that the language barrier limited them to what they could observe of us with their eyes. Those lads learning Wersgor had, as yet, mastered too few words for intelligible conversation. Many a commoner—or even warrior, it may be—would have blurted his own terror and ignorance, begged them to take him home again, had he been able. As it was, all detailed speech with the English must be filtered through myself. And I relayed Sir Roger's cheerful arrogance.

He did not hide from them that an avenging Wersgor fleet would soon fall on Darova. Rather, he boasted of it. His trap was set, he claimed. If Boda and the other starfaring planets would not help him spring it, he must call England for reinforcements.

The idea of an armada from a totally unknown realm, entering their region of space, disquieted the Jair leaders. I make no doubt that some of them took us for mere adventurers, outlaws perhaps, who could actually count on no help from our birthplace. But then others must have argued:

"Dare we stand by and take no hand in what is to happen? Even if they are pirates, these newcomers have conquered a planet, and show no fear of the whole Wersgor Empire. In every case, we must arm ourselves against the possibility that England is—despite their denials—as aggressive as the blueface nation. So would it not be best to strengthen ourselves by helping this Roger, occupying many planets and taking much booty? The only alternative seems to be to make alliance with Wersgor against him, and that is unthinkable!"

Furthermore, the imagination of the Jair people was captured. They saw Sir Roger and his brilliant companions gallop down their sedate avenues. They heard of the defeat he had inflicted on their old enemies. Their folklore, which had long based itself on the fact that they knew only the smallest portion of the universe, predisposed them to believe that older and stronger races existed beyond their maps. Thus, when they heard that he urged war, they took fire and clamored for it. Boda was a true republic, not a sham one such as the Wersgor had. This popular voice rang loud in the parliament.

The Wersgor ambassador protested. He threatened destruction. But he was far from home, the dispatches he sent would take time to arrive, and meanwhile crowds stoned his residence.

Sir Roger himself conferred with two other emissaries. These were the representatives of the other starfaring nations, Ashenkoghli and Pr?*tans. The odd letters in the latter name are my own, standing respectively for a whistle and a grunt. I will let one such conversation stand for the many that took place.

As usual, it was in the Wersgor language. I had more trouble interpreting than I was wont, since the Pr?*tan was in a box which maintained the heat and poisonous air he needed, and talked through a loud-speaker with an accent worse than my own. I never even tried to know his personal name or rank, for these involved concepts more subtle to the human mind than the books of Maimonides. I thought of him as Tertiary Eggmaster of the Northwest Hive, and privately I named him Ethelbert.

We visitors were seated in a cool blue room, far above the city. While Ethelbert's tentacled shape, dimly seen through glass, labored with formal courtesies, Sir Roger glanced out at the view. "Open windows, broad as a sally port," he muttered. "What an opportunity! How I'd love to attack this place!"

When our talk was begun, Ethelbert said: "I cannot commit the Hives to any policy. I can only send a recommendation. However, since our people have minds less individualistic than average, I may add that my recommendation will carry great weight. At the same time, I am correspondingly hard to convince."

We had already been given to understand this. As for the Ashenkoghli, they were divided into clans; their ambassador here was chief of one and could raise its fleet on his own authority. This so simplified our negotiations that we saw God's purpose revealed. I daresay the confidence we gained thereby was itself a powerful asset to us.

"Surely you, good sir, are aware of the arguments we've given the Jairs," Sir Roger said. "They're no less applicable to Pur—Pur—whatever your by-our-lady planet is called."

I felt an exasperation, that he should throw on me the whole burden of pronunciation and polite rephrasing, and set myself a rosary in penance. Wersgor was so barbarous that I could still not think properly in it. Accordingly, when interpreting Sir Roger's French, I first put the gist into my own boyhood English, then into stately Latin periods, on which firm foundation I could erect a Wersgor structure that Ethelbert mentally translated into Pr?*tan. Marvelous are the works of God.

"The Hives have suffered," admitted the ambassador. "The Wersgorix limit our space fleet and extraplanetary possessions;

they exact a heavy tribute of rare metals. However, our home world is useless to them, so we have no fear of ultimate conquest like Boda and Ashenk. Why should we provoke their wrath?"

"I suppose these creatures have no idea of honor," the baron grumbled to me, "so tell him he'll be free of those restrictions and tribute, once Wersgorixan is overthrown."

"Obviously," was the cold reply. "Yet the gain is too small, in comparison with the risk that our planet and its colonies may be bombarded."

"That risk will be much lessened, if all Wersgorixan's foes act together. The enemy'll be kept too busy to take offensive action."

"But no such alliance exists."

"I've reason to believe the Ashenkoghli lord here on Boda plans to join us. Then many other clans of theirs are sure to do likewise, if only to keep him from gaining too much power."

"Sire," I protested in English, "you know that he of Ashenk is less than ready to stake his fleet on this gamble."

"Tell the monster here what I said, anyhow."

"My lord, it isn't true!"

"Ah, but we'll make it come true; so 'tis no lie after all."

I choked on the casuistry but rendered it as required of me. Ethelbert shot back: "What makes you think so? He of Ashenk is known to be a cautious one."

"Certes." It was a shame that the blandness of Sir Roger's tone was wasted on those nonhuman ears. "Therefore he's not about to announce his intention openly. But his staff . . . some of 'em blab, or can't resist dropping a hint—"

"This must be investigated!" said Ethelbert. I could all but read his thoughts. He would set his own spies, hireling Jairs, to work.

We hied ourselves elsewhere and resumed some talks Sir Roger had been having with a young Ashenkogh. This fiery centaur was himself eager for a war in which he might win fame and wealth. He explained the details of organization, record-keeping, communication, which Sir Roger needed to know. Then the baron instructed him what documents to forge and leave for Ethelbert's agents to find, what words to let fall in drunkenness, what clumsy attempts to make at bribing Jair officials. . . . Erelong everyone but the Ashenkoghli ambassador himself knew that he was planning to join us.

So Ethelbert sent a recommendation of war to Pr?*t. It went secretly, of course, but Sir Roger bribed the Jair inspector who passed diplomatic messages out in special boxes to the mailships. The inspector was promised an entire archipelago on Tharixan. That was a shrewd investment of my lord's, for it won him the right to show the Ashenkoghli chief that dispatch ere it continued on its way. Since Ethelbert had so much confidence in our cause, the chief sent for his own fleet and wrote letters inviting the lords of allied clans to do likewise.

By now, the military intelligence of Boda knew what was going on. They could certainly not allow Pr?*t and Ashenk to reap so rich a harvest while their planet remained insignificant. Accordingly, they recommended that the Jairs also join the alliance. Thus urged, the parliament declared war on Wersgorixan.

Sir Roger grinned all over his face. "'Twas easy to do," he said when his captains praised him. "I needed but to inquire the way in which things are done hereabouts, which was never secret. Then the star-folk tumbled into snares which would not have fooled a half-witted prince of Germans."

"But how could that be, sire?" asked Sir Owain. "They're older and stronger and wiser than we."

"The first two, granted," nodded the baron. His humor was so good that he addressed even this knight with frank fellowship. "But the third, no. Where it comes to intrigue, I'm no master of it myself, no Italian. But the star-folk are like children.

"And why? Well, on Earth there've been many nations and lords for many centuries, all at odds with each other, under a feudal system nigh too complicated to remember. Why've we fought so many wars in France? Because the Duke of Anjou was on the one hand the sovereign king of England and on the other hand a Frenchman! Think you what that led to; and yet 'tis really a minor example. On our Earth, we've perforce learned all the knavery there is to know.

"But up here, for centuries, the Wersgorix have been the only real power. They conquered by only one method, crude obliteration of races which had not weapons to fight back. By sheer force—the accident that they had the largest domain

—they imposed their will on the three other nations which possessed such military arts. These, being impotent, never even tried to plot against Wersgorixan. None of this has called for more statecraft or generalship than a snowball fight. It took no skill for me to play on simplicity, greed, dawning fear, and mutual rivalry."

"You are too modest, sire." Sir Owain smiled.

"Argh!" The baron's pleasure vanished. "Satan take such matters. The only important thing now is: here we sit, stewing, until the fleet is raised. And meanwhile the enemy is on his way!"

Indeed, that was a nightmare time. We could not leave Boda to join our women and children in the fortress, for the alliance was still unstable. A hundred times Sir Roger must patch it up, often using means that would cost him dearly in the next life. The rest of us spent our time studying history, languages, geography (or should I say astrology?), and the witchlike mechanic arts. This latter must be done on pretext of comparing local engines with those of our home, to the detriment of the former. Luckily, though not unnaturally—Sir Roger had extracted the information from officers and documents, ere we left Tharixan—certain of the arms we captured there were secret. Thus we could demonstrate an especially effective handgun or explosive ball and claim it was English, taking care that none of our allies got too close a look at it.

The night the Jair liaison ship returned from Tharixan, with word that the enemy armada had arrived, Sir Roger went alone into his bedchamber. I do not know what happened, but next morning his sword needed sharpening and all the furniture lay in splinters.

God granted, though, that we had not much longer to wait. The Bodavant fleet was already gathered in orbit. Now several dozen lean battlecraft from Ashenk arrived, and soon thereafter the boxlike vessels of Pr?*t lumbered in from their poisonous home world. We embarked and roared off to war.

Our first glimpse of Darova, after we had fought past outlying Wersgor ships and into Tharixan's atmosphere, made me doubt that aught was left to rescue. For hundreds of miles around the land lay black, ripped, and desolated. Rock bubbled molten wherever a shell had newly struck. That subtle death which can only be sensed with instruments had lain waste this entire continent, and would linger for years.

But Darova was built to withstand such forces, and Lady Catherine had provisioned it well. I glimpsed a Wersgor flotilla as it screamed low above her force-field. Their missiles burst close, causing the near-solid stone of the aboveground structures to flow on the outside—but leaving the interiors unharmed. The seared earth opened; bombards thrust out like viper tongues, spat lightning, and retracted ere fresh explosives could smite. Three Wersgor ships tumbled in ruin. Their wrecks were added to the carnage which was left from an attempt to storm this place on the ground.

Then I saw no more of smoke-veiled Darova. For the Wersgorix were upon us in force, and the combat moved up again into space.

Strange was that battle. It was fought at unimaginable distances with fire-beams, cannon shells, unmanned missiles. Ships maneuvered under direction from artificial brains, so fast that only the weight-making fields prevented their crews from being smeared across the bulkheads. Hulls were blown open by near-misses, yet could not sink in airless space: the wounded portions sealed themselves off, and the remainder continued to shoot.

Such was the usual way of space war. Sir Roger made an innovation. It had horrified the Jair admirals when he first proposed it, but he had insisted it was a standard English tactic —which it was, in a way. Actually, of course, he did it for fear that his men would otherwise betray their clumsiness with the hell-weapons.

So he disposed them in numerous small, exceedingly fast craft. Our over-all plan of battle was made highly unorthodox, for no other reason than to maneuver the enemy into certain positions. When that chance came, Sir Roger's boats flitted into the heart of the Wersgor fleet. He lost some few, but the others continued their outrageous orbit, to the very flagship of the foe. It was a monstrous thing, almost a mile long, even big enough to carry force-field generators. But the English used explosives to punch through its hull. Then, in space armor, atop which the knights planted their crests—carrying sword, ax, halberd, and bow, as well as handguns—they boarded.

They were not enough to seize that entire labyrinth of corridors and cabins. Yet they enjoyed themselves, suffered small loss (sailors out here being untrained in hand-to-hand fighting), and threw matters into a confusion which vastly aided our general assault. Eventually the crew abandoned that ship. Sir Roger saw them doing so and withdrew his own troop just before the hull was blown to bits.

Only God and the more warlike saints know if his action proved decisive. The allied fleet was outnumbered and very much outgunned, so every gain we made was valuable out of proportion. On the other hand, our attack had come as a surprise. And we had boxed the foe between ourselves and Darova, whose largest missiles flew into space itself to destroy Wersgor craft.

I cannot describe the vision of St. George, for it was not my privilege to observe this. However, many a sober, trustworthy man-at-arms swore that he saw the holy knight ride down the Milky Way in a foam of stars and impale enemy ships on his lance like so many dragons. Be this as it may, after many hours which I remember but dimly, the Wersgorix gave up. They withdrew in good order, having lost perhaps a fourth of their fleet, and we did not pursue them far.

Instead, we hovered above blackened Darova. Sir Roger and the chiefs of his allies went down in a boat. In the central underground hall, the English garrison, grimy and exhausted from days of battle, gave a feeble cheer. Lady Catherine took time to bathe and garb herself in her best, for honor's sake. She swept out like a queen to greet the captains.

But when she saw her husband, standing in dinted space armor against the chilly glow-light, her stride faltered. "My lord—"

He took off his glazed helmet. The air tubes got somewhat in the way of his knightly gesture, as he tucked it under an arm and went to one knee before her. "No," he cried aloud. "Say not that. Let me rather say, 'My lady and love.'"

She advanced like a sleepwalker. "Is the victory yours?"

"No. Yours."

"And now—"

He rose, grimacing as the necessities clamped back down on him. "Conferences," he said. "Repair of battle damage.

Making of new ships, raising of more armies. Intrigues among allies, heads to knock together, laggards to hearten. And fighting to do, always fighting. Until, God willing, the bluefaces are whipped back to their home planet and submit—" He stopped. Her face had lost its quick lovely color. "But for tonight, my lady," he said, unskillfully, though he must have rehearsed it many times, "I think we've earned the right to be alone, that I may praise you."

She drew a shaken breath. "Did Sir Owain Montbelle live?" she asked. When he did not say no, she crossed herself, and a tiny smile flickered on her lips. Then she bade the alien captains welcome and held out her hand for them to kiss.

Chapter XVII

I COME now to a grievous part of this history, and the most difficult to write. Nor was I present, save at the very end.

This was because Sir Roger hurled himself into his crusade as if he fled from something—which in a way was true—and I was dragged with him like a leaf whirled along in a gale. I was his interpreter, but at every moment when we had naught else to do I became his teacher and would instruct him in Wersgor until my poor weak flesh could endure no more. My last glimpse, ere I toppled into sleep, would be of candlelight guttering on my lord's haggard face. Then he would often as not summon a doctor of the Jair language, who would teach him until dawn. At this rate, it was not many weeks before he could curse hideously in both tongues.

Meanwhile, he drove his allies nigh as hard as he did himself. The Wersgorix must be given no chance to recover. Planet after planet must be attacked, reduced, and garrisoned, so that the foe always fought off balance, on the defensive. In this task, we had much help from enslaved native populations. As a rule, these need only be given arms and leadership. Then they attacked their masters in such hordes, with such ferocity, that the latter fled to us for protection. Jairs, Ashenkoghli, and Pr?*tans were horrified. They had no experience in such matters; whereas Sir Roger had encountered the Jacquerie in France. In their bewilderment, his fellow chieftains came more and more to accept his unquestioned leadership.

The ins and outs of what happened are too complex, too various from world to world, for this paltry record. But in essence, on each inhabited planet, the Wersgorix had destroyed whatever original civilization existed. Now the Wersgor system in turn was toppled. Into this vacuum—unreligion, anarchy, banditry, famine, the ever-present menace of a blueface return, the necessity of training the natives themselves to eke out our thin garrisons—Sir Roger stepped. He had a solution to these problems, one hammered out in Europe during those not dissimilar centuries after Rome fell: the feudal system.

But just when he was thus laying the cornerstone of victory, it crumbled for him. God rest his soul! No more gallant knight ever lived. Even now, a lifetime later, tears dim my old eyes, and I were fain to hurry over this part of the chronicle. Since I witnessed so little, it would be excusable for me to do so.

However, those who betrayed their lord did not rush into it. They stumbled. Had Sir Roger not been blind to all warning signs, it would never have happened. Therefore I shall not set it down in cold words, but fall back on the earlier (and, I think, truer) practice of inventing whole scenes, that folk now dust may live again and be known, not as abstract villainies, but as fallible souls: on whom perhaps God, at the very last, had mercy.

We begin on Tharixan. The fleet had just departed to seize the first Wersgor colony of its long campaign. A Jair garrison occupied Darova. But those English women, children, and grandsires who had so valiantly held fast, were given what reward lay in Sir Roger's power. He moved them to that island where our kine were pastured. There they could dwell in woods and fields, erecting houses, herding, hunting, sowing and reaping, almost as if it were home. Lady Catherine was set to rule over them. She kept Branithar, of the Wersgor captives, as much to prevent his revealing too much to the Jairs as to continue giving instruction in his language. She also had a small fast spaceship for emergency use. Visits from the Jairs across the sea were discouraged, lest they observe too closely.

It was a peaceful time, save in my lady's heart.

For her the great grief began the day after Sir Roger embarked. She walked across a flowery meadow, hearing wind sough in the trees. A pair of her maids followed behind. Through the woods came voices, the ring of an ax, the bark of a dog, but to her they seemed of dreamlike remoteness.

Suddenly she halted. For a moment she could only stare. Then one hand stole to the crucifix on her breast. "Mary, have pity." Her maids, well-trained, slipped back out of earshot.

Sir Owain Montbelle hobbled from the glade. He was in his gayest garb, nothing but a sword to remind her of war. The crutch on which he leaned hardly interfered with his gracefulness as he swept off his plumed bonnet in a bow.

"Ah," he cried, "this instant the place has become Arcady,

and old Hob the swineherd whom I just met is heathen Apollo, harping a hymn to the great witch Venus."

"What's this?" Catherine's eyes were blue dismay. "Has the fleet returned?"

"Nay." Sir Owain shrugged. "Blame my own awkwardness yestre'en. I was frolicking about, playing ball, when I stumbled. My ankle twisted, and remains so weak and tender that I'd be useless in battle. Perforce I deputed my command to young Hugh Thorne and flitted hither in an aircraft. Now I must wait till I am healed, then borrow a ship and a Jair pilot to rejoin my comrades."

Catherine tried desperately to speak sober words. "In . . . in his language lessons . . . Branithar has mentioned that the star folk have s-s-strange chirurgic arts." She flushed like fire. "Their lenses can look . . . even inside a living body . . . and they inject simples which heal the worst wound in days."

"I thought of that," said Sir Owain. "For of course I would not be a laggard in war. But then I remembered my lord's strict orders, that our entire hope depends for the nonce on convincing these demon races we are as learned as they."

She clasped the crucifix still tighter.

"So I dared not ask help of their physicians," he continued. "I told them instead that I remain behind to attend certain matters of moment, and carry this crutch as a penance for sin. When nature has healed me, I will depart. Though in truth, 'twill be like tearing out my own heart, to go from you."

"Does Sir Roger know?"

He nodded. They passed hastily to something else. That nod was a black lie. Sir Roger did not know. None of his men dared tell him. I might have ventured it, for he would not strike a man of the cloth, but I was also ignorant. Since the baron avoided Sir Owain's company these days, and had enough else to occupy his mind, he never thought of it. I suppose in his inmost soul he did not want to think of it.

Whether Sir Owain really hurt his ankle, I dare not say. But it would be a strange coincidence. However, I doubt if he had planned his final treason in detail. Most likely his wish was to continue certain talks with Branithar and see what developed.

He leaned close to Catherine. His laughter rang out. "Until I go," he said, "I feel free to bless the accident."

She looked away, and trembled. "Why?"

"I think you know." He took her hand.

She withdrew it. "I beg you, remember my husband is at war."

"Misdoubt me not!" he exclaimed. "I would sooner lie dead than be dishonored in your eyes."

"I could never . . . misdoubt . . . so courteous a knight."

"Is that all I am? Courteous only? Amusing? A jester for your weary moments? Well-a-day, better Catherine's fool than Venus' lover. So let me then entertain you." And he lifted his clear voice in a roundel to her praise.

"No—" She moved from him, like a doe edging clear of the hunter. "I am . . . I gave pledges—"

"In the courts of Love," he said, "there is only one pledge, Love itself." The sunlight burnished his hair.

"I have two children to think of," she begged.

He grew somber. "Indeed, my lady. I've often dandled Robert and little Matilda on my knee. I hope I may do it again, while God allows."

She faced him afresh, almost crouching. "What do you mean?"

"Oh— Nay." He looked into the murmurous woods, whose leaves were of no shape or color ever seen on Earth. "I would not voice disloyalty."

"But the children!" This time it was she who seized his hand. "In Christ's holy name, Owain, if you know aught, speak!"

He kept his face turned from her. He had a fine profile. "I am not privy to any secrets, Catherine," he said. "Belike you can judge the question better than I. For you know the baron best."

"Does anyone know him?" she asked in bitterness.

He said, very low, "It seems to me that his dreams grow with each new turn of fate. At first he was content to fly to France and join the King. Then he would liberate the Holy Land. Brought here by evil fortune, he responded nobly; none can deny that. But having gained a respite, has he sought Terra again? No, he took this whole world. Now he is off to conquer suns. Where will it end?"

"Where—" She could not continue. Nor could she pull her gaze from Sir Owain.

The knight said, "God puts bounds to all things. Unlimited ambition is the egg of Satan, from which only woe can hatch. Does it not seem to you, my lady, when you lie sleepless at night, that we will overreach ourselves and be ruined?"

After a long while he added: "Wherefore I say, Christ and His Mother help all the little children."

"What can we do?" she cried in her anguish. "We've lost our way to Earth!"

"It might be found again," he said.

"In a hundred years of search?"

He watched her in silence for a while before he answered:

"I would not raise false hopes in so sweet a bosom. But from time to time I've conversed a little with Branithar. Our knowledge of each other's tongues is but scant, and certes he does not trust any human overmuch. Yet . . . a few things he has said . . . make me think that perhaps the road home might be found."

"What?" Both her frantic hands seized him. "How? Where? Owain, are you gone mad?"

"No," he said with studied roughness. "But let us suppose this be true, then Branithar can guide us despite all. He'll not do so without a price, I suppose. Do you think Sir Roger would renounce his crusade and go quietly back to England?"

"He—why—"

"Has he not said again and yet again: while the Wersgor power remains, England lies in mortal danger? Would not the rediscovery of Terra only lead him to redouble his efforts? Nay, what use is it to learn our way back? The war would still continue, until it ended in our destruction."

She shuddered and crossed herself.

"Since I am here," Sir Owain finished, "I may as well try to learn if the homeward route can indeed be found. Perhaps you can think of some means to use that knowledge, ere it is too late."

He bade her a courtly good day, which she did not hear, and limped on into the forest.

Chapter XVIII

MANY LONG Tharixanian days passed: weeks of Earth time. Having taken the first planet he aimed at, Sir Roger went on to the next. Here, while his allies distracted the enemy gunners, he stormed the main castle afoot, using foliage to conceal his approach. This was the place where Red John Hameward actually did rescue a captive princess. True, she had green hair and feathery antennae, nor was there any possibility of issue between her species and our own. But the human-likeness, and exceeding gratitude, of the Vashtunari—who had just been in process of being conquered—did much to cheer lonely Englishmen. Whether or not the prohibitions of Leviticus are applicable is still being hotly debated.

The Wersgorix counterattacked from space, basing their fleet in a ring of planetoids. Sir Roger had taken an opportunity while en route to turn off the artificial weight aboard ship and let his men practice movement under such conditions. So now, armored against vacuum, our bowmen made that famous raid called the Battle of the Meteors. Cloth-yard shafts pierced many a Wersgor spacesuit without fire-flash or magnetic force-pulse to give away a man's position. With their base thus depleted of manpower, the enemy withdrew from the entire system. Admiral Beljad had grabbed off three other suns while they were occupied with this one, so their new retreat was a long one.

And on Tharixan, Sir Owain Montbelle made himself pleasant to Lady Catherine. And he and Branithar felt each other out, cautiously, under pretext of language study. At last they thought they had touched mutual understanding.

It remained to convince the baroness.

I believe both moons had risen. Treetops were hoar with that radiance; double shadows reached across grass where dew glittered; by now, the night sounds had become familiar and peaceful. Lady Catherine left her pavilion, as often after her children were fallen asleep and she unable to. Wrapped in a hooded mantle, she walked down a lane intended for the street of the new village, past half-finished wattle huts that were blocks of shadow under the moons, and out onto a meadow through which ran a brook. The water flowed and sparkled with light; it chimed on rocks. She drank a warm strange smell of flowers, and remembered English hawthorn when they crowned the May Queen. She remembered standing on the pebble beach at Dover, newly wed, when her husband had embarked on a summer's campaign, and waving and waving until the last sail was vanished. Now the stars were a colder shore, and no one would see her kerchief if it fluttered. She bent her head and told herself she would not weep.

Harp strings jingled in the dark. Sir Owain trod forth. He had discarded his crutch, though he still affected a limp. A massy silver chain caught moonlight across his black velvet tunic, and she saw him smile. "Oho," he said softly, "the nymphs and dryads are out!"

"Nay." Despite all resolutions, she felt gladdened. His banter and flattery had lightened so many sad hours; they brought back her courtly girlhood. She fluttered protesting hands, knew she was being coy, but could not stop. "Nay, good knight, this is unseemly."

"Beneath such a sky, and in such a presence, nothing is unseemly," he told her. "For we are assured there is no sin in Paradise."

"Speak not so!" Her pain came back redoubled. "If we have wandered anywhere, 'tis into hell."

"Wherever my lady is, there is Paradise."

"Is this any place to hold a Court of Love?" she gibed bitterly.

"No." He grew solemn in his turn. "Indeed, a tent—or a log cabin, when they complete it—is no place for her to dwell who commands all hearts. Nor are these marches a fit home for you . . . or your children. You should sit among roses as Queen of Love and Beauty, with a thousand knights breaking lances in your honor and a thousand minstrels singing your charms."

She tried to protest, "'Twould be enough to see England again—" but her voice would go no further.

He stood gazing into the brook where twin moonpaths glided and shivered. At last he reached beneath his cloak. She saw steel gleam in his hand. An instant she shrank away. But he raised the crosshilt upward and said, in those rich tones he well knew how to use: "By this token of my Saviour and my honor, I swear you shall have your wish!"

His blade sank. He stared at it. She could scarcely hear him when he added, "If you truly wish it."

"What do you mean?" She drew her mantle tight, as if the air were cold. Sir Owain's gaiety was not the hoarse boisterousness of Sir Roger, and his present gravity was more eloquent than her husband's stammering protestations. Yet briefly she felt afraid of Sir Owain, and would have given all her jewels to see the baron clank from the forest.

"You never say plainly what you mean," she whispered.

He turned a face of disarming boyish ruefulness on her. "Mayhap I never learned the difficult art of blunt speech. But if now I hesitate, 'tis because I am loath to tell my lady that which is hard."

She straightened. For a moment, in the unreal light, she looked strangely like Sir Roger; it was his gesture. Then she was only Catherine, who said with forlorn courage, "Tell me anyhow."

"Branithar can find Terra again," he said.

She was not one to faint. But the stars wavered. She regained awareness leaning against Sir Owain's breast. His arms enclosed her waist, and his lips moved along her cheek toward her mouth. She drew a little away, and he did not pursue his kiss. But she felt too weak to leave his embrace.

"I call this hard news," he said, "for reasons I've discussed erenow. Sir Roger will not give up his war."

"But he could send *us* home!" she gasped.

Sir Owain looked bleak. "Think you he will? He needs every human soul to maintain his garrisons and keep up an appearance of strength. You recall what he proclaimed ere the fleet left Tharixan. As soon as a planet seems strongly enough held, he will send for some people of this village to join those few men he has newly created dukes and knights. As for himself —oh, aye, he talks of ending England's peril, but has he never spoken of making you a queen?"

She could only sigh, remembering a few words let slip.

"Branithar himself shall explain." Sir Owain whistled.

The Wersgor stepped from a canebrake where he had waited.

He could move about freely enough, since he had no hope of escaping the island. His stocky form was well clad in plundered raiment, which glittered as with a thousand tiny pearls. The round, hairless, long-eared, snouted face no longer seemed ugly; the yellow eyes were even gay. By now Catherine could follow his language well enough for him to address her.

"My lady will wonder how I could ever find my way back along a zigzag route taken through swarming uncharted stars," he said. "When the navigator's notes were lost at Ganturath, I myself despaired. So many suns, even of the type of your own, lie within the radius of our cruise, that random search might require a thousand years. This is the more true since nebulosities in space hide numbers of stars until one chances fairly close to them. To be sure, if any deck officers of my ship had survived, they could have narrowed down the search somewhat. But my own work was with the engines. I saw stars only in casual glimpses, and they meant nothing to me. When I tricked your people—rue the day!—all I did was push an emergency control which instructed an automaton to pilot us hither."

A lift of excitement brought back impatience to Catherine. She pulled free of Sir Owain's arms and snapped, "I'm not altogether a fool. My lord respected me enough to try to explain these things to me, however ill I listened. What new have you discovered?"

"Not discovered," said Branithar. "Remembered. 'Tis an idea which should have occurred to me erenow, but there was so much happening— Well . . .

"Know, then, my lady, that there are certain beacon stars, brilliant enough to be visible throughout the spiral arm of the Via Galactica. They are used in navigation. Thus, if the suns called (by us) Ulovarna, Yariz, and Gratch, are seen to form a certain configuration with respect to each other, one must be in a certain region of space. Even a crude visual estimate of the angles would fix one's position within twenty or so light-years. This is not too large a sphere to find a given yellow-dwarf sun like your own."

She nodded, slowly and thoughtfully. "Aye. Belike you think of bright stars like Sirius and Rigel. . . ."

"The major stars in the sky of a planet may not be the ones I mean," he warned. "They may simply happen to lie close by.

Actually, a navigator would need a good sketch of your constellations, with numerous bright stars indicated by color (as seen from airless space). Given enough data, he could analyze and determine which *must* be the beacon giants. Then their relative positions would tell him where they had been observed from."

"I think I could draw the Zodiac for you," said Lady Catherine uncertainly.

"It would be of no use, mistress," Branithar told her. "You have no skill in identifying stellar types by eye. I admit I have little enough: no training at all, merely the casual hearsay about other people's special crafts which one picks up. And while I did chance to be in the control turret once, while our ship was orbiting about Terra making long-range observations, I paid no special heed to the constellations. I have no memory of what they looked like."

Her heart tumbled downward. "But then we're still lost!"

"Not quite so. I should say, I have no conscious memory. Yet we Wersgorix have long known that the mind is composed of more than the self-aware portion."

"True," agreed Catherine wisely. "There is the soul."

"Er . . . that's not exactly what I meant. There is an unconscious or half-conscious depth in the mind, the source of dreams and— Well, anyhow, let it suffice that this unawareness never forgets. It records even the most trivial things which ever impinged on the senses. If I were thrown into a trance and given proper guidance, I could draw quite an accurate picture of the Terrestrial sky, as glimpsed by myself.

"Then a skilled navigator, his star tables at hand, could winnow this crop with his arts mathematic. It would require time. Many blue stars might be Gratch, for example, and only detailed study could eliminate those which are in an impossible relationship to (shall we say) the globular cluster assumed to be Torgelta. Eventually, however, he would narrow the possibilities down to that smallish region whereof I spoke. Then he could flit thither, with a space pilot to aid him, and they could visit all yellow dwarf stars in the neighborhood until they found Sol."

Catherine smote her hands together. "But this is wonderful!"

she cried. "Oh, Branithar, what reward do you wish? My lord will bestow a kingdom on you!"

He planted his thick legs wide, looked up into her shadowed face, and said with the surly valor we had come to know:

"What joy would a kingdom give me, built from the shards of my people's empire? Why should I help find your England again, if it only brings more Englishmen ravening hither?"

She clenched her fists and said with Norman bleakness, "You'll not withhold your knowledge from One-Eyed Hubert."

He shrugged. "The unaware mind is not readily evoked, my lady. Your barbarous tortures might set up an impassable barrier." He reached beneath his tunic. Suddenly a knife gleamed in his hand. "Not that I would endure them. Stand back! Owain gave me this. I know well enough where my own heart lies."

Catherine whirled about with a tiny shriek.

The knight laid both hands on her shoulders. "Hear me before you judge," he said swiftly. "For weeks I've been trying to sound out Branithar. He dropped hints. I dropped hints in turn. We bargained like two Saracen merchants, never openly admitting that we bargained. At last he named that dagger as the price of spreading out his wares for me to see. I could not imagine him harming any of us with it. Even our children now go about with better weapons than a knife. I took it on myself to agree. Then he told me what he has now told you."

The tautness shuddered out of her. She had taken too many shocks in all this time, with too much fear and solitude in between. Her strength was drained.

"What do you require?" she asked.

Branithar ran a thumb along his knife blade, nodded, and sheathed it again. He spoke quite gently. "First, you must obtain a good Wersgor mind-physician. I can find one with the help of this planet's Domesday Book, which is kept at Darova. You can borrow it from the Jairs on some pretext. This physician has to work together with a skilled Wersgor navigator, who can tell him what questions to ask of me and guide my pencil as I draw the map in my trance. Later we will also need a space pilot; and I insist on a pair of gunners as well. These can also be found somewhere on Tharixan. You can tell your allies you want them to help search out technical secrets of the enemy."

"When you have your star map, what?"

"Well, I shall not turn it freely over to your husband! I suggest that we go secretly aboard your spaceship. There will be a fair balance of power: you humans holding the weapons, we Wersgorix the knowledge. We will stand ready to destroy those notes, and ourselves, if you betray us. At long range, we can haggle with Sir Roger. Your own pleas ought to sway him. If he withdraws from the war, transportation home can be arranged, and our nation will undertake to leave yours alone hereafter."

"If he won't agree?" Her voice remained dull.

Sir Owain leaned close, to whisper in French: "Then you and the children . . . and myself . . . will nonetheless be returned. But Sir Roger must not be told this, of course."

"I cannot think." She covered her face. "Father in Heaven, I know not what to do!"

"If your folk persist in this lunatic war," Branithar said, "it can only end in their destruction."

Sir Owain had told her the same thing, over and over, all this time when he was the only one of her station on this planet, the only one to whom she could freely talk. She remembered scorched corpses in the fortress ruins; she thought how small Matilda had screamed during the siege of Darova, each time a shellburst rocked the walls; she thought of green English woods where she had gone hawking with her lord in the first years of their marriage, and of the years he now expected to spend fighting for a goal she could not understand. She lifted her face to the moons, light ran cold along her tears, and she said, "Yes."

Chapter XIX

I CANNOT tell what drove Sir Owain to his treachery. Two souls had ever striven in his breast; his deepest heart must always have remembered how his mother's people had suffered at the hands of his father's. In part, no doubt, his feelings were truly what he claimed to Catherine: horror at the situation, doubt of our victory, love for her person, and concern for her safety. And in part there was a less honorable motive, which may have begun as an idle thought but waxed with time—what might not be done on Terra with a few Wersgor weapons! Reader of my chronicle, when you pray for the souls of Sir Roger and Lady Catherine, say a little word for unhappy Sir Owain Montbelle.

Whatever took place in his secret self, the recreant acted with outward boldness and intelligence. He kept close watch upon the Wersgorix gotten to assist Branithar. During the weeks of their toil, while that which Branithar had forgotten was extracted from his dreams and studied with mathematic devices of more than Arabian cunning, the knight quietly prepared the spaceship to go. And always he must keep up the heart of his fellow conspirator, the baroness.

She wavered in her resolve, wept, stormed, yelled at him to depart her presence. Once a vessel arrived with orders for so-and-so many people to come settle on yet another captured planet. Aboard it was a letter which Sir Roger had sent his wife. He dictated this to me, for his spelling was not always under control, and I took it on myself to polish his phrases a little, so that through their stiffness might come some hint of a humble and enduring love. Catherine at once wrote a reply, admitting her actions and imploring forgiveness. But Sir Owain anticipated this, got the letter ere the ship departed again, burned it, and persuaded her to abide by their scheme. It was, he swore, the best for all concerned, even for her lord.

Finally she gave her dwindled village some excuse about joining her husband. She embarked with the children and two maidservants. Sir Owain had learned enough space arts to send the ship to some known, clear destination—a mere matter of pressing the correct buttons—so he could also join them openly. The night before, he had smuggled the Wersgorix aboard: Branithar, the physician, the pilot, the navigator, and a couple of soldiers trained to use those bombards projecting out of the hull.

Those were useless within the ship, where Owain and Catherine bore the only guns. Extra hand weapons were stowed in the clothes chest in her bedchamber, and one maid was always stationed there. The girls were so terrified of the bluefaces that had any attempted to come take a gun, the screaming would have brought Sir Owain in haste.

Nonetheless, knight and lady must watch their associates like wolves. For the obvious thing for Branithar to do was steer to Wersgorixan itself, where he could inform the emperor of Terra's location. With all England a hostage, Sir Roger must submit. Even the knowledge that we were not from a great space-traveling civilization, but simple and innocent Christian folk, mere lambs led to this slaughter, would have so heartened the Wersgorix and demoralized our allies, that Branithar must on no account be allowed to communicate the secret.

Not until Sir Owain's plans had reached fruition. Perhaps never. I am sure Branithar himself foresaw a certain awkwardness at the moment when he had deposited his human comrade on English soil. No doubt he made his own devious plans against it. But for the present, their interests ran in the same channel.

These considerations alone will disprove certain sniggering canards about Lady Catherine. She and Sir Owain dared never be at ease simultaneously. They must stand watch on watch, gun at hip, the entire voyage, lest their crew overwhelm them. It was the most effective chaperonage in history. Not that she would have misbehaved in any event. Confused and frightened she might become, but she was never faithless.

Sir Owain felt reasonably confident that Branithar's data were honest. But he insisted on proof. The boat flew for some ten days, to the indicated region of space. Another couple of weeks were spent casting about, examining various hopeful stars. I shall not try to chronicle what the humans felt, as constellations gradually became familiar again; nor that single aerial glimpse which their bargain with distrustful Branithar vouchsafed them, when Dover castle fluttered its pennons above white cliffs. I do not believe they ever spoke about it.

Their ship screamed from atmosphere and lined out again for the hostile stars.

Chapter XX

SIR ROGER had established himself on the planet we named New Avalon. Our folk needed a rest, and he needed time to settle many questions of securing that vast kingdom which has already fallen to him. He was furthermore in secret negotiation with the Wersgor governor of an entire star cluster. This person seemed willing to yield up all he controlled, could we give him suitable bribes and guarantees. The haggling went slowly, but Sir Roger felt confident of its outcome.

"They know so little about the detection and use of traitors out here," he remarked to me, "that I can buy this fellow for less than an Italian city. Our allies never attempted this, for they imagined that the Wersgor nation must be as solid as their own. Yet isn't it logic, that so vast a sprawl of estates, separated by days and weeks of travel, must in many ways resemble a European country? Though even more corruptible—"

"Since they lack the true Faith," I said.

"Hm, well, yes, no doubt. Though I've never found Christians who refused a bribe on religious grounds. I was thinking that the Wersgor type of government commands no fealty."

At any rate, we had a little while of peace, camped in a dale beneath dizzyingly tall cliffs. A waterfall rushed arrow-straight into a lake more clear than glass, ringed with trees. Even our sprawling, brawling English camp could not hurt so much beauty.

I had settled down outside my own little tent, at ease in a rustic chair. My hard studies laid aside for a moment, I indulged myself with a book from home, a relaxing chronicle of the miracles of St. Cosmas. As if from far off, I heard the crackle of fire-gun practice, the *zap* of archery, the cheerful clatter of quarterstaff play. I was almost asleep, when feet thudded to a halt beside me.

Startled, I blinked upward at the terrified face of a baronial esquire. "Brother Parvus!" he said. "In God's name, come at once!"

"Ugh, uh, whoof?" I said in my drowsiness.

"Exactly," he groaned.

I gathered my cassock and trotted at his heels. Sunlight and blossoming bowers and birdsong overhead were suddenly remote. I knew only the leap of my heart and the realization of how few and weak and far from home we were. "What's awry?"

"I know not," said the esquire. "A message came on the far-speaker, relayed from space by one of our patrol ships. Sir Owain Montbelle desired private talk with my lord. I know not what was spoken on the narrow beam. But Sir Roger came staggering out like a blind man and roared for you. Oh, Brother Parvus, it was horrible to see!"

I thought that I should pray for us all, doomed if the baron's strength and cunning could no longer uphold us. But I was at once too full of pity for him alone. He had borne too much, too long, with never a soul to share the burden. All brave saints, I thought, stand by him now.

Red John Hameward mounted guard outside the portable Jair shelter. He had spied his master's strickenness, and dashed thither from the target range. With strung bow, he bellowed at the crowd that milled and muttered: "Get you back! Back to your places! God's death, I'll put this arrow through the first by-our-lady sod to pester my lord, and break the by-our-lady neck o' the next! Go, I say!"

I brushed the giant aside and entered. It was hot within the shelter. Sunlight filtered through its translucency had a thick color. Mostly it was furnished with homely things, leather, tapestry, armor. But one shelf held instruments of alien manufacture, and a large far-speaker set was placed on the floor.

Sir Roger slumped in a chair before this, chin on breast, his big hands hanging limp. I stole up behind him and laid my own hand on his shoulder. "What is the matter, sire?" I asked, as softly as might be.

He hardly moved. "Go away," he said.

"You called for me."

"I knew not what I was doing. This is between myself and— Go away."

His voice was flat, but it took my whole small stock of courage to walk around in front of him and say, "I presume your receiver inscribed the message as usual?"

"Aye. No doubt. I'd best wipe out that record."

"No."

His gray gaze lifted toward me. I remembered a wolf I had once seen trapped, when the townsfolk closed in to make an end of it. "I don't want to harm you, Brother Parvus," he said.

"Then don't," I answered brusquely, and stooped to turn on the playback.

He gathered his powers, in great weariness. "If you see that message," he warned, "I must kill you for my honor."

I thought back to my boyhood. There had been various short, pungent, purely English words in common use. I selected one and pronounced it. From the corner of an eye, as I squatted by the dials, I saw his jaw fall. He sank back into his chair. I pronounced another English word for good measure.

"Your honor lies in the well-being of your people," I added. "You're not fit to judge anything which can so shake you as this. Sit down and let me hear it."

He huddled into himself. I turned a switch. Sir Owain's face leaped into the screen. I saw that he was also gaunt, the handsomeness less evident, the eyes dry and burning. He spoke in formal, courteous wise, but could not hide his exultation.

I cannot remember his exact words. Nor do they matter. He told his lord what had happened. He was now in space, with the stolen ship. He had approached close to New Avalon to beam this call but taken to his heels again immediately it was spoken. There was no hope of finding him in that vastness. If we yielded, he said, he would arrange the transportation home of our folk, and Branithar assured him the Wersgor emperor would promise to keep hands off Terra. If we did not yield, the recreant would go to Wersgorixan and reveal the truth about us. Then, if necessary, the foe could recruit enough French or Saracen mercenaries to destroy us; but probably the demoralization of our allies, as they learned our weakness, would suffice to bring them to terms. In either case, Sir Roger would never see his wife and children again.

Lady Catherine entered the screen. I recall her words. But I do not choose to write them down. When the record was ended, I wiped it out myself.

We were silent awhile, my lord and I.

At last: "Well," he said, like an old man.

I stared at my feet. "Montbelle said they would re-enter communication range at a certain hour tomorrow, to hear your decision," I mumbled. "'Twould be possible to send numerous unmanned ships, loaded with explosive fused by a magnetic nose, along that far-speaker beam. Belike he could be destroyed."

"You've already asked much of me, Brother Parvus," said Sir Roger. Still his words had no life in them. "Ask me not to slay my lady and children . . . unshriven."

"Aye. Ah, could the vessel be captured? No," I answered myself. "'Twould be a practical impossibility. Any single shot which struck close enough to a little ship like that would more likely make dust of it than merely disable its engines. Or else the damage would be small, and he would at once flee faster than light."

The baron raised his congealed face. "Whatever happens," he said, "no one is to know my lady's part in this. D' you understand? She's not in her right mind. Some fiend has possessed her."

I regarded him with a pity still greater than before. "You're too brave to hide behind such foolishness," I said.

"Well, what can I do?" he growled.

"You can fight on—"

"Hopelessly, once Montbelle has gone to Wersgorixan."

"Or you can accept the terms offered."

"Ha! How long d' you think the blueskins would actually leave Terra in peace?"

"Sir Owain must have some reason to believe they will," I said cautiously.

"He's a fool." Sir Roger's fist smote the arm of the chair. He sat up straight, and the harshness of his voice was a lonely token of hopefulness to me. "Or else he's a blacker Judas than he has even confessed, and hopes to become viceroy after the conquest. See you not, 'tis more than the wish for land which'll force the Wersgorix to overrun our planet. 'Tis the fact that our race has proven itself mortally dangerous. As yet, men are helpless at home. But given a few centuries to prepare, men might well build their own spaceships and overwhelm the universe."

"The Wersgorix have suffered in this war," I argued feebly. "They'll need time to regain what they have lost, even if our allies surrender all occupied worlds. They might very likely find it expedient to leave Terra alone for a hundred years or so."

"Till we're safely dead?" Sir Roger nodded heavily. "Aye, there's the great temptation. The real bribe. Yet would we not burn in hell, if we thus broke faith with unborn children?"

"It may be the best we can do for our race," I said. "Whatever lies beyond our own power is in the charge of God."

"But no, no, no." He twisted his hands together. "I can't. Better to die now like men. . . . Yet Catherine—"

After another stillness, I said, "It may not be too late to dissuade Sir Owain. No soul is irredeemably lost while this life remains. You could recall his honor, and point out to him how foolish it is to rely on Wersgor promises, and offer him forgiveness and great position—"

"And the use of my wife?" he jeered.

But in a moment: "It may be. I'd far liefer spill his evil brains. But perhaps . . . aye, perhaps a talk . . . I would even try to humble myself. Will you aid me, Brother Parvus? I must not curse him to his face. Will you strengthen my spirit?"

Chapter XXI

T HE NEXT evening, we departed New Avalon.
Sir Roger and I went alone, in a tiny unarmed space
lifeboat. We ourselves were but little stronger. I had my cassock and rosary as always: no more. He was clad in a yeoman's
doublet and hose, though he wore sword and dagger and his
gilt spurs were on his boots. His big form sat the pilot chair
as it were a saddle, but his eyes, turned heavenward, were full
of winter.

We had told our captains that this was only a short flight
to view some special thing Sir Owain had fetched. The camp
sensed a lie and rumbled with unease. Red John broke two
quarterstaffs before he restored order. It seemed to me as I
embarked that our enterprise was suddenly rusted. Men sat so
quiet. It was a windless evening, our banners drooped on their
staffs, and I noticed how faded and torn they were.

Our boat split the blue sky and entered blackness, like Lu-
cifer expelled. Briefly I glimpsed a battleship, patrolling in orbit, and would have been much comforted to have those great
guns at my back. But we must take only this helpless splinter. Sir Owain had made that clear, when we talked a second
time along the far-speaker beam. "If you wish, de Tourneville,
we'll receive you for a parley. But you must come alone, in a
plain lifeboat, and unarmed. . . . Oh, very well, you can have
your friar, too. . . . I shall tell you what orbit to assume. At a
certain point thereof, my ship will meet you. If my telescopes
and detectors show any sign of treachery on your part, I'll go
straight to Wersgorixan instead."

We accelerated outward through a silence that thickened.
Once I ventured to say, "If you two can be reconciled, it will
put heart back in our people. I think then they would be truly
invincible."

"Catherine and I?" barked Sir Roger.

"Why, I-I-I meant you and Sir Owain—" I stammered. But
the truth opened up before me: I had indeed been thinking
of the lady. Owain was nothing in himself. Sir Roger was the

one on whom our whole fate rested. Yet he could not continue much longer, sundered from her who possessed his soul.

She, and the children they had had together, were the reason he came so meekly to beg Owain's indulgence.

Outward and outward we fled. The planet shrank to a tarnished coin behind us. I had not felt so alone before, not even when we were first borne from our Earth.

But at last a few of the many stars were obscured. I saw the lean black form of the spaceship grow, as it matched velocities. We could have tossed a bombshell by hand and destroyed it. But Sir Owain knew well we would never do that, while Catherine and Robert and Matilda were aboard. Presently a magnetic grapnel clanked against our hull. The ships drew together, portal to portal, a cold kiss. We opened our own gates and waited.

Branithar himself stepped through. Victory flamed in him. He recoiled when he saw Sir Roger's glaive and misericord. "You were to have no weapons!" he rasped.

"Oh? Oh, aye. Aye." The baron looked dully down at the blades. "I never thought . . . they're like my spurs, insignia of what I am . . . naught more."

"Give them over," said Branithar.

Sir Roger unbelted both and handed them to the Wersgor in their sheaths. Branithar passed them to another blue and searched our bodies himself. "No hidden guns," he decided. I felt my cheeks burn at the insult, but Sir Roger hardly seemed to notice. "Very well," said Branithar, "follow me."

We went down a corridor to the salon cabin. Sir Owain sat behind a table of inlaid wood. He himself was somber in black velvet, but jewels flashed on the hand which covered a firegun laid in front of him. Lady Catherine wore a gray gown and wimple. She had overlooked a stray lock of hair, which fell across her brow like smoldering fire.

Sir Roger halted just within the cabin door. "Where are the children?" he said.

"They are in my bedchamber with the maidservants." His wife spoke like a machine. "They are well."

"Be seated, sire," urged Sir Owain glibly. His gaze flickered about the room. Branithar had laid the sword and dagger down by him, and stood on his right hand. The other Wersgor, and a third one who had waited here, stood with folded arms by the entrance, just behind us. I took them to be the physician and navigator which had been mentioned; the two gunners must be at their turrets, the pilot up by his controls, in case aught went amiss. Lady Catherine stood, a waxen image, against the rear wall to Owain's left.

"You bear no grudges, I trust," said the recreant. "All's fair in love and war."

Catherine lifted a hand to protest. "In war only." She could scarce be heard. The hand fell down again.

Sir Roger and I kept our feet. He spat on the deck.

Owain reddened. "Look you," he exclaimed, "let's have no cant about broken vows. Your own position is more than doubtful. You've arrogated to yourself the right of creating noblemen out of peasants and serfs, disposing of fiefs, dealing with foreign kings. Why, you'd make yourself king if you could! What then of your pledges to sovereign Edward?"

"I've done naught to his harm," Sir Roger answered, shaken of voice. "If ever I find Terra, I'll add my conquests to his domain. Until then, we must manage somehow, and have no choice but to establish our own feudality."

"That may have been the case hitherto," Sir Owain admitted. His smile returned. "But you should thank me, Roger, that I've lifted this necessity from you. We can go back home!"

"As Wersgor cattle?"

"I think not. But do be seated, you two. I shall have wine and cakes brought. You're my guests now, you know."

"Nay. I'll not break bread with you."

"Then you'll starve to death," said Sir Owain merrily.

Roger became like stone. I noticed for the first time that Lady Catherine wore a holster but that it was empty. Owain must have gotten her weapon on some pretext. Now he alone was armed.

He turned grave as he read our expressions. "My lord," he said, "when you offered to come parley, you could not expect me to refuse such a chance. You'll remain with us."

Catherine stirred. "Owain, no!" she cried. "You never told me—you said he'd be free to leave this ship if—"

He turned his fine profile to her view and said gently, "Think, my lady. Was it not your highest wish, to save him? But you

wept, fearing his pride would never let him yield. Now he is a
prisoner. Your wish is granted. All the dishonor is on myself. I
bear that burden lightly, since 'tis for my lady's dear sake."

She trembled so I could see it. "I had no part in this, Roger,"
she pleaded. "I never imagined—"

Her husband did not look at her. His voice chopped hers off.
"What d' you plan, Montbelle?"

"This new situation has given me new hopes," answered the
other knight. "I confess I was never overly joyed at thought of
bargaining with the Wersgorix. Now 'tis not needful. We can
go directly home. The weapons and chests of gold aboard this
vessel will win me as much as I care to possess."

Branithar, the only nonhuman there who understood his
English, barked: "Hoy, what of me and my friends here?"

Owain answered coolly, "Why should you not accompany
us? Without Sir Roger de Tourneville, the English cause must
soon collapse, so you'll have done your duty to your own
people. I've studied your way of thinking—a particular place
means nothing to you. We'll pick up some females of your race
along the way. As my loyal vassals, you can win as much power
and land on Terra as anywhere else; your descendants will share
the planet with mine. True, you sacrifice a certain amount of
wonted social intercourse, but on the other hand, you gain a
degree of liberty your own government never allowed you."

He had the weapons. Yet I think Branithar yielded to the
argument itself, and that his slow mumble of agreement was
honest.

"And us?" breathed Lady Catherine.

"You and Roger shall have your estate in England," pledged
Sir Owain. "I'll add thereto one at Winchester."

Perhaps he was also honest. Or perhaps he thought, once he
was the overlord of Europe, he could do as he wished with her
husband and herself. She was too shaken to foresee the latter
chance. I saw her suddenly enclouded with dream. She faced
Sir Roger, smiling and weeping. "My love, we can go home
again!"

He glanced at her, once. "But what of the folk we led
hither?" he asked.

"Nay, I cannot risk taking them with us." Sir Owain
shrugged. "They're lowborn anyway."

Sir Roger nodded. "Ah," he said. "So."

Once more he looked at his wife. Then he kicked backward. The spur of knighthood struck into the belly of the Wersgor behind him. He ripped downward.

Falling with the same motion, he rolled across the deck. Sir Owain yelled and leaped up. His fire gun blasted the air. It missed. The baron was too quick, reached upward, seized the other stupefied Wersgor and pulled him down on top. The second fire blast struck that living shield.

Sir Roger heaved the corpse before him, rising and advancing in one gigantic surge of motion. Owain had time for a last shot, which charred the dead flesh. Then Roger threw the body across the table, into the other man's face.

Owain went down beneath it. Sir Roger snatched for his sword. Branithar had already put a hand on it. Sir Roger got the dagger instead. It flared from the sheath. I heard the *thunk* as he drove it through Branithar's hand, into the table, to the very hilt.

"Wait there for me!" snarled Sir Roger. He drew the sword. "Haro! God send the right!"

Sir Owain had scrambled free and risen, still clutching the gun. I found myself a-pant just across the table from him. He aimed squarely at the baron's midriff. I promised the saints many candles and smacked my rosary across the traitor's wrist. He howled. The gun fell from his hand and skidded across the table. Sir Roger's great glaive whistled. Owain was barely fast enough to dodge. The edged steel crashed into the wood. A moment Sir Roger must struggle to free it. The fire gun lay on the deck. I dove for it. So did Lady Catherine, who had dashed around the table. Our brows met. When my wits came back, I was sitting up and Roger was chasing Owain out the door.

Catherine screamed.

Roger stopped as if noosed. She rose in a swirl of garments. "The children, my lord! They're aft, in the bedchamber—where the extra weapons are—"

He cursed and sped out. She followed. I picked myself up, a trifle groggily, the gun which they had both forgotten in my grasp. Branithar bared teeth at me. He tugged against the knife that pinioned him, but only made the blood run faster. I judged him safely held. My attention was elsewhere. The

Wersgor whom my master had disemboweled was still alive, but would not remain so for long. A moment I hesitated . . . where did my duty lie, to my lord and his lady or to a dying heathen? . . . I bent above the contorted blue face. "Father," he gasped. I know not who, or Who, he called upon, but I led him through such poor rites as the circumstances allowed and held him while he died. I pray he may at least have won to Limbo.

Sir Roger came back, wiping his sword. He grinned all over, I have rarely seen such joy in a man. "The little wolf!" he whooped. "Aye, Norman blood is ever easy to tell!"

"What happened?" I asked, rising in my soiled raiment.

"Owain didn't make for the arms chest after all," Sir Roger told me. "He must have turned forward instead, to the control turret. But the other crewmen, the gunners, had heard the fight. Judging the chance ripe and the need clear, they went to equip themselves. I saw one of them pass through the boudoir door. The other was at his heels, armed with a long wrench. I fell upon him with my sword, but he fought well and it took a while to get him slain. Meantime Catherine pursued the first and fought him barehanded till he struck her down. Those chicken-headed maidservants did naught but cower and scream, as expected. But then! Listen, Brother Parvus! My son Robert opened the weapon chest, took forth a gun and plugged that Wersgor as neatly as Red John could have. Oh, the little devil-cub!"

My lady entered. Her braids hung loose, and one fair cheek was purpled with a bruise. But she said as impersonally as any sergeant reporting an assignment of pickets: "I quieted the children down."

"Poor tiny Matilda," murmured her husband. "Was she very much frightened?"

Lady Catherine looked indignant. "They both wanted to come fight!"

"Wait here," he said. "I'll go deal with Owain and the pilot."

She drew a shaken breath. "Must I forever hide away when my lord goes into peril?"

He stopped still and looked upon her. "But I thought—" he began, oddly helpless.

"That I betrayed you merely to win home again? Aye." She

stared at the deck. "I think you'll forgive me for that long ere I can ever forgive myself. Yet I did what seemed best . . . for you, too. . . . I was confused. 'Twas like a fever dream. You should not have left me alone so long, my lord. I missed you too much."

Very slowly he nodded. "'Tis I who must beg pardon," he said. "God grant me years enough to become worthy of you."

Clasping her shoulders: "But remain here. 'Tis needful you guard yon blueface. If I should kill Owain and the pilot—"

"Do that!" she cried in upsurging fury.

"I'd liefer not," he said with the same gentleness as he used toward her. "Looking upon you, I can understand him so well. But—if worst come to worst—Branithar can guide us home. So watch him."

She took the gun from me and sat down. The nailed captive stood rigid with defiance.

"Come, Brother Parvus," said Sir Roger. "I may need your skill with words."

He carried his sword and had thrust a fire gun from the weapon chest into his belt. We made our way along a corridor, up a ramp, and so to the entrance of the control turret. Its door was shut, locked from within.

Sir Roger beat upon it with the pommel of his glaive. "You two in there!" he shouted. "Yield yourselves!"

"And if we do not?" Owain's voice drifted faintly through the panels.

"If naught else," said Roger starkly, "I'll wreck the engines and depart in my boat, leaving you adrift. But see here: I've rid myself of anger. Everything has ended for the best, and we shall indeed go home—*after* these stars have been made safe for Englishmen. You and I were friends once, Owain. Give me your hand again. I swear no harm shall come to you."

Silence lay heavy.

Until the man behind the door said: "Aye. You were never one to break an oath, were you? Very well, come on through, Roger."

I heard the bolt click down. The baron put his hand to the door. I know not what impelled me to say, "Wait, sire," and shove myself before him with unheard-of ill manners.

"What is it?" He blinked, bemused in his gladness.

I opened the door and stepped over the threshold. Two iron bars smashed down on my head.

The rest of this adventure must needs be told from hearsay, for I was not to come to my senses for a week. I toppled in blood, and Sir Roger thought me slain.

The moment they saw it was not the baron they had gotten, Owain and the pilot attacked him. They were armed with two unscrewed stanchions, as long and heavy as swords. Sir Roger's blade flashed. The pilot threw up his club. The blade glanced off in a shower of sparks. Sir Roger howled so the walls echoed. "*You murderers of innocence*—" His second blow knocked the bar out of a numbed hand. At his third, the blue head sprang from its shoulders and bounced down the ramp.

Catherine heard the uproar. She went to the door of the salon and looked forward, as if terror could sharpen her eyes to pierce the walls between. Branithar set his teeth together. He seized the misericord with his free hand. Muscles jumped forth in his shoulders. Few men could have drawn that blade, but Branithar did.

My lady heard the noise and whirled. Branithar was rounding the table. His right hand hung torn, astream with blood, but the knife gleamed in his left.

She raised her gun. "Back!" she yelled.

"Put that down," he said scornfully. "You'd never use it. You never saw enough stars at Terra, with wise enough vision. If anything goes wrong in the bows, I am your only way home."

She looked into the eyes of her husband's enemy, and shot him dead. Then she ran toward the turret.

Sir Owain Montbelle had scampered back into that chamber. He could not fend off the sheer fury of Sir Roger's assault. The baron drew his gun. Owain snatched up a book and held it before his breast.

"Have a care!" he panted. "This is the ship's log. It has the notes on Terra's position. There are no others."

"You lie. There's Branithar's mind." Nonetheless, Sir Roger thrust the gun back in his belt as he stalked forward. "I'm sorry to outrage clean steel with your blood. For you killed Brother Parvus and you're going to die."

Owain poised. His stanchion was a clumsy weapon. But he raised his arm and hurled it. Struck across the brow, Sir Roger lurched backward. Owain sprang, snatched the gun from the stunned man's belt, and dodged a feeble sword-slash. He scuttled clear, yelling his triumph. Roger stumbled toward him. Owain took aim.

Catherine appeared in the door. Her gun flamed. The book of her journey vanished in smoke and ash. Owain screamed in anguish. Coldly, she fired again, and he fell.

She flung herself into Roger's arms and wept. He comforted her. Yet I wonder which of them gave the most strength to the other.

Afterward he said ruefully: "I fear we've managed ill. Now the way home is indeed lost."

"It doesn't matter," she whispered. "Where you are, there is England."

Epilogue

A NOISE of trumpets and cloven air broke loose. The captain laid the typescript down and pressed an intercom button. "What's going on?" he snapped.

"That eight-legged seneschal up at the castle finally got hold of his boss, sir," answered the voice of the sociotech. "As near as I can make out, the planetary duke was out on safari, and it took all this while to locate him. He uses a whole continent for his hunting preserve. Anyhow, he's just now arriving. Come see the show. A hundred antigrav aircraft—good Lord!—the ones that've landed are disgorging horsemen!"

"Ceremonial, no doubt. Just a minute and I'll be there." The captain glared at the typescript. He had read about halfway through it. How could he talk intelligently to this fantastic overlord without some inkling of what had really developed out here?

He skimmed hastily, page after page. The chronicle of the Wersgor Crusade was long and thunderous. Suffice it to read the conclusion, how King Roger I was crowned by the Archbishop of New Canterbury, and reigned for many fruitful years.

But what had *happened*? Oh, sure, one way or another the English won their battles. Eventually they acquired enough actual strength to be independent of their leader's luck and cunning. But their society! How could even their language, let alone their institutions, have survived contact with old and sophisticated civilizations? Hang it, why had the sociotech translated this long-winded Brother Parvus at all, unless some significant data were included? . . . Wait. Yes. A passage near the end caught the captain's eye. He read:

". . . I have remarked that Sir Roger de Tourneville established the feudal system on newly conquered worlds given into his care by the allies. Some latter-day mockers of my noble master have implied he did this only because he knew nothing better to do. I refute this. As I said before, the collapse of Wersgorixan was not unlike the collapse of Rome, and similar problems found a similar answer. His advantage lay in having that answer ready to hand, the experience of many Terrestrial centuries.

"To be sure, each planet was a separate case requiring separate treatment. However, most of them had certain important things in common. The native populations were eager to follow the behest of us, their liberators. Quite apart from gratitude, they were poor ignorant folk, their own civilizations long ago obliterated; they needed guidance in all things. By embracing the Faith, they proved they had souls. This forced our English clergy to ordain converts in great haste. Father Simon found texts of Scripture and the Church Fathers to support this practical necessity—indeed, while he himself never claimed so, it would seem that the veritable God consecrated him a bishop by sending him so far out *in partibus infidelium*. Once this is granted, it follows that he did not exceed his authority in planting the seed of our own Catholic church. Of course, in his day we were always careful to speak of the Archbishop of New Canterbury as 'our' Pope, or the 'Popelet,' to remind us that this was a mere agent of the true Holy Father, whom we could not find. I deplore the carelessness of the younger generations in this matter of titles.

"Oddly enough, no few Wersgorix soon came to accept the new order. Their central government had always been a distant thing to them, a mere collector of taxes and enforcer of arbitrary laws. Many a blueskin found his imagination captured by our rich ceremonial and by a government of individual nobles whom he could meet face to face. Moreover, by loyally serving these overlords, he might hope to regain an estate, or even a title. Of the Wersgorix who have repented their sins and become valuable Christian Englishmen, I need only mention our one-time foe Huruga, whom all this world of Yorkshire honors as Archbishop William.

"But there was nothing disingenuous in Sir Roger's proceedings. He never betrayed his allies, as some have charged. He dealt with them shrewdly, but except for the necessary concealment of our true origin (which mask he dropped as soon as we had waxed strong enough not to fear exposure) he was aboveboard. It was not his fault that God always favors the English.

"Jairs, Ashenkoghli, and Pr?*tans fell in with his proposals readily enough. They had no real concept of empire. If they could have whatever planets without natives we seized, they were quite happy to leave us humans the immensely troublesome task of governing that larger number where a slave population existed. They turned hypocritical eyes away from the often bloody necessities of such government. I am sure that many of their politicians secretly rejoiced that each new responsibility of this sort thinned out the force of their enigmatic associate; for he must create a duke and lesser gentility for it, then leave that small garrison to train the aborigines. Uprisings, internecine war, Wersgor counterattacks, reduced these tiny cadres still further. Having little military tradition of their own, the Jairs, Ashenkoghli, and Pr?*tans did not realize how those cruel years welded bonds of loyalty between native peasants and English aristocrats. Also, being somewhat effete, they did not foresee how lustily humans would breed.

"So in the end, when all these facts were pikestaff plain, it was too late. Our allies were still only three nations, each with its own language and way of life. Springing up around them were a hundred races, united in Christendom, the English tongue, and the English crown. Even if we humans had wished, we could not have changed this. Indeed, we were about as surprised as anyone.

"As proof that Sir Roger never plotted against his allies, consider how easily he could have overrun them in his old age, when he ruled the mightiest nation ever seen among these stars. But he leaned backward to be generous. It was not his doing that their own younger generation, awestruck by our successes, began more and more to imitate our ways. . . ."

The captain put the pages aside and hurried out to the main airlock entrance. The ramp had been let down, and a red-haired human giant was striding up to greet him. Fantastically clad, bearing a florid ornamental sword, he also carried a businesslike blast gun. Behind him an honor guard of riflemen in Lincoln green stood at attention. Over their heads fluttered a banner with the arms of a cadet branch of the great Hameward family.

The captain's hand was engulfed in a hairy ducal paw. The sociotech translated a distorted English: "At last! God be praised, they've finally learned to build spaceships on Old Earth! Welcome, good sir!"

"But why did you never find us . . . er . . . your grace?" stammered the captain. When it had been translated, the duke shrugged and answered:

"Oh, we searched. For generations every young knight went looking for Earth, unless he chose to look for the Holy Grail. But you know how bloody many suns there are. And even more toward the center of the galaxy—where we encountered still other starfaring peoples. Commerce, exploration, war, everything drew us inward, away from this thinly starred spiral arm. You realize this is only a poor outlying province you've come upon. The King and the Pope dwell away off in the Seventh Heaven. . . . Finally the quest petered out. In past centuries, Old Earth has become little more than a tradition." His big face beamed. "But now it's all turned topsy-turvy. *You* found *us*! Most wonderful! Tell me at once, has the Holy Land been liberated from the paynim?"

"Well," said Captain Yeshu haLevy, who was a loyal citizen of the Israeli Empire, "yes."

"Too bad. I'd have loved a fresh crusade. Life's been dull since we conquered the Dragons ten years ago. They say, however, that the royal expeditions to the Sagittarian star clouds have turned up some very promising planets— But see here! You must come over to the castle. I'll entertain you as best as I can, and outfit you for the trip to the King. That's tricky navigation, but I'll furnish you with an astrologer who knows the way."

"Now what did he say?" asked Captain haLevy, when the bass burble had stopped.

The sociotech explained.

Captain haLevy turned fire color. "No astrologer is going to touch my ship!"

The sociotech sighed. He'd have a lot of work to do in the coming years.

WAY STATION

Clifford D. Simak

1

THE NOISE was ended now. The smoke drifted like thin, gray wisps of fog above the tortured earth and the shattered fences and the peach trees that had been whittled into toothpicks by the cannon fire. For a moment silence, if not peace, fell upon those few square miles of ground where just a while before men had screamed and torn at one another in the frenzy of old hate and had contended in an ancient striving and then had fallen apart, exhausted.

For endless time, it seemed, there had been belching thunder rolling from horizon to horizon and the gouted earth that had spouted in the sky and the screams of horses and the hoarse bellowing of men; the whistling of metal and the thud when the whistle ended; the flash of searing fire and the brightness of the steel; the bravery of the colors snapping in the battle wind.

Then it all had ended and there was a silence.

But silence was an alien note that held no right upon this field or day, and it was broken by the whimper and the pain, the cry for water, and the prayer for death—the crying and the calling and the whimpering that would go on for hours beneath the summer sun. Later the huddled shapes would grow quiet and still and there would be an odor that would sicken all who passed, and the graves would be shallow graves.

There was wheat that never would be harvested, trees that would not bloom when spring came round again, and on the slope of land that ran up to the ridge the words unspoken and the deeds undone and the sodden bundles that cried aloud the emptiness and the waste of death.

There were proud names that were the prouder now, but now no more than names to echo down the ages—the Iron Brigade, the 5th New Hampshire, the 1st Minnesota, the 2nd Massachusetts, the 16th Maine.

And there was Enoch Wallace.

He still held the shattered musket and there were blisters on his hands. His face was smudged with powder. His shoes were caked with dust and blood.

He was still alive.

2

DR. ERWIN HARDWICKE rolled the pencil back and forth between his palms, an irritating business. He eyed the man across the desk from him with some calculation.

"What I can't figure out," said Hardwicke, "is why you should come to us."

"Well, you're the National Academy and I thought . . ."

"And you're Intelligence."

"Look, Doctor, if it suits you better, let's call this visit unofficial. Pretend I'm a puzzled citizen who dropped in to see if you could help."

"It's not that I wouldn't like to help, but I don't see how I can. The whole thing is so hazy and so hypothetical."

"Damn it, man," Claude Lewis said, "you can't deny the proof—the little that I have."

"All right, then," said Hardwicke, "let's start over once again and take it piece by piece. You say you have this man . . ."

"His name," said Lewis, "is Enoch Wallace. Chronologically, he is one hundred and twenty-four years old. He was born on a farm a few miles from the town of Millville in Wisconsin, April 22, 1840, and he is the only child of Jedediah and Amanda Wallace. He enlisted among the first of them when Abe Lincoln called for volunteers. He was with the Iron Brigade, which was virtually wiped out at Gettysburg in 1863. But Wallace somehow managed to get transferred to another fighting outfit and fought down across Virginia under Grant. He was in on the end of it at Appomattox . . ."

"You've run a check on him."

"I've looked up his records. The record of enlistment at the State Capitol in Madison. The rest of it, including discharge, here in Washington."

"You say he looks like thirty."

"Not a day beyond it. Maybe even less than that."

"But you haven't talked with him."

Lewis shook his head.

"He may not be the man. If you had fingerprints . . ."

"At the time of the Civil War," said Lewis, "they'd not thought of fingerprints."

"The last of the veterans of the Civil War," said Hardwicke, "died several years ago. A Confederate drummer boy, I think. There must be some mistake."

Lewis shook his head. "I thought so myself, when I was assigned to it."

"How come you were assigned? How does Intelligence get involved in a deal like this?"

"I'll admit," said Lewis, "that it's a bit unusual. But there were so many implications . . ."

"Immortality, you mean."

"It crossed our mind, perhaps. The chance of it. But only incidentally. There were other considerations. It was a strange setup that bore some looking into."

"But Intelligence . . ."

Lewis grinned. "You are thinking, why not a scientific outfit? Logically, I suppose it should have been. But one of our men ran afoul of it. He was on vacation. Had relatives back in Wisconsin. Not in that particular area, but some thirty miles away. He heard a rumor—just the vaguest rumor, almost a casual mention. So he nosed around a bit. He didn't find out too much, but enough to make him think there might be something to it."

"That's the thing that puzzles me," said Hardwicke. "How could a man live for one hundred and twenty-four years in one locality without becoming a celebrity that the world would hear about? Can you imagine what the newspapers could do with a thing like this?"

"I shudder," Lewis said, "when I think about it."

"You haven't told me how."

"This," said Lewis, "is a bit hard to explain. You'd have to know the country and the people in it. The southwestern corner of Wisconsin is bounded by two rivers, the Mississippi on the west, the Wisconsin on the north. Away from the rivers there is flat, broad prairie land, rich land, with prosperous farms and towns. But the land that runs down to the river is rough and rugged; high hills and bluffs and deep ravines and cliffs, and there are certain areas forming bays or pockets that are isolated. They are served by inadequate roads and the small, rough farms are inhabited by a people who are closer, perhaps, to the pioneer days of a hundred years ago than they are to the twentieth century. They have cars, of course, and radios, and someday soon, perhaps, even television. But in spirit they are conservative and clannish—not all the people, of course, not even many of them, but these little isolated neighborhoods.

"At one time there were a lot of farms in these isolated pockets, but today a man can hardly make a living on a farm of that sort. Slowly the people are being squeezed out of the areas by economic circumstances. They sell their farms for whatever they can get for them and move somewhere else, to the cities mostly, where they can make a living."

Hardwicke nodded. "And the ones that are left, of course, are the most conservative and clannish."

"Right. Most of the land now is held by absentee owners who make no pretense of farming it. They may run a few head of cattle on it, but that is all. It's not too bad as a tax write-off for someone who needs that sort of thing. And in the land-bank days a lot of the land was put into the bank."

"You're trying to tell me these backwoods people—is that what you'd call them?—engaged in a conspiracy of silence."

"Perhaps not anything," said Lewis, "as formal or elaborate as that. It is just their way of doing things, a holdover from the old, stout pioneer philosophy. They minded their own business. They didn't want folks interfering with them and they interfered with no one else. If a man wanted to live to be a thousand, it might be a thing of wonder, but it was his own damned business. And if he wanted to live alone and be let alone while he was doing it, that was his business, too. They might talk about it among themselves, but to no one else. They'd resent it if some outsider tried to talk about it.

"After a time, I suppose, they came to accept the fact that Wallace kept on being young while they were growing old. The wonder wore off it and they probably didn't talk about it a great deal, even among themselves. New generations accepted it because their elders saw in it nothing too unusual—and anyhow no one saw much of Wallace because he kept strictly to himself.

"And in the nearby areas the thing, when it was thought of at all, grew to be just a sort of legend—another crazy tale that wasn't worth looking into. Maybe just a joke among those

folks down Dark Hollow way. A Rip Van Winkle sort of business that probably didn't have a word of truth in it. A man
might look ridiculous if he went prying into it."

"But your man looked into it."

"Yes. Don't ask me why."

"Yet he wasn't assigned to follow up the job."

"He was needed somewhere else. And besides he was known
back there."

"And you?"

"It took two years of work."

"But now you know the story."

"Not all of it. There are more questions now than there were
to start with."

"You've seen this man."

"Many times," said Lewis. "But I've never talked with him. I
don't think he's ever seen me. He takes a walk each day before
he goes to get the mail. He never moves off the place, you see.
The mailman brings out the little stuff he needs. A bag of flour,
a pound of bacon, a dozen eggs, cigars, and sometimes liquor."

"But that must be against the postal regulations."

"Of course it is. But mailmen have been doing it for years.
It doesn't hurt a thing until someone screams about it. And no
one's going to. The mailmen probably are the only friends he
has ever had."

"I take it this Wallace doesn't do much farming."

"None at all. He has a little vegetable garden, but that is all
he does. The place has gone back pretty much to wilderness."

"But he has to live. He must get money somewhere."

"He does," said Lewis. "Every five or ten years or so he ships
off a fistful of gems to an outfit in New York."

"Legal?"

"If you mean, is it hot, I don't think so. If someone wanted
to make a case of it, I suppose there are illegalities. Not to start
with, when he first started sending them, back in the old days.
But laws change and I suspect both he and the buyer are in
defiance of any number of them."

"And you don't mind?"

"I checked on this firm," said Lewis, "and they were rather
nervous. For one thing, they'd been stealing Wallace blind. I
told them to keep on buying. I told them that if anyone came

around to check, to refer them straight to me. I told them to keep their mouths shut and not change anything."

"You don't want anyone to scare him off," said Hardwicke.

"You're damned right, I don't. I want the mailman to keep on acting as a delivery boy and the New York firm to keep on buying gems. I want everything to stay just the way it is. And before you ask me where the stones come from, I'll tell you I don't know."

"He maybe has a mine."

"That would be quite a mine. Diamonds and rubies and emeralds, all out of the same mine."

"I would suspect, even at the prices that he gets from them, he picks up a fair income."

Lewis nodded. "Apparently he only sends a shipment in when he runs out of cash. He wouldn't need too much. He lives rather simply, to judge from the grub he buys. But he subscribes to a lot of daily papers and news magazines and to dozens of scientific journals. He buys a lot of books."

"Technical books?"

"Some of them, of course, but mostly keeping up with new developments. Physics and chemistry and biology—all that sort of stuff."

"But I don't . . ."

"Of course you don't. Neither do I. He's no scientist. Or at least he has no formal education in the sciences. Back in the days when he went to school there wasn't much of it—not in the sense of today's scientific education. And whatever he learned then would be fairly worthless now in any event. He went through grade school—one of those one-room country schools—and spent one winter at what was called an academy that operated for a year or two down in Millville village. In case you don't know, that was considerably better than par back in the 1850s. He was, apparently, a fairly bright young man."

Hardwicke shook his head. "It sounds incredible. You've checked on all of this?"

"As well as I could. I had to go at it gingerly. I wanted no one to catch on. And one thing I forgot—he does a lot of writing. He buys these big, bound record books, in lots of a dozen at the time. He buys ink by the pint."

Hardwicke got up from his desk and paced up and down the room.

"Lewis," he said, "if you hadn't shown me your credentials and if I hadn't checked on them, I'd figure all of this to be a very tasteless joke."

He went back and sat down again. He picked up the pencil and started rolling it between his palms once more.

"You've been on the case two years," he said. "You have no ideas?"

"Not a one," said Lewis. "I'm entirely baffled. That is why I'm here."

"Tell me more of his history. After the war, that is."

"His mother died," said Lewis, "while he was away. His father and the neighbors buried her right there on the farm. That was the way a lot of people did it then. Young Wallace got a furlough, but not in time to get home for the funeral. There wasn't much embalming done in those days and the traveling was slow. Then he went back to the war. So far as I can find, it was his only furlough. The old man lived alone and worked the farm, batching it and getting along all right. From what I can pick up, he was a good farmer, an exceptionally good farmer for his day. He subscribed to some farm journals and was progressive in his ideas. He paid attention to such things as crop rotation and the prevention of erosion. The farm wasn't much of a farm by modern standards, but it made him a living and a little extra he managed to lay by.

"Then Enoch came home from the war and they farmed the place together for a year or so. The old man bought a mower —one of those horse-drawn contraptions with a sickle bar to cut hay or grain. It was the progressive thing to do. It beat a scythe all hollow.

"Then one afternoon the old man went out to mow a hay-field. The horses ran away. Something must have scared them. Enoch's father was thrown off the seat and forward, in front of the sickle bar. It was not a pretty way to die."

Hardwicke made a grimace of distaste. "Horrible," he said.

"Enoch went out and gathered up his father and got the body to the house. Then he took a gun and went hunting for the horses. He found them down in the corner of the pasture and he shot the two of them and he left them. I mean exactly that. For years their skeletons lay there in the pasture, where he'd killed them, still hitched to the mower until the harness rotted.

"Then he went back to the house and laid his father out. He washed him and he dressed him in the good black suit and laid him on a board, then went out to the barn and carpentered a coffin. And after that, he dug a grave beside his mother's grave. He finished it by lantern light, then went back to the house and sat up with his father. When morning came, he went to tell the nearest neighbor and that neighbor notified the others and someone went to get a preacher. Late in the afternoon they had the funeral, and Enoch went back to the house. He has lived there ever since, but he never farmed the land. Except the garden, that is."

"You told me these people wouldn't talk to strangers. You seem to have learned a lot."

"It took two years to do it. I infiltrated them. I bought a beat-up car and drifted into Millville and I let it out that I was a ginseng hunter."

"A what?"

"A ginseng hunter. Ginseng is a plant."

"Yes, I know. But there's been no market for it for years."

"A small market and an occasional one. Exporters will take on some of it. But I hunted other medicinal plants as well and pretended an extensive knowledge of them and their use. 'Pretended' isn't actually the word; I boned up plenty on them."

"The kind of simple soul," said Hardwicke, "those folks could understand. A sort of cultural throwback. And inoffensive, too. Perhaps not quite right in the head."

Lewis nodded. "It worked even better than I thought. I just wandered around and people talked to me. I even found some ginseng. There was one family in particular—the Fisher family. They live down in the river bottoms below the Wallace farm, which sits on the ridge above the bluffs. They've lived there almost as long as the Wallace family, but a different stripe entirely. The Fishers are a coon-hunting, catfishing, moonshine-cooking tribe. They found a kindred spirit in me. I was just as shiftless and no-account as they were. I helped them with their moonshine, both in the making and the drinking and once in a while the peddling. I went fishing with them and hunting with them and I sat around and talked and they showed me a place or two where I might find some ginseng—'sang' is what they call it. I imagine a social scientist might find a gold mine in the Fishers. There is one girl—a deaf-mute, but a pretty thing, and she can charm off warts . . ."

"I recognize the type," said Hardwicke. "I was born and raised in the southern mountains."

"They were the ones who told me about the team and mower. So one day I went up in that corner of the Wallace pasture and did some digging. I found a horse's skull and some other bones."

"But no way of knowing if it was one of the Wallace horses."

"Perhaps not," said Lewis. "But I found part of the mower as well. Not much left of it, but enough to identify."

"Let's get back to the history," suggested Hardwicke. "After the father's death, Enoch stayed on at the farm. He never left it?"

Lewis shook his head. "He lives in the same house. Not a thing's been changed. And the house apparently has aged no more than the man."

"You've been in the house?"

"Not in it. At it. I will tell you how it was."

3

HE HAD an hour. He knew he had an hour, for he had timed Enoch Wallace during the last ten days. And from the time he left the house until he got back with his mail, it had never been less than an hour. Sometimes a little longer, when the mailman might be late, or they got to talking. But an hour, Lewis told himself, was all that he could count on.

Wallace had disappeared down the slope of ridge, heading for the point of rocks that towered above the bluff face, with the Wisconsin River running there below. He would climb the rocks and stand there, with the rifle tucked beneath his arm, to gaze across the wilderness of the river valley. Then he would go back down the rocks again and trudge along the wooded path to where, in proper season, the pink lady's-slippers grew, and from there up the hill again to the spring that gushed out of the hillside just below the ancient field that had lain fallow for a century or more, and then along the slope until he hit the almost overgrown road and so down to the mailbox.

In the ten days that Lewis had watched him, his route had never varied. It was likely, Lewis told himself, that it had not varied through the years. Wallace did not hurry. He walked as if he had all the time there was. And he stopped along the way to renew acquaintances with old friends of his—a tree, a squirrel, a flower. He was a rugged man and there still was much of the soldier in him—old tricks and habits left from the bitter years of campaigning under many leaders. He walked with his head held high and his shoulders back and he moved with the easy stride of one who had known hard marches.

Lewis came out of the tangled mass of trees that once had been an orchard and in which a few trees, twisted and gnarled and gray with age, still bore their pitiful and bitter crop of apples.

He stopped at the edge of the copse and stood for a moment to stare up at the house on the ridge above, and for a single instant it seemed to him the house stood in a special light, as if a rare and more distilled essence of the sun had crossed the gulf of space to shine upon this house and to set it apart from all other houses in the world. Bathed in that light, the house was somehow unearthly, as if, indeed, it might be set apart as a very special thing. And then the light, if it ever had been there, was gone and the house shared the common sunlight of the fields and woods.

Lewis shook his head and told himself that it had been foolishness, or perhaps a trick of seeing. For there was no such thing as special sunlight and the house was no more than a house, although wondrously preserved.

It was the kind of house one did not see too often in these days. It was rectangular; long and narrow and high, with old-fashioned gingerbread along the eaves and gables. It had a certain gauntness that had nothing to do with age; it had been gaunt the day it had been built—gaunt and plain and strong, like the people that it sheltered. But gaunt as it might be, it stood prim and neat, with no peeling paint, with no sign of weathering, and no hint of decay.

Against one end of it was a smaller building, no more than a shed, as if it were an alien structure that had been carted in from some other place and shoved against its end, covering the side door of the house. Perhaps the door, thought Lewis, that led into the kitchen. The shed undoubtedly had been used as a place to hang outdoor clothing and to leave overshoes and boots, with a bench for milk cans and buckets, and perhaps a basket in which to gather eggs. From the top of it extended some three feet of stovepipe.

Lewis went up to the house and around the shed and there, in the side of it, was a door ajar. He stepped up on the stoop and pushed the door wide open and stared in amazement at the room.

For it was not a simple shed. It apparently was the place where Wallace lived.

The stove from which the stovepipe projected stood in one corner, an ancient cookstove, smaller than the old-fashioned kitchen range. Sitting on its top was a coffeepot, a frying pan, and a griddle. Hung from hooks on a board behind it were other cooking implements. Opposite the stove, shoved against the wall, was a three-quarter-size four-poster bed, covered with a lumpy quilt, quilted in one of the ornate patterns of many pieces of many-colored cloth, such as had been the delight of ladies of a century before. In another corner was a table and a chair, and above the table, hung against the wall, a small open cupboard in which were stacked some dishes. On the table stood a kerosene lantern, battered from much usage, but with its chimney clean, as if it had been washed and polished as recently as this morning.

There was no door into the house, no sign there had ever been a door. The clapboard of the house's outer wall ran unbroken to form the fourth wall of the shed.

This was incredible, Lewis told himself—that there should be no door, that Wallace should live here, in this shed, when there was a house to live in. As if there were some reason he should not occupy the house, and yet must stay close by it. Or perhaps that he might be living out a penance of some sort, living here in this shed as a medieval hermit might have lived in a woodland hut or in a desert cave.

He stood in the center of the shed and looked around him,

hoping that he might find some clue to this unusual circumstance. But there was nothing, beyond the bare, hard fact of living, the very basic necessities of living—the stove to cook his food and heat the place, the bed to sleep on, the table to eat on, and the lantern for its light. Not even so much as an extra hat (although, come to think of it, Wallace never wore a hat) or an extra coat.

No sign of magazines or papers, and Wallace never came home from the mailbox empty-handed. He subscribed to the New York *Times*, the *Wall Street Journal*, the *Christian Science Monitor*, and the Washington *Star*, as well as many scientific and technical journals. But there was no sign of them here, nor of the many books he bought. No sign, either, of the bound record books. Nothing at all on which a man could write.

Perhaps, Lewis told himself, this shed, for some baffling reason, was no more than a show place, a place staged most carefully to make one think that this was where Wallace lived. Perhaps, after all, he lived in the house. Although, if that were the case, why all this effort, not too successful, to make one think he didn't?

Lewis turned to the door and walked out of the shed. He went around the house until he reached the porch that led up to the front door. At the foot of the steps, he stopped and looked around. The place was quiet. The sun was midmorning-high and the day was warming up and this sheltered corner of the earth stood relaxed and hushed, waiting for the heat.

He looked at his watch and he had forty minutes left, so he went up the steps and across the porch until he came to the door. Reaching out his hand, he grasped the knob and turned—except he didn't turn it; the knob stayed exactly where it was and his clenched fingers went half around it in the motion of a turn.

Puzzled, he tried again and still he didn't turn the knob. It was as if the knob were covered with some hard, slick coating, like a coat of brittle ice, on which the fingers slipped without exerting any pressure on the knob.

He bent his head close to the knob and tried to see if there were any evidence of coating, and there was no evidence. The knob looked perfectly all right—too all right, perhaps. For it was clean, as if someone had wiped and polished it. There was no dust upon it, and no weather specks.

He tried a thumbnail on it, and the thumbnail slipped but left no mark behind it. He ran his palm over the outer surface of the door and the wood was slick. The rubbing of the palm set up no friction. The palm slid along the wood as if the palm were greased, but there was no sign of grease. There was no indication of anything to account for the slickness of the door.

Lewis moved from the door to the clapboard and the clapboard also was slick. He tried palm and thumbnail on it and the answer was the same. There was something covering this house which made it slick and smooth—so smooth that dust could not cling upon its surface nor could weather stain it.

He moved along the porch until he came to a window, and now, as he stood facing the window, he realized something he had not noticed before, something that helped make the house seem gaunter than it really was. The windows were black. There were no curtains, no drapes, no shades; they were simply black rectangles, like empty eyes staring out of the bare skull of the house.

He moved closer to the window and put his face up to it, shading the sides of his face, next to the eyes, with his upheld hands to shield out the sunlight. But even so, he could not see into the room beyond. He stared, instead, into a pool of blackness, and the blackness, curiously enough, had no reflective qualities. He could not see himself reflected in the glass. He could see nothing but the blackness, as if the light hit the window and was absorbed by it, sucked in and held by it. There was no bouncing back of light once it had hit that window.

He left the porch and went slowly around the house, examining it as he went. The windows were all blank, black pools that sucked in the captured light, and all the exterior was slick and hard.

He pounded the clapboard with his fist, and it was like the pounding of a rock. He examined the stone walls of the basement where they were exposed, and the walls were smooth and slick. There were mortar gaps between the stones and in the stones themselves one could see uneven surfaces, but the hand rubbed across the wall could detect no roughness.

An invisible something had been laid over the roughness of the stone, just enough of it to fill in the pits and uneven surfaces. But one could not detect it. It was almost as if it had no substance.

Straightening up from his examination of the wall, Lewis looked at his watch. There were only ten minutes left. He must be getting on.

He walked down the hill toward the tangle of old orchard. At its edge he stopped and looked back, and now the house was different. It was no longer just a structure. It wore a personality, a mocking, leering look, and there was a malevolent chuckle bubbling inside of it, ready to break out.

Lewis ducked into the orchard and worked his way in among the trees. There was no path and beneath the trees the grass and weeds grew tall. He ducked the drooping branches and walked around a tree that had been uprooted in some windstorm of many years before.

He reached up as he went along, picking an apple here and there, scrubby things and sour, taking a single bite out of each one of them, then throwing it away, for there was none of them that was fit to eat, as if they might have taken from the neglected soil a certain basic bitterness.

At the far side of the orchard he found the fence and the graves that it enclosed. Here the weeds and grass were not so high and the fence showed signs of repair made rather recently, and at the foot of each grave, opposite the three crude native limestone headstones, was a peony bush, each a great straggling mass of plants that had grown, undisciplined, for years.

Standing before the weathered picketing, he knew that he had stumbled on the Wallace family burial plot.

But there should have been only the two stones. What about the third?

He moved around the fence to the sagging gate and went into the plot. Standing at the foot of the graves, he read the legends on the stones. The carving was angular and rough, giving evidence of having been executed by unaccustomed hands. There were no pious phrases, no lines of verse, no carvings of angels or of lambs or of other symbolic figures such as had been customary in the 1860s. There were just the names and dates.

On the first stone: Amanda Wallace 1821–1863

And on the second stone: Jedediah Wallace 1816–1866

And on the third stone——

4

"GIVE ME that pencil, please," said Lewis.

Hardwicke quit rolling it between his palms and handed it across.

"Paper, too?" he asked.

"If you please," said Lewis.

He bent above the desk and drew rapidly.

"Here," he said, handing back the paper.

Hardwicke wrinkled his brow.

"But it makes no sense," he said. "Except for that figure underneath."

"The figure eight, lying on its side. Yes, I know. The symbol for infinity."

"But the rest of it?"

"I don't know," said Lewis. "It is the inscription on the tombstone. I copied it . . ."

"And you know it now by heart."

"I should. I've studied it enough."

"I've never seen anything like it in my life," said Hardwicke. "Not that I'm an authority. I really know little at all in this field."

"You can put your mind at rest. It's nothing that anyone knows anything about. It bears no resemblance, not even the remotest, to any language or any known inscription. I checked with men who know. Not one, but a dozen of them. I told them I'd found it on a rocky cliff. I am sure that most of them think I am a crackpot. One of those people who are trying to prove that the Romans or the Phoenicians or the Irish or what-not had pre-Columbian settlements in America."

Hardwicke put down the sheet of paper.

"I can see what you mean," he said, "when you say you have more questions now than when you started. Not only the question of a young man more than a century old, but likewise the matter of the slickness of the house and the third gravestone with the undecipherable inscription. You say you've never talked with Wallace?"

"No one talks to him. Except the mailman. He goes out on his daily walks and he packs this gun."

"People are afraid to talk with him?"

"Because of the gun, you mean."

"Well, yes, I suppose that was in the back of my mind. I wondered why he carried it."

Lewis shook his head. "I don't know. I've tried to tie it in, to find some reason he always has it with him. He has never fired the rifle so far as I can find. But I don't think the rifle is the reason no one talks with him. He's an anachronism, something living from another age. No one fears him, I am sure of that. He's been around too long for anyone to fear him. Too familiar. He's a fixture of the land, like a tree or boulder. And yet no one feels quite comfortable with him, either. I would imagine that most of them, if they should come face to face with him, would feel uncomfortable. For he's something they are not—something greater than they are and at the same time a good deal less. As if he were a man who had walked away from his own humanity. I think that, secretly, many of his neighbors may be a bit ashamed of him, shamed because he has, somehow, perhaps ignobly, sidestepped growing old, one of the penalties, but perhaps, as well, one of the rights of all humankind. And perhaps this secret shame may contribute in some part to their unwillingness to talk about him."

"You spent a good deal of time watching him?"

"There was a time I did. But now I have a crew. They watch on regular shifts. We have a dozen spots we watch from, and we keep shifting them around. There isn't an hour, day in, day out, that the Wallace house isn't under observation."

"This business really has you people bugged."

"I think with reason," Lewis said. "There is still one other thing."

He bent over and picked up the brief case he had placed beside his chair. Unsnapping it, he took out a sheaf of photographs and handed them to Hardwicke.

"What do you make of these?" he asked.

Hardwicke picked them up. Suddenly he froze. The color drained out of his face. His hands began to tremble and he laid the pictures carefully on the desk. He had looked at only the top one; not any of the others.

Lewis saw the question in his face.

"In the grave," he said. "The one beneath the headstone with the funny writing."

5

THE MESSAGE machine whistled shrilly, and Enoch Wallace put away the book in which he had been writing and got up from his desk. He walked across the room to the whistling machine. He punched a button and shoved a key and the whistling stopped.

The machine built up its hum and the message began to form on the plate, faint at first and then becoming darker until it stood out clearly. It read:

NO. 406301 TO STATION 18327. TRAVELER AT 16097.38. NATIVE THUBAN VI. NO BAGGAGE. NO. 3 LIQUID TANK. SOLUTION 27. DEPART FOR STATION 12892 AT 16439.16. CONFIRM.

Enoch glanced up at the great galactic chronometer hanging on the wall. There was almost three hours to go.

He touched a button, and a thin sheet of metal bearing the message protruded from the side of the machine. Beneath it the duplicate fed itself into the record file. The machine chuckled and the message plate was clear once more and waiting.

Enoch pulled out the metal plate, threaded the holes in it through the double filing spindle and then dropped his fingers to the keyboard and typed: NO. 406301 RECEIVED. CON-FIRM MOMENTARILY. The message came into being on the plate and he left it there.

Thuban VI? Had there been, he wondered, one of them before? As soon as he got his chores done, he would go to the filing cabinet and check.

It was a liquid tank case and those, as a rule, were the most uninteresting of all. They usually were hard ones to strike up a conversation with, because too often their concept of language was too difficult to handle. And as often, too, their very thinking processes proved too divergent to provide much common ground for communication.

Although, he recalled, that was not always true. There had been that tank traveler several years ago, from somewhere in Hydra (or had it been the Hyades?), he'd sat up the whole night with and almost failed of sending off on time, yarning through the hours, their communication (you couldn't call it words) tumbling over one another as they packed into the little time they had a lot of fellowship and, perhaps, some brotherhood.

He, or she, or it—they'd never got around to that—had not come back again. And that was the way it was, thought Enoch; very few came back. By far the greater part of them were just passing through.

But he had he, or she, or it (whichever it might be) down in black and white, as he had all of them, every single blessed one of them, down in black and white. It had taken him, he remembered, almost the entire following day, crouched above his desk, to get it written down; all the stories he'd been told, all the glimpses he had caught of a far and beautiful and tantalizing land (tantalizing because there was so much of it he could not understand), all the warmth and comradeship that had flowed between himself and this misshapen, twisted, ugly living being from another world. And any time he wished, any day he wished, he could take down the journal from the row of journals and relive that night again. Although he never had. It was strange, he thought, how there was never time, or never seemed to be the time, to thumb through and reread in part what he'd recorded through the years.

He turned from the message machine and rolled a No. 3 liquid tank into place beneath the materializer, positioning it exactly and locking it in place. Then he pulled out the retracting hose and thumbed the selector over to No. 27. He filled the tank and let the hose slide back into the wall.

Back at the machine, he cleared the plate and sent off his confirmation that all was ready for the traveler from Thuban, got back double confirmation from the other end, then threw the machine to neutral, ready to receive again.

He went from the machine to the filing cabinet that stood next to his desk and pulled out a drawer jammed with filing cards. He looked and Thuban VI was there, keyed to August 22, 1931. He walked across the room to the wall filled with books and rows of magazines and journals, filled from floor to ceiling, and found the record book he wanted. Carrying it, he walked back to his desk.

August 22, 1931, he found, when he located the entry, had been one of his lighter days. There had been one traveler only, the one from Thuban VI. And although the entry for the day filled almost a page in his small, crabbed writing, he had devoted no more than one paragraph to the visitor.

Came today [it read] *a blob from Thuban VI. There is no other way in which one might describe it. It is simply a mass of matter, presumably of flesh, and this mass seems to go through some sort of rhythmic change in shape, for periodically it is globular, then begins to flatten out until it lies in the bottom of the tank, somewhat like a pancake. Then it begins to contract and to pull in upon itself, until finally it is a ball again. This change is rather slow and definitely rhythmic, but only in the sense that it follows the same pattern. It seems to have no relation to time. I tried timing it and could detect no time pattern. The shortest period needed to complete the cycle was seven minutes and the longest was eighteen. Perhaps over a longer period one might be able to detect a time rhythm, but I didn't have the time. The semantic translator did not work with it, but it did emit for me a series of sharp clicks, as if it might be clicking claws together, although it had no claws that I could see. When I looked this up in the pasimology manual I learned that what it was trying to say was that it was all right, that it needed no attention, and please leave it alone. Which I did thereafter.*

And at the end of the paragraph, jammed into the little space that had been left, was the notation: *See Oct. 16, 1931.*

He turned the pages until he came to October 16 and that had been one of the days, he saw, that Ulysses had arrived to inspect the station.

His name, of course, was not Ulysses. As a matter of fact, he had no name at all. Among his people there was no need of names; there was other identifying terminology which was far more expressive than mere names. But this terminology, even the very concept of it, was such that it could not be grasped, much less put to use, by human beings.

"I shall call you Ulysses," Enoch recalled telling him, the first time they had met. "I need to call you something."

"It is agreeable," said the then strange being (but no longer strange). "Might one ask why the name Ulysses?"

"Because it is the name of a great man of my race."

"I am glad you chose it," said the newly christened being. "To my hearing it has a dignified and noble sound and, between the two of us, I shall be glad to bear it. And I shall call you Enoch, for the two of us shall work together for many of your years."

And it had been many years, thought Enoch, with the record book open to that October entry of more than thirty years ago. Years that had been satisfying and enriching in a way that one could not have imagined until it had all been laid out before him.

And it would go on, he thought, much longer than it already had gone on—for many centuries more, for a thousand years, perhaps. And at the end of that thousand years, what would he know then?

Although, perhaps, he thought, the knowing was not the most important part of it.

And none of it, he knew, might come to pass, for there was interference now. There were watchers, or at least a watcher, and before too long whoever it might be might start closing in. What he'd do or how he'd meet the threat, he had no idea until that moment came. It was something that had been almost bound to happen. It was something he had been prepared to have happen all these years. There was some reason to wonder, he knew, that it had not happened sooner.

He had told Ulysses of the danger of it that first day they'd met. He'd been sitting on the steps that led up to the porch, and thinking of it now, he could remember it as clearly as if it had been only yesterday.

6

HE WAS sitting on the steps and it was late afternoon. He was watching the great white thunderheads that were piling up across the river beyond the Iowa hills. The day was hot and sultry and there was not a breath of moving air. Out in the barnyard a half a dozen bedraggled chickens scratched listlessly, for the sake, it seemed, of going through the motions rather than from any hope of finding food. The sound of the sparrows' wings, as they flew between the gable of the barn

and the hedge of honeysuckle that bordered the field beyond
the road, was a harsh, dry sound, as if the feathers of their
wings had grown stiff with heat.

And here he sat, he thought, staring at the thunderheads
when there was work to do—corn to be plowed and hay to be
gotten in and wheat to reap and shock.

For despite whatever might have happened, a man still had a
life to live, days to be gotten through the best that one could
manage. It was a lesson, he reminded himself, that he should
have learned in all its fullness in the last few years. But war,
somehow, was different from what had happened here. In war
you knew it and expected it and were ready when it happened,
but this was not the war. This was the peace to which he had
returned. A man had a right to expect that in the world of
peace there really would be peace fencing out the violence and
the horror.

Now he was alone, as he'd never been alone before. Now, if
ever, could be a new beginning; now, perhaps, there had to be
a new beginning. But whether it was here, on the homestead
acres, or in some other place, it still would be a beginning of
bitterness and anguish.

He sat on the steps, with his wrists resting on his knees, and
watched the thunderheads piling in the west. It might mean
rain and the land could use the rain—or it might be nothing,
for above the merging river valleys the air currents were erratic
and there was no way a man could tell where those clouds
might flow.

He did not see the traveler until he turned in at the gate.
He was a tall and gangling one and his clothes were dusty and
from the appearance of him he had walked a far way. He came
up the path and Enoch sat waiting for him, watching him, but
not stirring from the steps.

"Good day, sir," Enoch finally said. "It's a hot day to be
walking. Why don't you sit a while."

"Quite willingly," said the stranger. "But first, I wonder,
could I have a drink of water?"

Enoch got up to his feet. "Come along," he said. "I'll pump
a fresh one for you."

He went down across the barnyard until he reached the
pump. He unhooked the dipper from where it hung upon a

bolt and handed it to the man. He grasped the handle of the pump and worked it up and down.

"Let it run a while," he said. "It takes a time for it to get real cool."

The water splashed out of the spout, running on the boards that formed the cover of the well. It came in spurts as Enoch worked the handle.

"Do you think," the stranger asked, "that it is about to rain?"

"A man can't tell," said Enoch. "We have to wait and see."

There was something about this traveler that disturbed him. Nothing, actually, that one could put a finger on, but a certain strangeness that was vaguely disquieting. He watched him narrowly as he pumped and decided that probably this stranger's ears were just a bit too pointed at the top, but put it down to his imagination, for when he looked again they seemed to be all right.

"I think," said Enoch, "that the water should be cold by now."

The traveler put down the dipper and waited for it to fill. He offered it to Enoch. Enoch shook his head.

"You first. You need it worse than I do."

The stranger drank greedily and with much slobbering.

"Another one?" asked Enoch.

"No, thank you," said the stranger. "But I'll catch another dipperful for you if you wish me to."

Enoch pumped, and when the dipper was full the stranger handed it to him. The water was cold and Enoch, realizing for the first time that he had been thirsty, drank it almost to the bottom.

He hung the dipper back on its bolt and said to the man, "Now, let's get in that sitting."

The stranger grinned. "I could do with some of it," he said. Enoch pulled a red bandanna from his pocket and mopped his face. "The air gets close," he said, "just before a rain."

And as he mopped his face, quite suddenly he knew what it was that had disturbed him about the traveler. Despite his bedraggled clothes and his dusty shoes, which attested to long walking, despite the heat of this time-before-a-rain, the stranger was not sweating. He appeared as fresh and cool as if he had been lying at his ease beneath a tree in springtime.

Enoch put the bandanna back into his pocket and they walked back to the steps and sat there, side by side.

"You've traveled a far way," said Enoch, gently prying.

"Very far, indeed," the stranger told him. "I'm a right smart piece from home."

"And you have a far way yet to go?"

"No," the stranger said, "I believe that I have gotten to the place where I am going."

"You mean . . ." asked Enoch, and left the question hanging.

"I mean right here," said the stranger, "sitting on these steps. I have been looking for a man and I think that man is you. I did not know his name nor where to look for him, but yet I knew that one day I would find him."

"But me," Enoch said, astonished. "Why should you look for me?"

"I was looking for a man of many different parts. One of the things about him was that he must have looked up at the stars and wondered what they were."

"Yes," said Enoch, "that is something I have done. On many nights, camping in the field, I have lain in my blankets and looked up at the sky, looking at the stars and wondering what they were and how they'd been put up there and, most important of all, why they had been put up there. I have heard some say that each of them is another sun like the sun that shines on Earth, but I don't know about that. I guess there is no one who knows too much about them."

"There are some," the stranger said, "who know a deal about them."

"You, perhaps," said Enoch, mocking just a little, for the stranger did not look like a man who'd know much of anything.

"Yes, I," the stranger said. "Although I do not know as much as many others do."

"I've sometimes wondered," Enoch said, "if the stars are other suns, might there not be other planets and other people, too."

He remembered sitting around the campfire of a night, jawing with the other fellows to pass away the time. And once he'd mentioned this idea of maybe other people on other planets circling other suns and the fellows all had jeered him and for days afterward had made fun of him, so he had never mentioned it again. Not that it mattered much, for he had no real belief in it himself; it had never been more than campfire speculation.

And now he'd mentioned it again and to an utter stranger. He wondered why he had.

"You believe that?" asked the stranger.

Enoch said, "It was just an idle notion."

"Not so idle," said the stranger. "There are other planets and there are other people. I am one of them."

"But you . . ." cried Enoch, then was stricken into silence.

For the stranger's face had split and began to fall away and beneath it he caught the glimpse of another face that was not a human face.

And even as the false human face sloughed off that other face, a great sheet of lightning went crackling across the sky and the heavy crash of thunder seemed to shake the land and from far off he heard the rushing of the rain as it charged across the hills.

7

THAT WAS how it started, Enoch thought, almost a hundred years ago. The campfire fantasy had turned into fact and the Earth now was on galactic charts, a way station for many different peoples traveling star to star. Strangers once, but now there were no strangers. There were no such things as strangers. In whatever form, with whatever purpose, all of them were people.

He looked back at the entry for October 16, 1931, and ran through it swiftly. There, near the end of it was the sentence:

Ulysses says the Thubans from planet VI are perhaps the greatest mathematicians in the galaxy. They have developed, it seems, a numeration system superior to any in existence, especially valuable in the handling of statistics.

He closed the book and sat quietly in the chair, wondering if the statisticians of Mizar X knew of the Thubans' work. Perhaps they did, he thought, for certainly some of the math they used was unconventional.

He pushed the record book to one side and dug into a desk drawer, bringing out his chart. He spread it flat on the desk before him and puzzled over it. If he could be sure, he thought. If he only knew the Mizar statistics better. For the last ten years or more he had labored at the chart, checking and rechecking all the factors against the Mizar system, testing again and again to determine whether the factors he was using were the ones he should be using.

He raised a clenched fist and hammered at the desk. If he only could be certain. If he could only talk with someone. But that had been something that he had shrunk from doing, for it would be equivalent to showing the very nakedness of the human race.

He still was human. Funny, he thought, that he should stay human, that in a century of association with these beings from the many stars he should have, through it all, remained a man of Earth.

For in many ways, his ties with Earth were cut. Old Winslowe Grant was the only human he ever talked with now. His neighbors shunned him, and there were no others, unless one could count the watchers, and those he seldom saw—only glimpses of them, only the places they had been.

Only old Winslowe Grant and Mary and the other people from the shadow who came occasionally to spend lonely hours with him.

That was all of Earth he had, old Winslowe and the shadow people and the homestead acres that lay outside the house—but not the house itself, for the house was alien now.

He shut his eyes and remembered how the house had been in the olden days. There had been a kitchen, in this same area where he was sitting, with the iron cookstove, black and monstrous, in its corner, showing its row of fiery teeth along the slit made by the grate. Pushed against the wall had been the table where the three of them had eaten, and he could remember how the table looked, with the vinegar cruet and the glass that held the spoons and the Lazy Susan with the mustard, horseradish, and chili sauce sitting in a group, a sort of centerpiece in the middle of the red checkered cloth that the table wore.

There had been a winter night and he had been, it seemed, no more than three or four. His mother was busy at the stove with supper. He was sitting on the floor in the center of the kitchen, playing with some blocks, and outside he could hear the muffled howling of the wind as it prowled along the eaves. His father had come in from milking at the barn, and a gust of wind and a swirl of snow had come into the room with him. Then he'd shut the door and the wind and snow were gone, shut outside this house, condemned to the outer darkness and the wilderness of night. His father had set the pail of milk that he had been carrying on the kitchen sink and Enoch saw that his beard and eyebrows were coated with snow and there was frost on the whiskers all around his mouth.

He held that picture still, the three of them like historic manikins posed in a cabinet in a museum—his father with the frost upon his whiskers and the great felt boots that came up to his knees; his mother with her face flushed from working at the stove and with the lace cap upon her head, and himself upon the floor, playing with the blocks.

There was one other thing that he remembered, perhaps more clearly than all the rest of it. There was a great lamp sitting on the table, and on the wall behind it hung a calendar, and the glow of the lamp fell like a spotlight upon the picture on the calendar. There was old Santa Claus, riding in his sleigh along a woodland track and all the little woodland people had turned out to watch him pass. A great moon hung above the trees and there was thick snow on the ground. A pair of rabbits sat there, gazing soulfully at Santa, and a deer beside the rabbits, with a raccoon just a little distance off, ringed tail wrapped about his feet, and a squirrel and chickadee side by side upon an overhanging branch. Old Santa had his whip raised high in greeting and his cheeks were red and his smile was merry and the reindeer hitched to his sled were fresh and spirited and proud.

Through all the years this mid-nineteenth-century Santa had ridden down the snowy aisles of time, with his whip uplifted in happy greeting to the woodland creatures. And the golden lamplight had ridden with him, still bright upon the wall and the checkered tablecloth.

So, thought Enoch, some things do endure—the memory and the thought and the snug warmness of a childhood kitchen on a stormy winter night.

But the endurance was of the spirit and the mind, for nothing else endured. There was no kitchen now, nor any sitting room with its old-fashioned sofa and the rocking chair; no back parlor with its stuffy elegance of brocade and silk, no guest bedroom on the first and no family bedrooms on the second floor.

It all was gone and now one room remained. The second-story floor and all partitions had been stripped away. Now the house was one great room. One side of it was the galactic station and the other side the living space for the keeper of the station. There was a bed over in one corner and a stove that worked on no principle known on Earth and a refrigerator that was of alien make. The walls were lined with cabinets and shelves, stacked with magazines and books and journals.

There was just one thing left from the early days, the one thing Enoch had not allowed the alien crew that had set up the station to strip away—the massive old fireplace of brick and native stone that had stood against one wall of the sitting room. It still stood there, the one reminder of the days of old, the one thing left of Earth, with its great, scarred oak mantel that his father had carved out with a broadax from a massive log and had smoothed by hand with plane and draw-shave.

On the fireplace mantel and strewn on shelf and table were articles and artifacts that had no earthly origin and some no earthly names—the steady accumulation through the years of the gifts from friendly travelers. Some of them were functional and others were to look at only, and there were other things that were entirely useless because they had little application to a member of the human race or were inoperable on Earth, and many others of the purpose of which he had no idea, accepting them, embarrassed, with many stumbling thanks, from the well-meaning folks who had brought them to him.

And on the other side of the room stood the intricate mass of machinery, reaching well up into the open second story, that wafted passengers through the space that stretched from star to star.

An inn, he thought, a stopping place, a galactic crossroads.

He rolled up the chart and put it back into the desk. The record book he put away in its proper place among all the other record books upon the shelf.

He glanced at the galactic clock upon the wall and it was time to go.

He pushed the chair tight against the desk and shrugged into the jacket that hung upon the chair back. He picked the rifle off the supports that held it on the wall and then he faced the wall itself and said the single word that he had to say. The wall slid back silently and he stepped through it into the little shed with its sparse furnishings. Behind him the section of the wall slid back and there was nothing there to indicate it was anything but a solid wall.

Enoch stepped out of the shed and it was a beautiful late summer day. In a few weeks now, he thought, there'd be the signs of autumn and a strange chill in the air. The first goldenrods were blooming now and he'd noticed, just the day before, that some of the early asters down in the ancient fence row had started to show color.

He went around the corner of the house and headed toward the river, striding down the long deserted field that was overrun with hazel brush and occasional clumps of trees.

This was the Earth, he thought—a planet made for Man. But not for Man alone, for it was as well a planet for the fox and owl and weasel, for the snake, the katydid, the fish, for all the other teeming life that filled the air and earth and water. And not these natives alone, but for other beings that called other earths their home, other planets that far light-years distant were basically the same as Earth. For Ulysses and the Hazers and all the rest of them who could live upon this planet, if need be, if they wished, with no discomfort and no artificial aids.

Our horizons are so far, he thought, and we see so little of them. Even now, with flaming rockets striving from Canaveral to break the ancient bonds, we dream so little of them.

The ache was there, the ache that had been growing, the ache to tell all mankind those things that he had learned. Not so much the specific things, although there were some of them that mankind well could use, but the general things, the unspecific, central fact that there was intelligence throughout the universe, that Man was not alone, that if he only found the way he need never be alone again.

He went down across the field and through the strip of woods and came out on the great outthrust of rock that stood atop the cliff that faced the river. He stood there, as he had stood on thousands of other mornings, and stared out at the river, sweeping in majestic blue-and-silverness through the wooded bottom land.

Old, ancient water, he said, talking silently to the river, you have seen it happen—the mile-high faces of the glaciers that came and stayed and left, creeping back toward the pole inch by stubborn inch, carrying the melting water from those very glaciers in a flood that filled this valley with a tide such as now is never known; the mastodon and the sabertooth and the bear-sized beaver that ranged these olden hills and made the night clamorous with trumpeting and screaming; the silent little bands of men who trotted in the woods or clambered up the cliffs or paddled on your surface, woods-wise and water-wise, weak in body, strong in purpose, and persistent in a way no other thing ever was persistent, and just a little time ago that other breed of men who carried dreams within their skulls and cruelty in their hands and the awful sureness of an even greater purpose in their hearts. And before that, for this is ancient country beyond what is often found, the other kinds of life and the many turns of climate and the changes that came upon the Earth itself. And what think you of it? he asked the river. For yours is the memory and the perspective and the time and by now you should have the answers, or at least some of the answers.

As Man might have some of the answers had he lived for several million years—as he might have the answers several million years from this very summer morning if he still should be around.

I could help, thought Enoch. I could not give the answers, but I could help Man in his scramble after them. I could give him faith and hope and I could give purpose such as he has not had before.

But he knew he dare not do it.

Far below a hawk swung in lazy circles above the highway of the river. The air was so clear that Enoch imagined, if he strained his eyes a little, he could see every feather in those outspread wings.

There was almost a fairy quality to this place, he thought. The far look and the clear air and the feeling of detachment that touched almost on greatness of the spirit. As if this were a special place, one of those special places that each man must seek out for himself, and count himself as lucky if he ever found it, for there were those who sought and never found it. And worst of all, there were even those who never hunted for it.

He stood upon the rock and stared out across the river, watching the lazy hawk and the sweep of water and the green carpeting of trees, and his mind went up and out to those other places until his mind was dizzy with the thought of it. And then he called it home.

He turned slowly and went back down the rock and moved off among the trees, following the path he'd beaten through the years.

He considered going down the hill a way to look in on the patch of pink lady's-slippers, to see how they might be coming, to try to conjure up the beauty that would be his again in June, but decided that there'd be little point to it, for they were well hidden in an isolated place, and nothing could have harmed them. There had been a time, a hundred years ago, when they had bloomed on every hill and he had come trailing home with great armloads of them, which his mother had put in the great brown jug she had, and for a day or two the house had been filled with the heaviness of their rich perfume. But they were hard to come by now. The trampling of pastured cattle and flower-hunting humans had swept them from the hills.

Some other day, he told himself, some day before first frost, he would visit them again and satisfy himself that they'd be there in the spring.

He stopped a while to watch a squirrel as it frolicked in an oak. He squatted down to follow a snail which had crossed his path. He stopped beside a massive tree and examined the pattern of the moss that grew upon its trunk. And he traced the wanderings of a silent, flitting songbird as it fluttered tree to tree.

He followed the path out of the woods and along the edge of field until he came to the spring that bubbled from the hillside.

Sitting beside the spring was a woman and he recognized her as Lucy Fisher, the deaf-mute daughter of Hank Fisher, who lived down in the river bottoms.

He stopped and watched her and thought how full she was of grace and beauty, the natural grace and beauty of a primitive and lonely creature.

She was sitting by the spring and one hand was uplifted and she held in it, at the tips of long and sensitive fingers, something that glowed with color. Her head was held high, with a sharp look of alertness, and her body was straight and slender, and it also had that almost startled look of quiet alertness.

Enoch moved slowly forward and stopped not more than three feet behind her, and now he saw that the thing of color on her fingertips was a butterfly, one of those large gold and red butterflies that come with the end of summer. One wing of the insect stood erect and straight, but the other was bent and crumpled and had lost some of the dust that lent sparkle to the color.

She was, he saw, not actually holding the butterfly. It was standing on one fingertip, the one good wing fluttering very slightly every now and then to maintain its balance.

But he had been mistaken, he saw, in thinking that the second wing was injured, for now he could see that somehow it had been simply bent and distorted in some way. For now it was straightening slowly and the dust (if it ever had been gone) was back on it again, and it was standing up with the other wing.

He stepped around the girl so that she could see him and when she saw him there was no start of surprise. And that, he knew, would be quite natural, for she must be accustomed to it—someone coming up behind her and suddenly being there.

Her eyes were radiant and there was, he thought, a holy look upon her face, as if she had experienced some ecstasy of the soul. And he found himself wondering again, as he did each time he saw her, what it must be like for her, living in a world of two-way silence, unable to communicate. Perhaps not entirely unable to communicate, but at least barred from that free flow of communication which was the birthright of the human animal.

There had been, he knew, several attempts to establish her in a state school for the deaf, but each had been a failure. Once she'd run away and wandered days before being finally found and returned to her home. And on other occasions she had gone on disobedience strikes, refusing to co-operate in any of the teaching.

Watching her as she sat there with the butterfly, Enoch thought he knew the reason. She had a world, he thought, a world of her very own, one to which she was accustomed and knew how to get along in. In that world she was no cripple, as she most surely would have been a cripple if she had been pushed, part way, into the normal human world.

What good to her the hand alphabet or the reading of the lips if they should take from her some strange inner serenity of spirit?

She was a creature of the woods and hills, of springtime flower and autumn flight of birds. She knew these things and lived with them and was, in some strange way, a specific part of them. She was one who dwelt apart in an old and lost apartment of the natural world. She occupied a place that Man long since had abandoned, if, in fact, he'd ever held it.

And there she sat, with the wild red and gold of the butterfly poised upon her finger, with the sense of alertness and expectancy and, perhaps, accomplishment shining on her face. She was alive, thought Enoch, as no other thing he knew had ever been alive.

The butterfly spread its wings and floated off her finger and went fluttering, unconcerned, unfrightened, up across the wild grass and the goldenrod of the field.

She pivoted to watch it until it disappeared near the top of the hill up which the old field climbed, then she turned to Enoch. She smiled and made a fluttery motion with her hands, like the fluttering of the red and golden wings, but there was something else in it, as well—a sense of happiness and an expression of well-being, as if she might be saying that the world was going fine.

If, Enoch thought, I could only teach her the pasimology of

my galactic people—then we could talk, the two of us, almost as well as with the flow of words on the human tongue. Given the time, he thought, it might not be too hard, for there was a natural and a logical process to the galactic sign language that made it almost instinctive once one had caught the underlying principle.

Throughout the Earth as well, in the early days, there had been sign languages, and none so well developed as that one which obtained among the aborigines of North America, so that an Amerindian, no matter what his tongue, could express himself among many other tribes.

But even so the sign language of the Indian was, at best, a crutch that allowed a man to hobble when he couldn't run. Whereas that of the galaxy was in itself a language, adaptable to many different means and methods of expression. It had been developed through millennia, with many different peoples making contributions, and through the centuries it had been refined and shaken down and polished until today it was a communications tool that stood on its own merits.

There was need for such a tool, for the galaxy was Babel. Even the galactic science of pasimology, polished as it might be, could not surmount all the obstacles, could not guarantee, in certain cases, the basic minimum of communication. For not only were there millions of tongues, but those other languages as well which could not operate on the principle of sound because the races were incapable of sound. And even sound itself failed of efficiency when the race talked in ultrasonics others could not hear. There was telepathy, of course, but for every telepath there were a thousand races that had telepathic blocks. There were many who got along on sign languages alone and others who could communicate only by a written or pictographic system, including some who carried chemical blackboards built into their bodies. And there was that sightless, deaf, and speechless race from the mystery stars of the far side of the galaxy who used what was perhaps the most complicated of all the galactic languages—a code of signals routed along their nervous systems.

Enoch had been at the job almost a century, and even so, he thought, with the aid of the universal sign language and the semantic translator, which was little more than a pitiful (although complicated) mechanical contrivance, he still was hard put at times to know what many of them said.

Lucy Fisher picked up a cup that was standing by her side —a cup fashioned of a strip of folded birch bark—and dipped it in the spring. She held it out to Enoch and he stepped close to take it, kneeling down to drink from it. It was not entirely watertight, and water ran from it down across his arm, wetting the cuff of shirt and jacket.

He finished drinking and handed back the cup. She took it in one hand and reached out the other, to brush across his forehead with the tip of gentle fingers in what she might have thought of as a benediction.

He did not speak to her. Long ago he had ceased talking to her, sensing that the movement of his mouth, making sounds she could not hear, might be embarrassing.

Instead he put out a hand and laid his broad palm against her cheek, holding it there for a reassuring moment as a gesture of affection. Then he got to his feet and stood staring down at her and for a moment their eyes looked into the other's eyes and then turned away.

He crossed the little stream that ran down from the spring and took the trail that led from the forest's edge across the field, heading for the ridge. Halfway up the slope, he turned around and saw that she was watching him. He held up his hand in a gesture of farewell and her hand gestured in reply.

It had been, he recalled, twelve years or more ago that he first had seen her, a little fairy person of ten years or so, a wild thing running in the woods. They had become friends, he recalled, only after a long time, although he saw her often, for she roamed the hills and valley as if they were a playground for her—which, of course, they were.

Through the years he had watched her grow and had often met her on his daily walks, and between the two of them had grown up an understanding of the lonely and the outcast, but understanding based on something more than that—on the fact that each had a world that was their own and worlds that had given them an insight into something that others seldom saw. Not that either, Enoch thought, ever told the other, or tried to tell the other, of these private worlds, but the fact of these private worlds was there, in the consciousness of each, providing a firm foundation for the building of a friendship.

He recalled the day he'd found her at the place where the pink lady's-slippers grew, just kneeling there and looking at them, not picking any of them, and how he'd stopped beside her and been pleased she had not moved to pick them, knowing that in the sight of them, the two, he and she, had found a joy and a beauty that was beyond possession.

He reached the ridgetop and turned down the grass-grown road that led down to the mailbox.

And he'd not been mistaken back there, he told himself, no matter how it may have seemed on second look. The butterfly's wing had been torn and crumpled and drab from the lack of dust. It had been a crippled thing and then it had been whole again and had flown away.

8

WINSLOWE GRANT was on time.

Enoch, as he reached the mailbox, sighted the dust raised by his old jalopy as it galloped along the ridge. It had been a dusty year, he thought, as he stood beside the box. There had been little rain and the crops had suffered. Although, to tell the truth, there were few crops on the ridge these days. There had been a time when comfortable small farms had existed, almost cheek by jowl, all along the road, with the barns all red and the houses white. But now most of the farms had been abandoned and the houses and the barns were no longer red or white, but gray and weathered wood, with all the paint peeled off and the ridgepoles sagging and the people gone.

It would not be long before Winslowe would arrive and Enoch settled down to wait. The mailman might be stopping at the Fisher box, just around the bend, although the Fishers, as a rule, got but little mail, mostly just the advertising sheets and other junk that was mailed out indiscriminately to the rural boxholders. Not that it mattered to the Fishers, for sometimes days went by in which they did not pick up their mail. If it were not for Lucy, they perhaps would never get it, for it was mostly Lucy who thought to pick it up.

The Fishers were, for a fact, Enoch told himself, a truly shiftless outfit. Their house and all the buildings were ready to fall in upon themselves and they raised a grubby patch of corn that was drowned out, more often than not, by a flood rise of the river. They mowed some hay off a bottom meadow and they had a couple of raw-boned horses and a half-dozen scrawny cows and a flock of chickens. They had an old clunk of a car and a still hidden out somewhere in the river bottoms and they hunted and fished and trapped and were generally no-account. Although, when one considered it, they were not bad neighbors. They tended to their business and never bothered anyone except that periodically they went around, the whole tribe of them, distributing pamphlets and tracts through the neighborhood for some obscure fundamentalist sect that Ma Fisher had become a member of at a tent revival meeting down in Millville several years before.

Winslowe didn't stop at the Fisher box, but came boiling around the bend in a cloud of dust. He braked the panting machine to a halt and turned off the engine.

"Let her cool a while," he said.

The block crackled as it started giving up its heat.

"You made good time today," said Enoch.

"Lots of people didn't have any mail today," said Winslowe. "Just went sailing past their boxes."

He dipped into the pouch on the seat beside him and brought out a bundle tied together with a bit of string for Enoch—several daily papers and two journals.

"You get a lot of stuff," said Winslowe, "but hardly ever letters."

"There is no one left," said Enoch, "who would want to write to me."

"But," said Winslowe, "you got a letter this time."

Enoch looked, unable to conceal surprise, and could see the end of an envelope peeping from between the journals.

"A personal letter," said Winslowe, almost smacking his lips. "Not one of them advertising ones. Nor a business one."

Enoch tucked the bundle underneath his arm, beside the rifle stock.

"Probably won't amount to much," he said.

"Maybe not," said Winslowe, a sly glitter in his eyes.

He pulled a pipe and pouch from his pocket and slowly filled the pipe. The engine block continued its crackling and popping. The sun beat down out of a cloudless sky. The vegetation alongside the road was coated with dust and an acrid smell rose from it.

"Hear that ginseng fellow is back again," said Winslowe, conversationally, but unable to keep out a conspiratorial tone. "Been gone for three, four days."

"Maybe off to sell his sang."

"You ask me," the mailman said, "he ain't hunting sang. He's hunting something else."

"Been at it," Enoch said, "for a right smart time."

"First of all," said Winslowe, "there's barely any market for the stuff and even if there was, there isn't any sang. Used to be a good market years ago. Chinese used it for medicine, I guess. But now there ain't no trade with China. I remember when I was a boy we used to go hunting it. Not easy to find, even then. But most days a man could locate a little of it."

He leaned back in the seat, puffing serenely at his pipe.

"Funny goings on," he said.

"I never saw the man," said Enoch.

"Sneaking through the woods," said Winslowe. "Digging up different kinds of plants. Got the idea myself he maybe is a sort of magic-man. Getting stuff to make up charms and such. Spends a lot of his time yarning with the Fisher tribe and drinking up their likker. You don't hear much of it these days, but I still hold with magic. Lots of things science can't explain. You take that Fisher girl, the dummy, she can charm off warts."

"So I've heard," said Enoch.

And more than that, he thought. She can fix a butterfly.

Winslowe hunched forward in his seat.

"Almost forgot," he said. "I have something else for you."

He lifted a brown paper parcel from the floor and handed it to Enoch.

"This ain't mail," he said. "It's something that I made for you."

"Why, thank you," Enoch said, taking it from him.

"Go ahead," Winslowe said, "and open it up."

Enoch hesitated.

"Ah, hell," said Winslowe, "don't be bashful."

Enoch tore off the paper and there it was, a full-figure wood carving of himself. It was in a blond, honey-colored wood and some twelve inches tall. It shone like golden crystal in the sun.

He was walking, with his rifle tucked beneath his arm and a wind was blowing, for he was leaning slightly into it and there were wind-flutter ripples on his jacket and his trousers.

Enoch gasped, then stood staring at it.

"Wins," he said, "that's the most beautiful piece of work I have ever seen."

"Did it," said the mailman, "out of that piece of wood you gave me last winter. Best piece of whittling stuff I ever ran across. Hard and without hardly any grain. No danger of splitting or of nicking or of shredding. When you make a cut, you make it where you want to and it stays the way you cut it. And it takes polish as you cut. Just rub it up a little is all you need to do."

"You don't know," said Enoch, "how much this means to me."

"Over the years," the mailman told him, "you've given me an awful lot of wood. Different kinds of wood no one's ever seen before. All of it top-grade stuff and beautiful. It was time I was carving something for you."

"And you," said Enoch, "have done a lot for me. Lugging things from town."

"Enoch," Winslowe said, "I like you. I don't know what you are and I ain't about to ask, but anyhow I like you."

"I wish that I could tell you what I am," said Enoch.

"Well," said Winslowe, moving over to plant himself behind the wheel, "it don't matter much what any of us are, just so we get along with one another. If some of the nations would only take a lesson from some small neighborhood like ours—a lesson in how to get along—the world would be a whole lot better."

Enoch nodded gravely. "It doesn't look too good, does it?"

"It sure don't," said the mailman, starting up the car.

Enoch stood and watched the car move off, down the hill, building up its cloud of dust as it moved along.

Then he looked again at the wooden statuette of himself.

It was as if the wooden figure were walking on a hilltop, naked to the full force of the wind and bent against the gale.

Why? He wondered. What was it the mailman had seen in him to portray him as walking in the wind?

9

HE LAID the rifle and the mail upon a patch of dusty grass and carefully rewrapped the statuette in the piece of paper. He'd put it, he decided, either on the mantelpiece or, perhaps better yet, on the coffee table that stood beside his favorite chair in the corner by the desk. He wanted it, he admitted to himself, with some quiet embarrassment, where it was close at hand, where he could look at it or pick it up any time he wished. And he wondered at the deep, heart-warming, soul-satisfying pleasure that he got from the mailman's gift.

It was not, he knew, because he was seldom given gifts. Scarcely a week went past that the alien travelers did not leave several with him. The house was cluttered and there was a wall of shelves down in the cavernous basement that were crammed with the stuff that had been given him. Perhaps it was, he told himself, because this was a gift from Earth, from one of his own kind.

He tucked the wrapped statuette beneath his arm and, picking up the rifle and the mail, headed back for home, following the brush-grown trail that once had been the wagon road leading to the farm.

Grass had grown into thick turf between the ancient ruts, which had been cut so deep into the clay by the iron tires of the old-time wagons that they still were no more than bare, impacted earth in which no plant as yet had gained a root-hold. But on each side the clumps of brush, creeping up the field from the forest's edge, grew man-high or better, so that now one moved down an aisle of green.

But at certain points, quite unexplainably—perhaps due to the character of the soil or to the mere vagaries of nature—the growth of brush had faltered, and here were vistas where one might look out from the ridgetop across the river valley.

It was from one of these vantage points that Enoch caught the flash from a clump of trees at the edge of the old field, not too far from the spring where he had found Lucy.

He frowned as he saw the flash and stood quietly on the path, waiting for its repetition. But it did not come again.

It was one of the watchers, he knew, using a pair of binoculars to keep watch upon the station. The flash he had seen had been the reflection of the sun upon the glasses.

Who were they? he wondered. And why should they be watching? It had been going on for some time now but, strangely, there had been nothing but the watching. There had been no interference. No one had attempted to approach him, and such approach, he realized, could have been quite simple and quite natural. If they—whoever they might be—had wished to talk with him, a very casual meeting could have been arranged during any one of his morning walks.

But apparently as yet they did not wish to talk.

What, then, he wondered, did they wish to do? Keep track of him, perhaps. And in that regard, he thought, with a wry inner twinge of humor, they could have become acquainted with the pattern of his living in their first ten days of watching.

Or perhaps they might be waiting for some happening that would provide them with a clue to what he might be doing. And in that direction there lay nothing but certain disappointment. They could watch for a thousand years and gain no hint of it.

He turned from the vista and went plodding up the road, worried and puzzled by his knowledge of the watchers.

Perhaps, he thought, they had not attempted to contact him because of certain stories that might be told about him. Stories that no one, not even Winslowe, would pass on to him. What kind of stories, he wondered, might the neighborhood by now have been able to fabricate about him—fabulous folk tales to be told in bated breath about the chimney corner?

It might be well, he thought, that he did not know the stories, although it would seem almost a certainty that they would exist. And it also might be as well that the watchers had not attempted contact with him. For so long as there was no contact, he still was fairly safe. So long as there were no questions, there need not be any answers.

Are you really, they would ask, that same Enoch Wallace who marched off in 1861 to fight for old Abe Lincoln? And there was one answer to that, there could only be one answer. Yes, he'd have to say, I am that same man.

And of all the questions they might ask him that would be

the only one of all he could answer truthfully. For all the others there would necessarily be silence or evasion.

They would ask how come that he had not aged—how he could stay young when all mankind grew old. And he could not tell them that he did not age inside the station, that he only aged when he stepped out of it, that he aged an hour each day on his daily walks, that he might age an hour or so working in his garden, that he could age for fifteen minutes sitting on the steps to watch a lovely sunset. But that when he went back indoors again the aging process was completely canceled out.

He could not tell them that. And there was much else that he could not tell them. There might come a time, he knew, if they once contacted him, that he'd have to flee the questions and cut himself entirely from the world, remaining isolated within the station's walls.

Such a course would constitute no hardship physically, for he could live within the station without any inconvenience. He would want for nothing, for the aliens would supply everything he needed to remain alive and well. He had bought human food at times, having Winslowe purchase it and haul it out from town, but only because he felt a craving for the food of his own planet, in particular those simple foods of his childhood and his campaigning days.

And, he told himself, even these foods might well be supplied by the process of duplication. A slab of bacon or a dozen eggs could be sent to another station and remain there as a master pattern for the pattern impulses, being sent to him on order as he needed them.

But there was one thing the aliens could not provide—the human contacts he'd maintained through Winslowe and the mail. Once shut inside the station, he'd be cut off completely from the world he knew, for the newspapers and the magazines were his only contact. The operation of a radio in the station was made impossible by the interference set up by the installations.

He would not know what was happening in the world, would know no longer how the outside might be going. His chart would suffer from this and would become largely useless;

although, he told himself, it was nearly useless now, since he could not be certain of the correct usage of the factors.

But aside from all of this, he would miss this little outside world that he had grown to know so well, this little corner of the world encompassed by his walks. It was the walks, he thought, more than anything, perhaps, that had kept him human and a citizen of Earth.

He wondered how important it might be that he remain, intellectually and emotionally, a citizen of Earth and a member of the human race. There was, he thought, perhaps no reason that he should. With the cosmopolitanism of the galaxy at his fingertips, it might even be provincial of him to be so intent upon his continuing identification with the old home planet. He might be losing something by this provincialism.

But it was not in himself, he knew, to turn his back on Earth. It was a place he loved too well—loving it more, most likely, than those other humans who had not caught his glimpse of far and unguessed worlds. A man, he told himself, must belong to something, must have some loyalty and some identity. The galaxy was too big a place for any being to stand naked and alone.

A lark sailed out of a grassy plot and soared high into the sky, and seeing it, he waited for the trill of liquid song to spray out of its throat and drip out of the blue. But there was no song, as there would have been in spring.

He plodded down the road and now, ahead of him, he saw the starkness of the station, reared upon its ridge.

Funny, he thought, that he should think of it as station rather than as home, but it had been a station longer than it had been a home.

There was about it, he saw, a sort of ugly solidness, as if it might have planted itself upon that ridgetop and meant to stay forever.

It would stay, of course, if one wanted it, as long as one wanted it. For there was nothing that could touch it.

Even should he be forced some day to remain within its walls, the station still would stand against all of mankind's watching, all of mankind's prying. They could not chip it and they could not gouge it and they could not break it down. There was nothing they could do. All his watching, all his speculating, all his analyzing, would gain Man nothing beyond the knowledge that a highly unusual building existed on that ridgetop. For it could survive anything except a thermonuclear explosion— and maybe even that.

He walked into the yard and turned around to look back toward the clump of trees from which the flash had come, but there was nothing now to indicate that anyone was there.

10

INSIDE THE station, the message machine was whistling plaintively.

Enoch hung up his gun, dropped the mail and statuette upon his desk and strode across the room to the whistling machine. He pushed the button and punched the lever and the whistling stopped.

Upon the message plate he read:

NO. 406,302 TO STATION 18327. WILL ARRIVE EARLY EVENING YOUR TIME. HAVE THE COFFEE HOT. ULYSSES.

Enoch grinned. Ulysses and his coffee! He was the only one of the aliens who had ever liked any of Earth's foods or drinks. There had been others who had tried them, but not more than once or twice.

Funny about Ulysses, he thought. They had liked each other from the very first, from that afternoon of the thunderstorm when they had been sitting on the steps and the mask of human form had peeled off the alien's face.

It had been a grisly face, graceless and repulsive. The face, Enoch had thought, of a cruel clown. Wondering, even as he thought it, what had put that particular phrase into his head, for clowns were never cruel. But here was one that could be —the colored patchwork of the face, the hard, tight set of jaw, the thin slash of the mouth.

Then he saw the eyes and they canceled all the rest. They were large and had a softness and the light of understanding in them, and they reached out to him, as another being might hold out its hands in friendship.

The rain had come hissing up the land to thrum across the machine-shed roof, and then it was upon them, slanting sheets of rain that hammered angrily at the dust which lay across the yard, while surprised, bedraggled chickens ran frantically for cover.

Enoch sprang to his feet and grasped the other's arm, pulling him to the shelter of the porch.

They stood facing one another, and Ulysses had reached up and pulled the split and loosened mask away, revealing a bullet head without a hair upon it—and the painted face. A face like a wild and rampaging Indian, painted for the warpath, except that here and there were touches of the clown, as if the entire painting job had been meant to point up the inconsistent grotesqueries of war. But even as he stared, Enoch knew it was not paint, but the natural coloration of this thing which had come from somewhere among the stars.

Whatever other doubt there was, or whatever wonder, Enoch had no doubt at all that this strange being was not of the Earth. For it was not human. It might be in human form, with a pair of arms and legs, with a head and face. But there was about it an essence of inhumanity, almost a negation of humanity.

In olden days, perhaps, he thought, it might have been a demon, but the days were past (although, in some areas of the country, not entirely past) when one believed in demons or in ghosts or in any of the others of that ghastly tribe which, in man's imagination, once had walked the Earth.

From the stars, he'd said. And perhaps he was. Although it made no sense. It was nothing one ever had imagined even in the purest fantasy. There was nothing to grab hold of, nothing to hang on to. There was no yardstick for it and there were no rules. And it left a sort of blank spot in one's thinking that might fill in, come time, but now was no more than a tunnel of great wonder that went on and on forever.

"Take your time," the alien said. "I know it is not easy. And I do not know of a thing that I can do to make it easier. There is, after all, no way for me to prove I am from the stars."

"But you talk so well."

"In your tongue, you mean. It was not too difficult. If you only knew of all the languages in the galaxy, you would realize how little difficult. Your language is not hard. It is a basic one and there are many concepts with which it need not deal."

And, Enoch conceded, that could be true enough.

"If you wish," the alien said, "I can walk off somewhere for a day or two. Give you time to think. Then I could come back. You'd have thought it out by then."

Enoch smiled, woodenly, and the smile had an unnatural feel upon his face.

"That would give me time," he said, "to spread alarm throughout the countryside. There might be an ambush waiting for you."

The alien shook its head. "I am sure you wouldn't do it. I would take the chance. If you want me to . . ."

"No," said Enoch, so calmly he surprised himself. "No, when you have a thing to face, you face it. I learned that in the war."

"You'll do," the alien said. "You will do all right. I did not misjudge you and it makes me proud."

"Misjudge me?"

"You do not think I just came walking in here cold? I know about you, Enoch. Almost as much, perhaps, as you know about yourself. Probably even more."

"You know my name?"

"Of course I do."

"Well, that is fine," said Enoch. "And what about your own?"

"I am seized with great embarrassment," the alien told him. "For I have no name as such. Identification, surely, that fits the purpose of my race, but nothing that the tongue can form."

Suddenly, for no reason, Enoch remembered that slouchy figure perching on the top rail of a fence, with a stick in one hand and a jackknife in the other, whittling placidly while the cannon balls whistled overhead and less than half a mile away the muskets snarled and crackled in the billowing powder smoke that rose above the line.

"Then you need a name to call you by," he said, "and it shall be Ulysses. I need to call you something."

"It is agreeable," said that strange one. "But might one ask why the name Ulysses?"

"Because it is the name," said Enoch, "of a great man of my race."

It was a crazy thing, of course. For there was no resemblance

between the two of them—that slouchy Union general whittling as he perched upon the fence and this other who stood
upon the porch.

"I am glad you chose it," said this Ulysses, standing on the
porch. "To my hearing it has a dignified and noble sound and,
between the two of us, I shall be glad to bear it. And I shall call
you Enoch, as friends of the first names, for the two of us shall
work together for many of your years."

It was beginning to come straight now and the thought was
staggering. Perhaps it was as well, Enoch told himself, that it
had waited for a while, that he had been so dazed it had not
come on him all at once.

"Perhaps," said Enoch, fighting back the realization that was
crowding in on him, crowding in too fast, "I could offer you
some victuals. I could cook up some coffee . . ."

"Coffee," said Ulysses, smacking his thin lips. "Do you have
the coffee?"

"I'll make a big pot of it. I'll break in an egg so it will settle
clear . . ."

"Delectable," Ulysses said. "Of all the drinks that I have
drunk on all the planets I have visited, the coffee is the best."

They went into the kitchen and Enoch stirred up the coals
in the kitchen range and then put in new wood. He took the
coffeepot over to the sink and ladled in some water from the
water pail and put it on to boil. He went into the pantry to get
some eggs and down into the cellar to bring up the ham.

Ulysses sat stiffly in a kitchen chair and watched him as he
worked.

"You eat ham and eggs?" asked Enoch.

"I eat anything," Ulysses said. "My race is most adaptable.
That is the reason I was sent to this planet as a—what do you
call it?—a looker-out, perhaps."

"A scout," suggested Enoch.

"That is it, a scout."

He was an easy thing to talk with, Enoch told himself—
almost like another person, although, God knows, he looked
little like a person. He looked, instead, like some outrageous
caricature of a human being.

"You have lived here, in this house," Ulysses said, "for a
long, long time. You feel affection for it."

"It has been my home," said Enoch, "since the day that I was born. I was gone from it for almost four years, but it was always home."

"I'll be glad," Ulysses told him, "to be getting home again myself. I've been away too long. On a mission such as this one, it always is too long."

Enoch put down the knife he had been using to cut a slice of ham and sat down heavily in a chair. He stared at Ulysses, across the table from him.

"You?" he asked. "You are going home?"

"Why, of course," Ulysses told him. "Now that my job is nearly done. I have got a home. Did you think I hadn't?"

"I don't know," said Enoch weakly. "I had never thought of it."

And that was it, he knew. It had not occurred to him to connect a being such as this with a thing like home. For it was only human beings that had a place called home.

"Some day," Ulysses said, "I shall tell you about my home. Some day you may even visit me."

"Out among the stars," said Enoch.

"It seems strange to you now," Ulysses said. "It will take a while to get used to the idea. But as you come to know us —all of us—you will understand. And I hope you like us. We are not bad people, really. Not any of the many different kinds of us."

The stars, Enoch told himself, were out there in the loneliness of space and how far they were he could not even guess, nor what they were nor why. Another world, he thought— no, that was wrong—many other worlds. There were people there, perhaps many other people; a different kind of people, probably, for every different star. And one of them sat here in this very kitchen, waiting for the coffeepot to boil, for the ham and eggs to fry.

"But why?" he asked. "But why?"

"Because," Ulysses said, "we are a traveling people. We need a travel station here. We want to turn this house into a station and you to keep the station."

"This house?"

"We could not build a station, for then we'd have people asking who was building it and what it might be for. So we are forced to use an existing structure and change it for our needs. But the inside only. We leave the outside as it is, in appearance, that is. For there must be no questions asked. There must be . . ."

"But traveling . . ."

"From star to star," Ulysses said. "Quicker than the thought of it. Faster than a wink. There is what you would call machinery, but it is not machinery—not the same as the machinery you think of."

"You must excuse me," Enoch said, confused. "It seems so impossible."

"You remember when the railroad came to Millville?"

"Yes, I can remember that. I was just a kid."

"Then think of it this way. This is just another railroad and the Earth is just another town and this house will be the station for this new and different railroad. The only difference is that no one on Earth but you will know the railroad's here. For it will be no more than a resting and a switching point. No one on the Earth can buy a ticket to travel on the railroad."

Put that way, of course, it had a simple sound, but it was, Enoch sensed, very far from simple.

"Railroad cars in space?" he asked.

"Not railroad cars," Ulysses told him. "It is something else. I do not know how to begin to tell you . . ."

"Perhaps you should pick someone else. Someone who would understand."

"There is no one on this planet who could remotely understand. No, Enoch, we'll do with you as well as anyone. In many ways, much better than with anyone."

"But . . ."

"What is it, Enoch?"

"Nothing," Enoch said.

For he remembered now how he had been sitting on the steps thinking how he was alone and about a new beginning, knowing that he could not escape a new beginning, that he must start from scratch and build his life anew.

And here, suddenly, was that new beginning—more wondrous and fearsome than anything he could have dreamed even in an insane moment.

11

ENOCH FILED the message and sent his confirmation:

NO. 406,302 RECEIVED. COFFEE ON THE FIRE.
ENOCH.

Clearing the machine, he walked over to the No. 3 liquid
tank he'd prepared before he left. He checked the temperature
and the level of the solution and made certain once again that
the tank was securely positioned in relation to the materializer.

From there he went to the other materializer, the official and
emergency materializer, positioned in the corner, and checked
it over closely. It was all right, as usual. It always was all right,
but before each of Ulysses's visits he never failed to check it.
There was nothing he could have done about it had there been
something wrong other than send an urgent message to Galactic Central. In which case someone would have come in on the
regular materializer and put it into shape.

For the official and emergency materializer was exactly what
its name implied. It was used only for official visits by personnel
of Galactic Center or for possible emergencies and its operation was entirely outside that of the local station.

Ulysses, as an inspector for this and several other stations,
could have used the official materializer at any time he wished
without prior notice. But in all the years that he had been coming to the station he had never failed, Enoch remembered with
a touch of pride, to message that he was coming. It was, he
knew, a courtesy which all the other stations on the great galactic network might not be accorded, although there were some
of them which might be given equal treatment.

Tonight, he thought, he probably should tell Ulysses about
the watch that had been put upon the station. Perhaps he
should have told him earlier, but he had been reluctant to admit that the human race might prove to be a problem to the
galactic installation.

It was a hopeless thing, he thought, this obsession of his to
present the people of the Earth as good and reasonable. For in
many ways they were neither good nor reasonable; perhaps because they had not as yet entirely grown up. They were smart

and quick and at times compassionate and even understanding, but they failed lamentably in many other ways.

But if they had the chance, Enoch told himself, if they ever got a break, if they only could be told what was out in space, then they'd get a grip upon themselves and they would measure up and then, in the course of time, would be admitted into the great cofraternity of the people of the stars.

Once admitted, they would prove their worth and would pull their weight, for they were still a young race and full of energy—at times, maybe, too much energy.

Enoch shook his head and went across the room to sit down at his desk. Drawing the bundle of mail in front of him, he slid it out of the string which Winslowe had used to tie it all together.

There were the daily papers, a news weekly, two journals— *Nature* and *Science*—and the letter.

He pushed the papers and the journals to one side and picked up the letter. It was, he saw, an air mail sheet and was postmarked London and the return address bore a name that was unfamiliar to him. He puzzled as to why an unknown person should be writing him from London. Although, he reminded himself, anyone who wrote from London, or indeed from anywhere, would be an unknown person. He knew no one in London nor elsewhere in the world.

He slit the air sheet open and spread it out on the desk in front of him, pulling the desk lamp close so the light would fall upon the writing.

> *Dear sir* [he read], *I would suspect I am unknown to you. I am one of the several editors of the British journal,* Nature, *to which you have been a subscriber for these many years. I do not use the journal's letterhead because this letter is personal and unofficial and perhaps not even in the best of taste.*
>
> *You are, it may interest you to know, our eldest subscriber. We have had you on our mailing lists for more than eighty years.*
>
> *While I am aware that it is no appropriate concern of mine, I have wondered if you, yourself, have subscribed to our publication for this length of time, or if it might be*

possible that your father or someone close to you may have been the original subscriber and you simply have allowed the subscription to continue in his name.

My interest undoubtedly constitutes an unwarranted and inexcusable curiosity and if you, sir, choose to ignore the query it is entirely within your rights and proper that you do so. But if you should not mind replying, an answer would be appreciated.

I can only say in my own defense that I have been associated for so long with our publication that I feel a certain sense of pride that someone has found it worth the having for more than eighty years. I doubt that many publications can boast such long time interest on the part of any man.

May I assure, you, sir, of my utmost respect.

Sincerely yours.

And then the signature.

Enoch shoved the letter from him.

And there it was again, he told himself. Here was another watcher, although discreet and most polite and unlikely to cause trouble.

But someone else who had taken notice, who had felt a twinge of wonder at the same man subscribing to a magazine for more than eighty years.

As the years went on, there would be more and more. It was not only the watchers encamped outside the station with whom he must concern himself, but those potential others. A man could be as self-effacing as he well could manage and still he could not hide. Soon or late the world would catch up with him and would come crowding around his door, agog to know why he might be hiding.

It was useless, he knew, to hope for much further time. The world was closing in.

Why can't they leave me alone? he thought. If he only could explain how the situation stood, they might leave him alone. But he couldn't explain to them. And even if he could, there would be some of them who'd still come crowding in.

Across the room the materializer beeped for attention and Enoch swung around.

The Thuban had arrived. He was in the tank, a shadowy

globular blob of substance, and above him, riding sluggishly in the solution, was a cube of something.

Luggage, Enoch wondered. But the message had said there would be no luggage.

Even as he hurried across the room, the clicking came to him—the Thuban talking to him.

"Presentation to you," said the clicking. "Deceased vegetation."

Enoch peered at the cube floating in the liquid.

"Take him," clicked the Thuban. "Bring him for you."

Fumblingly, Enoch clicked out his answer, using tapping fingers against the glass side of the tank: "I thank you, gracious one." Wondering as he did it, if he were using the proper form of address to this blob of matter. A man, he told himself, could get terribly tangled up on that particular point of etiquette. There were some of these beings that one addressed in flowery language (and even in those cases, the floweriness would vary) and others that one talked with in the simplest, bluntest terms.

He reached into the tank and lifted out the cube and he saw that it was a block of heavy wood, black as ebony and so close-grained it looked very much like stone. He chuckled inwardly, thinking how, in listening to Winslowe, he had grown to be an expert in the judging of artistic wood.

He put the wood upon the floor and turned back to the tank.

"Would you mind," clicked the Thuban, "revealing what you do with him? To us, very useless stuff."

Enoch hesitated, searching desperately through his memory. What, he wondered, was the code for "carve?"

"Well?" the Thuban asked.

"You must pardon me, gracious one. I do not use this language often. I am not proficient."

"Drop, please, the 'gracious one.' I am a common being."

"Shape it," Enoch tapped. "Into another form. Are you a visual being? Then I show you one."

"Not visual," said the Thuban. "Many other things, not visual."

It had been a globe when it had arrived and now it was beginning to flatten out.

"You," the Thuban clicked, "are a biped being."

"That is what I am."

"Your planet. It is a solid planet?"

Solid? Enoch wondered. Oh, yes, solid as opposed to liquid.
"One-quarter solid," he tapped. "The rest of it is liquid."

"Mine almost all liquid. Only little solid. Very restful world."

"One thing I want to ask you," Enoch tapped.

"Ask," the creature said.

"You are a mathematician. All you folks, I mean."

"Yes," the creature said. "Excellent recreation. Occupies the
mind."

"You mean you do not use it?"

"Oh, yes, once use it. But no need for use any more. Got all
we need to use, very long ago. Recreation now."

"I have heard of your system of numerical notation."

"Very different," clicked the Thuban. "Very better concept."
"You can tell me of it?"

"You know notation system used by people of Polaris VII?"
"No, I don't," tapped Enoch.

"Then no use to tell you of our own. Must know Polaris
first."

So that was that, thought Enoch. He might have known.
There was so much knowledge in the galaxy and he knew so
little of it, understood so little of the little that he knew.

There were men on Earth who could make sense of it. Men
who would give anything short of their very lives to know the
little that he knew, and could put it all to use.

Out among the stars lay a massive body of knowledge, some
of it an extension of what mankind knew, some of it concerning matters which Man had not yet suspected, and used in ways
and for purposes that Man had not as yet imagined. And never
might imagine, if left on his own.

Another hundred years, thought Enoch. How much would
he learn in another hundred years? In another thousand?

"I rest now," said the Thuban. "Nice to talk with you."

12

ENOCH TURNED from the tank and picked up the block of
wood. A little puddle of liquid had drained off it and lay glistening on the floor.

He carried the block across the room to one of the windows

and examined it. It was heavy and black and close-grained and at one corner of it a bit of bark remained. It had been sawed. Someone had cut it into a size that would fit the tank where the Thuban rested.

He recalled an article he had read in one of the daily papers just a day or two before in which a scientist had contended that no great intelligence ever could develop on a liquid world.

But that scientist was wrong, for the Thuban race had so developed and there were other liquid worlds which were members of the galactic cofraternity. There were a lot of things, he told himself, that Man would have to unlearn, as well as things to learn, if he ever should become aware of the galactic culture.

The limitation of the speed of light, for one thing.

For if nothing moved faster than the speed of light, then the galactic transport system would be impossible.

But one should not censure Man, he reminded himself, for setting the speed of light as a basic limitation. Observations were all that Man—or anyone, for that matter—could use as data upon which to base his premises. And since human science had so far found nothing which consistently moved faster than the speed of light, then the assumption must be valid that nothing could or did consistently move faster. But valid as an assumption only and no more than that.

For the impulse patterns which carried creatures star to star were almost instantaneous, no matter what the distance.

He stood and thought about it and it still was hard, he admitted to himself, for a person to believe.

Moments ago the creature in the tank had rested in another tank in another station and the materializer had built up a pattern of it—not only of its body, but of its very vital force, the thing that gave it life. Then the impulse pattern had moved across the gulfs of space almost instantaneously to the receiver of this station, where the pattern had been used to duplicate the body and the mind and memory and the life of that creature now lying dead many light years distant. And in the tank the new body and the new mind and memory and life had taken almost instant form—an entirely new being, but exactly like the old one, so that the identity continued and the consciousness (the very thought no more than momentarily interrupted), so that to all intent and purpose the being was the same.

There were limitations to the impulse patterns, but this had nothing to do with speed, for the impulses could cross the entire galaxy with but little lag in time. But under certain conditions the patterns tended to break down and this was why there must be many stations—many thousands of them. Clouds of dust or gas or areas of high ionization seemed to disrupt the patterns and in those sectors of the galaxy where these conditions were encountered, the distance jumps between the stations were considerably cut down to keep the pattern true. There were areas that had to be detoured because of high concentrations of the distorting gas and dust.

Enoch wondered how many dead bodies of the creature that now rested in the tank had been left behind at other stations in the course of the journey it was making—as this body in a few hours' time would lie dead within this tank when the creature's pattern was sent out again, riding on the impulse waves.

A long trail of dead, he thought, left across the stars, each to be destroyed by a wash of acid and flushed into deep-lying tanks, but with the creature itself going on and on until it reached its final destination to carry out the purpose of its journey.

And those purposes, Enoch wondered—the many purposes of the many creatures who passed through the stations scattered wide in space? There had been certain instances when, chatting with the travelers, they had told their purpose, but with the most of them he never learned the purpose—nor had he any right to learn it. For he was the keeper only.

Mine host, he thought, although not every time, for there were many creatures that had no use for hosts. But the man, at any rate, who watched over the operation of the station and who kept it going, who made ready for the travelers and who sent them on their way again when that time should come. And who performed the little tasks and courtesies of which they might stand in need.

He looked at the block of wood and thought how pleased Winslowe would be with it. It was very seldom that one came upon a wood that was as black or fine-grained as this.

What would Winslowe think, he wondered, if he could only know that the statuettes he carved were made of woods that had grown on unknown planets many light years distant.

Winslowe, he knew, must have wondered many times where the wood came from and how his friend could have gotten it. But he had never asked. And he knew as well, of course, that there was something very strange about this man who came out to the mailbox every day to meet him. But he had never asked that, either.

And that was friendship, Enoch told himself.

This wood, too, that he held in his hands, was another evidence of friendship—the friendship of the stars for a very humble keeper of a remote and backwoods station stuck out in one of the spiral arms, far from the center of the galaxy.

The word had spread, apparently, through the years and throughout space, that this certain keeper was a collector of exotic woods—and so the woods came in. Not only from those races he thought of as his friends, but from total strangers, like the blob that now rested in the tank.

He put the wood down on a table top and went to the refrigerator. From it he took a slab of aged cheese that Winslowe had bought for him several days ago, and a small package of fruit that a traveler from Sirrah X had brought the day before.

"Analyzed," it had told him, "and you can eat it without hurt. It will play no trouble with your metabolism. You've had it before, perhaps? So you haven't. I am sorry. It is most delicious. Next time, you like it, I shall bring you more."

From the cupboard beside the refrigerator he took out a small, flat loaf of bread, part of the ration regularly provided him by Galactic Central. Made of a cereal unlike any known on Earth, it had a distinctly nutty flavor with the faintest hint of some alien spice.

He put the food on what he called the kitchen table, although there was no kitchen. Then he put the coffee maker on the stove and went back to his desk.

The letter still lay there, spread out, and he folded it together and put it in a drawer.

He stripped the brown folders off the papers and put them in a pile. From the pile he selected the New York *Times* and moved to his favorite chair to read.

NEW PEACE CONFERENCE AGREED UPON, said the lead-off headline.

The crisis had been boiling for a month or more, the newest

of a long series of crises which had kept the world on edge for years. And the worst of it, Enoch told himself, was that the most of them were manufactured crises, with one side or the other pushing for advantage in the relentless chess game of power politics which had been under way since the end of World War II.

The stories in the *Times* bearing on the conference had a rather desperate, almost fatalistic, ring, as if the writers of the stories, and perhaps the diplomats and all the rest involved, knew the conference would accomplish nothing—if, in fact, it did not serve to make the crisis deeper.

> *Observers in this capital* [wrote one of the *Times*'s Washington bureau staff] *are not convinced the conference will serve, in this instance, as similar conferences sometimes have served in the past, to either delay a showdown on the issues or to advance the prospects for a settlement. There is scarcely concealed concern in many quarters that the conference will, instead, fan the flames of controversy higher without, by way of compensation, opening any avenues by which a compromise might seem possible. A conference is popularly supposed to provide a time and place for the sober weighing of the facts and points of argument, but there are few who see in the calling of this conference any indications that this may be the case.*

The coffee maker was going full blast now and Enoch threw the paper down and strode to the stove to snatch it off. From the cupboard he got a cup and went to the table with it.

But before he began to eat, he went back to the desk and, opening a drawer, got out his chart and spread it on the table. Once again he wondered just how valid it might be, although in certain parts of it, at times, it seemed to make a certain sort of sense.

He had based it on the Mizar theory of statistics and had been forced, because of the nature of his subject, to shift some of the factors, to substitute some values. He wondered now, for the thousandth time, if he had made an error somewhere. Had his shifting and substitution destroyed the validity of the system? And if so, how could he correct the errors to restore validity?

Here the factors were, he thought: the birth rate and the total population of the Earth, the death rate, the values of currencies, the spread of living costs, attendance of places of worship, medical advances, technological developments, industrial indices, the labor market, world trade trends—and many others, including some that at first glance might not seem too relevant: the auction price of art objects, vacation preferences and movements, the speed of transportation, the incidence of insanity.

The statistical method developed by the mathematicians of Mizar, he knew, would work anywhere, on anything, if applied correctly. But he had been forced to twist it in translating an alien planet's situation to fit the situation here on Earth—and in consequence of that twisting, did it still apply?

He shuddered as he looked at it. For if he'd made no mistake, if he'd handled everything correctly, if his translations had done no violence to the concept, then the Earth was headed straight for another major war, for a holocaust of nuclear destruction.

He let loose of the corners of the chart and it rolled itself back into a cylinder.

He reached for one of the fruits the Sirrah being had brought him and bit into it. He rolled it on his tongue, savoring the delicacy of the taste. It was, he decided, as good as that strange, birdlike being had guaranteed it would be.

There had been a time, he remembered, when he had held some hope that the chart based on the Mizar theory might show, if not a way to end all war, at least a way to keep the peace. But the chart had never given any hint of the road to peace. Inexorably, relentlessly, it had led the way to war.

How many other wars, he wondered, could the people of the Earth endure?

No man could say, of course, but it might be just one more. For the weapons that would be used in the coming conflict had not as yet been measured and there was no man who could come close to actually estimating the results these weapons would produce.

War had been bad enough when men faced one another with their weapons in their hands, but in any present war great payloads of destruction would go hurtling through the skies to engulf whole cities—aimed not at military concentrations, but at total populations.

He reached out his hand for the chart again, then pulled it back. There was no further need of looking at it. He knew it all by heart. There was no hope in it. He might study it and puzzle over it until the crack of doom and it would not change a whit. There was no hope at all. The world was thundering once again, in a blind red haze of fury and of helplessness, down the road to war.

He went on with his eating and the fruit was even better than it had been at first bite. "Next time," the being had said, "I will bring you more." But it might be a long time before he came again, and he might never come. There were many of them who passed through only once, although there were a few who showed up every week or so—old, regular travelers who had become close friends.

And there had been, he recalled, that little group of Hazers who, years ago, had made arrangements for extra long stop-overs at the station so they could sit around this very table and talk the hours away, arriving laden with hampers and with baskets of things to eat and drink, as if it were a picnic.

But finally they had stopped their coming and it had been years since he'd seen any one of them. And he regretted it, for they'd been the best of companions.

He drank an extra cup of coffee, sitting idly in the chair, thinking about those good old days when the band of Hazers came.

His ears caught the faint rustling and he glanced quickly up to see her sitting on the sofa, dressed in the demure hoop skirts of the 1860s.

"Mary!" he said, surprised, rising to his feet.

She was smiling at him in her very special way and she was beautiful, he thought, as no other woman ever had been beautiful.

"Mary," he said, "it's so nice to have you here."

And now, leaning on the mantelpiece, dressed in Union blue, with his belted saber and his full black mustache, was another of his friends.

"Hello, Enoch," David Ransome said. "I hope we don't intrude."

"Never," Enoch told him. "How can two friends intrude?"

He stood beside the table and the past was with him, the good and restful past, the rose-scented and unhaunted past that had never left him.

Somewhere in the distance was the sound of fife and drum and the jangle of the battle harness as the boys marched off to war, with the colonel glorious in his full-dress uniform upon the great black stallion, and the regimental flags snapping in the stiff June breeze.

He walked across the room and over to the sofa. He made a little bow to Mary.

"With your permission, ma'am," he said.

"Please do," she said. "If you should happen to be busy . . ."

"Not at all," he said. "I was hoping you would come."

He sat down on the sofa, not too close to her, and he saw her hands were folded, very primly, in her lap. He wanted to reach out and take her hands in his and hold them for a moment, but he knew he couldn't.

For she wasn't really there.

"It's been almost a week," said Mary, "since I've seen you. How is your work going, Enoch?"

He shook his head. "I still have all the problems. The watchers still are out there. And the chart says war."

David left the mantel and came across the room. He sat down in a chair and arranged his saber.

"War, the way they fight it these days," he declared, "would be a sorry business. Not the way we fought it, Enoch."

"No," said Enoch, "not the way we fought it. And while a war would be bad enough itself, there is something worse. If Earth fights another war, our people will be barred, if not forever, at least for many centuries, from the cofraternity of space."

"Maybe that's not so bad," said David. "We may not be ready to join the ones in space."

"Perhaps not," Enoch admitted. "I rather doubt we are. But we could be some day. And that day would be shoved far into the future if we fight another war. You have to make some pretense of being civilized to join those other races."

"Maybe," Mary said, "they might never know. About a war, I mean. They go no place but this station."

Enoch shook his head. "They would know. I think they're watching us. And anyhow, they would read the papers."

"The papers you subscribe to?"

"I save them for Ulysses. That pile over in the corner. He takes them back to Galactic Central every time he comes. He's very interested in Earth, you know, from the years he spent here. And from Galactic Central, once he's read them, I have a hunch they travel to the corners of the galaxy."

"Can you imagine," David asked, "what the promotion departments of those newspapers might have to say about it if they only knew their depth of circulation."

Enoch grinned at the thought of it.

"There's that paper down in Georgia," David said, "that covers Dixie like the dew. They'd have to think of something that goes with galaxy."

"Glove," said Mary quickly. "Covers the galaxy like a glove. What do you think of that?"

"Excellent," said David.

"Poor Enoch," Mary said contritely. "Here we make our jokes and Enoch has his problems."

"Not mine to solve, of course," Enoch told her. "I'm just worried by them. All I have to do is stay inside the station and there are no problems. Once you close the door here, the problems of the world are securely locked outside."

"But you can't do that."

"No, I can't," said Enoch.

"I think you may be right," said David, "in thinking that these other races may be watching us. With an eye, perhaps, to some day inviting the human race to join them. Otherwise, why would they have wanted to set up a station here on Earth?"

"They're expanding the network all the time," said Enoch. "They needed a station in this solar system to carry out their extension into this spiral arm."

"Yes, that's true enough," said David, "but it need not have been the Earth. They could have built a station out on Mars and used an alien for a keeper and still have served their purpose."

"I've often thought of that," said Mary. "They wanted a station on the Earth and an Earthman as its keeper. There must be a reason for it."

"I had hoped there was," Enoch told her, "but I'm afraid they came too soon. It's too early for the human race. We aren't grown up. We still are juveniles."

"It's a shame," said Mary. "We'd have so much to learn. They know so much more than we. Their concept of religion, for example."

"I don't know," said Enoch, "whether it's actually a religion. It seems to have few of the trappings we associate with religion. And it is not based on faith. It doesn't have to be. It is based on knowledge. These people know, you see."

"You mean the spiritual force."

"It is there," said Enoch, "just as surely as all the other forces that make up the universe. There is a spiritual force, exactly as there is time and space and gravitation and all the other factors that make up the immaterial universe. It is there and they can establish contact with it . . ."

"But don't you think," asked David, "that the human race may sense this? They don't know it, but they sense it. And are reaching out to touch it. They haven't got the knowledge, so they must do the best they can with faith. And that faith goes back a far way. Back, perhaps, deep into the prehistoric days. A crude faith, then, but a sort of faith, a grasping for a faith."

"I suppose so," Enoch said. "But it actually wasn't the spiritual force I was thinking of. There are all the other things, the material things, the methods, the philosophies that the human race could use. Name almost any branch of science and there is something there for us, more than what we have."

But his mind went back to that strange business of the spiritual force and the even stranger machine which had been built eons ago, by means of which the galactic people were able to establish contact with the force. There was a name for that machine, but there was no word in the English language which closely approximated it. "Talisman" was the closest, but Talisman was too crude a word. Although that had been the word that Ulysses had used when, some years ago, they had talked of it.

There were so many things, so many concepts, he thought, out in the galaxy which could not be adequately expressed in any tongue on Earth. The Talisman was more than a talisman and the machine which had been given the name was more than a mere machine. Involved in it, as well as certain mechanical concepts, was a psychic concept, perhaps some sort of psychic energy that was unknown on Earth. That and a great deal more. He had read some of the literature on the spiritual force and on the Talisman and had realized, he remembered, in the reading of it, how far short he fell, how far short the human race must fall, in an understanding of it.

The Talisman could be operated only by certain beings with certain types of minds and something else besides (could it be, he wondered, with certain kinds of souls?). "Sensitives" was the word he had used in his mental translation of the term for these kinds of people, but once again, he could not be sure if the word came close to fitting. The Talisman was placed in the custody of the most capable, or the most efficient, or the most devoted (whichever it might be) of the galactic sensitives, who carried it from star to star in a sort of eternal progression. And on each planet the people came to make personal and individual contact with the spiritual force through the intervention and the agency of the Talisman and its custodian.

He found that he was shivering at the thought of it—the pure ecstasy of reaching out and touching the spirituality that flooded through the galaxy and, umdoubtedly, through the universe. The assurance would be there, he thought, the assurance that life had a special place in the great scheme of existence, that one, no matter how small, how feeble, how insignificant, still did count for something in the vast sweep of space and time.

"What is the trouble, Enoch?" Mary asked.

"Nothing," he said. "I was just thinking. I am sorry. I will pay attention now."

"You were talking," David said, "about what we could find in the galaxy. There was, for one thing, that strange sort of math. You were telling us of it once and it was something . . ."

"The Arcturus math, you mean," said Enoch. "I know little more than when I told you of it. It is too involved. It is based on behavior symbolism."

There was some doubt, he told himself, that you could even call it math, although, by analysis, that was probably what it was. It was something that the scientists of Earth, no doubt, could use to make possible the engineering of the social sciences as logically and as efficiently as the common brand of math had been used to build the gadgets of the Earth.

"And the biology of that race out in Andromeda," Mary said. "The ones who colonized all those crazy planets."

"Yes, I know. But Earth would have to mature a bit in its intellectual and emotional outlook before we'd venture to use it as the Andromedans did. Still, I suppose that it would have its applications."

He shuddered inwardly as he thought of how the Andromedans used it. And that, he knew, was proof that he still was a man of Earth, kin to all the bias and the prejudice and the shibboleths of the human mind. For what the Andromedans had done was only common sense. If you cannot colonize a planet in your present shape, why, then you change your shape. You make yourself into the sort of being that can live upon the planet and then you take it over in that alien shape into which you have changed yourself. If you need to be a worm, then you become a worm—or an insect or a shellfish or whatever it may take. And you change not your body only, but your mind as well, into the kind of mind that will be necessary to live upon that planet.

"There are all the drugs," said Mary, "and the medicines. The medical knowledge that could apply to Earth. There was that little package Galactic Central sent you."

"A packet of drugs," said Enoch, "that could cure almost every ill on Earth. That, perhaps, hurts me most of all. To know they're up there in the cupboard, actually on this planet, where so many people need them."

"You could mail out samples," David said, "to medical associations or to some drug concern."

Enoch shook his head. "I thought of that, of course. But I have the galaxy to consider. I have an obligation to Galactic Central. They have taken great precautions that the station not be known. There are Ulysses and all my other alien friends. I cannot wreck their plans. I cannot play the traitor to them. For when you think of it, Galactic Central and the work it's doing is more important than the Earth."

"Divided loyalties," said David with slight mockery in his tone.

"That is it, exactly. There had been a time, many years ago, when I thought of writing papers for submissions to some of the scientific journals. Not the medical journals, naturally, for I know nothing about medicine. The drugs are there, of course, lying on the shelf, with directions for their use, but they are merely so many pills or powders or ointments, or whatever they may be. But there were other things I knew of, other things I'd learned. Not too much about them, naturally, but at least some hints in some new directions. Enough that someone could pick them up and go on from there. Someone who might know what to do with them."

"But look here," David said, "that wouldn't have worked out. You have no technical nor research background, no educational record. You're not tied up with any school or college. The journals just don't publish you unless you can prove yourself."

"I realize that, of course. That's why I never wrote the papers. I knew there was no use. You can't blame the journals. They must be responsible. Their pages aren't open to just anyone. And even if they had viewed the papers with enough respect to want to publish them, they would have had to find out who I was. And that would have led straight back to the station."

"But even if you could have gotten away with it," David pointed out, "you'd still not have been clear. You said a while ago you had a loyalty to Galactic Central."

"If," said Enoch, "in this particular case I could have got away with it, it might have been all right. If you just threw out ideas and let some Earth scientists develop them, there'd be no harm done Galactic Central. The main problem, of course, would be not to reveal the source."

"Even so," said David, "there'd be little you actually could tell them. What I mean is that generally you haven't got enough to go on. So much of this galactic knowledge is off the beaten track."

"I know," said Enoch. "The mental engineering of Mankalinen III, for one thing. If the Earth could know of that, our people undoubtedly could find a clue to the treatment of the neurotic and the mentally disturbed. We could empty all the institutions and we could tear them down or use them for something else. There'd be no need of them. But no one other than the people out on Mankalinen III could ever tell us of it. I only know they are noted for their mental engineering, but that is all I know. I haven't the faintest inkling of what it's all about. It's something that you'd have to get from the people out there."

"What you are really talking of," said Mary, "are all the nameless sciences—the ones that no human has ever thought about."

"Like us, perhaps," said David.

"David!" Mary cried.

"There is no sense," said David angrily, "in pretending we are people."

"But you are," said Enoch tensely. "You are people to me. You are the only people that I have. What is the matter, David?"

"I think," said David, "that the time has come to say what we really are. That we are illusion. That we are created and called up. That we exist only for one purpose, to come and talk with you, to fill in for the real people that you cannot have."

"Mary," Enoch cried, "you don't think that way, too! You can't think that way!"

He reached out his arms to her and then he let them drop —terrified at the realization of what he'd been about to do. It was the first time he'd ever tried to touch her. It was the first time, in all the years, that he had forgotten.

"I am sorry, Mary. I should not have done that."

Her eyes were bright with tears.

"I wish you could," she said. "Oh, how I wish you could!"

"David," he said, not turning his head.

"David left," said Mary.

"He won't be back," said Enoch.

Mary shook her head.

"What is the matter, Mary? What is it all about? What have I done!"

"Nothing," Mary said, "except that you made us too much like people. So that we became more human, until we were entirely human. No longer puppets, no longer pretty dolls, but really actual people. I think David must resent it—not that he is people, but that being people, he is still a shadow. It did not matter when we were dolls or puppets, for we were not human then. We had no human feeling."

"Mary, please," he said. "Mary, please forgive me."

She leaned toward him and her face was lighted by deep tenderness. "There is nothing to forgive," she said. "Rather, I suppose, we should thank you for it. You created us out of a love of us and a need of us and it is wonderful to know that you are loved and needed."

"But I don't create you any more," Enoch pleaded. "There was a time, long ago, I had to. But not any longer. Now you come to visit me of your own free will."

How many years? he wondered. It must be all of fifty. And Mary had been the first, and David had been second. Of all the others of them, they had been the first and were the closest and the dearest.

And before that, before he'd even tried, he'd spent other years in studying that nameless science stemming from the thaumaturgists of Alphard XXII.

There had been a day and a state of mind when it would have been black magic, but it was not black magic. Rather, it was the orderly manipulation of certain natural aspects of the universe as yet quite unsuspected by the human race. Perhaps aspects that Man never would discover. For there was not, at least at the present moment, the necessary orientation of the scientific mind to initiate the research that must precede discovery.

"David felt," said Mary, "that we could not go on forever, playing out our little sedate visits. There had to be a time when we faced up to what we really are."

"And the rest of them?"

"I am sorry, Enoch. The rest of them as well."

"But you? How about you, Mary?"

"I don't know," she said. "It is different with me. I love you very much."

"And I . . ."

"No, that's not what I mean. Don't you understand! I'm in love with you."

He sat stricken, staring at her, and there was a great roaring in the world, as if he were standing still and the world and time were rushing swiftly past him.

"If it only could have stayed," she said, "the way it was at first. Then we were glad of our existence and our emotions were so shallow and we seemed to be so happy. Like little happy children, running in the sun. But then we all grew up. And I think I the most of all."

She smiled at him and tears were in her eyes.

"Don't take it so hard, Enoch. We can . ."

"My dear," he said, "I've been in love with you since the first day that I saw you. I think maybe even before that."

He reached out a hand to her, then pulled it back, remembering.

"I did not know," she said. "I should not have told you. You could live with it until you knew I loved you, too."

He nodded dumbly.

She bowed her head. "Dear God, we don't deserve this. We have done nothing to deserve it."

She raised her head and looked at him. "If I could only touch you."

"We can go on," he said, "as we have always done. You can come to see me any time you want. We can . ."

She shook her head. "It wouldn't work," she said. "There could neither of us stand it."

He knew that she was right. He knew that it was done. For fifty years she and the others had been dropping in to visit. And they'd come no more. For the fairyland was shattered and the magic spell was broken. He'd be left alone—more alone than ever, more alone than before he'd ever known her.

She would not come again and he could never bring himself to call her up again, even if he could, and his shadow world and his shadow love, the only love he'd ever really had, would be gone forever.

"Good bye, my dear," he said.

But it was too late. She was already gone.

And from far off, it seemed, he heard the moaning whistle that said a message had come in.

13

SHE HAD said that they must face up to the kind of things they were.

And what were they? Not, what did he think they were, but what were they, actually? What did they think themselves to be? For perhaps they knew much better than did he.

Where had Mary gone? When she left this room, into what kind of limbo did she disappear? Did she still exist? And if so, what kind of an existence would it be? Would she be stored away somewhere as a little girl would store away her doll in a box pushed back into the closet with all the other dolls?

He tried to imagine limbo and it was a nothingness, and if that were true, a being pushed into limbo would be an existence within a non-existence. There would be nothing—not space nor time, nor light, nor air, no color and no vision, just a never ending nothing that of necessity must lie at some point outside the universe.

Mary! he cried inside himself. *Mary, what have I done to you?*

And the answer lay there, hard and naked.

He had dabbled in a thing which he had not understood. And had, furthermore, committed that greater sin of thinking that he did understand. And the fact of the matter was that he had just barely understood enough to make the concept work, but had not understood enough to be aware of its consequences.

With creation went responsibility and he was not equipped to assume more than the moral responsibility for the wrong that he had done, and moral responsibility, unless it might be coupled with the ability to bring about some mitigation, was an entirely useless thing.

They hated him and resented him and he did not blame them, for he'd led them out and shown them the promised land of humanity and then had led them back. He had given them everything that a human being had with the one exception of that most important thing of all—the ability to exist within the human world.

They all hated him but Mary, and for Mary it was worse than hate. For she was condemned, by the very virtue of the humanity he had given her, to love the monster who had created her.

Hate me, Mary, he pleaded. *Hate me like the others!*

He had thought of them as shadow people, but that had been just a name he'd thought up for himself, for his own convenience, a handy label that he had tagged them with so that he would have some way of identifying them when he thought of them.

But the label had been wrong, for they were not shadowy or ghostlike. To the eyes they were solid and substantial, as real as any people. It was only when you tried to touch them that they were not real—for when you tried to touch them, there was nothing there.

A figment of his mind, he'd thought at first, but now he was not sure. At first they'd come only when he'd called them up, using the knowledge and the techniques that he had acquired in his study of the work done by the thaumaturgists of Alphard XXII. But in recent years he had not called them up. There had been no occasion to. They had anticipated him and come before he could call them up. They sensed his need of them before he knew the need himself. And they were there, waiting for him, to spend an hour or evening.

Figments of his mind in one sense, of course, for he had shaped them, perhaps at the time unconsciously, not knowing why he shaped them so, but in recent years he'd known, although he had tried not to know, would have been better satisfied if he had not known. For it was a knowledge that he had not admitted, but kept pushed back, far within his mind. But now, when all was gone, when it no longer mattered, he finally did admit it.

David Ransome was himself, as he had dreamed himself to be, as he had wished himself to be—but, of course, as he had never been. He was the dashing Union officer, of not so high a rank as to be stiff and stodgy, but a fair cut above the man of ordinary standing. He was trim and debonair and definitely daredevilish, loved by all the women, admired by all the men. He was a born leader and a good fellow all at once, at home alike in the field or drawing room.

And Mary? Funny, he thought, he had never called her anything but Mary. There had never been a surname. She had been simply Mary.

And she was at least two women, if not more than that. She was Sally Brown, who had lived just down the road—and how long had it been, he wondered, since he'd thought of Sally Brown? It was strange, he knew, that he had not thought of her, that he now was shocked by the memory of a one-time neighbor girl named Sally Brown. For the two of them once had been in love, or only thought, perhaps, that they had been in love. For even in the later years, when he still remembered her, he had never been quite certain, even through the romantic mists of time, if it had been love or no more than the romanticism of a soldier marching off to war. It had been a shy and fumbling, an awkward sort of love, the love of the farmer's daughter for the next-door farmer's son. They had decided to be married when he came home from war, but a few days after Gettysburg he had received the letter, then more than three weeks written, which told him that Sally Brown was dead of diphtheria. He had grieved, he now recalled, but he could not recall how deeply, although it probably had been deeply, for to grieve long and deeply was the fashion in those days.

So Mary very definitely was partly Sally Brown, but not entirely Sally. She was as well that tall, stately daughter of the South, the woman he had seen for a few moments only as he marched a dusty road in the hot Virginia sun. There had been a mansion, one of those great plantation houses, set back from the road, and she had been standing on the portico, beside one of the great white pillars, watching the enemy march past. Her hair was black and her complexion whiter than the pillar and she had stood so straight and proud, so defiant and imperious, that he had remembered her and thought of her and dreamed of her—although he never knew her name—through all the dusty, sweaty, bloody days of war. Wondering as he thought and dreamed of her if the thinking and the dreaming might be unfaithful to his Sally. Sitting around the campfire, when the talk grew quiet, and again, rolled in his blankets, staring at the stars, he had built up a fantasy of how, when the war was ended, he'd go back to that Virginia house and find her. She might be there no longer, but he still would roam the South and find her. But he never did; he had never really meant to find her. It had been a campfire dream.

So Mary had been both of these—she had been Sally Brown and the unknown Virginia belle standing by the pillar to watch the troops march by. She had been the shadow of them and perhaps of many others as yet unrealized by him, a composite of all he had ever known or seen or admired in women. She had been an ideal and perfection. She had been his perfect woman, created in his mind. And now, like Sally Brown, resting in her grave; like the Virginia belle, lost in the mists of time; like all the others who may have contributed to his molding of her, she was gone from him.

And he had loved her, certainly, for she had been a compounding of his loves—a cross section, as it were, of all the women he had ever loved (if he actually had loved any) or the ones he had thought he loved, even in the abstract.

But that she should love him was something that had never crossed his mind. And until he knew her love for him, it had been quite possible to nurse his love of her close inside the heart, knowing that it was a hopeless love and impossible, but the best that he could manage.

He wondered where she might be now, where she had retreated—into the limbo he had attempted to imagine or into some strange non-existence, waiting all unknowing for the time she'd come to him again.

He put up his hands and lowered his head into them and sat in utter misery and guilt, with his face cupped in his fingers.

She would never come again. He prayed she'd never come. It would be better for the both of them if she never came.

If he only could be sure, he thought, of where she might be now. If he only could be certain that she was in a semblance of death and untortured by her thoughts. To believe that she was sentient was more than one could bear.

He heard the hooting of the whistle that said a message waited and he took his head out of his hands. But he did not get up off the sofa.

Numbly his hand reached out to the coffee table that stood before the sofa, its top covered with some of the more colorful of the gewgaws and gimcracks that had been left as gifts by travelers.

He picked up a cube of something that might have been some strange sort of glass or of translucent stone—he had never been able to decide which it was, if either—and cupped it in his hands. Staring into it, he saw a tiny picture, three-dimensional and detailed, of a faery world. It was a prettily grotesque place set inside what might have been a forest glade surrounded by what appeared to be flowering toadstools, and drifting down through the air, as if it might have been a part of the air itself, came what looked for all the world like a shower of jeweled snow, sparkling and glinting in the violet light of a great blue sun. There were things dancing in the glade and they looked more like flowers than animals, but they moved with a grace and poetry that fired one's blood to watch. Then the faery place was wiped out and there was another place—a wild and dismal place, with grim, gaunt, beetling cliffs rearing high against a red and angry sky, while great flying things that looked like flapping dishrags beat their way up and down the cliffs, and there were others of them roosting, most obscenely, upon the scraggly projections that must have been some sort of misshapen trees growing from the very wall of rock. And from far below, from some distance that one could only guess, came the lonesome thundering of a rushing river.

He put the cube back upon the table. He wondered what it was that one saw within its depths. It was like turning the pages of a book, with each page a picture of a different place, but never anything to tell where that place might be. When he first had been given it, he had spent fascinated hours, watching the pictures change as he held it in his hands. There had never been a picture that looked even faintly like any other picture and there was no end to them. One got the feeling that these were not pictures, actually, but that one was looking at the scene itself and that at any moment one might lose his perch upon wherever he was roosting and plunge head first down into the place itself.

But it had finally palled upon him, for it had been a senseless business, gawking at a long series of places that had no identity. Senseless to him, of course, he thought, but not senseless, certainly, to that native of Enif V who had given it to him. It might, for all he knew, Enoch told himself, be of great significance and a treasure of great value.

That was the way it was with so many of the things he had. Even the ones that had given pleasure, he knew, he might be using wrongly, or, at least, in a way that had not been intended.

But there were some—a few, perhaps—that did have a value he could understand and appreciate, although in many instances their functions were of little use to him. There was the tiny clock that gave the local times for all the sectors of the galaxy, and while it might be intriguing, and even essential under certain circumstances, it had little value to him. And there was the perfume mixer, which was as close as he could come in naming it, which allowed a person to create the specific scent desired. Just get the mixture that one wanted and turn it on and the room took on that scent until one should turn it off. He'd had some fun with it, remembering that bitter winter day when, after long experimenting, he had achieved the scent of apple blossoms, and had lived a day in spring while a blizzard howled outside.

He reached out and picked up another piece—a beautiful thing that always had intrigued him, but for which he had never found a use—if, indeed, it had a use. It might be, he told himself, no more than a piece of art, a pretty thing that was meant to look at only. But it had a certain feel (if that were the word) which had led him to believe that it might have some specific function.

It was a pyramid of spheres, succeeding smaller spheres set on larger spheres. Some fourteen inches tall, it was a graceful piece, with each of the spheres a different color—and not just a color painted on, but each color so deep and true that one knew instinctively the color was intrinsic to each sphere, that the entire sphere, from the center of it out to the surface, was all of its particular color.

There was nothing to indicate that any gluelike medium had been used to mount the spheres and hold them in their places. It looked for all the world as if someone had simply piled the spheres, one atop the other, and they had stayed that way.

Holding it in his hands, he tried to recall who had given it to him, but he had no memory of it.

The whistle of the message machine still was calling and there was work to do. He could not sit here, he told himself, mooning the afternoon away. He put the pyramid of spheres back on the table top, and rising, went across the room.

The message said:

NO. 406,302 TO STATION 18327. NATIVE OF VEGA XXI ARRIVING AT 16532.82. DEPARTURE INDETERMINATE. NO LUGGAGE. CABINET ONLY, LOCAL CONDITIONS. CONFIRM.

Enoch felt a glow of happiness, looking at the message. It would be good to have a Hazer once again. It had been a month or more since one had passed through the station.

He could remember back to that first day he had ever met a Hazer, when the five of them had come. It must have been, he thought, back in 1914 or maybe 1915. World War I, which everyone then was calling the Great War, was under way, he knew.

The Hazer would be arriving at about the same time as Ulysses and the three of them could spend a pleasant evening. It was not too often that two good friends ever visited here at once.

He stood a bit aghast at thinking of the Hazer as a friend, for more than likely the being itself was one he had never met. But that made little difference, for a Hazer, any Hazer, would turn out to be a friend.

He got the cabinet in position beneath a materializer unit and double-checked to be sure that everything was exactly as it should be, then went back to the message machine and sent off the confirmation.

And all the time his memory kept on nagging at him. Had it been 1914, or perhaps a little later?

At the catalogue cabinet, he pulled out a drawer and found Vega XXI and the first date listed was July 12, 1915. He found the record book on the shelf and pulled it out and brought it to the desk. He leafed through it rapidly until he found the date.

14

JULY 12, 1915—Arrived this afternoon (3:20 P.M.) five beings from Vega XXI, the first of their kind to pass through this station. They are biped and humanoid, and one gains the impression that they are not made of flesh—that flesh would be too gross for the kind of things they are—but, of course, they are made of flesh the same as anyone. They glow, not with a visible light, but there is about them an aura that goes with them wherever they may be.

They were, I gathered, a sexual unit, the five of them, although I am not so certain I understand, for it is most confusing. They were happy and friendly and they carried with them an air of faint amusement, not at anything in particular, but at the universe itself, as if they might have enjoyed some sort of cosmic and very private joke that was known to no one else. They were on a holiday and were en route to a festival (although that may not be the precise word for it) on another planet, where other life forms were gathering for a week of carnival. Just how they had been invited or why they had been invited I was unable to determine. It must surely have been a great honor for them to be going there, but so far as I could see they did not seem to think so, but took it as their right. They were very happy and without a care and extremely self-assured and poised, but thinking back on it, I would suppose that they are always that way. I found myself just a little envious at not being able to be as carefree and gay as they were, and trying to imagine how fresh life and the universe must seem to them, and a little resentful that they could be, so unthinkingly, as happy as they were.

I had, according to instructions, hung hammocks so that they could rest, but they did not use them. They brought with them hampers that were filled with food and drink and sat down at my table and began to talk and feast. They asked me to sit with them and they chose two dishes and a bottle, which they assured me would be safe for me to eat and drink, the rest of their fare being somewhat doubtful for a metabolism such as mine. The food was delicious and of a kind I had never tasted —one dish being rather like the rarest and most delicate of old cheeses, and the other of a sweetness that was heavenly. The drink was somewhat like the finest of brandies, yellow in color and no heavier than water.

They asked me about myself and about my planet and they were courteous and seemed genuinely interested and they were quick of understanding in the things I told them. They told me they were headed for a planet the name of which I had not heard before, and they talked among themselves, gaily and happily, but in such a way that I did not seem to be left out. From their talk I gained the fact that some form of art was being presented at the festival on this planet. The art form was not alone of music or painting, but was composed of sound and color and emotion and form and other qualities for which there seem to be no words in the language of the Earth, and which I do not entirely recognize, only gaining the very faintest inkling of what they were talking of in this particular regard. I gained the impression of a three-dimensional symphony, although this is not entirely the right expression, which had been composed, not by a single being, but by a team of beings. They talked of the art form enthusiastically and I seemed to understand that it would last for not only several hours, but for days, and that it was an experience rather than a listening or seeing and that the spectators or audience did not merely sit and listen, but could, if they wished, and must, to get the most out of it, be participants. But I could not understand how they participated and felt I should not ask. They talked of the people they would meet and when they had met them last and gossiped considerably about them, although in kindly fashion, leaving the impression that they and many other people went from planet to planet for some happy purpose. But whether there was any purpose other than enjoyment in their going, I could not determine. I gathered that there might be.

They spoke of other festivals and not all of them were concerned with the one art form, but with other more specialized aspects of the arts, of which I could gain no adequate idea. They seemed to find a great and exuberant happiness in the festivals and it seemed to me that some certain significances aside from the art itself contributed to that happiness. I did not join in this part of their conversation, for, frankly, there was no opportunity. I would have liked to ask some questions, but I had no chance. I suppose that if I had, my questions must have sounded stupid to them, but given the chance, that would not have bothered me too much. And yet in spite of this, they managed somehow to make me feel I was included in their conversation. There was no obvious attempt to do this, and yet they made me feel I was one with them and not simply a station keeper they would spend a short time with. At times they spoke briefly in the language of their planet, which is one of the most beautiful I have ever heard, but for the most part they conversed in the vernacular used by a number of the humanoid races, a sort of pidgin language made up for convenience, and I suspect that this was done out of courtesy to me, and a great courtesy it was. I believe that they were truly the most civilized people I have ever met.

I have said they glowed and I think by that I mean they glowed in spirit. It seemed that they were accompanied, somehow, by a sparkling golden haze that made happy everything it touched—almost as if they moved in some special world that no one else had found. Sitting at the table with them, I seemed to be included in this golden haze and I felt strange, quiet, deep currents of happiness flowing in my veins. I wondered by what route they and their world had arrived at this golden state and if my world could, in some distant time, attain it.

But back of this happiness was a great vitality, the bubbling, effervescent spirit with an inner core of strength and a love of living that seemed to fill every pore of them and every instant of their time.

They had only two hours' time and it passed so swiftly that I had to finally warn them it was time to go. Before they left, they placed two packages on the table and said they were for me and thanked me for my table (what a strange way for them to put it); then they said good bye and stepped into the cabinet (the extra-large one) and I sent them on their way. Even after they were gone, the golden haze seemed to linger in the room and it was hours before all of it was gone. I wished that I might have gone with them to that other planet and its festival.

One of the packages they left contained a dozen bottles of the brandy-like liquor and the bottles themselves were each a piece of art, no two of them alike, being formed of what I am convinced is diamond, but whether fabricated diamond or carved from some great stones, I have no idea. At any rate, I would estimate that each of them is priceless, and each carved in a disturbing variety of symbolisms, each of which, however, has a special beauty of its own. And in the other box was a —well, I suppose that, for lack of other name, you might call it a music box. The box itself is ivory, old yellow ivory that is as smooth as satin, and covered by a mass of diagrammatic carving which must have some significance which I do not understand. On the top of it is a circle set inside a graduated scale and when I turned the circle to the first graduation there was music and through all the room an interplay of many-colored light, as if the entire room was filled with different kinds of color, and through it all a far-off suggestion of that golden haze. And from the box came, too, perfumes that filled the room, and feeling, emotion—whatever one may call it—but something that took hold of one and made one sad or happy or whatever might go with the music and the color and perfume.

Out of that box came a world in which one lived out the com-
position or whatever it might be—living it with all that one had
in him, all the emotion and belief and intellect of which one is
capable. And here, I am quite certain, was a recording of that
art form of which they had been talking. And not one com-
position alone, but 206 of them, for that is the number of the
graduation marks and for each mark there is a separate compo-
sition. In the days to come I shall play them all and make notes
upon each of them and assign them names, perhaps, according
to their characteristics, and from them, perhaps, can gain some
knowledge as well as entertainment.

15

THE TWELVE diamond bottles, empty long ago, stood in a sparkling row upon the fireplace mantel. The music box, as one of
his choicest possessions, was stored inside one of the cabinets,
where no harm could come to it. And Enoch thought rather
ruefully, in all these years, despite regular use of it, he had not
as yet played through the entire list of compositions. There
were so many of the early ones that begged for a replaying
that he was not a great deal more than halfway through the
graduated markings.

The Hazers had come back, the five of them, time and time
again, for it seemed that they found in this station, perhaps
even in the man who operated it, some quality that pleased
them. They had helped him learn the Vegan language and had
brought him scrolls of Vegan literature and many other things,
and had been, without any doubt, the best friends among the
aliens (other than Ulysses) that he had ever had. Then one day
they came no more and he wondered why, asking after them
when other Hazers showed up at the station. But he had never
learned what had happened to them.

He knew far more now about the Hazers and their art forms,
their traditions and their customs and their history, than he'd
known that first day he'd written of them, back in 1915. But
he still was far from grasping many of the concepts that were
commonplace with them.

There had been many of them since that day in 1915 and there was one he remembered in particular—the old, wise one, the philosopher, who had died on the floor beside the sofa.

They had been sitting on the sofa, talking, and he even could remember the subject of their talk. The old one had been telling of the perverse code of ethics, at once irrational and comic, which had been built up by that curious race of social vegetables he had encountered on one of his visits to an off-track planet on the other side of the galactic rim. The old Hazer had a drink or two beneath his belt and he was in splendid form, relating incident after incident with enthusiastic gusto.

Suddenly, in mid-sentence, he had stopped his talking, and had slumped quietly forward. Enoch, startled, reached for him, but before he could lay a hand upon him, the old alien had slid slowly to the floor.

The golden haze had faded from his body and slowly flickered out and the body lay there, angular and bony and obscene, a terribly alien thing there upon the floor, a thing that was at once pitiful and monstrous. More monstrous, it seemed to Enoch, than anything in alien form he had ever seen before.

In life it had been a wondrous creature, but now, in death, it was an old bag of hideous bones with a scaly parchment stretched to hold the bones together. It was the golden haze, Enoch told himself, gulping, in something near to horror, that had made the Hazer seem so wondrous and so beautiful, so vital, so alive and quick, so filled with dignity. The golden haze was the life of them and when the haze was gone, they became mere repulsive horrors that one gagged to look upon.

Could it be, he wondered, that the goldenness was the Hazers' life force and that they wore it like a cloak, as a sort of over-all disguise? Did they wear their life force on the outside of them while all other creatures wore it on the inside?

A piteous little wind was lamenting in the gingerbread high up in the gables and through the windows he could see battalions of tattered clouds fleeing in ragged retreat across the moon, which had climbed halfway up the eastern sky.

There was a coldness and a loneliness in the station—a far-reaching loneliness that stretched out and out, farther than mere Earth loneliness could go.

Enoch turned from the body and walked stiffly across the

room to the message machine. He put in a call for a connection direct with Galactic Central, then stood waiting, gripping the sides of the machine with both his hands.

GO AHEAD, said Galactic Central.

Briefly, as objectively as he was able, Enoch reported what had happened.

There was no hesitation and there were no questions from the other end. Just the simple directions (as if this was something that happened all the time) of how the situation should be handled. The Vegan must remain upon the planet of its death, its body to be disposed of according to the local customs obtaining on that planet. For that was the Vegan law, and, likewise, a point of honor. A Vegan, when he fell, must stay where he fell, and that place became, forever, a part of Vega XXI. There were such places, said Galactic Central, all through the galaxy.

THE CUSTOM HERE [typed Enoch] IS TO INTER THE DEAD.

THEN INTER THE VEGAN.

WE READ A VERSE OR TWO FROM OUR HOLY BOOK.

READ ONE FOR THE VEGAN, THEN. YOU CAN DO ALL THIS?

YES. BUT WE USUALLY HAVE IT DONE BY A PRACTITIONER OF RELIGION. UNDER THE PRESENT CIRCUMSTANCES, HOWEVER, THAT MIGHT BE UNWISE.

AGREED [said Galactic Central] YOU CAN DO AS WELL YOURSELF?

I CAN.

IT IS BEST, THEN, THAT YOU DO.

WILL THERE BE RELATIVES OR FRIENDS ARRIVING FOR THE RITES?

NO.

YOU WILL NOTIFY THEM?

FORMALLY, OF COURSE. BUT THEY ALREADY KNOW.

HE ONLY DIED A MOMENT OR TWO AGO.

NEVERTHELESS, THEY KNOW.

WHAT ABOUT A DEATH CERTIFICATE?
NONE IS NEEDED. THEY KNOW OF WHAT HE
DIED.
HIS LUGGAGE? THERE IS A TRUNK.
KEEP IT. IT IS YOURS. IT IS A TOKEN FOR THE
SERVICES YOU PERFORM FOR THE HONORED
DEAD. THAT ALSO IS THE LAW.
BUT THERE MAY BE IMPORTANT MATTERS
IN IT.
YOU WILL KEEP THE TRUNK. TO REFUSE
WOULD INSULT THE MEMORY OF THE DEAD.
ANYTHING ELSE? [asked Enoch] THAT IS ALL?
THAT IS ALL. PROCEED AS IF THE VEGAN
WERE ONE OF YOUR OWN.

Enoch cleared the machine and went back across the room.
He stood above the Hazer, getting up his nerve to bend and
lift the body to place it on the sofa. He shrank from touching
it. It was so unclean and terrible, such a travesty on the shining
creature that had sat there talking with him.

Since he met the Hazers he had loved them and admired
them, had looked forward to each visit by them—by any one
of them. And now he stood, a shivering coward who could not
touch one dead.

It was not the horror only, for in his years as keeper of the
station, he had seen much of pure visual horror as portrayed in
alien bodies. And yet he had learned to submerge that sense of
horror, to disregard the outward appearance of it, to regard all
life as brother life, to meet all things as people.

It was something else, he knew, some other unknown factor
quite apart from horror, that he felt. And yet this thing, he
reminded himself, was a friend of his. And as a dead friend, it
demanded honor from him, it demanded love and care.

Blindly he drove himself to the task. He stooped and lifted
it. It had almost no weight at all, as if in death it had lost a
dimension of itself, had somehow become a smaller thing and
less significant. Could it be, he wondered, that the golden haze
might have a weight all of its own?

He laid the body on the sofa and straightened it as best he

could. Then he went outside and, lighting the lantern in the shed, went down to the barn.

It had been years since he had been there, but nothing much had changed. Protected by a tight roof from the weather, it had stayed snug and dry. There were cobwebs hanging from the beams and dust was everywhere. Straggling clumps of ancient hay, stored in the mow above, hung down through the cracks in the boards that floored the mow. The place had a dry, sweet, dusty smell about it, all the odors of animals and manure long gone.

Enoch hung the lantern on the peg behind the row of stanchions and climbed the ladder to the mow. Working in the dark, for he dared not bring the lantern into this dust heap of dried-out hay, he found the pile of oaken boards far beneath the eaves.

Here, he remembered, underneath these slanting eaves, had been a pretended cave in which, as a boy, he had spent many happy rainy days when he could not be outdoors. He had been Robinson Crusoe in his desert island cave, or some now nameless outlaw hiding from a posse, or a man holed up against the threat of scalp-hunting Indians. He had had a gun, a wooden gun that he had sawed out of a board, working it down later with draw-shave and knife and a piece of glass to scrape it smooth. It had been something he had cherished through all his boyhood days—until that day, when he had been twelve, that his father, returning home from a trip to town, had handed him a rifle for his very own.

He explored the stack of boards in the dark, determining by feel the ones that he would need. These he carried to the ladder and carefully slid down to the floor below.

Climbing down the ladder, he went up the short flight of stairs to the granary, where the tools were stored. He opened the lid of the great tool chest and found that it was filled with long deserted mice nests. Pulling out handfuls of the straw and hay and grass that the rodents had used to set up their one-time housekeeping, he uncovered the tools. The shine had gone from them, their surface grayed by the soft patina that came from long disuse, but there was no rust upon them and the cutting edges still retained their sharpness.

Selecting the tools he needed, he went back to the lower part of the barn and fell to work. A century ago, he thought, he had done as he was doing now, working by lantern light to construct a coffin. And that time it had been his father lying in the house.

The oaken boards were dry and hard, but the tools still were in shape to handle them. He sawed and planed and hammered and there was the smell of sawdust. The barn was snug and silent, the depth of hay standing in the mow drowning out the noise of the complaining wind outside.

He finished the coffin and it was heavier than he had figured, so he found the old wheelbarrow, leaning against the wall back of the stalls that once had been used for horses, and loaded the coffin on it. Laboriously, stopping often to rest, he wheeled it down to the little cemetery inside the apple orchard.

And here, beside his father's grave, he dug another grave, having brought a shovel and a pickax with him. He did not dig it as deep as he would have liked to dig, not the full six feet that was decreed by custom, for he knew that if he dug it that deep he never would be able to get the coffin in. So he dug it slightly less than four, laboring in the light of the lantern, set atop the mound of dirt to cast its feeble glow. An owl came up from the woods and sat for a while, unseen, somewhere in the orchard, muttering and gurgling in between its hoots. The moon sank toward the west and the ragged clouds thinned out to let the stars shine through.

Finally it was finished, with the grave completed and the casket in the grave and the lantern flickering, the kerosene almost gone, and the chimney blacked from the angle at which the lantern had been canted.

Back at the station, Enoch hunted up a sheet in which to wrap the body. He put a Bible in his pocket and picked up the shrouded Vegan and, in the first faint light that preceded dawn, marched down to the apple orchard. He put the Vegan in the coffin and nailed shut the lid, then climbed from the grave.

Standing on the edge of it, he took the Bible from his pocket and found the place he wanted. He read aloud, scarcely needing to strain his eyes in the dim light to follow the text, for it was from a chapter that he had read many times:

*In my Father's house are many mansions; if it were not
so, I would have told you . . .*

Thinking, as he read it, how appropriate it was; how there
must need be many mansions in which to house all the souls
in the galaxy—and of all the other galaxies that stretched, perhaps interminably, through space. Although if there were understanding, one might be enough.

He finished reading and recited the burial service, from
memory, as best he could, not being absolutely sure of all the
words. But sure enough, he told himself, to make sense out of
it. Then he shoveled in the dirt.

The stars and moon were gone and the wind had died. In
the quietness of the morning, the eastern sky was pearly pink.

Enoch stood beside the grave, with the shovel in his hand.

"Good bye, my friend," he said.

Then he turned and, in the first flush of the morning, went
back to the station.

16

ENOCH GOT up from his desk and carried the record book back
to the shelf and slid it into place.

He turned around and stood hesitantly.

There were things that he should do. He should read his
papers. He should be writing up his journal. There were a couple of papers in the latest issues of the *Journal of Geophysical
Research* that he should be looking at.

But he didn't feel like doing any of them. There was too
much to think about, too much to worry over, too much to
mourn.

The watchers still were out there. He had lost his shadow
people. And the world was edging in toward war.

Although, perhaps, he should not be worrying about what
happened to the world. He could renounce the world, could
resign from the human race any time he wished. If he never
went outside, if he never opened up the door, then it would
make no difference to him what the world might do or what

might happen to it. For he had a world. He had a greater world than anyone outside this station had ever dreamed about. He did not need the Earth.

But even as he thought it, he knew he could not make it stick. For, in a very strange and funny way, he still did need the Earth.

He walked over to the door and spoke the phrase and the door came open. He walked into the shed and it closed behind him.

He went around the corner of the house and sat down on the steps that led up to the porch.

This, he thought, was where it all had started. He had been sitting here that summer day of long ago when the stars had reached out across vast gulfs of space and put the finger on him.

The sun was far down the sky toward the west and soon it would be evening. Already the heat of the day was falling off, with a faint, cool breeze creeping up out of the hollow that ran down to the river valley. Down across the field, at the edge of the woods, crows were wheeling in the sky and cawing.

It would be hard to shut the door, he knew, and keep it shut. Hard never to feel the sun or wind again, to never know the smell of the changing seasons as they came across the Earth. Man, he told himself, was not ready for that. He had not as yet become so totally a creature of his own created environment that he could divorce entirely the physical characteristics of his native planet. He needed sun and soil and wind to remain a man.

He should do this oftener, Enoch thought, come out here and sit, doing nothing, just looking, seeing the trees and the river to the west and the blue of the Iowa hills across the Mississippi, watching the crows wheeling in the skies and the pigeons strutting on the ridgepole of the barn.

It would be worth while each day to do it, for what was another hour of aging? He did not need to save his hours—not now he didn't. There might come a time when he'd become very jealous of them and when that day came, he could hoard the hours and minutes, even the seconds, in as miserly a fashion as he could manage.

He heard the sound of the running feet as they came around

the farther corner of the house, a stumbling, exhausted running, as if the one who ran might have come a far way.

He leapt to his feet and strode out into the yard to see who it might be and the runner came stumbling toward him, with her arms outstretched. He put out an arm and caught her as she came close to him, holding her close against him so she would not fall.

"Lucy!" he cried. "Lucy! What has happened, child?"

His hands against her back were warm and sticky and he took one of them away to see that it was smeared with blood. The back of her dress, he saw, was soaked and dark.

He grabbed her by the shoulders and shoved her away from him so he could see her face. It was wet with crying and there was terror in the face—and pleading with the terror.

She pulled away from him and turned around. Her hands came up and slipped her dress off her shoulders and let it slide halfway down her back. The flesh of the shoulders was ribboned by long slashes that still were oozing blood.

She pulled the dress up again and turned to face him. She made a pleading gesture and pointed backward down the hill, in the direction of the field that ran down to the woods.

There was motion down there, someone coming through the woods, almost at the edge of the old deserted field.

She must have seen it, too, for she came close against him, shivering, seeking his protection.

He bent and lifted her in his arms and ran for the shed. He spoke the phrase and the door came open and he stepped into the station. Behind him he heard the door go sliding shut.

Once inside, he stood there, with Lucy Fisher cradled in his arms, and knew that what he'd done had been a great mistake —that it was something that, in a sober moment, he never would have done, that if he'd given it a second thought, he would not have done it.

But he had acted on an impulse, with no thought at all. The girl had asked protection and here she had protection, here nothing in the world ever could get at her. But she was a human being and no human being, other than himself, should have ever crossed the threshold.

But it was done and there was no way to change it. Once across the threshold, there was no way to change it.

He carried her across the room and put her on the sofa, then stepped back. She sat there, looking up at him, smiling very faintly, as if she did not know if she were allowed to smile in a place like this. She lifted a hand and tried to brush away the tears that were upon her cheeks.

She looked quickly around the room and her mouth made an O of wonder.

He squatted down and patted the sofa and shook a finger at her, hoping that she might understand that he meant she should stay there, that she must go nowhere else. He swept an arm in a motion to take in all the remainder of the station and shook his head as sternly as he could.

She watched him, fascinated, then she smiled and nodded, as if she might have understood.

He reached out and took one of her hands in his own, and holding it, patted it as gently as he could, trying to reassure her, to make her understand that everything was all right if she only stayed exactly where she was.

She was smiling now, not wondering, apparently, if there were any reason that she should not smile.

She reached out her free hand and made a little fluttering gesture toward the coffee table, with its load of alien gadgets.

He nodded and she picked up one of them, turning it admiringly in her hand.

He got to his feet and went to the wall to take down the rifle.

Then he went outside to face whatever had been pursuing her.

17

TWO MEN were coming up the field toward the house and Enoch saw that one of them was Hank Fisher, Lucy's father. He had met the man, rather briefly, several years ago, on one of his walks. Hank had explained, rather sheepishly and when no explanation had been necessary, that he was hunting for a cow which had strayed away. But from his furtive manner, Enoch had deduced that his errand, rather than the hunting of a cow, had been somewhat on the shady side, although he could not imagine what it might have been.

The other man was younger. No more, perhaps, than sixteen or seventeen. More than likely, Enoch told himself, he was one of Lucy's brothers.

Enoch stood by the porch and waited.

Hank, he saw, was carrying a coiled whip in his hand, and looking at it, Enoch understood those wounds on Lucy's shoulders. He felt a swift flash of anger, but tried to fight it down. He could deal better with Hank Fisher if he kept his temper.

The two men stopped three paces or so away.

"Good afternoon," said Enoch.

"You seen my gal?" asked Hank.

"And if I have?" asked Enoch.

"I'll take the hide off of her," yelled Hank, flourishing the whip.

"In such a case," said Enoch, "I don't believe I'll tell you anything."

"You got her hid," charged Hank.

"You can look around," said Enoch.

Hank took a quick step forward, then thought better of it.

"She got what she had coming to her," he yelled. "And I ain't finished with her yet. There ain't no one, not even my own flesh and blood, can put a hex on me."

Enoch said nothing. Hank stood, undecided.

"She meddled," he said. "She had no call to meddle. It was none of her damn' business."

The young man said, "I was just trying to train Butcher. Butcher," he explained to Enoch, "is a coon hound pup."

"That is right," said Hank. "He wasn't doing nothing wrong. The boys caught a young coon the other night. Took a lot of doing. Roy, here, had staked out the coon—tied it to a tree. And he had Butcher on a leash. He was letting Butcher fight the coon. Not hurting anything. He'd pull Butcher off before any damage could be done and let them rest a while. Then he'd let Butcher at the coon again."

"It's the best way in the world," said Roy, "to get a coon dog trained."

"That is right," said Hank. "That is why they caught the coon."

"We needed it," said Roy, "to train this Butcher pup."

"This all is fine," said Enoch, "and I am glad to hear it. But what has it got to do with Lucy?"

"She interfered," said Hank. "She tried to stop the training. She tried to grab Butcher away from Roy, here."

"For a dummy," Roy said, "she is a mite too uppity."

"You hush your mouth," his father told him sternly, swinging around on him.

Roy mumbled to himself, falling back a step.

Hank turned back to Enoch.

"Roy knocked her down," he said. "He shouldn't have done that. He should have been more careful."

"I didn't mean to," Roy said. "I just swung my arm out to keep her away from Butcher."

"That is right," said Hank. "He swung a bit too hard. But there wasn't any call for her doing what she did. She tied Butcher up in knots so he couldn't fight that coon. Without laying a finger on him, mind you, she tied him up in knots. He couldn't move a muscle. That made Roy mad."

He appealed to Enoch, earnestly, "Wouldn't that have made you mad?"

"I don't think it would," said Enoch. "But then, I'm not a coon-dog man."

Hank stared in wonder at this lack of understanding.

But he went on with his story. "Roy got real mad at her. He'd raised that Butcher. He thought a lot of him. He wasn't going to let no one, not even his own sister, tie that dog in knots. So he went after her and she tied him up in knots, just like she did to Butcher. I never seen a thing like it in all my born days. Roy just stiffened up and then he fell down to the ground and his legs pulled up against his belly and he wrapped his arms around himself and he laid there on the ground, pulled into a ball. Him and Butcher, both. But she never touched that coon. She never tied him in no knots. Her own folks is all she touched."

"It didn't hurt," said Roy. "It didn't hurt at all."

"I was sitting there," said Hank, "braiding this here bull whip. Its end had frayed and I fixed a new one on it. And I seen it all, but I didn't do a thing until I saw Roy there, tied up on the ground. And I figured then it had gone far enough. I am a broad-minded man; I don't mind a little wart-charming and other piddling things like that. There have been a lot of people who have been able to do that. It ain't no disgrace at all. But this thing of tying dogs and people into knots . . ."

"So you hit her with the whip," said Enoch.

"I did my duty," Hank told him solemnly. "I ain't about to have no witch in any family of mine. I hit her a couple of licks and her making that dumb show of hers to try to get me stopped. But I had my duty and I kept on hitting. If I did enough of it, I figured, I'd knock it out of her. That was when she put the hex on me. Just like she did on Roy and Butcher, but in a different way. She turned me blind—she blinded her own father! I couldn't see a thing. I just stumbled around the yard, yelling and clawing at my eyes. And then they got all right again, but she was gone. I saw her running through the woods and up the hill. So Roy and me, we took out after her."

"And you think I have her here?"

"I know you have," said Hank.

"O.K.," said Enoch. "Have a look around."

"You can bet I will," Hank told him grimly. "Roy, take the barn. She might be hiding there."

Roy headed for the barn. Hank went into the shed, came out almost immediately, strode down to the sagging chicken house.

Enoch stood and waited, the rifle cradled on his arm.

He had trouble here, he knew—more trouble than he'd ever had before. There was no such thing as reasoning with a man of Hank Fisher's stripe. There was no approach, right now, that he would understand. All that he could do, he knew, was to wait until Hank's temper had cooled off. Then there might be an outside chance of talking sense to him.

The two of them came back.

"She ain't nowhere around," said Hank. "She is in the house."

Enoch shook his head. "There can't anyone get into that house."

"Roy," said Hank, "climb them there steps and open up that door."

Roy looked fearfully at Enoch.

"Go ahead," said Enoch.

Roy moved forward slowly and went up the steps. He crossed the porch and put his hand upon the front door knob and turned. He tried again. He turned around.

"Pa," he said, "I can't turn it. I can't get it open."

"Hell," said Hank, disgusted, "you can't do anything."

Hank took the steps in two jumps, paced wrathfully across the porch. His hand reached out and grasped the knob and wrenched at it powerfully. He tried again and yet again. He turned angrily to face Enoch.

"What is going on here?" he yelled.

"I told you," Enoch said, "that you can't get in."

"The hell I can't!" roared Hank.

He tossed the whip to Roy and came down off the porch, striding over to the woodpile that stood beside the shed. He wrenched the heavy, double-bitted ax out of the chopping block.

"Careful with that ax," warned Enoch. "I've had it for a long time and I set a store by it."

Hank did not answer. He went up on the porch and squared off before the door.

"Stand off," he said to Roy. "Give me elbow room."

Roy backed away.

"Wait a minute," Enoch said. "You mean to chop down that door?"

"You're damned right I do."

Enoch nodded gravely.

"Well?" asked Hank.

"It's all right with me if you want to try."

Hank took his stance, gripping the handle of the ax. The steel flashed swiftly, up over his shoulder, then down in a driven blow.

The edge of the steel struck the surface of the door and turned, deflected by the surface, changed its course, bouncing from the door. The blade came slicing down and back. It missed Hank's spraddled leg by no more than an inch and the momentum of it spun him half around.

He stood there, foolishly, arms outstretched, hands still gripping the handle of the ax. He stared at Enoch.

"Try again," invited Enoch.

Rage flowed over Hank. His face was flushed with anger.

"By God, I will!" he yelled.

He squared off again and this time he swung the ax, not at the door, but at the window set beside the door.

The blade struck and there was a high singing sound as pieces of sun-bright steel went flying through the air.

Ducking away, Hank dropped the ax. It fell to the floor of the porch and bounced. One blade was broken, the metal sheared away in jagged breaks. The window was intact. There was not a scratch upon it.

Hank stood there for a moment, staring at the broken ax, as if he could not quite believe it.

Silently he stretched out his hand and Roy put the bull whip in it.

The two of them came down the stairs.

They stopped at the bottom of them and looked at Enoch. Hank's hand twitched on the whip.

"If I were you," said Enoch, "I wouldn't try it, Hank. I can move awfully fast."

He patted the gun butt. "I'd have the hand off you before you could swing that whip."

Hank breathed heavily. "There's the devil in you, Wallace," he said. "And there's the devil in her, too. You're working together, the two of you. Sneaking around in the woods, meeting one another."

Enoch waited, watching the both of them.

"God help me," cried Hank. "My own daughter is a witch!"

"I think," said Enoch, "you should go back home. If I happen to find Lucy, I will bring her there."

Neither of them made a move.

"You haven't heard the last of this," yelled Hank. "You have my daughter somewhere and I'll get you for it."

"Any time you want," said Enoch, "but not now."

He made an imperative gesture with the rifle barrel.

"Get moving," he said. "And don't come back. Either one of you."

They hesitated for a moment, looking at him, trying to gauge him, trying to guess what he might do next.

Slowly they turned and, walking side by side, moved off down the hill.

18

HE SHOULD have killed the two of them, he thought. They were not fit to live.

He glanced down at the rifle and saw that his hands had such a tense grip on the gun that his fingers stood out white and stiff against the satin brownness of the wood.

He gasped a little in his effort to fight down the rage that boiled inside him, trying to explode. If they had stayed here any longer, if he'd not run them off, he knew he'd have given in to that towering rage.

And it was better, much better, the way that it had been. He wondered a little dully how he had managed to hold in.

And was glad he had. For even as it stood, it would be bad enough.

They would say he was a madman; that he had run them off at gunpoint. They might even say that he had kidnaped Lucy and was holding her against her will. They would stop at nothing to make him all the trouble that they could.

He had no illusions about what they might do, for he knew the breed, vindictive in their smallness—little vicious insects of the human race.

He stood beside the porch and watched them down the hill, wondering how a girl so fine as Lucy could spring from such decadent stock. Perhaps her handicap had served as a bulwark against the kind of folks they were; had kept her from becoming another one of them. Perhaps if she could have talked with them or listened, she would in time have become as shiftless and as vicious as any one of them.

It had been a great mistake to get mixed up in a thing like this. A man in his position had no business in an involvement such as this. He had too much to lose; he should have stood aside.

And yet what could he have done? Could he have refused to give Lucy his protection, with the blood soaking through her dress from the lashes that lay across her shoulders? Should he have ignored the frantic, helpless pleading in her face?

He might have done it differently, he thought. There might have been other, smarter ways in which to handle it. But there had been no time to think of any smarter way. There only had been time to carry her to safety and then go outside to meet them.

And now, that he thought of it, perhaps the best thing would have been not to go outside at all. If he'd stayed inside the station, nothing would have happened.

It had been impulsive, that going out to face them. It had been, perhaps, the human thing to do, but it had not been wise. But he had done it and it was over now and there was no turning back. If he had it to do again, he would do it differently, but you got no second chance.

He turned heavily around and went back inside the station.

Lucy was still sitting on the sofa and she held a flashing object in her hand. She was staring at it raptly and there was in her face again that same vibrant and alert expression he had seen that morning when she'd held the butterfly.

He laid the rifle on the desk and stood quietly there, but she must have caught the motion of him, for she looked quickly up. And then her eyes once more went back to the flashing thing she was holding in her hands.

He saw that it was the pyramid of spheres and now all the spheres were spinning slowly, in alternating clockwise and counterclockwise motions, and that as they spun they shone and glittered, each in its own particular color, as if there might be, deep inside each one of them, a source of soft, warm light.

Enoch caught his breath at the beauty and the wonder of it—the old, hard wonder of what this thing might be and what it might be meant to do. He had examined it a hundred times or more and had puzzled at it and there had been nothing he could find that was of significance. So far as he could see, it was only something that was meant to be looked at, although there had been that persistent feeling that it had a purpose and that, perhaps, somehow, it was meant to operate.

And now it was in operation. He had tried a hundred times to get it figured out and Lucy had picked it up just once and had got it figured out.

He noticed the rapture with which she was regarding it. Was it possible, he wondered, that she knew its purpose?

He went across the room and touched her arm and she lifted her face to look at him and in her eyes he saw the gleam of happiness and excitement.

He made a questioning gesture toward the pyramid, trying to ask if she knew what it might be. But she did not understand him. Or perhaps she knew, but knew as well how impossible it would be to explain its purpose. She made that happy, fluttery motion with her hand again, indicating the table with its load of gadgets and she seemed to try to laugh—there was, at least, a sense of laughter in her face.

Just a kid, Enoch told himself, with a box heaped high with new and wondrous toys. Was that all it was to her? Was she happy and excited merely because she suddenly had become aware of all the beauty and the novelty of the things stacked there on the table?

He turned wearily and went back to the desk. He picked up the rifle and hung it on the pegs.

She should not be in the station. No human being other than himself should ever be inside the station. Bringing her here, he had broken that unspoken understanding he had with the aliens who had installed him as a keeper. Although, of all the humans he could have brought, Lucy was the one who could possibly be exempt from the understood restriction. For she could never tell the things that she had seen.

She could not remain, he knew. She must be taken home. For if she were not taken, there would be a massive hunt for her, a lost girl—a beautiful deaf-mute.

A story of a missing deaf-mute girl would bring in newspapermen in a day or two. It would be in all the papers and on television and on radio and the woods would be swarming with hundreds of searchers.

Hank Fisher would tell how he'd tried to break into the house and couldn't and there'd be others who would try to break into the house and there'd be hell to pay.

Enoch sweated, thinking of it.

All the years of keeping out of people's way, all the years of being unobtrusive would be for nothing then. This strange house upon a lonely ridge would become a mystery for the world, and a challenge and a target for all the crackpots of the world.

He went to the medicine cabinet, to get the healing ointment that had been included in the drug packet provided by Galactic Central.

He found it and opened the little box. More than half of it remained. He'd used it through the years, but sparingly. There was, in fact, little need to use a great deal of it.

He went across the room to where Lucy sat and stood back of the sofa. He showed her what he had and made motions to show her what it was for. She slid her dress off her shoulders and he bent to look at the slashes.

The bleeding had stopped, but the flesh was red and angry.

Gently he rubbed ointment into the stripes that the whip had made.

She had healed the butterfly, he thought; but she could not heal herself.

On the table in front of her the pyramid of spheres still was flashing and glinting, throwing a flickering shadow of color all about the room.

It was operating, but what could it be doing?

It was finally operating, but not a thing was happening as a result of that operation.

19

ULYSSES CAME as twilight was deepening into night.

Enoch and Lucy had just finished with their supper and were sitting at the table when Enoch heard his footsteps.

The alien stood in shadow and he looked, Enoch thought, more than ever like the cruel clown. His lithe, flowing body had the look of smoked, tanned buckskin. The patchwork color of his hide seemed to shine with a faint luminescence and the sharp, hard angles of his face, the smooth baldness of his head, the flat, pointed ears pasted tight against the skull lent him a vicious fearsomeness.

If one did not know him for the gentle character that he was, Enoch told himself, he would be enough to scare a man out of seven years of growth.

"We had been expecting you," said Enoch. "The coffeepot is boiling."

Ulysses took a slow step forward, then paused.

"You have another with you. A human, I would say."

"There is no danger," Enoch told him.

"Of another gender. A female, is it not? You have found a mate?"

"No," said Enoch. "She is not my mate."

"You have acted wisely through the years," Ulysses told him. "In a position such as yours, a mate is not the best."

"You need not worry. There is a malady upon her. She has no communication. She can neither hear nor speak."

"A malady?"

"Yes, from the moment she was born. She has never heard or spoken. She can tell of nothing here."

"Sign language?"

"She knows no sign language. She refused to learn it."

"She is a friend of yours."

"For some years," said Enoch. "She came seeking my protection. Her father used a whip to beat her."

"This father knows she's here?"

"He thinks she is, but he cannot know."

Ulysses came slowly out of the darkness and stood within the light.

Lucy was watching him, but there was no terror on her face. Her eyes were level and untroubled and she did not flinch.

"She takes me well," Ulysses said. "She does not run or scream."

"She could not scream," said Enoch, "even if she wished."

"I must be most repugnant," Ulysses said, "at first sight to any human."

"She does not see the outside only. She sees inside of you as well."

"Would she be frightened if I made a human bow to her?"

"I think," said Enoch, "she might be very pleased."

Ulysses made his bow, formal and exaggerated, with one hand upon his leathery belly, bowing from the waist.

Lucy smiled and clapped her hands.

"You see," Ulysses cried, delighted, "I think that she may like me."

"Why don't you sit down, then," suggested Enoch, "and we all will have some coffee."

"I had forgotten of the coffee. The sight of this other human drove coffee from my mind."

He sat down at the place where the third cup had been set

and waiting for him. Enoch started around the table, but Lucy rose and went to get the coffee.

"She understands?" Ulysses asked.

Enoch shook his head. "You sat down by the cup and the cup was empty."

She poured the coffee, then went over to the sofa.

"She will not stay with us?" Ulysses asked.

"She's intrigued by that tableful of trinkets. She set one of them to going."

"You plan to keep her here?"

"I can't keep her," Enoch said. "There'll be a hunt for her. I'll have to take her home."

"I do not like it," Ulysses said.

"Nor do I. Let's admit at once that I should not have brought her here. But at the time it seemed the only thing to do. I had no time to think it out."

"You've done no wrong," said Ulysses softly.

"She cannot harm us," said Enoch. "Without communication . . ."

"It's not that," Ulysses told him. "She's just a complication and I do not like further complications. I came tonight to tell you, Enoch, that we are in trouble."

"Trouble? But there's not been any trouble."

Ulysses lifted his coffee cup and took a long drink of it.

"That is good," he said. "I carry back the bean and make it at my home. But it does not taste the same."

"This trouble?"

"You remember the Vegan that died here several of your years ago."

Enoch nodded. "The Hazer."

"The being has a proper name . . ."

Enoch laughed. "You don't like our nicknames."

"It is not our way," Ulysses said.

"My name for them," said Enoch, "is a mark of my affection."

"You buried this Vegan."

"In my family plot," said Enoch. "As if he were my own. I read a verse above him."

"That is well and good," Ulysses said. "That is as it should be. You did very well. But the body's gone."

"Gone! It can't be gone!" cried Enoch.

"It has been taken from the grave."

"But you can't know," protested Enoch. "How could you know?"

"Not I. It's the Vegans. The Vegans are the ones who know."

"But they're light-years distant . . ."

And then he was not too sure. For on that night the wise old one had died and he'd messaged Galactic Central, he had been told that the Vegans had known the moment he had died. And there had been no need for a death certificate, for they knew of what he died.

It seemed impossible, of course, but there were too many impossibilities in the galaxy which turned out, after all, to be entirely possible for a man to ever know when he stood on solid ground.

Was it possible, he wondered, that each Vegan had some sort of mental contact with every other Vegan? Or that some central census bureau (to give a human designation to something that was scarcely understandable) might have some sort of official linkage with every living Vegan, knowing where it was and how it was and what it might be doing?

Something of the sort, Enoch admitted, might indeed be possible. It was not beyond the astounding capabilities that one found on every hand throughout the galaxy. But to maintain a similar contact with the Vegan dead was something else again.

"The body's gone," Ulysses said. "I can tell you that and know it is the truth. You're held accountable."

"By the Vegans?"

"By the Vegans, yes. And the galaxy."

"I did what I could," said Enoch hotly. "I did what was required. I filled the letter of the Vegan law. I paid the dead my honor and the honor of my planet. It is not right that the responsibility should go on forever. Not that I can believe the body can be really gone. There is no one who would take it. No one who knew of it."

"By human logic," Ulysses told him, "you, of course, are right. But not by Vegan logic. And in this case Galactic Central would tend to support the Vegans."

"The Vegans," Enoch said testily, "happen to be friends of mine. I have never met a one of them that I didn't like or couldn't get along with. I can work it out with them."

"If only the Vegans were concerned," said Ulysses, "I am quite sure you could. I would have no worry. But the situation gets complicated as you go along. On the surface it seems a rather simple happening, but there are many factors. The Vegans, for example, have known for some time that the body had been taken and they were disturbed, of course. But out of certain considerations, they had kept their silence."

"They needn't have. They could have come to me. I don't know what could have been done . . ."

"Silent not because of you. Because of something else."

Ulysses finished off his coffee and poured himself another cup. He filled Enoch's half-filled cup and set the pot aside.

Enoch waited.

"You may not have been aware of it," said Ulysses, "but at the time this station was established, there was considerable opposition to it from a number of races in the galaxy. There were many reasons cited, as is the case in all such situations, but the underlying reason, when you get down to basics, rests squarely on the continual contest for racial or regional advantage. A situation akin, I would imagine, to the continual bickering and maneuvering which you find here upon the Earth to gain an economic advantage for one group or another, or one nation and another. In the galaxy, of course, the economic considerations only occasionally are the underlying factors. There are many other factors than the economic."

Enoch nodded. "I had gained a hint of this. Nothing recently. But I hadn't paid too much attention to it."

"It's largely a matter of direction," Ulysses said. "When Galactic Central began its expansion into this spiral arm, it meant there was no time or effort available for expansions in other directions. There is one large group of races which has held a dream for many centuries of expanding into some of the nearby globular clusters. It does make a dim sort of sense, of course. With the techniques that we have, the longer jump across space to some of the closer clusters is entirely possible. Another thing—the clusters seem to be extraordinarily free of dust and gas, so that once we got there we could expand more rapidly throughout the cluster than we can in many parts of the galaxy. But at best, it's a speculative business, for we don't know what we'll find there. After we've made all the effort and spent all the time we may find little or nothing, except possibly some more real estate. And we have plenty of that in the galaxy. But the clusters have a vast appeal for certain types of minds."

Enoch nodded. "I can see that. It would be the first venturing out of the galaxy itself. It might be the first short step on the route that could lead us to other galaxies."

Ulysses peered at him. "You, too," he said. "I might have known."

Enoch said smugly: "I am that type of mind."

"Well, anyhow, there was this globular-cluster faction—I suppose you'd call it that—which contended bitterly when we began our move in this direction. You understand—certainly you do—that we've barely begun the expansion into this neighborhood. We have less than a dozen stations and we'll need a hundred. It will take centuries before the network is complete."

"So this faction is still contending," Enoch said. "There still is time to stop this spiral-arm project."

"That is right. And that's what worries me. For the faction is set to use this incident of the missing body as an emotion-charged argument against the extension of this network. It is being joined by other groups that are concerned with certain special interests. And these special interest groups see a better chance of getting what they want if they can wreck this project."

"Wreck it?"

"Yes, wreck it. They will start screaming, as soon as the body incident becomes open knowledge, that a planet so barbaric as the Earth is no fit location for a station. They will insist that this station be abandoned."

"But they can't do that!"

"They can," Ulysses said. "They will say it is degrading and unsafe to maintain a station so barbaric that even graves are rifled, on a planet where the honored dead cannot rest in peace. It is the kind of highly emotional argument that will gain wide acceptance and support in some sections of the galaxy. The Vegans tried their best. They tried to hush it up, for the sake of the project. They have never done a thing like that before. They are a proud people and they feel a slight to honor—perhaps more deeply than many other races—and yet, for the greater good, they were willing to accept dishonor. And would have if they could have kept it quiet. But the story leaked out somehow—by good espionage, no doubt. And they cannot stand the loss of face in advertised dishonor. The Vegan who will be arriving here this evening is an official representative charged with delivering an official protest."

"To me?"

"To you, and through you, to the Earth."

"But the Earth is not concerned. The Earth doesn't even know."

"Of course it doesn't. So far as Galactic Central is concerned, you are the Earth. You represent the Earth."

Enoch shook his head. It was a crazy way of thinking. But, he told himself, he should not be surprised. It was the kind of thinking he should have expected. He was too hidebound, he thought, too narrow. He had been trained in the human way of thinking and, even after all these years, that way of thought persisted. Persisted to a point where any way of thought that conflicted with it must automatically seem wrong.

This talk of abandoning Earth station was wrong, too. It made no sort of sense. For abandoning of the station would not wreck the project. Although, more than likely, it would wreck whatever hope he'd held for the human race.

"But even if you have to abandon Earth," he said, "you could go out to Mars. You could build a station there. If it's necessary to have a station in this solar system there are other planets."

"You don't understand," Ulysses told him. "This station is just one point of attack. It is no more than a toehold, just a bare beginning. The aim is to wreck the project, to free the time and effort that is expended here for some other project. If they can force us to abandon one station, then we stand discredited. Then all our motives and our judgment come up for review."

"But even if the project should be wrecked," Enoch pointed out, "there is no surety that any group would gain. It would only throw the question of where the time and energy should be used into an open debate. You say that there are many special interest factions banding together to carry on the fight against us. Suppose that they do win. Then they must turn around and start fighting among themselves."

"Of course that's the case," Ulysses admitted, "but then each of them has a chance to get what they want, or think they have a chance. The way it is they have no chance at all. Before any of them has a chance this project must go down the drain. There is one group on the far side of the galaxy that wants to move out into the thinly populated sections of one particular section of the rim. They still believe in an ancient legend which says that their race arose as the result of immigrants from another galaxy who landed on the rim and worked their way inward over many galactic years. They think that if they can get out to the rim they can turn that legend into history to their greater glory. Another group wants to go into a small spiral arm because of an obscure record that many eons ago their ancestors picked up some virtually undecipherable messages which they believed came from that direction. Through the years the story has grown, until today they are convinced a race of intellectual giants will be found in that spiral arm. And there is always the pressure, naturally, to probe deeper into the galactic core. You must realize that we have only started, that the galaxy still is largely unexplored, that the thousands of races who form Galactic Central still are pioneers. And as a result, Galactic Central is continually subjected to all sorts of pressures."

"You sound," said Enoch, "as if you have little hope of maintaining this station, here on Earth."

"Almost no hope at all," Ulysses told him. "But so far as you yourself are concerned, there will be an option. You can stay here and live out an ordinary life on Earth or you can be assigned to another station. Galactic Central hopes that you would elect to continue on with us."

"That sounds pretty final."

"I am afraid," Ulysses said, "it is. I am sorry, Enoch, to be the bearer of bad news."

Enoch sat numb and stricken. Bad news! It was worse than that. It was the end of everything.

He sensed the crashing down of not only his own personal world, but of all the hopes of Earth. With the station gone, Earth once more would be left in the backwaters of the galaxy, with no hope of help, no chance of recognition, no realization of what lay waiting in the galaxy. Standing alone and naked, the human race would go on in its same old path, fumbling its uncertain way toward a blind, mad future.

20

THE HAZER was elderly. The golden haze that enveloped him had lost the sparkle of its youthfulness. It was a mellow glow, deep and rich—not the blinding haze of a younger being. He carried himself with a solid dignity, and the flaring topknot that was neither hair nor feathers was white, a sort of saintly whiteness. His face was soft and tender, the softness and the tenderness which in a man might have been expressed in kindly wrinkles.

"I am sorry," he told Enoch, "that our meeting must be such as this. Although, under any circumstances, I am glad to meet you. I have heard of you. It is not often that a being of an outside planet is the keeper of a station. Because of this, young being, I have been intrigued with you. I have wondered what sort of creature you might turn out to be."

"You need have no apprehension of him," Ulysses said, a little sharply. "I will vouch for him. We have been friends for years."

"Yes, I forgot," the Hazer said. "You are his discoverer."

He peered around the room. "Another one," he said. "I did not know there were two of them. I only knew of one."

"It's a friend of Enoch's," Ulysses said.

"There has been contact, then. Contact with the planet."

"No, there has been no contact."

"Perhaps an indiscretion."

"Perhaps," Ulysses said, "but under provocation that I doubt either you or I could have stood against."

Lucy had risen to her feet and now she came across the room, moving quietly and slowly, as if she might be floating.

The Hazer spoke to her in the common tongue. "I am glad to meet you. Very glad to meet you."

"She cannot speak," Ulysses said. "Nor hear. She has no communication."

"Compensation," said the Hazer.

"You think so?" asked Ulysses.

"I am sure of it."

He walked slowly forward and Lucy waited.

"It—she, the female form, you called it—she is not afraid."

Ulysses chuckled. "Not even me," he said.

The Hazer reached out his hand to her and she stood quietly

for a moment, then one of her hands came up and took the Hazer's fingers, more like tentacles than fingers, in its grasp.

It seemed to Enoch, for a moment, that the cloak of golden haze reached out to wrap the Earth girl in its glow. Enoch blinked his eyes and the illusion, if it had been illusion, was swept away, and it only was the Hazer who had the golden cloak.

And how was it, Enoch wondered, that there was no fear in her, either of Ulysses or the Hazer? Was it because, in truth, as he had said, she could see beyond the outward guise, could somehow sense the basic humanity (God help me, I cannot think, even now, except in human terms!) that was in these creatures? And if that were true, was it because she herself was not entirely human? A human, certainly, in form and origin, but not formed and molded into the human culture—being, perhaps, what a human would be if he were not hemmed about so closely by the rules of behavior and outlook that through the years had hardened into law to comprise a common human attitude.

Lucy dropped the Hazer's hand and went back to the sofa.

The Hazer said, "Enoch Wallace."

"Yes."

"She is of your race?"

"Yes, of course she is."

"She is most unlike you. Almost as if there were two races."

"There are not two races. There is only one."

"Are there many others like her?"

"I would not know," said Enoch.

"Coffee," said Ulysses to the Hazer. "Would you like some coffee?"

"Coffee?"

"A most delicious brew. Earth's one great accomplishment."

"I am not acquainted with it," said the Hazer. "I don't believe I will."

He turned ponderously to Enoch.

"You know why I am here?" he asked.

"I believe so."

"It is a matter I regret," said the Hazer. "But I must . . ."

"If you'd rather," Enoch said, "we can consider that the protest has been made. I would so stipulate."

"Why not?" Ulysses said. "There is no need, it seems to me, to have the three of us go through a somewhat painful scene."

The Hazer hesitated.

"If you feel you must," said Enoch.

"No," the Hazer said. "I am satisfied if an unspoken protest be generously accepted."

"Accepted," Enoch said, "on just one condition. That I satisfy myself that the charge is not unfounded. I must go out and see."

"You do not believe me?"

"It is not a matter of belief. It is something that can be checked. I cannot accept either for myself or for my planet until I have done that much."

"Enoch," Ulysses said, "the Vegan has been gracious. Not only now, but before this happened. His race presses the charge most reluctantly. They suffered much to protect the Earth and you."

"And the feeling is that I would be ungracious if I did not accept the protest and the charge on the Vegan statement."

"I am sorry, Enoch," said Ulysses. "That is what I mean."

Enoch shook his head. "For years I've tried to understand and to conform to the ethics and ideas of all the people who have come through this station. I've pushed my own human instincts and training to one side. I've tried to understand other viewpoints and to evaluate other ways of thinking, many of which did violence to my own. I am glad of all of it, for it has given me a chance to go beyond the narrowness of Earth. I think I gained something from it all. But none of this touched Earth; only myself was involved. This business touches Earth and I must approach it from an Earthman's viewpoint. In this particular instance I am not simply the keeper of a galactic station."

Neither of them said a word. Enoch stood waiting and still there was nothing said.

Finally he turned and headed for the door.

"I'll be back," he told them.

He spoke the phrase and the door started to slide open.

"If you'll have me," said the Hazer quietly, "I'd like to go with you."

"Fine," said Enoch. "Come ahead."

It was dark outside and Enoch lit the lantern. The Hazer watched him closely.

"Fossil fuel," Enoch told him. "It burns at the tip of a saturated wick."

The Hazer said, in horror, "But surely you have better."

"Much better now," said Enoch. "I am just old-fashioned."

He led the way outside, the lantern throwing a small pool of light. The Hazer followed.

"It is a wild planet," said the Hazer.

"Wild here. There are parts of it are tame."

"My own planet is controlled," the Hazer said. "Every foot of it is planned."

"I know. I have talked to many Vegans. They described the planet to me."

They headed for the barn.

"You want to go back?" asked Enoch.

"No," said the Hazer. "I find it exhilarating. Those are wild plants over there?"

"We call them trees," said Enoch.

"The wind blows as it wishes?"

"That's right," said Enoch. "We do not know as yet how to control the weather."

The spade stood just inside the barn door and Enoch picked it up. He headed for the orchard.

"You know, of course," the Hazer said, "the body will be gone."

"I'm prepared to find it gone."

"Then why?" the Hazer asked.

"Because I must be sure. You can't understand that, can you?"

"You said back there in the station," the Hazer said, "that you tried to understand the rest of us. Perhaps, for a change, at least one of us should try understanding you."

Enoch led the way down the path through the orchard. They came to the rude fence enclosing the burial plot. The sagging gate stood open. Enoch went through it and the Hazer followed.

"This is where you buried him?"

"This is my family plot. My mother and my father are here and I put him with them."

He handed the lantern to the Vegan and, armed with the spade, walked up to the grave. He thrust the spade into the ground.

"Would you hold the lantern a little closer, please?"

The Hazer moved up a step or two.

Enoch dropped to his knees and brushed away the leaves that had fallen on the ground. Underneath them was the soft, fresh earth that had been newly turned. There was a depression and a small hole at the bottom of the depression. As he brushed at the earth, he could hear the clods of displaced dirt falling through the hole and striking on something that was not the soil.

The Hazer had moved the lantern again and he could not see. But he did not need to see. He knew there was no use of digging; he knew what he would find. He should have kept a watch. He should not have put up the stone to attract attention —but Galactic Central had said, "As if he were your own." And that was the way he'd done it.

He straightened, but remained upon his knees, felt the damp of the earth soaking through the fabric of his trousers.

"No one told me," said the Hazer, speaking softly.

"Told you what?"

"The memorial. And what is written on it. I was not aware that you knew our language."

"I learned it long ago. There were scrolls I wished to read. I'm afraid it's not too good."

"Two misspelled words," the Hazer told him, "and one little awkwardness. But those are things which do not matter. What matters, and matters very much, is that when you wrote, you thought as one of us."

Enoch rose and reached out for the lantern.

"Let's go back," he said sharply, almost impatiently. "I know now who did this. I have to hunt him out."

21

THE TREETOPS far above moaned in the rising wind. Ahead, the great clump of canoe birch showed whitely in the dim glow of the lantern's light. The birch clump, Enoch knew, grew on

the lip of a small cliff that dropped twenty feet or more and
here one turned to the right to get around it and continue
down the hillside.

Enoch turned slightly and glanced over his shoulder. Lucy
was following close behind. She smiled at him and made a
gesture to say she was all right. He made a motion to indicate
that they must turn to the right, that she must follow closely.
Although, he told himself, it probably wasn't necessary; she
knew the hillside as well, perhaps even better, than he did
himself.

He turned to the right and followed along the edge of the
rocky cliff, came to the break and clambered down to reach
the slope below. Off to the left he could hear the murmur of
the swiftly running creek that tumbled down the rocky ravine
from the spring below the field.

The hillside plunged more steeply now and he led a way that
angled across the steepness.

Funny, he thought, that even in the darkness he could recognize certain natural features—the crooked white oak that
twisted itself, hanging at a crazy angle above the slope of hill;
the small grove of massive red oaks that grew out of a dome
of tumbled rock, so placed that no axman had even tried to
cut them down; the tiny swamp, filled with cattails, that fitted
itself snugly into a little terrace carved into the hillside.

Far below he caught the gleam of window light and angled
down toward it. He looked back over his shoulder and Lucy
was following close behind.

They came to a rude fence of poles and crawled through it
and now the ground became more level.

Somewhere below a dog barked in the dark and another
joined him. More joined in and the pack came sweeping up
the slope toward them. They arrived in a rush of feet, veered
around Enoch and the lantern to launch themselves at Lucy
—suddenly transformed, at the sight of her, into a welcoming
committee rather than a company of guards. They reared upward, a tangled mass of dogs. Her hands went out and patted
at their heads. As if by signal, they went rushing off in a happy
frolic, circling to come back again.

A short distance beyond the pole fence was a vegetable garden and Enoch led the way across, carefully following a path

between the rows. Then they were in the yard and the house stood before them, a tumbledown, sagging structure, its outlines swallowed by the darkness, the kitchen windows glowing with a soft, warm lamplight.

Enoch crossed the yard to the kitchen door and knocked. He heard feet coming across the kitchen floor.

The door came open and Ma Fisher stood framed against the light, a great, tall, bony woman clothed in something that was more sack than dress.

She stared at Enoch, half frightened, half belligerent. Then, back of him, she saw the girl.

"Lucy!" she cried.

The girl came forward with a rush and her mother caught her in her arms.

Enoch set his lantern on the ground, tucked the rifle underneath his arm, and stepped across the threshold.

The family had been at supper, seated about a great round table set in the center of the kitchen. An ornate oil lamp stood in the center of the table. Hank had risen to his feet, but his three sons and the stranger were still seated.

"So you brung her back," said Hank.

"I found her," Enoch said.

"We quit hunting for her just a while ago," Hank told him. "We was going out again."

"You remember what you told me this afternoon?" asked Enoch.

"I told you a lot of things."

"You told me that I had the devil in me. Raise your hand against that girl once more and I promise you I'll show you just how much devil there is in me."

"You can't bluff me," Hank blustered.

But the man was frightened. It showed in the limpness of his face, the tightness of his body.

"I mean it," Enoch said. "Just try me out and see."

The two men stood for a moment, facing one another, then Hank sat down.

"Would you join us in some victuals?" he inquired.

Enoch shook his head.

He looked at the stranger. "Are you the ginseng man?" he asked.

The man nodded. "That is what they call me."

"I want to talk with you. Outside."

Claude Lewis stood up.

"You don't have to go," said Hank. "He can't make you go. He can talk to you right here."

"I don't mind," said Lewis. "In fact, I want to talk with him. You're Enoch Wallace, aren't you?"

"That's who he is," said Hank. "Should of died of old age fifty years ago. But look at him. He's got the devil in him. I tell you, him and the devil has a deal."

"Hank," Lewis said, "shut up."

Lewis came around the table and went out the door.

"Good night," Enoch said to the rest of them.

"Mr. Wallace," said Ma Fisher, "thanks for bringing back my girl. Hank won't hit her again. I can promise you. I'll see to that."

Enoch went outside and shut the door. He picked up the lantern. Lewis was out in the yard. Enoch went to him.

"Let's walk off a ways," he said.

They stopped at the edge of the garden and turned to face one another.

"You been watching me," said Enoch.

Lewis nodded.

"Official? Or just snooping?"

"Official, I'm afraid. My name is Claude Lewis. There is no reason I shouldn't tell you—I'm C.I.A."

"I'm not a traitor or a spy," Enoch said.

"No one thinks you are. We're just watching you."

"You know about the cemetery?"

Lewis nodded.

"You took something from a grave."

"Yes," said Lewis. "The one with the funny headstone."

"Where is it?"

"You mean the body. It's in Washington."

"You shouldn't have taken it," Enoch said, grimly. "You've caused a lot of trouble. You have to get it back. As quickly as you can."

"It will take a little time," said Lewis. "They'll have to fly it out. Twenty-four hours, maybe."

"That's the fastest you can make it."

"I might do a little better."

"Do the very best you can. It's important that you get that body back."

"I will, Wallace. I didn't know . . ."

"And, Lewis."

"Yes."

"Don't try to play it smart. Don't add any frills. Just do what I tell you. I'm trying to be reasonable because that's the only thing to be. But you try one smart move . . ."

He reached out a hand and grabbed Lewis's shirt front, twisting the fabric tight.

"You understand me, Lewis?"

Lewis was unmoved. He did not try to pull away.

"Yes," he said. "I understand."

"What the hell ever made you do it?"

"I had a job."

"Yeah, a job. Watching me. Not robbing graves."

He let loose of the shirt.

"Tell me," said Lewis, "that thing in the grave. What was it?"

"That's none of your damn' business," Enoch told him, bitterly. "Getting back that body is. You're sure that you can do it? Nothing standing in your way?"

Lewis shook his head. "Nothing at all. I'll phone as soon as I can reach a phone. I'll tell them that it's imperative."

"It's all of that," said Enoch. "Getting that body back is the most important thing you've ever done. Don't forget that for a minute. It affects everyone on Earth. You and me and everyone. And if you fail, you'll answer to me for it."

"With that gun?"

"Maybe," Enoch said. "Don't fool around. Don't imagine that I'd hesitate to kill you. In this situation, I'd kill anyone —anyone at all."

"Wallace, is there something you can tell me?"

"Not a thing," said Enoch.

He picked up the lantern.

"You're going home?"

Enoch nodded.

"You don't seem to mind us watching you."

"No," Enoch told him. "Not your watching. Just your interference. Bring back that body and go on watching if you want to. But don't push me any. Don't lean on me. Keep your hands off. Don't touch anything."

"But good God, man, there's something going on. You can tell me something."

Enoch hesitated.

"Some idea," said Lewis, "of what this is all about. Not the details, just . . ."

"You bring the body back," Enoch told him, slowly, "and maybe we can talk again."

"It will be back," said Lewis.

"If it's not," said Enoch, "you're as good as dead right now."

Turning, he went across the garden and started up the hill.

In the yard, Lewis stood for a long time, watching the lantern bobbing out of sight.

22

ULYSSES WAS alone in the station when Enoch returned. He had sent the Thuban on his way and the Hazer back to Vega.

A fresh pot of coffee was brewing and Ulysses was sprawled out on the sofa, doing nothing.

Enoch hung up the rifle and blew out the lantern. Taking off his jacket, he threw it on the desk. He sat down in a chair across from the sofa.

"The body will be back," he said, "by this time tomorrow."

"I sincerely hope," Ulysses said, "that it will do some good. But I'm inclined to doubt it."

"Maybe," said Enoch bitterly, "I should not have bothered."

"It will show good faith," Ulysses said. "It might have some mitigating effect in the final weighing."

"The Hazer could have told me," Enoch said, "where the body was. If he knew it had been taken from the grave, then he must have known where it could be found."

"I would suspect he did," Ulysses said, "but, you see, he couldn't tell you. All that he could do was to make his protest. The rest was up to you. He could not lay aside his dignity by suggesting what you should do about it. For the record, he must remain the injured party."

"Sometimes," said Enoch, "this business is enough to drive one crazy. Despite the briefings from Galactic Central, there are always some surprises, always yawning traps for you to tumble into."

"There may come a day," Ulysses said, "when it won't be like that. I can look ahead and see, in some thousands of years, the knitting of the galaxy together into one great culture, one huge area of understanding. The local and the racial variations still will exist, of course, and that is as it should be, but overriding all of these will be a tolerance that will make for what one might be tempted to call a brotherhood."

"You sound," said Enoch, "almost like a human. That is the sort of hope that many of our thinkers have held out."

"Perhaps," Ulysses said. "You know that a lot of Earth seems to have rubbed off on me. You can't spend as long as I did on your planet without picking up at least a bit of it. And by the way, you made a good impression on the Vegan."

"I hadn't noticed it," Enoch told him. "He was kind and correct, of course, but little more."

"That inscription on the gravestone. He was impressed by that."

"I didn't put it there to impress anyone. I wrote it out because it was the way I felt. And because I like the Hazers. I was only trying to make it right for them."

"If it were not for the pressure from the galactic factions," Ulysses said, "I am convinced the Vegans would be willing to forget the incident and that is a greater concession than you can realize. It may be that, even so, they may line up with us when the showdown comes."

"You mean they might save the station?"

Ulysses shook his head. "I doubt anyone can do that. But it will be easier for all of us at Galactic Central if they threw their weight with us."

The coffeepot was making sounds and Enoch went to get it. Ulysses had pushed some of the trinkets on the coffee table to one side to make room for two coffee cups. Enoch filled them and set the pot upon the floor.

Ulysses picked up his cup, held it for a moment in his hands, then put it back on the table top.

"We're in bad shape," he said. "Not like in the old days. It has Galactic Central worried. All this squabbling and haggling among the races, all the pushing and the shoving."

He looked at Enoch. "You thought it was all nice and cozy."

"No," said Enoch, "not that. I knew that there were conflicting viewpoints and I knew there was some trouble. But I'm afraid I thought of it as being on a fairly lofty plane—gentlemanly, you know, and good-mannered."

"That was the way it was at one time. There always have been differing opinions, but they were based on principles and ethics, not on special interests. You know about the spiritual force, of course—the universal spiritual force."

Enoch nodded. "I've read some of the literature. I don't quite understand, but I'm willing to accept it. There is a way, I know, to get in contact with the force."

"The Talisman," said Ulysses.

"That's it. The Talisman. A machine, of sorts."

"I suppose," Ulysses agreed, "you could call it that. Although the word, 'machine,' is a little awkward. More than mechanics went into the making of it. There is just the one. Only one was ever made, by a mystic who lived ten thousand of your years ago. I wish I could tell you what it is or how it is constructed, but there is no one, I am afraid, who can tell you that. There have been others who have attempted to duplicate the Talisman, but no one has succeeded. The mystic who made it left no blueprints, no plans, no specifications, not a single note. There is no one who knows anything about it."

"There is no reason, I suppose," said Enoch, "that another should not be made. No sacred taboos, I mean. To make another one would not be sacrilegious."

"Not in the least," Ulysses told him. "In fact, we need another badly. For now we have no Talisman. It has disappeared."

Enoch jerked upright in his chair.

"Disappeared?" he asked.

"Lost," said Ulysses. "Misplaced. Stolen. No one knows."

"But I hadn't . . ."

Ulysses smiled bleakly. "You hadn't heard. I know. It is not something that we talk about. We wouldn't dare. The people must not know. Not for a while, at least."

"But how can you keep it from them?"

"Not too hard to do. You know how it worked, how the custodian took it from planet to planet and great mass meetings were held, where the Talisman was exhibited and contact made through it with the spiritual force. There had never been a schedule of appearances; the custodian simply wandered. It might be a hundred of your years or more between the visits of the custodian to any particular planet. The people hold no expectations of a visit. They simply know there'll be one, sometime; that some day the custodian will show up with the Talisman."

"That way you can cover up for years."

"Yes," Ulysses said. "Without any trouble."

"The leaders know, of course. The administrative people."

Ulysses shook his head. "We have told very few. The few that we can trust. Galactic Central knows, of course, but we're a close-mouthed lot."

"Then why . . ."

"Why should I be telling you. I know; I shouldn't. I don't know why I am. Yes, I guess I do. How does it feel, my friend, to sit as a compassionate confessor?"

"You're worried," Enoch said. "I never thought I would see you worried."

"It's a strange business," Ulysses said. "The Talisman has been missing for several years or so. And no one knows about it—except Galactic Central and the—what would you call it?— the hierarchy, I suppose, the organization of mystics who take care of the spiritual setup. And yet, even with no one knowing, the galaxy is beginning to show wear. It's coming apart at the seams. In time to come, it may fall apart. As if the Talisman represented a force that all unknowingly held the races of the galaxy together, exerting its influence even when it remained unseen."

"But even if it's lost, it's somewhere," Enoch pointed out. "It still would be exerting its influence. It couldn't have been destroyed."

"You forget," Ulysses reminded him, "that without its proper custodian, without its sensitive, it is inoperative. For it's not the machine itself that does the trick. The machine merely acts as an intermediary between the sensitive and the spiritual force. It is an extension of the sensitive. It magnifies the capability of the sensitive and acts as a link of some sort. It enables the sensitive to perform his function."

"You feel that the loss of the Talisman has something to do with the situation here?"

"The Earth station. Well, not directly, but it is typical. What is happening in regard to the station is symptomatic. It involves the sort of petty quarreling and mean bickering that has broken out through many sections of the galaxy. In the old days it would have been—what did you say, gentlemanly and on a plane of principles and ethics."

They sat in silence for a moment, listening to the soft sound that the wind made as it blew through the gable gingerbread.

"Don't worry about it," Ulysses said. "It is not your worry. I should not have told you. It was indiscreet to do so."

"You mean I shouldn't pass it on. You can be sure I won't."

"I know you won't," Ulysses said. "I never thought you would."

"You really think relations in the galaxy are deteriorating?"

"Once," Ulysses said, "the races all were bound together. There were differences, naturally, but these differences were bridged, sometimes rather artificially and not too satisfactorily, but with both sides striving to maintain the artificial bridging and generally succeeding. Because they wanted to, you see. There was a common purpose, the forging of a great cofraternity of all intelligences. We realized that among us, among all the races, we had a staggering fund of knowledge and of techniques—that working together, by putting together all this knowledge and capability, we could arrive at something that would be far greater and more significant than any race, alone, could hope of accomplishing. We had our troubles, certainly, and as I have said, our differences, but we were progressing. We brushed the small animosities and the petty differences underneath the rug and worked only on the big ones. We felt that if we could get the big ones settled, the small ones would become so small they would disappear. But it is becoming different now. There is a tendency to pull the pettiness from underneath the rug and blow it beyond its size, meanwhile letting the major and the important issues fall away."

"It sounds like Earth," said Enoch.

"In many ways," Ulysses said. "In principle, although the circumstances would diverge immensely."

"You've been reading the papers I have been saving for you?"

Ulysses nodded. "It doesn't look too happy."

"It looks like war," said Enoch bluntly.

Ulysses stirred uneasily.

"You don't have wars," said Enoch.

"The galaxy, you mean. No, as we are set up now we don't have wars."

"Too civilized?"

"Stop being bitter," Ulysses told him. "There has been a time or two when we came very close, but not in recent years. There are many races now in the cofraternity that in their formative years had a history of war."

"There is hope for us, then. It's something you outgrow."

"In time, perhaps."

"But not a certainty?"

"No, I wouldn't say so."

"I've been working on a chart," said Enoch. "Based on the Mizar system of statistics. The chart says there is going to be war."

"You don't need the chart," Ulysses said, "to tell you that."

"But there was something else. It was not just knowing if there'd be a war. I had hoped that the chart might show how to keep the peace. There must be a way. A formula, perhaps. If we could only think of it or know where to look or whom to ask or . . ."

"There is a way," Ulysses said, "to prevent a war."

"You mean you know . . ."

"It's a drastic measure. It only can be used as a last resort."

"And we've not reached that last resort?"

"I think, perhaps, you have. The kind of war that Earth would fight could spell an end to thousands of years of advancement, could wipe out all the culture, everything but the feeble remnants of civilizations. It could, just possibly, eliminate most of the life upon the planet."

"This method of yours—it has been used?"

"A few times."

"And worked?"

"Oh, certainly. We'd not even consider it if it didn't work."

"It could be used on Earth?"

"You could apply for its application."

"I?"

"As a representative of the Earth. You could appear before Galactic Central and appeal for us to use it. As a member of your race, you could give testimony and you would be given a hearing. If there seemed to be merit in your plea, Central might name a group to investigate and then, upon the report of its findings, a decision would be made."

"You said I. Could anyone on Earth?"

"Anyone who could gain a hearing. To gain a hearing, you must know about Galactic Central and you're the only man on Earth who does. Besides, you're a part of Galactic Central's staff. You have served as a keeper for a long time. Your record has been good. We would listen to you."

"But one man alone! One man can't speak for an entire race."

"You're the only one of your race who is qualified."

"If I could consult some others of my race."

"You can't. And even if you could, who would believe you?"

"That's true," said Enoch.

Of course it was. To him there was no longer any strangeness in the idea of a galactic cofraternity, of a transportation network that spread among the stars—a sense of wonder at times, but the strangeness had largely worn off. Although, he remembered, it had taken years. Years even with the physical evidence there before his eyes, before he could bring himself to a complete acceptance of it. But tell it to any other Earthman and it would sound like madness.

"And this method?" he asked, almost afraid to ask it, braced to take the shock of whatever it might be.

"Stupidity," Ulysses said.

Enoch gasped. "Stupidity? I don't understand. We are stupid enough, in many ways, right now."

"You're thinking of intellectual stupidity and there is plenty of that, not only on Earth, but throughout the galaxy. What I am talking about is a mental incapacity. An inability to understand the science and the technique that makes possible the kind of war that Earth would fight. An inability to operate the machines that are necessary to fight that kind of war. Turning the people back to a mental position where they would not be able to comprehend the mechanical and technological and scientific advances they have made. Those who know would forget. Those who didn't know could never learn. Back to the simplicity of the wheel and lever. That would make your kind of war impossible."

Enoch sat stiff and straight, unable to speak, gripped by an icy terror, while a million disconnected thoughts went chasing one another in a circle through his brain.

"I told you it was drastic," Ulysses said. "It has to be. War is something that costs a lot to stop. The price is high."

"I couldn't!" Enoch said. "No one could."

"Perhaps you can't. But consider this: If there is a war . . ."

"I know. If there is a war, it could be worse. But it wouldn't stop war. It's not the kind of thing I had in mind. People still could fight, still could kill."

"With clubs," said Ulysses. "Maybe bows and arrows. Rifles, so long as they still had rifles, and until they ran out of ammunition. Then they wouldn't know how to make more powder or how to get the metal to make the bullets or even how to make the bullets. There might be fighting, but there'd be no holocaust. Cities would not be wiped out by nuclear warheads, for no one could fire a rocket or arm the warhead—perhaps wouldn't even know what a rocket or a warhead was. Communications as you know them would be gone. All but the simplest transportation would be gone. War, except on a limited local scale, would be impossible."

"It would be terrible," Enoch said.

"So is war," Ulysses said. "The choice is up to you."

"But how long?" asked Enoch. "How long would it last? We wouldn't have to go back to stupidity forever?"

"Several generations," said Ulysses. "By that time the effect of—what shall we call it? the treatment?—would gradually begin wearing off. The people slowly would shake off their moronic state and begin their intellectual climb again. They'd be given, in effect, a second chance."

"They could," said Enoch, "in a few generations after that arrive at exactly the same situation that we have today."

"Possibly. I wouldn't expect it, though. Cultural development would be most unlikely to be entirely parallel. There'd be a chance that you'd have a better civilization and a more peaceful people."

"It's too much for one man . . ."

"Something hopeful," Ulysses said, "that you might consider. The method is offered only to those races which seem to us to be worth the saving."

"You have to give me time," said Enoch.

But he knew there was no time.

23

A MAN would have a job and suddenly be unable to perform it. Nor could the men around him carry on their jobs. For they would not have the knowledge or the backgrounds to do the tasks that they had been doing. They might try, of course— they might keep on trying for a time, but perhaps for not too long. And because the jobs could not be done, the business or the corporation or factory or whatever it might be, would cease its operation. Although the going out of business would not be a formal nor a legal thing. It would simply stop. And not entirely because the jobs could not be done, because no one could muster the business sense to keep it operating, but also because the transportation and communications which made the business possible also would have stopped.

Locomotives could not be operated, nor could planes and ships, for there would be no one who would remember how to operate them. There would be men who at one time had possessed all the skills that had been necessary for their operation, but now the skills would have disappeared. There might be some who still would try, with tragic consequences. And there might be a few who could vaguely remember how to operate the car or truck or bus, for they were simple things to run and it would be almost second nature for a man to drive them. But once they had broken down, there would be no one with the knowledge of mechanics to repair them and they'd not run again.

In the space of a few hours' time the human race would be stranded in a world where distance once again had come to be a factor. The world would grow the larger and the oceans would be barriers and a mile would be long once more. And in a few days' time there would be a panic and a huddling and a fleeing and a desperation in the face of a situation that no one could comprehend.

How long, Enoch wondered, would it take a city to use the last of the food stacked in its warehouses and then begin to starve? What would happen when electricity stopped flowing through the wires? How long, under a situation such as this, would a silly symbolic piece of paper or a minted coin still retain its value?

Distribution would break down; commerce and industry would die; government would become a shadow, with neither the means nor the intelligence to keep it functioning; communications would cease; law and order would disintegrate; the world would sink into a new barbaric framework and would begin to slowly readjust. That readjustment would go on for years and in the process of it there would be death and pestilence and untold misery and despair. In time it would work out and the world would settle down to its new way of life, but in the process of shaking down there'd be many who would die and many others who would lose everything that had spelled out life for them and the purpose of that life.

But would it, bad as it might be, be as bad as war?

Many would die of cold and hunger and disease (for medicine would go the way of all the rest), but millions would not be annihilated in the fiery breath of nuclear reaction. There would be no poison dust raining from the skies and the waters still would be as pure and fresh as ever and the soil remain as fertile. There still would be a chance, once the initial phases of the change had passed, for the human race to go on living and rebuild society.

If one were certain, Enoch told himself, that there would be a war, that war was inescapable, then the choice might not be hard to make. But there was always the possibility that the world could avoid war, that somehow a frail, thin peace could be preserved, and in such a case the desperate need of the galactic cure for war would be unnecessary. Before one could decide, he told himself, one must be sure; and how could one be sure? The chart lying in the desk drawer said there would be a war; many of the diplomats and observers felt that the up-coming peace conference might serve no other purpose than to trigger war. Yet there was no surety.

And even if there were, Enoch asked himself, how could one man—one man, alone—take it upon himself to play the role of God for the entire race? By what right did one man make a decision that affected all the rest, all the billions of others? Could he, if he did, ever be able, in the years to come, to justify his choice?

How could a man decide how bad war might be and, in comparison, how bad stupidity? The answer seemed to be he couldn't. There was no way to measure possible disaster in either circumstance.

After a time, perhaps, a choice either way could be rationalized. Given time, a conviction might develop that would enable a man to arrive at some sort of decision which, while it might not be entirely right, he nevertheless could square with his conscience.

Enoch got to his feet and walked to the window. The sound of his footsteps echoed hollowly in the station. He looked at his watch and it was after midnight.

There were races in the galaxy, he thought, who could reach a quick and right decision on almost any question, cutting straight across all the tangled lines of thought, guided by rules of logic that were more specific than anything the human race might have. That would be good, of course, in the sense that it made decision possible, but in arriving at decision would it not tend to minimize, perhaps ignore entirely, some of those very facets of the situation that might mean more to the human race than the decision would itself?

Enoch stood at the window and stared out across the moon-lit fields that ran down to the dark line of the woods. The clouds had blown away and the night was peaceful. This particular spot, he thought, always would be peaceful, for it was off the beaten track, distant from any possible target in atomic war. Except for the remote possibility of some ancient and nonrecorded, long forgotten minor conflict in prehistoric days, no battle ever had been fought here or ever would be fought. And yet it could not escape the common fate of poisoned soil and water if the world should suddenly, in a fateful hour of fury, unleash the might of its awesome weapons. Then the skies would be filled with atomic ash, which would come sifting down, and it would make little difference where a man might be. Soon or late, the war would come to him, if not in a flash of monstrous energy, then in the snow of death falling from the skies.

He walked from the window to the desk and gathered up the newspapers that had come in the morning mail and put them in a pile, noticing as he did so that Ulysses had forgotten to take with him the stack of papers which had been saved for him. Ulysses was upset, he told himself, or he'd not have forgotten the papers. God save us both, he thought; for we have our troubles.

It had been a busy day. He had done no more, he realized, than read two or three of the stories in the *Times*, all touching on the calling of the conference. The day had been too full, too full of direful things.

For a hundred years, he thought, things had gone all right. There had been the good moments and the bad, but by and large his life had gone on serenely and without alarming incident. Then today had dawned and all the serene years had come tumbling down all about his ears.

There once had been a hope that Earth could be accepted as a member of the galactic family, that he might serve as the emissary to gain that recognition. But now that hope was shattered, not only by the fact that the station might be closed, but that its very closing would be based upon the barbarism of the human race. Earth was being used as a whipping boy, of course, in galactic politics, but the brand, once placed, could not soon be lifted. And in any event, even if it could be lifted, now the planet stood revealed as one against which Galactic Central, in the hope of saving it, might be willing to apply a drastic and degrading action.

There was something he could salvage out of all of it, he knew. He could remain an Earthman and turn over to the people of the Earth the information that he had gathered through the years and written down, in meticulous detail, along with personal happenings and impressions and much other trivia, in the long rows of record books which stood on the shelves against the wall. That and the alien literature he had obtained and read and hoarded. And the gadgets and the artifacts which came from other worlds. From all of this the people of the Earth might gain something which could help them along the road that eventually would take them to the stars and to that further knowledge and that greater understanding which would be their heritage—perhaps the heritage and right of all intelligence. But the wait for that day would be long—longer now, because of what had happened on this day, than it had ever been before. And the information that he held, gathered painfully over the course of almost a century, was so inadequate compared with that more complete knowledge which he could have gathered in another century (or a thousand years) that it seemed a pitiful thing to offer to his people.

If there could only be more time, he thought. But, of course, there never was. There was not the time right now and there would never be. No matter how many centuries he might be able to devote, there'd always be so much more knowledge than he'd gathered at the moment that the little he had gathered would always seem a pittance.

He sat down heavily in the chair before the desk and now, for the first time, he wondered how he'd do it—how he could leave Galactic Central, how he could trade the galaxy for a single planet, even if that planet still remained his own.

He drove his haggard mind to find the answer and the mind could find no answer.

One man alone, he thought.

One man alone could not stand against both Earth and galaxy.

24

THE SUN streaming through the window woke him and he stayed where he was, not stirring for a moment, soaking in its warmth. There was a good, hard feeling to the sunlight, a reassuring touch, and for a moment he held off the worry and the questioning. But he sensed its nearness and he closed his eyes again. Perhaps if he could sleep some more it might go away and lose itself somewhere and not be there when he awakened later.

But there was something wrong, something besides the worry and the questioning.

His neck and shoulders ached and there was a strange stiffness in his body and the pillow was too hard.

He opened his eyes again and pushed with his hands to sit erect and he was not in bed. He was sitting in a chair and his head, instead of resting on a pillow, had been laid upon the desk. He opened and shut his mouth to taste it, and it tasted just as bad as he knew it would.

He got slowly to his feet, straightening and stretching, trying to work out the kinks that had tied themselves into joints and muscles. As he stood there, the worry and the trouble and the dreadful need of answers seeped back into him, from wherever they'd been hiding. But he brushed them to one side, not an entirely successful brush, but enough to make them retreat a little and crouch there, waiting to close in again.

He went to the stove and looked for the coffeepot, then remembered that last night he'd set it on the floor beside the coffee table. He went to get it. The two cups still stood on the table, the dark brown dregs of coffee covering the bottoms of them. And in the mass of gadgets that Ulysses had pushed to one side to make room for the cups, the pyramid of spheres lay tilted on its side, but it still was sparkling and glinting, each successive sphere revolving in an opposite direction to its fellow spheres.

Enoch reached out and picked it up. His fingers carefully explored the base upon which the spheres were set, seeking something—some lever, some indentation, some trip, some button—by which it might be turned either on or off. But there was nothing he could find. He should have known, he told himself, that there would be nothing. For he had looked before. And yet yesterday Lucy had done something that had set it operating and it still was operating. It had operated for more than twelve hours now and no results had been obtained. Check that, he thought—no results that could be recognized.

He set it back on the table on its base and stacked the cups, one inside the other, and picked them up. He stooped to lift the coffeepot off the floor. But his eyes never left the pyramid of spheres.

It was maddening, he told himself. There was no way to turn it on and yet, somehow, Lucy had turned it on. And now there was no way to turn it off—although it probably did not matter if it were off or on.

He went back to the sink with the cups and coffeepot.

The station was quiet—a heavy, oppressive quietness; although, he told himself, the impression of oppressiveness probably was no more than his imagination.

He crossed the room to the message machine and the plate was blank. There had been no messages during the night. It was silly of him, he thought, to expect there would be, for if there were, the auditory signal would be functioning, would continue to sound off until he pushed the lever.

Was it possible, he wondered, that the station might already have been abandoned, that whatever traffic that happened to be moving was being detoured around it? That, however, was hardly possible, for the abandonment of Earth station would mean as well that those beyond it must also be abandoned. There were no shortcuts in the network extending out into the spiral arm to make rerouting possible. It was not unusual for many hours, even for a day, to pass without any traffic. The traffic was irregular and had no pattern to it. There were times when scheduled arrivals had to be held up until there were facilities to take care of them, and there were other times when there would be none at all, when the equipment would sit idle, as it was sitting now.

Jumpy, he thought. I am getting jumpy.

Before they closed the station, they would let him know. Courtesy, if nothing else, would demand that they do that.

He went back to the stove and started the coffeepot. In the refrigerator he found a package of mush made from a cereal grown on one of the Draconian jungle worlds. He took it out, then put it back again and took out the last two eggs of the dozen that Wins, the mailman, had brought out from town a week or so ago.

He glanced at his watch and saw that he had slept later than he thought. It was almost time for his daily walk.

He put the skillet on the stove and spooned in a chunk of butter. He waited for the butter to melt, then broke in the eggs.

Maybe, he thought, he'd not go on the walk today. Except for a time or two when a blizzard had been raging, it would be the first time he had ever missed his walk. But because he always did it, he told himself, contentiously, was no sufficient reason that he should always take it. He'd just skip the walk and later on go down and get the mail. He could use the time to catch up on all the things he'd failed to do yesterday. The papers still were piled upon the desk, waiting for his reading. He'd not written in his journal, and there was a lot to write, for he must record in detail exactly what had happened and there had been a good deal happening.

It had been a rule he'd set himself from the first day that the station had begun its operation—that he never skimped the journal. He might be a little late at times in getting it all down, but the fact that he was late or that he was pressed for time had never made him put down one word less than he had felt might be required to tell all there was to tell.

He looked across the room at the long rows of record books that were crowded on the shelves and thought, with pride and satisfaction, of the completeness of that record. Almost a century of writing lay between the covers of those books and there was not a single day that he had ever skipped.

Here was his legacy, he thought; here was his bequest to the world; here would be his entrance fee back into the human race; here was all he'd seen and heard and thought for almost a hundred years of association with those alien peoples of the galaxy.

Looking at the rows of books, the questions that he had shoved aside came rushing in on him and this time there was no denying them. For a short space of time he had held them off, the little time he'd needed for his brain to clear, for his body to become alive again. He did not fight them now. He accepted them, for there was no dodging them.

He slid the eggs out of the skillet onto the waiting plate. He got the coffeepot and sat down to his breakfast.

He glanced at his watch again.

There still was time to go on his daily walk.

25

THE GINSENG man was waiting at the spring.

Enoch saw him while still some distance down the trail and wondered, with a quick flash of anger, if he might be waiting there to tell him that he could not return the body of the Hazer, that something had come up, that he had run into unexpected difficulties.

And thinking that, Enoch remembered how he'd threatened the night before to kill anyone who held up the return of the body. Perhaps, he told himself, it had not been smart to say that. Wondering whether he could bring himself to kill a man —not that it would be the first man he had ever killed. But that had been long ago and it had been a matter then of kill or being killed.

He shut his eyes for a second and once again could see that slope below him, with the long lines of men advancing through the drifting smoke, knowing that those men were climbing up the ridge for one purpose only, to kill himself and those others who were atop the ridge.

And that had not been the first time nor had it been the last, but all the years of killing boiled down in essence to that single moment—not the time that came after, but that long and terrible instant when he had watched the lines of men purposefully striding up the slope to kill him.

It had been in that moment that he had realized the insanity of war, the futile gesture that in time became all but meaningless, the unreasoning rage that must be nursed long beyond the memory of the incident that had caused the rage, the sheer illogic that one man, by death or misery, might prove a right or uphold a principle.

Somewhere, he thought, on the long backtrack of history, the human race had accepted an insanity for a principle and had persisted in it until today that insanity-turned-principle stood ready to wipe out, if not the race itself, at least all of those things, both material and immaterial, that had been fashioned as symbols of humanity through many hard-won centuries.

Lewis had been sitting on a fallen log and now, as Enoch neared, he rose.

"I waited for you here," he said. "I hope that you don't mind."

Enoch stepped across the spring.

"The body will be here sometime in early evening," Lewis said. "Washington will fly it out to Madison and truck it here from there."

Enoch nodded. "I am glad to hear that."

"They were insistent," Lewis said, "that I should ask you once again what the body is."

"I told you last night," said Enoch, "that I can't tell you anything. I wish I could. I've been figuring for years how to get it told, but there's no way of doing it."

"The body is something from off this Earth," said Lewis. "We are sure of that."

"You think so," Enoch said, not making it a question.

"And the house," said Lewis, "is something alien, too."

"The house," Enoch told him, shortly, "was built by my father."

"But something changed it," Lewis said. "It is not the way he built it."

"The years change things," said Enoch.

"Everything but you."

Enoch grinned at him. "So it bothers you," he said. "You figure it's indecent."

Lewis shook his head. "No, not indecent. Not really anything. After watching you for years, I've come to an acceptance of you and everything about you. No understanding, naturally, but complete acceptance. Sometimes I tell myself I'm crazy, but that's only momentary. I've tried not to bother you. I've worked to keep everything exactly as it was. And now that I've met you, I am glad that is the way it was. But we're going at this wrong. We're acting as if we were enemies, as if we were strange dogs—and that's not the way to do it. I think that the two of us may have a lot in common. There's something going on and I don't want to do a thing that will interfere with it."

"But you did," said Enoch. "You did the worst thing that you could when you took the body. If you'd sat down and planned how to do me harm, you couldn't have done worse.

And not only me. Not really me, at all. It was the human race you harmed."

"I don't understand," said Lewis. "I'm sorry, but I don't understand. There was the writing on the stone . . ."

"That was my fault," said Enoch. "I should never have put up that stone. But at the time it seemed the thing to do. I didn't think that anyone would come snooping around and . . ."

"It was a friend of yours?"

"A friend of mine? Oh, you mean the body. Well, not actually. Not that particular person."

"Now that it's done," Lewis said, "I'm sorry."

"Sorry doesn't help," said Enoch.

"But isn't there something—isn't there anything that can be done about it? More than just bringing back the body?"

"Yes," Enoch told him, "there might be something. I might need some help."

"Tell me," Lewis said, quickly. "If it can be done . . ."

"I might need a truck," said Enoch. "To haul away some stuff. Records and other things like that. I might need it fast."

"I can have a truck," said Lewis. "I can have it waiting. And men to help you load."

"I might want to talk to someone in authority. High authority. The President. Secretary of State. Maybe the U.N. I don't know. I have to think it out. And not only would I need a way to talk to them, but some measure of assurance that they would listen to what I had to say."

"I'll arrange," said Lewis, "for mobile short-wave equipment. I'll have it standing by."

"And someone who will listen?"

"That's right," said Lewis. "Anyone you say."

"And one thing more."

"Anything," said Lewis.

"Forgetfulness," said Enoch. "Maybe I won't need any of these things. Not the truck or any of the rest of it. Maybe I'll have to let things go just as they're going now. And if that should be the case, could you and everyone else concerned forget I ever asked?"

"I think we could," said Lewis. "But I would keep on watching."

"I wish you would," said Enoch. "Later on I might need some help. But no further interference."

"Are you sure," asked Lewis, "that there is nothing else?"

Enoch shook his head. "Nothing else. All the rest of it I must do myself."

Perhaps, he thought, he'd already talked too much. For how could he be sure that he could trust this man? How could he be sure he could trust anyone?

And yet, if he decided to leave Galactic Central and cast his lot with Earth, he might need some help. There might be some objection by the aliens to his taking along his records and the alien gadgets. If he wanted to get away with them, he might have to make it fast.

But did he want to leave Galactic Central? Could he give up the galaxy? Could he turn down the offer to become the keeper of another station on some other planet? When the time should come, could he cut his tie with all the other races and all the mysteries of the other stars?

Already he had taken steps to do those very things. Here, in the last few moments, without too much thought about it, almost as if he already had reached his decision, he had arranged a setup that would turn him back to Earth.

He stood there, thinking, puzzled at the steps he'd taken.

"There'll be someone here," said Lewis. "Someone at this spring. If not myself, then someone else who can get in touch with me."

Enoch nodded absent-mindedly.

"Someone will see you every morning when you take your walk," said Lewis. "Or you can reach us here any time you wish."

Like a conspiracy, thought Enoch. Like a bunch of kids playing cops and robbers.

"I have to be getting on," he said. "It's almost time for mail. Wins will be wondering what has happened to me."

He started up the hill.

"Be seeing you," said Lewis.

"Yeah," said Enoch. "I'll be seeing you."

He was surprised to find the warm glow spreading in him —as if there had been something wrong and now it was all right, as if there had been something lost that now had been recovered.

26

ENOCH MET the mailman halfway down the road that led into the station. The old jalopy was traveling fast, bumping over the grassy ruts, swishing through the overhanging bushes that grew along the track.

Wins braked to a halt when he caught sight of Enoch and sat waiting for him.

"You got on a detour," Enoch said, coming up to him. "Or have you changed your route?"

"You weren't waiting at the box," said Wins, "and I had to see you."

"Some important mail?"

"Nope, it isn't mail. It's old Hank Fisher. He is down in Millville, setting up the drinks in Eddie's tavern and shooting off his face."

"It's not like Hank to be buying drinks."

"He's telling everyone that you tried to kidnap Lucy."

"I didn't kidnap her," Enoch said. "Hank had took a bull whip to her and I hid her out until he got cooled down."

"You shouldn't have done that, Enoch."

"Maybe. But Hank was set on giving her a beating. He already had hit her a lick or two."

"Hank's out to make you trouble."

"He told me that he would."

"He says you kidnaped her, then got scared and brought her back. He says you had her hid out in the house and when he tried to break in and get her, he couldn't do it. He says you have a funny sort of house. He says he broke an ax blade on a window pane."

"Nothing funny about it," Enoch said. "Hank just imagines things."

"It's all right so far," said the mailman. "None of them, in broad daylight and their right senses, will do anything about it. But come night they'll be liquored up and won't have good sense. There are some of them might be coming up to see you."

"I suppose he's telling them I've got the devil in me."

"That and more," said Wins. "I listened for a while before I started out."

He reached into the mail pouch and found the bundle of papers and handed them to Enoch.

"Enoch, there's something that you have to know. Something you may not realize. It would be easy to get a lot of people stirred up against you—the way you live and all. You are strange. No, I don't mean there's anything wrong with you —I know you and I know there isn't—but it would be easy for people who didn't know you to get the wrong ideas. They've let you alone so far because you've given them no reason to do anything about you. But if they get stirred up by all that Hank is saying . . ."

He did not finish what he was saying. He left it hanging in midair.

"You're talking about a posse," Enoch said.

Wins nodded, saying nothing.

"Thanks," said Enoch. "I appreciate your warning me."

"Is it true," asked the mailman, "that no one can get inside your house?"

"I guess it is," admitted Enoch. "They can't break into it and they can't burn it down. They can't do anything about it."

"Then, if I were you, I'd stay close tonight. I'd stay inside. I'd not go venturing out."

"Maybe I will. It sounds like a good idea."

"Well," said Wins, "I guess that about covers it. I thought you'd ought to know. Guess I'll have to back out to the road. No chance of turning around."

"Drive up to the house. There's room there."

"It's not far back to the road," said Wins. "I can make it easy."

The car started backing slowly.

Enoch stood watching.

He lifted a hand in solemn salute as the car began rounding a bend that would take it out of sight. Wins waved back and then the car was swallowed by the scrub that grew close against both sides of the road.

Slowly Enoch turned around and plodded back toward the station.

A mob, he thought—good God, a mob!

A mob howling about the station, hammering at the doors and windows, peppering it with bullets, would wipe out the

last faint chance—if there still remained a chance—of Galactic Central standing off the move to close the station. Such
a demonstration would add one more powerful argument to
the demand that the expansion into the spiral arm should be
abandoned.

Why was it, he wondered, that everything should happen all
at once? For years nothing at all had happened and now everything was happening within a few hours' time. Everything, it
seemed, was working out against him.

If the mob showed up, not only would it mean that the fate
of the station would be sealed, but it might mean, as well, that
he would have no choice but to accept the offer to become the
keeper of another station. It might make it impossible for him
to remain on Earth, even if he wished. And he realized, with a
start, that it might just possibly mean that the offer of another
station for him might be withdrawn. For with the appearance
of a mob howling for his blood, he, himself, would become
involved in the charge of barbarism now leveled against the
human race in general.

Perhaps, he told himself, he should go down to the spring
and see Lewis once again. Perhaps some measures could be
taken to hold off the mob. But if he did, he knew, there'd be an
explanation due and he might have to tell too much. And there
might not be a mob. No one would place too much credence
in what Hank Fisher said and the whole thing might peter out
without any action being taken.

He'd stay inside the station and hope for the best. Perhaps
there'd be no traveler in the station at the time the mob arrived
—if it did arrive—and the incident would pass with no galactic
notice. If he were lucky it might work out that way. And by the
law of averages, he was owed some luck. Certainly he'd had
none in the last few days.

He came to the broken gate that led into the yard and
stopped to look up at the house, trying, for some reason he
could not understand, to see it as the house he had known in
boyhood.

It stood the same as it had always stood, unchanged, except
that in the olden days there had been ruffled curtains at each
window. The yard around it had changed with the slow growth

of the years, with the clump of lilacs thicker and more rank and tangled with each passing spring, with the elms that his father had planted grown from six-foot whips into mighty trees, with the yellow rose bush at the kitchen corner gone, victim of a long-forgotten winter, with the flower beds vanished and the small herb garden, here beside the gate, overgrown and smothered out by grass.

The old stone fence that had stood on each side of the gate now was little more than a humpbacked mound. The heaving of a hundred frosts, the creep of vines and grasses, the long years of neglect, had done their work and in another hundred years, he thought, it would be level, with no trace of it left. Down in the field, along the slope where erosion had been at work, there were long stretches where it had entirely disappeared.

All of this had happened and until this moment he had scarcely noticed it. But now he noticed it and wondered why he did. Was it because he now might be returning to the Earth again—he who had never left its soil and sun and air, who had never left it physically, but who had, for a longer time than most men had allotted to them, walked not one, but many planets, far among the stars?

He stood there, in the late summer sun, and shivered in the cold wind that seemed to be blowing out of some unknown dimension of unreality, wondering for the first time (for the first time he ever had been forced to wonder at it) what kind of man he was. A haunted man who must spend his days neither completely alien nor completely human, with divided loyalties, with old ghosts to tramp the years and miles with him no matter which life he might choose, the Earth life or the stars? A cultural half-breed, understanding neither Earth nor stars, owing a debt to each, but paying neither one? A homeless, footless, wandering creature who could recognize neither right nor wrong from having seen so many different (and logical) versions of the right and wrong?

He had climbed the hill above the spring, filled with the rosy inner glow of a regained humanity, a member of the human race again, linked in a boylike conspiracy with a human team. But could he qualify as human—and if he qualified as human, or tried to qualify, then what about the implied hundred years' allegiance to Galactic Central? Did he, he wondered, even want to qualify as human?

He moved slowly through the gate, and the questions still kept hammering in his brain, that great, ceaseless flow of questions to which there were no answers. Although that was wrong, he thought. Not no answers, but too many answers.

Perhaps Mary and David and the rest of them would come visiting tonight and they could talk it over—then he suddenly remembered.

They would not be coming. Not Mary, not David, nor any of the others. They had come for years to see him, but they would come no longer, for the magic had been dimmed and the illusion shattered and he was alone.

As he had always been alone, he told himself, with a bitter taste inside his brain. It all had been illusion; it never had been real. For years he'd fooled himself—most eagerly and willingly he had fooled himself into peopling the little corner by the fireplace with these creatures of his imagination. Aided by an alien technique, driven by his loneliness for the sight and sound of humankind, he had brought them into a being that defied every sense except the solid sense of touch.

And defied as well every sense of decency.

Half-creatures, he thought. Poor pitiful half-creatures, neither of the shadow or the world.

Too human for the shadows, too shadowy for Earth.

Mary, if I had only known—if I had known, I never would have started. I'd have stayed with loneliness.

And he could not mend it now. There was nothing that would help.

What is the matter with me? he asked himself.

What has happened to me?

What is going on?

He couldn't even think in a straight line any more. He'd told himself that he'd stay inside the station to escape the mob that might be showing up—and he couldn't stay inside the station, for Lewis, sometime shortly after dark, would be bringing back the Hazer's body.

And if the mob showed up at the same time Lewis should

appear, bringing back the body, there'd be unsheeted hell to pay.

Stricken by the thought, he stood undecided.

If he alerted Lewis to the danger, then he might not bring the body. And he had to bring the body. Before the night was over the Hazer must be secure within the grave.

He decided that he would have to take a chance.

The mob might not show up. Even if it did, there had to be a way that he could handle it.

He'd think of something, he told himself.

He'd have to think of something.

27

THE STATION was as silent as it had been when he'd left it. There had been no messages and the machinery was quiet, not even muttering to itself, as it sometimes did.

Enoch laid the rifle across the desk top and dropped the bundle of papers beside it. He took off his jacket and hung it on the back of the chair.

There were still the papers to be read, not only today's, but yesterday's as well, and the journal to be gotten up, and the journal, he reminded himself, would take a lot of time. There would be several pages of it, even if he wrote it close, and he must write it logically and chronologically, so that it would appear he had written the happenings of yesterday yesterday and not a full day late. He must include each event and every facet of each happening and his own reactions to it and his thoughts about it. For that was the way he'd always done and that was the way he must do it now. He'd always been able to do it that way because he had created for himself a little special niche, not of the Earth, nor of the galaxy, but in that vague condition which one might call existence, and he had worked inside the framework of that special niche as a medieval monk had worked inside his cell. He had been an observer only, an intensely interested observer who had not been content with observance only, but who had made an effort to dig into what he had observed, but still basically and essentially an observer who was not vitally nor personally involved in what had gone on about him. But in the last two days, he realized, he had lost that observer status. The Earth and the galaxy had both intruded on him, and his special niche was gone and he was personally involved. He had lost his objective viewpoint and no longer could command that correct and coldly factual approach which had given him a solid basis upon which to do his writing.

He walked over to the shelf of journals and pulled out the current volume, fluttering its pages to find where he had stopped. He found the place and it was very near the end. There were only a few blank pages left, perhaps not enough of them to cover the events of which he'd have to write. More than likely, he thought, he'd come to an end of the journal before he had finished with it and would have to start a new one.

He stood with the journal in his hand and stared at the page where the writing ended, the writing that he'd done the day before yesterday. Just the day before yesterday and it now was ancient writing; it even had a faded look about it. And well it might, he thought, for it had been writing done in another age. It had been the last entry he had made before his world had come crashing down about him.

And what, he asked himself, was the use of writing further? The writing now was done, all the writing that would matter. The station would be closed and his own planet would be lost —no matter whether he stayed on or went to another station on another planet, the Earth would now be lost.

Angrily he slammed shut the book and put it back into its place upon the shelf. He walked back to the desk.

The Earth was lost, he thought, and he was lost as well, lost and angry and confused. Angry at fate (if there were such a thing as fate) and at stupidity. Not only the intellectual stupidity of the Earth, but at the intellectual stupidity of the galaxy as well, at the petty bickering which could still the march of the brotherhood of peoples that finally had extended into this galactic sector. As on Earth, so in the galaxy, the number and complexity of the gadget, the noble thought, the wisdom and erudition might make for a culture, but not for a civilization. To be truly civilized, there must be something far more subtle than the gadget or the thought.

He felt the tension in him, the tension to be doing something —to prowl about the station like a caged and pacing beast, to run outside and shout incoherently until his lungs were empty, to smash and break, to work off, somehow, his rage and disappointment.

He reached out a hand and snatched the rifle off the desk. He pulled out a desk drawer where he kept the ammunition, and took out a box of it, tearing it apart, emptying the cartridges in his pocket.

He stood there for a moment, with the rifle in his hand, and the silence of the room seemed to thunder at him and he caught the bleakness and the coldness of it and he laid the rifle back on the desk again.

What childishness, he thought, to take out his resentment and his rage on an unreality. And when there was no real reason for resentment or for rage. For the pattern of events was one that should be recognized and thus accepted. It was the kind of thing to which a human being should long since have become accustomed.

He looked around the station and the quietness and the waiting still was there, as if the very structure might be marking time for an event to come along on the natural flow of time.

He laughed softly and reached for the rifle once again.

Unreality or not, it would be something to occupy his mind, to snatch him for a while from this sea of problems which was swirling all about him.

And he needed the target practice. It had been ten days or more since he'd been on the rifle range.

28

THE BASEMENT was huge. It stretched out into a dim haze beyond the lights which he had turned on, a place of tunnels and rooms, carved deep into the rock that folded up to underlie the ridge.

Here were the massive tanks filled with the various solutions for the tank travelers; here the pumps and the generators, which operated on a principle alien to the human manner of generating electric power, and far beneath the floor of the basement itself those great storage tanks which held the acids and the soupy matter which once had been the bodies of those creatures which came traveling to the station, leaving behind them, as they went on to some other place, the useless bodies which then must be disposed of.

Enoch moved across the floor, past the tanks and generators, until he came to a gallery that stretched out into the darkness. He found the panel and pressed it to bring on the lights, then walked down the gallery. On either side were metal shelves which had been installed to accommodate the overflow of gadgets, of artifacts, of all sorts of gifts which had been brought him by the travelers. From floor to ceiling the shelves were jammed with a junkyard accumulation from all the corners of the galaxy. And yet, thought Enoch, perhaps not actually a junkyard, for there would be very little of this stuff that would be actual junk. All of it was serviceable and had some purpose, either practical or aesthetic, if only that purpose could be learned. Although perhaps not in every instance a purpose that would be applicable to humans.

Down at the end of the shelves was one section of shelving into which the articles were packed more systematically and with greater care, each one tagged and numbered, with cross-filing to a card catalogue and certain journal dates. These were the articles of which he knew the purpose and, in certain instances, something of the principles involved. There were some that were innocent enough and others that held great potential value and still others that had, at the moment, no connection whatsoever with the human way of life—and there were, as well, those few, tagged in red, that made one shudder to even think upon.

He went down the gallery, his footsteps echoing loudly as he trod through this place of alien ghosts.

Finally the gallery widened into an oval room and the walls here were padded with a thick gray substance that would entrap a bullet and prevent a ricochet.

Enoch walked over to a panel set inside a deep recess sunk into the wall. He reached in and thumbed up a tumbler, then stepped quickly out into the center of the room.

Slowly the room began to darken, then suddenly it seemed to flare and he was in the room no longer, but in another place, a place he had never seen before.

He stood on a little hillock and in front of him the land sloped down to a sluggish river bordered by a width of marsh. Between the beginning of the marsh and the foot of the hillock stretched a sea of rough, tall grass. There was no wind, but the grass was rippling and he knew that the rippling motion of the grass was caused by many moving bodies, foraging in the grass. Out of it came a savage grunting, as if a thousand angry hogs were fighting for choice morsels in a hundred swill troughs. And from somewhere farther off, perhaps from the river, came a deep, monotonous bellowing that sounded hoarse and tired.

Enoch felt the hair crawling on his scalp and he thrust the rifle out and ready. It was puzzling. He felt and knew the danger and as yet there was no danger. Still, the very air of this place —wherever it might be—seemed to crawl with danger.

He spun around and saw that close behind him the thick, dark woods climbed down the range of river hills, stopping at the sea of grass which flowed around the hillock on which he found himself. Off beyond the hills, dark purple in the air, loomed a range of mighty mountains that seemed to fade into the sky, but purple to their peaks, with no sign of snow upon them.

Two things came trotting from the woods and stopped at the edge of it. They sat down and grinned at him, with their tails wrapped neatly round their feet. They might have been wolves or dogs, but they were neither one. They were nothing he had ever seen or heard of. Their pelts glistened in the weak sunshine, as if they had been greased, but the pelts stopped at their necks, with their skulls and faces bare. Like evil old men, off on a masquerade, with their bodies draped in the hides of wolves. But the disguise was spoiled by the lolling tongues which spilled out of their mouths, glistening scarlet against the bone-white of their faces.

The woods was still. There were only the two gaunt beasts sitting on their haunches. They sat and grinned at him, a strangely toothless grin.

The woods was dark and tangled, the foliage so dark green that it was almost black. All the leaves had a shine to them, as if they had been polished to a special sheen.

Enoch spun around again, to look back towards the river, and crouched at the edge of the grass was a line of toadlike monstrosities, six feet long and standing three feet high, their bodies the color of a dead fish belly, and each with a single eye, or what seemed to be an eye, which covered a great part of the area just above the snout. The eyes were faceted and glowed in the dim sunlight, as the eyes of a hunting cat will glow when caught in a beam of light.

The hoarse bellowing still came from the river and in between the bellowing there was a faint, thin buzzing, an angry and malicious buzzing, as if a mosquito might be hovering for attack, although there was a sharper tone in it than in the noise of a mosquito.

Enoch jerked up his head to look into the sky and far in the depths of it he saw a string of dots, so high that there was no way of knowing what kind of things they were.

He lowered his head to look back at the line of squatting, toadlike things, but from the corner of his eye he caught the sense of flowing motion and swung back toward the woods.

The wolf-like bodies with the skull-like heads were coming up the hill in a silent rush. They did not seem to run. There was no motion of their running. Rather they were moving as if they had been squirted from a tube.

Enoch jerked up his rifle and it came into his shoulder, fitting there, as if it were a part of him. The bead settled in the rear-sight notch and blotted out the skull-like face of the leading beast. The gun bucked as he squeezed the trigger and, without waiting to see if the shot had downed the beast, the rifle barrel was swinging toward the second as his right fist worked the bolt. The rifle bucked again and the second wolf-like being somersaulted and slid forward for an instant, then began rolling down the hill, flopping as it rolled.

Enoch worked the bolt again and the spent brass case glittered in the sun as he turned swiftly to face the other slope.

The toadlike things were closer now. They had been creeping in, but as he turned they stopped and squatted, staring at him.

He reached a hand into his pocket and took out two cartridges, cramming them into the magazine to replace the shells he'd fired.

The bellowing down by the river had stopped, but now there was a honking sound that he could not place. Turning cautiously, he tried to locate what might be making it, but there was nothing to be seen. The honking sound seemed to be coming from the forest, but there was nothing moving.

In between the honking, he still could hear the buzzing and it seemed louder now. He glanced into the sky and the dots were larger and no longer in a line. They had formed into a circle and seemed to be spiraling downward, but they were still so high that he could not make out what kinds of things they were.

He glanced back toward the toadlike monsters and they were closer than they had been before. They had crept up again.

Enoch lifted the rifle and, before it reached his shoulder, pressed the trigger, shooting from the hip. The eye of one of the foremost of them exploded, like the splash a stone would make if thrown into water. The creature did not jump or flop. It simply settled down, flat upon the ground, as if someone had put his foot upon it and had exerted exactly force enough to squash it flat. It lay there, flat, and there was a big round hole where the eye had been and the hole was filling with a thick and ropy yellow fluid that may have been the creature's blood.

The others backed away, slowly, watchfully. They backed all the way off the hillock and only stopped when they reached the grass edge.

The honking was closer and the buzzing louder and there could be no doubt that the honking was coming from the hills.

Enoch swung about and saw it, striding through the sky, coming down the ridge, stepping through the trees and honking dolefully. It was a round and black balloon that swelled and deflated with its honking, and jerked and swayed as it walked along, hung from the center of four stiff and spindly legs that arched above it to the joint that connected this upper portion of the leg arrangement with the downward-spraddling legs that raised it high above the forest. It was walking jerkily, lifting its legs high to clear the massive treetops before putting them down again. Each time it put down a foot, Enoch could hear the crunching of the branches and the crashing of the trees that it broke or brushed aside.

Enoch felt the skin along his spine trying to roll up his back like a window shade, and the bristling of the hair along the base of his skull, obeying some primordial instinct in its striving to raise itself erect into a fighting ruff.

But even as he stood there, almost stiff with fright, some part of his brain remembered that one shot he had fired and his fingers dug into his pocket for another cartridge to fill the magazine.

The buzzing was much louder and the pitch had changed. The buzzing was now approaching at tremendous speed.

Enoch jerked up his head and the dots no longer were circling in the sky, but were plunging down toward him, one behind the other.

He flicked a glance toward the balloon, honking and jerking on its stiltlike legs. It still was coming on, but the plunging dots were faster and would reach the hillock first.

He shifted the rifle forward, outstretched and ready to slap against his shoulder, and watched the falling dots, which were dots no longer, but hideous streamlined bodies, each carrying a rapier that projected from its head. A bill of sorts, thought Enoch, for these things might be birds, but a longer, thinner, larger, more deadly bird than any earthly bird.

The buzzing changed into a scream and the scream kept mounting up the scale until it set the teeth on edge and through it, like a metronome measuring off a beat, came the hooting of the black balloon that strode across the hills.

Without knowing that he had moved his arms, Enoch had the rifle at his shoulder, waiting for that instant when the first of the plunging monsters was close enough to fire.

They dropped like stones out of the sky and they were bigger than he had thought they were—big and coming like so many arrows aimed directly at him.

The rifle thudded against his shoulder and the first one crumpled, lost its arrow shape, folding up and falling, no longer on its course. He worked the bolt and fired again and the second one in line lost its balance and began to tumble—and the bolt was worked once more and the trigger pressed. The third skidded in the air and went off at a slant, limp and ragged, fluttering in the wind, falling toward the river.

The rest broke off their dive. They made a shallow turn and beat their way up into the sky, great wings that were more like windmill vanes than wings thrashing desperately.

A shadow fell across the hillock and a mighty pillar came

down from somewhere overhead, driving down to strike to one side of the hillock. The ground trembled at the tread and the water that lay hidden by the grass squirted high into the air.

The honking was an engulfing sound that blotted out all else and the great balloon was zooming down, cradled on its legs.

Enoch saw the face, if anything so grotesque and so obscene could be called a face. There was a beak and beneath it a sucking mouth and a dozen or so other organs that might have been the eyes.

The legs were like inverted V's, with the inner stroke somewhat shorter than the outer and in the center of these inner joints hung the great balloon that was the body of the creature, with its face on the underside so that it could see all the hunting territory that might lie beneath it.

But now auxiliary joints in the outer span of legs were bending to let the body of the creature down so it could seize its prey.

Enoch was not conscious of putting up the rifle or of operating it, but it was hammering at his shoulder and it seemed to him that a second part of him stood off, apart, and watched the firing of the rifle—as if the figure that held and fired the weapon might be a second man.

Great gouts of flesh flew out of the black balloon and jagged rents suddenly tore across it and from these rents poured out a cloud of liquid that turned into a mist, with black droplets raining from it.

The firing pin clicked on an empty breech and the gun was empty, but there was no need of another shot. The great legs were folding, and trembling as they folded, and the shrunken body shivered convulsively in the heavy mist that was pouring out of it. There was no hooting now, and Enoch could hear the patter of the black drops falling from that cloud as they struck the short grass on the hill.

There was a sickening odor and the drops, where they fell on him, were sticky, running like cold oil, and above him the great structure that had been the stiltlike creature was toppling to the ground.

Then the world faded swiftly and was no longer there.

Enoch stood in the oval room in the faint glow of the bulbs. There was the heavy smell of powder and all about his feet, glinting in the light, lay the spent and shining cases that had been kicked out of the gun.

He was back in the basement once again. The target shoot was over.

29

ENOCH LOWERED the rifle and drew in a slow and careful breath. It always was like this, he thought. As if it were necessary for him to ease himself, by slow degrees, back to this world of his after the season of unreality.

One knew that it would be illusion when he kicked on the switch that set into motion whatever was to happen and one knew it had been illusion when it all had ended, but during the time that it was happening it was not illusion. It was as real and as substantial as if it all were true.

They had asked him, he remembered, when the station had been built, if he had a hobby—if there was any sort of recreational facility they could build into the station for him. And he had said that he would like a rifle range, expecting no more than a shooting gallery with ducks moving on a chain or clay pipes rotating on a wheel. But that, of course, would have been too simple for the screwball architects, who had designed, and the slap-happy crew of workmen who had built the station.

At first they had not been certain what he meant by a rifle range and he'd had to tell them what a rifle was and how it operated and for what it might be used. He had told them about hunting squirrels on sunny autumn mornings and shaking rabbits out of brush piles with the first coming of the snow (although one did not use a rifle, but a shotgun, on the rabbits), about hunting coons of an autumn night, and waiting for the deer along the run that went down to the river. But he was dishonest and he did not tell them about that other use to which he'd put a rifle during four long years.

He'd told them (since they were easy folks to talk with) about his youthful dream of some day going on a hunt in

Africa, although even as he told them he was well aware of how unattainable it was. But since that day he'd hunted (and been hunted by) beasts far stranger than anything that Africa could boast.

From what these beasts might have been patterned, if indeed they came from anywhere other than the imagination of those aliens who had set up the tapes which produced the target scene, he had no idea. There had not, so far in the thousands of times that he had used the range, been a duplication either in the scene nor in the beasts which rampaged about the scene. Although, perhaps, he thought, there might be somewhere an end of them, and then the whole sequence might start over and run its course once more. But it would make little difference now, for if the tapes should start rerunning there'd be but little chance of his recalling in any considerable detail those adventures he had lived so many years ago.

He did not understand the techniques nor the principle which made possible this fantastic rifle range. Like many other things, he accepted it without the need of understanding. Although, some day, he thought, he might find the clue which in time would turn blind acceptance into understanding—not only of the range, but of many other things.

He had often wondered what the aliens might think about his fascination with the rifle range, with that primal force that drove a man to kill, not for the joy of killing so much as to negate a danger, to meet force with a greater and more skillful force, cunning with more cunning. Had he, he wondered, given his alien friends concern in their assessment of the human character by his preoccupation with the rifle? For the understanding of an alien, how could one draw a line between the killing of other forms of life and the killing of one's own? Was there actually a differential that would stand up under logical examination between the sport of hunting and the sport of war? To an alien, perhaps, such a differentiation would be rather difficult, for in many cases the hunted animal would be more closely allied to the human hunter in its form and characteristics than would many of the aliens.

Was war an instinctive thing, for which each ordinary man was as much responsible as the policy makers and the so-called statesmen? It seemed impossible, and yet, deep in every man was the combative instinct, the aggressive urge, the strange sense of competition—all of which spelled conflict of one kind or another if carried to conclusion.

He put the rifle underneath his arm and walked over to the panel. Sticking from a slot in the bottom of it was a piece of tape.

He pulled it out and puzzled out the symbols. They were not reassuring. He had not done so well.

He had missed that first shot he had fired at the charging wolf-thing with the old man's face, and back there somewhere, in that dimension of unreality, it and its companion were snarling over the tangled, torn mass of ribboned flesh and broken bone that had been Enoch Wallace.

30

HE WENT back through the gallery, with its gifts stacked there as other gifts, in regular human establishments, might be stacked away in dry and dusty attics.

The tape nagged at him, the little piece of tape which said that while he had made all his other shots, he had missed that first one back there on the hillock. It was not often that he missed. And his training had been for that very type of shooting —the you-never-know-what-will-happen-next, the totally unexpected, the kill-or-be-killed kind of shooting that thousands of expeditions into the target area had taught him. Perhaps, he consoled himself, he had not been as faithful in his practice lately as he should have been. Although there actually was no reason that he should be faithful, for the shooting was for recreation only and his carrying of the rifle on his daily walks was from force of habit only and for no other reason. He carried the rifle as another man might take along a cane or walking stick. At the time he had first done it, of course, it had been a different kind of rifle and a different day. It then was no unusual thing for a man to carry a gun while out on a walk. But today was different and he wondered, with an inner grin, how much talk his carrying a gun might have furnished the people who had seen him with it.

Near the end of the gallery he saw the black bulk of a trunk projecting from beneath the lower shelf, too big to fit comfortably beneath it, jammed against the wall, but with a foot or two of it still projecting out beyond the shelf.

He went on walking past it, then suddenly turned around. That trunk, he thought—that was the trunk which had belonged to the Hazer who had died upstairs. It was his legacy from that being whose stolen body would be brought back to its grave this evening.

He walked over to the shelving and leaned his rifle against the wall. Stooping, he pulled the trunk clear of its resting place.

Once before, prior to carrying it down the stairs and storing it here beneath the shelves, he had gone through its contents, but at the time, he recalled, he'd not been too interested. Now, suddenly, he felt an absorbing interest in it.

He lifted the lid carefully and tilted it back against the shelves.

Crouching above the open trunk, and without touching anything to start with, he tried to catalogue the upper layer of its contents.

There was a shimmering cloak, neatly folded, perhaps some sort of ceremonial cloak, although he could not know. And atop the cloak lay a tiny bottle that was a blaze of reflected light, as if someone had taken a large-sized diamond and hollowed it out to make a bottle of it. Beside the cloak lay a nest of balls, deep violet and dull, with no shine at all, looking for all the world like a bunch of table-tennis balls that someone had cemented together to make a globe. But that was not the way it was, Enoch remembered, for that other time he had been entranced by them and had picked them up, to find that they were not cemented, but could be freely moved about, although never outside the context of their shape. One ball could not be broken from the mass, no matter how hard one might try, but would move about, as if buoyed in a fluid, among all the other balls. One could move any, or all, of the balls, but the mass remained the same. A calculator of some sort, Enoch wondered, but that seemed only barely possible, for one ball was entirely like another, there was no way in which they could be identified. Or at least, no way to identify them by the human eye. Was it possible, he wondered, that identification might be possible to a Hazer's eye? And if a calculator, what kind of a calculator? Mathematical? Or ethical? Or philosophical? Although that was slightly foolish, for who had ever heard of a calculator for ethics or philosophy? Or, rather, what human had ever heard? More than likely it was not a calculator, but something else entirely. Perhaps a sort of game—a game of solitaire?

Given time, a man might finally get it figured out. But there was no time and no incentive at the moment to spend upon one particular item any great amount of time when there were hundreds of other items equally fantastic and incomprehensible. For while one puzzled over a single item, the edges of his mind would always wonder if he might not be spending time on the most insignificant of the entire lot.

He was a victim of museum fatigue, Enoch told himself, overwhelmed by the many pieces of the unknown scattered all about him.

He reached out a hand, not for the globe of balls, but for the shining bottle that lay atop the cloak. As he picked it up and brought it closer, he saw that there was a line of writing engraved upon the glass (or diamond?) of the bottle. Slowly he studied out the writing. There had been a time, long ago, when he had been able to read the Hazer language, if not fluently, at least well enough to get along. But he had not read it for some years now and he had lost a good deal of it and he stumbled haltingly from one symbol to another. Translated very freely, the inscription on the bottle read: *To be taken when the first symptoms occur.*

A bottle of medicine! To be taken when the first symptoms occur. The symptoms, perhaps, that had come so quickly and built up so rapidly that the owner of this bottle could make no move to reach it and so had died, falling from the sofa.

Almost reverently, he put the bottle back in its place atop the cloak, fitting it back into the faint impression it had made from lying there.

So different from us in so many ways, thought Enoch, and then in other little ways so like us that it is frightening. For that bottle and the inscription on its face was an exact parallel of the prescription bottle that could be compounded by any corner drugstore.

Beside the globe of balls was a box, and he reached out and lifted it. It was made of wood and had a rather simple clasp to hold it shut. He flipped back the lid and inside he saw the metallic sheen of the material the Hazers used as paper.

Carefully he lifted out the first sheet and saw that it was not a sheet, but a long strip of the material folded in accordion fashion. Underneath it were more strips, apparently of the same material.

There was writing on it, faint and faded, and Enoch held it close to read it.

To my ——, —— *friend:* (although it was not "friend." "Blood brother," perhaps, or "colleague." And the adjectives which preceded it were such as to escape his sense entirely.)

The writing was hard to read. It bore some resemblance to the formalized version of the language, but apparently bore the imprint of the writer's personality, expressed in curlicues and flourishes which obscured the form. Enoch worked his way slowly down the paper, missing much of what was there, but picking up the sense of much that had been written.

The writer had been on a visit to some other planet, or possibly just some other place. The name of the place or planet was one that Enoch did not recognize. While he had been there he had performed some sort of function (although exactly what it was was not entirely clear) which had to do with his approaching death.

Enoch, startled, went back over the phrase again. And while much of the rest of what was written was not clear, that part of it was. *My approaching death*, he had written, and there was no room for mistranslation. All three of the words were clear.

He urged that his good (friend?) do likewise. He said it was a comfort and made clear the road.

There was no further explanation, no further reference. Just the calm declaration that he had done something which he felt must be arranged about his death. As if he knew that death was near and was not only unafraid, but almost unconcerned.

The next passage (for there were no paragraphs) told about someone he had met and how they'd talked about a certain matter which made no sense at all to Enoch, who found himself lost in a terminology he did not recognize.

And then: *I am most concerned about the mediocrity* (incompetence? inability? weakness?) *of the recent custodian of* (and then that cryptic symbol which could be translated, roughly, as the Talisman). *For* (a word, which from the context, seemed to mean a great length of time), *ever since the death of the last custodian, the Talisman has been but poorly served. It has been, in all reality,* (another long time term), *since a true* (sensitive?) *has been found to carry out its purpose. Many have been tested and none has qualified, and for the lack of such a one the galaxy has lost its close identification with the ruling principle of life. We here at the* (temple? sanctuary?) *all are greatly concerned that without a proper linkage between the people and* (several words that were not decipherable) *the galaxy will go down in chaos* (and another line that he could not puzzle out).

The next sentence introduced a new subject—the plans that were going forward for some cultural festival which concerned a concept that, to Enoch, was hazy at the best.

Enoch slowly folded up the letter and put it back into the box. He felt a faint uneasiness in reading what he had, as if he'd pried into a friendship that he had no right to know. *We here at the temple*, the letter had said. Perhaps the writer had been one of the Hazer mystics, writing to his old friend, the philosopher. And the other letters, quite possibly, were from that same mystic—letters that the dead old Hazer had valued so highly that he took them along with him when he went traveling.

A slight breeze seemed to be blowing across Enoch's shoulders; not actually a breeze, but a strange motion and a coldness to the air.

He glanced back into the gallery and there was nothing stirring, nothing to be seen.

The wind had quit its blowing, if it had ever blown. Here one moment, gone the next. Like a passing ghost, thought Enoch.

Did the Hazer have a ghost?

The people back on Vega XXI had known the moment he had died and all the circumstances of his death. They had known again about the body disappearing. And the letter had spoken calmly, much more calmly than would have been in the capacity of most humans, about the writer's near approach to death.

Was it possible that the Hazers knew more of life and death than had ever been spelled out? Or had it been spelled out, put down in black and white, in some depository or depositories in the galaxy?

Was the answer there? he wondered.

Squatting there, he thought that perhaps it might be, that someone already knew what life was for and what its destiny. There was a comfort in the thought, a strange sort of personal comfort in being able to believe that some intelligence might have solved the riddle of that mysterious equation of the universe. And how, perhaps, that mysterious equation might tie in with the spiritual force that was idealistic brother to time and space and all those other elemental factors that held the universe together.

He tried to imagine what one might feel if he were in contact with the force, and could not. He wondered if even those who might have been in contact with it could find the words to tell. It might, he thought, be impossible. For how could one who had been in intimate contact all his life with space and time tell what either of these meant to him or how they felt?

Ulysses, he thought, had not told him all the truth about the Talisman. He had told him that it had disappeared and that the galaxy was without it, but he had not told him that for many years its power and glory had been dimmed by the failure of its custodian to provide a proper linkage between the people and the force. And all that time the corrosion occasioned by that failure had eaten away at the bonds of the galactic cofraternity. Whatever might be happening now had not happened in the last few years; it had been building up for a longer time than most aliens would admit. Although, come to think of it, most aliens probably did not know.

Enoch closed the box lid and put it back into the trunk. Some day, he thought, when he was in the proper frame of mind, when the pressure of events made him less emotional, when he could dull the guilt of prying, he would achieve a scholarly and conscientious translation of those letters. For in them, he felt certain, he might find further understanding of that intriguing race. He might, he thought, then be better able to gauge *their* humanity—not humanity in the common and accepted sense of being a member of the human race of Earth, but in the sense that certain rules of conduct must underlie all racial concepts even as the thing called humanity in its narrow sense underlay the human concept.

He reached up to close the lid of the trunk and then he hesitated.

Some day, he had said. And there might not be a some day. It was a state of mind to be always thinking *some day*, a state of mind made possible by the conditions inside this station. For here there were endless days to come, forever and forever there were days to come. A man's concept of time was twisted out of shape and reason and he could look ahead complacently down a long, almost never ending, avenue of time. But that might be all over now. Time might suddenly snap back into its rightful focus. Should he leave this station, the long procession of days to come would end.

He pushed back the lid again until it rested against the shelves. Reaching in, he lifted out the box and set it on the floor beside him. He'd take it upstairs, he told himself, and put it with the other stuff that he must be prepared immediately to take along with him if he should leave the station.

If? he asked himself. Was there a question any longer? Had he, somehow, made that hard decision? Had it crept upon him unaware, so that he now was committed to it?

And if he had actually arrived at that decision, then he must, also, have arrived at the other one. If he left the station, then he could no longer be in a position to appear before Galactic Central to plead that Earth be cured of war.

You are the representative of the Earth, Ulysses had told him. You are the only one who can represent the Earth. But could he, in reality, represent the Earth? Was he any longer a true representative of the human race? He was a nineteenth-century man and how could he, being that, represent the twentieth? How much, he wondered, does the human character change with each generation? And not only was he of the nineteenth century, but he had, as well, lived for almost a hundred years under a separate and a special circumstance.

He knelt there, regarding himself with awe, and a little pity, too, wondering what he was, if he were even human, if, unknown to himself, he had absorbed so much of the mingled alien viewpoint to which he had been subjected that he had become some strange sort of hybrid, a queer kind of galactic half-breed.

Slowly he pulled the lid down and pushed it tight. Then he shoved the trunk back underneath the shelves.

He tucked the box of letters underneath his arm and rose, picking up his rifle, and headed for the stairs.

31

HE FOUND some empty cartons stacked in the kitchen corner, boxes that Winslowe had used to bring out from town the supplies that he had ordered, and began to pack.

The journals, stacked neatly in order, filled one large box and a part of another. He took a stack of old newspapers and carefully wrapped the twelve diamond bottles off the mantel and packed them in another box, thickly padded, to guard against their breakage. Out of the cabinet he got the Vegan music box and wrapped it as carefully. He pulled out of another cabinet the alien literature that he had and piled it in the fourth box. He went through his desk, but there wasn't too much there, only odds and ends tucked here and there throughout the drawers. He found his chart and, crumpling it, threw it in the wastebasket that stood beside his desk.

The already filled boxes he carried across the room and stacked beside the door for easy reaching. Lewis would have a truck, but once he let him know he needed it, it still might take a while for it to arrive. But if he had the important stuff all packed, he told himself, he could get it out himself and have it waiting for the truck.

The important stuff, he thought. Who could judge importance? The journals and the alien literature, those first of all, of course. But the rest of it? Which of the rest of it? It was all important; every item should be taken. And that might be possible. Given time and with no extra complications, it might be possible to haul it all away, all that was in this room and stored down in the basement. It all was his and he had a right to it, for it had been given him. But that did not mean, he knew, that Galactic Central might not object most strenuously to his taking any of it.

And if that should happen, it was vital that he should be able to get away with those most important items. Perhaps he should go down into the basement and lug up those tagged articles of which he knew the purpose. It probably would be better to take material about which something might be known than a lot of stuff about which there was nothing known.

He stood undecided, looking all about the room. There were all the items on the coffee table and those should be taken, too, including the little flashing pyramid of globes that Lucy had set to working.

He saw that the Pet once again had crawled off the table and fallen on the floor. He stooped and picked it up and held it in his hands. It had grown an extra knob or two since the last time he had looked at it and it was now a faint and delicate pink, whereas the last time he had noticed it had been a cobalt blue.

He probably was wrong, he told himself, in calling it the Pet. It might not be alive. But if it were, it was a sort of life he could not even guess at. It was not metallic and it was not stone, but very close to both. A file made no impression on it and he'd been tempted a time or two to whack it with a hammer to see what that might do, although he was willing to bet it would have no effect at all. It grew slowly, and it moved, but there was no way of knowing how it moved. But leave it and come back and it would have moved—a little, not too much. It knew it was being watched and it would not move while watched. It did not eat so far as he could see and it seemed to have no wastes. It changed colors, but entirely without season and with no visible reason for the change.

A being from somewhere in the direction of Sagittarius had given it to him just a year or two ago, and the creature, Enoch recalled, had been something for the books. He probably wasn't actually a walking plant, but that was what he'd looked like—a rather spindly plant that had been shorted on good water and cheated on good soil, but which had sprouted a crop of dime-store bangles that rang like a thousand silver bells when he made any sort of motion.

Enoch remembered that he had tried to ask the being what the gift might be, but the walking plant had simply clashed its bangles and filled the place with ringing sound and didn't try to answer.

So he had put the gift on one end of the desk and hours later, after the being was long gone, he found that it had moved to the other end of the desk. But it had seemed too crazy to think that a thing like that could move, so he finally convinced himself that he was mistaken as to where he'd put it. It was not until days later that he was able to convince himself it moved.

He'd have to take it when he left and Lucy's pyramid and the cube that showed you pictures of other worlds when you looked inside of it and a great deal of other stuff.

He stood with the Pet held in his hand and now, for the first time, he wondered at why he might be packing.

He was acting as if he'd decided he would leave the station, as if he'd chosen Earth as against the galaxy. But when and how, he wondered, had he decided it? Decision should be based on weighing and on measuring and he had weighed and measured nothing. He had not posed the advantages and the disadvantages and tried to strike a balance. He had not thought it out. Somehow, somewhere, it had sneaked up on him—this decision which had seemed impossible, but now had been reached so easily.

Was it, he wondered, that he had absorbed, unconsciously, such an odd mixture of alien thought and ethics that he had evolved, unknown to himself, a new way in which to think, perhaps some subconscious way of thought that had lain inoperative until now, when it had been needed.

There was a box or two out in the shed and he'd go and get them and finish up the packing of what he'd pick out here. Then he'd go down into the basement and start lugging up the stuff that he had tagged. He glanced toward the window and realized, with some surprise, that he would have to hurry, for the sun was close to setting. It would be evening soon.

He remembered that he'd forgotten lunch, but he had no time to eat. He could get something later.

He turned to put the Pet back on the table and as he did a faint sound caught his ear and froze him where he stood.

It was the slight chuckle of a materializer operating and he could not mistake it. He had heard the sound too often to be able to mistake it.

And it must be, he knew, the official materializer, for no one could have traveled on the other without the sending of a message.

Ulysses, he thought. Ulysses coming back again. Or perhaps some other member of Galactic Central. For if Ulysses had been coming, he would have sent a message.

He took a quick step forward so he could see the corner where the materializer stood and a dark and slender figure was stepping out from the target circle.

"Ulysses!" Enoch cried, but even as he spoke he realized it was not Ulysses.

For an instant he had the impression of a top hat, of white tie and tails, of a jauntiness, and then he saw that the creature was a rat that walked erect, with sleek, dark fur covering its body and a sharp, axlike rodent face. For an instant, as it turned its head toward him, he caught the red glitter of its eyes. Then it turned back toward the corner and he saw that its hand was lifted and was pulling out of a harnessed holster hung about its middle something that glinted with a metallic shimmer even in the shadow.

There was something very wrong about it. The creature should have greeted him. It should have said hello and come out to meet him. But instead it had thrown him that one red-eyed glance and then turned back to the corner.

The metallic object came out of the holster and it could only be a gun, or at least some sort of weapon that one might think of as a gun.

And was this the way, thought Enoch, that they would close the station? One quick shot, without a word, and the station keeper dead upon the floor. With someone other than Ulysses, because Ulysses could not be trusted to kill a long-time friend.

The rifle was lying across the desk top and there wasn't any time.

But the ratlike creature was not turning toward the room. It still was facing toward the corner and its hand was coming up, with the weapon glinting in it.

An alarm twanged within Enoch's brain and he swung his arm and yelled, hurling the Pet toward the creature in the corner, the yell jerked out of him involuntarily from the bottom of his lungs.

For the creature, he realized, had not been intent on the killing of the keeper, but the disruption of the station. The only thing there was to aim at in the corner was the control complex, the nerve center of the station's operation. And if that should be knocked out, the station would be dead. To set it in operation once again it would be necessary to send a crew of technicians out in a spaceship from the nearest station—a trip that would require many years to make.

At Enoch's yell, the creature jerked around, dropping toward a crouch, and the flying Pet, tumbling end for end, caught it in the belly and drove it back against the wall.

Enoch charged, arms outspread to grapple with the creature. The gun flew from the creature's hand and pinwheeled across the floor. Then Enoch was upon the alien and even as he closed with it, his nostrils were assailed by its body stench—a sickening wave of nastiness.

He wrapped his arms about it and heaved, and it was not as heavy as he had thought it might be. His powerful wrench jerked it from the corner and swung it around and sent it skidding out across the floor.

It crashed against a chair and came to a stop and then like a steel coil it rose off the floor and pounced for the gun.

Enoch took two great strides and had it by the neck, lifting it and shaking it so savagely that the recovered gun flew from its hand again and the bag it carried on a thong across its shoulder pounded like a vibrating trip hammer against its hairy ribs.

The stench was thick, so thick that one could almost see it, and Enoch gagged on it as he shook the creature. And suddenly it was worse, much worse, like a fire raging in one's throat and a hammer in one's head. It was like a physical blow that hit one in the belly and shoved against the chest. Enoch let go his hold upon the creature and staggered back, doubled up and retching. He lifted his hands to his face and tried to push the stench away, to clear his nostrils and his mouth, to rub it from his eyes.

Through a haze he saw the creature rise and, snatching up the gun, rush toward the door. He did not hear the phrase that the creature spoke, but the door came open and the creature spurted forward and was gone. And the door slammed shut again.

32

ENOCH WOBBLED across the room to the desk and caught at it for support. The stench was diminishing and his head was clearing and he scarcely could believe that it all had happened. For it was incredible that a thing like this should happen. The creature had traveled on the official materializer, and no one but a member of Galactic Central could travel by that route. And no member of Galactic Central, he was convinced, would have acted as the ratlike creature had. Likewise, the creature had known the phrase that would operate the door. No one but himself and Galactic Central would have known that phrase.

He reached out and picked up his rifle and hefted it in his fist.

It was all right, he thought. There was nothing harmed. Except that there was an alien loose upon the Earth and that was something that could not be allowed. The Earth was barred to aliens. As a planet which had not been recognized by the galactic cofraternity, it was off-limit territory.

He stood with the rifle in his hand and knew what he must do—he must get that alien back, he must get it off the Earth.

He spoke the phrase aloud and strode toward the door and out and around the corner of the house.

The alien was running across the field and had almost reached the line of woods.

Enoch ran desperately, but before he was halfway down the field, the ratlike quarry had plunged into the woods and disappeared.

The woods was beginning to darken. The slanting rays of light from the setting sun still lighted the upper canopy of the foliage, but on the forest floor the shadows had begun to gather.

As he ran into the fringe of the woods, Enoch caught a glimpse of the creature angling down a small ravine and plunging up the other slope, racing through a heavy cover of ferns that reached almost to its middle.

If it kept on in that direction, Enoch told himself, it might work out all right, for the slope beyond the ravine ended in a clump of rocks that lay above an outthrust point that ended in a cliff, with each side curving in, so that the point and its mass of boulders lay isolated, a place hung out in space. It might be a little rough to dig the alien from the rocks if it took refuge there, but at least it would be trapped and could not get away. Although, Enoch reminded himself, he could waste no time, for the sun was setting and it would soon be dark.

Enoch angled slightly westward to go around the head of the small ravine, keeping an eye on the fleeing alien. The creature kept on up the slope and Enoch, observing this, put on an extra burst of speed. For now he had the alien trapped. In its fleeing, it had gone past the point of no return. It could no longer turn around and retreat back from the point. Soon it would reach the cliff edge and then there'd be nothing it could do but hole up in the patch of boulders.

Running hard, Enoch crossed the area covered by the ferns and came out on the sharper slope some hundred yards or so below the boulder clump. Here the cover was not so dense. There was a scant covering of spotty underbrush and a scattering of trees. The soft loam of the forest floor gave way to a footing of shattered rock which through the years had been chipped off the boulders by the winters' frost, rolling down the slope. They lay there now, covered with thick moss, a treacherous place to walk.

As he ran, Enoch swept the boulders with a glance, but there was no sign of the alien. Then, out of the corner of his vision, he saw the motion, and threw himself forward to the ground behind a patch of hazel brush, and through the network of the bushes he saw the alien outlined against the sky, its head pivoting back and forth to sweep the slope below, the weapon half lifted and set for instant use.

Enoch lay frozen, with his outstretched hand gripping the rifle. There was a slash of pain across one set of knuckles and he knew that he had skinned them on the rock as he had dived for cover.

The alien dropped from sight behind the boulders and Enoch slowly pulled the rifle back to where he would be able to handle it should a shot present itself.

Although, he wondered, would he dare to fire? Would he dare to kill an alien?

The alien could have killed him back there at the station, when he had been knocked silly by the dreadful stench. But it had not killed him; it had fled instead. Was it, he wondered, that the creature had been so badly frightened that all that it could think of had been to get away? Or had it, perhaps, been as reluctant to kill a station keeper as he himself was to kill an alien?

He searched the rocks above him and there was no motion and not a thing to see. He must move up that slope, and quickly, he told himself, for time would work against him and to the advantage of the alien. Darkness could not be more than thirty minutes off and before dark had fallen this issue must be settled. If the alien got away, there'd be little chance to find it.

And why, asked a second self, standing to one side, should you worry about alien complications? For are you yourself not prepared to inform the Earth that there are alien peoples in the galaxy and to hand to Earth, unauthorized, as much of that alien lore and learning as may be within your power? Why should you have stopped this alien from the wrecking of the station, insuring its isolation for many years—for if that had been done, then you'd have been free to do as you might wish with all that is within the station? It would have worked to your advantage to have allowed events to run their course.

But I couldn't, Enoch cried inside himself. *Don't you see I couldn't? Don't you understand?*

A rustle in the bushes to his left brought him around with the rifle up and ready.

And there was Lucy Fisher, not more than twenty feet away.

"Get out of here!" he shouted, forgetting that she could not hear him.

But she did not seem to notice. She motioned to the left and made a sweeping motion with her hand and pointed toward the boulders.

Go away, he said underneath his breath. *Go away from here.*

And made rejection motions to indicate that she should go back, that this was no place for her.

She shook her head and sprang away, in a running crouch, moving further to the left and up the slope.

Enoch scrambled to his feet, lunging after her, and as he did the air behind him made a frying sound and there was the sharp bite of ozone in the air.

He hit the ground, instinctively, and farther down the slope he saw a square yard of ground that boiled and steamed, with the ground cover swept away by a fierce heat and the very soil and rock turned into a simmering pudding.

A laser, Enoch thought. The alien's weapon was a laser, packing a terrific punch in a narrow beam of light.

He gathered himself together and made a short rush up the hillside, throwing himself prone behind a twisted birch clump.

The air made the frying sound again and there was an instant's blast of heat and the ozone once again. Over on the reverse slope a patch of ground was steaming. Ash floated down and settled on Enoch's arms. He flashed a quick glance upward and saw that the top half of the birch clump was gone, sheared off by the laser and reduced to ash. Tiny coils of smoke rose lazily from the severed stumps.

No matter what it may have done, or failed to do, back there at the station, the alien now meant business. It knew that it was cornered and it was playing vicious.

Enoch huddled against the ground and worried about Lucy. He hoped that she was safe. The little fool should have stayed out of it. This was no place for her. She shouldn't even have been out in the woods at this time of day. She'd have old Hank out looking for her again, thinking she was kidnaped. He wondered what the hell had gotten into her.

The dusk was deepening. Only the far peak of the treetops caught the last rays of the sun. A coolness came stealing up the ravine from the valley far below and there was a damp, lush smell that came out of the ground. From some hidden hollow a whippoorwill called out mournfully.

Enoch darted out from behind the birch clump and rushed up the slope. He reached the fallen log he'd picked as a barricade and threw himself behind it. There was no sign of the alien and there was not another shot from the laser gun.

Enoch studied the ground ahead. Two more rushes, one to that small pile of rock and the next to the edge of the boulder area itself, and he'd be on top of the hiding alien. And once he got there, he wondered, what was he to do.

Go in and rout the alien out, of course.

There was no plan that could be made, no tactics that could be laid out in advance. Once he got to the edge of the boulders, he must play it all by ear, taking advantage of any break that might present itself. He was at a disadvantage in that he must not kill the alien, but must capture it instead and drag it back, kicking and screaming, if need be, to the safety of the station.

Perhaps, here in the open air, it could not use its stench defense as effectively as it had in the confines of the station, and that, he thought, might make it easier. He examined the clump of boulders from one edge to the other and there was nothing that might help him to locate the alien.

Slowly he began to snake around, getting ready for the next rush up the slope, moving carefully so that no sound would betray him.

Out of the tail of his eye he caught the moving shadow that came flowing up the slope. Swiftly he sat up, swinging the rifle. But before he could bring the muzzle round, the shadow was upon him, bearing him back, flat upon the ground, with one great splay-fingered hand clamped upon his mouth.

"Ulysses!" Enoch gurgled, but the fearsome shape only hissed at him in a warning sound.

Slowly the weight shifted off him and the hand slid from his mouth.

Ulysses gestured toward the boulder pile and Enoch nodded.

Ulysses crept closer and lowered his head toward Enoch's. He whispered with his mouth inches from the Earthman's ear: "The Talisman! He has the Talisman!"

"The Talisman!" Enoch cried aloud, trying to strangle off the cry even as he made it, remembering that he should make no sound to let the watcher up above know where they might be.

From the ridge above a loose stone rattled as it was dislodged and began to roll, bouncing down the slope. Enoch hunkered closer to the ground behind the fallen log.

"Down!" he shouted to Ulysses. "Down! He has a gun."

But Ulysses's hand gripped him by the shoulder.

"Enoch!" he cried. "Enoch, look!"

Enoch jerked himself erect and atop the pile of rock, dark against the skyline, were two grappling figures.

"Lucy!" he shouted.

For one of them was Lucy and the other was the alien.

She sneaked up on him, he thought. That damn' little fool,

she sneaked up on him! While the alien had been distracted with watching the slope, she had slipped up close and then had tackled him. She had a club of some sort in her hand, an old dead branch, perhaps, and it was raised above her head, ready for a stroke, but the alien had a grip upon her arm and she could not strike.

"Shoot," said Ulysses, in a flat, dead voice.

Enoch raised the rifle and had trouble with the sights because of the deepening darkness. And they were so close together! They were too close together.

"Shoot!" yelled Ulysses.

"I can't," sobbed Enoch. "It's too dark to shoot."

"You have to shoot," Ulysses said, his voice tense and hard. "You have to take the chance."

Enoch raised the rifle once again and the sights seemed clearer now and he knew the trouble was not so much the darkness as that shot which he had missed back there in the world of the honking thing that had strode its world on stilts. If he had missed then, he could as well miss now.

The bead came to rest upon the head of the ratlike creature, and then the head bobbed away, but was bobbing back again.

"Shoot!" Ulysses yelled.

Enoch squeezed the trigger and the rifle coughed and up atop the rocks the creature stood for a second with only half a head and with tattered gouts of flesh flying briefly like dark insects zooming against the half-light of the western sky.

Enoch dropped the gun and sprawled upon the earth, clawing his fingers into the thin and mossy soil, sick with the thought of what could have happened, weak with the thankfulness that it had not happened, that the years on that fantastic rifle range had at last paid off.

How strange it is, he thought, how so many senseless things shape our destiny. For the rifle range had been a senseless thing, as senseless as a billiard table or a game of cards—designed for one thing only, to please the keeper of the station. And yet the hours he'd spent there had shaped toward this hour and end, to this single instant on this restricted slope of ground.

The sickness drained away into the earth beneath him and a peace came stealing in upon him—the peace of trees and woodland soil and the first faint hush of nightfall. As if the sky and stars and very space itself had leaned close above him and was whispering his essential oneness with them. And it seemed for a moment that he had grasped the edge of some great truth and with this truth had come a comfort and a greatness he'd never known before.

"Enoch," Ulysses whispered. "Enoch, my brother . . ."

There was something like a hidden sob in the alien's voice and he had never, until this moment, called the Earthman brother.

Enoch pulled himself to his knees and up on the pile of tumbled boulders was a soft and wondrous light, a soft and gentle light, as if a giant firefly had turned on its lamp and had not turned it off, but had left it burning.

The light was moving down across the rocks toward them and he could see Lucy moving with the light, as if she were walking toward them with a lantern in her hand.

Ulysses's hand reached out of the darkness and closed hard on Enoch's arm.

"Do you see?" he asked.

"Yes, I see. What is . . ."

"It is the Talisman," Ulysses said, enraptured, his breath rasping in his throat. "And she is our new custodian. The one we've hunted through the years."

33

YOU DID not become accustomed to it, Enoch told himself as they tramped up through the woods. There was not a moment you were not aware of it. It was something that you wanted to hug close against yourself and hold it there forever, and even when it was gone from you, you'd probably not forget it, ever.

It was something that was past all description—a mother's love, a father's pride, the adoration of a sweetheart, the closeness of a comrade, it was all of these and more. It made the farthest distance near and turned the complex simple and it swept away all fear and sorrow, for all of there being a certain feeling of deep sorrow in it, as if one might feel that never in his lifetime would he know an instant like this, and that in another instant he would lose it and never would be able to hunt it out again. But that was not the way it was, for this ascendant instant kept going on and on.

Lucy walked between them and she held the bag that contained the Talisman close against her breast, with her two arms clasped about it, and Enoch, looking at her, in the soft glow of its light, could not help but think of a little girl carrying her beloved pussy cat.

"Never for a century," said Ulysses, "perhaps for many centuries, perhaps never, has it glowed so well. I myself cannot remember when it was like this. It is wonderful, is it not?"

"Yes," said Enoch. "It is wonderful."

"Now we shall be one again," Ulysses said. "Now we shall feel again. Now we shall be a people instead of many people."

"But the creature that had it . . ."

"A clever one," Ulysses said. "He was holding it for ransom."

"It had been stolen, then."

"We do not know all the circumstances," Ulysses told him. "We will find out, of course."

They tramped on in silence through the woods and far in the east one could see, through the treetops, the first flush in the sky that foretold the rising moon.

"There is something," Enoch said.

"Ask me," said Ulysses.

"How could that creature back there carry it and not feel —feel no part of it? For if he could have, he would not have stolen it."

"There is only one in many billions," Ulysses said, "who can —how do you say it?—tune in on it, perhaps. To you and I it would be nothing. It would not respond to us. We could hold it in our hands forever and there would nothing happen. But let that one in many billions lay a finger on it and it becomes alive. There is a certain rapport, a sensitivity—I don't know how to say it—that forms a bridge between this strange machine and the cosmic spiritual force. It is not the machine, itself, you understand, that reaches out and taps the spiritual force. It is the living creature's mind, aided by the mechanism, that brings the force to us."

A machine, a mechanism, no more than a tool—technological brother to the hoe, the wrench, the hammer—and yet as far a cry from these as the human brain was from that first amino acid which had come into being on this planet when the Earth was very young. One was tempted, Enoch thought, to say that this was as far as a tool could go, that it was the ultimate in the ingenuity possessed by any brain. But that would be a dangerous way of thinking, for perhaps there was no limit, there might, quite likely, be no such condition as the ultimate; there might be no time when any creature or any group of creatures could stop at any certain point and say, this is as far as we can go, there is no use of trying to go farther. For each new development produced, as side effects, so many other possibilities, so many other roads to travel, that with each step one took down any given road there were more paths to follow. There'd never be an end, he thought—no end to anything.

They reached the edge of the field and headed up across it toward the station. From its upper edge came the sound of running feet.

"Enoch!" a voice shouted out of the darkness. "Enoch, is that you?"

Enoch recognized the voice.

"Yes, Winslowe. What is wrong?"

The mailman burst out of the darkness and stopped, panting with his running, at the edge of light.

"Enoch, they are coming! A couple of carloads of them. But I put a crimp in them. Where the road turns off into your lane —that narrow place, you know. I dumped two pounds of roofing nails along the ruts. That'll hold them for a while."

"Roofing nails?" Ulysses asked.

"It's a mob," Enoch told him. "They are after me. The nails . . ."

"Oh, I see," Ulysses said. "The deflation of the tires."

Winslowe took a slow step closer, his gaze riveted on the glow of the shielded Talisman.

"That's Lucy Fisher, ain't it?"

"Of course it is," said Enoch.

"Her old man came roaring into town just a while ago and said she was gone again. Up until then everything had quieted down and it was all right. But old Hank, he got them stirred up again. So I went down to the hardware store and got them roofing nails and I beat them here."

"This mob?" Ulysses asked. "I don't . . ."

Winslowe interrupted him, gasping in his eagerness to tell all his information. "That ginseng man is up there, waiting at the house for you. He has a panel truck."

"That," said Enoch, "would be Lewis with the Hazer's body."

"He is some upset," said Winslowe. "He said you were expecting him."

"Perhaps," suggested Ulysses, "we shouldn't just be standing here. It seems to my poor intellect that many things, indeed, may be coming to a crisis."

"Say," the mailman yelled, "what is going on here? What is that thing Lucy has and who's this fellow with you?"

"Later," Enoch told him. "I'll tell you later. There's no time to tell you now."

"But, Enoch, there's the mob."

"I'll deal with them," said Enoch grimly, "when I have to deal with them. Right now there's something more important."

They ran up the slope, the four of them, dodging through the waist-high clumps of weeds. Ahead of them the station reared dark and angular against the evening sky.

"They're down there at the turnoff," Winslowe gasped, wheezing with his running. "That flash of light down the ridge. That was the headlights of a car."

They reached the edge of the yard and ran toward the house. The black bulk of the panel truck glimmered in the glow cast by the Talisman. A figure detached itself from the shadow of the truck and hurried out toward them.

"Is that you, Wallace?"

"Yes," said Enoch. "I'm sorry that I wasn't here."

"I was a bit upset," said Lewis, "when I didn't find you waiting."

"Something unforeseen," said Enoch. "Something that must be taken care of."

"The body of the honored one?" Ulysses asked. "It is in the truck?"

Lewis nodded. "I am happy that we can restore it."

"We'll have to carry him down to the orchard," Enoch said. "You can't get a car in there."

"The other time," Ulysses said, "you were the one who carried him."

Enoch nodded.

"My friend," the alien said, "I wonder if on this occasion I could be allowed the honor."

"Why, yes, of course," said Enoch. "He would like it that way."

And the words came to his tongue, but he choked them back, for it would not have done to say them—the words of thanks for lifting from him the necessity of complete recompense, for the gesture which released him from the utter letter of the law.

At his elbow, Winslowe said: "They are coming. I can hear them down the road."

He was right.

From down the road came the soft sound of footsteps padding in the dust, not hurrying, with no need to hurry, the insulting and deliberate treading of a monster so certain of its prey that it need not hurry.

Enoch swung around and half lifted his rifle, training it toward the padding that came out of the dark.

Behind him, Ulysses spoke softly: "Perhaps it would be most proper to bear him to the grave in the full glory and unshielded light of our restored Talisman."

"She can't hear you," Enoch said. "You must remember she is deaf. You will have to show her."

But even as he said it, a blaze leaped out that was blinding in its brightness.

With a strangled cry Enoch half turned back to face the little group that stood beside the truck, and the bag that had enclosed the Talisman, he saw, lay at Lucy's feet and she held the glowing brightness high and proudly so that it spread its light across the yard and the ancient house, and some of it as well spilled out into the field.

There was a quietness. As if the entire world had caught its breath and stood attentive and in awe, waiting for a sound that did not come, that would never come but would always be expected.

And with the quietness came an abiding sense of peace that seemed to seep into the very fiber of one's being. It was no synthetic thing—not as if someone had invoked a peace and peace then was allowed to exist by sufferance. It was a present and an actual peace, the peace of mind that came with the calmness of a sunset after a long, hot day, or the sparkling, ghost-like shimmer of a springtime dawn. You felt it inside of you and all about you, and there was the feeling that it was not only here but that the peace extended on and out in all directions, to the farthest reaches of infinity, and that it had a depth which would enable it to endure until the final gasp of all eternity.

Slowly, remembering, Enoch turned back to face the field and the men were there, at the edge of the light cast by the Talisman, a gray, huddled group, like a pack of chastened wolves that slunk at the faint periphery of a campfire's light.

And as he watched, they melted back—back into the deeper dark from which they had padded in the dust track of the road.

Except for one who turned and bolted, plunging down the hill in the darkness toward the woods, howling in maddened terror like a frightened dog.

"There goes Hank," said Winslowe. "That is Hank running down the hill."

"I am sorry that we frightened him," said Enoch soberly. "No man should be afraid of this."

"It is himself that he is frightened of," the mailman said. "He lives with a terror in him."

And that was true, thought Enoch. That was the way with Man; it had always been that way. He had carried terror with him. And the thing he was afraid of had always been himself.

34

THE GRAVE was filled and mounded and the five of them stood for a moment more, listening to the restless wind that stirred in the moon-drenched apple orchard, while from far away, down in the hollows above the river valley, the whippoorwills talked back and forth through the silver night.

In the moonlight Enoch tried to read the graven line upon the rough-hewn tombstone, but there was not light enough. Although there was no need to read it; it was in his mind:

> *Here lies one from a distant star, but the soil is not alien to him, for in death he belongs to the universe.*

When you wrote that, the Hazer diplomat had told him, just the night before, you wrote as one of us. And he had not said so, but the Vegan had been wrong. For it was not a Vegan sentiment alone; it was human, too.

The words were chiseled awkwardly and there was a mistake or two in spelling, for the Hazer language was not an easy one to master. The stone was softer than the marble or the granite most commonly used for gravestones and the lettering would not last. In a few more years the weathering of sun and rain and frost would blur the characters, and in some years after that they would be entirely gone, with no more than the roughness of the stone remaining to show that words had once been written there. But it did not matter, Enoch thought, for the words were graven on more than stone alone.

He looked across the grave at Lucy. The Talisman was in its bag once more and the glow was softer. She still held it clasped tight against herself and her face was still exalted and unnoticing—as if she no longer lived in the present world, but had entered into some other place, some other far dimension where she dwelled alone and was forgetful of all past.

"Do you think," Ulysses asked, "that she will go with us? Do you think that we can have her? Will the Earth . . ."

"The Earth," said Enoch, "has not a thing to say. We Earth people are free agents. It is up to her."

"You think that she will go?"

"I think so," Enoch said. "I think maybe this has been the moment she had sought for all her life. I wonder if she might not have sensed it, even with no Talisman."

For she always had been in touch with something outside of human ken. She had something in her no other human had. You sensed it, but you could not name it, for there was no name for this thing she had. And she had fumbled with it, trying to use it, not knowing how to use it, charming off the warts and healing poor hurt butterflies and only God knew what other acts that she performed unseen.

"Her parent?" Ulysses asked. "The howling one that ran away from us?"

"I'll handle him," said Lewis. "I'll have a talk with him. I know him fairly well."

"You want her to go back with you to Galactic Central?" Enoch asked.

"If she will," Ulysses said. "Central must be told at once."

"And from there throughout the galaxy?"

"Yes," Ulysses said. "We need her very badly."

"Could we, I wonder, borrow her for a day or two."

"Borrow her?"

"Yes," said Enoch. "For we need her, too. We need her worst of all."

"Of course," Ulysses said. "But I don't . . ."

"Lewis," Enoch asked, "do you think our government— the Secretary of State, perhaps—might be persuaded to appoint one Lucy Fisher as a member of our peace conference delegation?"

Lewis stammered, made a full stop, then began again: "I think it could possibly be managed."

"Can you imagine," Enoch asked, "the impact of this girl and the Talisman at the conference table?"

"I think I can," said Lewis. "But the Secretary undoubtedly would want to talk with you before he arrived at his decision."

Enoch half turned toward Ulysses, but he did not need to phrase his question.

"By all means," Ulysses said to Lewis. "Let me know and I'll sit in on the meeting. And you might tell the good Secretary, too, that it would not be a bad idea to begin the formation of a world committee."

"A world committee?"

"To arrange," Ulysses said, "for the Earth becoming one of us. We cannot accept a custodian, can we, from an outside planet?"

35

IN THE moonlight the tumbled boulder pile gleamed whitely, like the skeleton of some prehistoric beast. For here, near the edge of the cliff that towered above the river, the heavy trees thinned out and the rocky point stood open to the sky.

Enoch stood beside one of the massive boulders and gazed down at the huddled figure that lay among the rocks. Poor, tattered bungler, he thought, dead so far from home and, so far as he, himself, must be concerned, to so little purpose.

Although perhaps neither poor nor tattered, for in that

brain, now broken and spattered beyond recovery, must surely have lain a scheme of greatness—the kind of scheme that the brain of an earthly Alexander or Xerxes or Napoleon may have held, a dream of some great power, cynically conceived, to be attained and held at whatever cost, the dimensions of it so grandiose that it shoved aside and canceled out all moral considerations.

He tried momentarily to imagine what the scheme might be, but knew, even as he tested his imagination, how foolish it was to try, for there would be factors, he was sure, that he would not recognize and considerations that might lie beyond his understanding.

But however that might be, something had gone wrong, for in the plan itself Earth could have had no place other than as a hideout which could be used if trouble struck. This creature's lying here, then, was a part of desperation, a last-ditch gamble that had not worked out.

And, Enoch thought, it was ironic that the key of failure lay in the fact that the creature, in its fleeing, had carried the Talisman into the backyard of a sensitive, and on a planet, too, where no one would have thought to look for a sensitive. For, thinking back on it, there could be little doubt that Lucy had sensed the Talisman and had been drawn to it as truly as a magnet would attract a piece of steel. She had known nothing else, perhaps, than that the Talisman had been there and was something she must have, that it was something she had waited for in all her loneliness, without knowing what it was or without hope of finding it. Like a child who sees, quite suddenly, a shiny, glorious bauble on a Christmas tree and knows that it's the grandest thing on Earth and that it must be hers.

This creature lying here, thought Enoch, must have been able and resourceful. For it would have taken great ability and resourcefulness to have stolen the Talisman to start with, to keep it hidden for years, to have penetrated into the secrets and the files of Galactic Central. Would it have been possible, he wondered, if the Talisman had been in effective operation? With an energetic Talisman would the moral laxity and the driving greed have been possible to motivate the deed?

But that was ended now. The Talisman had been restored and a new custodian had been found—a deaf-mute girl of

Earth, the humblest of humans. And there would be peace on Earth and in time the Earth would join the cofraternity of the galaxy.

There were no problems now, he thought. No decisions to be made. Lucy had taken the decisions from the hands of everyone.

The station would remain and he could unpack the boxes he had packed and put the journals back on the shelves again. He could go back to the station once again and settle down and carry on his work.

I am sorry, he told the huddled shape that lay among the boulders. *I am sorry that mine was the hand that had to do it to you.*

He turned away and walked out to where the cliff dropped straight down to the river flowing at its foot. He raised the rifle and held it for a moment motionless and then he threw it out and watched it fall, spinning end for end, the moonlight glinting off the barrel, saw the tiny splash it made as it struck the water. And far below, he heard the smug, contented gurgling of the water as it flowed past this cliff and went on, to the further ends of Earth.

There would be peace on Earth, he thought; there would be no war. With Lucy at the conference table, there could be no thought of war. Even if some ran howling from the fear inside themselves, a fear and guilt so great that it overrode the glory and the comfort of the Talisman, there still could be no war.

But it was a long trail yet, a long and lonesome way, before the brightness of real peace would live in the hearts of man.

Until no man ran howling, wild with fear (any kind of fear), would there be actual peace. Until the last man threw away his weapon (any sort of weapon), the tribe of Man could not be at peace. And a rifle, Enoch told himself, was the least of the weapons of the Earth, the least of man's inhumanity to man, no more than a symbol of all the other and more deadly weapons.

He stood on the rim of the cliff and looked out across the river and the dark shadow of the wooded valley. His hands felt strangely empty with the rifle gone, but it seemed that somewhere, back there just a way, he had stepped into another field of time, as if an age or day had dropped away and he had come into a place that was shining and brand new and unsullied by any past mistakes.

The river rolled below him and the river did not care. Nothing mattered to the river. It would take the tusk of mastodon, the skull of sabertooth, the rib cage of a man, the dead and sunken tree, the thrown rock or rifle and would swallow each of them and cover them in mud or sand and roll gurgling over them, hiding them from sight.

A million years ago there had been no river here and in a million years to come there might be no river—but in a million years from now there would be, if not Man, at least a caring thing. And that was the secret of the universe, Enoch told himself—a thing that went on caring.

He turned slowly from the cliff edge and clambered through the boulders, to go walking up the hill. He heard the tiny scurrying of small life rustling through the fallen leaves and once there was the sleepy peeping of an awakened bird and through the entire woods lay the peace and comfort of that glowing light—not so intense, not so deep and bright and so wonderful as when it actually had been there, but a breath of it still left.

He came to the edge of the woods and climbed the field and ahead of him the station stood foursquare upon its ridgetop. And it seemed that it was no longer a station only, but his home as well. Many years ago it had been a home and nothing more and then it had become a way station to the galaxy. But now, although way station still, it was home again.

36

HE CAME into the station and the place was quiet and just a little ghostly in the quietness of it. A lamp burned on his desk and over on the coffee table the little pyramid of spheres was flashing, throwing its many-colored lights, like the crystal balls they'd used in the Roaring Twenties to turn a dance hall into a place of magic. The tiny flickering colors went flitting all about the room, like the dance of a zany band of Technicolor fireflies.

He stood for a moment, indecisive, not knowing what to do. There was something missing and all at once he realized what it was. During all the years there'd been a rifle to hang upon its pegs or to lay across the desk. And now there was no rifle.

He'd have to settle down, he told himself, and get back to work. He'd have to unpack and put the stuff away. He'd have to get the journals written and catch up with his reading. There was a lot to do.

Ulysses and Lucy had left an hour or two before, bound for Galactic Central, but the *feeling* of the Talisman still seemed to linger in the room. Although, perhaps, he thought, not in the room at all, but inside himself. Perhaps it was a feeling that he'd carry with him no matter where he went.

He walked slowly across the room and sat down on the sofa. In front of him the pyramid of spheres was splashing out its crystal shower of colors. He reached out a hand to pick it up, then drew it slowly back. What was the use, he asked himself, of examining it again? If he had not learned its secret the many times before, why should he expect to now?

A pretty thing, he thought, but useless.

He wondered how Lucy might be getting on and knew she was all right. She'd get along, he told himself, anywhere she went.

Instead of sitting here, he should be getting back to work. There was a lot of catching up to do. And his time would not be his own from now on, for the Earth would be pounding at the door. There would be conferences and meetings and a lot of other things and in a few hours more the newspapers might be here. But before it happened, Ulysses would be back to help him, and perhaps there would be others, too.

In just a little while he'd rustle up some food and then he'd get to work. If he worked far into the night, he could get a good deal done.

Lonely nights, he told himself, were good for work. And it was lonely now, when it should not be lonely. For he no longer was alone, as he had thought he was alone just a few short hours before. Now he had the Earth and the galaxy, Lucy and Ulysses, Winslowe and Lewis and the old philosopher out in the apple orchard.

He rose and walked to the desk and picked up the statuette Winslowe had carved of him. He held it beneath the desk lamp and turned it slowly in his hands. There was, he saw now, a loneliness in that figure, too—the essential loneliness of a man who walked alone.

But he'd had to walk alone. There'd been no other way. There had been no choice. It had been a one-man job. And now the job was—no, not done, for there still was much that must be done. But the first phase of it now was over and the second phase was starting.

He set the statuette back on the desk and remembered that he had not given Winslowe the piece of wood the Thuban traveler had brought. Now he could tell Winslowe where all the wood had come from. They could go through the journals and find the dates and the origin of every stick of it. That would please old Winslowe.

He heard the silken rustle and swung swiftly round.

"Mary!" he cried.

She stood just at the edge of shadow and the flitting colors from the flashing pyramid made her seem like someone who had stepped from fairyland. And that was right, he was thinking wildly, for his lost fairyland was back.

"I had to come," she said. "You were lonely, Enoch, and I could not stay away."

She could not stay away—and that might be true, he thought. For within the conditioning he'd set up there might have been the inescapable compulsion to come whenever she was needed.

It was a trap, he thought, from which neither could escape. There was no free will here, but instead the deadly precision of this blind mechanism he had shaped himself.

She should not come to see him and perhaps she knew this as well as he, but could not help herself. Would this be, he wondered, the way that it would be, forever and forever?

He stood there, frozen, torn by the need of her and the emptiness of her unreality, and she was moving toward him.

She was close to him and in a moment she would stop, for she knew the rules as well as he; she, no more than he, could admit illusion.

But she did not stop. She came so close that he could smell the apple-blossom fragrance of her. She put out a hand and laid it on his arm.

It was no shadow touch and it was no shadow hand. He could feel the pressure of her fingers and the coolness of them.

He stood rigid, with her hand upon his arm.

The flashing light! he thought. The pyramid of spheres!

For now he remembered who had given it to him—one of those aberrant races of the Alphard system. And it had been from the literature of that system that he had learned the art of fairyland. They had tried to help him by giving him the pyramid and he had not understood. There had been a failure of communication—but that was an easy thing to happen. In the Babel of the galaxy, it was easy to misunderstand or simply not to know.

For the pyramid of spheres was a wonderful, and yet a simple, mechanism. It was the fixation agent that banished all illusion, that made a fairyland for real. You made something as you wanted it and then turned on the pyramid and you had what you had made, as real as if it had never been illusion.

Except, he thought, in some things you couldn't fool yourself. You knew it was illusion, even if it should turn real.

He reached out toward her tentatively, but her hand dropped from his arm and she took a slow step backward.

In the silence of the room—the terrible, lonely silence—they stood facing one another while the colored lights ran like playing mice as the pyramid of spheres twirled its everlasting rainbow.

"I am sorry," Mary said, "but it isn't any good. We can't fool ourselves."

He stood mute and shamed.

"I waited for it," she said. "I thought and dreamed about it."

"So did I," said Enoch. "I never thought that it would happen."

And that was it, of course. So long as it could not happen, it was a thing to dream about. It was romantic and far-off and impossible. Perhaps it had been romantic only because it had been so far-off and so impossible.

"As if a doll had come to life," she said, "or a beloved Teddy bear. I am sorry, Enoch, but you could not love a doll or a Teddy bear that had come to life. You always would remember them the way they were before. The doll with the silly, painted smile; the Teddy bear with the stuffing coming out of it."

"No!" cried Enoch. "No!"

"Poor Enoch," she said. "It will be so bad for you. I wish that I could help. You'll have so long to live with it."

"But you!" he cried. "But you? What can you do now?"

It had been she, he thought, who had the courage. The courage that it took to face things as they were.

How, he wondered, had she sensed it? How could she have known?

"I shall go away," she said. "I shall not come back. Even when you need me, I shall not come back. There is no other way."

"But you can't go away," he said. "You are trapped the same as I."

"Isn't it strange," she said, "how it happened to us. Both of us victims of illusion . . ."

"But you," he said. "Not you."

She nodded gravely. "I, the same as you. You can't love the doll you made or I the toymaker. But each of us thought we did; each of us still think we should and are guilty and miserable when we find we can't."

"We could try," said Enoch. "If you would only stay."

"And end up by hating you? And, worse than that, by your hating me. Let us keep the guilt and misery. It is better than the hate."

She moved swiftly and the pyramid of spheres was in her hand and lifted.

"No, not that!" he shouted. "No, Mary . . ."

The pyramid flashed, spinning in the air, and crashed against the fireplace. The flashing lights went out. Something—glass? metal? stone?—tinkled on the floor.

"Mary!" Enoch cried, striding forward in the dark.

But there was no one there.

"Mary!" he shouted, and the shouting was a whimper.

She was gone and she would not be back.

Even when he needed her, she would not be back.

He stood quietly in the dark and silence, and the voice of a century of living seemed to speak to him in a silent language.

All things are hard, it said. There is nothing easy.

There had been the farm girl living down the road, and the

southern beauty who had watched him pass her gate, and now there was Mary, gone forever from him.

He turned heavily in the room and moved forward, groping for the table. He found it and switched on the light.

He stood beside the table and looked about the room. In this corner where he stood there once had been a kitchen, and there, where the fireplace stood, the living room, and it all had changed—it had been changed for a long time now. But he still could see it as if it were only yesterday.

All the days were gone and all the people in them.

Only he was left.

He had lost his world. He had left his world behind him.

And, likewise, on this day, had all the others—all the humans that were alive this moment.

They might not know it yet, but they, too, had left their world behind them. It would never be the same again.

You said good bye to so many things, to so many loves, to so many dreams.

"Good bye, Mary," he said. "Forgive me and God keep you."

He sat down at the table and pulled the journal that lay upon its top in front of him. He flipped it open, searching for the pages he must fill.

He had work to do.

Now he was ready for it.

He had said his last good bye.

FLOWERS FOR ALGERNON

Daniel Keyes

For my mother
And in memory of my father

Any one who has common sense will remember that the bewilderments of the eyes are of two kinds, and arise from two causes, either from coming out of the light or from going into the light, which is true of the mind's eye, quite as much as of the bodily eye; and he who remembers this when he sees any one whose vision is perplexed and weak, will not be too ready to laugh; he will first ask whether that soul of man has come out of the brighter life, and is unable to see because unaccustomed to the dark, or having turned from darkness to the day is dazzled by excess of light. And he will count the one happy in his condition and state of being, and he will pity the other; or, if he have a mind to laugh at the soul which comes from below into the light, there will be more reason in this than in the laugh which greets him who returns from above out of the light into the den.

Plato, The Republic

progris riport 1   martch 3

D R STRAUSS says I shoud rite down what I think and re-membir and evrey thing that happins to me from now on. I dont no why but he says its importint so they will see if they can use me. I hope they use me becaus Miss Kinnian says mabye they can make me smart. I want to be smart. My name is Charlie Gordon I werk in Donners bakery where Mr Donner gives me 11 dollers a week and bred or cake if I want. I am 32 yeres old and next munth is my brithday. I tolld dr Strauss and perfesser Nemur I cant rite good but he says it dont matter he says I shud rite just like I talk and like I rite compushishens in Miss Kinnians class at the beekmin collidge center for retarted adults where I go to lern 3 times a week on my time off. Dr. Strauss says to rite a lot evrything I think and evrything that happins to me but I cant think anymor because I have nothing to rite so I will close for today . . . yrs trulie Charlie Gordon.

progris riport 2—martch 4

I had a test today. I think I faled it and I think mabye now they wont use me. What happind is I went to Prof Nemurs office on my lunch time like they said and his secertery took me to a place that said psych dept on the door with a long hall and alot of littel rooms with onley a desk and chares. And a nice man was in one of the rooms and he had some wite cards with ink spilld all over them. He sed sit down Charlie and make yourself cunfortible and rilax. He had a wite coat like a docter but I dont think he was no docter because he dint tell me to opin my mouth and say ah. All he had was those wite cards. His name is Burt. I fergot his last name because I dont remembir so good.

I dint know what he was gonna do and I was holding on tite to the chair like sometimes when I go to a dentist onley Burt aint no dentist neither but he kept telling me to rilax and that gets me skared because it always means its gonna hert.

So Burt sed Charlie what do you see on this card. I saw the spilld ink and I was very skared even tho I got my rabits foot in my pockit because when I was a kid I always faled tests in school and I spilld ink to.

I tolld Burt I saw ink spilld on a wite card. Burt said yes and he smild and that maid me feel good. He kept terning all the cards and I tolld him somebody spilld ink on all of them red and black. I thot that was a easy test but when I got up to go Burt stoppd me and said now sit down Charlie we are not thru yet. Theres more we got to do with these cards. I dint understand about it but I remembir Dr Strauss said do anything the testor telld me even if it dont make no sense because thats testing.

I dont remembir so good what Burt said but I remembir he wantid me to say what was in the ink. I dint see nothing in the ink but Burt sed there was picturs there. I coudnt see no picturs. I reely tryed to see. I holded the card up close and then far away. Then I said if I had my eye glassis I coud probaly see better I usully only ware my eyeglassis in the movies or to watch TV but I sed maybe they will help me see the picturs in the ink. I put them on and I said now let me see the card agan I bet I find it now.

I tryed hard but I still coudnt find the picturs I only saw the ink. I tolld Burt mabey I need new glassis. He rote somthing down on a paper and I got skared of faling the test. So I tolld him it was a very nice pictur of ink with pritty points all around the eges but he shaked his head so that wasnt it neither. I asked him if other pepul saw things in the ink and he sed yes they imagen picturs in the inkblot. He tolld me the ink on the card was calld inkblot.

Burt is very nice and he talks slow like Miss Kinnian dose in her class where I go to lern reeding for slow adults. He explained me it was a *raw shok test*. He sed pepul see things in the ink. I said show me where. He dint show me he just kept saying *think* imagen theres something on the card. I tolld him I imaggen a inkblot. He shaked his head so that wasnt rite eather. He said what does it remind you of pretend its something. I closd my eyes for a long time to pretend and then I said I pretend a bottel of ink spilld all over a wite card. And thats when the point on his pencel broke and then we got up and went out.

I dont think I passd the *raw shok test*.

3d progris riport

martch 5—Dr Strauss and prof Nemur say it dont matter about the ink on the cards. I tolld them I dint spill the ink on them and I coudnt see anything in the ink. They said maybe they will still use me. I tolld Dr Strauss that Miss Kinnian never gave me tests like that only riting and reeding. He said Miss Kinnian tolld him I was her bestist pupil in the Beekman School for retarted adults and I tryed the hardist becaus I reely wantd to lern I wantid it more even then pepul who are smarter even then me.

Dr Strauss askd me how come you went to the Beekman School all by yourself Charlie. How did you find out about it. I said I dont remembir.

Prof Nemur said but why did you want to lern to reed and spell in the frist place. I tolld him because all my life I wantid to be smart and not dumb and my mom always tolld me to try and lern just like Miss Kinnian tells me but its very hard to be smart and even when I lern something in Miss Kinnians class at the school I ferget alot.

Dr Strauss rote some things on a peice of paper and prof Nemur talkd to me very sereus. He said you know Charlie we are not shure how this experamint will werk on pepul because we onley tried it up to now on animils. I said thats what Miss Kinnian tolld me but I dont even care if it herts or anything because Im strong and I will werk hard.

I want to get smart if they will let me. They said they got to get permissen from my familie but my uncle Herman who use to take care of me is ded and I dont rimember about my familie. I dint see my mother or father or my littel sister Norma for a long long long time. Mabye their ded to. Dr. Strauss askd me where they use to live. I think in brooklin. He sed they will see if mabye they can find them.

I hope I dont have to rite to much of these progris riports

because it takes along time and I get to sleep very late and Im tired at werk in the morning. Gimpy hollered at me because I droppd a tray full of rolles I was carrying over to the oven. They got derty and he had to wipe them off before he put them in to bake. Gimpy hollers at me all the time when I do something rong, but he reely likes me because hes my frend. Boy if I get smart wont he be serprised.

progris riport 4

mar 6—I had more crazy tests today in case they use me. That same place but a differnt littel testing room. The nice lady who give it to me tolld me the name and I askd her how do you spell it so I can put it down rite in my progris riport. THEMATIC APPERCEPTION TEST. I dont know the frist 2 werds but I know what test means. You got to pass it or you get bad marks.

This test lookd easy because I coud see the picturs. Only this time she dint want me to tell what I saw in the picturs. That mixd me up. I tolld her yesterday Burt said I shoud tell what I saw in the ink. She said that dont make a difrence because this test is something else. Now you got to make up storys about the pepul in the picturs.

I said how can I tell storys about pepul I dont know. She said make beleeve but I tolld her thats lies. I never tell lies any more because when I was a kid I made lies and I always got hit. I got a pictur in my walet of me and Norma with Uncle Herman who got me the job to be janiter at Donners bakery before he dyed.

I said I coud make storys about them because I livd with Uncle Herman along time but the lady dint want to hear about them. She said this test and the other one the *raw shok* was for getting persinality. I laffd. I tolld her how can you get that thing from cards that sombody spilld ink on and fotos of pepul you dont even no. She lookd angrey and took the picturs away. I dont care.

I gess I faled that test too.

Then I drawed some picturs for her but I dont drawer so good. Later the other testor Burt in the wite coat came back his name is Burt Selden and he took me to a diferent place on

the same 4th floor in the Beekman University that said PSY-
CHOLOGY LABORATORY on the door. Burt said PSYCHOLOGY
means minds and LABORATORY meens a place where they make
spearamints. I thot it ment like where they made the chooing
gum but now I think its puzzels and games because thats what
we did.

I coudnt werk the puzzels so good because it was all broke
and the peices coudnt fit in the holes. One game was a paper
with lines in all derections and lots of boxs. On one side it said
START and on the other end it said FINISH. He told me that
game was *amazed* and I shoud take the pencil and go from
where it said START to where it said FINISH withowt crossing
over any of the lines.

I dint understand the amazed and we used up a lot of papers. Then Burt said look Ill show you something lets go to
the sperimental lab mabye youll get the idea. We went up to
the 5th floor to another room with lots of cages and animils
they had monkys and some mouses. It had a funny smel like
old garbidge. And there was other pepul in wite coats playing
with the animils so I thot it was like a pet store but their wasnt
no customers. Burt took a wite mouse out of the cage and
showd him to me. Burt said thats Algernon and he can do this
amazed very good. I tolld him you show me how he does that.

Well do you know he put Algernon in a box like a big tabel
with alot of twists and terns like all kinds of walls and a START
and a FINISH like the paper had. Only their was a skreen over
the big tabel. And Burt took out his clock and lifted up a slid-
ding door and said lets go Algernon and the mouse sniffd 2 or
3 times and startid to run. First he ran down one long row and
then when he saw he coudnt go no more he came back where
he startid from and he just stood there a minit wiggeling his
wiskers. Then he went off in the other derection and startid to
run again.

It was just like he was doing the same thing Burt wanted
me to do with the lines on the paper. I was laffing because I
thot it was going to be a hard thing for a mouse to do. But
then Algernon kept going all the way threw that thing all the
rite ways till he came out where it said FINISH and he made a
squeek. Burt says that means he was happy because he did the
thing rite.

Boy I said thats a smart mouse. Burt said woud you like to race against Algernon. I said sure and he said he had a differnt kind of amaze made of wood with rows skratched in it and an electrik stick like a pencil. And he coud fix up Algernons amaze to be the same like that one so we could both be doing the same kind.

He moved all the bords around on Algernons tabel because they come apart and he could put them together in differnt ways. And then he put the skreen back on top so Algernon woudnt jump over any rows to get to the FINISH. Then he gave me the electrik stick and showd me how to put it in between the rows and Im not suppose to lift it off the bord just follow the little skratches until the pencil cant move any more or I get a little shock.

He took out his clock and he was trying to hide it. So I tryed not to look at him and that made me very nervus.

When he said go I tryed to go but I dint know where to go. I didnt know the way to take. Then I herd Algernon squeeking from the box on the tabel and his feet skratching like he was runing alredy. I startid to go but I went in the rong way and got stuck and a littel shock in my fingers so I went back to the START but evertime I went a differnt way I got stuck and a shock. It didnt hert or anything just made me jump a littel and Burt said it was to show me I did the wrong thing. I was haffway on the bord when I herd Algernon squeek like he was happy again and that means he won the race.

And the other ten times we did it over Algernon won evry time because I coudnt find the right rows to get to where it says FINISH. I dint feel bad because I watched Algernon and I lernd how to finish the amaze even if it takes me along time.

I dint know mice were so smart.

progris riport 5   mar 6

They found my sister Norma who lives with my mother in Brooklin and she gave permissen for the operashun. So their going to use me. Im so exited I can hardley rite it down. But then Prof Nemur and Dr Strauss had a argament about it frist. I was sitting in Prof Nemurs office when Dr Strauss and Burt

Selden came in. Prof Nemur was worryed about using me but Dr Strauss tolld him I looked like the best one they testid so far. Burt tolld him Miss Kinnian rekemmended me the best from all the people who she was teaching at the center for retarted adults. Where I go.

Dr Strauss said I had something that was very good. He said I had a good motor-vation. I never even knowed I had that. I felt good when he said not everbody with an eye-Q of 68 had that thing like I had it. I dont know what it is or where I got it but he said Algernon had it too. Algernons motor-vation is the chees they put in his box. But it cant be only that because I dint have no chees this week.

Prof Nemur was worryd about my eye-Q getting too high from mine that was too low and I woud get sick from it. And Dr Strauss tolld Prof Nemur somthing I dint understand so wile they was talking I rote down some of the words in my notebook for keeping my progris riports.

He said Harold thats Prof Nemurs frist name I know Charlie is not what you had in mind as the frist of your new breed of intelek** coudnt get the word *** superman. But most people of his low ment** are host** and uncoop** they are usally dull and apathet** and hard to reach. Charlie has a good natcher and hes intristed and eeger to pleese.

Then prof Nemur said remembir he will be the first human beeing ever to have his intelijence increesd by sergery. Dr Strauss said thats exakly what I ment. Where will we find another retarted adult with this tremendus motor-vation to lern. Look how well he has lerned to reed and rite for his low mentel age. A tremen** achev**

I dint get all the werds and they were talking to fast but it sounded like Dr Strauss and Burt was on my side and Prof Nemur wasnt.

Burt kept saying Alice Kinnian feels he has an overwhelm** desir to lern. He aktually beggd to be used. And thats true because I wantid to be smart. Dr Strauss got up and walkd around and said I say we use Charlie. And Burt noded. Prof Nemur skratchd his head and rubbd his nose with his thum and said mabye your rite. We will use Charlie. But weve got to make him understand that a lot of things can go wrong with the experamint.

When he said that I got so happy and exited I jumpd up and shaked his hand for being so good to me. I think he got skared when I did that.

He said Charlie we werked on this for a long time but only on animils like Algernon. We are sure thers no fisical danger for you but there are other things we cant tell untill we try it. I want you to understand this mite fale and then nothing woud happen at all. Or it mite even sucseed temperary and leeve you werse off then you are now. Do you understand what that meens. If that happins we will have to send you bak to the Warren state home to live.

I said I dint care because I aint afraid of nothing. Im very strong and I always do good and beside I got my luky rabits foot and I never breakd a mirrir in my life. I droppd some dishis once but that dont count for bad luk.

Then Dr Strauss said Charlie even if this fales your making a grate contribyushun to sience. This experimint has been sucessful on lots of animils but its never bin tride on a humen beeing. You will be the first.

I told him thanks doc you wont be sorry for giving me my 2nd chanse like Miss Kinnian says. And I meen it like I tolld them. After the operashun Im gonna try to be smart. Im gonna try awful hard.

progris riport 6th Mar 8

Im skared. Lots of pepul who werk at the collidge and the pepul at the medicil school came to wish me luk. Burt the tester brot me some flowers he said they were from the pepul at the psych departmint. He wished me luk. I hope I have luk. I got my rabits foot and my luky penny and my horshoe. Dr Strauss said dont be so superstishus Charlie. This is sience. I dont no what sience is but they all keep saying it so mabye its something that helps you have good luk. Anyway Im keeping my rabits foot in one hand and my luky penny in the other hand with the hole in it. The penny I meen. I wish I coud take the horshoe with me to but its hevy so Ill just leeve it in my jaket.

Joe Carp from the bakery brot me a chokilat cake from Mr Donner and the folks at the bakery and they hope I get better soon. At the bakery they think Im sick becaus thats what Prof

Nemur said I shoud tell them and nothing about an operashun for getting smart. Thats a secrit until after in case it dont werk or something goes wrong.

Then Miss Kinnian came to see me and she brout me some magizenes to reed, and she lookd kind of nervus and skared. She fixd up the flowres on my tabel and put evrything nice and neet not messd up like I made it. And she fixd the pilow under my hed. She likes me alot becaus I try very hard to lern evrything not like some of the pepul at the adult center who dont reely care. She wants me to get smart. I know.

Then Prof Nemur said I cant have any more visiters becaus I got to rest. I askd Prof Nemur if I coud beet Algernon in the race after the operashun and he sayd mabye. If the operashun werks good Ill show that mouse I can be as smart as he is even smarter. Then Ill be abel to reed better and spell the werds good and know lots of things and be like other pepul. Boy that woud serprise everyone. If the operashun werks and I get smart mabye Ill be abel to find my mom and dad and sister and show them. Boy woud they be serprised to see me smart just like them and my sister.

Prof Nemur says if it werks good and its perminent they will make other pepul like me smart also. Mabye pepul all over the werld. And he said that meens Im doing somthing grate for sience and Ill be famus and my name will go down in the books. I dont care so much about beeing famus. I just want to be smart like other pepul so I can have lots of frends who like me.

They dint give me anything to eat today. I dont know what eating got to do with geting smart and Im hungry. Prof Nemur took away my choklate cake. That Prof Nemur is a growch. Dr. Strauss says I can have it back after the operashun. You cant eat before a operashun. Not even cheese.

PROGRESS REPORT 7   MARCH 11

The operashun dint hert. Dr. Strauss did it while I was sleeping. I dont know how because I dint see but there was bandiges on my eyes and my head for 3 days so I coudnt make no PROGRESS REPORT til today. The skinny nerse who wached me riting says I spelld PROGRESS rong and she tolld me how to spell it and REPORT to and MARCH. I got to remembir that. I have a very

bad memary for speling. Anyway they took off the bandiges
from my eyes today so I can make a PROGRESS REPORT now.
But there is still some bandigis on my head.

I was skared when they came in and tolld me it was time to
go for the operashun. They maid me get out of the bed and on
another bed that has weels on it and they rolld me out of the
room and down the hall to the door that says sergery. Boy was
I serprised that it was a big room with green walls and lots of
docters sitting around up high all around the room waching
the operashun. I dint no it was going to be like a show.

A man came up to the tabel all in wite and with a wite cloth
on his face like in TV shows and rubber glovs and he said rilax
Charlie its me Dr Strauss. I said hi doc Im skared. He said
theres nothing to be skared about Charlie he said youll just go
to sleep. I said thats what Im skared about. He patted my head
and then 2 other men waring wite masks too came and straped
my arms and legs down so I coudnt move them and that maid
me very skared and my stomack feeled tite like I was gone to
make all over but I dint only wet a littel and I was gone to cry
but they put a rubber thing on my face for me to breeth in and
it smelld funny. All the time I herd Dr Strauss talking out loud
about the operashun telling evrybody what he was gonna do.
But I dint understand anything about it and I was thinking
mabye after the operashun Ill be smart and Ill understand all
the things hes talking about. So I breethed deep and then I
gess I was very tired becase I went to sleep.

When I waked up I was back in my bed and it was very
dark. I coudnt see nothing but I herd some talking. It was the
nerse and Burt and I said whats the matter why dont you put
on the lites and when are they gonna operate. And they laffed
and Burt said Charlie its all over. And its dark because you got
bandijis over your eyes.

Its a funny thing. They did it while I was sleeping.

Burt comes in to see me evry day to rite down all the things
like my tempertur and my blud preshur and the other things
about me. He says its on acount of the sientific methid. They
got to keep reckerds about what happins so they can do it agen
when they want to. Not to me but to the other pepul like me
who aint smart.

Thats why I got to do these ~~progris~~ *progress reports*. Burt says
its part of the esperimint and they will make fotastats of the ~~rip~~

reports to study them so they will know what is going on in my mind. I dont see how they will know what is going on in my mind by looking at these reports. I read them over and over a lot of times to see what I rote and I dont no whats going on in my mind so how are they going to.

But anyway thats sience and I got to try to be smart like other pepul. Then when I am smart they will talk to me and I can sit with them and listen like Joe Carp and Frank and Gimpy do when they talk and have a discushen about importent things. While their werking they start talking about things like about god or about the truble with all the mony the presedint is spending or about the ripublicans and demicrats. And they get all excited like their gonna have a fite so Mr Donner got to come in and tell them to get back to baking or theyll all get canned union or no union. I want to talk about things like that.

If your smart you can have lots of frends to talk to and you never get lonley by yourself all the time.

Prof Nemur says its ok to tell about all the things that happin to me in the progress reports but he says I shoud rite more about what I feel and what I think and remembir about the past. I tolld him I dont know how to think or remembir and he said just try.

All the time the bandiges were on my eyes I tryed to think and remembir but nothing happined. I dont know what to think or remembir about. Maybe if I ask him he will tell me how I can think now that Im suppose to get smart. What do smart pepul think about or remembir. Fancy things I bet. I wish I new some fancy things alredy.

March 12—I dont have to rite PROGRESS REPORT on top evry day just when I start a new batch after Prof Nemur takes the old ones away. I just have to put the date on top. That saves time. Its a good idea. I can sit up in bed and look out the window at the gras and trees outside. The skinney nerses name is Hilda and she is very good to me. She brings me things to eat and she fixes my bed and she says I was a very brave man to let them do things to my hed. She says she woud never let them do things to her branes for all the tea in china. I tolld her it wasnt for tea in china. It was to make me smart. And she said mabey they got no rite to make me smart because if god wantid me to be smart he would have made me born that way. And what about Adem and Eev and the sin with the tree of nowlege and eating the appel and the fall. And mabey Prof Nemur and Dr Strauss was tampiring with things they got no rite to tampir with.

She's very skinney and when she talks her face gets all red. She says mabey I better prey to god to ask him to forgiv what they done to me. I dint eat no appels or do nothing sinful. And now Im skared. Mabey I shoudnt of let them oparate on my branes like she said if its agenst god. I dont want to make god angrey.

March 13—They changed my nerse today. This one is pritty. Her name is Lucille she showd me how to spell it for my prog-ress report and she got yellow hair and blew eyes. I askd her where was Hilda and she said Hilda wasnt werking in that part of the hospitil no more. Only in the matirnity ward by the babys where it dont matter if she talks too much.

When I askd her about what was matirnity she said its about having babys but when I askd her how they have them she got red in the face just the same like Hilda and she said she got to take sombodys temperchure. Nobody ever tells me about the babys. Mabye if this thing werks and I get smart Ill find out.

Miss Kinnian came to see me today and she said Charlie you look wonderful. I tolld her I feel fine but I dont feel smart yet. I thot that when the operashun was over and they took the bandijis off my eyes Id be smart and no a lot of things so I coud read and talk about importent things like evryebody else.

She said thats not the way it werks Charlie. It comes slowley and you have to werk very hard to get smart.

I dint no that. If I got to werk hard anyway what did I have to have the operashun for. She said she wasnt sure but the operashun was to make it so that when I did werk hard to get smart it woud stick with me and not be like it was before when it dint stick so good.

Well I tolld her that made me kind of feel bad because I thot I was going to be smart rite away and I coud go back to show the guys at the bakery how smart I am and talk with them about things and mabye even get to be an assistint baker. Then I was gone to try and find my mom and dad. They woud be serprised

to see how smart I got because my mom always wanted me too
be smart to. Mabey they woudnt send me away no more if they
see how smart I am. I tolld Miss Kinnian I woud try hard to be
smart as hard as I can. She pattid my hand and said I no you
will. I have fayth in you Charlie.

PROGRESS REPORT 8

March 15—Im out of the hospitil but not back at werk yet.
Nothing is happining. I had lots of tests and differint kinds of
races with Algernon. I hate that mouse. He always beets me.
Prof Nemur says I got to play those games and I got to take
those tests over and over agen.

Those amazes are stoopid. And those picturs are stoopid to.
I like to drawer the picturs of a man and woman but I wont
make up lies about pepul.

And I cant do the puzzels good.

I get headakes from trying to think and remembir so much.
Dr Strauss promised he was going to help me but he dont. He
dont tell me what to think or when Ill get smart. He just makes
me lay down on a couch and talk.

Miss Kinnian comes to see me at the collidge too. I tolld her
nothing was happining. When am I going to get smart. She
said you got to be pashent Charlie these things take time. It
will happin so slowley you wont know its happening. She said
Burt tolld her I was comming along fine.

I still think those races and those tests are stoopid and I
think riting these progress reports are stoopid to.

March 16—I ate lunch with Burt at the collidge resterant. They
got all kinds of good food and I dont have to pay for it neither.
I like to sit and wach the collidge boys and girls. They fool
around somtimes but mostly they talk about all kinds of things
just like the bakers do at Donners bakery. Burt says its about
art and polatics and riligon. I dont know what those things are
about but I know riligon is god. Mom use to tell me all about
him and the things he done to make the world. She said I
shoud always love god and prey to him. I dont remembir how
to prey to him but I think mom use to make me prey to him a

lot when I was a kid that he shoud make me get better and not be sick. I dont rimember how I was sick. I think it was about me not being smart.

Anyway Burt says if the experimint werks Ill be able to understand all those things the studints are talking about and I said do you think Ill be smart like them and he laffed and said those kids arent so smart youll pass them as if their standing still.

He interduced me to alot of the studints and some of them look at me funny like I dont belong in a collidge. I almost forgot and started to tell them I was going to be very smart soon like them but Burt intirupted and he tolld them I was cleaning the psych departmint lab. Later he explaned to me their mussent be any publisity. That meens its a seecrit.

I dont reely understand why I got to keep it a seecrit. Burt says its in case theirs a faleure Prof Nemur dont want everbody to laff espeshully the pepul from the Welberg foundashun who gave him the mony for the projekt. I said I dont care if pepul laff at me. Lots of pepul laff at me and their my frends and we have fun. Burt put his arm on my sholder and said its not you Nemurs worryd about. He dont want pepul to laff at him.

I dint think pepul would laff at Prof Nemur because hes a sientist in a collidge but Bert said no sientist is a grate man to his colleegs and his gradulate studints. Burt is a gradulate studint and he is a majer in *psychology* like the name on the door to the lab. I dint know they had majers in collidge. I thot it was onley in the army.

Anyway I hope I get smart soon because I want to lern everything there is in the werld like the collidge boys know. All about art and politiks and god.

March 17—When I waked up this morning rite away I thot I was gone to be smart but Im not. Evry morning I think Im gone to be smart but nothing happins. Mabye the experimint dint werk. Maby I wont get smart and Ill have to go live at the Warren home. I hate the tests and I hate the amazeds and I hate Algernon.

I never new before that I was dumber than a mouse. I dont feel like riting any more progress reports. I forget things and even when I rite them in my notbook sometimes I cant reed my own riting and its very hard. Miss Kinnian says have pashents but I feel sick and tired. And I get headakes all the time. I want to go back to werk in the bakery and not rite ~~progris~~ *progess* reports any more.

March 20—Im going back to werk at the bakery. Dr Strauss told Prof Nemur it was better I shoud go back to werk but I still cant tell anyone what the operashun was for and I have to come to the lab for 2 hrs evry nite after werk for my tests and keep riting these dumb reports. They are going to pay me evry week like for a part time job because that was part of the arraingment when they got the mony from the Welberg foundashun. I still dont know what that Welberg thing is. Miss Kinnian explaned me but I still dont get it. So if I dint get smart why are they paying me to rite these dumb things. If their gonna pay me Ill do it. But its very hard to rite.

Im glad Im going back to werk because I miss my job at the bakery and all my frends and all the fun we have.

Dr. Strauss says I shoud keep a notbook in my pockit for things I remembir. And I dont have to do the progress reports every day just when I think of somthing or somthing speshul happins. I told him nothing speshul ever happins to me and it dont look like this speshul experimint is going to happin neither. He says dont get discouriged Charlie because it takes a long time and it happins slow and you cant notise it rite away. He explaned how it took a long time with Algernon before he got 3 times smarter then he was before.

Thats why Algernon beats me all the time in that amaze race because he had that operashun too. Hes a speshul mouse the 1st animil to stay smart so long after the operashun. I dint know he was a speshul mouse. That makes it diffrint. I coud probaly do that amazed faster then a reglar mouse. Maybe some day Ill beat Algernon. Boy woud that be somthing. Dr Strauss says that so far Algernon looks like he mite be smart permanint and he says thats a good sine becaus we both had the same kind of operashun.

March 21—We had a lot of fun at the bakery today. Joe Carp said hey look where Charlie had his operashun what did they do Charlie put some brains in. I was going to tell him about me getting smart but I remembered Prof Nemur said no. Then Frank Reilly said what did you do Charlie open a door the hard way. That made me laff. Their my frends and they really like me.

Their is a lot of werk to catch up. They dint have anyone to clean out the place because that was my job but they got a new boy Ernie to do the diliveries that I always done. Mr. Donner said he decided not to fire him for a while to give me a chanse to rest up and not werk so hard. I told him I was alright and I can make my diliveries and clean up like I always done but Mr. Donner says we will keep the boy.

I said so what am I gonna do. And Mr. Donner patted me on the shoulder and says Charlie how old are you. I told him 32 years going on 33 my next brithday. And how long you been here he said. I told him I dint know. He said you came here seventeen years ago. Your Uncle Herman god rest his sole was my best frend. He brout you in here and he askd me to let you werk here and look after you as best I coud. And when he died 2 years later and your mother had you comited to the Warren home I got them to releese you on outside werk placmint. Seventeen years its been Charlie and I want you to know that the bakery bisness is not so good but like I always said you got a job here for the rest of your life. So dont worry about me bringing in somebody to take your place. Youll never have to go back to that Warren home.

I aint worryd only what does he need Ernie for to diliver and werk around here when I was always deliviring the packiges good. He says the boy needs the mony Charlie so Im going to keep him on as an aprentise to lern him to be a baker. You can be his asistent and help him out on diliverys when he needs it.

I never was a asistent before. Ernie is very smart but the other pepul in the bakery dont like him so much. Their all my good frends and we have lots of jokes and laffs here.

Some times somebody will say hey lookit Frank, or Joe or even Gimpy. He really pulled a Charlie Gordon that time. I dont know why they say it but they always laff and I laff too. This morning Gimpy hes the head baker and he has a bad foot and he limps he used my name when he shouted at Ernie because Ernie losst a birthday cake. He said Ernie for godsake you trying to be a Charlie Gordon. I dont know why he said that. I never lost any packiges.

I askd Mr Donner if I coud lern to be an aprentise baker like Ernie. I told him I coud lern it if he gave me a chanse.

Mr Donner looked at me for a long time funny because I gess I dont talk so much most of the time. And Frank herd me and he laffed and laffed until Mr Donner told him to shut up and go tend to his oven. Then Mr Donner said to me theirs lots of time for that Charlie. A bakers werk is very importint and very complikated and you shoudnt worry about things like that.

I wish I coud tell him and all the other people about my real operashun. I wish it woud reely work alredy so I coud get smart like evrybody else.

March 24—Prof Nemur and Dr Strauss came to my room to-night to see why I dont come in to the lab like I am suppose to. I told them I dont want to race with Algernon no more. Prof Nemur said I dont have to for a while but I shoud come in any way. He brout me a presint only it wasnt a presint but just for lend. He said its a teeching mashine that werks like TV. It talks and makes picturs and I got to tern it on just before I go to sleep. I said your kidding. Why shoud I tern on a TV before I go to sleep. But Prof Nemur said if I want to get smart I got to do what he says. So I told him I dint think I was goin to get smart anyway.

Then Dr. Strauss came over and put his hand on my sholder and said Charlie you dont know it yet but your getting smarter all the time. You wont notise it for a while like you dont notise how the hour hand on a clock moves. Thats the way it is with the changes in you. They are happining so slow you cant tell. But we can follow it from the tests and the way you act and talk and your progress reports. He said Charlie youve got to have fayth in us and in yourself. We cant be sure it will be per-manint but we are confidant that soon your going to be a very intellijent young man.

I said okay and Prof Nemur showed me how to werk the TV that reely wasnt a TV. I askd him what did it do. First he lookd sore again because I asked him to explane me and he said I shoud just do what he told me. But Dr Strauss said he shoud explane it to me because I was beginning to questien autho-rety. I dont no what that meens but Prof Nemur looked like he was going to bite his lip off. Then he explaned me very slow that the mashine did lots of things to my mind. Somethings it did just before I fall asleep like teach me things when Im very sleepy and a littel while after I start to fall asleep I still hear the talk even if I dont see the picturs anymore. Other things is at nite its suppose to make me have dreams and remembir things that happened a long time ago when I was a very littel kid.

Its scary.

Oh yes I forgot. I asked Prof Nemur when I can go back to Miss Kinnians class at the adult center and he said soon Miss Kinnian will come to the collidge testing center to teach me speshul. I am glad about that. I dint see her so much ever since the operashun but she is nice.

March 25—That crazy TV kept me up all nite. How can I sleep with something yelling crazy things all night in my ears. And the nutty picturs. Wow. I dont know what it says when Im up so how am I going to know when Im sleeping. I asked Burt about it and he says its ok. He says my branes are lerning just before I got to sleep and that will help me when Miss Kinnian starts my lessons at the testing center. The testing center isnt a hospitil for animils like I thougt before. Its a labortory for sience. I dont know what sience is exept Im helping it with this experimint.

Anyway I dont know about that TV. I think its crazy. If you can get smart when your going to sleep why do pepul go to school. I dont think that thing will werk. I use to watch the late show and the late late show on TV all the time before I went to sleep and it never made me smart. Maybe only certin movies make you smart. Maybe like quizz shows.

March 26—How am I gonna work in the daytime if that thing keeps waking me up at nite. In the middel of the nite I woke up and I coudnt go back to sleep because it kept saying *remembir . . . remembir . . . remembir. . . .* So I think I re-membird something. I dont remembir exackly but it was about Miss Kinnian and the school where I lerned about reading. And how I went their.

A long time ago once I asked Joe Carp how he lerned to read and if I coud lern to read to. He laffed like he always done when I say somthing funny and he says to me Charlie why waste your time they cant put any branes in where there aint none. But Fanny Birden herd me and she askd her cusin who is a collidge studint at Beekman and she told me about the adult center for retarted pepul at the Beekman collidge.

She rote the name down on a paper and Frank laffed and said dont go getting so eddicated that you wont talk to your old frends. I said dont worry I will always keep my old frends even if I can read and rite. He was laffing and Joe Carp was laffing but Gimpy came in and told them to get back to making rolls. They are all good frends to me.

After werk I walked over six blocks to the school and I was scared. I was so happy I was going to lern to read that I bougt a newspaper to take home with me and read after I lerned.

When I got their it was a big long hall with lots of pepul. I got scared of saying somthing wrong to sombody so I startid to go home. But I dont know why I terned around and went inside agen.

I wated until most everbody went away exept some pepul going over by a big timeclock like the one we have at the bakery and I asked the lady if I coud lern to read and rite because I wanted to read all the things in the newspaper and I showed it to her. She was Miss Kinnian but I dint know it then. She said if you come back tomorow and rejister I will start to teach you how to read. But you got to understand it will take a long time maybe years to lern to read. I told her I dint know it took so long but I wantid to lern anyway because I made believe a lot of times. I meen I pretend to pepul I know how to read but it aint true and I wantid to lern.

She shaked my hand and said glad to meet you Mistre Gordon. I will be your teacher. My name is Miss Kinnian. So thats wear I went to lern and thats how I met Miss Kinnian.

Thinking and remembiring is hard and now I dont sleep so good any more. That TV is too loud.

March 27—Now that Im starting to have those dreams and remembiring Prof Nemur says I got to go to theripy sesions with Dr Strauss. He says theripy sesions is like when you feel bad you talk to make it better. I tolld him I dont feel bad and I do plenty of talking all day so why do I have to go to theripy but he got sore and says I got to go anyway.

What theripy is is that I got to lay down on a couch and Dr. Strauss sits in a chair near me and I talk about anything that

comes into my head. For a long time I dint say nothing because I coudnt think of nothing to say. Then I told him about
the bakery and the things they do there. But its silly for me to
go to his office and lay down on the couch to talk because I
rite it down in the progress reports anyway and he could read
it. So today I brout the progress report with me and I told
him maybe he could just read it and I could take a nap on the
couch. I was very tired because that TV kept me up all nite but
he said no it dont work that way. I got to talk. So I talked but
then I fell asleep on the couch anyway—rite in the middle.

March 28—I got a headake. Its not from that TV this time. Dr
Strauss showed me how to keep the TV turned low so now
I can sleep. I dont hear a thing. And I still dont understand
what it says. A few times I play it over in the morning to find
out what I lerned before I fell asleep and while I was sleeping
and I dont even know the words. Maybe its another langwidge
or something. But most times it sounds american. But it talks
too fast.

I askd Dr Strauss what good is it to get smart in my sleep if
I want to be smart when Im awake. He says its the same thing
and I have two minds. Theres the SUBCONSCIOUS *and the* CON-
SCIOUS (thats how you spell it) and one dont tell the other one
what its doing. They dont even talk to each other. Thats why I
dream. And boy have I been having crazy dreams. Wow. Ever
since that night TV. The late late late late late movie show.

I forgot to ask Dr Strauss if it was only me or if everybody
has two minds like that.

(I just looked up the word in the dicshunery Dr Strauss gave
me. SUBCONSCIOUS. *adj. Of the nature of mental operations yet
not present in consciousness; as, subconscious conflict of desires.*)
Theres more but I still dont know what it meens. This isnt a
very good dicshunery for dumb people like me.

Anyway the headake is from the party. Joe Carp and Frank
Reilly invited me to go with them after work to Hallorans Bar
for some drinks. I dont like to drink wiskey but they said we
will have lots of fun. I had a good time. We played games with
me doing a dance on the top of the bar with a lampshade on
my head and everyone laffing.

Then Joe Carp said I shoud show the girls how I mop out

the toilet in the bakery and he got me a mop. I showed them and everyone laffed when I told them that Mr Donner said I was the best janiter and errand boy he ever had because I like my job and do it good and never come late or miss a day exept for my operashun.

I said Miss Kinnian always told me Charlie be proud of the work you do because you do your job good.

Everybody laffed and Frank said that Miss Kinnian must be some cracked up piece if she goes for Charlie and Joe said hey Charlie are you making out with her. I said I dint know what that meens. They gave me lots of drinks and Joe said Charlie is a card when hes potted. I think that means they like me. We have some good times but I cant wait to be smart like my best frends Joe Carp and Frank Reilly.

I dont remember how the party was over but they asked me to go around the corner to see if it was raining and when I came back there was no one their. Maybe they went to find me. I looked for them all over till it was late. But I got lost and I felt bad at myself for getting lost because I bet Algernon coud go up and down those streets a hundrid times and not get lost like I did.

Then I dont remember so good but Mrs Flynn says a nice poleecman brought me back home.

That same nite I dreamed about my mother and father only I coudnt see her face it was all wite and she was blurry. I was crying because we were in a big departmint store and I was losst and I coudnt find them and I ran up and down the rows around all the big cownters in the store. Then a man came and took me in a big room with benches and gave me a lolypop and tolld me a big boy like me shoudnt cry because my mother and father woud come to find me.

Anyway thats the dream and I got a headake and a big lump on my head and black and blue marks all over. Joe Carp says mabye I got rolled or the cop let me have it. I dont think poleecmen do things like that. But anyway I dont think Ill drink wiskey anymore.

March 29—I beet Algernon. I dint even know I beet him until Burt Selden told me. Then the second time I lost because I got so exited. But after that I beet him 8 more times. I must be getting smart to beat a smart mouse like Algernon. But I dont feel smarter.

I wanted to race some more but Burt said thats enough for one day. He let me hold Algernon for a minit. Algernon is a nice mouse. Soft like cotton. He blinks and when he opens his eyes their black and pink on the eges.

I asked can I feed him because I felt bad to beat him and I wanted to be nice and make frends. Burt said no Algernon is a very speshul mouse with an operashun like mine. He was the first of all the animals to stay smart so long and he said that Algernon is so smart he has to solve a problem with a lock that changes every time he goes in to eat so he has to lern something new to get his food. That made me sad because if he coudnt lern he woudnt be able to eat and he woud be hungry.

I dont think its right to make you pass a test to eat. How woud Burt like to have to pass a test every time he wants to eat. I think Ill be frends with Algernon.

That reminds me. Dr Strauss says I shoud write down all my dreams and the things I think so when I come to his office I can tell them. I tolld him I dont know how to think yet but he says he means more things like what I wrote about my mom and dad and about when I started school at Miss Kinnians or anything that happened before the operation is thinking and I wrote them in my progress report.

I didnt know I was thinking and remembering. Maybe that means something is happining to me. I dont feel different but Im so exited I cant sleep.

Dr Strauss gave me some pink pills to make me sleep good. He says I got to get lots of sleep because thats when most of the changes happin in my brane. It must be true because Uncle Herman use to sleep in our house all the time when he was out of werk on the old sofa in the parler. He was fat and it was hard for him to get a job because he use to paint pepuls houses and he got very slow going up and down the ladder.

When I once tolld my mom I wantid to be a painter like Uncle Herman my sister Norma said yeah Charlies going to be the artist of the family. And dad slappd her face and tolld her not to be so goddam nasty to her brother. I dont no what a artist is but if Norma got slappd for saying it I gess its not a nice thing. I always feeled bad when Norma got slappd for beeing meen to me. When I get smart Ill go visit her.

March 30—Tonite after werk Miss Kinnian came to the teeching room near the labatory. She looked glad to see me but nervus. She looks yunger then I remembired her. I tolld her I was trying very hard to be smart. She said I have confidense in you Charlie the way you strugled so much to reed and rite better then all the others. I know you can do it. At werst you will have it all for a little wile and your doing somthing for other retarded pepul.

We startid to reed a very hard book. I never red such a hard book before. Its called Robinson Crusoe about a man who gets merooned on a dessert iland. Hes smart and figgers out all kinds of things so he can have a house and food and hes a good swimmer. Only I feel sorry for him because hes all alone and he has no frends. But I think their must be sombody else on the iland because theres a picture of him with his funny umbrela looking at feetprints. I hope he gets a frend and not be so lonely.

March 31—Miss Kinnian teeches me how to spel better. She says look at a werd and close your eyes and say it over and over again until you remember. I have lots of truble with *through* that you say THREW and *enough* and *tough* that you dont say ENEW and TEW. You got to say ENUFF and TUFF. Thats how I use to rite it before I started to get smart. Im mixd up but Miss Kinnian says dont worry spelling is not suppose to make sence.

PROGRESS REPORT 9

April 1—Everbody in the bakery came to see me today where I started my new job working by the dough-mixer. It happined like this. Oliver who works on the mixer quit yesterday. I use to help him out before bringing the bags of flour over for him to put in the mixer. Anyway I dint know that I knew how to work the mixer. Its very hard and Oliver went to bakers school for one year before he could learn how to be an assistint baker.

But Joe Carp hes my friend he said Charlie why dont you take over Olivers job. Everybody on the floor came around and they were ~~laff~~ *laughing* and Frank Reilly said yes Charlie you been here long ~~enuff~~ *enough*. Go ahead. Gimpy aint around and he wont know you tryed it. I was scared because Gimpy is the head baker and he told me never to go near the mixer because I would get hurt. Everyone said do it exept Fannie Birden who said stop it why dont you leave the poor man alone.

Frank Reilly said shut up Fanny its April fools day and if Charlie works on the mixer he might fix it good so we will all have the day off. I said I coudnt fix the mashine but I could work it because I been watching Oliver ever since I got back.

I worked the dough-mixer and everybody was surprised es-peshully Frank Reilly. Fanny Birden got exited because she said it took Oliver 2 years to learn how to mix the dough right and he went to bakers school. Bernie Bates who helps on the mashine said I did it faster then Oliver did and better. Nobody laffed. When Gimpy came back and Fanny told him he got sore at me for working on the mixer.

But she said watch him and see how he does it. They were playing him for an April Fool joke and he foold them instead. Gimpy watched and I knew he was sore at me because he dont like when people dont do what he tells them just like Prof Nemur. But he saw how I worked the mixer and he skratched his head and said I see it but I dont believe it. Then he called Mr Donner and told me to work it again so Mr Donner could see it.

I was scared he was going to be angry and holler at me so after I was finished I said can I go back to my own job now. I got to sweep out the front of the bakery behind the counter. Mr Donner looked at me funny for a long time. Then he said this must be some kind of April fools joke you guys are playing on me. Whats the catch.

Gimpy said thats what I thought it was some kind of a gag. He limped all around the mashine and he said to Mr Donner I dont understand it either but Charlie knows how to handle it and I got to admit it he does a better job then Oliver.

Everybody was crowded around and talking about it and I got scared because they all looked at me funny and they were exited. Frank said I told you there is something peculier lately about Charlie. And Joe Carp says yeah I know what you mean. Mr Donner sent everybody back to work and he took me out to the front of the store with him.

He said Charlie I dont know how you done it but it looks like you finally learned something. I want you to be carefull

and do the best you can do. You got yourself a new job with a
5 doller raise.

I said I dont want a new job because I like to clean up and
sweep and deliver and do things for my friends but Mr Donner
said never mind your friends I need you for this job. I dont
think much of a man who dont want to advance.

I said whats advance mean. He scratched his head and looked
at me over his glasses. Never mind that Charlie. From now on
you work that mixer. Thats advance.

So now instead of delivering packiges and washing out the
toilets and dumping the garbage. Im the new mixer. Thats advance. Tomorrow I will tell Miss Kinnian. I think she will be
happy but I dont know why Frank and Joe are mad at me. I
asked Fanny and she said never mind those fools. This is April
Fools day and the joke backfired and made them the fools instead of you.

I asked Joe to tell me what was the joke that backfired and
he said go jump in the lake. I guess their mad at me because
I worked the mashine but they didnt get the day off like they
thought. Does that mean Im getting smarter.

April 3—Finished Robinson Crusoe. I want to find out more
about what happens to him but Miss Kinnian says thats all
there is. WHY.

April 4—Miss Kinnian says Im learning fast. She read some of
my progress reports and she looked at me kind of funny. She
says Im a fine person and Ill show them all. I asked her why.
She said never mind but I shouldnt feel bad if I find out that
everybody isnt nice like I think. She said for a person who God
gave so little to you did more than a lot of people with brains
they never even used. I said that all my friends are smart people
and their good. They like me and they never did anything that
wasnt nice. Then she got something in her eye and she had to
run out to the ladys room.

While I was sitting in the teaching room waiting for her I
was wondering about how Miss Kinnian was a nice lady like my
mother use to be. I think I remember my mother told me to be
good and always be freindly to people. She said but always be
careful because some people dont understand and they might
think you are trying to make trouble.

That makes me remember when mom had to go away and they put me to stay in Mrs Leroys house who lived next door. Mom went to the hospital. Dad said she wasnt sick or nothing but she went to the hospital to bring me back a baby sister or a brother. (I still dont know how they do that) I told them I want a baby brother to play with and I dont know why they got me a sister instead but she was nice like a doll. Only she cryd all the time.

I never hurt her or nothing.

They put her in a crib in their room and once I heard Dad say dont worry Charlie wouldnt harm her.

She was like a bundle all pink and screaming sometimes that I couldnt sleep. And when I went to sleep she woke me up in the nighttime. One time when they were in the kitchen and I was in my bed she was crying. I got up to pick her up and hold her to get quiet the way mom does. But then Mom came in yelling and took her away. And she slapped me so hard I fell on the bed.

Then she startid screaming. Dont you ever touch her again. Youll hurt her. Shes a baby. You got no business touching her. I dint know it then but I guess I know it now that she thought I was going to hurt the baby because I was too dumb to know what I was doing. Now that makes me feel bad because I would never of hurt the baby.

When I go to Dr Straus office I got to tell him about that.

April 6—Today, I learned, the *comma*, this is, a, comma (,) a period, with, a tail, Miss Kinnian, says its, importent, because, it makes writing, better, she said, somebody, could lose, a lot, of money, if a comma, isnt in, the right, place, I got, some money, that I, saved from, my job, and what, the foundation, pays me, but not, much and, I dont, see how, a comma, keeps, you from, losing it,

But, she says, everybody, uses commas, so Ill, use them, too,,,,

April 7—I used the comma wrong. Its *punctuation*. Miss Kinnian told me to look up long words in the dictionary to learn to spell them. I said whats the difference if you can read it anyway. She said its part of your education so from now on Ill look up all the words Im not sure how to spell. It takes a long time to write that way but I think Im remembering more and more.

Anyway thats how come I got the word *punctuation* right. Its that way in the dictionary. Miss Kinnian says a period is punctuation too, and there are lots of other marks to learn. I told her I thought she meant all the periods had to have tails and be called commas. But she said no.

She said; You, got. to-mix?them!up: She showd? me" how, to mix! them; up, and now! I can. mix(up all? kinds of punctuation — in, my. writing! There" are lots, of rules; to learn? but. Im' get'ting them in my head:

One thing? I, like: about, Dear Miss Kinnian: (thats, the way? it goes; in a business, letter (if I ever go! into business?) is that, she: always; gives me' a reason" when—I ask. She"s a gen'ius! I wish? I cou'd be smart-like-her;

Punctuation, is? fun!

April 8—What a dope I am! I didn't even understand what she was talking about. I read the grammar book last night and it explains the whole thing. Then I saw it was the same way as Miss Kinnian was trying to tell me, but I didn't get it. I got up in the middle of the night and the whole thing straightened out in my mind.

Miss Kinnian said that the TV working, just before I fell asleep and during the night, helped out. She said I reached a *plateau.* That's like the flat top of a hill.

After I figured out how punctuation worked, I read over all my old progress reports from the beginning. Boy, did I have crazy spelling and punctuation! I told Miss Kinnian I ought to go over the pages and fix all the mistakes, but she said, "No, Charlie, Professor Nemur wants them just as they are. That's why he lets you keep them after they're photostated—to see your own progress. You're coming along fast, Charlie."

That made me feel good. After the lesson I went down and played with Algernon. We don't race any more.

April 10—I feel sick. Not like for a doctor, but inside my chest it feels empty, like getting punched and a heartburn at the same time.

I wasn't going to write about it, but I guess I got to, because it's important. Today was the first day I ever stayed home from work on purpose.

Last night Joe Carp and Frank Reilly invited me to a party. There were lots of girls and Gimpy was there and Ernie too. I remembered how sick I got last time I drank too much, so I told Joe I didn't want to drink anything. He gave me a plain coke instead. It tasted funny, but I thought it was just a bad taste in my mouth.

We had a lot of fun for a while.

"Dance with Ellen," Joe said. "She'll teach you the steps." Then he winked at her like he had something in his eye.

She said, "Why don't you leave him alone?"

He slapped me on the back. "This is Charlie Gordon, my buddy, my pal. He's no ordinary guy—he's been promoted to working on the dough-mixing machine. All I did was ask you to dance with him and give him a good time. What's wrong with that?"

He pushed me up close against her. So she danced with me. I fell three times and I couldn't understand why because no one else was dancing besides Ellen and me. And all the time I was tripping because somebody's foot was always sticking out.

They were all around in a circle watching and laughing at the way we were doing the steps. They laughed harder every time I fell, and I was laughing too because it was so funny. But the last time it happened I didn't laugh. I picked myself up and Joe pushed me down again.

Then I saw the look on Joe's face and it gave me a funny feeling in my stomach.

"He's a scream," one of the girls said. Everybody was laughing.

"Oh, you were right, Frank," choked Ellen. "He's a one man side show." Then she said, "Here, Charlie, have a fruit." She gave me an apple, but when I bit into it, it was fake.

Then Frank started laughing and he said, "I told ya he'd eat it. C'n you imagine anyone dumb enough to eat wax fruit?"

Joe said, "I ain't laughed so much since we sent him around the corner to see if it was raining that night we ditched him at Halloran's."

Then I saw a picture that I remembered in my mind when I

was a kid and the children in the block let me play with them, hide-and-go-seek and I was IT. After I counted up to ten over and over on my fingers I went to look for the others. I kept looking until it got cold and dark and I had to go home.

But I never found them and I never knew why.

What Frank said reminded me. That was the same thing that happened at Halloran's. And that was what Joe and the rest of them were doing. Laughing at me. And the kids playing hide-and-go-seek were playing tricks on me and they were laughing at me too.

The people at the party were a bunch of blurred faces all looking down and laughing at me.

"Look at him. His face is red."

"He's blushing. Charlie's blushing."

"Hey, Ellen, what'd you do to Charlie? I never saw him act like this before."

"Boy, Ellen sure got him worked up."

I didn't know what to do or where to turn. Her rubbing up against me made me feel funny. Everyone was laughing at me and all of a sudden I felt naked. I wanted to hide myself so they wouldn't see. I ran out of the apartment. It was a large apartment house with lots of halls and I couldn't find my way to the staircase. I forgot all about the elevator. Then, after, I found the stairs and ran out into the street and walked for a long time before I went to my room. I never knew before that Joe and Frank and the others liked to have me around just to make fun of me.

Now I know what they mean when they say "to pull a Charlie Gordon."

I'm ashamed.

And another thing. I dreamed about that girl Ellen dancing and rubbing up against me and when I woke up the sheets were wet and messy.

April 13—Still didn't go back to work at the bakery. I told Mrs. Flynn, my landlady, to call and tell Mr. Donner I'm sick. Mrs. Flynn looks at me lately like she's scared of me.

I think it's a good thing about finding out how everybody laughs at me. I thought about it a lot. It's because I'm so dumb and I don't even know when I'm doing something dumb.

People think it's funny when a dumb person can't do things the same way they can.

Anyway, now I know I'm getting a little smarter every day. I know punctuation, and I can spell good. I like to look up all the hard words in the dictionary and I remember them. And I try to write these progress reports very careful but that's hard to do. I am reading a lot now, and Miss Kinnian says I read very fast. And I even understand a lot of the things I'm reading about, and they stay in my mind. There are times when I can close my eyes and think of a page and it all comes back like a picture.

But other things come into my head too. Sometimes I close my eyes and I see a clear picture. Like this morning just after I woke up, I was laying in bed with my eyes open. It was like a big hole opened up in the walls of my mind and I can just walk through. I think its far back . . . a long time ago when I first started working at Donner's Bakery. I see the street where the bakery is. Fuzzy at first and then it gets patchy with some things so real they are right here now in front of me, and other things stay blurred, and I'm not sure. . . .

A little old man with a baby carriage made into a pushcart with a charcoal burner, and the smell of roasting chestnuts, and snow on the ground. A young fellow, skinny with wide eyes and a scared look on his face looking up at the store sign. What does it say? Blurred letters in a way that don't make sense. I know *now* that the sign says DONNER'S BAKERY, but looking back in my memory at the sign I can't read the words through his eyes. None of the signs make sense. I think that fellow with the scared look on his face is me.

Bright neon lights. Christmas trees and sidewalk peddlers. People bundled in coats with collars up and scarves around their necks. But he has no gloves. His hands are cold and he puts down a heavy bundle of brown paper bags. He's stopping to watch the little mechanical toys that the peddler winds up —the tumbling bear, the dog jumping, the seal spinning a ball on its nose. Tumbling, jumping, spinning. If he had those toys for himself he would be the happiest person in the world.

He wants to ask the red-faced peddler, with his fingers sticking through the brown cotton gloves, if he can hold the tumbling bear for a minute, but he is afraid. He picks up the bundle of paper bags and puts it on his shoulder. He is skinny but he is strong from many years of hard work.

"Charlie! Charlie! . . . fat head barley!"

Children circle around him laughing and teasing him like little dogs snapping at his feet. Charlie smiles at them. He would like to put down his bundle and play games with them, but when he thinks about it the skin on his back twitches and he feels the way the older boys throw things at him.

Coming back to the bakery he sees some boys standing in the door of a dark hallway.

"Hey look, there's Charlie!"

"Hey, Charlie. What you got there? Want to shoot some craps?"

"C'mere. We won't hurtya."

But there is something about the doorway—the dark hall, the laughing, that makes his skin twitch again. He tries to know what it is but all he can remember is their dirt and piss all over his clothes, and Uncle Herman shouting when he came home all covered with filth, and how Uncle Herman ran out with a hammer in his hand to find the boys who did that to him. Charlie backs away from the boys laughing in the hallway, drops the bundle. Picks it up again and runs the rest of the way to the bakery.

"What took you so long, Charlie?" shouts Gimpy from the doorway to the back of the bakery.

Charlie pushes through the swinging doors to the back of the bakery and sets down the bundle on one of the skids. He leans against the wall shoving his hands into his pockets. He wishes he had his spinner.

He likes it back here in the bakery where the floors are white with flour—whiter than the sooty walls and ceiling. The thick soles of his own high shoes are crusted with white and there is white in the stitching and lace-eyes, and under his nails and in the cracked chapped skin of his hands.

He relaxes here—squatting against the wall—leaning back in a way that tilts his baseball cap with the *D* forward over his eyes. He likes the smell of flour, sweet dough, bread and cakes and rolls baking. The oven is crackling and makes him sleepy.

Sweet . . . warm . . . sleep . . .

Suddenly, falling, twisting, head hitting against the wall. Someone has kicked his legs out from under him.

That's all I can remember. I can see it all clearly, but I don't know why it happened. It's like when I used to go to the movies. The first time I never understood because they went too fast but after I saw the picture three or four times I used to understand what they were saying. I've got to ask Dr. Strauss about it.

April 14—Dr. Strauss says the important thing is to keep recalling memories like the one I had yesterday and to write them down. Then when I come into his office we can talk about them.

Dr. Strauss is a psychiatrist and a neurosurgeon. I didn't know that. I thought he was just a plain doctor. But when I went to his office this morning, he told me about how important it is for me to learn about myself so that I can understand my problems. I said I didn't have any problems.

He laughed and then he got up from his chair and went to the window. "The more intelligent you become the more problems you'll have, Charlie. Your intellectual growth is going to outstrip your emotional growth. And I think you'll find that as you progress, there will be many things you'll want to talk to me about. I just want you to remember that this is the place for you to come when you need help."

I still don't know what it's all about, but he said even if I don't understand my dreams or memories or why I have them, some time in the future they're all going to connect up, and I'll learn more about myself. He said the important thing is to find out what those people in my memories are saying. It's all about me when I was a boy and I've got to remember what happened.

I never knew about these things before. It's like if I get intelligent enough I'll understand all the words in my mind, and I'll know about those boys standing in the hallway, and about my Uncle Herman and my parents. But what he means is then I'm going to feel bad about it all and I might get sick in my mind.

So I've got to come into his office twice a week now to talk about the things that bother me. We just sit there, and I talk, and Dr. Strauss listens. It's called therapy, and that means talking about things will make me feel better. I told him one of the things that bothers me is about women. Like dancing with that girl Ellen got me all excited. So we talked about it and I got a funny feeling while I was talking, cold and sweaty, and a buzzing inside my head and I thought I was going to throw up. Maybe because I always thought it was dirty and bad to talk about that. But Dr. Strauss said what happened to me after the party was a wet dream, and it's a natural thing that happens to boys.

So even if I'm getting intelligent and learning a lot of new things, he thinks I'm still a boy about women. It's confusing, but I'm going to find out all about my life.

April 15—I'm reading a lot these days and almost everything is staying in my mind. Besides history and geography and arithmetic, Miss Kinnian says I should start learning foreign languages. Prof. Nemur gave me some more tapes to play while I sleep. I still don't know how the conscious and unconscious mind works, but Dr. Strauss says not to worry yet. He made me promise that when I start learning college subjects in a couple of weeks I won't read any books on psychology—that is, until he gives me permission. He says it will confuse me and make me think about psychological theories instead of about my own ideas and feelings. But it's okay to read novels. This week I read *The Great Gatsby*, *An American Tragedy*, and *Look Homeward, Angel*. I never knew about men and women doing things like that.

April 16—I feel a lot better today, but I'm still angry that all the time people were laughing and making fun of me. When I become intelligent the way Prof. Nemur says, with much more than twice my I.Q. of 70, then maybe people will like me and be my friends.

I'm not sure what I.Q. is anyway. Prof. Nemur said it was something that measured how intelligent you were—like a scale in the drugstore weighs pounds. But Dr. Strauss had a big argument with him and said an I.Q. didn't *weigh* intelligence at all. He said an I.Q. showed how much intelligence you could get, like the numbers on the outside of a measuring cup. You still had to fill the cup up with stuff.

When I asked Burt Seldon, who gives me my intelligence tests and works with Algernon, he said that some people would say both of them were wrong and according to the things he's been reading up on, the I.Q. measures a lot of different things including some of the things you learned already and it really isn't a good measure of intelligence at all.

So I still don't know what I.Q. is, and everybody says it's something different. Mine is about a hundred now, and it's going to be over a hundred and fifty soon, but they'll still have to fill me up with the stuff. I didn't want to say anything, but I don't see how if they don't know *what* it is, or *where* it is—how they know *how much* of it you've got.

Prof Nemur says I have to take a *Rorschach Test* the day after tomorrow. I wonder what that is.

April 17—I had a nightmare last night, and this morning, after I woke up, I free-associated the way Dr. Strauss told me to do when I remember my dreams. Think about the dream and just let my mind wander until other thoughts come up in my mind. I keep on doing that until my mind goes blank. Dr. Strauss says that it means I've reached a point where my subconscious is trying to block my conscious from remembering. It's a wall between the present and the past. Sometimes the wall stays up and sometimes it breaks down and I can remember what's behind it.

Like this morning.

The dream was about Miss Kinnian reading my progress reports. In the dream I sit down to write but I can't write or read any more. It's all gone. I get frightened so I ask Gimpy at the bakery to write for me. But when Miss Kinnian reads the report she gets angry and tears the pages up because they've got dirty words in them.

When I get home Prof. Nemur and Dr. Strauss are waiting for me and they give me a beating for writing dirty things in the progress report. When they leave me I pick up the torn pages but they turn into lace valentines with blood all over them.

It was a horrible dream but I got out of bed and wrote it all down and then I started to free associate.

Bakery . . . baking . . . the urn . . . someone kicking me . . . fall down . . . bloody all over . . . writing . . . . . . big pencil on a red valentine . . . a little gold heart . . . a locket . . . a chain . . . all covered with blood . . . and he's laughing at me . . .

The chain is from a locket . . . spinning around . . . flashing the sunlight into my eyes. And I like to watch it spin . . . watch the chain . . . all bunched up and twisting and spinning . . . and a little girl is watching me.

Her name is Miss Kin—I mean Harriet.

"Harriet . . . Harriet . . . we all love Harriet."

And then there's nothing. It's blank again.

Miss Kinnian reading my progress reports over my shoulder.

Then we're at the Adult Center for the Retarded, and she's reading over my shoulder as I write my ~~composishuns~~ *compositions.*

School changes into P.S. 13 and I'm eleven years old and Miss Kinnian is eleven years old too, but now she's not Miss Kinnian. She's a little girl with dimples and long curls and her name is Harriet. We all love Harriet. It's Valentines Day.

I remember . . .

I remember what happened at P.S. 13 and why they had to change my school and send me to P.S. 222. It was because of Harriet.

I see Charlie—eleven years old. He has a little gold-color locket he once found in the street. There's no chain, but he has it on a string, and he likes to twirl the locket so that it bunches up the string, and then watch it unwind, spinning around with the sun flicking into his eyes.

Sometimes when the kids play catch they let him play in the middle and he tries to get the ball before one of them catches it. He likes to be in the middle—even if he never catches the ball—and once when Hymie Roth dropped the ball by mistake and he picked it up they wouldn't let him throw it but he had to go in the middle again.

When Harriet passes by, the boys stop playing and look at her. All the boys love Harriet. When she shakes her head her curls bounce up and down, and she has dimples. Charlie doesn't know why they make such a fuss about a girl and why they always want to talk to her (he'd rather play ball or kick-the-can, or ringo-levio than talk to a girl) but all the boys are in love with Harriet so he is in love with her too.

She never teases him like the other kids, and he does tricks for her. He walks on the desks when the teacher isn't there. He throws erasers out the window, scribbles all over the blackboard and walls. And Harriet always screeches and giggles, "Oh, lookit Charlie. Ain't he funny? Oh, ain't he silly?"

It's Valentine's Day, and the boys are talking about valentines they're going to give Harriet, so Charlie says, "I'm gonna give Harriet a valentime too."

They laugh and Barry says, "Where you gonna get a valentime?"

"I'm gonna get her a pretty one. You'll see."

But he doesn't have any money for a valentine, so he decides to give Harriet his locket that is heart-shaped like the valentines in the store windows. That night he takes tissue paper from his mother's drawer, and it takes a long time to wrap and tie it with a piece of red ribbon. Then he takes it to Hymie Roth the next day during lunch period in school and asks Hymie to write on the paper for him.

He tells Hymie to write: *"Dear Harriet, I think you are the most prettiest girl in the whole world. I like you very much and I love you. I want you to be my valentime. Your friend, Charlie Gordon."*

Hymie prints very carefully in large letters on the paper, laughing all the time, and he tells Charlie, "Boy, this will knock her eyes out. Wait'll she sees this."

Charlie is scared, but he wants to give Harriet that locket, so he follows her home from school and waits until she goes into her house. Then he sneaks into the hall and hangs the package on the inside of the doorknob. He rings the bell twice and runs across the street to hide behind the tree.

When Harriet comes down she looks around to see who rang the bell. Then she sees the package. She takes it and goes upstairs. Charlie goes home from school and he gets a spanking because he took the tissue paper and ribbon out of his mother's drawer without telling her. But he doesn't care. Tomorrow

Harriet will wear the locket and tell all the boys he gave it to her. Then they'll see.

The next day he runs all the way to school, but it's too early. Harriet isn't there yet, and he's excited.

But when Harriet comes in she doesn't even look at him. She isn't wearing the locket. And she looks sore.

He does all kinds of things when Mrs. Janson isn't watching: He makes funny faces. He laughs out loud. He stands up on his seat and wiggles his fanny. He even throws a piece of chalk at Harold. But Harriet doesn't look at him even once. Maybe she forgot. Maybe she'll wear it tomorrow. She passes by in the hallway, but when he comes over to ask her she pushes past him without saying a word.

Down in the schoolyard her two big brothers are waiting for him.

Gus pushes him. "You little bastard, did you write this dirty note to my sister?"

Charlie says he didn't write any dirty notes. "I just gave her a valentime."

Oscar who was on the football team before he graduated from high school grabs Charlie's shirt and tears off two buttons. "You keep away from my kid sister, you degenate. You don't belong in this school anyway."

He pushes Charlie over to Gus who catches him by the throat. Charlie is scared and starts to cry.

Then they start to hurt him. Oscar punches him in the nose, and Gus knocks him on the ground and kicks him in the side and then both of them kick him, one and then the other, and some of the other kids in the yard—Charlie's friends—come running screaming and clapping hands: "Fight! Fight! They're beating up Charlie!"

His clothes are torn and his nose is bleeding and one of his teeth is broken, and after Gus and Oscar go away he sits on the sidewalk and cries. The blood tastes sour. The other kids just laugh and shout: "Charlie got a licking! Charlie got a licking!" And then Mr. Wagner, one of the caretakers from the school, comes and chases them away. He takes Charlie into the boys' room and tells him to wash off the blood and dirt from his face and hands before he goes back home. . . .

I guess I was pretty dumb because I believed what people told me. I shouldn't have trusted Hymie or anyone.

I never remembered any of this before today, but it came back to me after I thought about the dream. It has something to do with the feeling about Miss Kinnian reading my progress reports. Anyway, I'm glad now I don't have to ask anyone to write things for me. Now I can do it for myself.

But I just realized something. Harriet never gave me back my locket.

April 18—I found out what a Rorschach is. It's the test with the inkblots, the one I took before the operation. As soon as I saw what it was, I got frightened. I knew Burt was going to ask me to find the pictures, and I knew I wouldn't be able to. I was thinking, if only there was some way of knowing what kind of pictures were hidden there. Maybe there weren't any pictures at all. Maybe it was just a trick to see if I was dumb enough to look for something that wasn't there. Just thinking about it made me sore at him.

"All right, Charlie," he said, "you've seen these cards before, remember?"

"Of course, I remember."

The way I said it, he knew I was angry, and he looked up at me surprised.

"Anything wrong, Charlie?"

"No, nothing's wrong. Those inkblots upset me."

He smiled and shook his head. "Nothing to be upset about. This is just one of the standard personality tests. Now I want you to look at this card. What might this be? What do you see on this card? People see all sorts of things in these inkblots. Tell me what it might be for you—what it makes you think of."

I was shocked. I stared at the card and then at him. That wasn't what I had expected him to say at all. "You mean there are no pictures hidden in those inkblots?"

Burt frowned and took off his glasses. "What?"

"Pictures! Hidden in the inkblots! Last time you told me that everyone could see them and you wanted me to find them too."

"No, Charlie. I couldn't have said that."

"What do you mean?" I shouted at him. Being so afraid of the inkblots had made me angry at myself and at Burt too. "That's what you said to me. Just because you're smart enough to go to college doesn't mean you have to make fun of me. I'm sick and tired of everybody laughing at me."

I don't recall ever being so angry before. I don't think it was at Burt himself, but suddenly everything exploded. I tossed the Rorschach cards on the table and walked out. Professor Nemur was passing by in the hall, and when I rushed past him without saying hello he knew something was wrong. He and Burt caught up with me as I was about to go down in the elevator.

"Charlie," said Nemur, grabbing my arm. "Wait a minute. What is this all about?"

I shook free and nodded at Burt. "I'm sick and tired of people making fun of me. That's all. Maybe before I didn't know any better, but now I do, and I don't like it."

"Nobody's making fun of you here, Charlie," said Nemur.

"What about the inkblots? Last time Burt told me there were pictures in the ink—that everyone could see, and I—"

"Look, Charlie, would you like to hear the exact words Burt said to you, and your answers as well? We have a tape-recording of that testing session. We can replay it and let you hear exactly what was said."

I went back with them to the psych office with mixed feelings. I was sure they had made fun of me and tricked me when I was too ignorant to know better. My anger was an exciting feeling, and I didn't give it up easily. I was ready to fight.

As Nemur went to the files to get the tape, Burt explained: "Last time, I used almost the exact words I used today. It's a requirement of these tests that the procedure be the same each time it's administered."

"I'll believe that when I hear it."

A look passed between them. I felt the blood rush to my face again. They were laughing at me. But then I realized what I had just said, and hearing myself I understood the reason for the look. They weren't laughing. They knew what was happening to me. I had reached a new level, and anger and suspicion were my first reactions to the world around me.

Burt's voice boomed over the tape recorder:

"Now I want you to look at this card, Charlie. What might this be? What do you see on this card? People see all kinds of things in these inkblots. Tell me what it makes you think of . . ."

The same words, almost the same tone of voice he had used minutes ago in the lab. And then I heard my answers—childish, impossible things. And I dropped limply into the chair beside Professor Nemur's desk. "Was that really me?"

I went back to the lab with Burt, and we went on with the Rorschach. We went through the cards slowly. This time my responses were different. I "saw" things in the inkblots. A pair of bats tugging at each other. Two men fencing with swords. I imagined all sorts of things. But even so, I found myself not trusting Burt completely any more. I kept turning the cards around, checking the backs to see if there was anything there I was supposed to catch.

I peeked, while he was making his notes. But it was all in code that looked like this:

WF + A DdF-Ad orig. WF – A SF + obj

The test still doesn't make sense. It seems to me that anyone could make up lies about things he didn't really see. How could they know I wasn't making fools of them by saying things I didn't really imagine?

Maybe I'll understand it when Dr. Strauss lets me read up on psychology. It's getting harder for me to write down all my thoughts and feelings because I know that people are reading them. Maybe it would be better if I could keep some of these reports private for a while. I'm going to ask Dr. Strauss. Why should it suddenly start to bother me?

PROGRESS REPORT 10

April 21—I figured out a new way to set up the mixing machines in the bakery to speed up production. Mr. Donner says he will save labor costs and increase profits. He gave me a fifty-dollar bonus and a ten-dollar-a-week raise.

I wanted to take Joe Carp and Frank Reilly out to lunch to celebrate, but Joe had to buy some things for his wife, and

Frank was meeting his cousin for lunch. I guess it will take time for them to get used to the changes in me.

Everyone seems frightened of me. When I went over to Gimpy and tapped him on the shoulder to ask him something, he jumped up and dropped his cup of coffee all over himself. He stares at me when he thinks I'm not looking. Nobody at the place talks to me any more, or kids around the way they used to. It makes the job kind of lonely.

Thinking about it makes me remember the time I fell asleep standing up and Frank kicked my legs out from under me. The warm sweet smell, the white walls, the roar of the oven when Frank opens the door to shift the loaves.

Suddenly falling . . . twisting . . . everything out from under me and my head cracking against the wall.

It's me, and yet it's like someone else lying there—another Charlie. He's confused . . . rubbing his head . . . staring up at Frank, tall and thin, and then at Gimpy nearby, massive, hairy, gray-faced Gimpy with bushy eyebrows that almost hide his blue eyes.

"Leave the kid alone," says Gimp. "Jesus, Frank, why do you always gotta pick on him?"

"It don't mean nothing," laughs Frank. "It don't hurt him. He don't know any better. Do you, Charlie?"

Charlie rubs his head and cringes. He doesn't know what he's done to deserve this punishment, but there is always the chance that there will be more.

"But you know better," says Gimpy, clumping over on his orthopedic boot, "so what the hell you always picking on him for?" The two men sit down at the long table, the tall Frank and the heavy Gimp shaping the dough for the rolls that have to be baked for the evening orders.

They work in silence for a while, and then Frank stops and tips his white cap back. "Hey, Gimp, think Charlie could learn to bake rolls?"

Gimp leans an elbow on the worktable. "Why don't we just leave him alone?"

"No, I mean it, Gimp—seriously. I bet he could learn something simple like making rolls."

The idea seems to appeal to Gimpy who turns to stare at

Charlie. "Maybe you got something there. Hey, Charlie, come here a minute."

As he usually does when people are talking about him, Charlie has been keeping his head down, staring at his shoelaces. He knows how to lace and tie them. He could make rolls. He could learn to pound, roll, twist and shape the dough into the small round forms.

Frank looks at him uncertainly. "Maybe we shouldn't, Gimp. Maybe it's wrong. If a moron can't learn maybe we shouldn't start anything with him."

"You leave this to me," says Gimpy who has now taken over Frank's idea. "I think maybe he can learn. Now listen, Charlie. You want to learn something? You want me to teach you how to make rolls like me and Frank are doing?"

Charlie stares at him, the smile melting from his face. He understands what Gimpy wants, and he feels cornered. He wants to please Gimpy, but there is something about the words *learn* and *teach*, something to remember about being punished severely, but he doesn't recall what it is—only a thin white hand upraised, hitting him to make him learn something he couldn't understand.

Charlie backs away but Gimpy grabs his arm. "Hey, kid, take it easy. We ain't gonna hurt you. Look at him shaking like he's gonna fall apart. Look, Charlie. I got a nice new shiny good-luck piece for you to play with." He holds out his hand and reveals a brass chain with a shiny brass disc that says STA-BRITE METAL POLISH. He holds the chain by one end and the gleaming gold disc rotates slowly, catching the light of the fluorescent bulbs. The pendant is a brightness that Charlie remembers but he doesn't know why or what.

He doesn't reach for it. He knows you get punished if you reach out for other people's things. If someone puts it into your hand that is all right. But otherwise it's wrong. When he sees that Gimpy is offering it to him, he nods and smiles again.

"That he knows," laughs Frank. "Give him something bright and shiny." Frank, who has let Gimpy take over the experiment, leans forward excitedly. "Maybe if he wants that piece of junk bad enough and you tell him he'll get it if he learns to shape the dough into rolls—maybe it'll work."

As the bakers set to the task of teaching Charlie, others from the shop gather around. Frank clears an area between them on the table, and Gimpy pulls off a medium sized piece of dough for Charlie to work with. There is talk of betting on whether or not Charlie can learn to make rolls.

"Watch us carefully," says Gimpy, putting the pendant beside him on the table where Charlie can see it. "Watch and do everything we do. If you learn how to make rolls, you'll get this shiny good-luck piece."

Charlie hunches over on his stool, intently watching Gimpy pick up the knife and cut off a slab of dough. He studies each movement as Gimpy rolls out the dough into a long roll, breaks it off and twists it into a circle, pausing now and then to sprinkle it with flour.

"Now watch me," says Frank, and he repeats Gimpy's performance. Charlie is confused. There are differences. Gimpy holds his elbows out as he rolls the dough, like a bird's wings, but Frank keeps his arms close to his sides. Gimpy keeps his thumbs together with the rest of his fingers as he kneads the dough, but Frank works with the flat of his palms, keeping thumbs apart from his other fingers and up in the air.

Worrying about these things makes it impossible for Charlie to move when Gimpy says, "Go ahead, try it."

Charlie shakes his head.

"Look, Charlie, I'm gonna do it again slow. Now you watch everything I do, and do each part along with me. Okay? But try to remember everything so then you'll be able to do the whole thing alone. Now come on—like this."

Charlie frowns as he watches Gimpy pull off a section of dough and roll it into a ball. He hesitates, but then he picks up the knife and slices off a piece of dough and sets it down in the center of the table. Slowly, keeping his elbows out exactly as Gimpy does, he rolls it into a ball.

He looks from his own hands to Gimpy's, and he is careful to keep his fingers exactly the same way, thumbs together with the rest of his fingers—slightly cupped. He has to do it right, the way Gimpy wants him to do it. There are echoes inside him that say, do it right and they will like you. And he wants Gimpy and Frank to like him.

When Gimpy has finished working his dough into a ball, he stands back, and so does Charlie. "Hey, that's great. Look, Frank, he made it into a ball."

Frank nods and smiles. Charlie sighs and his whole frame trembles as the tension builds. He is unaccustomed to this rare moment of success.

"All right now," says Gimpy. "Now we make a roll." Awkwardly, but carefully, Charlie follows Gimpy's every move. Occasionally, a twitch of his hand or arm mars what he is doing, but in a little while he is able to twist off a section of the dough and fashion it into a roll. Working beside Gimpy he makes six rolls, and sprinkling them with flour he sets them carefully alongside Gimpy's in the large flour-covered tray.

"All right, Charlie." Gimpy's face is serious. "Now, let's see you do it by yourself. Remember all the things you did from the beginning. Now, go ahead."

Charlie stares at the huge slab of dough and at the knife that Gimpy has pushed into his hand. And once again panic comes over him. What did he do first? How did he hold his hand? His fingers? Which way did he roll the ball? . . . A thousand confusing ideas burst into his mind at the same time and he stands there smiling. He wants to do it, to make Frank and Gimpy happy and have them like him, and to get the bright good-luck piece that Gimpy has promised him. He turns the smooth, heavy piece of dough around and around on the table, but he cannot bring himself to start. He cannot cut into it because he knows he will fail and he is afraid.

"He forgot already," says Frank. "It don't stick."

He wants it to stick. He frowns and tries to remember: first you start to cut off a piece. Then you roll it out into a ball. But how does it get to be a roll like the ones in the tray? That's something else. Give him time and he'll remember. As soon as the fuzziness passes away he'll remember. Just another few seconds and he'll have it. He wants to hold on to what he's learned—for a little while. He wants it so much.

"Okay, Charlie," sighs Gimpy, taking the cutter out of his hand. "That's all right. Don't worry about it. It's not your work anyway."

Another minute and he'll remember. If only they wouldn't rush him. Why does everything have to be in such a hurry?

"Go ahead, Charlie. Go sit down and look at your comic book. We got to get back to work."

Charlie nods and smiles, and pulls the comic book out of his back pocket. He smooths it out, and puts it on his head as a make-believe hat. Frank laughs and Gimpy finally smiles.

"Go on, you big baby," snorts Gimpy. "Go sit down there until Mr. Donner wants you."

Charlie smiles at him and goes back to the flour sacks in the corner near the mixing machines. He likes to lean back against them while he sits on the floor cross-legged and looks at the pictures in his comic book. As he starts to turn the pages, he feels like crying, but he doesn't know why. What is there to feel sad about? The fuzzy cloud comes and goes, and now he looks forward to the pleasure of the brightly colored pictures in the comic book that he has gone through thirty, forty times. He knows all of the figures in the comic—he has asked their names over and over again (of almost everyone he meets)—and he understands that the strange forms of letters and words in the white balloons above the figures mean that they are saying something. Would he ever learn to read what was in the balloons? If they gave him enough time—if they didn't rush him or push him too fast—he would get it. But nobody has time.

Charlie pulls his legs up and opens the comic book to the first page where the Batman and Robin are swinging up a long rope to the side of a building. Someday, he decides, he is going to read. And then he will be able to read the story. He feels a hand on his shoulder and he looks up. It is Gimpy holding out the brass disc and chain, letting it swing and twirl around so that it catches the light.

"Here," he says gruffly, tossing it into Charlie's lap, and then he limps away. . . .

I never thought about it before, but that was a nice thing for him to do. Why did he? Anyway, that is my memory of the time, clearer and more complete than anything I have ever experienced before. Like looking out of the kitchen window early when the morning light is still gray. I've come a long way since then, and I owe it all to Dr. Strauss and Professor Nemur, and the other people here at Beekman. But what must Frank and Gimpy think and feel now, seeing how I've changed?

April 22—People at the bakery are changing. Not only ignoring me. I can feel the hostility. Donner is arranging for me to join the baker's union, and I've gotten another raise. The rotten thing is that all of the pleasure is gone because the others resent me. In a way, I can't blame them. They don't understand what has happened to me, and I can't tell them. People are not proud of me the way I expected—not at all.

Still, I've got to have someone to talk to. I'm going to ask Miss Kinnian to go to a movie tomorrow night to celebrate my raise. If I can get up the nerve.

April 24—Professor Nemur finally agreed with Dr. Strauss and me that it will be impossible for me to write down everything if I know it's immediately read by people at the lab. I've tried to be completely honest about everything, no matter who I was talking about, but there are things I can't put down unless I can keep them private—at least for a while.

Now, I'm allowed to keep back some of these more personal reports, but before the final report to the Welberg Foundation, Professor Nemur will read through everything to decide what part of it should be published.

What happened today at the lab was very upsetting.

I dropped by the office earlier this evening to ask Dr. Strauss or Professor Nemur if they thought it would be all right for me to ask Alice Kinnian out to a movie, but before I could knock I heard them arguing with each other. I shouldn't have stayed, but it's hard to break the habit of listening because people have always spoken and acted as if I weren't there, as if they never cared what I overheard.

I heard someone bang on the desk, and then Professor Nemur shouted: "I've already informed the convention committee that we will present the paper at Chicago."

Then I heard Dr. Strauss' voice: "But you're wrong, Harold. Six weeks from now is still too soon. He's still changing."

And then Nemur: "We've predicted the pattern correctly so far. We're justified in making an interim report. I tell you, Jay, there's nothing to be afraid of. We've succeeded. It's all positive. Nothing can go wrong now."

Strauss: "This is too important to all of us to bring it out into the open prematurely. You're taking the authority on yourself—"

Nemur: "You forget that I'm the senior member of this project."

Strauss: "And you forget that you're not the only one with a reputation to consider. If we claim too much now, our whole hypothesis will come under fire."

Nemur: "I'm not afraid of regression any more. I've checked and rechecked everything. An interim report will do no harm. I feel sure nothing can go wrong now."

The argument went on that way with Strauss saying that Nemur had his eye on the Chair of Psychology at Hallston, and Nemur saying that Strauss was riding on the coattails of his psychological research. Then Strauss said that the project had as much to do with his techniques in psychosurgery and enzyme-injection patterns, as with Nemur's theories, and that someday thousands of neurosurgeons all over the world would be using *his* methods, but at this point Nemur reminded him that those new techniques would never have come about if not for *his* original theory.

They called each other names—*opportunist, cynic, pessimist* —and I found myself frightened. Suddenly, I realized I no longer had the right to stand there outside the office and listen to them without their knowing it. They might not have cared when I was too feeble-minded to know what was going on, but now that I could understand they wouldn't want me to hear it. I left without waiting for the outcome.

It was dark, and I walked for a long time trying to figure out why I was so frightened. I was seeing them clearly for the first time—not gods or even heroes, but just two men worried about getting something out of their work. Yet, if Nemur is right and the experiment is a success, what does it matter? There's so much to do, so many plans to make.

I'll wait until tomorrow to ask them about taking Miss Kinnian to a movie to celebrate my raise.

April 26—I know I shouldn't hang around the college when I'm through at the lab, but seeing the young men and women going back and forth carrying books and hearing them talk about all the things they're learning in their classes excites me.

I wish I could sit and talk with them over coffee in the Campus
Bowl Luncheonette when they get together to argue about
books and politics and ideas. It's exciting to hear them talking
about poetry and science and philosophy—about Shakespeare
and Milton; Newton and Einstein and Freud; about Plato and
Hegel and Kant, and all the other names that echo like great
church bells in my mind.

Sometimes I listen in on the conversations at the tables
around me, and pretend I'm a college student, even though
I'm a lot older than they are. I carry books around, and I've
started to smoke a pipe. It's silly, but since I belong at the lab I
feel as if I'm a part of the university. I hate to go home to that
lonely room.

April 27—I've made friends with some of the boys at the Campus Bowl. They were arguing about whether or not Shakespeare really wrote Shakespeare's plays. One of the boys—the
fat one with the sweaty face—said that Marlowe wrote all of
Shakespeare's plays. But Lenny, the short kid with the dark
glasses, didn't believe that business about Marlowe, and he said
that everyone knew that Sir Francis Bacon wrote the plays because Shakespeare had never been to college and never had the
education that shows up in those plays. That's when the one
with the freshman beanie said he had heard a couple of guys
in the men's room talking about how Shakespeare's plays were
really written by a lady.

And they talked about politics and art and God. I never before heard anyone say that there might not be a God. That
frightened me, because for the first time I began to think about
what God means.

Now I understand one of the important reasons for going
to college and getting an education is to learn that the things
you've believed in all your life aren't true, and that nothing is
what it appears to be.

All the time they talked and argued, I felt the excitement
bubble up inside me. This was what I wanted to do—go to
college and hear people talk about important things.

I spend most of my free time at the library now, reading and
soaking up what I can from books. I'm not concentrating on anything in particular, just reading a lot of fiction now—Dostoevski,

Flaubert, Dickens, Hemingway, Faulkner—everything I can get my hands on—feeding a hunger that can't be satisfied.

April 28—In a dream last night I heard Mom screaming at Dad and the teacher at the elementary school P.S. 13 (my first school before they transferred me to P.S. 222). . . .

"He's normal! He's normal! He'll grow up like other people. Better than others." She was trying to scratch the teacher, but Dad was holding her back. "He'll go to college someday. He'll be *somebody*." She kept screaming it, clawing at Dad so he'd let go of her. "He'll go to college someday and he'll be somebody."

We were in the principal's office and there were a lot of people looking embarrassed, but the assistant principal was smiling and turning his head so no one would see it.

The principal in my dream had a long beard, and was floating around the room and pointing at me. "He'll have to go to a special school. Put him into the Warren State Home and Training School. We can't have him here."

Dad was pulling Mom out of the principal's office, and she was shouting and crying too. I didn't see her face, but her big red teardrops kept splashing down on me. . . .

This morning I could recall the dream, but now there's more than that—I can remember through the blur, back to when I was six years old and it all happened. Just before Norma was born. I see Mom, a thin, dark-haired woman who talks too fast and uses her hands too much. As always her face is blurred. Her hair is up in a bun, and her hand goes to touch it, pat it smooth, as if she has to make sure it's still there. I remember that she was always fluttering like a big, white bird—around my father, and he too heavy and tired to escape her pecking.

I see Charlie, standing in the center of the kitchen, playing with his spinner, bright colored beads and rings threaded on a string. He holds the string up in one hand and turns the rings so they wind and unwind in bright spinning flashes. He spends long hours watching his spinner. I don't know who made it for him, or what became of it, but I see him standing there fascinated as the string untwists and sets the rings spinning. . . .

She is screaming at him—no, she's screaming at his father. "I'm not going to take him. There's nothing wrong with him!"

"Rose, it won't do any good pretending any longer that nothing is wrong. Just look at him, Rose. Six years old, and—"

"He's not a dummy. He's normal. He'll be just like everyone else."

He looks sadly at his son with the spinner and Charlie smiles and holds it up to show him how pretty it is when it goes around and around.

"Put that thing away!" Mom shrieks and suddenly she knocks the spinner from Charlie's hand, and it crashes across the kitchen floor. "Go play with your alphabet blocks."

He stands there, frightened by the sudden outburst. He cowers, not knowing what she will do. His body begins to shake. They're arguing, and the voices back and forth make a squeezing pressure inside him and a sense of panic.

"Charlie, go to the bathroom. Don't you dare do it in your pants."

He wants to obey her, but his legs are too soft to move. His arms go up automatically to ward off blows.

"For God's sake, Rose. Leave him alone. You've got him terrified. You always do this, and the poor kid—"

"Then why don't you help me? I have to do it all by myself. Every day I try to teach him—to help him catch up to the others. He's just slow, that's all. But he can learn like everyone else."

"You're fooling yourself, Rose. It's not fair to us or to him. Pretending he's normal. Driving him as if he were an animal that could learn to do tricks. Why don't you leave him alone?"

"Because I want him to be like everyone else."

As they argue, the feeling that grips Charlie's insides becomes greater. His bowels feel as if they will burst and he knows he should go to the bathroom as she has told him so often. But he can't walk. He feels like sitting down right there in the kitchen, but it is wrong and she will slap him.

He wants his spinner. If he has his spinner and he watches it going round and round, he will be able to control himself and not make in his pants. But the spinner is all apart with some of the rings under the table and some under the sink, and the cord is near the stove.

It is very strange that although I can recall the voices clearly their faces are still blurred, and I can see only general outlines. Dad massive and slumped. Mom thin and quick. Hearing them now, arguing with each other across the years, I have the impulse to shout at them: "Look at him. There, down there! Look at Charlie. He has to go to the toilet!"

Charlie stands clutching and pulling at his red checkered shirt as they argue over him. The words are angry sparks between them—an anger and a guilt he can't identify.

"Next September he's going to go back to P.S. 13 and do the term's work over again."

"Why can't you let yourself see the truth? The teacher says he's not capable of doing the work in a regular class."

"That bitch a teacher? Oh, I've got better names for her. Let her start with me again and I'll do more than just write to the board of education. I'll scratch that dirty slut's eyes out. Charlie, why are you twisting like that? Go to the bathroom. Go by yourself. You know how to go."

"Can't you see he wants you to take him? He's frightened."

"Keep out of this. He's perfectly capable of going to the bathroom himself. The book says it gives him confidence and a feeling of achievement."

The terror that waits in that cold tile room overwhelms him. He is afraid to go there alone. He reaches up for her hand and sobs out: "Toi— toi . . ." and she slaps his hand away.

"No more," she says sternly. "You're a big boy now. You can go by yourself. Now march right into that bathroom and pull your pants down the way I taught you. I warn you, if you make in your pants you'll get spanked."

I can almost feel it now, the stretching and knotting in his intestines as the two of them stand over him waiting to see what he will do. His whimper becomes a soft crying as suddenly he can control no longer, and he sobs and covers his face with his hands as he dirties himself.

It is soft and warm and he feels the confusion of relief and fear. It is his, but she will take it away from him as she always does. She will take it away and keep it for herself. And she will spank him. She comes toward him, screaming that he is a bad boy, and Charlie runs to his father for help.

Suddenly, I remember that her name is Rose and his name is Matt. It's odd to have forgotten your parents' names. And what about Norma? Strange I haven't thought about them all for a long time. I wish I could see Matt's face now, to know what he was thinking at that moment. All I remember is that as she began to spank me, Matt Gordon turned and walked out of the apartment.

I wish I could see their faces more clearly.

PROGRESS REPORT 11

May 1—Why haven't I ever noticed how beautiful Alice Kinnian is? She has pigeon-soft brown eyes and feathery brown hair down to the hollow of her neck. When she smiles, her full lips look as if she's pouting.

We went to a movie and then to dinner. I didn't see much of the first picture because I was too conscious of her sitting next to me. Twice her bare arm touched mine on the armrest, and both times the fear that she would become annoyed made me pull back. All I could think about was her soft skin just inches away. Then I saw, two rows ahead of us, a young man with his arm around his girl, and I wanted to put my arm around Miss Kinnian. Terrifying. But if I did it slowly . . . first resting my arm on the back of her seat . . . moving up . . . inch by inch . . . to rest near her shoulders and the back of her neck . . . casually . . .

I didn't dare.

The best I could do was rest my elbow on the back of her seat, but by the time I got there I had to shift position to wipe the perspiration off my face and neck.

Once, her leg accidentally brushed against mine.

It became such an ordeal—so painful—that I forced myself to take my mind off her. The first picture had been a war film, and all I caught was the ending where the G.I. goes back to Europe to marry the woman who saved his life. The second picture interested me. A psychological film about a man and woman apparently in love but actually destroying each other. Everything suggests that the man is going to kill his wife but at the last moment, something she screams out in a nightmare makes him recall something that happened to him during his childhood. The sudden memory shows him that his hatred is really directed at a depraved governess who had terrified him with frightening stories and left a flaw in his personality. Excited at discovering this, he cries out with joy so that his wife awakens. He takes her in his arms and the implication is that all his problems have been solved. It was pat and cheap, and I must have shown my anger because Alice wanted to know what was wrong. "It's a lie," I explained, as we walked out into the lobby. "Things just don't happen that way."

"Of course not." She laughed. "It's a world of make-believe."

"Oh, no! That's no answer." I insisted. "Even in the world of make-believe there have to be rules. The parts have to be consistent and belong together. This kind of picture is a lie. Things are forced to fit because the writer or the director or somebody wanted something in that didn't belong. And it doesn't feel right."

She looked at me thoughtfully as we walked out into the bright dazzling night-lights of Times Square. "You're coming along fast."

"I'm confused. I don't know what I know any more."

"Never mind that," she insisted. "You're beginning to see and understand things." She waved her hand to take in all of the neon and glitter around us as we crossed over to Seventh Avenue. "You're beginning to see what's behind the surface of things. What you say about the parts having to belong together —that was a pretty good insight."

"Oh, come on now. I don't feel as if I'm accomplishing anything. I don't understand about myself or my past. I don't even know where my parents are, or what they look like. Do you know that when I see them in a flash of memory or in a dream the faces are a blur? I want to see their expressions. I can't understand what's going on unless I can see their faces—"

"Charlie, calm down." People were turning to stare. She slipped her arm through mine and pulled me close to restrain me. "Be patient. Don't forget you're accomplishing in weeks what takes others a lifetime. You're a giant sponge soaking in knowledge. Soon you'll begin to connect things up, and you'll see how all the different worlds of learning are related. All the levels, Charlie, like steps on a giant ladder. And you'll climb higher and higher to see more and more of the world around you."

As we entered the cafeteria on Forty-fifth Street and picked up our trays, she spoke animatedly. "Ordinary people," she said, "can see only a little bit. They can't change much or go any higher than they are, but you're a genius. You'll keep going up and up, and see more and more. And each step will reveal worlds you never even knew existed."

People on the line who heard her turned to stare at me, and only when I nudged her to stop did she lower her voice. "I just hope to God," she whispered, "that you don't get hurt."

For a little while after that I didn't know what to say. We ordered our food at the counter and carried it to our table and ate without talking. The silence made me nervous. I knew what she meant about her fear, so I joked about it.

"Why should I get hurt? I couldn't be any worse off than I was before. Even Algernon is still smart, isn't he? As long as he's up there I'm in good shape." She toyed with her knife making circular depressions in a pat of butter and the movement hypnotized me. "And besides," I told her, "I overheard something—Professor Nemur and Dr. Strauss were arguing, and Nemur said he's positive that nothing can go wrong."

"I hope so," she said. "You have no idea how afraid I've been that something might go wrong. I feel partly responsible." She saw me staring at the knife and she put it down carefully beside her plate.

"I never would have done it but for you," I said.

She laughed and it made me tremble. That's when I saw that her eyes were soft brown. She looked down at the tablecloth quickly and blushed.

"Thank you, Charlie," she said, and took my hand.

It was the first time anyone had ever done that, and it made me bolder. I leaned forward, holding on to her hand, and the words came out. "I like you very much." After I said it, I was afraid she'd laugh, but she nodded and smiled.

"I like you too, Charlie."

"But it's more than liking. What I mean is . . . oh, hell! I don't know what I mean." I knew I was blushing, and I didn't know where to look or what to do with my hands. I dropped a fork, and when I tried to retrieve it, I knocked over a glass of water and it spilled on her dress. Suddenly, I had become clumsy and awkward again, and when I tried to apologize I found my tongue had become too large for my mouth.

"That's all right, Charlie," she tried to reassure me. "It's only water. Don't let it upset you this way."

In the taxi on the way home, we were silent for a long time, and then she put down her purse and straightened my tie and puffed up my breast pocket handkerchief. "You were very upset tonight, Charlie."

"I feel ridiculous."

"I upset you by talking about it. I made you self-conscious."

"It's not that. What bothers me is that I can't put into words the way I feel."

"These feelings are new to you. Not everything has to . . . be put into words."

I moved closer to her and tried to take her hand again, but she pulled away. "No, Charlie. I don't think this is good for you. I've upset you, and it might have a negative effect."

When she put me off, I felt awkward and ridiculous at the same time. It made me angry with myself and I pulled back to my side of the seat and stared out the window. I hated her as I had never hated anyone before—with her easy answers and maternal fussing. I wanted to slap her face, to make her crawl, and then to hold her in my arms and kiss her.

"Charlie, I'm sorry if I've upset you."

"Forget it."

"But you've got to understand what's happening."

"I understand," I said, "and I'd rather not talk about it."

By the time the cab reached her apartment on Seventy-seventh Street, I was thoroughly miserable.

"Look," she said, "this is my fault. I shouldn't have gone out with you tonight."

"Yes, I see that now."

"What I mean is, we have no right to put this on a personal . . . emotional level. You have so much to do. I have no right to come into your life at this time."

"That's my worry, isn't it?"

"Is it? This isn't your private affair any more, Charlie. You've got obligations now—not only to Professor Nemur and Dr. Strauss, but to the millions who may follow in your footsteps."

The more she talked that way, the worse I felt. She highlighted my awkwardness, my lack of knowledge about the right things to say and do. I was a blundering adolescent in her eyes, and she was trying to let me down easy.

As we stood at the door to her apartment, she turned and smiled at me and for a moment I thought she was going to invite me in, but she just whispered: "Good night, Charlie. Thank you for a wonderful evening."

I wanted to kiss her good night. I had worried about it earlier. Didn't a woman expect you to kiss her? In the novels I'd read and the movies I'd seen, the man makes the advances. I had decided last night that I would kiss her. But I kept thinking: what if she turns me down?

I moved closer and reached for her shoulders, but she was too quick for me. She stopped me and took my hand in hers. "We'd better just say good night this way, Charlie. We can't let this get personal. Not yet."

And before I could protest, or ask what she meant by *not yet*, she started inside. "Good night, Charlie, and thank you again for a lovely . . . lovely time." And closed the door.

I was furious at her, myself, and the world, but by the time I got home, I realized she was right. Now, I don't know whether she cares for me or if she was just being kind. What could she possibly see in me? What makes it so awkward is that I've never experienced anything like this before. How does a person go about learning how to act toward another person? How does a man learn how to behave toward a woman?

The books don't help much.

But next time, I'm going to kiss her good night.

May 3—One of the things that confuses me is never really knowing when something comes up from my past, whether it really happened that way, or if that was the way it seemed to be at the time, or if I'm inventing it. I'm like a man who's been half-asleep all his life, trying to find out what he was like before he woke up. Everything is strangely slow-motion and blurred.

I had a nightmare last night, and when I woke up I remembered something.

First the nightmare: I'm running down a long corridor, half blinded by the swirls of dust. At times I run forward and then I float around and run backwards, but I'm afraid because I'm hiding something in my pocket. I don't know what it is or where I got it, but I know they want to take it away from me and that frightens me.

The wall breaks down and suddenly there is a red-haired girl with her arms outstretched to me—her face is a blank mask. She takes me into her arms, kisses and caresses me, and I want to hold her tightly but I'm afraid. The more she touches me, the more frightened I become because I know I must never touch a girl. Then, as her body rubs up against mine, I feel a strange bubbling and throbbing inside me that makes me warm. But when I look up I see a bloody knife in her hands.

I try to scream as I run, but no sound comes out of my throat, and my pockets are empty. I search in my pockets but I don't know what it is I've lost or why I was hiding it. I know only that it's gone, and there is blood on my hands too.

When I woke up, I thought of Alice, and I had the same feeling of panic as in the dream. What am I afraid of? Something about the knife.

I made myself a cup of coffee and smoked a cigarette. I'd never had a dream like it before, and I knew it was connected with my evening with Alice. I have begun to think of her in a different way.

Free association is still difficult, because it's hard not to control the direction of your thoughts . . . just to leave your mind open and let anything flow into it . . . ideas bubbling to the surface like a bubble bath . . . a woman bathing . . . a girl . . . Norma taking a bath . . . I am watching through the keyhole . . . and when she gets out of the tub to dry herself I see that her body is different from mine. Something is missing.

Running down the hallway . . . somebody chasing me . . . not a person . . . just a big flashing kitchen knife . . . and I'm scared and crying but no voice comes out because my neck is cut and I'm bleeding . . .

"Mama, Charlie is peeking at me through the keyhole . . ."
Why is she different? What happened to her? . . . blood
. . . bleeding . . . a dark cubbyhole . . .

> Three blind mice . . . three blind mice,
> See how they run! See how they run!
> They all run after the farmer's wife,
> She cut off their tails with a carving knife,
> Did you ever see such a sight in your life,
> As three . . . blind . . . mice?

Charlie, alone in the kitchen early in the morning. Everyone
else asleep, and he amuses himself playing with his spinner.
One of the buttons pops off his shirt as he bends over, and it
rolls across the intricate line-pattern of the kitchen linoleum. It
rolls towards the bathroom and he follows, but then he loses
it. Where is the button? He goes into the bathroom to find it.
There is a closet in the bathroom where the clothes hamper is,
and he likes to take out all the clothes and look at them. His
father's things and his mother's . . . and Norma's dresses. He
would like to try them on and make believe he is Norma, but
once when he did that his mother spanked him for it. There
in the clothes hamper he finds Norma's underwear with dried
blood. What had she done wrong? He was terrified. Whoever
had done it might come looking for him. . . .

Why does a memory like that from childhood remain with me
so strongly, and why does it frighten me now? Is it because of
my feelings for Alice?

Thinking about it now, I can understand why I was taught
to keep away from women. It was wrong for me to express
my feelings to Alice. I have no right to think of a woman that
way—not yet.

But even as I write these words, something inside shouts
that there is more. I'm a person. I was somebody before I went
under the surgeon's knife. And I have to love someone.

May 8—Even now that I have learned what has been going on
behind Mr. Donner's back, I find it hard to believe. I first noticed something was wrong during the rush hour two days ago.
Gimpy was behind the counter wrapping a birthday cake for

one of our regular customers—a cake that sells for $3.95. But when Gimpy rang up the sale the register showed only $2.95. I started to tell him he had made a mistake, but in the mirror behind the counter I saw a wink and smile that passed from the customer to Gimpy and the answering smile on Gimpy's face. And when the man took his change, I saw the flash of a large silver coin left behind in Gimpy's hand, before his fingers closed on it, and the quick movement with which he slipped the half-dollar into his pocket.

"Charlie," said a woman behind me, "are there any more of those cream-filled éclairs?"

"I'll go back and find out."

I was glad of the interruption because it gave me time to think about what I had seen. Certainly, Gimpy had not made a mistake. He had deliberately undercharged the customer, and there had been an understanding between them.

I leaned limply against the wall not knowing what to do. Gimpy had worked for Mr. Donner for over fifteen years. Donner—who always treated his workers like close friends, like relatives—had invited Gimpy's family to his house for dinner more than once. He often put Gimpy in charge of the shop when he had to go out, and I had heard stories of the times Donner gave Gimpy money to pay his wife's hospital bills.

It was incredible that anyone would steal from such a man. There had to be some other explanation. Gimpy had really made a mistake in ringing up the sale, and the half-dollar was a tip. Or perhaps Mr. Donner had made some special arrangement for this one customer who regularly bought cream cakes. Anything rather than believe that Gimpy was stealing. Gimpy had always been so nice to me.

I no longer wanted to know. I kept my eyes averted from the register as I brought out the tray of éclairs and sorted out the cookies, buns, and cakes.

But when the little red-haired woman came in—the one who always pinched my cheek and joked about finding a girl friend for me—I recalled that she came in most often when Donner was out to lunch and Gimpy was behind the counter. Gimpy had often sent me out to deliver orders to her house.

Involuntarily, my mind totaled her purchases to $4.53. But

I turned away so that I would not see what Gimpy rang up on the cash register. I wanted to know the truth, and yet I was afraid of what I might learn.

"Two forty-five, Mrs. Wheeler," he said.

The ring of the sale. The counting of change. The slam of the drawer. "Thank you, Mrs. Wheeler." I turned just in time to see him putting his hand into his pocket, and I heard the faint clink of coins.

How many times had he *used me* as a go-between to deliver packages to her, undercharging her so that later they could split the difference? Had he used me all these years to help him steal?

I couldn't take my eyes off Gimpy as he clomped around behind the counter, perspiration streaming down from under his paper cap. He seemed animated and good-natured, but looking up he caught my eye, frowned and turned away.

I wanted to hit him. I wanted to go behind the counter and smash his face in. I don't remember ever hating anyone before —but this morning I hated Gimpy with all my heart.

Pouring this all out on paper in the quiet of my room has not helped. Every time I think of Gimpy stealing from Mr. Donner I want to smash something. Fortunately, I don't think I'm capable of violence. I don't think I ever hit anyone in my life.

But I still have to decide what to do. Tell Donner that his trusted employee has been stealing from him all these years? Gimpy would deny it, and I could never prove it was true. And what would it do to Mr. Donner? I don't know what to do.

May 9—I can't sleep. This has gotten to me. I owe Mr. Donner too much to stand by and see him robbed this way. I'd be as guilty as Gimpy by my silence. And yet, is it my place to inform on him? The thing that bothers me most is that when he sent me on deliveries he used *me* to help him steal from Donner. Not knowing about it, I was outside it—not to blame. But now that I know, by my silence I am as guilty as he is.

Yet, Gimpy is a co-worker. Three children. What will he do if Donner fires him? He might not be able to get another job —especially with his club foot.

Is that my worry?

What's right? Ironic that all my intelligence doesn't help me solve a problem like this.

May 10—I asked Professor Nemur about it, and he insists that I'm an innocent bystander and there's no reason for me to become involved in what would be an unpleasant situation. The fact that I've been used as a go-between doesn't seem to bother him at all. If I didn't understand what was happening at the time, he says, then it doesn't matter. I'm no more to blame than the knife is to blame in a stabbing, or the car in a collision.

"But I'm not an inanimate object," I argued. "I'm a *person*."

He looked confused for a moment and then laughed. "Of course, Charlie. But I wasn't referring to now. I meant before the operation."

Smug, pompous—I felt like hitting him too. "I was a person before the operation. In case you forgot—"

"Yes, of course, Charlie. Don't misunderstand. But it was different . . ." And then he remembered that he had to check some charts in the lab.

Dr. Strauss doesn't talk much during our psychotherapy sessions, but today when I brought it up, he said that I was morally obligated to tell Mr. Donner. But the more I thought about it the less simple it became. I had to have someone else to break the tie, and the only one I could think of was Alice. Finally, at ten thirty I couldn't hold out any longer. I dialed three times, broke off in the middle each time, but on the fourth try, I managed to hold on until I heard her voice.

At first she didn't think she should see me, but I begged her to meet me at the cafeteria where we had dinner together. "I respect you—you've always given me good advice." And when she still wavered, I insisted. "You *have* to help me. You're partly responsible. You said so yourself. If not for you I would never have gone into this in the first place. You just can't shrug me off now."

She must have sensed the urgency because she agreed to meet me. I hung up and stared at the phone. Why was it so important for me to know what *she* thought, how *she* felt? For more than a year at the Adult Center the only thing that mattered was pleasing her. Was that why I had agreed to the operation in the first place?

I paced up and back in front of the cafeteria until the policeman began to eye me suspiciously. Then I went in and bought coffee. Fortunately, the table we had used last time was empty. She would think of looking for me back there.

She saw me and waved to me, but stopped at the counter for coffee before she came over to the table. She smiled and I knew it was because I had chosen the same table. A foolish, romantic gesture.

"I know it's late," I apologized, "but I swear I was going out of my mind. I had to talk to you."

She sipped her coffee and listened quietly as I explained how I had found out about Gimpy's cheating, my own reaction, and the conflicting advice I'd gotten at the lab. When I finished, she sat back and shook her head.

"Charlie, you amaze me. In some ways you're so advanced, and yet when it comes to making a decision, you're still a child. I can't decide for you, Charlie. The answer can't be found in books—or be solved by bringing it to other people. Not unless you want to remain a child all your life. You've got to find the answer inside you—*feel* the right thing to do. Charlie, you've got to learn to trust yourself."

At first, I was annoyed at her lecture, but then—suddenly—it began to make sense. "You mean, *I've* got to decide?"

She nodded.

"In fact," I said, "now that I think of it, I believe I've already decided some of it! I think Nemur and Strauss are both wrong!"

She was watching me closely, excitedly. "Something is happening to you, Charlie. If you could only see your face."

"You're damned right, something is happening! A cloud of smoke was hanging in front of my eyes, and with one breath you blew it away. A simple idea. Trust *myself*. And it never occurred to me before."

"Charlie, you're wonderful."

I caught her hand and held it. "No, it's you. You touch my eyes and make me see."

She blushed and pulled her hand back.

"The last time we were here," I said, "I told you I liked you. I should have trusted myself to say I love you."

"Don't, Charlie. Not yet."

"*Not yet?*" I shouted. "That's what you said last time. Why not yet?"

"Shhhh . . . Wait a while, Charlie. Finish your studies. See where they lead you. You're changing too fast."

"What does that have to do with it? My feeling for you won't change because I'm becoming intelligent. I'll only love you more."

"But you're changing emotionally too. In a peculiar sense I'm the first woman you've ever been really aware of—in this way. Up to now I've been your teacher—someone you turn to for help and advice. You're bound to think you're in love with me. See other women. Give yourself more time."

"What you're saying is that young boys are always falling in love with their teachers, and that emotionally I'm still just a boy."

"You're twisting my words around. No, I don't think of you as a boy."

"Emotionally retarded then."

"No."

"Then, why?"

"Charlie, don't push me. I don't know. Already, you've gone beyond my intellectual reach. In a few months or even weeks, you'll be a different person. When you mature intellectually, we may not be able to communicate. When you mature emotionally, you may not even want me. I've got to think of myself too, Charlie. Let's wait and see. Be patient."

She was making sense, but I wasn't letting myself listen. "The other night—" I choked out, "you don't know how much I looked forward to that date. I was out of my mind wondering how to behave, what to say, wanting to make the best impression, and terrified I might say something to make you angry."

"You didn't make me angry. I was flattered."

"Then, when can I see you again?"

"I have no right to let you get involved."

"But I *am* involved!" I shouted, and then seeing people turn to look, I lowered my voice until it trembled with anger. "I'm a person—a man—and I can't live with just books and tapes and electronic mazes. You say, 'see other women.' How can I when I don't know any other women? Something inside is burning me up, and all I know is it makes me think of you. I'm in the middle of a page and I see your face on it—not blurred like those in my past, but clear and alive. I touch the page and your face is gone and I want to tear the book apart and throw it away."

"Please, Charlie . . ."

"Let me see you again."

"Tomorrow at the lab."

"You know that's not what I mean. Away from the lab. Away from the university. Alone."

I could tell she wanted to say yes. She was surprised by my insistence. I was surprised at myself. I only knew that I couldn't stop pressing her. And yet there was a terror in my throat as I begged her. My palms were damp. Was I afraid she'd say *no*, or afraid she'd say *yes*? If she hadn't broken the tension by answering me, I think I would have fainted.

"All right, Charlie. Away from the lab and the university, but not alone. I don't think we should be alone together."

"Anywhere you say," I gasped. "Just so I can be with you and not think of tests . . . statistics . . . questions . . . answers . . ."

She frowned for a moment. "All right. They have free spring concerts in Central Park. Next week you can take me to one of the concerts."

When we got to her doorway, she turned quickly and kissed my cheek. "Good night, Charlie. I'm glad you called me. I'll see you at the lab." She closed the door and I stood outside the building and looked at the light in her apartment window until it went out.

There is no question about it now. I'm in love.

May 11—After all this thinking and worrying, I realized Alice was right. I had to trust my intuition. At the bakery, I watched Gimpy more closely. Three times today, I saw him undercharging customers and pocketing his portion of the difference as the customers passed money back to him. It was only with certain regular customers that he did it, and it occurred to me that these people were as guilty as he. Without their agreement this could never take place. Why should Gimpy be the scapegoat?

That's when I decided on the compromise. It might not be the perfect decision, but it was my decision, and it seemed to be the best answer under the circumstances. I would tell Gimpy what I knew and warn him to stop.

I got him alone back by the washroom, and when I came up to him he started away. "I've got something important to talk to you about," I said. "I want your advice for a friend who has a problem. He's discovered that one of his fellow employees is cheating his boss, and he doesn't know what to do about it. He doesn't like the idea of informing and getting the guy into trouble, but he won't stand by and let his boss—who has been good to both of them—be cheated."

Gimpy looked at me hard. "What does this friend of yours plan to do about it?"

"That's the trouble. He doesn't want to do anything. He feels if the stealing stops there would be nothing gained by doing anything at all. He would forget about it."

"Your friend ought to keep his nose in his own business," said Gimpy, shifting off his club foot. "He ought to keep his eyes closed to things like that and know who *his* friends are. A boss is a boss, and working people got to stick together."

"My friend doesn't feel that way."

"It's none of his business."

"He feels that if he knows about it he's partly responsible. So he's decided that if the thing stops, he's got nothing more to say. Otherwise, he'll tell the whole story. I wanted to ask your opinion. Do you think that under the circumstances the stealing will stop?"

It was a strain for him to conceal his anger. I could see that he wanted to hit me, but he just kept squeezing his fist.

"Tell your friend the guy doesn't seem to have any choice."

"That's fine," I said. "That will make my friend very happy."

Gimpy started away, and then he paused and looked back. "Your friend—could it be maybe he's interested in a cut? Is that his reason?"

"No, he just wants the whole thing to stop."

He glared at me. "I can tell you, you'll be sorry you stuck your nose in. I always stood up for you. I should of had my head examined." And then he limped off.

Perhaps I ought to have told Donner the whole story and

had Gimpy fired—I don't know. Doing it this way has something to be said for it. It's over and done with. But how many people are there like Gimpy who use other people that way?

May 15—My studies are going well. The university library is my second home now. They've had to get me a private room because it takes me only a second to absorb the printed page, and curious students invariably gather around me as I flip through my books.

My most absorbing interests at the present time are etymologies of ancient languages, the newer works on the calculus of variations, and Hindu history. It's amazing the way things, apparently disconnected, hang together. I've moved up to another plateau, and now the streams of the various disciplines seem to be closer to each other as if they flow from a single source.

Strange how when I'm in the college cafeteria and hear the students arguing about history or politics or religion, it all seems so childish.

I find no pleasure in discussing ideas any more on such an elementary level. People resent being shown that they don't approach the complexities of the problem—they don't know what exists beyond the surface ripples. It's just as bad on a higher level, and I've given up any attempt to discuss these things with the professors at Beekman.

Burt introduced me to an economics professor at the faculty cafeteria, one well known for his work on the economic factors affecting interest rates. I had long wanted to talk to an economist about some of the ideas I had come across in my reading. The moral aspects of the military blockade as a weapon in times of peace had been bothering me. I asked him what he thought of the suggestion by some senators that we begin using such tactics as "blacklisting" and reinforcement of the navicert controls that had been used in World Wars I and II, against some of the smaller nations which now oppose us.

He listened quietly, staring off into space, and I assumed he was collecting his thoughts for an answer, but a few minutes later he cleared his throat and shook his head. That, he explained apologetically, was outside his area of specialization. His interest was in interest rates, and he hadn't given military economics much thought. He suggested I see Dr. Wessey, who once did a paper on War Trade Agreements during World War II. He might be able to help me.

Before I could say anything else, he grabbed my hand and shook it. He had been glad to meet me, but there were some notes he had to assemble for a lecture. And then he was gone.

The same thing happened when I tried to discuss Chaucer with an American literature specialist, questioned an Orientalist about the Trobriand Islanders, and tried to focus on the problems of automation-caused unemployment with a social psychologist who specialized in public opinion polls on adolescent behavior. They would always find excuses to slip away, afraid to reveal the narrowness of their knowledge.

How different they seem to be now. And how foolish I was ever to have thought that professors were intellectual giants. They're people—and afraid the rest of the world will find out. And Alice is a person too—a woman, not a goddess—and I'm taking her to the concert tomorrow night.

May 17—Almost morning and I can't fall asleep. I've got to understand what happened to me last night at the concert.

The evening started out well enough. The Mall at Central Park had filled up early, and Alice and I had to pick our way among the couples stretched out on the grass. Finally, far back from the path, we found an unused tree where—out of the range of lamplight—the only evidence of other couples was the protesting female laughter and the glow of lit cigarettes.

"This will be fine," she said. "No reason to be right on top of the orchestra."

"What's that they're playing now?" I asked.

"Debussy's *La Mer*. Do you like it?"

I settled down beside her. "I don't know much about this kind of music. I have to think about it."

"Don't think about it," she whispered. "Feel it. Let it sweep over you like the sea without trying to understand." She lay back on the grass and turned her face in the direction of the music.

I had no way of knowing what she expected of me. This was far from the clear lines of problem-solving and the systematic acquisition of knowledge. I kept telling myself that the sweating palms, the tightness in my chest, the desire to put my arms around her were merely biochemical reactions. I even traced the pattern of stimulus-and-reaction that caused my nervousness and excitement. Yet everything was fuzzy and uncertain. Should I put my arm around her or not? Was she waiting for me to do it? Would she get angry? I could tell I was still behaving like an adolescent and it angered me.

"Here," I choked, "why don't you make yourself more comfortable? Rest on my shoulder." She let me put my arm around her, but she didn't look at me. She seemed to be too absorbed in the music to realize what I was doing. Did she want me to hold her that way, or was she merely tolerating it? As I slipped my arm down to her waist, I felt her tremble, but still she kept staring in the direction of the orchestra. She was pretending to be concentrating on the music so that she wouldn't have to respond to me. She didn't want to know what was happening. As long as she looked away, and listened, she could pretend that my closeness, my arms around her, were without her knowledge or consent. She wanted me to make love to her body while she kept her mind on higher things. I reached over roughly and turned her chin. "Why don't you look at me? Are you pretending I don't exist?"

"No, Charlie," she whispered. "I'm pretending *I* don't exist."

When I touched her shoulder she stiffened and trembled, but I pulled her toward me. Then it happened. It started as a hollow buzzing in my ears . . . an electric saw . . . far away. Then the cold: arms and legs prickly, and fingers numbing. Suddenly, I had the feeling I was being watched.

A sharp switch in perception. I saw, from some point in the darkness behind a tree, the two of us lying in each other's arms.

I looked up to see a boy of fifteen or sixteen, crouching nearby. "Hey!" I shouted. As he stood up, I saw his trousers were open and he was exposed.

"What's the matter?" she gasped.

I jumped up, and he vanished into the darkness. "Did you see him?"

"No," she said, smoothing her skirt nervously. "I didn't see anyone."

"Standing right here. Watching us. Close enough to touch you."

"Charlie, where are you going?"

"He couldn't have gotten very far."

"Leave him alone, Charlie. It doesn't matter."

But it mattered to me. I ran into the darkness, stumbling over startled couples, but there was no way to tell where he had gone.

The more I thought about him, the worse became the queasy feeling that comes before fainting. Lost and alone in a great wilderness. And then I caught hold of myself and found my way back to where Alice was sitting.

"Did you find him?"

"No, but he was there. I saw him."

She looked at me strangely. "Are you all right?"

"I will be . . . in a minute . . . Just that damned buzzing in my ears."

"Maybe we'd better go."

All the way back to her apartment, it was on my mind that the boy had been crouching there in the darkness, and for one second I had caught a glimpse of what he was seeing—the two of us lying in each other's arms.

"Would you like to come in? I could make some coffee."

I wanted to, but something warned me against it. "Better not. I've got a lot of work to do tonight."

"Charlie, is it anything I said or did?"

"Of course not. Just that kid watching us upset me."

She was standing close to me, waiting for me to kiss her. I put my arm around her, but it happened again. If I didn't get away quickly, I would pass out.

"Charlie, you look sick."

"Did you see him, Alice? The truth . . ."

She shook her head. "No. It was too dark. But I'm sure—"

"I've got to go. I'll call you." And before she could stop me, I pulled away. I had to get out of that building before everything caved in.

Thinking about it now, I'm certain it was a hallucination. Dr. Strauss feels that emotionally I'm still in that adolescent state where being close to a woman, or thinking of sex, sets off anxiety, panic, even hallucinations. He feels that my rapid intellectual development has deceived me into thinking I could live a normal emotional life. But I've got to accept the fact that the fears and blocks triggered in these sexual situations reveal that emotionally I'm still an adolescent—sexually retarded. I guess he means I'm not ready for a relationship with a woman like Alice Kinnian. Not yet.

May 20—I've been fired from my job at the bakery. I know it was foolish of me to hang on to the past, but there was something about the place with its white brick walls browned by oven heat . . . It was home to me.

What did I do to make them hate me so?

I can't blame Donner. He's got to think of his business and the other employees. And yet, he's been closer to me than a father.

He called me into his office, cleared the statements and bills off the solitary chair beside his roll-top desk, and without looking up at me, he said, "I've been meaning to talk to you. Now is as good a time as any."

It seems foolish now, but as I sat there staring at him—short, chubby, with the ragged light-brown moustache comically drooping over his upper lip—it was as if both of me, the old Charlie and the new, were sitting on that chair, frightened at what Old Mr. Donner was going to say.

"Charlie, your Uncle Herman was a good friend of mine. I kept my promise to him to keep you on the job, good times and bad, so that you didn't ever want for a dollar in your pocket and a place to lay your head without being put away in that home."

"The bakery is my home—"

"And I treated you like my own son who gave up his life for his country. And when Herman died—how old were you? seventeen? more like a six-year-old boy—I swore to myself . . . I said, Arthur Donner, as long as you got a bakery and a business over your head, you're going to look after Charlie. He is going to have a place to work, a bed to sleep in, and bread in his mouth. When they committed you to that Warren place, I told them how you would work for me, and I would take care of you. You didn't spend even one night in that place. I got you a room and I looked after you. Now, have I kept that solemn promise?"

I nodded, but I could see by the way he was folding and unfolding his bills that he was having trouble. And as much as I didn't want to know—I knew. "I've tried my best to do a good job. I've worked hard. . . ."

"I know, Charlie. Nothing's wrong with your work. But something happened to you, and I don't understand what it means. Not only me. Everyone has been talking about it. I've had them in here a dozen times in the last few weeks. They're all upset. Charlie, I got to let you go."

I tried to stop him but he shook his head.

"There was a delegation in to see me last night. Charlie, I got my business to hold together."

He was staring at his hands, turning the paper over and over as if he hoped to find something on it that was not there before. "I'm sorry, Charlie."

"But where will I go?"

He peered up at me for the first time since we'd walked into his cubbyhole office. "You know as well as I do that you don't *need* to work here any more."

"Mr. Donner, I've never worked anywhere else."

"Let's face it. You're not the Charlie who came in here seventeen years ago—not even the same Charlie of four months ago. You haven't talked about it. It's your own affair. Maybe a miracle of some kind—who knows? But you've changed into a very smart young man. And operating the dough mixer and delivering packages is no work for a smart young man."

He was right, of course, but something inside me wanted to make him change his mind.

"You've got to let me stay, Mr. Donner. Give me another chance. You said yourself that you promised Uncle Herman I would have a job here for as long as I needed it. Well, I still need it, Mr. Donner."

"You don't, Charlie. If you did then I'd tell them I don't care about their delegations and their petitions, and I'd stick up for you against all of them. But as it is now, they're all scared to death of you. I got to think of my own family too."

"What if they change their minds? Let me try to convince them." I was making it harder for him than he expected. I knew I should stop, but I couldn't control myself. "I'll make them understand," I pleaded.

"All right," he sighed finally. "Go ahead, try. But you're only going to hurt yourself."

As I came out of his office, Frank Reilly and Joe Carp walked by me, and I knew what he had said was true. Having me around to look at was too much for them. I made them all uncomfortable.

Frank had just picked up a tray of rolls and both he and Joe turned when I called. "Look, Charlie, I'm busy. Maybe later—"

"No," I insisted. "Now—right now. Both of you have been avoiding me. Why?"

Frank, the fast talker, the ladies' man, the arranger, studied me for a moment and then set the tray down on the table. "Why? I'll tell you why. Because all of a sudden you're a big shot, a know-it-all, a brain! Now you're a regular whiz kid, an egghead. Always with a book—always with all the answers. Well, I'll tell you something. You think you're better than the rest of us here? Okay, go someplace else."

"But what did I do to you?"

"What did he do? Hear that, Joe? I'll tell you what you did, *Mister* Gordon. You come pushing in here with your ideas and suggestions and make the rest of us all look like a bunch of dopes. But I'll tell you something. To me you're still a moron. Maybe I don't understand some of them big words or the names of the books, but I'm as good as you are—better even."

"Yeah." Joe nodded, turning to emphasize the point to Gimpy who had just come up behind him.

"I'm not asking you to be my friends," I said, "or have anything to do with me. Just let me keep my job. Mr. Donner says it's up to you."

Gimpy glared at me and then shook his head in disgust. "You got a nerve," he shouted. "You can go to hell!" Then he turned and limped off heavily.

And so it went. Most of them felt the way Joe and Frank and Gimpy did. It had been all right as long as they could laugh at me and appear clever at my expense, but now they were feeling inferior to the moron. I began to see that by my astonishing growth I had made them shrink and emphasized their inadequacies. I had betrayed them, and they hated me for it.

Fanny Birden was the only one who didn't think I should be forced to leave, and despite their pressure and threats, she had been the only one not to sign the petition.

"Which don't mean to say," she remarked, "that I don't think there's something mighty strange about you, Charlie. The way you've changed! I don't know. You used to be a good, dependable man—ordinary, not too bright maybe, but honest—and who knows what you done to yourself to get so smart all of a sudden. Like everybody's been saying—it ain't right."

"But what's wrong with a person wanting to be more intelligent, to acquire knowledge, and understand himself and the world?"

"If you'd read your Bible, Charlie, you'd know that it's not meant for man to know more than was given to him to know by the Lord in the first place. The fruit of that tree was forbidden to man. Charlie, if you done anything you wasn't supposed to—you know, like with the devil or something—maybe it ain't too late to get out of it. Maybe you could go back to being the good simple man you was before."

"There's no going back, Fanny. I haven't done anything wrong. I'm like a man born blind who has been given a chance to see light. That can't be sinful. Soon there'll be millions like me all over the world. Science can do it, Fanny."

She stared down at the bride and groom on the wedding cake she was decorating and I could see her lips barely move as she whispered: "It was evil when Adam and Eve ate from the *tree of knowledge.* It was evil when they saw they was naked, and learned about lust and shame. And they was driven out of Paradise and the gates was closed to them. If not for that none of us would have to grow old and be sick and die."

There was nothing more to say, to her or to the rest of them. None of them would look into my eyes. I can still feel the hostility. Before, they had laughed at me, despising me for my ignorance and dullness; now, they hated me for my knowledge and understanding. Why? What in God's name did they want of me?

This intelligence has driven a wedge between me and all the people I knew and loved, driven me out of the bakery. Now, I'm more alone than ever before. I wonder what would happen if they put Algernon back in the big cage with some of the other mice. Would *they* turn against him?

May 25—So this is how a person can come to despise himself —knowing he's doing the wrong thing and not being able to stop. Against my will I found myself drawn to Alice's apartment. She was surprised but she let me in.

"You're soaked. The water is streaming down your face."

"It's raining. Good for the flowers."

"Come on in. Let me get you a towel. You'll catch pneumonia."

"You're the only one I can talk to," I said. "Let me stay."

"I've got a pot of fresh coffee on the stove. Go ahead and dry yourself and then we can talk."

I looked around while she went to get the coffee. It was the first time I had ever been inside her apartment. I felt a sense of pleasure, but there was something disturbing about the room.

Everything was neat. The porcelain figurines were in a straight line on the window-ledge, all facing the same way. And the throw-pillows on the sofa hadn't been thrown at all, but were regularly spaced on the clear plastic covers that protected the upholstery. Two of the end tables had magazines, neatly stacked so that the titles were clearly visible. On one table: *The Reporter, The Saturday Review, The New Yorker*; on the other: *Mademoiselle, House Beautiful,* and *Reader's Digest.*

On the far wall, across from the sofa, hung an ornately framed reproduction of Picasso's "Mother and Child," and directly opposite, above the sofa, was a painting of a dashing Renaissance courtier, masked, sword in hand, protecting a frightened, pink-cheeked maiden. Taken all together, it was wrong. As if Alice couldn't make up her mind who she was and which world she wanted to live in.

"You haven't been to the lab for a few days," she called from the kitchen. "Professor Nemur is worried about you."

"I couldn't face them," I said. "I know there's no reason for me to be ashamed, but it's an empty feeling not going in to work every day—not seeing the shop, the ovens, the people. It's too much. Last night and the night before, I had nightmares of drowning."

She set the tray in the center of the coffee table—the napkins folded into triangles, and the cookies laid out in a circular display pattern. "You mustn't take it so hard, Charlie. It has nothing to do with you."

"It doesn't help to tell myself that. Those people—for all these years—were my family. It was like being thrown out of my own home."

"That's just it," she said. "This has become a symbolic repetition of experiences you had as a child. Being rejected by your parents . . . being sent away . . ."

"Oh, Christ! Never mind giving it a nice neat label. What matters is that before I got involved in this experiment I had friends, people who cared for me. Now I'm afraid—"

"You've still got friends."

"It's not the same."

"Fear is a normal reaction."

"It's more than that. I've been afraid before. Afraid of being strapped for not giving in to Norma, afraid of passing Howells Street where the gang used to tease me and push me around. And I was afraid of the schoolteacher, Mrs. Libby, who tied my hands so I wouldn't fidget with things on my desk. But those things were real—something I was justified in being afraid of. This terror at being kicked out of the bakery is vague, a fear I don't understand."

"Get hold of yourself."

"*You* don't feel the panic."

"But, Charlie, it's to be expected. You're a new swimmer forced off a diving raft and terrified of losing the solid wood under your feet. Mr. Donner *was* good to you, and you *were* sheltered all these years. Being driven out of the bakery this way is an even greater shock than you expected."

"Knowing it intellectually doesn't help. I can't sit alone in my room any more. I wander into the streets at all hours of the day or night, not knowing what I'm looking for . . . walking until I'm lost . . . finding myself outside the bakery. Last night I walked all the way from Washington Square to Central Park, and I slept in the park. What the hell am I searching for?"

The more I talked, the more upset she became. "What can I do to help you, Charlie?"

"I don't know. I'm like an animal who's been locked out of his nice, safe cage."

She sat beside me on the couch. "They're pushing you too fast. You're confused. You want to be an adult, but there's still a little boy inside you. Alone and frightened." She put my head on her shoulder, trying to comfort me, and as she stroked my hair I knew that she needed me the way I needed her.

"Charlie," she whispered after a while, "whatever you want . . . don't be afraid of me. . . ."

I wanted to tell her I was waiting for the panic.

Once—during a bakery delivery—Charlie had nearly fainted when a middle-aged woman, just out of the bath, amused herself by opening her bathrobe and exposing herself. Had he ever seen a woman without clothes on? Did he know how to make love? His terror—his whining—must have frightened her because she clutched her robe together and gave him a quarter to forget what had happened. She was only testing him, she warned, to see if he was a good boy.

He tried to be good, he told her, and not look at women, because his mother used to beat him whenever that happened in his pants. . . .

Now he had the clear picture of Charlie's mother, screaming at him, holding a leather belt in her hand, and his father trying to hold her back. "Enough, Rose! You'll kill him! Leave him alone!" His mother straining forward to lash at him, just out of reach now so that the belt swishes past his shoulder as he writhes and twists away from it on the floor.

"Look at him!" Rose screams. "He can't learn to read and write, but he knows enough to look at a girl that way. I'll beat that filth out of his mind."

"He can't help it if he gets an erection. It's normal. He didn't do anything."

"He's got no business to think that way about girls. A friend of his sister's comes to the house and he starts thinking like that! I'll teach him so he never forgets. Do you hear? If you ever touch a girl, I'll put you away in a cage, like an animal, for the rest of your life. Do you hear me? . . ."

I still hear her. But perhaps I had been released. Maybe the fear and nausea was no longer a sea to drown in, but only a pool of water reflecting the past alongside the now. Was I free?

If I could reach Alice in time—without thinking about it,

before it overwhelmed me—maybe the panic wouldn't happen. If only I could make my mind a blank. I managed to choke out: "You . . . you do it! Hold me!" And before I knew what she was doing, she was kissing me, holding me closer than anyone had ever held me before. But at the moment I should have come closest of all, it started: the buzzing, the chill, and the nausea. I turned away from her.

She tried to soothe me, to tell me it didn't matter, that there was no reason to blame myself. But ashamed, and no longer able to control my anguish, I began to sob. There in her arms I cried myself to sleep, and I dreamed of the courtier and the pink-cheeked maiden. But in my dream it was the maiden who held the sword.

PROGRESS REPORT 12

June 5—Nemur is upset because I haven't turned in any progress reports in almost two weeks (and he's justified because the Welberg Foundation has begun paying me a salary out of the grant so that I won't have to look for a job). The International Psychological Convention at Chicago is only a week away. He wants his preliminary report to be as full as possible, since Algernon and I are the prime exhibits for his presentation.

Our relationship is becoming increasingly strained. I resent Nemur's constant references to me as a laboratory specimen. He makes me feel that before the experiment I was not really a human being.

I told Strauss that I was too involved in thinking, reading, and digging into myself, trying to understand who and what I am, and that writing was such a slow process it made me impatient to get my ideas down. I followed his suggestion that I learn to type, and now that I can type nearly seventy-five words a minute, it's easier to get it all down on paper.

Strauss again brought up my need to speak and write simply and directly so that people will understand me. He reminds me that language is sometimes a barrier instead of a pathway. Ironic to find myself on the other side of the intellectual fence.

I see Alice occasionally, but we don't discuss what happened. Our relationship remains platonic. But for three nights after I left the bakery there were the nightmares. Hard to believe it was two weeks ago.

I am pursued down the empty streets at night by ghostly figures. Though I always run to the bakery, the door is locked, and the people inside never turn to look at me. Through the window, the bride and groom on the wedding cake point at me and laugh—the air becomes charged with laughter until I can't stand it—and the two cupids wave their flaming arrows. I scream. I pound on the door, but there is no sound. I see Charlie staring back at me from inside. Is it only a reflection? Things clutch at my legs and drag me away from the bakery down into the shadows of the alleyway, and just as they begin to ooze over me I wake up.

Other times the window of the bakery opens into the past and looking through it I see other things and other people.

It's astonishing how my power of recall is developing. I cannot control it completely yet, but sometimes when I'm busy reading or working on a problem, I get a feeling of intense clarity.

I know it's some kind of subconscious warning signal, and now instead of waiting for the memory to come to me, I close my eyes and reach out for it. Eventually, I'll be able to bring this recall completely under control, to explore not only the sum of my past experiences, but also all of the untapped faculties of the mind.

Even now, as I think about it, I feel the sharp stillness. I see the bakery window . . . reach out and touch it . . . cold and vibrating, and then the glass becomes warm . . . hotter . . . fingers burning. The window reflecting my image becomes bright, and as the glass turns into a mirror, I see little Charlie Gordon—fourteen or fifteen—looking out at me through the window of his house, and it's doubly strange to realize how different he was. . . .

He has been waiting for his sister to come from school, and when he sees her turn the corner onto Marks Street, he waves and calls her name and runs out onto the porch to meet her.

Norma waves a paper. "I got an *A* in my history test. I knew all the answers. Mrs. Baffin said it was the best paper in the whole class."

She is a pretty girl with light brown hair carefully braided and coiled about her head in a crown, and as she looks up at her big brother the smile turns to a frown and she skips away, leaving him behind as she darts up the steps into the house.

Smiling, he follows her.

His mother and father are in the kitchen, and Charlie, bursting with the excitement of Norma's good news, blurts it out before she has a chance.

"She got an *A*! She got an *A*!"

"No!" shrieks Norma. "Not you. You don't tell. It's my mark, and I'm going to tell."

"Now wait a minute, young lady." Matt puts his newspaper down and addresses her sternly. "That's no way to talk to your brother."

"He had no right to tell!"

"Never mind." Matt glares at her over his warning finger. "He meant no harm by it, and you mustn't shout at him that way."

She turns to her mother for support. "I got an *A*—the best mark in class. Now I can have a dog? You promised. You said if I got a good mark in my test. And I got an *A*. A brown dog with white spots. And I'm going to call him Napoleon because that was the question I answered best on the test. Napoleon lost the battle of Waterloo."

Rose nods. "Go out on the porch and play with Charlie. He's been waiting over an hour for you to come home from school."

"I don't want to play with him."

"Go out on the porch," says Matt.

Norma looks at her father and then at Charlie. "I don't have to. Mother said I don't have to play with him if I don't want to."

"Now, young lady"—Matt rises out of his chair and comes toward her—"you just apologize to your brother."

"I don't have to," she screeches, rushing behind her mother's chair. "He's like a baby. He can't play Monopoly or checkers or anything . . . he gets everything all mixed up. I won't play with him any more."

"Then go to your room!"

"Can I have a dog now, Mama?"

Matt hits the table with his fist. "There'll be no dog in this house as long as you take this attitude, young lady."

"I promised her a dog if she did well in school—"

"A brown one with white spots!" adds Norma.

Matt points to Charlie standing near the wall. "Did you forget you told your son he couldn't have one because we didn't have the room, and no one to take care of it. Remember? When he asked for a dog? Are you going back on what you said to him?"

"But I can take care of my own dog," insists Norma. "I'll feed him, and wash him, and take him out . . ."

Charlie, who has been standing near the table, playing with his large red button at the end of a string, suddenly speaks out.

"I'll help her take care of the dog! I'll help her feed it and brush it and I won't let the other dogs bite it!"

But before either Matt or Rose can answer, Norma shrieks: "No! It's going to be my dog. Only my dog!"

Matt nods. "You see?"

Rose sits beside her and strokes her braids to calm her. "But we have to share things, dear. Charlie can help you take care of it."

"No! Only mine! . . . I'm the one who got the *A* in history —not him! He never gets good marks like me. Why should he help with the dog? And then the dog will like him more than me, and it'll be his dog instead of mine. No! If I can't have it for myself I don't want it."

"That settles it," says Matt picking up his newspaper and settling down in his chair again. "No dog."

Suddenly, Norma jumps off the couch and grabs the history test she had brought home so eagerly just a few minutes earlier. She tears it and throws the pieces into Charlie's startled face. "I hate you! I hate you!"

"Norma, stop that at once!" Rose grabs her but she twists away.

"And I hate school! I hate it! I'll stop studying, and I'll be a dummy like him. I'll forget everything I learned and then I'll be just like him." She runs out of the room, shrieking: "It's happening to me already. I'm forgetting everything . . . I'm forgetting . . . I don't remember anything I learned any more!"

Rose, terrified, runs after her. Matt sits there staring at the newspaper in his lap. Charlie, frightened by the hysteria and the screaming, shrinks into a chair whimpering softly. What has he done wrong? And feeling the wetness in his trousers and the trickling down his leg, he sits there waiting for the slap he knows will come when his mother returns.

The scene fades, but from that time Norma spent all her free moments with her friends, or playing alone in her room. She kept the door to her room closed, and I was forbidden to enter without her permission.

I recall once overhearing Norma and one of her girl friends playing in her room, and Norma shouting: "He is not my real brother! He's just a boy we took in because we felt sorry for him. My mamma told me, and she said I can tell everyone now that he's not really my brother at all."

I wish this memory were a photograph so that I could tear it up and throw it back into her face. I want to call back across the years and tell her I never meant to stop her from getting her dog. She could have had it all to herself, and I wouldn't have fed it, or brushed it, or played with it—and I would never have made it like me more than it liked her. I only wanted her to play games with me the way we used to. I never meant to do anything that would hurt her at all.

June 6—My first real quarrel with Alice today. My fault. I wanted to see her. Often, after a disturbing memory or dream, talking to her—just being with her—makes me feel better. But it was a mistake to go down to the Center to pick her up.

I had not been back to the Center for Retarded Adults since the operation, and the thought of seeing the place was exciting. It's on Twenty-third Street, east of Fifth Avenue, in an old schoolhouse that has been used by the Beekman University Clinic for the last five years as a center for experimental education—special classes for the handicapped. The sign outside on the doorway, framed by the old spiked gateway, is just a gleaming brass plate that says *C. R. A. Beekman Extension.*

Her class ended at eight, but I wanted to see the room where —not so long ago—I had struggled over simple reading and writing and learned to count change of a dollar.

I went inside, slipped up to the door, and, keeping out of sight, I looked through the window. Alice was at her desk, and in a chair beside her was a thin-faced woman I didn't recognize. She was frowning that open frown of unconcealed puzzlement, and I wondered what Alice was trying to explain.

Near the blackboard was Mike Dorni in his wheelchair, and there in his usual first-row first-seat was Lester Braun, who, Alice said, was the smartest in the group. Lester had learned easily what I had struggled over, but he came when he felt like it, or he stayed away to earn money waxing floors. I guess if he had cared at all—if it had been important to him as it was to me—they would have used him for this experiment. There were new faces, too, people I didn't know.

Finally, I got up the nerve to go in.

"It's Charlie!" said Mike, whirling his wheelchair around.

I waved to him.

Bernice, the pretty blonde with empty eyes, looked up and smiled dully. "Where ya been, Charlie? That's a nice suit."

The others who remembered me waved to me and I waved back. Suddenly, I could see by Alice's expression that she was annoyed.

"It's almost eight o'clock," she announced. "Time to put things away."

Each person had an assigned task, the putting away of chalk, erasers, papers, books, pencils, note paper, paints, and demonstration material. Each one knew his job and took pride in doing it well. They all started on their tasks except Bernice. She was staring at me.

"Why ain't Charlie been coming to school?" asked Bernice. "What's the matter, Charlie? Are you coming back?"

The others looked up at me. I looked to Alice, waiting for her to answer for me, but there was a long silence. What could I tell them that would not hurt them?

"This is just a visit," I said.

One of the girls started to giggle—Francine, whom Alice was always worried about. She had given birth to three children by the time she was eighteen, before her parents arranged for a hysterectomy. She wasn't pretty—not nearly as attractive as Bernice—but she had been an easy mark for dozens of men who bought her something pretty, or paid her way to the movies. She lived at a boarding house approved for outside work trainees by the Warren State Home, and was permitted out in the evenings to come to the Center. Twice she hadn't shown up—picked up by men on the way to school—and now she was allowed out only with an escort.

"He talks like a big shot now," she giggled.

"All right," said Alice, breaking in sharply. "Class dismissed. I'll see you all tomorrow night at six."

When they were gone, I could see by the way she was slamming her own things into her closet, that she was angry.

"I'm sorry," I said. "I was going to wait for you downstairs, and then I got curious about the old classroom. My *alma mater*. I just wanted to look through the window. And before I knew what I was doing I came in. What's bothering you?"

"Nothing—nothing's bothering me."

"Come on. Your anger is all out of proportion to what's happened. Something's on your mind."

She slammed down a book she was holding. "All right. You want to know? You're different. You've changed. And I'm not talking about your I.Q. It's your attitude toward people—you're not the same kind of human being—"

"Oh, come on now! Don't—"

"Don't interrupt me!" The real anger in her voice pushed me back. "I mean it. There was something in you before. I don't know . . . a warmth, an openness, a kindness that made everyone like you and like to have you around. Now, with all your intelligence and knowledge, there are differences that—"

I couldn't let myself listen. "What did you expect? Did you think I'd remain a docile pup, wagging my tail and licking the foot that kicks me? Sure, all this has changed me and the way I think about myself. I no longer have to take the kind of crap that people have been handing me all my life."

"People have not been bad to you."

"What do you know about it? Listen, the best of them have been smug and patronizing—using me to make themselves superior and secure in their own limitations. Anyone can feel intelligent beside a moron."

After I said it, I knew she was going to take it the wrong way.

"You put me in that category too, I suppose."

"Don't be absurd. You know damned well I—"

"Of course, in a sense, I guess you're right. Next to you I am rather dull-witted. Nowadays every time we see each other, after I leave you I go home with the miserable feeling that I'm slow and dense about everything. I review things I've said, and come up with all the bright and witty things I should have said, and I feel like kicking myself because I didn't mention them when we were together."

"That's a common experience."

"I find myself wanting to impress you in a way I never thought about doing before, but being with you has undermined my self-confidence. I question my motives now, about everything I do."

I tried to get her off the subject, but she kept coming back to it. "Look, I didn't come here to argue with you," I finally said. "Will you let me take you home? I need someone to talk to."

"So do I. But these days I can't talk to you. All I can do is listen and nod my head and pretend I understand all about cultural variants, and neo-Boulean mathematics, and post-symbolic logic, and I feel more and more stupid, and when you leave the apartment, I have to stare in the mirror and scream at myself: 'No, you're not growing duller every day! You're not losing your intelligence! You're not getting senile and dull-witted. It's Charlie exploding forward so quickly that it makes it appear as if you're slipping backwards.' I say that to myself, Charlie, but whenever we meet and you tell me something and look at me in that impatient way, I know you're laughing.

"And when you explain things to me, and I can't remember them, you think it's because I'm not interested and don't want to take the trouble. But you don't know how I torture myself when you're gone. You don't know the books I've struggled over, the lectures I've sat in on at Beekman, and yet whenever I talk about something, I see how impatient you are, as if it were all childish. I wanted you to be intelligent. I wanted to help you and share with you—and now you've shut me out of your life."

As I listened to what she was saying, the enormity of it dawned on me. I had been so absorbed in myself and what was happening to me that I never thought about what was happening to her.

She was crying silently as we left the school, and I found

myself without words. All during the ride on the bus I thought to myself how upside-down the situation had become. She was terrified of me. The ice had broken between us and the gap was widening as the current of my mind carried me swiftly into the open sea.

She was right in refusing to torture herself by being with me. We no longer had anything in common. Simple conversation had become strained. And all there was between us now was the embarrassed silence and unsatisfied longing in a darkened room.

"You're very serious," she said, breaking out of her own mood and looking up at me.

"About us."

"It shouldn't make you so serious. I don't want to upset you. You're going through a great trial." She was trying to smile.

"But you did. Only I don't know what to do about it."

On the way from the bus stop to her apartment, she said, "I'm not going to the convention with you. I called Professor Nemur this morning and told him. There will be a lot for you to do there. Interesting people—the excitement of the spotlight for a while. I don't want to be in the way—"

"Alice—"

"—and no matter what you say about it now, I know that's how I'm going to *feel*, so if you don't mind, I'll hang on to my splintering ego—thank you."

"But you're making more of this than it is. I'm sure if you'll just—"

"You *know*? You're *sure*?" She turned and glared at me on the front steps of her apartment building. "Oh, how insufferable you've become. How do *you* know what I feel? You take liberties with other people's minds. You can't tell *how* I feel or *what* I feel or *why* I feel."

She started inside and then she looked back at me, her voice shaky: "I'll be here when you get back. I'm just upset, that's all, and I want both of us to have a chance to think this out while we're a good distance apart."

For the first time in many weeks she didn't ask me inside. I stared at the closed door with the anger mounting inside me. I wanted to create a scene, to bang on the door, to break it down. I wanted my anger to consume the building.

But as I walked away I felt a kind of simmering, then cooling, and finally a relief. I walked so fast I was drifting along the streets, and the feeling that hit my cheek was a cool breeze out of the summer night. Suddenly free.

I realize now that my feeling for Alice had been moving backwards against the current of my learning, from worship, to love, to fondness, to a feeling of gratitude and responsibility. My confused feeling for her had been holding me back, and I had clung to her out of my fear of being forced out on my own, and cut adrift.

But with the freedom came a sadness. I wanted to be in love with her. I wanted to overcome my emotional and sexual fears, to marry, have children, settle down.

Now it's impossible. I am just as far away from Alice with an I.Q. of 185 as I was when I had an I.Q. of 70. And this time we both know it.

June 8—What drives me out of the apartment to prowl through the city? I wander through the streets alone—not the relaxing stroll of a summer night, but the tense hurry to get—where? Down alleyways, looking into doorways, peering into half-shuttered windows, wanting someone to talk to and yet afraid to meet anyone. Up one street, and down another, through the endless labyrinth, hurling myself against the neon cage of the city. Searching . . . for what?

I met a woman in Central Park. She was sitting on a bench near the lake, with a coat clutched around her despite the heat. She smiled and motioned for me to sit beside her. We looked at the bright skyline on Central Park South, the honeycomb of lighted cells against the blackness, and I wished I could absorb them all.

Yes, I told her, I was from New York. No, I had never been to Newport News, Virginia. That's where she was from, and where she had married this sailor who was at sea now, and she hadn't seen him in two and a half years.

She twisted and knotted a handkerchief, using it from time to time to wipe the beaded sweat from her forehead. Even in the dim light reflected from the lake, I could see that she wore a great deal of make-up, but she looked attractive with her straight dark hair loose to her shoulders—except that her face was puffy and swollen as if she had just gotten up from sleep. She wanted to talk about herself, and I wanted to listen.

Her father had given her a good home, an education, everything a wealthy shipbuilder could give his only daughter—but not forgiveness. He would never forgive her elopement with the sailor.

She took my hand as she spoke, and rested her head on my shoulder. "The night Gary and I were married," she whispered, "I was a terrified virgin. And he just went crazy. First, he had to slap me and beat me. And then he took me with no love-making. That was the last time we were ever together. I never let him touch me again."

She could probably tell by the trembling of my hand that I was startled. It was too violent and intimate for me. Feeling my hand stir, she gripped it tighter as if she had to finish her story before she could let me go. It was important to her, and I sat quietly as one sits before a bird that feeds from your palm.

"Not that I don't like men," she assured me with wide-eyed openness. "I've been with other men. Not him, but lots of others. Most men are gentle and tender with a woman. They make love slowly, with caresses and kisses first." She looked at me meaningfully, and let her open palm brush back and forth against mine.

It was what I had heard about, read about, dreamed about. I didn't know her name, and she didn't ask mine. She just wanted me to take her someplace where we could be alone. I wondered what Alice would think.

I caressed her awkwardly and kissed her still more hesitantly so that she looked up at me. "What's the matter?" she whispered. "What are you thinking?"

"About you."

"Do you have a place we can go?"

Each step forward was caution. At what point would the ground give way and plunge me into anxiety? Something kept me moving ahead to test my footing.

"If you don't have a place, the Mansion Hotel on Fifty-third doesn't cost too much. And they don't bother you about luggage if you pay in advance."

"I have a room—"

She looked at me with new respect. "Well, that's fine."

Still nothing. And that in itself was curious. How far could I go without being overwhelmed by symptoms of panic? When we were alone in the room? When she undressed? When I saw her body? When we were lying together?

Suddenly, it was important to know if I could be like other men, if I could ever ask a woman to share a life with me. Having intelligence and knowledge wasn't enough. I wanted this, too. The sense of release and looseness was strong now with the feeling that it *was* possible. The excitement that came over me when I kissed her again communicated itself, and I was sure I could be normal with her. She was different from Alice. She was the kind of woman who had been around.

Then her voice changed, uncertain. "Before we go . . . Just one thing . . ." She stood up and took a step toward me in the spray of lamplight, opening her coat, and I could see the shape of her body as I had not imagined it all the time we were sitting next to each other in the shadows. "Only the fifth month," she said. "It doesn't make any difference. You don't mind, do you?"

Standing there with her coat open, she was superimposed as a double exposure on the picture of the middle-aged woman just out of the bathtub, holding open her bathrobe for Charlie to see. And I waited, as a blasphemer waits for lightning. I looked away. It was the last thing I had expected, but the coat wrapped tightly around her on such a hot night should have warned me that something was wrong.

"It's not my husband's," she assured me. "I wasn't lying to you about what I said before. I haven't seen him for years. It was a salesman I met about eight months ago. I was living with him. I'm not going to see him any more, but I'm going to keep the baby. We've just got to be careful—not rough or anything like that. But otherwise you don't have to worry."

Her voice ran down when she saw my anger. "That's filthy!" I shouted. "You ought to be ashamed of yourself."

She drew away, wrapping her coat quickly around her to protect what lay within.

As she made that protective gesture, I saw the second double image: my mother, heavy with my sister, in the days when she was holding me less, warming me less with her voice and touch, protecting me less against anyone who dared to say I was subnormal.

I think I grabbed her shoulder—I'm not sure, but then she was screaming, and I was sharply back to reality with the sense of danger. I wanted to tell her I had meant no harm—I would never hurt her or anyone. "Please, don't scream!"

But she was screaming, and I heard the running footsteps on the darkened path. This was something no one would understand. I ran into the darkness, to find an exit from the park, zig-zagging across one path and down another. I didn't know the park, and suddenly I crashed into something that threw me backwards. A wire-mesh fence—a dead end. Then I saw the swings and slides and realized it was a children's playground locked up for the night. I followed the fence, and kept going, half-running, stumbling over twisted roots. At the lake that curved around near the playground, I doubled back, found another path, went over the small footbridge and then around and under it. No exit.

"What is it? What happened, lady?"

"A maniac?"

"You all right?"

"Which way did he go?"

I had circled back to where I had started from. I slipped behind the huge outcropping of a rock and a screen of bramble and dropped flat on my stomach.

"Get a cop. There's never a cop when you need one."

"What happened?"

"A degenerate tried to rape her."

"Hey, some guy down there is chasing him. There he goes!"

"Come on! Get the bastard before he gets outta the park!"

"Careful. He's got a knife and a gun. . . ."

It was obvious that the shouting had flushed out the night crawlers because the cry of "there he goes!" was echoed from behind me, and looking out from behind the rock I could see a lone runner being chased down the lamplit path into the darkness. Seconds later, another one passed in front of the rock and disappeared into the shadows. I pictured myself being caught by this eager mob and beaten and torn by them. I deserved it. I almost wanted it.

I stood up, brushed the leaves and dirt from my clothing and walked slowly down the path in the direction from which I had come. I expected every second to be grabbed from behind and pulled down into the dirt and darkness, but soon I saw the bright lights of Fifty-ninth Street and Fifth Avenue, and I came out of the park.

Thinking about it now, in the security of my room, I am shaken with the rawness that touched me. Remembering how my mother looked before she gave birth to my sister is frightening. But even more frightening is the feeling that I wanted them to catch me and beat me. Why did I want to be punished? Shadows out of the past clutch at my legs and drag me down. I open my mouth to scream, but I am voiceless. My hands are trembling, I feel cold, and there is a distant humming in my ears.

PROGRESS REPORT 13

June 10—We're on a Strato-jet about to take off for Chicago. I owe this progress report to Burt who had the bright idea that I could dictate this on a transistor tape recorder and have a public stenographer in Chicago type it up. Nemur likes the idea. In fact, he wants me to use the recorder up to the last minute. He feels it will add to the report if they play the most recent tape at the end of the session.

So here I am, sitting off by myself in our private section of a jet on the way to Chicago, trying to get used to thinking aloud, and to the sound of my own voice. I suppose the typist can get rid of all the *uhm's*, *er's* and *ah's*, and make it all seem natural on paper (I can't help the paralysis that comes over me when I think hundreds of people are going to listen to the words I'm saying now).

My mind is a blank. At this point my feelings are more important than anything else.

The idea of going up in the air terrifies me.

As far as I can tell, in the days before the operation, I never really understood what planes were. I never connected the movies and TV close-ups of planes with the things that I saw zooming overhead. Now that we're about to take off I can think only of what might happen if we crash. A cold feeling, and the thought that I don't want to die. Brings to mind those discussions about God.

I've thought about death often in recent weeks, but not really about God. My mother took me to church occasionally —but I don't recall ever connecting that up with the thought of God. She mentioned Him quite often, and I had to pray to Him at night, but I never thought much about it. I remember Him as a distant uncle with a long beard on a throne (like Santa Claus in the department store on his big chair, who picks you up on his knee and asks you if you've been good, and what would you like him to give you?). She was afraid of Him, but asked favors anyway. My father never mentioned Him—it was as if God was one of Rose's relatives he'd rather not get involved with.

* * *

"We're ready to take off, sir. May I help you fasten your seat belt?"

"Do I have to? I don't like to be strapped down."

"Until we're airborne."

"I'd rather not, unless it's necessary. I've got this fear of being strapped in. It'll probably make me sick."

"It's regulations, sir. Here, let me help you."

"No! I'll do it myself."

"No . . . that one goes through here."

"Wait, uh. . . . Okay."

* * *

Ridiculous. There's nothing to be afraid of. Seat belt isn't too tight—doesn't hurt. Why should putting on the damned seat belt be so terrifying? That, and the vibrations of the plane taking off. Anxiety all out of proportion to the situation . . . so it must be something . . . what? . . . flying up into and through dark clouds . . . fasten your seat belts . . . strapped down . . . straining forward . . . odor of sweaty leather . . . vibrations and a roaring sound in my ears.

Through the window—in the clouds—I see Charlie. Age is difficult to tell, about five years old. Before Norma . . .

"Are you two ready yet?" His father comes to the doorway, heavy, especially in the sagging fleshiness of his face and neck. He has a tired look. "I said, are you ready?"

"Just a minute," answers Rose. "I'm getting my hat on. See if his shirt is buttoned, and tie his shoelaces."

"Come on, let's get this thing over with."

"Where?" asks Charlie. "Where . . . Charlie . . . go?"

His father looks at him and frowns. Matt Gordon never knows how to react to his son's questions.

Rose appears in the doorway of her bedroom, adjusting the half-veil of her hat. She is a birdlike woman, and her arms—up to her head, elbows out—look like wings. "We're going to the doctor who is going to help you get smart."

The veil makes it look as if she were peering down at him through a wire screen. He is always frightened when they dress up to go out this way, because he knows he will have to meet other people and his mother will become upset and angry.

He wants to run, but there is no place for him to go.

"Why do you have to tell him that?" says Matt.

"Because it's the truth. Dr. Guarino can help him."

Matt paces the floor like a man who has given up hope but will make one last attempt to reason. "How do you know? What do you know about this man? If there was anything that could be done, the doctors would have told us long ago."

"Don't say that," she screeches. "Don't tell me there's nothing they can do." She grabs Charlie and presses his head against her bosom. "He's going to be normal, whatever we have to do, whatever it costs."

"It's not something money can buy."

"It's Charlie I'm talking about. Your son . . . your only child." She rocks him from side to side, near hysteria now. "I won't listen to that talk. They don't know, so they say nothing can be done. Dr. Guarino explained it all to me. They won't sponsor his invention, he says, because it will prove they're wrong. Like it was with those other scientists, Pasteur and Jennings, and the rest of them. He told me all about your fine medical doctors afraid of progress."

Talking back to Matt this way, she becomes relaxed and sure of herself again. When she lets go of Charlie, he goes to the corner and stands against the wall frightened and shivering.

"Look," she says, "you got him upset again."

"Me?"

"You always start these things in front of him."

"Oh, Christ! Come on, let's get this damned thing over with."

All the way to Dr. Guarino's office they avoid speaking to each other. Silence on the bus, and silence walking three blocks from the bus to the downtown office building. After about fifteen minutes, Dr. Guarino comes out to the waiting room to greet them. He is fat and balding, and he looks as if he would pop through his white lab jacket. Charlie is fascinated by the thick white eyebrows and white moustache that twitch from time to time. Sometimes the moustache twitches first, followed by the raising of both eyebrows, but sometimes the brows go up first and the moustache twitch follows.

The large white room into which Guarino ushers them smells recently painted, and it is almost bare—two desks on one side of the room, and on the other, a huge machine with rows of dials and four long arms like dentist's drills. Nearby is a black leather examination table with thick, webbed, restraining straps.

"Well, well, well," says Guarino, raising his eyebrows, "so this is Charlie." He grips the boy's shoulders firmly. "We're going to be friends."

"Can you really do anything for him, Dr. Guarino?" says Matt. "Have you ever treated this kind of thing before? We don't have much money."

The eyebrows come down like shutters as Guarino frowns. "Mr. Gordon, have I said anything yet about what I could do? Don't I have to examine him first? Maybe something can be done, maybe not. First there will have to be physical and mental tests to determine the causes of the pathology. There will be enough time later to talk of prognosis. Actually, I'm very busy these days. I only agreed to look into this case because I'm doing a special study of this type of neural retardation. Of course, if you have qualms, then perhaps . . ."

His voice trails off sadly, and he turns away, but Rose Gordon jabs at Matt with her elbow. "My husband doesn't mean that at all, Dr. Guarino. He talks too much." She glares at Matt again to warn him to apologize.

Matt sighs. "If there is any way you can help Charlie, we'll do anything you ask. Things are slow these days. I sell barber-shop supplies, but whatever I have I'll be glad to—"

"Just one thing I must insist on," says Guarino, pursing his lips as if making a decision. "Once we start, the treatment must continue all the way. In cases of this type, the results often come suddenly after long months without any sign of improvement. Not that I am promising you success, mind you. Nothing is guaranteed. But you must give the treatment a chance, otherwise you're better off not starting at all."

He frowns at them to let his warning sink in, and his brows are white shades from under which his bright blue eyes stare. "Now, if you'll just step outside and let me examine the boy."

Matt hesitates to leave Charlie alone with him, but Guarino nods. "This is the best way," he says, ushering them both outside to the waiting room. "The results are always more significant if the patient and I are alone when the psychosubstantiation tests are performed. External distractions have a deleterious effect on the ramified scores."

Rose smiles at her husband triumphantly, and Matt follows her meekly outside.

Alone with Charlie, Dr. Guarino pats him on the head. He has a kindly smile.

"Okay, kid. On the table."

When Charlie doesn't respond, he lifts him gently onto the leather-padded table and straps him down securely with heavy webbed straps. The table smells of deeply ingrained sweat, and leather.

"Maaaa!"

"She's outside. Don't worry, Charlie. This won't hurt a bit."

"Want Ma!" Charlie is confused at being restrained this way. He has no sense of what is being done to him, but there have been other doctors who were not so gentle after his parents left the room.

Guarino tries to calm him. "Take it easy, kid. Nothing to be scared of. You see this big machine here? Know what I'm going to do with it?"

Charlie cringes, and then he recalls his mother's words. "Make me smart."

"That's right. At least you know what you're here for. Now, just close your eyes and relax while I turn on these switches. It'll make a loud noise, like an airplane, but it won't hurt you. And we'll see if we can make you a little bit smarter than you are now."

Guarino snaps on the switch that sets the huge machine humming, red and blue lights blinking on and off. Charlie is terrified. He cringes and shivers, straining against the straps that hold him fast to the table.

He starts to scream, but Guarino quickly pushes a wad of cloth into his mouth. "Now, now, Charlie. None of that. You be a good little boy. I told you it won't hurt."

He tries to scream again, but all that comes out is a muffled choking that makes him want to throw up. He feels the wetness and the stickiness around his legs, and the odor tells him that his mother will punish him with the spanking and the corner for making in his pants. He could not control it. Whenever he feels trapped and panic sets in, he loses control and dirties himself. Choking . . . sick . . . nausea . . . and everything goes black . . .

There is no way of knowing how much time passes, but when Charlie opens his eyes, the cloth is out of his mouth, and the straps have been removed. Dr. Guarino pretends he does not smell the odor. "Now that didn't hurt you a bit, did it?"

"N-no . . ."

"Well, then what are you trembling like that for? All I did was use that machine to make you smarter. How does it feel to be smarter now than you were before?"

Forgetting his terror, Charlie stares wide-eyed at the machine. "Did I get smart?"

"Of course you did. Uh, stand back over there. How does it feel?"

"Feels wet. I made."

"Yes, well—uh—you won't do that next time, will you? You won't be scared any more, now that you know it doesn't hurt. Now I want you to tell your mom how smart you feel, and she'll bring you here twice a week for shortwave encephalo-reconditioning, and you'll get smarter, and smarter, and smarter."

Charlie smiles. "I can walk backwards."

"You can? Let's see," says Guarino closing his folder in mock excitement. "Let me see."

Slowly, and with great effort, Charlie takes several steps backward, stumbling against the examination table as he goes. Guarino smiles and nods. "Now that's what I call something. Oh, you wait. You're going to be the smartest boy on your block before we're through with you."

Charlie flushes with pleasure at this praise and attention. It is not often that people smile at him and tell him he has done something well. Even the terror of the machine, and of being strapped down to the table, begins to fade.

"On the whole block?" The thought fills him as if he cannot take enough air into his lungs no matter how he tries. "Even smarter than Hymie?"

Guarino smiles again and nods. "Smarter than Hymie."

Charlie looks at the machine with new wonder and respect. The machine will make him smarter than Hymie who lives two doors away and knows how to read and write and is in the Boy Scouts. "Is that your machine?"

"Not yet. It belongs to the bank. But soon it'll be mine, and then I'll be able to make lots of boys like you smart." He pats Charlie's head and says, "You're a lot nicer than some of the normal kids whose mothers bring them here hoping I can make geniuses out of them by raising their I.Q.'s."

"Do they be jean-asses if you raise their eyes?" He puts his hands to his face to see if the machine had done anything to raise his eyes. "You gonna make me a jean-ass?"

Guarino's laugh is friendly as he squeezes Charlie's shoulder. "No, Charlie. Nothing for you to worry about. Only nasty little donkeys become jean-asses. You'll stay just the way you are—a nice kid." And then, thinking better of it, he adds: "Of course, a little smarter than you are now."

He unlocks the door and leads Charlie out to his parents. "Here he is, folks. None the worse for the experience. A good boy. I think we're going to be good friends, eh, Charlie?"

Charlie nods. He wants Dr. Guarino to like him, but he is terrified when he sees the expression on his mother's face. "Charlie! What did you do?"

"Just an accident, Mrs. Gordon. He was frightened the first

time. But don't blame him or punish him. I wouldn't want him to connect punishment with coming here."

But Rose Gordon is sick with embarrassment. "It's disgusting. I don't know what to do, Dr. Guarino. Even at home he forgets—and sometimes when we have people in the house. I'm so ashamed when he does that."

The look of disgust on his mother's face sets him trembling. For a short while he had forgotten how bad he is, how he makes his parents suffer. He doesn't know how, but it frightens him when she says he makes her suffer, and when she cries and screams at him, he turns his face to the wall and moans softly to himself.

"Now don't upset him, Mrs. Gordon, and don't worry. Bring him to me on Tuesday and Thursday each week at the same time."

"But will this really do any good?" asks Matt. "Ten dollars is a lot of—"

"Matt!" she clutches at his sleeve. "Is that anything to talk about at a time like this? Your own flesh and blood, and maybe Dr. Guarino can make him like other children, with the Lord's help, and you talk about money!"

Matt Gordon starts to defend himself, but then, thinking better of it, he pulls out his wallet.

"Please . . ." sighs Guarino, as if embarrassed at the sight of money. "My assistant at the front desk will take care of all the financial arrangements. Thank you." He half bows to Rose, shakes Matt's hand and pats Charlie on the back. "Nice boy. Very nice." Then, smiling again, he disappears behind the door to the inner office.

They argue all the way home, Matt complaining that barber supply sales have fallen off, and that their savings are dwindling, Rose screeching back that making Charlie normal is more important than anything else.

Frightened by their quarreling, Charlie whimpers. The sound of anger in their voices is painful to him. As soon as they enter the apartment, he pulls away and runs to the corner of the kitchen, behind the door and stands with his forehead pressed against the tile wall, trembling and moaning.

They pay no attention to him. They have forgotten that he has to be cleaned and changed.

"I'm not hysterical. I'm just sick of you complaining every time I try to do something for your son. You don't care. You just don't care."

"That's not true! But I realize there's nothing we can do. When you've got a child like him it's a cross, and you bear it, and love it. Well, I can bear him, but I can't stand your foolish ways. You've spent almost all our savings on quacks and phonies—money I could have used to set me up in a nice business of my own. Yes. Don't look at me that way. For all the money you've thrown down the sewer to do something that can't be done, I could have had a barbershop of my own instead of eating my heart out selling for ten hours a day. My own place with people working for *me*!"

"Stop shouting. Look at him, he's frightened."

"The hell with you. Now I know who's the dope around here. Me! For putting up with you." He storms out, slamming the door behind him.

* * *

"Sorry to interrupt you, sir, but we're going to be landing in a few minutes. You'll have to fasten your seat belt again . . . Oh, you have it on, sir. You've had it on all the way from New York. Close to two hours . . ."

"I forgot all about it. I'll just leave it on until we land. It doesn't seem to bother me any more."

* * *

Now I can see where I got the unusual motivation for becoming *smart* that so amazed everyone at first. It was something Rose Gordon lived with day and night. Her fear, her guilt, her shame that Charlie was a moron. Her dream that something could be done. The urgent question always: whose fault was it, hers or Matt's? Only after Norma proved to her that she was capable of having normal children, and that I was a freak, did she stop trying to make me over. But I guess I never stopped wanting to be the smart boy she wanted me to be, so that she would love me.

A funny thing about Guarino. I should resent him for what he did to me, and for taking advantage of Rose and Matt, but somehow I can't. After that first day, he was always pleasant to me. There was always the pat on the shoulder, the smile, the encouraging word that came my way so rarely.

He treated me—even then—as a human being.

It may sound like ingratitude, but that is one of the things that I resent here—the attitude that I am a guinea pig. Nemur's constant references to having *made me what I am*, or that someday there will be others like me who *will become real human beings*.

How can I make him understand that he did not create me?

He makes the same mistake as the others when they look at a feeble-minded person and laugh because they don't understand there are human feelings involved. He doesn't realize that I was a person before I came here.

I am learning to control my resentment, not to be so impatient, to wait for things. I guess I'm growing up. Each day I learn more and more about myself, and the memories that began as ripples now wash over me in high-breaking waves. . . .

June 11—The confusion began from the moment we arrived at the Chalmers Hotel in Chicago and discovered that by error our rooms would not be vacant until the next night and until then we would have to stay at the nearby Independence Hotel. Nemur was furious. He took it as a personal affront and quarrelled with everyone in the line of hotel command from the bellhop to the manager. We waited in the lobby as each hotel official went off in search of his superior to see what could be done.

In the midst of all the confusion—luggage drifting in and piling up all around the lobby, bellboys hustling back and forth with their little baggage carts, members who hadn't seen each other in a year, recognizing and greeting each other—we stood there feeling increasingly embarrassed as Nemur tried to collar officials connected with the International Psychological Association.

Finally, when it became apparent that nothing could be done about it, he accepted the fact that we would have to spend our first night in Chicago at the Independence.

As it turned out, most of the younger psychologists were staying at the Independence, and that was where the big first-night parties were. Here, people had heard about the experiment, and most of them knew who I was. Wherever we went, someone came up and asked my opinions on everything from the effects of the new tax to the latest archaeological discoveries in Finland. It was challenging, and my storehouse of general knowledge made it easy for me to talk about almost anything. But after a while I could see that Nemur was annoyed at all the attention I was getting.

When an attractive young clinician from Falmouth College asked me if I could explain some of the causes of my own retardation, I told her that Professor Nemur was the man to answer that.

It was the chance he had been waiting for to show his authority, and for the first time since we'd known each other he put his hand on my shoulder. "We don't know exactly what causes the type of phenylketonuria that Charlie was suffering from as a child—some unusual biochemical or genetic situation, possibly ionizing radiation or natural radiation or even a virus attack on the fetus—whatever it was resulted in a defective gene which produces a, shall we say, 'maverick enzyme' that creates defective biochemical reactions. And, of course, newly produced amino acids compete with the normal enzymes causing brain damage."

The girl frowned. She had not expected a lecture, but Nemur had seized the floor and he went on in the same vein. "I call it *competitive inhibition of enzymes.* Let me give you an example of how it works. Think of the enzyme produced by the defective gene as *a wrong key which fits* into the chemical lock of the central nervous system—*but won't turn.* Because it's there, the true key—the right enzyme—can't even enter the lock. It's blocked. Result? Irreversible destruction of proteins in the brain tissue."

"But if it is irreversible," intruded one of the other psychologists who had joined the little audience, "how is it possible that Mr. Gordon here is no longer retarded?"

"Ah!" crowed Nemur, "I said the destruction to the tissue was irreversible, not the process itself. Many researchers have been able to reverse the process through injections of chemicals which combine with the defective enzymes, changing the molecular shape of the interfering key, as it were. This is central to our own technique as well. But first, we remove the damaged portions of the brain and permit the implanted brain tissue which has been chemically revitalized to produce brain proteins at a supernormal rate—"

"Just a minute, Professor Nemur," I said, interrupting him at the height of his peroration. "What about Rahajamati's work in that field?"

He looked at me blankly. "Who?"

"Rahajamati. His article attacks Tanida's theory of enzyme fusion—the concept of changing the chemical structure of the enzyme blocking the step in the metabolic pathway."

He frowned. "Where was that article translated?"

"It hasn't been translated yet. I read it in the *Hindu Journal of Psychopathology* just a few days ago."

He looked at his audience and tried to shrug it off. "Well, I don't think we have anything to worry about. Our results speak for themselves."

"But Tanida himself first propounded the theory of blocking the maverick enzyme through combination, and now he points out that—"

"Oh, come now, Charlie. Just because a man is the first to come forth with a theory doesn't make him the final word on its experimental development. I think everyone here will agree that the research done in the United States and Britain far outshines the work done in India and Japan. We still have the best laboratories and the best equipment in the world."

"But that doesn't answer Rahajamati's point that—"

"This is not the time or place to go into that. I'm certain all of these points will be adequately dealt with in tomorrow's session." He turned to talk to someone about an old college friend, cutting me off completely, and I stood there dumbfounded.

I managed to get Strauss off to one side, and I started questioning him. "All right, now. You've been telling me I'm too sensitive to him. What did I say that upset him that way?"

"You're making him feel inferior and he can't take it."

"I'm serious, for God's sake. Tell me the truth."

"Charlie, you've got to stop thinking that everyone is laughing at you. Nemur couldn't discuss those articles because he hasn't read them. He can't read those languages."

"Not read Hindi and Japanese? Oh, come on now."

"Charlie, not everyone has your gift for languages."

"But then how can he refute Rahajamati's attack on this method, and Tanida's challenge to the validity of this kind of control? He must know about those—"

"No . . . ," said Strauss thoughtfully. "Those papers must be recent. There hasn't been time to get translations made."

"You mean you haven't read them either?"

He shrugged. "I'm an even worse linguist than he is. But I'm certain before the final reports are turned in, all the journals will be combed for additional data."

I didn't know what to say. To hear him admit that both of them were ignorant of whole areas in their own fields was terrifying. "What languages do you know?" I asked him.

"French, German, Spanish, Italian, and enough Swedish to get along."

"No Russian, Chinese, Portuguese?"

He reminded me that as a practicing psychiatrist and neurosurgeon he had very little time for languages. And the only ancient languages that he could read were Latin and Greek. Nothing of the ancient Oriental tongues.

I could see he wanted to end the discussion at that point, but somehow I couldn't let go. I had to find out just how much he knew.

I found out.

Physics: nothing beyond the quantum theory of fields. Geology: nothing about geomorphology or stratigraphy or even petrology. Nothing about the micro- or macroeconomic theory. Little in mathematics beyond the elementary level of calculus of variations, and nothing at all about Banach algebra or Riemannian manifolds. It was the first inkling of the revelations that were in store for me this weekend.

I couldn't stay at the party. I slipped away to walk and think this out. Frauds—both of them. They had pretended to be geniuses. But they were just ordinary men working blindly, pretending to be able to bring light into the darkness. Why is it that everyone lies? No one I know is what he appears to be. As I turned the corner I caught a glimpse of Burt coming after me.

"What's the matter?" I said as he caught up to me. "Are you following me?"

He shrugged and laughed uncomfortably. "Exhibit *A*, star of the show. Can't have you run down by one of these motorized Chicago cowboys or mugged and rolled on State Street."

"I don't like being kept in custody."

He avoided my gaze as he walked beside me, his hands deep in his pockets. "Take it easy, Charlie. The old man is on edge. This convention means a lot to him. His reputation is at stake."

"I didn't know you were so close to him," I taunted, recalling all the times Burt had complained about the professor's narrowness and pushing.

"I'm not close to him." He looked at me defiantly. "But he's put his whole life into this. He's no Freud or Jung or Pavlov or Watson, but he's doing something important and I respect his dedication—maybe even more because he's just an ordinary man trying to do a great man's work, while the great men are all busy making bombs."

"I'd like to hear you call him ordinary to his face."

"It doesn't matter what he thinks of himself. Sure he's egotistic, so what? It takes that kind of ego to make a man attempt a thing like this. I've seen enough of men like him to know that mixed in with that pompousness and self-assertion is a goddamned good measure of uncertainty and fear."

"And phoniness and shallowness," I added. "I see them now as they really are, phonies. I suspected it of Nemur. He always seemed frightened of something. But Strauss surprised me."

Burt paused and let out a long stream of breath. We turned into a luncheonette for coffee, and I didn't see his face, but the sound revealed his exasperation.

"You think I'm wrong?"

"Just that you've come a long way kind of fast," he said. "You've got a superb mind now, intelligence that can't really be calculated, more knowledge absorbed by now than most people pick up in a long lifetime. But you're lopsided. You know things. You see things. But you haven't developed understanding, or—I hate to use the word—tolerance. You call them phonies, but when did either of them ever claim to be perfect, or superhuman? They're ordinary people. You're the genius."

He broke off awkwardly, suddenly aware that he was preaching at me.

"Go ahead."

"Ever meet Nemur's wife?"

"No."

"If you want to understand why he's under tension all the time, even when things are going well at the lab and in his lectures, you've got to know Bertha Nemur. Did you know she got him his professorship? Did you know she used her father's influence to get him the Welberg Foundation grant? Well, now she's pushed him into this premature presentation at the convention. Until you've had a woman like her riding you, don't think you can understand the man who has."

I didn't say anything, and I could see he wanted to get back to the hotel. All the way back we were silent.

Am I a genius? I don't think so. Not yet anyway. As Burt would put it, mocking the euphemisms of educational jargon, I'm *exceptional*—a democratic term used to avoid the damning labels of *gifted* and *deprived* (which used to mean *bright* and *retarded*) and as soon as *exceptional* begins to mean anything to anyone they'll change it. The idea seems to be: use an expression only as long as it doesn't mean anything to anybody. *Exceptional* refers to both ends of the spectrum, so all my life I've been exceptional.

Strange about learning; the farther I go the more I see that I never knew even existed. A short while ago I foolishly thought I could learn everything—all the knowledge in the world. Now I hope only to be able to know of its existence, and to understand one grain of it.

Is there time?

Burt is annoyed with me. He finds me impatient and the others must feel the same. But they hold me back and try to keep me in my place. What is my place? Who and what am I now? Am I the sum of my life or only of the past months? Oh, how impatient they get when I try to discuss it with them. They don't like to admit that they don't know. It's paradoxical that an ordinary man like Nemur presumes to devote himself to making other people geniuses. He would like to be thought of as the discoverer of new laws of learning—the Einstein of psychology. And he has the teacher's fear of being surpassed by the student, the master's dread of having the disciple discredit his work. (Not that I am in any real sense Nemur's student or disciple as Burt is.)

I guess Nemur's fear of being revealed as a man walking on stilts among giants is understandable. Failure at this point would destroy him. He is too old to start all over again.

As shocking as it is to discover the truth about men I had respected and looked up to, I guess Burt is right. I must not be too impatient with them. Their ideas and brilliant work made the experiment possible. I've got to guard against the natural tendency to look down on them now that I have surpassed them.

I've got to realize that when they continually admonish me to speak and write simply so that people who read these reports will be able to understand me, they are talking about themselves as well. But still it's frightening to realize that my fate is in the hands of men who are not the giants I once thought them to be, men who don't know all the answers.

June 13—I'm dictating this under great emotional strain. I've walked out on the whole thing. I'm on a plane headed back to New York alone, and I have no idea what I'm going to do when I get there.

At first, I admit, I was in awe at the picture of an international convention of scientists and scholars, gathered for an exchange of ideas. Here, I thought, was where it all really happened. Here it would be different from the sterile college discussions, because these were the men on the highest levels of psychological research and education, the scientists who wrote the books and delivered the lectures, the authorities people quoted. If Nemur and Strauss were ordinary men working beyond their abilities, I felt sure it would be different with the others.

When it was time for the meeting, Nemur steered us through the gigantic lobby with its heavy baroque furnishings and huge curving marble staircases, and we moved through the thickening knots of handshakers, nodders, and smilers. Two other professors from Beekman who had arrived in Chicago just this morning joined us. Professors White and Clinger walked a little to the right and a step or two behind Nemur and Strauss, while Burt and I brought up the rear.

Standees parted to make a path for us into the Grand Ballroom, and Nemur waved to the reporters and photographers who had come to hear at first hand about the startling things that had been done with a retardate adult in just a little over three months.

Nemur had obviously sent out advance publicity releases.

Some of the psychological papers delivered at the meeting were impressive. A group from Alaska showed how stimulation of various portions of the brain caused a significant development in learning ability, and a group from New Zealand had mapped out those portions of the brain that controlled perception and retention of stimuli.

But there were other kinds of papers too—P. T. Zellerman's study on the difference in the length of time it took white rats to learn a maze when the corners were curved rather than angular, or Worfel's paper on the effect of intelligence level on the reaction-time of rhesus monkeys. Papers like these made me angry. Money, time, and energy squandered on the detailed analysis of the trivial. Burt was right when he praised Nemur and Strauss for devoting themselves to something important and uncertain rather than to something insignificant and safe.

If only Nemur would look at me as a human being.

After the chairman announced the presentation from Beekman University, we took our seats on the platform behind the long table—Algernon in his cage between Burt and me. We were the main attraction of the evening, and when we were settled, the chairman began his introduction. I half expected to hear him boom out: *Laideezzz and gentulmennnnnn. Step right this way and see the side show! An act never before seen in the scientific world! A mouse and a moron turned into geniuses before your very eyes!*

I admit I had come here with a chip on my shoulder.

All he said was: "The next presentation really needs no introduction. We have all heard about the startling work being done at Beekman University, sponsored by the Welberg Foundation grants, under the direction of the chairman of the psychology department, Professor Nemur, in co-operation with Dr. Strauss of the Beekman Neuropsychiatric Center. Needless to say, this is a report we have all been looking forward to with great interest. I turn the meeting over to Professor Nemur and Dr. Strauss."

Nemur nodded graciously at the chairman's introductory praise and winked at Strauss in the triumph of the moment.

The first speaker from Beekman was Professor Clinger.

I was becoming irritated, and I could see that Algernon, upset by the smoke, the buzzing, the unaccustomed surroundings, was moving around in his cage nervously. I had the strangest compulsion to open his cage and let him out. It was an absurd thought—more of an itch than a thought—and I tried to ignore it. But as I listened to Professor Clinger's stereotyped paper on "The effects of left-handed goal boxes in a T-maze versus right-handed goal boxes in a T-maze," I found myself toying with the release-lock mechanism of Algernon's cage.

In a short while (before Strauss and Nemur would unveil their crowning achievement) Burt would read a paper describing the procedures and results of administering intelligence and learning tests he had devised for Algernon. That would be followed by a demonstration as Algernon was put through his paces of solving a problem in order to get his meal (something I have never stopped resenting!).

Not that I had anything against Burt. He had always been straightforward with me—more so than most of the others—but when he described the white mouse who had been given intelligence, he was as pompous and artificial as the others. As if he were trying on the mantle of his teachers. I restrained myself at that point more out of friendship for Burt than anything else. Letting Algernon out of his cage would throw the meeting into chaos, and after all this was Burt's debut into the rat-race of academic preferment.

I had my finger on the cage door release, and as Algernon watched the movement of my hand with his pink-candy eyes, I'm certain he knew what I had in mind. At that moment Burt took the cage for his demonstration. He explained the complexity of the shifting lock, and the problem-solving required each time the lock was to be opened. (Thin plastic bolts fell into place in varying patterns and had to be controlled by the mouse, who depressed a series of levers in the same order.) As Algernon's intelligence increased, his problem-solving speed increased—that much was obvious. But then Burt revealed one thing I had *not* known.

At the peak of his intelligence, Algernon's performance had become variable. There were times, according to Burt's report, when Algernon refused to work at all—even when apparently hungry—and other times when he would solve the problem but, instead of taking his food reward, would hurl himself against the walls of his cage.

When someone from the audience asked Burt if he was suggesting that this erratic behavior was directly caused by increased intelligence, Burt ducked the question. "As far as I am concerned," he said, "there's not enough evidence to warrant that conclusion. There are other possibilities. It is possible that both the increased intelligence and the erratic behavior at this level were created by the original surgery, instead of one being a function of the other. It's also possible that this erratic behavior is unique to Algernon. We didn't find it in any of the other mice, but then none of the others achieved as high a level of intelligence nor maintained it for as long as Algernon has."

I realized immediately that this information had been withheld from me. I suspected the reason, and I was annoyed, but that was nothing to the anger I felt when they brought out the films.

I had never known that my early performances and tests in the laboratory were filmed. There I was, at the table beside Burt, confused and open-mouthed as I tried to run the maze with the electric stylus. Each time I received a shock, my expression changed to an absurd wide-eyed stare, and then that foolish smile again. Each time it happened the audience roared. Race after race, it was repeated, and each time they found it funnier than before.

I told myself they were not gawking curiosity seekers, but scientists here in search of knowledge. They couldn't help finding these pictures funny—but still, as Burt caught the spirit and made amusing comments on the films, I was overcome with a sense of mischief. It would be even funnier to see Algernon escape from his cage, and to see all these people scattering and crawling around on their hands and knees trying to retrieve a small, white, scurrying genius.

But I controlled myself, and by the time Strauss took the podium the impulse had passed.

Strauss dealt largely with the theory and techniques of neurosurgery, describing in detail how pioneer studies on the mapping of hormone control centers enabled him to isolate and stimulate these centers while at the same time removing the hormone-inhibitor producing portion of the cortex. He explained the enzyme-block theory and went on to describe my physical condition before and after surgery. Photographs (I didn't know they had been taken) were passed around and commented on, and I could see by the nods and smiles that most people there agreed with him that the "dull, vacuous facial expression" had been transformed into an "alert, intelligent appearance." He also discussed in detail the pertinent aspects of our therapy sessions—especially my changing attitudes toward free association on the couch.

I had come there as part of a scientific presentation, and I had expected to be put on exhibition, but everyone kept talking about me as if I were some kind of newly created thing they were presenting to the scientific world. No one in this room considered me an individual—a human being. The constant juxtaposition of "Algernon and Charlie," and "Charlie and Algernon," made it clear that they thought of both of us as a couple of experimental animals who had no existence outside the laboratory. But, aside from my anger, I couldn't get it out of my mind that something was wrong.

Finally, it was Nemur's turn to speak—to sum it all up as the head of the project—to take the spotlight as the author of a brilliant experiment. This was the day he had been waiting for.

He was impressive as he stood up there on the platform, and, as he spoke, I found myself nodding with him, agreeing with things I knew to be true. The testing, the experiment, the surgery, and my subsequent mental development were described at length, and his talk was enlivened by quotations from my progress reports. More than once I found myself hearing something personal or foolish read to this audience. Thank God I had been careful to keep most of the details about Alice and myself in my private file.

Then, at one point in his summary, he said it: "We who

have worked on this project at Beekman University have the
satisfaction of knowing we have taken one of nature's mistakes
and by our new techniques created a superior human being.
When Charlie came to us he was outside of society, alone in
a great city without friends or relatives to care about him,
without the mental equipment to live a normal life. No past,
no contact with the present, no hope for the future. It might
be said that Charlie Gordon did not really exist before this
experiment. . . ."

I don't know why I resented it so intensely to have them
think of me as something newly minted in their private trea-
sury, but it was—I am certain—echoes of that idea that had
been sounding in the chambers of my mind from the time we
had arrived in Chicago. I wanted to get up and show everyone what a fool he was, to shout at him: *I'm a human being,
a person—with parents and memories and a history—and I was
before you ever wheeled me into that operating room!*

At the same time deep in the heat of my anger there was
forged an overwhelming insight into the thing that had disturbed me when Strauss spoke and again when Nemur am-
plified his data. They had made a mistake—of course! The
statistical evaluation of the waiting period necessary to prove
the permanence of the change had been based on earlier experiments in the field of mental development and learning, on
waiting periods with normally dull or normally intelligent animals. But it was obvious that the waiting period would have to
be extended in those cases where an animal's intelligence had
been increased two or three times.

Nemur's conclusions had been premature. For both Algernon and myself, it would take more time to see if this change
would stick. The professors had made a mistake, and no one
else had caught it. I wanted to jump up and tell them, but I
couldn't move. Like Algernon, I found myself behind the mesh
of the cage they had built around me.

Now there would be a question period, and before I would
be allowed to have my dinner, I would be required to perform
before this distinguished gathering. No. I had to get out of
there.

". . . In one sense, he is the result of modern psychological
experimentation. In place of a feeble-minded shell, a burden

on the society that must fear his irresponsible behavior, we have a man of dignity and sensitivity, ready to take his place as a contributing member of society. I should like you all to hear a few words from Charlie Gordon. . . ."

God damn him. He didn't know what he was talking about. At that point, the compulsion overwhelmed me. I watched in fascination as my hand moved, independent of my will, to pull down the latch on Algernon's cage. As I opened it he looked up at me and paused. Then he turned, darted out of his cage, and scampered across the long table.

At first, he was lost against the damask tablecloth, a blur of white on white, until a woman at the table screamed, knocking her chair backwards as she leaped to her feet. Beyond her, pitchers of water overturned, and then Burt shouted. "Algernon's loose!" Algernon jumped down from the table, onto the platform and then to the floor.

"Get him! Get him!" Nemur screeched as the audience, divided in its aims, became a tangle of arms and legs. Some of the women (non-experimentalists?) tried to stand on the unstable folding chairs while others, trying to help corner Algernon, knocked them over.

"Close those back doors!" shouted Burt, who realized Algernon was smart enough to head in that direction.

"Run," I heard myself shout. "The side door!"

"He's gone out the side door," someone echoed.

"Get him! Get him!" begged Nemur.

The crowd surged out of the Grand Ballroom into the corridor, as Algernon, scampering along the maroon carpeted hallway, led them a merry chase. Under Louis XIV tables, around potted palms, up stairways, around corners, down stairways, into the main lobby, picking up other people as we went. Seeing them all running back and forth in the lobby, chasing a white mouse smarter than many of them, was the funniest thing that had happened in a long time.

"Go ahead, laugh!" snorted Nemur, who nearly bumped into me, "but if we don't find him, the whole experiment is in danger."

I pretended to be looking for Algernon under a waste basket. "Do you know something?" I said. "You've made a mistake. And after today, maybe it just won't matter at all."

Seconds later, half a dozen women came screaming out of the powder room, skirts clutched frantically around their legs.

"He's in there," someone yelled. But for a moment, the searching crowd was stayed by the handwriting on the wall —*Ladies*. I was the first to cross the invisible barrier and enter the sacred gates.

Algernon was perched on top of one of the washbasins, glaring at his reflection in the mirror.

"Come on," I said. "We'll get out of here together."

He let me pick him up and put him into my jacket pocket. "Stay in there quietly until I tell you."

The others came bursting through the swinging doors —looking guiltily as if they expected to see screaming nude females. I walked out as they searched the washroom, and I heard Burt's voice. "There's a hole in that ventilator. Maybe he went up there."

"Find out where it leads to," said Strauss.

"You go up to the second floor," said Nemur, waving to Strauss. "I'll go down to the basement."

At this point they burst out of the ladies' room and the forces split. I followed behind the Strauss contingent up to the second floor as they tried to discover where the ventilator led to. When Strauss and White and their half-dozen followers turned right down Corridor B, I turned left up Corridor C and took the elevator to my room.

I closed the door behind me, and patted my pocket. A pink snout and white fuzz poked out and looked around. "I'll just get my things packed," I said, "and we'll take off—just you and me—a couple of man-made geniuses on the run."

I had the bellhop put the bags and the tape-recorder into a waiting taxi, paid my hotel bill, and walked out the revolving door with the object of the search nestling in my jacket pocket. I used my return-flight ticket to New York.

Instead of going back to my place, I plan to stay at a hotel here in the city for one or two nights. We'll use that as a base of operations while I look for a furnished apartment, somewhere midtown. I want to be near Times Square.

Talking all this out makes me feel a lot better—even a little silly. I don't really know why I got so upset, or what I'm doing on a jet heading back to New York with Algernon in a shoebox under the seat. I mustn't panic. The mistake doesn't necessarily mean anything serious. It's just that things are not as definite as Nemur believed. But where do I go from here?

First, I've got to see my parents. As soon as I can.

I may not have all the time I thought I had. . . .

PROGRESS REPORT 14

June 15—Our escape hit the papers yesterday, and the tabloids had a field day. On the second page of the *Daily Press* there was an old picture of me and a sketch of a white mouse. The headline read: *Moron-Genius and Mouse Go Berserk*. Nemur and Strauss are reported as saying I had been under tremendous strain and that I would undoubtedly return soon. They offered a five-hundred-dollar reward for Algernon, not realizing we were together.

When I turned to the later story on the fifth page, I was stunned to find a picture of my mother and sister. Some reporter had obviously done his legwork.

SISTER UNAWARE OF MORON-GENIUS' WHEREABOUTS
(*Special to the Daily Press*)

Brooklyn, N.Y., June 14—Miss Norma Gordon, who lives with her mother, Rose Gordon, at 4136 Marks Street, Brooklyn, N.Y., denied any knowledge of her brother's whereabouts. Miss Gordon said, "We haven't seen him or heard from him in more than seventeen years."

Miss Gordon says she believed her brother dead until last March, when the head of the psychology department at Beekman University approached her for permission to use Charlie in an experiment.

"My mother told me he had been sent to the Warren place," (Warren State Home and Training School, in Warren, Long Island) said Miss Gordon, "and that he died there a few years later. I had no idea then that he was still alive."

Miss Gordon requests that anyone who has any news about her brother's whereabouts communicate with the family at their home address.

The father, Matthew Gordon, who is not living with his wife and daughter, now operates a barbershop in the Bronx.

I stared at the news story for a while, and then I turned back and looked at the picture again. How can I describe them?

I can't say I remember Rose's face. Although the recent photograph is a clear one, I still see it through the gauze of childhood. I knew her, and I didn't know her. Had we passed on the street, I would not have recognized her, but now, knowing she is my mother, I can make out the faint details—yes!

Thin, drawn into exaggerated lines. Sharp nose and chin. And I can almost hear her chatter and bird-screech. Hair done up in a bun, severely. Piercing me with her dark eyes. I want her to take me into her arms and tell me I am a good boy, and at the same time I want to turn away to avoid a slap. Her picture makes me tremble.

And Norma—thin-faced too. Features not so sharp, pretty, but very much like my mother. Her hair worn down to her shoulders softens her. The two of them are sitting on the living room couch.

It was Rose's face that brought back the frightening memories. She was two people to me, and I never had any way of knowing which she would be. Perhaps she would reveal it to others by a gesture of hand, a raised eyebrow, a frown—my sister knew the storm warnings, and she would always be out of range whenever my mother's temper flared—but it always caught me unawares. I would come to her for comforting, and her anger would break over me.

And other times there would be tenderness and holding-close like a warm bath, and hands stroking my hair and brow, and the words carved above the cathedral of my childhood:

> *He's like all the other children.*
> *He's a good boy.*

I see back through the dissolving photograph, myself and father leaning over a bassinet. He's holding me by the hand and saying, "There she is. You mustn't touch her because she's very little, but when she gets bigger you'll have a sister to play with."

I see my mother in the huge bed nearby, bleached and pasty, arms limp on the orchid-figured comforter, raising her head anxiously. "Watch him, Matt—"

That was before she had changed towards me, and now I

realize it was because she had no way of knowing yet if Norma would be like me or not. It was later on, when she was sure her prayers had been answered, and Norma showed all signs of normal intelligence, that my mother's voice began to sound different. Not only her voice, but her touch, her look, her very presence—all changed. It was as if her magnetic poles had reversed and where they had once attracted now repelled. I see now that when Norma flowered in our garden I became a weed, allowed to exist only where I would not be seen, in corners and dark places.

Seeing her face in the newspaper, I suddenly hated her. It would have been better if she had ignored the doctors and teachers and others who were so in a hurry to convince her that I was a moron, turning her away from me so that she gave me less love when I needed more.

What good would it do to see her now? What could she tell me about myself? And yet, I'm curious. How would she react?

To see her and trace back to learn what I was? Or to forget her? Is the past worth knowing? Why is it so important for me to say to her: "Mom, look at me. I'm not retarded any more. I'm normal. Better than normal. I'm a genius"?

Even as I try to get her out of my mind, the memories seep back from the past to contaminate the here and now. Another memory—when I was much older.

A quarrel.

Charlie lying in bed, with the covers pulled up around him. The room dark, except for the thin line of yellow light from the door ajar that penetrates the darkness to join both worlds. And he hears things, not understanding but feeling, because the rasp of their voices is linked to their talk of him. More and more, each day, he comes to associate that tone with a frown when they speak of him.

He had been almost asleep when through the bar of light the soft voices were raised to the pitch of argument—his mother's voice sharp with the threat of one used to having her way through hysteria. "He's got to be sent away. I don't want him in the house any more with her. Call Dr. Portman and tell him we want to send Charlie to the Warren State Home."

My father's voice is firm, steadying. "But you know Charlie

wouldn't harm her. It can't make any difference to her at this age."

"How do we know? Maybe it has a bad effect on a child to grow up with . . . someone like him in the house."

"Dr. Portman said—"

"Portman said! Portman said! I don't care what he said! Think of what it will be like for her to have a brother like that. I was wrong all these years, trying to believe he would grow up like other children. I admit it now. Better for him to be put away."

"Now that you've got her, you've decided you don't want him any more. . . ."

"Do you think this is easy? Why are you making it harder for me? All these years everyone telling me he should be put away. Well, they were right. Put him away. Maybe at the Home with his own kind he'll have something. I don't know what's right or wrong any more. All I know is I'm not going to sacrifice my daughter for him now."

And though Charlie has not understood what passed between them, he is afraid and sinks beneath the covers, eyes open, trying to pierce the darkness that surrounds him.

As I see him now, he is not really afraid, just withdrawing, as a bird or squirrel backs off from the brusque movements of the feeder—involuntary, instinctive. The light through that door ajar comes to me again in luminous vision. Seeing Charlie huddled beneath the covers I wish I could give him comfort, explain to him that he has done nothing wrong, that it is beyond him to change his mother's attitude back to what it was before his sister came. There on the bed, Charlie did not understand what they were saying, but now it hurts. If I could reach out into the past of my memories, I would make her see how much she was hurting me.

This is no time to go to her. Not until I've had time to work it out for myself.

Fortunately, as a precaution, I withdrew my savings from the bank as soon as I arrived in New York. Eight hundred and eighty-six dollars won't last long, but it will give me time to get my bearings.

I've checked into the Camden Hotel on 41st Street, a block from Times Square. New York! All the things I've read about it! Gotham . . . the melting pot . . . Baghdad-on-the-Hudson. City of light and color. Incredible that I've lived and worked all my life just a few stops away on the subway and been to Times Square only once—with Alice.

It's hard to keep from calling her. I've started and stopped myself several times. I've got to keep away from her.

So many confusing thoughts to get down. I tell myself that as long as I keep taping my progress reports, nothing will be lost; the record will be complete. Let them be in the dark for a while; I was in the dark for more than thirty years. But I'm tired now. Didn't get to sleep on the plane yesterday, and I can't keep my eyes open. I'll pick up at this point tomorrow.

June 16—Called Alice, but hung up before she answered. Today I found a furnished apartment. Ninety-five dollars a month is more than I planned to spend, but it's on Forty-third and Tenth Avenue and I can get to the library in ten minutes to keep up with my reading and study. The apartment is on the fourth floor, four rooms, and there's a rented piano in it. The landlady says that one of these days the rental service will pull it out, but maybe by that time I can learn to play it.

Algernon is a pleasant companion. At mealtimes he takes his place at the small gateleg table. He likes pretzels, and today he took a sip of beer while we watched the ball game on TV. I think he rooted for the Yankees.

I'm going to move most of the furniture out of the second bedroom and use the room for Algernon. I plan to build him a three-dimensional maze out of scrap plastic that I can pick up cheaply downtown. There are some complex maze variations I'd like him to learn to be sure he keeps in shape. But I'm going to see if I can find some motivation other than food. There must be other rewards that will induce him to solve problems.

Solitude gives me a chance to read and think, and now that the memories are coming through again—to rediscover my past, to find out who and what I really am. If anything should go wrong, I'll have at least that.

June 19—Met Fay Lillman, my neighbor across the hall. When I came back with an armful of groceries, I discovered I had locked myself out, and I remembered that the front fire escape connected my living room window and the apartment directly across the hall.

The radio was on loud and brassy, so I knocked—softly at first, and then louder.

"Come on in! Door's open!"

I pushed the door, and froze, because standing in front of an easel, painting, was a slender blonde in pink bra and panties.

"Sorry!" I gasped, closing the door again. From outside, I shouted. "I'm your neighbor across the hall. I locked myself out, and I wanted to use the fire escape to get over to my window."

The door swung open and she faced me, still in her underwear, a brush in each hand and hands on her hips. "Didn't you hear me say come in?" She waved me into the apartment, pushing away a carton full of trash. "Just step over that pile of junk there."

I thought she must have forgotten—or not realized—she was undressed, and I didn't know which way to look. I kept my eyes averted, looking at the walls, ceiling, everywhere but at her.

The place was a shambles. There were dozens of little folding snack-tables, all covered with twisted tubes of paint, most of them crusted dry like shriveled snakes, but some of them alive and oozing ribbons of color. Tubes, brushes, cans, rags, and parts of frames and canvas were strewn everywhere. The place was thick with the odor compounded of paint, linseed oil, and turpentine—and after a few moments the subtle aroma of stale beer. Three overstuffed chairs and a mangy green couch were piled high with discarded clothing, and on the floor lay shoes, stockings and underthings, as if she were in the habit of undressing as she walked and flinging her clothes as she went. A fine layer of dust covered everything.

"Well, you're Mr. Gordon," she said, looking me over. "I've been dying to get a peek at you ever since you moved in. Have a seat." She scooped up a pile of clothing from one of the chairs and dumped it onto the crowded sofa. "So you finally decided to visit your neighbors. Get you a drink?"

"You're a painter," I burbled, for want of something to say. I was unnerved by the thought that any moment she would realize she was undressed and would scream and dash for the bedroom. I tried to keep my eyes moving, looking everywhere but at her.

"Beer or ale? Nothing else in the place right now except cooking sherry. You don't want cooking sherry, do you?"

"I can't stay," I said, getting hold of myself and fixing my gaze at the beauty mark on the left side of her chin. "I've locked myself out of my apartment. I wanted to go across the fire escape. It connects our windows."

"Any time," she assured me. "Those lousy patent locks are a pain in the ass. I locked myself out of this place three times the first week I lived here—and once I was out in the hall stark naked for half an hour. Stepped out to get the milk, and the goddamned door swung shut behind me. I ripped the goddamned lock off and I haven't had one on my door since."

I must have frowned, because she laughed. "Well, you see what the damned locks do. They lock you out, and they don't protect much, do they? Fifteen burglaries in this goddamned building in the past year and every one of them in apartments that were locked. No one ever broke in here, even though the door was always open. They'd have a rotten time finding anything valuable here anyway."

When she insisted again on my having a beer with her, I accepted. While she was getting it from the kitchen, I looked around the room again. What I hadn't noticed before was that the part of the wall behind me had been cleared away—all the furniture pushed to one side of the room or the center, so that the far wall (the plaster of which had been torn off to expose the brick) served as an art gallery. Paintings were crowded to the ceiling and others were stacked against each other on the floor. Several of them were self-portraits, including two nudes. The painting she had been working on when I came in, the one on the easel, was a half-length nude of herself, showing her hair long (not the way she wore it now, up in blonde braids coiled around her head like a crown) down to her shoulders with part of her long tresses twisted around the front and resting between her breasts. She had painted her breasts uptilted and firm with the nipples an unrealistic lollipop-red. When I heard her coming back with the beer, I spun away from the easel quickly, stumbled over some books, and pretended to be interested in a small autumn landscape on the wall.

I was relieved to see that she had slipped into a thin ragged housecoat—even though it had holes in all the wrong places—and I could look directly at her for the first time. Not exactly beautiful, but her blue eyes and pert snub nose gave her a catlike quality that contrasted with her robust, athletic movements. She was about thirty-five, slender and well proportioned. She set the beers on the hardwood floor, curled up beside them in front of the sofa, and motioned for me to do the same.

"I find the floor more comfortable than chairs," she said, sipping the beer from the can. "Don't you?"

I told her I hadn't thought about it, and she laughed and said I had an honest face. She was in the mood to talk about herself. She avoided Greenwich Village, she said, because there, instead of painting, she would be spending all her time in bars and coffee shops. "It's better up here, away from the phonies and the dilettantes. Here I can do what I want and no one comes to sneer. You're not a sneerer, are you?"

I shrugged, trying not to notice the gritty dust all over my trousers and my hands. "I guess we all sneer at something. You're sneering at the phonies and dilettantes, aren't you?"

After a while, I said I'd better be getting over to my own apartment. She pushed a pile of books away from the window —and I climbed over newspapers and paper bags filled with empty quart beer bottles. "One of these days," she sighed, "I've got to cash them in."

I climbed onto the window sill and out to the fire escape. When I got my window open, I came back for my groceries, but before I could say thanks and good-bye, she started out onto the fire escape after me. "Let's see your place. I've never been there. Before you moved in, the two little old Wagner sisters wouldn't even say good morning to me." She crawled through my window behind me and sat on the ledge.

"Come on in," I said, putting the groceries on the table.

"I don't have any beer, but I can make you a cup of coffee." But she was looking past me, her eyes wide in disbelief.

"My God! I've never seen a place as neat as this. Who would dream that a man living by himself could keep a place so orderly?"

"I wasn't always that way," I apologized. "It's just since I moved in here. It was neat when I moved in, and I've had the compulsion to keep it that way. It upsets me now if anything is out of place."

She got down off the window sill to explore the apartment.

"Hey," she said, suddenly, "do you like to dance? You know—" She held out her arms and did a complicated step as she hummed a Latin beat. "Tell me you dance and I'll bust."

"Only the fox trot," I said, "and not very good at that."

She shrugged. "I'm nuts about dancing, but nobody I ever meet—that I like—is a good dancer. I've got to get myself all dolled up once in a while and go downtown to the Stardust Ballroom. Most of the guys hanging around there are kind of creepy, but they can dance."

She sighed as she looked around. "Tell you what I don't like about a place so goddamned orderly like this. As an artist . . . it's the lines that get me. All the straight lines in the walls, on the floors, in the corners that turn into boxes—like coffins. The only way I can get rid of the boxes is to take a few drinks. Then all the lines get wavy and wiggly, and I feel a lot better about the whole world. When things are all straight and lined up this way I get morbid. Ugh! If I lived here I would have to stay drunk all the time."

Suddenly, she swung around and faced me. "Say, could you let me have five until the twentieth? That's when my alimony check comes. I usually don't run short, but I had a problem last week."

Before I could answer, she screeched and started over to the piano in the corner. "I used to play the piano. I heard you fooling around with it a few times, and I said to myself that guy's goddamned good. That's how I knew I wanted to meet you even before I saw you. I haven't played in such a goddamned long time." She was picking away at the piano as I went into the kitchen to make coffee.

"You're welcome to practice on it any time," I said. I don't know why I suddenly became so free with my place, but there was something about her that demanded complete unselfishness. "I don't leave the front door open yet, but the window isn't locked, and if I'm not here all you've got to do is climb in through the fire escape. Cream and sugar in your coffee?"

When she didn't answer, I looked back into the living room. She wasn't there, and as I started towards the window, I heard her voice from Algernon's room.

"Hey, what's this?" She was examining the three dimensional plastic maze I had built. She studied it and then let out another squeal. "Modern sculpture! All boxes and straight lines!"

"It's a special maze," I explained. "A complex learning device for Algernon."

But she was circling around it, excited. "They'll go mad for it at the Museum of Modern Art."

"It's not sculpture," I insisted. I opened the door to Algernon's living-cage attached to the maze, and let him into the maze opening.

"My God!" she whispered. "Sculpture with a *living element.* Charlie, it's the greatest thing since junkmobiles and tincannia."

I tried to explain, but she insisted that the living element would make sculpture history. Only when I saw the laughter in her eyes did I realize she was teasing me. "It could be self-perpetuating art," she went on, "a creative experience for the art lover. You get another mouse and when they have babies, you always keep one to reproduce the living element. Your work of art attains immortality, and all the fashionable people buy copies for conversation pieces. What are you going to call it?"

"All right," I sighed. "I surrender. . . ."

"No," she snorted, tapping the plastic dome where Algernon had found his way into the goal-box. "*I surrender* is too much of a cliché. How about: *Life is just a box of mazes?*"

"You're a nut!" I said.

"Naturally!" She spun around and curtsied. "I was wondering when you'd notice."

About then the coffee boiled over.

Halfway through the cup of coffee, she gasped and said she had to run because she had a date a half-hour earlier with someone she met at an art exhibit.

"You wanted some money," I said.

She reached into my half open wallet and pulled out a five-dollar bill. "Till next week," she said, "when the check comes. Thanks a mill." She crumpled the money, blew Algernon a kiss, and before I could say anything she was out the window onto the fire escape, and out of sight. I stood there foolishly looking after her.

So damned attractive. So full of life and excitement. Her voice, her eyes—everything about her was an invitation. And she lived out the window and just a fire escape away.

June 20—Perhaps I should have waited before going to see Matt; or not gone to see him at all. I don't know. Nothing turns out the way I expect it to. With the clue that Matt had opened a barbershop somewhere in the Bronx, it was a simple matter to find him. I remembered he had sold for a barber supply company in New York. That led me to Metro Barber Shop Supplies who had a barbershop account under the name of *Gordons Barber Shop* on Wentworth Street in the Bronx.

Matt had often talked about a barbershop of his own. How he hated selling! What battles they had about it! Rose screaming that a salesman was at least a dignified occupation, but she would never have a barber for a husband. And oh, wouldn't Margaret Phinney snicker at the "barber's wife." And what about Lois Meiner whose husband was a claims examiner for the Alarm Casualty Company? Wouldn't she stick her nose up in the air!

During the years he worked as a salesman, hating every day of it (especially after he saw the movie version of *Death of a Salesman*) Matt dreamed that he would someday become his own boss. That must have been in his mind in those days when he talked about saving money and gave me my haircuts down in the basement. They were good haircuts too, he boasted, a lot better than I'd get in that cheap barbershop on Scales Avenue. When he walked out on Rose, he walked out on selling too, and I admired him for that.

I was excited at the thought of seeing him. Memories were warm ones. Matt had been willing to take me as I was. Before Norma: the arguments that weren't about money or impressing the neighbors were about me—that I should be let alone instead of being pushed to do what other kids did. And after Norma: that I had a right to a life of my own even though I wasn't like other children. Always defending me. I couldn't wait to see the expression on his face. He was someone I'd be able to share this with.

Wentworth Street was a rundown section of the Bronx. Most of the stores on the street had "For Rent" signs in the windows, and others were closed for the day. But halfway down the block from the bus stop there was a barber pole reflecting a candy cane of light from the window.

The shop was empty except for the barber reading a magazine in the chair nearest the window. When he looked up at me, I recognized Matt—stocky, red-cheeked, a lot older and nearly bald with a fringe of gray hair bordering the sides of his head—but still Matt. Seeing me at the door, he tossed the magazine aside.

"No waiting. You're next."

I hesitated, and he misunderstood. "Usually not open at this hour, mister. Had an appointment with one of my regulars, but he didn't show. Just about to close. Lucky for you I sat down to rest my feet. Best haircut and shave in the Bronx."

As I let myself be drawn into the shop, he bustled around, pulling out scissors and combs and a fresh neckcloth.

"Everything sanitary, as you can see, which is more than I can say for most barbershops in this neighborhood. Haircut and shave?"

I eased myself into the chair. Incredible that he didn't recognize me when I knew him so plainly. I had to remind myself that he had not seen me in more than fifteen years, and that my appearance had changed even more in the past months. He studied me in the mirror now that he had me covered with the striped neckcloth, and I saw a frown of faint recognition.

"The works," I said, nodding at the union-shop price list, "haircut, shave, shampoo, sun-tan . . ."

His eyebrows went up.

"I've got to meet someone I haven't seen in a long time," I assured him, "and I want to look my best."

It was a frightening sensation, having him cut my hair again. Later, as he stropped the razor against leather the harsh whisper made me cringe. I bent my head under the gentle press of his hand and felt the blade scrape carefully across my neck. I closed my eyes and waited. It was as if I were on the operating table again.

My neck muscle knotted, and without warning it twitched. The blade nicked me just above the Adam's apple.

"Hey!" he shouted. "Jesus . . . take it easy. You moved. Hey, I'm awful sorry."

He dashed to wet a towel at the sink.

In the mirror I watched the bright red bubble and the thin line dripping down my throat. Excited and apologizing, he got to it before it reached the neckcloth.

Watching him move, adroit for such a short, heavy man, I felt guilty at the deception. I wanted to tell him who I was and have him put his arm around my shoulder, so we could talk about the old days. But I waited while he dabbed at the cut with styptic powder.

He finished shaving me silently, and then brought the suntan lamp over to the chair and put cool white pads of cotton soaked in witch hazel over my eyes. There, in the bright red inner darkness I saw what happened the night he took me away from the house for the last time. . . .

Charlie is asleep in the other room, but he wakens to the sound of his mother shrieking. He has learned to sleep through quarrels—they are an everyday occurrence in his house. But tonight there is something terribly wrong in that hysteria. He shrinks back into the pillow and listens.

"I can't help it! He's got to go! We've got her to think about. I won't have her come home from school crying every day like this because the children tease her. We can't destroy her chance for a normal life because of him."

"What do you want to do? Turn him out into the street?"

"Put him away. Send him to the Warren State Home."

"Let's talk it over in the morning."

"No. All you do is talk talk, and you don't do anything. I don't want him here another day. Now—tonight."

"Don't be foolish, Rose. It's too late to do anything . . . tonight. You're shouting so loud everyone will hear you."

"I don't care. He goes out tonight. I can't stand looking at him any more."

"You're being impossible, Rose. What are you doing?"

"I warn you. Get him out of here."

"Put that knife down."

"I'm not going to have her life destroyed."

"You're crazy. Put that knife away."

"He's better off dead. He'll never be able to live a normal life. He'll be better off—"

"You're out of your mind. For God's sake, control yourself!"

"Then take him away from here. Now—tonight."

"All right. I'll take him over to Herman tonight and maybe tomorrow we'll find out about getting him into the Warren State Home."

There is silence. From the darkness I feel the shudder pass over the house, and then Matt's voice, less panicky than hers. "I know what you've gone through with him, and I can't blame you for being afraid. But you've got to control yourself. I'll take him over to Herman. Will that satisfy you?"

"That's all I ask. Your daughter is entitled to a life too."

Matt comes into Charlie's room and dresses his son, and though the boy doesn't understand what is happening, he is afraid. As they go out the door, she looks away. Perhaps she is trying to convince herself that he has already gone out of her life—that he no longer exists. On the way out, Charlie sees on the kitchen table the long carving knife she cuts roasts with, and he senses vaguely that she wanted to hurt him. She wanted to take something away from him, and give it to Norma.

When he looks back at her, she has picked up a rag to wash the kitchen sink. . . .

When the haircut, shave, sun treatment, and the rest were over, I sat in the chair limply, feeling light, and slick, and clean, and Matt whisked the neckcloth off and offered me a second mirror to see the reflection of the back of my head. Seeing myself in the front mirror looking into the back mirror, as he held it for me, it tilted for an instant into the one angle that produced the illusion of depth; endless corridors of myself . . . looking at myself . . . looking at myself . . . looking at myself . . . looking . . .

Which one? Who was I?

I thought of not telling him. What good was it for him to know? Just go away and not reveal who I was. Then I remembered that I wanted him to know. He had to admit that I was alive, that I was someone. I wanted him to boast about me to the customers tomorrow as he gave haircuts and shaves. That would make it all real. If he knew I was his son, then I would be a person.

"Now that you've got the hair off my face, maybe you'll know me," I said as I stood up, waiting for a sign of recognition.

He frowned. "What is this? A gag?"

I assured him it was not a gag, and if he looked and thought hard enough he would know me. He shrugged and turned to put his combs and scissors away. "I got no time for guessing games. Got to close up. That'll be three-fifty."

What if he didn't remember me? What if this was only an absurd fantasy? His hand was out for the money, but I made no move toward my wallet. He had to remember me. He had to know me.

But no—of course not—and as I felt the sour taste in my mouth and the sweat in my palms, I knew that in a minute I would be sick. But I didn't want that in front of him.

"Hey, you all right?"

"Yes . . . just . . . wait . . ." I stumbled into one of the chrome chairs and bent forward gasping for breath, waiting for the blood to come back to my head. My stomach was churning. Oh, God, don't let me faint now. Don't let me look ridiculous in front of him.

"Water . . . some water, please . . ." Not so much for the drink as to make him turn away. I didn't want him to see me like this after all these years. By the time he returned with a glass, I felt a little better.

"Here, drink this. Rest a minute. You'll be okay." He stared at me as I sipped the cool water, and I could see him struggling with half-forgotten memories. "Do I really know you from somewhere?"

"No . . . I'm okay. I'll leave in a minute."

How could I tell him? What was I supposed to say? Here, look at me, I'm Charlie, the son you wrote off the books? Not that I blame you for it, but here I am, all fixed up better than ever. Test me. Ask me questions. I speak twenty languages, living and dead; I'm a mathematical whiz, and I'm writing a piano concerto that will make them remember me long after I'm gone.

How could I tell him?

How absurd I was sitting in his shop, waiting for him to pat me on the head and say, "Good boy." I wanted his approval, the old glow of satisfaction that came to his face when I learned to tie my own shoelaces and button my sweater. I had come here for that look in his face, but I knew I wouldn't get it.

"You want me to call a doctor?"

I wasn't his son. That was another Charlie. Intelligence and knowledge had changed me, and he would resent me—as the others from the bakery resented me—because my growth diminished him. I didn't want that.

"I'm okay," I said. "Sorry to be a nuisance." I got up and tested my legs. "Something I ate. I'll let you close up now."

As I headed towards the door, his voice called after me sharply. "Hey, wait a minute!" His eyes met mine with suspicion. "What are you trying to pull?"

"I don't understand."

His hand was out, rubbing his thumb and forefinger together. "You owe me three-fifty."

I apologized as I paid him, but I could see that he didn't believe it. I gave him five, told him to keep the change, and hurried out of his barbershop without looking back.

June 21—I've added time sequences of increasing complexity to the three dimensional maze, and Algernon learns them easily. There is no need to motivate him with food or water. He appears to learn for the sake of solving the problem—success appears to be its own reward.

But, as Burt pointed out at the convention, his behavior is erratic. Sometimes after, or even during a run, he will rage, throw himself against the walls of the maze, or curl up and refuse to work at all. Frustration? Or something deeper?

5:30 P.M.—That crazy Fay came in through the fire escape this afternoon with a female white mouse—about half Algernon's size—to keep him company, she said, on these lonely summer nights. She quickly overcame all my objections and convinced me that it would do Algernon good to have companionship. After I assured myself that little "Minnie" was of sound health and good moral character, I agreed. I was curious to see what he would do when confronted with a female. But once we had put Minnie into Algernon's cage, Fay grabbed my arm and pulled me out of the room.

"Where's your sense of romance?" she insisted. She turned on the radio, and advanced toward me menacingly. "I'm going to teach you the latest steps."

How can you get annoyed at a girl like Fay?

At any rate, I'm glad that Algernon is no longer alone.

June 23—Late last night the sound of laughter in the hallway and a tapping on my door. It was Fay and a man.

"Hi, Charlie," she giggled as she saw me. "Leroy, meet Charlie. He's my across-the-hall neighbor. A wonderful artist. He does sculpture with a living element."

Leroy caught hold of her and kept her from bumping into the wall. He looked at me nervously and mumbled a greeting.

"Met Leroy at the Stardust Ballroom," she explained. "He's a terrific dancer." She started into her apartment and then pulled him back. "Hey," she giggled, "why don't we invite Charlie over for a drink and make it a party?"

Leroy didn't think it was a good idea.

I managed an apology and pulled away. Behind my closed door, I heard them laughing their way into her apartment, and though I tried to read, the pictures kept forcing their way into my mind: a big white bed . . . white cool sheets and the two of them in each other's arms.

I wanted to phone Alice, but I didn't. Why torment myself? I couldn't even visualize Alice's face. I could picture Fay, dressed or undressed, at will, with her crisp blue eyes and her blonde hair braided and coiled around her head like a crown. Fay was clear, but Alice was wrapped in mist.

About an hour later I heard shouting from Fay's apartment, then her scream and the sound of things being thrown, but as I started out of bed to see if she needed help, I heard the door slam—Leroy cursing as he left. Then, a few minutes afterward,

I heard a tapping on my living room window. It was open, and Fay slipped in and sat on the ledge, a black silk kimono revealing lovely legs.

"Hi," she whispered, "got a cigareet?"

I handed her one and she slipped down from the window ledge to the couch. "Whew!" she sighed, "I can usually take care of myself, but there's one type that's so hungry it's all you can do to hold them off."

"Oh," I said, "you brought him up here to hold him off."

She caught my tone and looked up sharply. "You don't approve?"

"Who am I to disapprove? But if you pick up a guy in a public dance hall you've got to expect advances. He had the right to make a pass at you."

She shook her head. "I go to the Stardust Ballroom because I like to dance, and I don't see that because I let a guy bring me home I've got to go to bed with him. You don't think I went to bed with him, do you?"

My image of the two of them in each other's arms popped like soap bubbles.

"Now if you were the guy," she said, "it would be different."

"What is that supposed to mean?"

"Just what it sounds like. If you asked me, I'd go to bed with you."

I tried to keep my composure. "Thanks," I said. "I'll keep that in mind. Can I get you a cup of coffee?"

"Charlie, I can't figure you out. Most men like me or not, and I know it right away. But you seem afraid of me. You're not a homosexual, are you?"

"Hell, no!"

"I mean you don't have to hide it from me if you are, because then we could be just good friends. But I'd have to know."

"I'm not a homosexual. Tonight, when you went into your place with that guy, I wished it was me."

She leaned forward and the kimono open at the neck revealed her bosom. She slipped her arms around me, waiting for me to do something. I knew what was expected of me, and I told myself there was no reason not to. I had the feeling there would be no panic now—not with her. After all, I wasn't the one making the advances. And she was different from any woman I'd ever met before. Perhaps she was right for me at this emotional level.

I slipped my arms around her.

"That's different," she cooed. "I was beginning to think you didn't care."

"I care," I whispered, kissing her throat. But as I did it, I saw the two of us, as if I were a third person standing in the doorway. I was watching a man and woman in each other's arms. But seeing myself that way, from a distance, left me unresponsive. There was no panic, it was true, but there was also no excitement—no desire.

"Your place or mine?" she asked.

"Wait a minute."

"What's the matter?"

"Maybe we'd better not. I don't feel well this evening."

She looked at me wonderingly. "Is there anything else? . . . Anything you want me to do? . . . I don't mind . . ."

"No, that's not it," I said sharply. "I just don't feel well tonight." I was curious about the ways she had of getting a man excited, but this was no time to start experimenting. The solution to my problem lay elsewhere.

I didn't know what else to say to her. I wished she'd go away, but I didn't want to tell her to go. She was studying me, and then finally she said, "Look, do you mind if I spend the night here?"

"Why?"

She shrugged. "I like you. I don't know. Leroy might come back. Lots of reasons. If you don't want me to . . ."

She caught me off guard again. I might have found a dozen excuses to get rid of her, but I gave in.

"Got any gin?" she asked.

"No, I don't drink much."

"I've got some in my place. I'll bring it over." Before I could stop her she was out the window and a few minutes later she returned with a bottle about two-thirds full, and a lemon. She took two glasses from my kitchen and poured some gin into each. "Here," she said, "this'll make you feel better. It'll take the starch out of those straight lines. That's what's bugging you. Everything is too neat and straight and you're all boxed in. Like Algernon in his sculpture there."

I wasn't going to at first, but I felt so lousy that I figured why not. It couldn't make things any worse, and it might possibly dull the feeling that I was watching myself through eyes that didn't understand what I was doing.

She got me drunk.

I remember the first drink, and getting into bed, and her slipping in beside me with the bottle in her hand. And that was all until this afternoon when I got up with a hangover.

She was still asleep, face to the wall, her pillow bunched up under her neck. On the night table beside the ash tray over-flowing with crushed butts stood the empty bottle, but the last thing I remembered before the curtain came down was watching myself take the second drink.

She stretched and rolled toward me—nude. I moved back and fell out of bed. I grabbed a blanket to wrap around myself.

"Hi," she yawned. "You know what I want to do one of these days?"

"What?"

"Paint you in the nude. Like Michelangelo's 'David.' You'd be beautiful. You okay?"

I nodded. "Except for a headache. Did I—uh—drink too much last night?"

She laughed and propped herself up on one elbow. "You were loaded. And boy did you act queer—I don't mean fairyish or anything like that but strange."

"What"—I said, struggling to work the blanket around so that I could walk—"is that supposed to mean? What did I do?"

"I've seen guys get happy, or sad, or sleepy, or sexy, but I never saw anyone act the way you did. It's a good thing you don't drink often. Oh, my God, I only wish I had a camera. What a short subject you'd have made."

"Well, for Christ's sake, what'd I do?"

"Not what I expected. No sex, or anything like that. But you were phenomenal. What an act! The weirdest. You'd be great on the stage. You'd wow them at the Palace. You went all con-fused and silly. You know, as if a grown man starts acting like a kid. Talking about how you wanted to go to school and learn to read and write so you could be smart like everyone else.

Crazy stuff like that. You were a different person—like they do with method-acting—and you kept saying you couldn't play with me because your mother would take away your peanuts and put you in a cage."

"Peanuts?"

"Yeah! So help me!" she laughed, scratching her head. "And you kept saying I couldn't have your peanuts. The weirdest. But I tell you, the way you talked! Like those dimwits on street corners, who work themselves up by just *looking* at a girl. A different guy completely. At first I thought you were just kidding around, but now I think you're compulsive or something. All this neatness and worrying about everything."

It didn't upset me, although I would have expected it to. Somehow, getting drunk had momentarily broken down the conscious barriers that kept the old Charlie Gordon hidden deep in my mind. As I suspected all along, he was not really gone. Nothing in our minds is ever really gone. The operation had covered him over with a veneer of education and culture, but emotionally he was there—watching and waiting.

What was he waiting for?

"You okay now?"

I told her I was fine.

She grabbed the blanket I was wrapped in, and pulled me back into bed. Before I could stop her she slipped her arms around me and kissed me. "I was scared last night, Charlie. I thought you flipped. I've heard about guys who are impotent, how it suddenly gets them and they become maniacs."

"How come you stayed?"

She shrugged. "Well, you were like a scared little kid. I was sure you wouldn't hurt me, but I thought you might hurt yourself. So I figured I'd hang around. I felt so sorry. Anyway, I kept this handy, just in case . . ." She pulled out a heavy book end she had wedged between the bed and the wall.

"I guess you didn't have to use it."

She shook her head. "Boy, you must have liked peanuts when you were a kid."

She got out of bed and started to dress. I lay there for a while watching her. She moved in front of me with no shyness or inhibition. Her breasts were full as she had painted them in that self-portrait. I longed to reach out for her, but

I knew it was futile. In spite of the operation Charlie was still with me.

And Charlie was afraid of losing his peanuts.

June 24—Today I went on a strange kind of anti-intellectual binge. If I had dared to, I would have gotten drunk, but after the experience with Fay, I knew it would be dangerous. So, instead, I went to Times Square, from movie house to movie house, immersing myself in westerns and horror movies—the way I used to. Each time, sitting through the picture, I would find myself whipped with guilt. I'd walk out in the middle of the picture and wander into another one. I told myself I was looking for something in the make-believe screen world that was missing from my new life.

Then, in a sudden intuition, right outside the Keno Amusement Center, I knew it wasn't the movies I wanted, but *the audiences*. I wanted to be with the people around me in the darkness.

The walls between people are thin here, and if I listen quietly, I hear what is going on. Greenwich Village is like that too. Not just being close—because I don't feel it in a crowded elevator or on the subway during the rush—but on a hot night when everyone is out walking, or sitting in the theater, there is a rustling, and for a moment I brush against someone and sense the connection between the branch and trunk and the deep root. At such moments my flesh is thin and tight, and the unbearable hunger to be part of it drives me out to search in the dark corners and blind alleys of the night.

Usually, when I'm exhausted from walking, I go back to the apartment and drop off into a deep sleep, but tonight instead of going up to my own place I went to the diner. There was a new dishwasher, a boy of about sixteen, and there was something familiar about him, his movements, the look in his eyes. And then, clearing away the table behind me, he dropped some dishes.

They crashed to the floor, shattering and sending bits of white china under the tables. He stood there, dazed and frightened, holding the empty tray in his hand. The whistles and catcalls from the customers (cries of "hey, there go the profits!" . . . "*Mazel tov!*" . . . and "well, *he* didn't work here very long . . ." which invariably seem to follow the breaking of dishware in a public restaurant) confused him.

When the owner came to see what the excitement was about, the boy cowered—threw up his arms as if to ward off a blow.

"All right! All right, you dope," shouted the man, "don't just stand there! Get the broom and sweep up that mess. A broom . . . a broom! you idiot! It's in the kitchen. Sweep up all the pieces."

When the boy saw that he was not going to be punished, his frightened expression disappeared, and he smiled and hummed as he came back with the broom. A few of the rowdier customers kept up the remarks, amusing themselves at his expense.

"Here, sonny, over here. There's a nice piece behind you . . ."

"C'mon, do it again . . ."

"He's not so dumb. It's easier to break 'em than to wash 'em . . ."

As the boy's vacant eyes moved across the crowd of amused onlookers, he slowly mirrored their smiles and finally broke into an uncertain grin at the joke which he did not understand.

I felt sick inside as I looked at his dull, vacuous smile—the wide, bright eyes of a child, uncertain but eager to please, and I realized what I had recognized in him. They were laughing at him because he was retarded.

And at first I had been amused along with the rest.

Suddenly, I was furious at myself and all those who were smirking at him. I wanted to pick up the dishes and throw them. I wanted to smash their laughing faces. I jumped up and shouted: "Shut up! Leave him alone! He can't understand. He can't help what he is . . . but for God's sake, have some respect! *He's a human being!*"

The restaurant grew silent. I cursed myself for losing control and creating a scene, and I tried not to look at the boy as I paid my check and walked out without touching my food. I felt ashamed for both of us.

How strange it is that people of honest feelings and sensibility, who would not take advantage of a man born without arms or legs or eyes—how such people think nothing of abusing a man born with low intelligence. It infuriated me to remember that not too long ago I—like this boy—had foolishly played the clown.

And I had almost forgotten.

Only a short time ago, I learned that people laughed at me. Now I can see that unknowingly I joined them in laughing at myself. That hurts most of all.

I have often reread my early progress reports and seen the illiteracy, the childish naïveté, the mind of low intelligence peering from a dark room, through the keyhole, at the dazzling light outside. In my dreams and memories I've seen Charlie smiling happily and uncertainly at what people around him were saying. Even in my dullness I knew I was inferior. Other people had something I lacked—something denied me. In my mental blindness, I had believed it was somehow connected with the ability to read and write, and I was sure that if I could get those skills I would have intelligence too.

Even a feeble-minded man wants to be like other men.

A child may not know how to feed itself, or what to eat, yet it knows hunger.

This day was good for me. I've got to stop this childish worrying about myself—*my* past and *my* future. Let me give something of myself to others. I've got to use my knowledge and skills to work in the field of increasing human intelligence. Who is better equipped? Who else has lived in both worlds?

Tomorrow, I'm going to get in touch with the board of directors at the Welberg Foundation and ask for permission to do some independent work on the project. If they'll let me, I may be able to help them. I have some ideas.

There is so much that can be done with this technique, if it is perfected. If I could be made into a genius, what about the more than five million mentally retarded in the United States? What about the countless millions all over the world, and those yet unborn destined to be retarded? What fantastic levels might be achieved by using this technique on normal people? On geniuses?

There are so many doors to open I am impatient to apply my own knowledge and skills to the problem. I've got to make them all see that this is something important for me to do. I'm sure the Foundation will grant me permission.

But I can't be alone any more. I have to tell Alice about it.

June 25—I called Alice today. I was nervous, and I must have sounded incoherent, but it was good to hear her voice, and she sounded happy to hear from me. She agreed to see me, and I took a taxi uptown, impatient at the slowness with which we moved.

Before I could knock, she opened the door and threw her arms around me. "Charlie, we've been so worried about you. I had horrible visions of you dead in an alleyway, or wandering around skid row with amnesia. Why didn't you let us know you were all right? You could have done that."

"Don't scold me. I had to be alone for a while to find some answers."

"Come in the kitchen. I'll make some coffee. What have you been doing?"

"Days—I've been thinking, reading, and writing; and nights —wandering in search of myself. And I've discovered that Charlie is watching me."

"Don't talk like that," she shuddered. "This business about being watched isn't real. You've built it up in your mind."

"I can't help feeling that I'm not me. I've usurped his place and locked him out the way they locked me out of the bakery. What I mean to say is that Charlie Gordon exists in the past, and the past is real. You can't put up a new building on a site until you destroy the old one, and the old Charlie can't be destroyed. He exists. At first I was searching for him: I went to see his—my—father. All I wanted to do was prove that Charlie existed as a person in the past, so that I could justify my own existence. I was insulted when Nemur said he created me. But I've discovered that not only did Charlie exist in the past, he exists now. In me and around me. He's been coming between us all along. I thought my intelligence created the barrier—my pompous, foolish pride, the feeling we had nothing in common because I had gone beyond you. You put that idea into my head. But that's not it. It's Charlie, the little boy who's afraid of women because of things his mother did to him. Don't you see? All these months while I've been growing up intellectually, I've still had the emotional wiring of the childlike Charlie. And every time I came close to you, or thought about making love to you, there was a short circuit."

I was excited, and my voice pounded at her until she began to quiver. Her face became flushed. "Charlie," she whispered, "can't I do anything? Can't I help?"

"I think I've changed during these weeks away from the lab," I said. "I couldn't see how to do it at first, but tonight, while I was wandering around the city, it came to me. The foolish thing was trying to solve the problem all by myself. But the deeper I get tangled up in this mass of dreams and memories the more I realize that emotional problems can't be solved as intellectual problems are. That's what I discovered about myself last night. I told myself I was wandering around like a lost soul, and then I saw that I *was* lost.

"Somehow I've become separated emotionally from everyone and everything. And what I was really searching for out there in the dark streets—the last damned place I could ever find it—was a way to make myself a part of people again emotionally, while still retaining my freedom intellectually. I've got to grow up. For me it means everything. . . ."

I talked on and on, spewing out of myself every doubt and fear that bubbled to the surface. She was my sounding board and she sat there hypnotized. I felt myself grow warm, feverish, until I thought my body was on fire. I was burning out the infection in front of someone I cared about, and that made all the difference.

But it was too much for her. What had started as trembling became tears. The picture over the couch caught my eye—the cringing, red-cheeked maiden—and I wondered what Alice was feeling just then. I knew she would give herself to me, and I wanted her, but what about Charlie?

Charlie might not interfere if I wanted to make love to Fay. He would probably just stand in the doorway and watch. But the moment I came close to Alice, he panicked. Why was he afraid to let me love Alice?

She sat on the couch, looking at me, waiting to see what I would do. And what could I do? I wanted to take her in my arms and . . .

As I began to think of it, the warning came.

"Are you all right, Charlie? You're so pale."

I sat down on the couch beside her. "Just a little dizzy. It'll pass." But I knew it would only get worse as long as Charlie felt there was danger I'd make love to her.

And then I got the idea. It disgusted me at first, but suddenly I realized the only way to overcome this paralysis was to outwit him. If for some reason Charlie was afraid of Alice but not of Fay, then I would turn out the lights, and pretend I was making love to Fay. He would never know the difference.

It was wrong—disgusting—but if it worked it would break Charlie's strangle hold on my emotions. I would know afterwards that I had loved Alice, and that this was the only way.

"I'm all right now. Let's sit in the dark for a while," I said, turning off the lights and waiting to collect myself. It wasn't going to be easy. I had to convince myself, visualize Fay, hypnotize myself into believing that the woman sitting beside me was Fay. And even if he separated himself from me to watch from outside my body, it would do him no good because the room would be dark.

I waited for some sign that he suspected—the warning symptoms of panic. But nothing. I felt alert and calm. I put my arm around her.

"Charlie, I—"

"*Don't talk!*" I snapped, and she shrank from me. "Please," I reassured her, "don't say anything. Just let me hold you quietly in the dark." I brought her close to me, and there under the darkness of my closed lids, I conjured up the picture of Fay— with her long blonde hair and fair skin. Fay, as I had seen her last beside me. I kissed Fay's hair, Fay's throat, and finally came to rest upon Fay's lips. I felt Fay's arms stroking the muscles on my back, my shoulders, and the tightness inside me built up as it had never before done for a woman. I caressed her slowly at first and then with impatient, mounting excitement that would soon tell.

The hairs on my neck began to tingle. Someone else was in the room, peering through the darkness, trying to see. And feverishly I thought the name over and over to myself. Fay! Fay! FAY! I imagined her face sharply and clearly so that nothing could come between us. And then, as she gripped me closer, I cried out and pushed her away.

"Charlie!" I couldn't see Alice's face, but her gasp mirrored the shock.

"No, Alice! I can't. You don't understand."

I jumped up from the couch and turned on the light. I almost expected to see him standing there. But of course not.

We were alone. It was all in my mind. Alice was lying there, her blouse open where I had unbuttoned it, her face flushed, eyes wide in disbelief. "I love you . . ." the words choked out of me, "but I can't do it. Something I can't explain, but if I hadn't stopped, I would hate myself for the rest of my life. Don't ask me to explain, or you'll hate me too. It has to do with Charlie. For some reason, he won't let me make love to you."

She looked away and buttoned her blouse. "It was different tonight," she said. "You didn't get nausea or panic or anything like that. You wanted me."

"Yes, I wanted you, but I wasn't really making love to *you*. I was going to use you—in a way—but I can't explain. I don't understand it myself. Let's just say I'm not ready yet. And I can't fake it or cheat or pretend it's all right when it's not. It's just another blind alley."

I got up to go.

"Charlie, don't run away again."

"I'm through running. I've got work to do. Tell them I'll be back to the lab in a few days—as soon as I get control of myself."

I left the apartment in a frenzy. Downstairs, in front of the building, I stood, not knowing which way to go. No matter which path I took I got a shock that meant another mistake. Every path was blocked. But, God . . . everything I did, everywhere I turned, doors were closed to me.

There was no place to enter. No street, no room, no woman.

Finally, I stumbled down into the subway and took it down to Forty-ninth Street. Not many people, but there was a blonde with long hair who reminded me of Fay. Heading toward the crosstown bus, I passed a liquor store, and without thinking about it, I went in and bought a fifth of gin. While I waited for the bus, I opened the bottle in the bag as I had seen bums do, and I took a long, deep drink. It burned all the way down, but it felt good. I took another—just a sip—and by the time the bus came, I was bathed in a powerful tingling sensation. I didn't take any more. I didn't want to get drunk now.

When I got to the apartment, I knocked at Fay's door. There was no answer. I opened the door and looked in. She hadn't come in yet, but all the lights were on in the place. She didn't give a damn about anything. Why couldn't I be that way?

I went to my own place to wait. I undressed, took a shower and put on a robe. I prayed that this wouldn't be one of the nights that someone came home with her.

About two thirty in the morning I heard her coming up the steps. I took my bottle, climbed out onto the fire escape and slipped over to her window just as her front door opened. I hadn't intended to crouch there and watch. I was going to tap on the window. But as I raised my hand to make my presence known, I saw her kick her shoes off and twirl around happily. She went to the mirror, and slowly, piece by piece, began to pull off her clothes in a private strip tease. I took another drink. But I couldn't let her know I had been watching her.

I went through my own apartment without turning on the lights. At first I thought of inviting her over to my place, but everything was too neat and orderly—too many straight lines to erase—and I knew it wouldn't work here. So I went out into the hallway. I knocked at her door, softly at first and then louder.

"Door's open!" she shouted.

She was in her underwear, lying on the floor, arms outstretched and legs up against the couch. She tilted her head back and looked at me upside down. "Charlie, darling! Why are you standing on your head?"

"Never mind," I said, pulling the bottle out of the paper bag. "The lines and boxes are too straight, and I thought you'd join me in erasing some of them."

"Best stuff in the world for that," she said. "If you concentrate on the warm spot that starts in the pit of your stomach, all the lines begin to melt."

"That's what's happening."

"Wonderful!" She jumped to her feet. "Me too. I danced with too many squares tonight. Let's melt 'em all down." She picked up a glass and I filled it for her.

As she drank, I slipped my arm around her and toyed with the skin of her bare back.

"Hey, there, boy! Whoa! What's up?"

"Me. I was waiting for you to come home."

She backed away. "Oh, wait a minute, Charlie boy. We've been through all this before. You know it doesn't do any good. I mean, you know I think a lot of you, and I'd drag you into bed in a minute if I thought there was a chance. But I don't want to get all worked up for nothing. It's not fair, Charlie."

"It'll be different tonight. I swear it." Before she could protest, I had her in my arms, kissing her, caressing her, overwhelming her with all the built-up excitement that was ready to tear me apart. I tried to unhook her brassière, but I pulled too hard and the hook tore out.

"For God's sake, Charlie, my bra—"

"Don't worry about your bra . . ." I choked, helping her to take it off. "I'll buy you a new one. I'm going to make up for the other times. I'm going to make love to you all night long."

She pulled away from me. "Charlie, I've never heard you talk like that. And stop looking at me as if you want to swallow me whole." She swept up a blouse from one of the chairs, and held it in front of her. "Now you're making me feel undressed."

"I want to make love to you. Tonight I can do it. I know it . . . I feel it. Don't turn me away, Fay."

"Here," she whispered, "have another drink."

I took one and poured another for her, and while she drank it, I covered her shoulder and neck with kisses. She began to breathe heavily as my excitement communicated itself to her.

"God, Charlie, if you get me started and disappoint me again I don't know what I'll do. I'm human too, you know."

I pulled her down beside me on the couch, on top of the pile of her clothing and underthings.

"Not here on the couch, Charlie," she said, struggling to her feet. "Let's go to bed."

"Here," I insisted, pulling the blouse away from her.

She looked down at me, set her glass on the floor, and stepped out of her underwear. She stood there in front of me, nude. "I'll turn out the lights," she whispered.

"No," I said, pulling her down onto the couch again. "I want to look at you."

She kissed me deeply and held me tightly in her arms. "Just don't disappoint me this time, Charlie. You'd better not."

Her body moved slowly, reaching for me, and I knew that this time nothing would interfere. I knew what to do and how to do it. She gasped and sighed and called my name.

For one moment I had the cold feeling he was watching. Over the arm of the couch, I caught a glimpse of his face

staring back at me through the dark beyond the window—
where just a few minutes earlier I had been crouching. A switch
in perception, and I was out on the fire escape again, watching
a man and a woman inside, making love on the couch.

Then, with a violent effort of the will, I was back on the
couch with her, aware of her body and my own urgency and
potency, and I saw the face against the window, hungrily
watching. And I thought to myself, go ahead, you poor bastard
—watch. I don't give a damn any more.

And his eyes went wide as he watched.

June 29—Before I go back to the lab I'm going to finish the
projects I've started since I left the convention. I phoned
Landsdoff at the New Institute for Advanced Study, about the
possibility of utilizing the pair-production nuclear photoeffect
for exploratory work in biophysics. At first he thought I was a
crackpot, but after I pointed out the flaws in his article in the
New Institute Journal he kept me on the phone for nearly an
hour. He wants me to come to the Institute to discuss my ideas
with his group. I might take him up on it after I've finished
my work at the lab—if there is time. That's the problem, of
course. I don't know how much time I have. A month? A year?
The rest of my life? That depends on what I find out about the
psychophysical side-effects of the experiment.

June 30—I've stopped wandering the streets now that I have
Fay. I've given her a key to my place. She kids me about my
locking the door, and I kid her about the mess her place is
in. She's warned me not to try to change her. Her husband
divorced her five years ago because she couldn't be bothered
about picking things up and taking care of her home.

That's the way she is about most things that seem unim-
portant to her. She just can't or won't bother. The other day I
discovered a stack of parking tickets in a corner behind a chair
—there must have been forty or fifty of them. When she came
in with the beer, I asked her why she was collecting them.

"Those!" she laughed. "As soon as my ex-husband sends me
my goddamned check, I've got to pay some of them. You have
no idea how bad I feel about those tickets. I keep them behind
that chair because otherwise I get an attack of guilt feelings

every time I see them. But what is a girl supposed to do? Everywhere I go they've got signs all over the place—don't park here! don't park there!—I just can't be bothered stopping to read a sign every time I want to get out of the car."

So I've promised I won't try to change her. She's exciting to be with. A great sense of humor. But most of all she's a free and independent spirit. The only thing that may become wearing after a while is her craze for dancing. We've been out every night this week until two or three in the morning. I don't have that much energy left.

It's not love—but she's important to me. I find myself listening for her footsteps down the hallway whenever she's been out.

Charlie has stopped watching us.

July 5—I dedicated my first piano concerto to Fay. She was excited by the idea of having something dedicated to her, but I don't think she really liked it. Just goes to show that you can't have everything you want in one woman. One more argument for polygamy.

The important thing is that Fay is bright and good-hearted. I learned today why she ran out of money so early this month. The week before she met me, she had befriended a girl she'd met at the Stardust Ballroom. When the girl told Fay she had no family in the city, was broke, and had no place to sleep, Fay invited her to move in. Two days later the girl found the two hundred and thirty-two dollars that Fay kept in her dresser drawer, and disappeared with the money. Fay hadn't reported it to the police—and as it turned out, she didn't even know the girl's last name.

"What good would it do to notify the police?" she wanted to know. "I mean this poor bitch must have needed the money pretty badly to do it. I'm not going to ruin her life over a few hundred bucks. I'm not rich or anything, but I'm not going after her skin—if you know what I mean."

I knew what she meant.

I have never met anyone as open and trusting as Fay is. She's what I need most of all right now. I've been starved for simple human contact.

July 8—Not much time for work—between the nightly club-hopping and the morning hangovers. It was only with aspirin and something Fay concocted for me that I was able to finish my linguistic analysis of Urdu verb forms and send the paper to the *International Linguistics Bulletin*. It will send the linguists back to India with their tape recorders, because it undermines the critical superstructure of their methodology.

I can't help but admire the structural linguists who have carved out for themselves a linguistic discipline based on the deterioration of written communication. Another case of men devoting their lives to studying more and more about less and less—filling volumes and libraries with the subtle linguistic analysis of the *grunt*. Nothing wrong with that, but it should not be used as an excuse to destroy the stability of language.

Alice called today to find out when I am coming back to work at the lab. I told her I wanted to finish the projects I had started, and that I was hoping to get permission from the Welberg Foundation for my own special study. She's right though —I've got to take time into consideration.

Fay still wants to go out dancing all the time. Last night started out with us drinking and dancing at the White Horse Club, and from there to Benny's Hideaway, and then on to the Pink Slipper . . . and after that I don't remember many of the places, but we danced until I was ready to drop. My tolerance for liquor must have increased because I was pretty far gone before Charlie made his appearance. I can only recall him doing a silly tap dance on the stage of the Allakazam Club. He got a great hand before the manager threw us out, and Fay said everyone thought I was a wonderful comedian and everyone liked my moron act.

What the hell happened then? I know I strained my back. I thought it was from all the dancing, but Fay says I fell off the goddamned couch.

Algernon's behavior is becoming erratic again. Minnie seems to be afraid of him.

July 9—A terrible thing happened today. Algernon bit Fay. I had warned her against playing with him, but she always liked to feed him. Usually when she came into his room, he'd perk up and run to her. Today it was different. He was at the far side, curled up into a white puff. When she put her hand in through the top trap door, he cringed and forced himself back into the corner. She tried to coax him, by opening the barrier to the maze, and before I could tell her to leave him alone, she made the mistake of trying to pick him up. He bit her thumb. Then he glared at both of us and scurried back into the maze.

We found Minnie at the other end in the reward box. She was bleeding from a gash in her chest, but she was alive. As I reached in to take her out Algernon came into the reward box and snapped at me. His teeth caught my sleeve and he hung on until I shook him loose.

He calmed down after that. I observed him for more than an hour afterward. He seems listless and confused, and though he still learns new problems without external rewards, his performance is peculiar. Instead of the careful, determined movements down the maze corridors, his actions are rushed and out of control. Time and again he turns a corner too quickly and crashes into a barrier. There is a strange sense of urgency in his behavior.

I hesitate to make a snap judgment. It could be many things. But now I've got to get him back to the lab. Whether or not I hear from the Foundation about my special grant, I'm going to call Nemur in the morning.

PROGRESS REPORT 15

July 12—Nemur, Strauss, Burt, and a few of the others on the project were waiting for me in the psych office. They tried to make me feel welcome, but I could see how anxious Burt was to take Algernon, and I turned him over. No one said anything, but I knew that Nemur would not soon forgive me for going over his head and getting in touch with the Foundation. But it had been necessary. Before I returned to Beekman, I had to be assured they would permit me to begin an independent study of the project. Too much time would be wasted if I had to account to Nemur for everything I did.

He had been informed of the Foundation's decision, and my reception was a cold and formal one. He held out his hand, but there was no smile on his face. "Charlie," he said, "we're all glad you're back and going to work with us. Jayson called and told me the Foundation was putting you to work on the project. This staff and the lab are at your disposal. The computer center has assured us that your work will have priority—and of course if I can help in any way . . ."

He was doing his utmost to be cordial, but I could see by his face that he was skeptical. After all, what experience did I have with experimental psychology? What did I know about the techniques that he had spent so many years developing? Well, as I say, he appeared cordial, and willing to suspend judgment. There isn't much else he can do now. If I don't come up with an explanation for Algernon's behavior, all of his work goes down the drain, but if I solve the problem I bring in the whole crew with me.

I went into the lab where Burt was watching Algernon in one of the multiple problem boxes. He sighed and shook his head. "He's forgotten a lot. Most of his complex responses seem to have been wiped out. He's solving problems on a much more primitive level than I would have expected."

"In what way?" I asked.

"Well, in the past he was able to figure out simple patterns —in that blind-door run, for example: every other door, every third door, red doors only, or the green doors only—but now he's been through that run three times and he's still using trial and error."

"Could it be because he was away from the lab for so long?"

"Could be. We'll let him get used to things again and see how he works out tomorrow."

I had been in the lab many times before this, but now I was here to learn everything it had to offer. I had to absorb procedures in a few days that the others had taken years to learn. Burt and I spent four hours going through the lab section by section, as I tried to familiarize myself with the total picture. When we were all through I noticed one door we had not looked into.

"What's in there?"

"The freeze and the incinerator." He pushed open the heavy door and turned on the light. "We freeze our specimens before we dispose of them in the incinerator. It helps cut down the odors if we control decomposition." He turned to leave, but I stood there for a moment.

"Not Algernon," I said. "Look . . . if and . . . when . . . I mean I don't want him dumped in there. Give him to me. I'll take care of him myself." He didn't laugh. He just nodded. Nemur had told him that from now on I could have anything I wanted.

Time was the barrier. If I was going to find out the answers for myself I had to get to work immediately. I got lists of books from Burt, and notes from Strauss and Nemur. Then, on the way out, I got a strange notion.

"Tell me," I asked Nemur, "I just got a look at your incinerator for disposing of experimental animals. What plans have been made for me?"

My question stunned him. "What do you mean?"

"I'm sure that from the beginning you planned for all exigencies. So what happens to me?"

When he was silent I insisted: "I have a right to know everything that pertains to the experiment, and that includes my future."

"No reason why you shouldn't know." He paused and lit an already lit cigarette. "You understand, of course, that from the beginning we had the highest hopes of permanence, and we still do . . . we definitely do—"

"I'm sure of that," I said.

"Of course, taking you on in this experiment was a serious responsibility. I don't know how much you remember or how much you've pieced together about things in the beginning of the project, but we tried to make it clear to you that there was a strong chance it might be only temporary."

"I had that written down in my progress reports, at the time," I agreed, "though I didn't understand at the time what you meant by it. But that's beside the point because I'm aware of it now."

"Well, we decided to risk it with you," he went on, "because we felt there was very little chance of doing you any serious harm, and we were sure there was a great chance of doing you some good."

"You don't have to justify that."

"But you realize we had to get permission from someone in your immediate family. You were incompetent to agree to this yourself."

"I know all about that. You're talking about my sister, Norma. I read about it in the papers. From what I remember of her, I imagine she'd have given you approval for my execution."

He raised his eyebrows, but let it pass. "Well, as we told her, in the event that the experiment failed, we couldn't send you back to the bakery or to that room where you came from."

"Why not?"

"For one thing, you might not be the same. Surgery and injections of hormones might have had effects not immediately evident. Experiences since the operation might have left their mark on you. I mean, possibly emotional disturbances to complicate the retardation; you couldn't possibly be the same kind of person—"

"That's great. As if one cross weren't enough to bear."

"And for another thing, there's no way of knowing if you would go back to the same mental level. There might be regression to an even more primitive level of functioning."

He was letting me have the worst of it—getting the weight off his mind. "I might as well know everything," I said, "while I'm still in a position to have some say about it. What plans have you made for me?"

He shrugged. "The Foundation has arranged to send you to the Warren State Home and Training School."

"What the hell!"

"Part of the agreement with your sister was that all the home's fees would be assumed by the Foundation, and you would receive a regular monthly income to be used for your personal needs for the rest of your life."

"But why there? I was always able to manage on my own on the outside, even when they committed me there, after Uncle Herman died. Donner was able to get me out right away, to work and live on the outside. Why do I have to go back?"

"If you can take care of yourself on the outside, you won't have to stay in Warren. The less severe cases are permitted to live off the grounds. But we had to make provision for you —just in case."

He was right. There was nothing for me to complain about. They had thought of everything. Warren was the logical place —the deep freeze where I could be put away for the rest of my days.

"At least it's not the incinerator," I said.

"What?"

"Never mind. A private joke." Then I thought of something. "Tell me, is it possible to visit Warren, I mean go through the place and look it over as a visitor?"

"Yes, I think they have people coming down all the time —regular tours through the home as a kind of public relations thing. But why?"

"Because I want to see. I've got to know what's going to happen while I'm still enough in control to be able to do something about it. See if you can arrange it—as soon as possible."

I could see he was upset about the idea of my visiting Warren. As if I were ordering my coffin to sit in before I died. But then, I can't blame him because he doesn't realize that finding out who I really am—the meaning of my total existence involves knowing the possibilities of my future as well as my past, where I'm going as well as where I've been. Although we know the end of the maze holds death (and it is something I have not always known—not long ago the adolescent in me thought death could happen only to other people), I see now that the path I choose through that maze makes me what I am. I am not only a thing, but also a way of being—one of many ways —and knowing the paths I have followed and the ones left to take will help me understand what I am becoming.

That evening and for the next few days I immersed myself in psychology texts: clinical, personality, psychometrics, learning, experimental psychology, animal psychology, physiological psychology, behaviorist, gestalt, analytical, functional, dynamic, organismic, and all the rest of the ancient and modern factions, schools, and systems of thought. The depressing thing is that so many of the ideas on which our psychologists base their beliefs about human intelligence, memory, and learning are all wishful thinking.

Fay wants to come down and visit the lab, but I've told her not to. All I need now is for Alice and Fay to run into each other. I've enough to worry about without that.

PROGRESS REPORT 16

July 14—It was a bad day to go out to Warren—gray and drizzly—and that may account for the depression that grips me when I think about it. Or perhaps I'm kidding myself and it was the idea of possibly being sent there that bothered me. I borrowed Burt's car. Alice wanted to come along, but I had to see it alone. I didn't tell Fay I was going.

It was an hour-and-a-half drive out to the farmland community of Warren, Long Island, and I had no trouble finding the place: a sprawling gray estate revealed to the world only by an entrance of two concrete pillars flanking a narrow side-road and a well-polished brass plate with the name *Warren State Home and Training School.*

The roadside sign said 15 MPH, so I drove slowly past the blocks of buildings looking for the administrative offices.

A tractor came across the meadow in my direction, and in addition to the man at the wheel there were two others hanging on the rear. I stuck out my head and called: "Can you tell me where Mr. Winslow's office is?"

The driver stopped the tractor and pointed to the left and ahead. "Main hospital. Turn left and bear to your right."

I couldn't help noticing the staring young man riding at the rear of the tractor, hanging on to a handrail. He was unshaven, and there was the trace of an empty smile. He had on a sailor's hat with the brim pulled down childishly to shield his eyes, although there was no sun out. I caught his glance for a moment —his eyes wide, inquiring—but I had to look away. When the tractor started forward again, I could see in the rear view mirror that he was looking after me, curiously. It upset me . . . because he reminded me of Charlie.

I was startled to find the head psychologist so young, a tall, lean man with a tired look on his face. But his steady blue eyes suggested a strength behind the youthful expression.

He drove me around the grounds in his own car, and pointed out the recreation hall, hospital, school, administrative offices, and the two-story brick buildings he called *cottages* where the patients lived.

"I didn't notice a fence around Warren," I said.

"No, only a gate at the entrance and hedges to keep out curiosity seekers."

"But how do you keep . . . them . . . from wandering off . . . from leaving the grounds?"

He shrugged and smiled. "We can't, really. Some of them do wander off, but most of them return."

"Don't you go after them?"

He looked at me as if trying to guess what was behind my question. "No. If they get into trouble, we soon know about it from the people in town—or the police bring them back."

"And if not?"

"If we don't hear about them, or from them, we assume they've made some satisfactory adjustment on the outside. You've got to understand, Mr. Gordon, this isn't a prison. We are required by the state to make all reasonable efforts to get our patients back, but we're not equipped to closely supervise four thousand people at all times. The ones who manage to leave are all high-moron types—not that we're getting many of those any more. Now we get more of the brain-damaged cases who require constant custodial care—but the high-morons can move around more freely, and after a week or so on the outside most of them come back when they find there's nothing for them out there. The world doesn't want them and they soon know it."

We got out of the car and walked over to one of the *cottages*. Inside, the walls were white tile, and the building had a disinfectant smell to it. The first-floor lobby opened up to a recreation room filled with some seventy-five boys sitting around waiting for the lunch bell to be sounded. What caught my eye immediately was one of the bigger boys on a chair in the corner, cradling one of the other boys—fourteen or fifteen years old—cuddling him in his arms. They all turned to look as we entered, and some of the bolder ones came over and stared at me.

"Don't mind them," he said, seeing my expression. "They won't hurt you."

The woman in charge of the floor, a large-boned, handsome woman, with rolled up shirt sleeves and a denim apron over her starched white skirt, came up to us. At her belt was a ring of keys that jangled as she moved, and only when she turned did I see that the left side of her face was covered by a large, wine-colored birthmark.

"Didn't expect any company today, Ray," she said. "You usually bring your visitors on Thursdays."

"This is Mr. Gordon, Thelma, from Beekman University. He just wants to look around and get an idea of the work we're doing here. I knew it wouldn't make any difference with you, Thelma. Any day is all right with you."

"Yeah," she laughed strongly, "but Wednesday we turn the mattresses. It smells a lot better here on Thursday."

I noticed that she kept to my left so that the blotch on her face was hidden. She took me through the dormitory, the laundry, the supply rooms, and the dining hall—now set and waiting for the food to be delivered from the central commissary. She smiled as she talked, and her expression and the hair piled in a bun high on her head made her look like a Lautrec dancer but she never looked straight at me. I wondered what it would be like living here with her to watch over me.

"They're pretty good here in this building," she said. "But you know what it is. Three hundred boys—seventy-five on a floor—and only five of us to look after them. It's not easy to keep them under control. But it's a lot better than the *untidy* cottages. The staff *there* doesn't last very long. With babies you don't mind so much, but when they get to be adults and still can't care for themselves, it can be a nasty mess."

"You seem to be a very nice person," I said. "The boys are fortunate to have you as their house-supervisor."

She laughed heartily still looking straight ahead, and showed her white teeth. "No better or worse than the rest. I'm very fond of my boys. It's not easy work, but it's rewarding when you think how much they need you." The smile left her for a moment. "Normal kids grow up too soon, stop needing you . . . go off on their own . . . forget who loved them and took care of them. But these children need all you can give—all of their lives." She laughed again, embarrassed at her seriousness. "It's hard work here, but worth it."

Back downstairs, where Winslow was waiting for us, the dinner bell sounded, and the boys filed into the dining room. I noticed that the big boy who had held the smaller one in his lap was now leading him to the table by the hand.

"Quite a thing," I said, nodding in that direction.

Winslow nodded too. "Jerry's the big one, and that's Dusty.

We see that sort of thing often here. When there's no one else who has time for them, sometimes they know enough to seek human contact and affection from each other."

As we passed one of the other cottages on our way to the school, I heard a shriek followed by a wailing, picked up and echoed by two or three other voices. There were bars on the windows.

Winslow looked uncomfortable for the first time that morning. "Special security cottage," he explained. "Emotionally disturbed retardates. When there's a chance they'll harm themselves or others, we put them in Cottage K. Locked up at all times."

"Emotionally disturbed patients here? Don't they belong in psychiatric hospitals?"

"Oh, sure," he said, "but it's a difficult thing to control. Some, the borderline emotionally disturbed, don't break down until after they've been here for a while. Others were committed by the courts, and we had no choice but to admit them even though there's really no room for them. The real problem is that there's no room for anyone anywhere. Do you know how long our own waiting list is? Fourteen hundred. And we *may* have room for twenty-five or thirty of them by the end of the year."

"Where are those fourteen hundred now?"

"Home. On the outside, waiting for an opening here or in some other institution. You see, our space problem is not like the usual hospital overcrowding. Our patients usually come here to stay for the rest of their lives."

As we arrived at the new school building, a one-story glass-and-concrete structure with large picture windows, I tried to imagine what it would be like walking through these corridors as a patient. I visualized myself in the middle of a line of men and boys waiting to enter a classroom. Perhaps I'd be one of those pushing another boy in a wheelchair, or guiding someone else by the hand, or cuddling a smaller boy in my arms.

In one of the woodworking classrooms, where a group of older boys were making benches under a teacher's supervision, they clustered around us, eyeing me curiously. The teacher put down the saw and came towards us.

"This is Mr. Gordon from Beekman University," said Winslow. "Wants to look over some of our patients. He's thinking of buying the place."

The teacher laughed and waved at his pupils. "Well, if he b-buys it, he's g-got to t-take us with it. And he's g-got to get us some more w-wood to w-work with."

As he showed me around the shop, I noticed how strangely quiet the boys were. They went on with their work of sanding or varnishing the newly finished benches, but they didn't talk.

"These are my s-silent b-boys, you know," he said, as if he sensed my unspoken question. "D-deaf m-mutes."

We have a hundred and six of them here," explained Winslow, "as a special study sponsored by the federal government."

What an incredible thing! How much less they had than other human beings. Mentally retarded, deaf, mute—and still eagerly sanding benches.

One of the boys who had been tightening a block of wood in a vise, stopped what he was doing, tapped Winslow on the arm, and pointed to the corner where a number of finished objects were drying on display shelves. The boy pointed to a lamp base on the second shelf, and then to himself. It was a poor job, unsteady, the patches of wood-filler showing through, and the varnish heavy and uneven. Winslow and the teacher praised it enthusiastically, and the boy smiled proudly and looked at me, waiting for my praise too.

"Yes," I nodded, mouthing the words exaggeratedly, "very good . . . very nice." I said it because he needed it, but I felt hollow. The boy smiled at me, and when we turned to leave he came over and touched my arm as a way of saying good-bye. It choked me up, and I had a great deal of difficulty controlling my emotions until we were out in the corridor again.

The principal of the school was a short, plump, motherly lady who sat me down in front of a neatly lettered chart, showing the various types of patients, the number of faculty assigned to each category, and the subjects they studied.

"Of course," she explained, "we don't get many of the upper I.Q.'s any more. They're taken care of—the sixty and seventy I.Q.'s—more and more in the city schools in special classes, or else there are community facilities for caring for them. Most of the ones we get are able to live out, in foster homes, or boarding houses, and do simple work on the farms or in a menial capacity in factories or laundries—"

"Or bakeries," I suggested.

She frowned. "Yes, I guess they might be able to do that. Now, we also classify our children (I call them all children, no matter what their ages are, they're all children here), we classify them as *tidy* or *untidy*. It makes the administration of their cottages a lot easier if they can be kept with their own levels. Some of the *untidies* are severely brain-damaged cases, kept in cribs, and they will be cared for that way for the rest of their lives . . ."

"Or until science finds a way to help them."

"Oh," she smiled, explaining to me carefully, "I'm afraid these are beyond help."

"No one is beyond help."

She peered at me, uncertainly now. "Yes, yes, of course, you're right. We must have hope."

I made her nervous. I smiled to myself at the thought of how it would be if they brought me back here as one of her children. Would I be *tidy* or not?

Back at Winslow's office, we had coffee as he talked about his work. "It's a good place," he said. "We have no psychiatrists on our staff—only an outside consulting man who comes in once every two weeks. But it's just as well. Every one on the psych staff is dedicated to his work. I could have hired a psychiatrist, but at the price I'd have to pay I'm able to hire two psychologists—men who aren't afraid to give away a part of themselves to these people."

"What do you mean by 'a part of themselves'?"

He studied me for a moment, and then through the tiredness flashed an anger. "There are a lot of people who will give money or materials, but very few who will give time and affection. That's what I mean." His voice grew harsh, and he pointed to an empty baby bottle on the bookshelf across the room.

"You see that bottle?"

I told him I had wondered about it when we came into his office.

"Well, how many people do you know who are prepared to take a grown man into his arms and let him nurse with the bottle? And take the chance of having the patient urinate or defecate all over him? You look surprised. You can't understand it, can you, from way up there in your research ivory tower? What do you know about being shut out from every human experience as our patients have been?"

I couldn't restrain a smile, and he apparently misunderstood, because he stood up and ended the conversation abruptly. If I come back here to stay, and he finds out the whole story, I'm sure he'll understand. He's the kind of man who would.

As I drove out of Warren, I didn't know what to think. The feeling of cold grayness was everywhere around me—a sense of resignation. There had been no talk of rehabilitation, of cure, of someday sending these people out into the world again. No one had spoken of hope. The feeling was of living death— or worse, of never having been fully alive and knowing. Souls withered from the beginning, and doomed to stare into the time and space of every day.

I wondered about the house-mother with her red-blotched face, and the stuttering shop teacher, and the motherly principal, and youthful tired-looking psychologist, and wished I knew how they had found their way here to work and dedicate themselves to these silent minds. Like the boy who held the younger one in his arms, each had found a fulfillment in giving away a part of himself to those who had less.

And what about the things I wasn't shown?

I may soon be coming to Warren, to spend the rest of my life with the others . . . waiting.

July 15—I've been putting off a visit to my mother. I want to see her and I don't. Not until I'm sure what is going to happen to me. Let's see first how the work goes and what I discover.

Algernon refuses to run the maze any more; general motivation has decreased. I stopped off again today to see him, and this time Strauss was there too. Both he and Nemur looked disturbed as they watched Burt force-feed him. Strange to see the little puff of white clamped down on the worktable and Burt forcing the food down his throat with an eye-dropper.

If it keeps up this way, they'll have to start feeding him by injection. Watching Algernon squirm under those tiny bands this afternoon, I felt them around my own arms and legs. I started to gag and choke, and I had to get out of the lab for fresh air. I've got to stop identifying with him.

I went down to Murray's Bar and had a few drinks. And then I called Fay and we made the rounds. Fay is annoyed that I've stopped taking her out dancing, and she got angry and walked out on me last night. She has no idea of my work and no interest in it, and when I do try to talk to her about it she makes no attempt to hide her boredom. She just can't be bothered, and I can't blame her. She's interested in only three things that I can see: dancing, painting, and sex. And the only thing we really have in common is sex. It's foolish of me to try to interest her in my work. So she goes dancing without me. She told me that the other night she dreamed she had come into the apartment and set fire to all my books and notes, and that we went off dancing around the flames. I've got to watch out. She's becoming possessive. I just realized tonight that my own place is starting to resemble her apartment—a mess. I've got to cut down on the drinking.

July 16—Alice met Fay last night. I'd been concerned about what would happen if they came face to face. Alice came to see me after she found out about Algernon from Burt. She knows what it may mean, and she still feels responsible for having encouraged me in the first place.

We had coffee and we talked late. I knew that Fay had gone out dancing at the Stardust Ballroom, so I didn't expect her home so early. But at about one forty-five in the morning we were startled by Fay's sudden appearance on the fire-escape. She tapped, pushed open the half-open window and came waltzing into the room with a bottle in her hand.

"Crashing the party," she said. "Brought my own refreshments."

I had told her about Alice working on the project at the university, and I had mentioned Fay to Alice earlier—so they weren't surprised to meet. But after a few seconds of sizing each other up, they started talking about art and me, and for all they cared I could have been anywhere else in the world. They liked each other.

"I'll get the coffee," I said, and wandered out to the kitchen to leave them alone.

When I came back, Fay had taken off her shoes and was sitting on the floor, sipping gin out of the bottle. She was explaining to Alice that as far as she was concerned there was nothing more valuable to the human body than sunbathing, and that nudist colonies were the answer to the world's moral problems.

Alice was laughing hysterically at Fay's suggestion that we all join a nudist colony, and she leaned over and accepted a drink that Fay poured for her.

We sat and talked until dawn, and I insisted on seeing Alice home. When she protested that it wasn't necessary, Fay insisted that she would be a fool to go out alone in the city at this hour. So I went down and hailed a cab.

"There's something about her," said Alice on the way home. "I don't know what it is. Her frankness, her open trust, her unselfishness . . ."

I agreed.

"And she loves you," said Alice.

"No. She loves everyone," I insisted. "I'm just the neighbor across the hall."

"Aren't you in love with her?"

I shook my head. "You're the only woman I've ever loved."

"Let's not talk about that."

"Then you've cut me off from an important source of conversation."

"Only one thing I'm worried about, Charlie. The drinking. I've heard about some of those hangovers."

"Tell Burt to confine his observations and reports to the experimental data. I won't have him poisoning you against me. I can handle the drinks."

"I've heard that one before."

"But never from me."

"That's the only thing I have against her," she said. "She's got you drinking and she's interfering with your work."

"I can handle that too."

"This work is important now, Charlie. Not only to the world and millions of unknown people, but to you. Charlie, you've got to solve this thing for yourself as well. Don't let anyone tie your hands."

"So, now the truth comes out," I teased. "You'd like me to see less of her."

"That's not what I said."

"It's what you meant. If she's interfering with my work we both know I've got to cut her out of my life."

"No, I don't think you should cut her out of your life. She's good for you. You need a woman who's been around as she has."

"You would be good for me."

She turned her face away. "Not in the same way she is." She looked back at me. "I came here tonight prepared to hate her. I wanted to see her as a vile, stupid whore you'd gotten mixed up with, and I had big plans about coming between you and saving you from her in spite of yourself. But now that I've met her, I realize I have no right to judge her behavior. I think she's good for you. So that really lets the air out of me. I like her even if I disapprove. But in spite of that, if you've got to drink with her and spend all of your time with her in night clubs and cabarets dancing, then she's in your way. And that's a problem only you can solve."

"Another one of those?" I laughed.

"Are you up to this one? You're deeply involved with her. I can tell."

"Not all that deep."

"Have you told her about yourself?"

"No."

Imperceptibly, I could see her relax. By keeping the secret about myself, I had somehow not committed myself to Fay completely. We both knew that, wonderful as she was, Fay would never understand.

"I needed her," I said, "and in a way she needed me, and living right across from each other, well it was just handy, that's all. But I wouldn't call it love—not the same thing that exists between us."

She looked down at her hands and frowned. "I'm not sure I know what does exist between us."

"Something so deep and significant that Charlie inside me is terrified whenever there seems to be any chance of my making love to you."

"And not with her?"

I shrugged. "That's how I know it's not important with her. It doesn't mean enough for Charlie to panic."

"Great!" she laughed. "And ironic as hell. When you talk about him that way, I hate him for coming between us. Do you think he'll ever let you . . . let us . . ."

"I don't know. I hope so."

I left her at the door. We shook hands, and yet, strangely, it was much closer and more intimate than an embrace would have been.

I went home and made love to Fay, but kept thinking of Alice.

July 27—Working around the clock. Over Fay's protests, I've had a cot moved into the lab. She's become too possessive and resentful of my work. I think she could tolerate another woman, but not this complete absorption in something she can't follow. I was afraid it would come to this, but I have no patience with her now. I'm jealous of every moment away from the work—impatient with anyone who tries to steal my time.

Though most of my writing time is spent on notes which I keep in a separate folder, from time to time I have to put down my moods and thoughts out of sheer habit.

The calculus of intelligence is a fascinating study. In a sense this is the problem I've been concerned with all my life. Here is the place for the application of all the knowledge I have acquired.

Time assumes another dimension now—work and absorption in the search for an answer. The world around me and my past seem far away and distorted, as if time and space were taffy being stretched and looped and twisted out of shape. The only real things are the cages and the mice and the lab equipment here on the fourth floor of the main building.

There is no night or day. I've got to cram a lifetime of research into a few weeks. I know I should rest, but I can't until I know the truth about what is happening.

Alice is a great help to me now. She brings me sandwiches and coffee, but she makes no demands.

About my perception: everything is sharp and clear, each sensation heightened and illuminated so that reds and yellows and blues glow. Sleeping here has a strange effect. The odors of the laboratory animals, dogs, monkeys, mice, spin me back into memories, and it is difficult to know whether I am experiencing a new sensation or recalling the past. It is impossible to tell what proportion is memory and what exists here and now—so that a strange compound is formed of memory and reality; past and present; response to stimuli stored in my brain centers, and response to stimuli in this room. It's as if all the things I've learned have fused into a crystal universe spinning before me so that I can see all the facets of it reflected in gorgeous bursts of light. . . .

A monkey sitting in the center of his cage, staring at me out of sleepy eyes, rubbing his cheeks with little old-man shriveled hands . . . *chee* . . . *cheee* . . . *cheeeee* . . . and bouncing off the cage wire, up to the swing overhead where the other monkey sits staring dumbly into space. Urinating, defecating, passing wind, staring at me and laughing . . . *cheeee* . . . *cheeeee* . . . *cheeeee*. . . .

And bouncing around, leap, hop, up around and down, he swings and tries to grab the other monkey's tail, but the one on the bar keeps swishing it away, without fuss, out of his grasp. Nice monkey . . . pretty monkey . . . with big eyes and swishy tail. Can I feed him a peanut? . . . No, the man'll holler. That sign says do not feed the animals. That's a chimpanzee. Can I pet him? No. I want to pet the chip-a-zee. Never mind, come and look at the elephants.

Outside, crowds of bright sunshiny people are dressed in spring.

Algernon lies in his own dirt, unmoving, and the odors are stronger than ever before. And what about me?

July 28—Fay has a new boy friend. I went home last night to be with her. I went to my room first to get a bottle and then headed over on the fire escape. But fortunately I looked before going in. They were together on the couch. Strange, I don't really care. It's almost a relief.

I went back to the lab to work with Algernon. He has moments out of his lethargy. Periodically, he will run a shifting maze, but when he fails and finds himself in a dead-end, he reacts violently. When I got down to the lab, I looked in. He was alert and came up to me as if he knew me. He was eager to work, and when I set him down through the trap door in the wire mesh of the maze, he moved swiftly along the pathways to the reward box. Twice he ran the maze successfully. The third time, he got halfway through, paused at an intersection, and then with a twitching movement took the wrong turn. I could see what was going to happen, and I wanted to reach down and take him out before he ended up in a blind alley. But I restrained myself and watched.

When he found himself moving along the unfamiliar path, he slowed down, and his actions became erratic: start, pause, double back, turn around and then forward again, until finally he was in the cul-de-sac that informed him with a mild shock that he had made a mistake. At this point, instead of turning back to find an alternate route, he began to move in circles, squeaking like a phonograph needle scratched across the grooves. He threw himself against the walls of the maze, again and again, leaping up, twisting over backwards and falling, and throwing himself again. Twice he caught his claws in the overhead wire mesh, screeching wildly, letting go, and trying hopelessly again. Then he stopped and curled himself up into a small, tight ball.

When I picked him up, he made no attempt to uncurl, but remained in that state much like a catatonic stupor. When I moved his head or limbs, they stayed like wax. I put him back into his cage and watched him until the stupor wore off and he began to move around normally.

What eludes me is the reason for his regression—is it a special case? An isolated reaction? Or is there some general principle of failure basic to the whole procedure? I've got to work out the rule.

If I can find that out, and if it adds even one jot of information to whatever else has been discovered about mental retardation and the possibility of helping others like myself, I will be satisfied. Whatever happens to me, I will have lived a thousand normal lives by what I might add to others not yet born.

That's enough.

July 31—I'm on the edge of it. I sense it. They all think I'm killing myself at this pace, but what they don't understand is that I'm living at a peak of clarity and beauty I never knew existed. Every part of me is attuned to the work. I soak it up into my pores during the day, and at night—in the moments before I pass off into sleep—ideas explode into my head like fireworks. There is no greater joy than the burst of solution to a problem.

Incredible that anything could happen to take away this bubbling energy, the zest that fills everything I do. It's as if all the knowledge I've soaked in during the past months has coalesced and lifted me to a peak of light and understanding. This is beauty, love, and truth all rolled into one. This is joy. And now that I've found it, how can I give it up? Life and work are the most wonderful things a man can have. I am in love with what I am doing, because the answer to this problem is right here in my mind, and soon—very soon—it will burst into consciousness. Let me solve this one problem. I pray God it is the answer I want, but if not I will accept any answer at all and try to be grateful for what I had.

Fay's new boy friend is a dance instructor from the Stardust Ballroom. I can't really blame her since I have so little time to be with her.

August 11—Blind alley for the past two days. Nothing. I've taken a wrong turn somewhere, because I get answers to a lot of questions, but not to the most important question of all: How does Algernon's regression affect the basic hypothesis of the experiment?

Fortunately, I know enough about the processes of the mind not to let this block worry me too much. Instead of panicking and giving up (or what's even worse, pushing hard for answers that won't come) I've got to take my mind off the problem for a while and let it stew. I've gone as far as I can on a conscious level, and now it's up to those mysterious operations below the level of awareness. It's one of those inexplicable things, how everything I've learned and experienced is brought to bear on the problem. Pushing too hard will only make things freeze up. How many great problems have gone unsolved because men didn't know enough, or have enough faith in the creative process and in themselves, to let go for the *whole* mind to work at it?

So I decided yesterday afternoon to put the work aside for a while and go to Mrs. Nemur's cocktail party. It was in honor of the two men on the board of the Welberg Foundation who had been instrumental in getting her husband the grant. I planned to take Fay, but she said she had a date and she'd rather go dancing.

I started out the evening with every intention of being pleasant and making friends. But these days I have trouble getting through to people. I don't know if it's me or them, but any attempt at conversation usually fades away in a minute or two, and the barriers go up. Is it because they are afraid of me? Or is it that deep down they don't care and I feel the same about them?

I took a drink and wandered around the big room. There were little knots of people sitting in conversation groups, the kind I find it impossible to join. Finally, Mrs. Nemur cornered me and introduced me to Hyram Harvey, one of the board members. Mrs. Nemur is an attractive woman, early forties, blonde hair, lots of make-up and long red nails. She had her arm through Harvey's. "How is the research coming?" she wanted to know.

"As well as can be expected. I'm trying to solve a tough problem right now."

She lit a cigarette and smiled at me. "I know that everyone on the project is grateful that you've decided to pitch in and help out. But I imagine you'd much rather be working on something of your own. It must be rather dull taking up someone else's work rather than something you've conceived and created yourself."

She was sharp, all right. She didn't want Hyram Harvey to forget that her husband had the credit coming. I couldn't resist tossing it back at her. "No one really starts anything new, Mrs. Nemur. Everyone builds on other men's failures. There is nothing really original in science. What each man contributes to the sum of knowledge is what counts."

"Of course," she said, talking to her elderly guest rather than to me. "It's a shame Mr. Gordon wasn't around earlier to help solve these little final problems." She laughed. "But then— oh, I forgot, you weren't in any position to do psychological experimentation."

Harvey laughed, and I thought I'd better keep quiet. Bertha Nemur was not going to let me get the last word in, and if things went any further it would really get nasty.

I saw Dr. Strauss and Burt talking to the other man from the Welberg Foundation—George Raynor. Strauss was saying: "The problem, Mr. Raynor, is getting sufficient funds to work on projects like these, without having strings tied to the money. When amounts are earmarked for specific purposes, we can't really operate."

Raynor shook his head and waved a big cigar at the small group around him. "The real problem is convincing the board that this kind of research has practical value."

Strauss shook his head. "The point I've been trying to make is that this money is intended for research. No one can ever know in advance if a project is going to result in something useful. Results are often negative. We learn what something is not—and that is as important as a positive discovery to the man who is going to pick up from there. At least he knows what not to do."

As I approached the group, I noticed Raynor's wife, to whom I had been introduced earlier. She was a beautiful, dark-haired woman of thirty or so. She was staring at me, or rather at the top of my head—as if she expected something to sprout. I stared back, and she got uncomfortable and turned back to Dr. Strauss. "But what about the present project? Do you anticipate being able to use these techniques on other retardates? Is this something the world will be able to use?"

Strauss shrugged and nodded towards me. "Still too early to tell. Your husband helped us put Charlie to work on the project, and a great deal depends on what he comes up with."

"Of course," Mr. Raynor put in, "we all understand the necessity for *pure* research in fields like yours. But it would be such a boon to our image if we could produce a really workable method for achieving permanent results outside the laboratory, if we could show the world that there is some tangible good coming out of it."

I started to speak, but Strauss, who must have sensed what I was going to say, stood up and put his arm on my shoulder. "All of us at Beekman feel that the work Charlie is doing is of the utmost importance. His job now is to find the truth wherever it leads. We leave it to your foundations to handle the public, to educate society."

He smiled at the Raynors and steered me away from them.

"That," I said, "is not at all what I was going to say."

"I didn't think you were," he whispered, holding onto my elbow. "But I could see by that gleam in your eye you were ready to cut them to pieces. And I couldn't allow that, could I?"

"Guess not," I agreed, helping myself to another martini.

"Is it wise of you to drink so heavily?"

"No, but I'm trying to relax and I seem to have come to the wrong place."

"Well, take it easy," he said, "and keep out of trouble tonight. These people are not fools. They know the way you feel about them, and even if you don't need them, we do."

I waved a salute at him. "I'll try, but you'd better keep Mrs. Raynor away from me. I'm going to goose her if she wiggles her fanny at me again."

"Shhhh!" he hissed. "She'll hear you."

"Shhhh!" I echoed. "Sorry. I'll just sit here in the corner and keep out of everyone's way."

The haze was coming over me, but through it I could see people staring at me. I guess I was muttering to myself—too audibly. I don't remember what I said. A little while later I had the feeling that people were leaving unusually early, but I didn't pay much attention until Nemur came up and stood in front of me.

"Just who the hell do you think you are, that you can behave that way? I have never seen such insufferable rudeness in my life."

I struggled to my feet. "Now, what makes you say that?"

Strauss tried to restrain him, but he spluttered and gasped out: "I say it, because you have no gratitude or understanding of the situation. After all, you are indebted to these people if not to us—in more ways than one."

"Since when is a guinea pig supposed to be grateful?" I shouted. "I've served your purposes, and now I'm trying to work out your mistakes, so how the hell does that make me indebted to anyone?"

Strauss started to move in to break it up, but Nemur stopped him. "Just a minute. I want to hear this. I think it's time we had this out."

"He's had too much to drink," said his wife.

"Not that much," snorted Nemur. "He's speaking pretty clearly. I've put up with a lot from him. He's endangered—if not actually destroyed—our work, and now I want to hear from his own mouth what he thinks his justification is."

"Oh, forget it," I said. "You don't really want to hear the truth."

"But I do, Charlie. At least your version of the truth. I want to know if you feel any gratitude for all the things that have been done for you—the abilities you've developed, the things you've learned, the experiences you've had. Or do you think possibly you were better off before?"

"In some ways, yes."

That shocked them.

"I've learned a lot in the past few months," I said. "Not only about Charlie Gordon, but about life and people, and I've discovered that nobody really cares about Charlie Gordon, whether he's a moron or a genius. So what difference does it make?"

"Oh," laughed Nemur. "You're feeling sorry for yourself. What did you expect? This experiment was calculated to raise your intelligence, not to make you popular. We had no control over what happened to your personality, and you've developed from a likeable, retarded young man into an arrogant, self-centered, antisocial bastard."

"The problem, dear professor, is that you wanted someone who could be made intelligent but still be kept in a cage and displayed when necessary to reap the honors you seek. The hitch is that I'm a person."

He was angry, and I could see he was torn between ending the fight and trying once more to beat me down. "You're being unfair, as usual. You know we've always treated you well—done everything we could for you."

"Everything but treat me as a human being. You've boasted time and again that I was nothing before the experiment, and I know why. Because if I was nothing, then you were responsible for creating me, and that makes you my lord and master. You resent the fact that I don't show my gratitude every hour of the day. Well, believe it or not, I am grateful. But what you did for me—wonderful as it is—doesn't give you the right to treat me like an experimental animal. I'm an individual now, and so was Charlie before he ever walked into that lab. You look shocked! Yes, suddenly we discover that I was always a person—even before—and that challenges your belief that someone with an I.Q. of less than 100 doesn't deserve consideration. Professor Nemur, I think when you look at me your conscience bothers you."

"I've heard enough," he snapped. "You're drunk."

"Ah, no," I assured him. "Because if I get drunk, you'll see a different Charlie Gordon from the one you've come to know. Yes, the other Charlie who walked in the darkness is still here with us. Inside me."

"He's gone out of his head," said Mrs. Nemur. "He's talking as if there were two Charlie Gordons. You'd better look after him, doctor."

Dr. Strauss shook his head. "No. I know what he means. It's come up recently in therapy sessions. A peculiar dissociation has taken place in the past month or so. He's had several experiences of perceiving himself as he was before the experiment —as a separate and distinct individual still functioning in his consciousness—as if the old Charlie were struggling for control of the body—"

"No! I never said that! Not struggling for control. Charlie is there, all right, but not struggling with me. Just waiting. He has never tried to take over or tried to prevent me from doing anything I wanted to do." Then, remembering about Alice, I modified it. "Well, almost never. The humble, self-effacing Charlie you were all talking about a while ago is just waiting patiently. I'll admit I'm like him in a number of ways, but humility and self-effacement are not among them. I've learned how little they get a person in this world."

"You've become cynical," said Nemur. "That's all this opportunity has meant to you. Your genius has destroyed your faith in the world and in your fellow men."

"That's not completely true," I said softly. "But I've learned that intelligence alone doesn't mean a damned thing. Here in your university, intelligence, education, knowledge, have all become great idols. But I know now there's one thing you've all overlooked: intelligence and education that hasn't been tempered by human affection isn't worth a damn."

I helped myself to another martini from the nearby side-board and continued my sermon.

"Don't misunderstand me," I said. "Intelligence is one of the greatest human gifts. But all too often a search for knowl-edge drives out the search for love. This is something else I've discovered for myself very recently. I present it to you as a hypothesis: Intelligence without the ability to give and receive affection leads to mental and moral breakdown, to neurosis, and possibly even psychosis. And I say that the mind absorbed in and involved in itself as a self-centered end, to the exclusion of human relationships, can only lead to vio-lence and pain.

"When I was retarded I had lots of friends. Now I have no one. Oh, I know lots of people. Lots and lots of people. But I don't have any real friends. Not like I used to have in the bak-ery. Not a friend in the world who means anything to me, and no one I mean anything to." I discovered that my speech was becoming slurred, and there was a lightness in my head. "That can't be right, can it?" I insisted. "I mean, what do you think? Do you think that's . . . that's right?"

Strauss came over and took my arm.

"Charlie, maybe you'd better lie down a while. You've had too much to drink."

"Why y'all looking at me like that? What did I say wrong? Did I say something wrong? I din't mean to say anything that wasn't right."

I heard the words thick in my mouth, as if my face had been shot full of novocaine. I was drunk—completely out of control. At that moment, almost with the flick of a switch, I was watch-ing the scene from the dining room doorway, and I could see myself as the other Charlie—there near the sideboard, drink in hand, eyes wide and frightened.

"I always try to do the right things. My mother always taught me to be nice to people because she said that way you won't get into trouble and you'll always have lots of friends."

I could see by the way he was twitching and writhing that he had to get to the bathroom. Oh, my God, not there in front of them. "Excuse me, please," he said, "I got to go . . ." Some-how, in that drunken stupor, I managed to turn him away from them and head him toward the bathroom.

He made it in time, and after a few seconds I was again in control. I rested my cheek against the wall, and then washed my face with cool water. Still groggy, but I knew I was going to be all right.

That's when I saw Charlie watching me from the mirror behind the washbasin. I don't know how I knew it was Charlie and not me. Something about the dull, questioning look in his face. His eyes, wide and frightened, as if at one word from me he would turn and run deep into the dimension of the mirrored world. But he didn't run. He just stared back at me, mouth open, jaw hanging loosely.

"Hello," I said, "so you've finally come face to face with me."

He frowned, just a bit, as if he didn't understand what I meant, as if he wanted an explanation but didn't know how to ask for it. Then, giving it up, he smiled wryly from the corner of his mouth.

"Stay there right in front of me," I shouted. "I'm sick and tired of your spying on me from doorways and dark places where I can't catch up with you."

He stared.

"Who are you, Charlie?"

Nothing but the smile.

I nodded and he nodded back.

"Then what do you want?" I asked.

He shrugged.

"Oh, come now," I said, "you must want something. You've been following me—"

He looked down and I looked at my hands to see what he was looking at. "You want these back, don't you? You want me out of here so you can come back and take over where you left off. I don't blame you. It's your body and your brain—and your life, even though you weren't able to make much use of it. I don't have the right to take it away from you. Nobody does. Who's to say that my light is better than your darkness? Who's to say death is better than your darkness? Who am I to say? . . .

"But I'll tell you something else, Charlie." I stood up and backed away from the mirror. "I'm not your friend. I'm your enemy. I'm not going to give up my intelligence without a struggle. I can't go back down into that cave. There's no place for *me* to go now, Charlie. So you've got to stay away. Stay inside my unconscious where you belong, and stop following me around. I'm not going to give up—no matter what they all think. No matter how lonely it is. I'm going to keep what they've given me and do great things for the world and for other people like you."

As I turned toward the door, I had the impression he was reaching out his hand toward me. But the whole damned thing was foolish. I was just drunk and that was my own reflection in the mirror.

When I came out, Strauss wanted to put me into a taxi, but I insisted I could get home all right. All I needed was a little fresh air, and I didn't want anyone to come with me. I wanted to walk by myself.

I was seeing myself as I really had become: Nemur had said it. I was an arrogant, self-centered bastard. Unlike Charlie, I was incapable of making friends or thinking about other people and their problems. I was interested in myself, and myself only. For one long moment in that mirror I had seen myself through Charlie's eyes—looked down at myself and saw what I had really become. And I was ashamed.

Hours later I found myself in front of the apartment house, and made my way upstairs and through the dimly lit hallway. Passing Fay's room, I could see there was a light on, and I started toward her door. But just as I was about to knock I heard her giggling, and a man's answering laugh.

It was too late for that.

I let myself into my apartment quietly and stood there for a while in the dark, not daring to move, not daring to turn on the light. Just stood there and felt the whirlpool in my eyes.

What has happened to me? Why am I so alone in the world?

4:30 A.M.—The solution came to me, just as I was dozing off. Illuminated! Everything fits together, and I see what I should have known from the beginning. No more sleep. I've got to get back to the lab and test this against the results from the computer. This, finally, is the flaw in the experiment. I've found it.

Now what becomes of me?

August 26—LETTER TO PROFESSOR NEMUR (COPY)
Dear Professor Nemur:

Under separate cover I am sending you a copy of my report entitled: "The Algernon-Gordon Effect: A Study of Structure and Function of Increased Intelligence," which may be published if you see fit.

As you know, my experiments are completed. I have included in my report all of my formulae, as well as mathematical analyses of the data in the appendix. Of course, these should be verified.

The results are clear. The more sensational aspects of my rapid climb cannot obscure the facts. The surgery-and-injection techniques developed by you and Dr. Strauss must be viewed as having little or no practical applicability, at the present time, to the increase of human intelligence.

Reviewing the data on Algernon: although he is still in his physical youth, he has regressed mentally. Motor activity impaired; general reduction of glandular functioning; accelerated loss of coordination; and strong indications of progressive amnesia.

As I show in my report, these and other physical and mental deterioration syndromes can be predicted with statistically significant results by the application of my new formula. Although the surgical stimulus to which we were both subjected resulted in an intensification and acceleration of all mental processes, the flaw, which I have taken the liberty of calling the "Algernon-Gordon Effect," *is the logical extension of the entire intelligence speed-up. The hypothesis here proved may be described most simply in the following terms:*

ARTIFICIALLY-INDUCED INTELLIGENCE DETERIORATES AT A RATE OF TIME DIRECTLY PROPORTIONAL TO THE QUANTITY OF THE INCREASE.

As long as I am able to write, I will continue to put down my thoughts and ideas in these progress reports. It is one of my few solitary pleasures and is certainly necessary to the completion of this research. However, by all indications, my own mental deterioration will be quite rapid.

I have checked and rechecked my data a dozen times in hope of finding an error, but I am sorry to say the results must stand. Yet, I am grateful for the little bit that I here add to the knowledge of the function of the human mind and of the laws governing the artificial increase of human intelligence.

The other night Dr. Strauss was saying that an experimental failure, *the* disproving of a theory, *was as important to the advancement of learning as a success would be. I know now that this is true. I am sorry, however, that my own contribution to the field must rest upon the ashes of the work of this staff, and especially those who have done so much for me.*

Yours truly,
Charles Gordon

encl: report
copy: Dr. Strauss
      The Welberg Foundation

September 1—I must not panic. Soon there will be signs of emotional instability and forgetfulness, the first symptoms of the burnout. Will I recognize these in myself? All I can do now is keep recording my mental state as objectively as possible, remembering that this psychological journal will be the first of its kind, and possibly the last.

This morning Nemur had Burt take my report and the statistical data down to Hallston University to have some of the top men in the field verify my results and the application of my formulas. All last week they had Burt going over my experiments and methodological charts. I shouldn't really be annoyed by their precautions. After all, I'm just a Charlie-come-lately, and it is difficult for Nemur to accept the fact that my work might be beyond him. He had come to believe in the myth of his own authority, and after all I am an outsider.

I don't really care any more what he thinks, or what any of them think for that matter. There isn't time. The work is done, the data is in, and all that remains is to see whether I have accurately projected the curve on the Algernon figures as a prediction of what will happen to me.

Alice cried when I told her the news. Then she ran out. I've got to impress on her that there is no reason for her to feel guilty about this.

September 2—Nothing definite yet. I move in a silence of clear white light. Everything around me is waiting. I dream of being alone on the top of a mountain, surveying the land around me, greens and yellows—and the sun directly above, pressing my shadow into a tight ball around my legs. As the sun drops into the afternoon sky, the shadow undrapes itself and stretches out toward the horizon, long and thin, and far behind me. . . .

I want to say here again what I've said already to Dr. Strauss. No one is in any way to blame for what has happened. This experiment was carefully prepared, extensively tested on animals, and statistically validated. When they decided to use me as the first human test, they were reasonably certain that there was no physical danger involved. There was no way to foresee the psychological pitfalls. I don't want anyone to suffer because of what happens to me.

The only question now is: How much can I hang on to?

September 15—Nemur says my results have been confirmed. It means that the flaw is central and brings the entire hypothesis into question. Someday there might be a way to overcome this problem, but that time is not yet. I have recommended that no further tests be made on human beings until these things are clarified by additional research on animals.

It is my own feeling that the most successful line of research will be that taken by the men studying enzyme imbalances. As with so many other things, time is the key factor—speed in discovering the deficiency, and speed in administering hormonal substitutes. I would like to help in that area of research, and in the search for radio-isotopes that may be used in local cortical control, but I know now that I won't have the time.

September 17—Becoming absent minded. Put things away on my desk or in the drawers of the lab tables, and when I can't find them I lose my temper and flare up at everyone. First signs?

Algernon died two days ago. I found him at four thirty in the morning when I came back to the lab after wandering around down at the waterfront—on his side, stretched out in the corner of his cage. As if he were running in his sleep.

Dissection shows that my predictions were right. Compared to the normal brain, Algernon's had decreased in weight and there was a general smoothing out of the cerebral convolutions as well as a deepening and broadening of brain fissures.

It's frightening to think that the same thing might be happening to me right now. Seeing it happen to Algernon makes it real. For the first time, I'm afraid of the future.

I put Algernon's body into a small metal container and took him home with me. I wasn't going to let them dump him into the incinerator. It's foolish and sentimental, but late last night I buried him in the back yard. I wept as I put a bunch of wild flowers on the grave.

September 21—I'm going to Marks Street to visit my mother tomorrow. A dream last night triggered off a sequence of memories, lit up a whole slice of the past and the important thing is to get it down on paper quickly before I forget it because I seem to forget things sooner now. It has to do with my mother, and now—more than ever—I want to understand her, to know what she was like and why she acted the way she did. I mustn't hate her.

I've got to come to terms with her *before* I see her so that I won't act harshly or foolishly.

September 27—I should have written this down right away, because it's important to make this record complete.

I went to see Rose three days ago. Finally, I forced myself to borrow Burt's car again. I was afraid, and yet I knew I had to go.

At first when I got to Marks Street I thought I had made a mistake. It wasn't the way I remembered it at all. It was a filthy street. Vacant lots where many of the houses had been torn down. On the sidewalk, a discarded refrigerator with its face ripped off, and on the curb an old mattress with wire intestines hanging out of its belly. Some houses had boarded up windows, and others looked more like patched-up shanties than homes. I parked the car a block away from the house and walked.

There were no children playing on Marks Street—not at all like the mental picture I had brought with me of children everywhere, and Charlie watching them through the front window (strange that most of my memories of the street are framed by the window, with me always inside watching the children play). Now there were only old people standing in the shade of tired porches.

As I approached the house, I had a second shock. My mother was on the front stoop, in an old brown sweater, washing the ground floor windows from the outside even though it was cold and windy. Always working to show the neighbors what a good wife and mother she was.

The most important thing had always been what other people thought—appearances before herself or her family. And righteous about it. Time and again Matt had insisted that what others thought about you wasn't the only thing in life. But it did no good. Norma had to dress well; the house had to have fine furniture; Charlie had to be kept inside so that other people wouldn't know anything was wrong.

At the gate, I paused to watch as she straightened up to catch her breath. Seeing her face made me tremble, but it was not the face I had struggled so hard to recall. Her hair had become white and streaked with iron, and the flesh of her thin cheeks was wrinkled. Perspiration made her forehead glisten. She caught sight of me and stared back.

I wanted to look away, to turn back down the street, but I couldn't—not after having come so far. I would just ask directions, pretending I was lost in a strange neighborhood. Seeing her had been enough. But all I did was stand there waiting for her to do something first. And all she did was stand there and look at me.

"Do you want something?" Her voice, hoarse, was an unmistakable echo down the corridors of memory.

I opened my mouth, but nothing came out. My mouth worked, I know, and I struggled to speak to her, to get something out, because in that moment I could see recognition in her eyes. This was not at all the way I wanted her to see me. Not standing there in front of her, dumbly, unable to make myself understood. But my tongue kept getting in the way, like a huge obstruction, and my mouth was dry.

Finally, something came out. Not what I had intended (I had planned something soothing and encouraging, to take control of the situation and wipe out all the past and pain with a few words) but all that came out of my cracked throat was: "Maaa . . ."

With all the things I had learned—in all the languages I had mastered—all I could say to her, standing on the porch staring at me, was, "*Maaaa*." Like a dry-mouthed lamb at the udder.

She wiped her forehead with the back of her arm and frowned

at me, as if she could not see me clearly. I stepped forward, past the gate to the walk, and then toward the steps. She drew back.

At first, I wasn't sure whether or not she really recognized me, but then she gasped: "*Charlie! . . .*" She didn't scream it or whisper it. She just gasped it as one might do coming out of a dream.

"Ma . . ." I started up the steps. "It's me . . ."

My movement startled her, and she stepped backwards, kicking over the bucket of soapy water, and the dirty suds rushed down the steps. "What are you doing here?"

"I just wanted to see you . . . talk to you . . ."

Because my tongue kept getting in my way, my voice came out of my throat differently, with a thick whining tone, as I might have spoken a long time ago. "Don't go away," I begged. "Don't run away from me."

But she had gone inside the vestibule and locked the door. A moment later I could see her peering at me from behind the sheer white curtain of the door window, her eyes terrified. Behind the window her lips moved soundlessly. "Go away! Leave me alone!"

Why? Who was she to deny me this way? By what right did she turn away from me?

"Let me in! I want to talk to you! Let me in!" I banged on the door against the glass so hard it cracked, and the crack spread a web that caught my skin for a moment and held it fast. She must have thought I was out of my mind and had come to harm her. She let go of the outer door and fled down the hallway that led into the apartment.

I pushed again. The hook gave way and, unprepared for the sudden yielding, I fell into the vestibule, off balance. My hand was bleeding from the glass I had broken, and not knowing what else to do, I put my hand into my pocket to prevent the blood from staining her freshly scrubbed linoleum.

I started in, past the stairs I had seen so often in my nightmares. I had often been pursued up that long, narrow staircase by demons who grabbed at my legs and pulled me down into the cellar below, while I tried to scream without voice, strangling on my tongue and gagging in silence. Like the silent boys at Warren.

The people who lived on the second floor—our landlord and landlady, the Meyers—had always been kind to me. They gave me sweets and let me come to sit in their kitchen and play with their dog. I wanted to see them, but without being told I knew they were gone and dead and that strangers lived upstairs. That path was now closed to me forever.

At the end of the hallway, the door through which Rose had fled was locked, and for a moment I stood—undecided.

"Open the door."

The answer was the high-pitched yapping of a small dog. It took me by surprise.

"All right," I said. "I don't intend to hurt you or anything, but I've come a long way, and I'm not leaving without talking to you. If you don't open the door, I'm going to break it down."

I heard her saying: "Shhhh, Nappie . . . Here, into the bedroom you go." A moment later I heard the click of the lock. The door opened and she stood there staring at me.

"Ma," I whispered, "I'm not going to do anything. I just want to talk to you. You've got to understand, I'm not the same as I was. I've changed. I'm normal now. Don't you understand? I'm not retarded any more. I'm not a moron. I'm just like anyone else. I'm normal—just like you and Matt and Norma."

I tried to keep talking, babbling so she wouldn't close the door. I tried to tell her the whole thing, all at once. "They changed me, performed an operation on me and made me different, the way you always wanted me to be. Didn't you read about it in the newspapers? A new scientific experiment that changes your capacity for intelligence, and I'm the first one they tried it on. Can't you understand? Why are you looking at me that way? I'm smart now, smarter than Norma, or Uncle Herman, or Matt. I know things even college professors don't know. Talk to me! You can be proud of me now and tell all the neighbors. You don't have to hide me in the cellar when company comes. Just talk to me. Tell me about things, the way it was when I was a little boy, that's all I want. I won't hurt you. I don't hate you. But I've got to know about myself, to understand myself before it's too late. Don't you see, I can't be a complete person unless I can understand myself, and you're the only one in the world who can help me now. Let me come in and sit down for a little while."

It was the way I spoke rather than what I said that hypnotized her. She stood there in the doorway and stared at me. Without thinking, I pulled my bloody hand out of my pocket and clenched it in my pleading. When she saw it her expression softened.

"You hurt yourself . . ." She didn't necessarily feel sorry for me. It was the sort of thing she might have felt for a dog that had torn its paw, or a cat that had been gashed in a fight. It wasn't because I was her Charlie, but in spite of it.

"Come in and wash it. I've got some bandage and iodine."

I followed her to the cracked sink with the corrugated drainboard at which she had so often washed my face and hands after I came in from the back yard, or when I was ready to eat or go to sleep. She watched me roll up my sleeves. "You shouldn't have broke the window. The landlord's gonna be sore, and I don't have enough money to pay for it." Then, as if impatient with the way I was doing it, she took the soap from me and washed my hand. As she did it, she concentrated so hard that I kept silent, afraid of breaking the spell. Occasionally she clucked her tongue, or sighed, "Charlie, Charlie, always getting yourself into a mess. When are you going to learn to take care of yourself?" She was back twenty-five years earlier when I was her little Charlie and she was willing to fight for my place in the world.

When the blood was washed off and she had dried my hands with paper toweling, she looked up into my face and her eyes went round with fright. "Oh, my God!" she gasped, and backed away.

I started talking again, softly, persuasively to convince her that nothing was wrong and I meant no harm. But as I spoke I could tell her mind was wandering. She looked around vaguely, put her hand to her mouth and groaned as she looked at me again. "The house is such a mess," she said. "I wasn't expecting company. Look at those windows, and that woodwork over there."

"That's all right, Ma. Don't worry about it."

"I've got to wax those floors again. It's got to be clean." She noticed some fingermarks on the door and taking up her washrag she scrubbed them away. When she looked up and saw me watching her, she frowned. "Have you come about the electric bill?"

Before I could say no, she wagged her finger, scolding, "I intend to send a check out the first of the month, but my husband is out of town on business. I told them all they don't have to worry about the money, because my daughter gets paid this week, and we'll be able to take care of all our bills. So there's no need bothering me for money."

"Is she your only child? Don't you have any other children?"

She started, and then her eyes looked far away. "I had a boy. So brilliant that all the other mothers were jealous of him. And they put the evil eye on him. They called it the *I.Q.* but it was the *evil-I.Q.* He would have been a great man, if not for that. He was really very bright—*exceptional*, they said. He could have been a genius . . ."

She picked up a scrub brush. "Excuse me now. I've got to get things ready. My daughter has a young man coming for dinner, and I've got to get this place clean." She got down on her knees and started to scrub the already shining floor. She didn't look up again.

She was muttering to herself now, and I sat down at the kitchen table. I would wait until she came out of it, until she recognized me and understood who I was. I couldn't leave until she knew that I was her Charlie. Somebody had to understand.

She had started humming sadly to herself, but she stopped, her rag poised midway between the bucket and the floor, as if suddenly aware of my presence behind her.

She turned, her face tired and her eyes glistening, and cocked her head. "How could it be? I don't understand. They told me you could never be changed."

"They performed an operation on me, and that changed me. I'm famous now. They've heard of me all over the world. I'm intelligent now, Mom. I can read and write, and I can—"

"Thank God," she whispered. "My prayers—all these years I thought He didn't hear me, but He was listening all the time, just waiting His own good time to do His will."

She wiped her face in her apron, and when I put my arm around her, she wept freely on my shoulder. All the pain was washed away, and I was glad I had come.

"I've got to tell everyone," she said, smiling, "all those teachers at the school. Oh, wait till you see their faces when I tell them. And the neighbors. And Uncle Herman—I've got to tell Uncle Herman. He'll be so pleased. And wait until your father comes home, and your sister! Oh, she'll be so happy to see you. You have no idea."

She hugged me, talking excitedly, making plans for the new life we were going to have together. I hadn't the heart to remind her that most of my childhood teachers were gone from this school, that the neighbors had long moved away, that Uncle Herman had died many years ago, and that my father had left her. The nightmare of all those years had been pain enough. I wanted to see her smiling and know I had been the one to make her happy. For the first time in my life, I had brought a smile to her lips.

Then after a while, she paused thoughtfully as if remembering something. I had the feeling her mind was going to wander. "No!" I shouted, startling her back to reality, "Wait, Ma! There's something else. Something I want you to have before I go."

"Go? You can't go away now."

"I have to go, Ma. I have things to do. But I'll write to you, and I'll send you money."

"But when will you come back?"

"I don't know—yet. But before I go, I want you to have this."

"A magazine?"

"Not exactly. It's a scientific report I wrote. Very technical. Look, it's called *The Algernon-Gordon Effect*. Something I discovered, and it's named partly after me. I want you to keep a copy of the report so that you can show people that your son turned out to be more than a dummy after all."

She took it and looked at it in awe. "It's . . . it's your name. I knew it would happen. I always said it would happen someday. I tried everything I could. You were too young to remember, but I tried. I told them all that you'd go to college and become a professional man and make your mark in the world. They laughed, but I told them."

She smiled at me through tears, and then a moment later she wasn't looking at me any more. She picked up her rag and began to wash the woodwork around the kitchen door, humming—more happily, I thought—as if in a dream.

The dog started barking again. The front door opened and closed and a voice called: "Okay, Nappie. Okay, it's me." The dog was jumping excitedly against the bedroom door.

I was furious at being trapped here. I didn't want to see Norma. We had nothing to say to each other, and I didn't want my visit spoiled. There was no back door. The only way would be to climb out the window into the back yard and go over the fence. But someone might mistake me for a burglar.

As I heard her key in the door, I whispered to my mother—I don't know why—"Norma's home." I touched her arm, but she didn't hear me. She was too busy humming to herself as she washed the woodwork.

The door opened. Norma saw me and frowned. She didn't recognize me at first—it was dim, the lights hadn't been turned on. Putting down the shopping bag she was carrying, she switched on the light. "Who are you? . . ." But before I could answer, her hand went over her mouth, and she slumped back against the door.

"Charlie!" She said it the same way my mother had, gasping. And she looked the way my mother used to look—thin, sharp features, birdlike, pretty. "Charlie! My God, what a shock! You might have gotten in touch and warned me. You should have called. I don't know what to say . . ." She looked at my mother, sitting on the floor near the sink. "Is she all right? You didn't shock her or anything . . ."

"She came out of it for a while. We had a little talk."

"I'm glad. She doesn't remember much these days. It's old age—senility. Dr. Portman wants me to put her into a nursing home, but I can't do it. I can't stand to think of her in one of those institutions." She opened the bedroom door to let the dog out, and when he jumped and whined joyously, she picked him up and hugged him. "I just can't do that to my own mother." Then she smiled at me uncertainly. "Well, what a surprise. I never dreamed. Let me look at you. I never would have recognized you. I'd have passed you by in the street. So different." She sighed. "I'm glad to see you, Charlie."

"Are you? I didn't think you'd want to see me again."

"Oh, Charlie!" She took my hands in hers. "Don't say that.

I *am* glad to see you. I've been expecting you. I didn't know when, but I knew someday you'd come back. Ever since I read that you had run away in Chicago." She pulled back to look up at me. "You don't know how I've thought about you and wondered where you were and what you were doing. Until that professor came here last—when was it? last March? just seven months ago?—I had no idea you were still alive. She told me you died in Warren. I believed it all these years. When they told me you were alive and they needed you for the experiment, I didn't know what to do. Professor . . . Nemur? —is that his name?—wouldn't let me see you. He was afraid to upset you before the operation. But when I saw in the papers that it worked and you had become a *genius*—oh, my!—you don't know what it felt like to read about that.

"I told all the people in my office, and the girls at my bridge club. I showed them your picture in the paper, and I told them you'd be coming back here to see us one day. And you have. You really have. You didn't forget us."

She hugged me again. "Oh, Charlie. Charlie . . . it's so wonderful to find all of a sudden I've got a big brother. You have no idea. Sit down—let me make you something to eat. You've got to tell me all about it and what your plans are. I . . . I don't know where to start asking questions. I must sound ridiculous—like a girl who has just found out her brother is a hero, or a movie star, or something."

I was confused. I had not expected a greeting like this from Norma. It had never occurred to me that all these years alone with my mother might change her. And yet it was inevitable. She was no longer the spoiled brat of my memories. She had grown up, had become warm and sympathetic and affectionate.

We talked. Ironic to sit there with my sister, the two of us talking about my mother—right there in the room with us—as if she wasn't there. Whenever Norma would refer to their life together, I'd look to see if Rose was listening, but she was deep in her own world, as if she didn't understand our language, as if none of it concerned her any more. She drifted around the kitchen like a ghost, picking things up, putting things away, without ever getting in the way. It was frightening.

I watched Norma feed her dog. "So you finally got him. Nappie—short for Napoleon, isn't it?"

She straightened up and frowned. "How did you know?"

I explained about my memory: the time she had brought home her test paper hoping to get the dog, and how Matt had forbidden it. As I told it, the frown became deeper.

"I don't remember any of it. Oh, Charlie, was I so mean to you?"

"There's one memory I'm curious about. I'm not really sure if it's a memory, or a dream, or if I just made it all up. It was the last time we played together as friends. We were in the basement, and we were playing a game with the lampshades on our heads, pretending we were Chinese coolies—jumping up and down on an old mattress. You were seven or eight, I think, and I was about thirteen. And, as I recall, you bounced off the mattress and hit your head against the wall. It wasn't very hard—just a bump—but Mom and Dad came running down because you were screaming, and you said I was trying to kill you.

"She blamed Matt for not watching me, for leaving us alone together, and she beat me with a strap until I was nearly unconscious. Do you remember it? Did it really happen that way?"

Norma was fascinated by my description of the memory, as if it awakened sleeping images. "It's all so vague. You know, I thought that was my dream. I remember us wearing the lamp-shades, and jumping up and down on the mattresses." She stared out of the window. "I hated you because they fussed over *you* all the time. They never spanked you for not doing your homework right, or for not bringing home the best marks. You skipped classes most of the time and played games, and I had to go to the hard classes in school. Oh, how I hated you. In school the other children scribbled pictures on the blackboard, a boy with a duncecap on his head, and they wrote *Norma's Brother* under it. And they scribbled things on the sidewalk in the schoolyard—*Moron's Sister* and *Dummy Gordon Family*. And then one day when I wasn't invited to Emily Raskin's birthday party, I knew it was because of you. And when we were playing there in the basement with those lampshades on our heads, I had to get even." She started to cry. "So I lied and said you hurt me. Oh, Charlie, what a fool I was—what a spoiled brat. I'm so ashamed—"

"Don't blame yourself. It must have been hard to face the

other kids. For me, this kitchen was my world—and that room there. The rest of it didn't matter as long as this was safe. You had to face the rest of the world."

"Why did they send you away, Charlie? Why couldn't you have stayed here and lived with us? I always wondered about that. Every time I asked her, she always said it was for your own good."

"In a way she was right."

She shook her head. "She sent you away because of *me*, didn't she? Oh, Charlie, why did it have to be? Why did all this happen to us?"

I didn't know what to tell her. I wished I could say that like the House of Atreus or Cadmus we were suffering for the sins of our forefathers, or fulfilling an ancient Greek oracle. But I had no answers for her, or for myself.

"It's past," I said. "I'm glad I met you again. It makes it a little easier."

She grabbed my arm suddenly. "Charlie, you don't know what I've been through all these years with her. The apartment, this street, my job. It's all been a nightmare, coming home each day, wondering if she's still here, if she's harmed herself, guilty for thinking about things like that."

I stood up and let her rest against my shoulder, and she wept. "Oh, Charlie. I'm glad you're back now. We've needed someone. I'm so tired. . . ."

I had dreamed of a time like this, but now that it was here, what good was it? I couldn't tell her what was going to happen to me. And yet, could I accept her affection on false pretenses? Why kid myself? If I had still been the old, feeble-minded, dependent Charlie, she wouldn't have spoken to me the same way. So what right did I have to it now? My mask would soon be ripped away.

"Don't cry, Norma. Everything will work out all right." I heard myself speaking in reassuring platitudes. "I'll try to take care of you both. I have a little money saved, and with what the Foundation has been paying me, I'll be able to send you some money regularly—for a while anyway."

"But you're not going away! You've got to stay with us now—"

"I've got to do some traveling, some research, make a few speeches, but I'll try to come back to visit you. Take care of her. She's been through a lot. I'll help you for as long as I can."

"Charlie! No, don't go!" She clung to me. "I'm frightened!"

The role I had always wanted to play—the big brother.

At that moment, I sensed that Rose, who had been sitting in the corner quietly, was staring at us. Something in her face had changed. Her eyes were wide, and she leaned forward on the edge of her seat. All I could think of was a hawk ready to swoop down.

I pushed Norma away from me, but before I could say anything, Rose was on her feet. She had taken the kitchen knife from the table and was pointing at me.

"What are you doing to her? Get away from her! I told you what I'd do to you if I ever caught you touching your sister again! Dirty mind! You don't belong with normal people!"

We both jumped back, and for some insane reason, I felt guilty, as if I had been caught doing something wrong, and I knew Norma felt the same way. It was as if my mother's accusation had made it true, that we were doing something obscene.

Norma screamed at her: "Mother! Put down that knife!"

Seeing Rose standing there with the knife brought back the picture of that night she had forced Matt to take me away. She was reliving that now. I couldn't speak or move. The nausea swept over me, the choking tension, the buzzing in my ears, my stomach knotting and stretching as if it wanted to tear itself out of my body.

She had a knife, and Alice had a knife, and my father had a knife, and Dr. Strauss had a knife. . . .

Fortunately, Norma had the presence of mind to take it away from her, but she couldn't erase the fear in Rose's eyes as she screamed at me. "Get him out of here! He's got no right to look at his sister with sex in his mind!"

Rose screamed and sank back into the chair, weeping.

I didn't know what to say, and neither did Norma. We were both embarrassed. Now she knew why I had been sent away.

I wondered if I had ever done anything to justify my mother's fear. There were no such memories, but how could I be sure there weren't horrible thoughts repressed behind the barriers of my tortured conscience? In the sealed-off passage-ways, beyond blind alleys, that I would never see. Possibly I will never know. Whatever the truth is, I must not hate Rose for protecting Norma. I must understand the way she saw it. Unless I forgive her, I will have nothing.

Norma was trembling.

"Take it easy," I said. "She doesn't know what she's doing. It wasn't me she was raving at. It was the old Charlie. She was afraid of what *he* might do to you. I can't blame her for want-ing to protect you. But we don't have to think about it now, because he's gone forever, isn't he?"

She wasn't listening to me. There was a dreamy expression on her face. "I've just had one of those strange experiences where something happens, and you have the feeling you know it's going to happen, as if it all took place before, the exact same way, and you watch it unfold again. . . ."

"A very common experience."

She shook her head. "Just now, when I saw her with that knife, it was like a dream I had a long time ago."

What was the use of telling her she had undoubtedly been awake that night as a child, and had seen the whole thing from her room—that it had been repressed and twisted until she imagined it as a fantasy. No reason for burdening her with the truth. She would have enough sadness with my mother in the days to come. I would gladly have taken the burden and the pain off her hands, but there was no sense in starting something I couldn't finish. I would have my own suffering to live with. There was no way to stop the sands of knowledge from slipping through the hourglass of my mind.

"I've got to go now," I said. "Take care of yourself, and of her." I squeezed her hand. As I went out, Napoleon barked at me.

I held it in for as long as I could, but when I reached the street it was impossible. It's hard to write it down, but people turned to look at me as I walked back to the car, crying like a child. I couldn't help myself, and I didn't care.

As I walked, the ridiculous words drummed themselves into my head over and over again, rising to the rhythm of a buzzing noise:

Three blind mice . . . three blind mice,
See how they run! See how they run!
They all run after the farmer's wife,
She cut off their tails with a carving knife,
Did you ever see such a sight in your life,
As three . . . blind . . . mice?

I tried to shut it out of my ears, but I couldn't, and once when I turned to look back at the house and the porch, I saw the face of a boy, staring at me, his cheek pressed against the window pane.

PROGRESS REPORT 17

October 3—Downhill. Thoughts of suicide to stop it all now while I am still in control and aware of the world around me. But then I think of Charlie waiting at the window. His life is not mine to throw away. I've just borrowed it for a while, and now I'm being asked to return it.

I must remember I'm the only person this ever happened to. As long as I can, I've got to keep putting down my thoughts and feelings. These progress reports are Charlie Gordon's contribution to mankind.

I have become edgy and irritable. Having fights with people in the building about playing the hi-fi set late at night. I've been doing that a lot since I've stopped playing the piano. It isn't right to keep it going all hours, but I do it to keep myself awake. I know I should sleep, but I begrudge every second of waking time. It's not just because of the nightmares; it's because I'm afraid of letting go.

I tell myself there'll be time enough to sleep later, when it's dark.

Mr. Vernor in the apartment below never used to complain, but now he's always banging on the pipes or on the ceiling of his apartment so that I hear the pounding beneath my feet. I ignored it at first, but last night he came up in his bathrobe. We quarreled, and I slammed the door in his face. An hour later he was back with a policeman who told me I couldn't play records that loudly at 4 A.M. The smile on Vernor's face so enraged me that it was all I could do to keep from hitting him. When they left I smashed all the records and the machine. I've been kidding myself anyway. I don't really like that kind of music any more.

October 4—Strangest therapy session I ever had. Strauss was upset. It was something he hadn't expected either.

What happened—I don't dare call it a memory—was a psychic experience or a hallucination. I won't attempt to explain or interpret it, but will only record what happened.

I was touchy when I came into his office, but he pretended not to notice. I lay down on the couch immediately, and he, as usual, took his seat to one side and a little behind me—just out of sight—and waited for me to begin the ritual of pouring out all the accumulated poisons of the mind.

I peered back at him over my head. He looked tired, and flabby, and somehow he reminded me of Matt sitting on his barber's chair waiting for customers. I told Strauss of the association and he nodded and waited.

"*Are* you waiting for customers?" I asked. "You ought to have this couch designed like a barber's chair. Then when you want free association, you could stretch your patient out the way the barber does to lather up his customer, and when the fifty minutes are up, you could tilt the chair forward again and hand him a mirror so he can see what he looks like on the outside after you've shaved his ego."

He said nothing, and while I felt ashamed at the way I was abusing him, I couldn't stop. "Then your patient could come in at each session and say, 'A little off the top of my anxiety, please,' or 'Don't trim the super-ego too close, if you don't mind,' or he might even come in for an egg shampoo—I mean, *ego shampoo*. Aha! Did you notice that slip of the tongue, doctor? Make a note of it. I said I wanted an *egg shampoo* instead of an *ego shampoo*. *Egg* . . . *ego* . . . close, aren't they? Does that mean I want to be washed clean of my sins? Reborn? Is it baptism symbolism? Or are we shaving too close? Does an *idiot* have an *id*?"

I waited for a reaction, but he just shifted in his chair.

"Are you awake?" I asked.

"I'm listening, Charlie."

"Only listening? Don't you ever get angry?"

"Why do you want me to be angry with you?"

I sighed. "Stolid Strauss—unmovable. I'll tell you something. I'm sick and tired of coming here. What's the sense of therapy any more? You know as well as I do what's going to happen."

"But I think you don't want to stop," he said. "You want to go on with it, don't you?"

"It's stupid. A waste of my time and yours."

I lay there in the dim light and stared at the pattern of squares on the ceiling . . . noise-absorbing tiles with thousands of tiny holes soaking up every word. Sound buried alive in little holes in the ceiling.

I found myself becoming lightheaded. My mind was a blank, and that was unusual because during therapy sessions I always had a great deal of material to bring out and talk about. Dreams . . . memories . . . associations . . . problems . . . But now I felt isolated and empty.

Only Stolid Strauss breathing behind me.

"I feel strange," I said.

"You want to talk about it?"

Oh, how brilliant, how subtle he was! What the hell was I doing there anyway, having my associations absorbed by little holes in the ceiling and big holes in my therapist?

"I don't know if I want to talk about it," I said. "I feel unusually hostile toward you today." And then I told him what I had been thinking.

Without seeing him, I could tell he was nodding to himself.

"It's hard to explain," I said. "A feeling I've had once or twice before, just before I fainted. A lightheadedness . . . everything intense . . . but my body feels cold and numb . . ."

"Go on." His voice had an edge of excitement. "What else?"

"I can't feel my body any more. I'm numb. I have the feeling that Charlie is close by. My eyes are open—I'm sure of that —are they?"

"Yes, wide open."

"And yet I see a blue-white glow from the walls and the ceiling gathering into a shimmering ball. Now it's suspended in midair. Light . . . forcing itself into my eyes . . . and my brain . . . Everything in the room is aglow . . . I have the feeling of floating . . . or rather *expanding* up and out . . . and yet without looking down I know my body is still here on the couch . . ."

Is this a hallucination?

"Charlie, are you all right?"

Or the things described by the mystics?

I hear his voice but I don't want to answer him. It annoys me that he is there. I've got to ignore him. Be passive and let this—whatever it is—fill me with the light and absorb me into itself.

"What do you see, Charlie? What's the matter?"

* * *

Upward, moving, like a leaf in an upcurrent of warm air. Spreading, the atoms of my body hurtling away from each other. I grow lighter, less dense, and larger . . . larger . . . exploding outward into the sun. I am an expanding universe swimming upward in a silent sea. Small at first, encompassing with my body, the room, the building, the city, the country, until I know that if I look down I will see my shadow blotting out the earth.

Light and unfeeling. Drifting and expanding through time and space.

And then, as I know I am about to pierce the crust of existence, like a flying fish leaping out of the sea, I feel the pull from below.

It annoys me. I want to shake it off. On the verge of blending with the universe I hear the whispers around the ridges of consciousness. And that ever-so-slight tug holds me to the finite and mortal world below.

Slowly, as waves recede, my expanding spirit shrinks back into earthly dimensions—not voluntarily, because I would prefer to lose myself, but I am pulled from below, back to myself, into myself, so that for just one moment I am on the couch again, fitting the fingers of my awareness into the glove of my flesh. And I know I can move this finger or wink that eye—if I want to. But I don't want to move. I will not move!

I wait, and leave myself open, passive, to whatever this experience means. Charlie doesn't want me to pierce the upper curtain of the mind. Charlie doesn't want to know what lies beyond.

Does he fear seeing God?

Or seeing nothing?

As I lie here waiting, the moment passes during which I *am* myself *in* myself, and again I lose all feeling of body or sensation. Charlie is drawing me down into myself. I stare inward in the center of my unseeing eye at the red spot that transforms itself into a multipetaled flower—the shimmering, swirling, luminescent flower that lies deep in the core of my unconscious.

I am shrinking. Not in the sense of the atoms of my body becoming closer and more dense, but a fusion—as the atoms of my-*self* merge into microcosm. There will be great heat and unbearable light—the hell within hell—but I don't look at the light, only at the flower, *un*multiplying, *un*dividing itself back from the many toward one. And for an instant the shimmering flower turns into the golden disk twirling on a string, and then to the bubble of swirling rainbows, and finally I am back in the cave where everything is quiet and dark and I swim the wet labyrinth searching for one to receive me . . . embrace me . . . absorb me . . . into *it*self.

That I may begin.

In the core I see the light again, an opening in the darkest of caves, now tiny and far away—through the wrong end of a telescope—brilliant, blinding, shimmering, and once again the multipetaled flower (swirling lotus—that floats near the entrance of the unconscious). At the entrance of that cave I will find the answer, if I dare go back and plunge through it into the grotto of light beyond.

Not yet!

I am afraid. Not of life, or death, or nothingness, but of wasting it as if I had never been. And as I start through the opening, I feel the pressure around me, propelling me in violent wavelike motions toward the mouth of the cave.

It's too small! I can't get through!

And suddenly I am hurled against the walls, again and again, and forced through the opening where the light threatens to burst my eyes. Again, I know I will pierce the crust into that holy light. More than I can bear. Pain as I have never known, and coldness, and nausea, and the great buzzing over my head flapping like a thousand wings. I open my eyes, blinded by the intense light. And flail the air and tremble and scream.

* * *

I came out of it at the insistence of a hand shaking me roughly. Dr. Strauss.

"Thank God," he said, when I looked into his eyes. "You had me worried."

I shook my head. "I'm all right."

"I think maybe that's all for today."

I got up and swayed as I regained my perspective. The room seemed very small. "Not only for today," I said. "I don't think I should have any more sessions. I don't want to see any more."

He was upset, but he didn't try to talk me out of it. I took my hat and coat and left.

And now—Plato's words mock me in the shadows on the ledge behind the flames:

> ". . . the men of the cave would say of him that up he went and down he came without his eyes. . . ."

October 5—Sitting down to type these reports is difficult, and I can't think with the tape recorder going. I keep putting it off for most of the day, but I know how important it is, and I've got to do it. I've told myself I won't have dinner until I sit down and write something—anything.

Professor Nemur sent for me again this morning. He wanted me at the lab for some tests, the kind I used to do. At first I figured it was only right, because they're still paying me, and it's important to have the record complete, but when I got down to Beekman and went through it all with Burt, I knew it would be too much for me.

First it was the paper and pencil maze. I remembered how it was before when I learned to do it quickly, and when I raced against Algernon. I could tell it was taking me a lot longer to solve the maze now. Burt had his hand out to take the paper, but I tore it up instead and threw the pieces into the waste basket.

"No more. I'm through running the maze. I'm in a blind alley now, and that's all there is to it."

He was afraid I'd run out, so he calmed me down. "That's all right, Charlie. Just take it easy."

"What do you mean 'take it easy'? You don't know what it's like."

"No, but I can imagine. We all feel pretty sick about it."

"Keep your sympathy. Just leave me alone."

He was embarrassed, and then I realized it wasn't his fault, and I was being lousy toward him. "Sorry I blew up," I said. "How's everything going? Got your thesis finished yet?"

He nodded. "Having it retyped now. I'll get my Ph.D. in February."

"Good boy." I slapped him on the shoulder to show him I wasn't angry with him. "Keep plugging. Nothing like an education. Look, forget what I said before. I'll do anything else you want. Just no more mazes—that's all."

"Well, Nemur wants a Rorschach check."

"To see what's happening down deep? What does he expect to find?"

I must have looked upset, because he started to back off. "We don't have to. You're here voluntarily. If you don't want to—"

"That's all right. Go ahead. Deal out the cards. But don't tell me what you find out."

He didn't have to.

I knew enough about the Rorschach to know that it wasn't what you saw in the cards that counted, but how you reacted to them. As wholes, or parts, with movement or just motionless figures, with special attention to the color spots or ignoring them, with lots of ideas or just a few stereotyped responses.

"It's not valid," I said. "I know what you're looking for. I know the kind of responses I'm supposed to have, to create a certain picture of what my mind is like. All I've got to do is . . ."

He looked up at me, waiting.

"All I've got to do is . . ."

But then it hit me like a fist against the side of my head that I didn't remember what I had to do. It was as if I had been looking at the whole thing clearly on the blackboard of my mind, but when I turned to read it, part of it had been erased and the rest didn't make sense.

At first, I refused to believe it. I went through the cards in a panic, so fast that I was choking on my words. I wanted to tear the inkblots apart to make them reveal themselves. Somewhere in those inkblots there were answers I had known just a little while ago. Not really in the inkblots, but in the part of my mind that would give form and meaning to them and project my imprint on them.

And I couldn't do it. I couldn't remember what I had to say. All missing.

"That's a woman . . ." I said, ". . . on her knees washing the floors. I mean—no—it's a man holding a knife." And even as I said it, I knew what I was saying and I switched away and started off in another direction. "Two figures tugging at something . . . like a doll . . . and each one is pulling so it looks as if they're going to tear it apart and—no!—I mean it's two faces staring at each other through the window, and—"

I swept the cards off the table and got up.

"No more tests. I don't want to take any more tests."

"All right, Charlie. We'll stop for today."

"Not just for today. I'm not coming back here any more. Whatever there is left in me that you need, you can get from the progress reports. I'm through running the maze. I'm not a guinea pig any more. I've done enough. I want to be left alone now."

"All right, Charlie. I understand."

"No, you don't understand because it isn't happening to you, and no one can understand but me. I don't blame you. You've got your job to do, and your Ph.D. to get, and—oh, yes, don't tell me, I know you're in this largely out of love of humanity, but still you've got your life to live and we don't happen to belong on the same level. I passed your floor on the way up, and now I'm passing it on the way down, and I don't think I'll be taking this elevator again. So let's just say good-bye here and now."

"Don't you think you should talk to Dr.—"

"Say good-bye to everyone for me, will you? I don't feel like facing any of them again."

Before he could say any more or try to stop me, I was out of the lab, and I caught the elevator down and out of Beekman for the last time.

October 7—Strauss tried to see me again this morning, but I wouldn't open the door. I want to be left to myself now.

It's a strange sensation to pick up a book you read and enjoyed just a few months ago and discover you don't remember it. I recall how wonderful I thought Milton was. When I picked up *Paradise Lost* I could only remember it was about Adam and Eve and the Tree of Knowledge, but now I couldn't make sense of it.

I stood up and closed my eyes and saw Charlie—myself—six or seven years old, sitting at the dinner table with a schoolbook, learning to read, saying the words over and over with my mother sitting beside him, beside me . . .

"Try it again."

"See Jack. See Jack run. See Jack see."

"No! Not *See* Jack *see*! It's *Run* Jack *run*!" Pointing with her rough-scrubbed finger.

"See Jack. See Jack run. Run Jack see."

"No! You're not trying. Do it again!"

Do it again . . . do it again . . . do it again . . .

"Leave the boy alone. You've got him terrified."

"He's got to learn. He's too lazy to concentrate."

Run Jack run . . . run Jack run . . . run Jack run . . . run Jack run . . .

"He's slower than the other children. Give him time."

"He's normal. There's nothing wrong with him. Just lazy. I'll beat it into him until he learns."

Run Jack run . . . run Jack run . . . run Jack run . . . run Jack run . . .

And then looking up from the table, it seems to me I saw myself, through Charlie's eyes, holding *Paradise Lost*, and I realized I was breaking the binding with the pressure of both hands as if I wanted to tear the book in half. I broke the back of it, ripped out a handful of pages, and flung them and the book across the room to the corner where the broken records were. I let it lay there and its torn white tongues were laughing because I couldn't understand what they were saying.

I've got to try to hold onto some of the things I've learned. Please, God, don't take it all away.

October 10—Usually at night I go out for walks, wander around the city. I don't know why. To see faces, I guess. Last night I couldn't remember where I lived. A policeman took me home. I have the strange feeling that this has all happened to me before—a long time ago. I don't want to write it down, but I keep reminding myself that I'm the only one in the world who can describe what happens when it goes this way.

Instead of walking I was floating through space, not clear and sharp, but with a gray film over everything. I know what's happening to me, but there is nothing I can do about it. I walk, or just stand on the sidewalk and watch people go by. Some of them look at me, and some of them don't but nobody says anything to me—except one night a man came up and asked if I wanted a girl. He took me to a place. He wanted ten dollars first and I gave it to him, but he never came back.

And then I remembered what a fool I was.

October 11—When I came into my apartment this morning, I found Alice there, asleep on the couch. Everything was cleaned up, and at first I thought I was in the wrong apartment, but then I saw she hadn't touched the smashed records or the torn books or the sheet music in the corner of the room. The floor creaked and she woke up and looked at me.

"Hi," she laughed. "Some night owl."

"Not an owl. More of a dodo. A dumb dodo. How'd you get in here?"

"Through the fire escape. Fay's place. I called her to find out about you and she said she was worried. She says you've been acting strangely—causing disturbances. So, I decided it was time for me to put in an appearance. I straightened up a bit. I didn't think you'd mind."

"I do mind . . . very much. I don't want anybody coming around feeling sorry for me."

She went to the mirror to comb her hair. "I'm not here because I feel sorry for you. It's because I feel sorry for me."

"What's that supposed to mean?"

"It doesn't mean," she shrugged. "It just is—like a poem. I wanted to see you."

"What's wrong with the zoo?"

"Oh, come off it, Charlie. Don't fence with me. I waited long enough for you to come and get me. I decided to come to you."

"Why?"

"Because there's still time. And I want to spend it with you."

"Is that a song?"

"Charlie, don't laugh at me."

"I'm not laughing. But I can't afford to spend my time with anyone—there's only enough left for myself."

"I can't believe you want to be completely alone."

"I do."

"We had a little time together before we got out of touch. We had things to talk about, and things to do together. It didn't last very long but it was something. Look, we've known this might happen. It was no secret. I didn't go away, Charlie, I've just been waiting. You're about at my level again, aren't you?"

I stormed around the apartment. "But that's crazy. There's nothing to look forward to. I don't dare let myself think ahead —only back. In a few months, weeks, days—who the hell knows?—I'll go back to Warren. You can't follow me there."

"No," she admitted, "and I probably won't even visit you there. Once you're in Warren I'll do my best to forget you. I'm not going to pretend otherwise. But until you go, there's no reason for either of us to be alone."

Before I could say anything, she kissed me. I waited, as she sat beside me on the couch, resting her head against my chest, but the panic didn't come. Alice was a woman, but perhaps now Charlie would understand that she wasn't his mother or his sister.

With the relief of knowing I had passed through a crisis, I sighed because there was nothing to hold me back. It was no time for fear or pretense, because it could never be this way with anyone else. All the barriers were gone. I had unwound the string she had given me, and found my way out of the labyrinth to where she was waiting. I loved her with more than my body.

I don't pretend to understand the mystery of love, but this time it was more than sex, more than using a woman's body. It was being lifted off the earth, outside fear and torment, being part of something greater than myself. I was lifted out of the dark cell of my own mind, to become part of someone else —just as I had experienced it that day on the couch in therapy. It was the first step outward to the universe—beyond the universe—because in it and with it we merged to recreate and perpetuate the human spirit. Expanding and bursting outward, and contracting and forming inward, it was the rhythm of being—of breathing, of heartbeat, of day and night—and the rhythm of our bodies set off an echo in my mind. It was the way it had been back there in that strange vision. The gray murk lifted from my mind, and through it the light pierced into my brain (how strange that light should blind!), and my body was absorbed back into a great sea of space, washed under in a strange baptism. My body shuddered with giving, and her body shuddered its acceptance.

This was the way we loved, until the night became a silent day. And as I lay there with her I could see how important physical love was, how necessary it was for us to be in each other's arms, giving and taking. The universe was exploding, each particle away from the next, hurtling us into dark and lonely space, eternally tearing us away from each other—child out of the womb, friend away from friend, moving from each other, each through his own pathway toward the goal-box of solitary death.

But this was the counterweight, the act of binding and holding. As when men to keep from being swept overboard in the storm clutch at each other's hands to resist being torn apart, so our bodies fused a link in the human chain that kept us from being swept into nothing.

And in the moment before I fell off into sleep, I remembered the way it had been between Fay and myself, and I smiled. No wonder that had been easy. It had been only physical. This with Alice was a mystery.

I leaned over and kissed her eyes.

Alice knows everything about me now, and accepts the fact that we can be together for only a short while. She has agreed to go away when I tell her to go. It's painful to think about that, but what we have, I suspect, is more than most people find in a lifetime.

October 14—I wake up in the morning and don't know where I am or what I'm doing here, and then I see her beside me and I remember. She senses when something is happening to me, and she moves quietly around the apartment, making breakfast, cleaning up the place, or going out and leaving me to myself, without any questions.

We went to a concert this evening, but I got bored and we left in the middle. Can't seem to pay much attention any more. I went because I know I used to like Stravinsky but somehow I no longer have the patience for it.

The only bad thing about having Alice here with me is that now I feel I should fight this thing. I want to stop time, freeze myself at this level and never let go of her.

October 17—Why can't I remember? I've got to try to resist this slackness. Alice tells me I lie in bed for days and don't seem to know who or where I am. Then it all comes back and I recognize her and remember what's happening. Fugues of amnesia. Symptoms of second childhood—what do they call it?—senility? I can watch it coming on.

All so cruelly logical, the result of speeding up all the processes of the mind. I learned so much so fast, and now my mind is deteriorating rapidly. What if I won't let it happen? What if I fight it? Think of those people at Warren, the empty smiles, the blank expressions, everyone laughing at them.

Little Charlie Gordon staring at me through the window—waiting. Please, not that again.

October 18—I'm forgetting things I learned recently. It seems to be following the classic pattern, the last things learned are first things forgotten. Or is that the pattern? Better look it up again.

Reread my paper on the *Algernon-Gordon Effect* and even though I know I wrote it, I keep feeling it was written by someone else. Most of it I don't even understand.

But why am I so irritable? Especially when Alice is so good to me? She keeps the place neat and clean, always putting my things away and washing dishes and scrubbing floors. I shouldn't have shouted at her the way I did this morning because it made her cry, and I didn't want that to happen. But she shouldn't have picked up the broken records and the music and the book and put them all neatly into a box. That made me furious. I don't want anyone to touch any of those things. I want to see them pile up. I want them to remind me of what I'm leaving behind. I kicked the box and scattered the stuff all over the floor and told her to leave them just where they were.

Foolish. No reason for it. I guess I got sore because I knew she thought it was silly to keep those things, and she didn't tell me she thought it was silly. She just pretended it was perfectly normal. She's humoring me. And when I saw that box I remembered the boy at Warren and the lousy lamp he made and the way we were all humoring him, pretending he had done something wonderful when he hadn't.

That was what she was doing to me, and I couldn't stand it.

When she went to the bedroom and cried I felt bad about it and I told her it was all my fault. I don't deserve someone as good as her. Why can't I control myself just enough to keep on loving her? Just enough.

October 19—Motor activity impaired. I keep tripping and dropping things. At first I didn't think it was me. I thought she was changing things around. The wastebasket was in my way, and so were the chairs, and I thought she had moved them.

Now I realize my coordination is bad. I have to move slowly to get things right. And it's increasingly difficult to type. Why do I keep blaming Alice? And why doesn't she argue? That irritates me even more because I see the pity in her face.

My only pleasure now is the TV set. I spend most of the day watching the quiz programs, the old movies, the soap operas, and even the kiddie shows and cartoons. And then I can't bring myself to turn it off. Late at night there are the old movies, the horror pictures, the late show, and the late-late show, and even the little sermon before the channel signs off for the night, and the "Star-Spangled Banner" with the flag waving in the background, and finally the channel test pattern that stares back at me through the little square window with its unclosing eye. . . .

Why am I always looking at life through a window?

And after it's all over I'm sick with myself because there is so little time left for me to read and write and think, and because I should know better than to drug my mind with this dishonest stuff that's aimed at the child in me. Especially me, because the child in me is reclaiming my mind.

I know all this, but when Alice tells me I shouldn't waste my time, I get angry and tell her to leave me alone.

I have a feeling I'm watching because it's important for me not to think, not to remember about the bakery, and my mother and father, and Norma. I don't want to remember any more of the past.

I had a terrible shock today. Picked up a copy of an article I had used in my research, Krueger's *Über Psychische Ganzheit*, to see if it would help me understand the paper I wrote and what I had done in it. First I thought there was something wrong with my eyes. Then I realized I could no longer read German. Tested myself in other languages. All gone.

October 21—Alice is gone. Let's see if I can remember. It started when she said we couldn't live like this with the torn books and papers and records all over the floor and the place in such a mess.

"Leave everything the way it is," I warned her.

"Why do you want to live this way?"

"I want everything where I put it. I want to see it all out here. You don't know what it's like to have something happening inside you, that you can't see and can't control, and know it's all slipping through your fingers."

"You're right. I never said I could understand the things that were happening to you. Not when you became too intelligent for me, and not now. But I'll tell you one thing. Before you had the operation, you weren't like this. You didn't wallow in your own filth and self-pity, you didn't pollute your own mind by sitting in front of the TV set all day and night, you didn't snarl and snap at people. There was something about you that made us respect you—yes, even as you were. You had something I had never seen in a retarded person before."

"I don't regret the experiment."

"Neither do I, but you've lost something you had before. You had a smile . . ."

"An empty, stupid smile."

"No, a warm, real smile, because you wanted people to like you."

"And they played tricks on me, and laughed at me."

"Yes, but even though you didn't understand why they were laughing, you sensed that if they could laugh at you they would like you. And you wanted them to like you. You acted like a child and you even laughed at yourself along with them."

"I don't feel like laughing at myself right now, if you don't mind."

She was trying to keep from crying. I think I wanted to make her cry. "Maybe that's why it was so important for me to learn. I thought it would make people like me. I thought I would have friends. That's something to laugh at, isn't it?"

"There's more to it than just having a high I.Q."

That made me angry. Probably because I didn't really understand what she was driving at. More and more these days she didn't come right out and say what she meant. She hinted at things. She talked around them and expected me to know what she was thinking. And I listened, pretending I understood but inside I was afraid she would see that I missed the point completely.

"I think it's time for you to leave."

Her face turned red. "Not yet, Charlie. It's not time yet. Don't send me away."

"You're making it harder for me. You keep pretending I can do things and understand things that are far beyond me now. You're pushing me. Just like my mother . . ."

"That's not true!"

"Everything you do says it. The way you pick up and clean up after me, the way you leave books around that you think will get me interested in reading again, the way you talk to me about the news to get me thinking. You say it doesn't matter, but everything you do shows how much it matters. Always the schoolteacher. I don't want to go to concerts or museums or foreign films or do anything that's going to make me struggle to think about life or about myself."

"Charlie—"

"Just leave me alone. I'm not myself. I'm falling apart, and I don't want you here."

That made her cry. This afternoon she packed her bags and left. The apartment feels quiet and empty now.

October 25—Deterioration progressing. I've given up using the typewriter. Coordination is too bad. From now on I'll have to write out these reports in longhand.

I thought a lot about the things Alice said, and then it hit me that if I kept on reading and learning *new* things, even while I was forgetting the old ones, I would be able to keep some of my intelligence. I was on a down escalator now. If I stood still I'd go all the way to the bottom, but if I started to run up maybe I could at least stay in the same place. The important thing was to keep moving upward no matter what happened.

So I went to the library and got out a lot of books to read. I've been reading a lot now. Most of the books are too hard for me, but I don't care. As long as I keep reading I'll learn new things and I won't forget how to read. That's the most important thing. If I keep reading, maybe I can hold my own.

Dr. Strauss came around the day after Alice left, so I guess she told him about me. He pretended all he wanted was the progress reports but I told him I would send them. I don't want him coming around here. I told him he doesn't have to be worried about me because when I think I won't be able to take care of myself any more I'll get on a train and go to Warren.

I told him I'd rather just go by myself when the time comes.

I tried to talk to Fay, but I can see she's afraid of me. I guess she figures I've gone out of my mind. Last night she came home with somebody—he looked very young.

This morning the landlady, Mrs. Mooney, came up with a bowl of hot chicken soup and some chicken. She said she just thought she would look in on me to see if I was doing all right. I told her I had lots of food to eat but she left it anyway and it was good. She pretended she was doing it on her own but I'm not that stupid yet. Alice or Strauss must have told her to look in on me and make sure I was all right. Well, that's okay. She's a nice old lady with an Irish accent and she likes to talk all about the people in the building. When she saw the mess on the floor inside my apartment she didn't say anything about it. I guess she's all right.

November 1—A week since I dared to write again. I don't know where the time goes. Todays Sunday I know because I can see through my window the people going into the church across the street. I think I laid in bed all week but I remember Mrs. Mooney bringing me food a few times and asking if I was sick.

What am I going to do with myself? I cant just hang around here all alone and look out the window. Ive got to get hold of myself. I keep saying over and over that Ive got to do something but then I forget or maybe its just easier not to do what I say Im going to do.

I still have some books from the library but a lot of them are too hard for me. I read a lot of mystery stories now and books about kings and queens from old times. I read a book about a man who thought he was a knight and went out on an old horse with his friend. But no matter what he did he always ended up getting beaten and hurt. Like when he thought the windmills were dragons. At first I thought it was a silly book because if he wasnt crazy he could see that windmills werent dragons and there is no such thing as sorcerers and enchanted castles but then I rememberd that there was something else it was all supposed to mean—something the story didnt say but only hinted at. Like there was other meanings. But I dont know what. That made me angry because I think I used to know. But Im keeping up with my reading and learning new things every day and I know its going to help me.

I know I should have written some progress reports before this so they will know whats happening to me. But writing is harder. I have to look up even simple words in the dictionary now and it makes me angry with myself.

November 2—I forgot to write in yesterdays report about the woman from the building across the alley one floor down. I saw her through my kitchen window last week. I dont know her name, or even what her top part looks like but every night about eleven oclock she goes into her bathroom to take a bath. She never pulls her shade down and thru my window when I put out my lights I can see her from the neck down when she comes out of the bath to dry herself.

It makes me excited, but when the lady turns out the light I feel let down and lonely. I wish I could see what she looks like sometimes, whether shes pretty or what. I know its not nice to watch a woman when shes like that but I cant help it. Anyway what difference does it make to her if she doesnt know Im watching.

Its nearly eleven oclock now. Time for her bath. So Id better go see . . .

Nov 5—Mrs Mooney is very worried about me. She says the way I lay around all day and dont do anything I remind her of her son before she threw him out of the house. She said she dont like loafters. If Im sick its one thing but if Im a loafter thats another thing and she has no use for me. I told her I think Im sick.

I try to read a little bit every day mostly stories but sometimes I have to read the same thing over and over again because I dont know what it means. And its hard to write. I know I should look up all the words in the dictionary but Im so tired all the time.

Then I got the idea that I would only use the easy words instead of the long hard ones. That saves time. Its getting chilly out but I still put flowers on Algernons grave. Mrs Mooney thinks Im silly to put flowers on a mouses grave but I told her that Algernon was a special mouse.

I went over to visit Fay across the hall. But she told me to go away and not come back. She put a new lock on her door.

Nov 9—Sunday again. I dont have anything to do to keep me busy now because the TV is broke and I keep forgetting to get it fixed. I think I lost this months check from the college. I dont remember.

I get awful headaches and asperin doesnt help much. Mrs. Mooney believes now that Im really sick and she feels very sory for me. She's a wonderful woman whenever someone is sick. Its getting so cold out now that Ive got to wear two sweaters.

The lady across the way pulls down her windowshade now, so I can't watch any more. My lousy luck.

Nov 10—Mrs Mooney called a strange doctor to see me. She was afraid I was going to die. I told the doctor I wasnt to sick and that I only forget sometimes. He asked me did I have any

friends or relatives and I said no I dont have any. I told him I
had a friend called Algernon once but he was a mouse and we
use to run races together. He looked at me kind of funny like
he thot I was crazy.

He smiled when I told him I use to be a genuis. He talked to
me like I was a baby and he winked at Mrs Mooney. I got mad
because he was making fun of me and laughing and I chased
him out and locked the door.

I think I know why I been haveing bad luck. Because I lost
my rabits foot and my horshoe. I got to get another rabits foot
fast.

Nov 11—Dr Strauss came to the door today and Alice to but I
didnt let them come in. I told them I didnt want anyone to see
me. I want to be left alone. Later Mrs Mooney came up with
some food and she told me they paid the rent and left money
for her to buy food and anything I need. I told her I dont want
to use there money any more. She said moneys money and
someone has to pay or I have to put you out. Then she said
why dont I get some job instead of just hanging around.

I dont know any work but the job I use to do at the bakery.
I dont want to go back their because they all knew me when I
was smart and maybe theyll laff at me. But I dont know what
else to do to get money. And I want to pay for everything myself. I am strong and I can werk. If I cant take care of myself Ill
go to Warren. I wont take charety from anybody.

Nov 15—I was looking at some of my old progress reports and
its very strange but I cant read what I wrote. I can make out
some of the words but they dont make sense. I think I wrote
them but I dont remember so good. I get tired very fast when
I try to read some of the books I baught in the drugstore. Exept the ones with the picturs of the pretty girls. I like to look
at them but I have funny dreams about them. Its not nice. I
wont buy them any more. I saw in one of those books they got
magic powder that can make you strong and smart and do lots
of things. I think mayby Ill send away and by some for myself.

Nov 16—Alice came to the door again but I said go away I dont
want to see you. She cryed and I cryed to but I woudnt let her
in because I didnt want her to laff at me. I told her I didnt like

her any more and I didnt want to be smart any more either. Thats not true but. I still love her and I still want to be smart but I had to say that so she woud go away. Mrs Mooney told me Alice brout some more money to look after me and for the rent. I dont want that. I got to get a job.

Please . . . please . . . dont let me forget how to reed and rite . . .

Nov 18—Mr Donner was very nice when I came back and askd him for my old job at the bakery. Frist he was very suspicius but I told him what happened to me and then he looked very sad and put his hand on my shoulder and said Charlie you got guts.

Evrybody looked at me when I came downstairs and started working in the toilet sweeping it out like I use to do. I said to myself Charlie if they make fun of you dont get sore because you remember their not so smart like you once thot they were. And besides they were once your frends and if they laffed at you that dont mean anything because they liked you to.

One of the new men who came to werk their after I went away his name is Meyer Klaus did a bad thing to me. He came up to me when I was loading the sacks of flower and he said hey Charlie I hear your a very smart fella—a real quiz kid. Say something inteligent. I felt bad because I could tell by the way he said it he was making fun of me. So I kept on with my werk. But then he came over and grabed me by the arm real hard and shouted at me. When I talk to you boy you better listen to me. Or I coud brake your arm for you. He twisted my arm so it hurt and I got scared he was going to brake it like he said. And he was laffing and twisting it, and I didnt know what to do. I got so afraid I felt like I was gonna cry but I didnt and then I had to go to the bathroom something awful. My stomack was all twisting inside like I was gonna bust open if I didnt go right away . . . because I couldnt hold it back.

I told him please let me go because I got to go to the toilet but he was just laffing at me and I dint know what to do. So I started crying. Let me go. Let me go. And then I made. It went in my pants and it smelled bad and I was crying. He let go of me then and made a sick face and he looked scared then. He said For gods sake I didnt mean anything Charlie.

But then Joe Carp came in and grabbed Klaus by the shirt

and said leave him alone you lousy bastard or Ill brake your neck. Charlie is a good guy and nobodys gonna start up with him without answering for it. I felt ashamed and I ran to the toilet to clean myself and change my cloths.

When I got back Frank was there to and Joe was telling him about it and then Gimpy came in and they told him about it and he said theyd get rid of Klaus. They were gonna tell Mr Donner to fire him. I told them I dint think he should be fired and have to find another job because he had a wife and a kid. And besides he said he was sorry for what he did to me. And I remember how sad I was when I had to get fired from the bakery and go away. I said Klaus shoud get a second chance because now he wouldnt do anything bad to me anymore.

Later Gimpy came over limping on his bad foot and he said Charlie if anyone bothers you or trys to take advantage you call me or Joe or Frank and we will set him strait. We all want you to remember that you got frends here and dont you ever forget it. I said thanks Gimpy. That makes me feel good.

Its good to have frends . . .

nov 21—I did a dumb thing today I forgot I wasnt in Miss Kinnians class at the adult center any more like I use to be. I went in and sat down in my old seat in the back of the room and she lookd at me funny and she said Charlie where have you been. So I said hello Miss Kinnian Im redy for my lessen today only I lossed the book we was using.

She started to cry and run out of the room and everbody looked at me and I saw alot of them wasnt the same pepul who use to be in my class.

Then all of a suddin I remembered some things about the operashun and me getting smart and I said holy smoke I reely pulled a Charlie Gordon that time. I went away before she came back to the room.

Thats why Im going away from here for good to the Warren Home school. I dont want to do nothing like that agen. I dont want Miss Kinnian to feel sorry for me. I know evrybody feels sorry for me at the bakery and I dont want that eather so Im going someplace where they are a lot of other pepul like me and nobody cares that Charlie Gordon was once a genus and now he cant even reed a book or rite good.

Im taking a cuple of books along and even if I cant reed them Ill practise hard and mabye Ill even get a littel bit smarter then I was before the operashun without an operashun. I got a new rabits foot and a luky penny and even a littel bit of that majic powder left and mabye they will help me.

If you ever reed this Miss Kinnian dont be sorry for me. Im glad I got a second chanse in life like you said to be smart because I lerned alot of things that I never even new were in this werld and Im grateful I saw it all even for a littel bit. And Im glad I found out all about my family and me. It was like I never had a family til I remembird about them and saw them and now I know I had a family and I was a person just like evryone.

I dont no why Im dumb agen or what I did rong. Mabye its because I dint try hard enuf or just some body put the evel eye on me. But if I try and practis very hard mabye Ill get a littel smarter and no what all the words are. I remembir a littel bit how nice I had a feeling with the blue book that I red with the toren cover. And when I close my eyes I think about the man who tored the book and he looks like me only he looks different and he talks different but I dont think its me because its like I see him from the window.

Anyway thats why Im gone to keep trying to get smart so I can have that feeling agen. Its good to no things and be smart and I wish I new evrything in the hole world. I wish I coud be smart agen rite now. If I coud I woud sit down and reed all the time.

Anyway I bet Im the frist dumb persen in the world who found out some thing inportent for sience. I did somthing but I dont remembir what. So I gess its like I did it for all the dumb pepul like me in Warren and all over the world.

Goodby Miss Kinnian and dr Strauss and evrybody . . .

P.S. please tel prof Nemur not to be such a grouch when pepul laff at him and he woud have more frends. Its easy to have frends if you let pepul laff at you. Im going to have lots of frends where I go.

P.S. please if you get a chanse put some flowrs on Algernons grave in the bak yard.

. . . AND CALL ME CONRAD
[THIS IMMORTAL]

Roger Zelazny

To Ben Jason

"YOU ARE a kallikanzaros," she announced suddenly.

I turned onto my left side and smiled through the darkness.

"I left my hooves and my horns at the Office."

"You've heard the story!"

"The name *is* 'Nomikos.'"

I reached for her, found her.

"Are you going to destroy the world this time around?"

I laughed and drew her to me.

"I'll think about it. If that's the way the Earth crumbles—"

"You know that children born here on Christmas are of the kallikanzaroi blood," she said, "and you once told me that your birthday—"

"All right!"

It had struck me that she was only half-joking. Knowing some of the things one occasionally meets in the Old Places, the Hot Places, you can almost believe in myths without extra effort—such as the story of those Pan-like sprites who gather together every spring to spend ten days sawing at the Tree of the World, only to be dispersed at the last moment by the ringing of the Easter bells. (*Ring-a-ding*, the bells, *gnash*, *gnash*, the teeth, *clackety-clack*, the hooves, etcetera.) Cassandra and I were not in the habit of discussing religion, politics, or Aegean folklore in bed—but, me having been born in these parts, the memories are still somehow alive.

"I am hurt," I said, only half-joking.

"You're hurting *me*, too. . . ."

"Sorry."

I relaxed again.

After a time I explained, "Back when I was a brat, the other brats used to push me around, called me 'Konstantin Kallikanzaros.' When I got bigger and uglier they stopped doing it. At least, they didn't say it to my face—"

"'Konstantin'? That was your name? I've wondered. . . ."

"It's 'Conrad' now, so forget it."

"But I like it. I'd rather call you 'Konstantin' than 'Conrad.'"

"If it makes you happy . . ."

545

The moon pushed her ravaged face up over the windowsill to mock me. I couldn't reach the moon, or even the window, so I looked away. The night was cold, was damp, was misty as it always is here.

"The Commissioner of Arts, Monuments and Archives for the planet Earth is hardly out to chop down the Tree of the World," I rasped.

"*My* kallikanzaros," she said too quickly, "I did not say that. But there are fewer bells every year, and it is not always desire that matters. I have this feeling that you *will* change things, somehow. Perhaps—"

"You are wrong, Cassandra."

"And I am afraid, and cold—"

And she was lovely in the darkness, so I held her in my arms to sort of keep her from the foggy foggy dew.

In attempting to reconstruct the affairs of these past six months, I realize now that as we willed walls of passion around our October and the isle of Kos, the Earth had already fallen into the hands of those powers which smash all Octobers. Marshaled from within and without, the forces of final disruption were even then goose-stepping amidst the ruins—faceless, ineluctable, arms upraised. Cort Myshtigo had landed at Port-au-Prince in the antique *Sol-Bus Nine*, which had borne him in from Titan along with a load of shirts and shoes, underwear, socks, assorted wines, medical supplies, and the latest tapes from civilization. A wealthy and influential galacto-journalist, he. Just how wealthy, we were not to learn for many weeks; just how influential, I found out only five days ago.

As we wandered among the olive groves gone wild, picked our way through the ruins of the Frankish castle, or mixed our tracks with the hieroglyph-prints of the herring-gulls, there on the wet sands of the beaches of Kos, we were burning time while waiting for a ransom which could not come, which should never, really, have been expected.

Cassandra's hair is the color of Katamara olives, and shiny. Her hands are soft, the fingers short, delicately webbed. Her eyes are very dark. She is only about four inches shorter than me, which makes her gracefulness something of an achievement, me being well over six feet. Of course, any woman looks graceful, precise and handsome when walking at my side, because I am none of these things: my left cheek was then a map of Africa done up in varying purples, because of that mutant fungus I'd picked up from a moldy canvas back when I'd been disinterring the Guggenheim for the New York Tour; my hairline peaks to within a fingerbreadth of my brow; my eyes are mismatched. (I glare at people through the cold blue one on the right side when I want to intimidate them; the brown one is for Glances Sincere and Honest.) I wear a reinforced boot because of my short right leg.

Cassandra doesn't require contrasting, though. She's beautiful.

I met her by accident, pursued her with desperation, married her against my will. (The last part was her idea.) I wasn't really thinking about it, myself—even on that day when I brought my caique into the harbor and saw her there, sunning herself like a mermaid beside the plane tree of Hippocrates, and decided that I wanted her. Kallikanzaroi have never been much the family sort. I just sort of slipped up, again.

It was a clean morning. It was starting our third month together. It was my last day on Kos—because of a call I'd received the evening before. Everything was still moist from the night's rain, and we sat out on the patio drinking Turkish coffee and eating oranges. Day was starting to lever its way into the world. The breeze was intermittent, was damp, goosepimpled us beneath the black bulk of our sweaters, skimmed the steam off the top of the coffee.

"'Rodos dactylos Aurora. . . .'" she said, pointing.

"Yeah," I said, nodding, "real rosy-fingered and nice."

"Let's enjoy it."

"Yeah. Sorry."

We finished our coffee, sat smoking.

"I feel crummy," I said.

"I know," she said. "Don't."

"Can't help it. Got to go away and leave you, and that's crummy."

"It may only be a few weeks. You said so yourself. Then you'll be back."

"Hope so," I said. "If it takes any longer, though, I'll send for you. Dunno where all I'll be, yet."

"Who is Cort Myshtigo?"

"Vegan actor, journalist. Important one. Wants to write

about what's left of Earth. So I've got to show it to him. Me. Personally. Damn!"

"Anybody who takes ten-month vacations to go sailing can't complain about being overworked."

"*I* can complain—and I will. My job is supposed to be a sinecure."

"Why?"

"Mainly because I made it that way. I worked hard for twenty years to make Arts, Monuments and Archives what it is, and ten years ago I got it to the point where my staff could handle just about everything. So I got me turned out to pasture, I got me told to come back occasionally to sign papers and to do whatever I damn pleased in the meantime. Now this—this bootlicking gesture!—having a Commissioner take a Vegan scribbler on a tour any staff guide could conduct! Vegans aren't gods!"

"Wait a minute, please," she said. "Twenty years? Ten years?"

Sinking feeling.

"You're not even thirty years old."

I sank further. I waited. I rose again.

"Uh—there's something I, well, in my own reticent way, sort of never quite got around to mentioning to you. . . . How old are you anyway, Cassandra?"

"Twenty."

"Uh-huh. Well . . . I'm around four times your age."

"I don't understand."

"Neither do I. Or the doctors. I just sort of stopped, somewhere between twenty and thirty, and I stayed that way. I guess that's a sort of, well—a part of my particular mutation, I guess. Does it make any difference?"

"I don't know. . . . Yes."

"You don't mind my limp, or my excessive shagginess, or even my face. Why should my age bother you? I *am* young, for all necessary purposes."

"It's just that it's not the same," she said with an unarguable finality. "What if you never grow old?"

I bit my lip. "I'm bound to, sooner or later."

"And if it's later? I love you. I don't want to out-age you."

"You'll live to be a hundred and fifty. There are the S-S treatments. You'll have them."

"But they won't keep me young—like you."

"I'm not really young. I was born old."

That one didn't work either. She started to cry.

"That's years and years away," I told her. "Who knows what will happen in the meantime?"

That only made her cry more.

I've always been impulsive. My thinking is usually pretty good, but I always seem to do it after I do my talking—by which time I've generally destroyed all basis for further conversation.

Which is one of the reasons I have a competent staff, a good radio, and am out to pasture most of the time.

There are some things you just can't delegate, though.

So I said, "Look, you have a touch of the Hot Stuff in you, too. It took me forty years to realize I wasn't forty years old. Maybe you're the same way. I'm just a neighborhood kid . . ."

"Do you know of any other cases like your own?"

"Well . . ."

"No, you don't."

"No. I don't."

I remember wishing then that I was back aboard my ship. Not the big blazeboat. Just my old hulk, the *Golden Vanitie*, out there in the harbor. I remember wishing that I was putting it into port all over again, and seeing her there for the first shiny time, and being able to start everything all over again from the same beginning—and either telling her all about it right there, or else working my way back up to the going-away time and keeping my mouth shut about my age.

It was a nice dream, but hell, the honeymoon was over.

I waited until she had stopped crying and I could feel her eyes on me again. Then I waited some more.

"Well?" I asked, finally.

"Pretty well, thanks."

I found and held her passive hand, raised it to my lips. "Rodos dactylos," I breathed, and she said, "Maybe it's a good idea —your going away—for awhile anyhow . . ." and the breeze that skimmed the steam came again, was damp, goosepimpled us, and made either her hand or my hand shake—I'm not sure which. It shook the leaves too, and they emptied over our heads.

"Did you exaggerate your age to me?" she asked. "Even a little bit?"

Her tone of voice suggested that agreement would be the wisest reply.

So, "Yes," I said, truthfully.

She smiled back then, somewhat reassured of my humanity. Ha!

So we sat there, holding hands and watching the morning. After awhile she began humming. It was a sad song, centuries old. A ballad. It told the story of a young wrestler named Themocles, a wrestler who had never been beaten. He eventually came to consider himself the greatest wrestler alive. Finally he called out his challenge from a mountaintop, and, that being too near home, the gods acted fast: the following day a crippled boy rode into the town, on the plated back of a huge wild dog. They wrestled for three days and three nights, Themocles and the boy, and on the fourth day the boy broke his back and left him there in the field. Wherever his blood fell, there sprang up the *strige-fleur*, as Emmet calls it, the blood-drinking flower that creeps rootless at night, seeking the lost spirit of the fallen champion in the blood of its victims. But Themocles' spirit is gone from the Earth, so they must creep, seeking, forever. Simpler than Aeschylus, but then we're a simpler people than we once were, especially the Mainlanders. Besides, that's not the way it really happened.

"Why are you weeping?" she asked me suddenly.

"I am thinking of the pictures on Achilleus' shield," I said, "and of what a terrible thing it is to be an educated beast—and I am not weeping. The leaves are dripping on me."

"I'll make some more coffee."

I washed out the cups while she was doing that, and I told her to take care of the *Vanitie* while I was gone, and to have it hauled up into drydock if I sent for her. She said that she would.

The sun wandered up higher into the sky, and after a time there came a sound of hammering from the yard of old Aldones, the coffin-maker. The cyclamen had come awake, and the breezes carried their fragrance to us from across the fields. High overhead, like a dark omen, a spiderbat glided across the sky toward the mainland. I ached to wrap my fingers around the stock of a thirty-oh-six, make loud noises, and watch it fall. The only firearms I knew of were aboard the *Vanitie*, though, so I just watched it vanish from sight.

"They say that they're not really native to Earth," she told me, watching it go, "and that they were brought here from Titan, for zoos and things like that."

"That's right."

". . . And that they got loose during the Three Days and went wild, and that they grow bigger here than they ever did on their own world."

"One time I saw one with a thirty-two foot wingspread."

"My great-uncle once told me a story he had heard in Athens," she recalled, "about a man killing one without any weapons. It snatched him up from off the dock he was standing on —at Piraeus—and the man broke its neck with his hands. They fell about a hundred feet into the bay. The man lived."

"That was a long time ago," I remembered, "back before the Office started its campaign to exterminate the things. There were a lot more around, and they were bolder in those days. They shy away from cities now."

"The man's name was Konstantin, as I recall the story. Could it have been you?"

"His last name was Karaghiosis."

"Are you Karaghiosis?"

"If you want me to be. Why?"

"Because he later helped to found the Returnist Radpol in Athens, and you have very strong hands."

"Are you a Returnist?"

"Yes. Are you?"

"I work for the Office. I don't have any political opinions."

"Karaghiosis bombed resorts."

"So he did."

"Are you sorry he bombed them?"

"No."

"I don't really know much about you, do I?"

"You know anything about me. Just ask. I'm really quite simple. —My air taxi is coming now."

"I don't hear anything."

"You will."

After a moment it came sliding down the sky toward Kos, homing in on the beacon I had set up at the end of the patio. I stood and drew her to her feet as it buzzed in low—a Radson Skimmer: a twenty-foot cockleshell of reflection and transparency; flat-bottomed, blunt-nosed.

"Anything you want to take with you?" she asked.

"You know it, but I can't."

The Skimmer settled and its side slid open. The goggled pilot turned his head.

"I have a feeling," she said, "that you are heading into some sort of danger."

"I doubt it, Cassandra."

Nor pressure, nor osmosis will restore Adam's lost rib, thank God.

"Goodbye, Cassandra."

"Goodbye, my kallikanzaros."

And I got into the Skimmer and jumped into the sky, breathing a prayer to Aphrodite. Below me, Cassandra waved. Behind me, the sun tightened its net of light. We sped westward, and this is the place for a smooth transition, but there isn't any. From Kos to Port-au-Prince was four hours, gray water, pale stars, and me mad. Watch the colored lights. . . .

The hall was lousy with people, a big tropical moon was shining fit to bust, and the reason I could see both was that I'd finally managed to lure Ellen Emmet out onto the balcony and the doors were mag-pegged open.

"Back from the dead again," she had greeted me, smiling slightly. "Gone almost a year, and not so much as a Get Well card from Ceylon."

"Were you ill?"

"I could have been."

She was small and, like all day-haters, creamy somewhere under her simicolor. She reminded me of an elaborate action-doll with a faulty mechanism—cold grace, and a propensity to kick people in the shins when they least expected it; and she had lots and lots of orangebrown hair, woven into a Gordian knot of a coif that frustrated me as I worked at untying it, mentally; her eyes were of whatever color it pleased the god of her choice on that particular day—I forget now, but they're always blue somewhere deep deep down inside. Whatever she was wearing was browngreen, and there was enough of it to go around a couple times and make her look like a shapeless weed, which was a dressmaker's lie if there ever was one, unless she was pregnant again, which I doubted.

"Well, get well," I said, "if you need to. I didn't make Ceylon. I was in the Mediterranean most of the time."

There was applause within. I was glad I was without. The players had just finished Graber's *Masque of Demeter*, which he had written in pentameter and honor of our Vegan guest; and the thing had been two hours long, and bad. Phil was all educated and sparsehaired, and he looked the part all right, but we had been pretty hard up for a laureate on the day we'd picked him. He was given to fits of Rabindranath Tagore and Chris Isherwood, the writing of fearfully long metaphysical epics, talking a lot about Enlightenment, and performing his daily breathing exercises on the beach. Otherwise, he was a fairly decent human being.

The applause died down, and I heard the glassy tinkle of thelinstra music and the sound of resuming voices.

Ellen leaned back on the railing.

"I hear you're somewhat married these days."

"True," I agreed; "also somewhat harried. Why did they call me back?"

"Ask your boss."

"I did. He said I'm going to be a guide. What I want to know, though, is *why*? —The real reason. I've been thinking about it and it's grown more puzzling."

"So how should I know?"

"You know everything."

"You overestimate me, dear. What's she like?"

I shrugged.

"A mermaid, maybe. Why?"

She shrugged.

"Just curious. What do you tell people I'm like?"

"I don't tell people you're like anything."

"I'm insulted. I must be like something, unless I'm unique."

"That's it, you're unique."

"Then why didn't you take me away with you last year?"

"Because you're a People person and you require a city around you. You could only be happy here at the Port."

"But I'm *not* happy here at the Port."

"You are less unhappy here at the Port than you'd be anywhere else on this planet."

"We could have tried," she said, and she turned her back

on me to look down the slope toward the lights of the harbor section.

"You know," she said after a time, "you're so damned ugly you're attractive. That must be it."

I stopped in mid-reach, a couple inches from her shoulder.

"You know," she continued, her voice flat, emptied of emotion, "you're a nightmare that walks like a man."

I dropped my hand, chuckled inside a tight chest.

"I know," I said. "Pleasant dreams."

I started to turn away and she caught my sleeve.

"Wait!"

I looked down at her hand, up at her eyes, then back down at her hand. She let go.

"You know I never tell the truth," she said. Then she laughed her little brittle laugh.

". . . And I *have* thought of something you ought to know about this trip. Donald Dos Santos is here, and I think he's going along."

"Dos Santos? That's ridiculous."

"He's up in the library now, with George and some big Arab."

I looked past her and down into the harbor section, watching the shadows, like my thoughts, move along dim streets, dark and slow.

"Big Arab?" I said, after a time. "Scarred hands? Yellow eyes? —Name of Hasan?"

"Yes, that's right. Have you met him?"

"He's done some work for me in the past," I acknowledged.

So I smiled, even though my blood was refrigerating, because I don't like people to know what I'm thinking.

"You're smiling," she said. "What are you thinking?"

She's like that.

"I'm thinking you take things more seriously than I thought you took things."

"Nonsense. I've often told you I'm a fearful liar. Just a second ago, in fact—and I was only referring to a minor encounter in a great war. And you're right about my being less unhappy here than anywhere else on Earth. So maybe you could talk to George—get him to take a job on Taler, or Bakab. Maybe? Huh?"

"Yeah," I said. "Sure. You bet. Just like that. After you've tried it for ten years. —How *is* his bug collection these days?"

She sort of smiled.

"Growing," she replied, "by leaps and bounds. Buzzes and crawls too—and some of those crawlies are radioactive. I say to him, 'George, why don't you run around with other women instead of spending all your time with those bugs?' But he just shakes his head and looks dedicated. Then I say, 'George, one day one of those uglies is going to bite you and make you impotent. What'll you do then?' Then he explains that that can't happen, and he lectures me on insect toxins. Maybe he's really a big bug himself, in disguise. I think he gets some kind of sexual pleasure out of watching them swarm around in those tanks. I don't know what else—"

I turned away and looked inside the hall then, because her face was no longer *her* face. When I heard her laugh a moment later I turned back and squeezed her shoulder.

"Okay, I know more than I knew before. Thanks. I'll see you sometime soon."

"Should I wait?"

"No. Good night."

"Good night, Conrad."

And I was away.

Crossing a room can be a ticklish and time-consuming business: if it's full of people, if the people all know you, if the people are all holding glasses, if you have even a slight tendency to limp.

It was, they did and they were, and I do. So . . .

Thinking inconspicuous thoughts, I edged my way along the wall just at the periphery of humanity for about twenty feet, until I reached the enclave of young ladies the old celibate always has hovering about him. He was chinless, nearly lipless, and going hairless; and the expression that had once lived in that flesh covering his skull had long ago retreated into the darkness of his eyes, and the eyes had it as they caught me—the smile of imminent outrage.

"Phil," said I, nodding, "not everybody can write a masque like that. I've heard it said that it's a dying art, but now I know better."

"You're still alive," he said, in a voice seventy years younger than the rest of him, "and late again, as usual."

"I abase myself in my contrition," I told him, "but I was detained at a birthday party for a lady aged seven, at the home of an old friend." (Which was true, but it has nothing to do with this story.)

"All your friends are old friends, aren't they?" he asked, and that was hitting below the belt, just because I had once known his barely-remembered parents, and had taken them around to the south side of the Erechtheum in order to show them the Porch of the Maidens and point out what Lord Elgin had done with the rest, all the while carrying their bright-eyed youngster on my shoulders and telling him tales that were old when the place was built.

". . . And I need your help," I added, ignoring the jibe and gently pushing my way through the soft, pungent circle of femininity. "It'll take me all night to cross this hall to where Sands is holding court with the Vegan—pardon me, Miss—and I don't have all night. —Excuse me, ma'am. —So I want you to run interference for me."

"You're Nomikos!" breathed one little lovely, staring at my cheek. "I've always wanted to—"

I seized her hand, pressed it to my lips, noted that her Camille-ring was glowing pink, said, "—and negative Kismet, eh?" and dropped it.

"So how about it?" I asked Graber. "Get me from here to there in a minimum of time in your typical courtier-like fashion, with a running conversation that no one would dare interrupt. Okay? Let's run."

He nodded brusquely.

"Excuse me, ladies. I'll be back."

We started across the room, negotiating alleys of people. High overhead, the chandeliers drifted and turned like faceted satellites of ice. The thelinstra was an intelligent Aeolian harp, tossing its shards of song into the air—pieces of colored glass. The people buzzed and drifted like certain of George Emmet's insects, and we avoided their swarms by putting one foot in front of another without pause and making noises of our own. We didn't step on anybody who squashed.

The night was warm. Most of the men wore the feather-weight, black dress-uniforms which protocol dictates the Staff suffer at these functions. Those who didn't weren't Staff.

Uncomfortable despite their lightness, the Dress Blacks mag-bind down the sides, leaving a smooth front whereon is displayed a green-blue-gray-white Earth insignia, about three inches in diameter, high up on the left breast; below, the symbol for one's department is worn, followed by the rank-sigil; on the right side goes every blessed bit of chicken manure that can be dreamt up to fake dignity—this, by the highly imaginative Office of Awards, Furbishments, Insigniae, Symbols and Heraldry (OAFISH, for short—its first Director appreciated his position). The collar has a tendency to become a garrot after the first ten minutes; at least mine does.

The ladies wore, or didn't, whatever they pleased, usually bright or accompanied by pastel simicoloring (unless they were Staff, in which case they were neatly packed into short-skirted Dress Blacks, but with bearable collars), which makes it some-what easier to tell some of the keepers from the kept.

"I hear Dos Santos is here," I said.

"So he is."

"Why?"

"I don't really know, or care."

"Tsk and tsk. What happened to your wonderful political consciousness? The Department of Literary Criticism used to praise you for it."

"At my age, the smell of death becomes more and more un-settling each time it's encountered."

"And Dos Santos smells?"

"He tends to reek."

"I've heard that he's employed a former associate of ours—from the days of the Madagascar Affair."

Phil cocked his head to one side and shot me a quizzical look.

"You hear things quite quickly. But then, you're a friend of Ellen's. Yes, Hasan is here. He's upstairs with Don."

"Whose karmic burden is he likely to help lighten?"

"As I said before, I don't really know or care about any of this."

"Want to venture a guess?"

"Not especially."

We entered a thinly-wooded section of the forest, and I paused to grab a rum-and-other from the dip-tray which had followed overhead until I could bear its anguish no longer, and had finally pressed the acorn which hung at the end of its tail. At this, it had dipped obligingly, smiled open, and revealed the treasures of its frosty interior.

"Ah, joy! Buy you a drink, Phil?"

"I thought you were in a hurry."

"I am, but I want to survey the situation some."

"Very well. I'll have a simicoke."

I squinted at him, passed him the thing. Then, as he turned away, I followed the direction of his gaze toward the easy chairs set in the alcove formed by the northeast corner of the room on two sides and the bulk of the thelinstra on the third. The thelinstra-player was an old lady with dreamy eyes. Earthdirector Lorel Sands was smoking his pipe. . . .

Now, the pipe is one of the more interesting facets of Lorel's personality. It's a real Meerschaum, and there aren't too many of them left in the world. As for the rest of him, his function is rather like that of an anti-computer: you feed him all kinds of carefully garnered facts, figures, and statistics and he translates them into garbage. Keen dark eyes, and a slow, rumbly way of speaking while he holds you with them; rarely given to gestures, but then very deliberate as he saws the air with a wide right hand or pokes imaginary ladies with his pipe; white at the temples and dark above; he is high of cheekbone, has a complexion that matches his tweeds (he assiduously avoids Dress Blacks), and he constantly strives to push his jaw an inch higher and further forward than seems comfortable. He is a political appointee, by the Earthgov on Taler, and he takes his work quite seriously, even to the extent of demonstrating his dedication with periodic attacks of ulcers. He is not the most intelligent man on Earth. He is my boss. He is also one of the best friends I have.

Beside him sat Cort Myshtigo. I could almost feel Phil hating him—from the pale blue soles of his six-toed feet to the pink upper-caste dye of his temple-to-temple hairstrip. Not hating him so much because he was him, but hating him, I was sure, because he was the closest available relative—grandson

—of Tatram Yshtigo, who forty years before had commenced to demonstrate that the greatest living writer in the English language was a Vegan. The old gent is still at it, and I don't believe Phil has ever forgiven him.

Out of the corner of my eye (the blue one) I saw Ellen ascending the big, ornate stairway on the other side of the hall. Out of the other corner of my other eye I saw Lorel looking in my direction.

"I," said I, "have been spotted, and I must go now to pay my respects to the William Seabrook of Taler. Come along?"

"Well . . . Very well," said Phil; "suffering is good for the soul."

We moved on to the alcove and stood before the two chairs, between the music and the noise, there in the place of power. Lorel stood slowly and shook hands. Myshtigo stood more slowly, and did not shake hands; he stared, amber-eyed, his face expressionless as we were introduced. His loose-hanging orange shirt fluttered constantly as his chambered lungs forced their perpetual exhalation out the anterior nostrils at the base of his wide ribcage. He nodded briefly, repeated my name. Then he turned to Phil with something like a smile.

"Would you care to have me translate your masque into English?" he asked, his voice sounding like a dying-down tuning fork.

Phil turned on his heel and walked away.

Then I thought the Vegan was ill for a second, until I recollected that a Vegan's laugh sounds something like a billy goat choking. I try to stay away from Vegans by avoiding the resorts.

"Sit down," said Lorel, looking uncomfortable behind his pipe.

I drew up a chair and set it across from them.

"Okay."

"Cort is going to write a book," said Lorel.

"So you've said."

"About the Earth."

I nodded.

"He expressed a desire that you be his guide on a tour of certain of the Old Places. . . ."

"I am honored," I said rather stiffly. "Also, I am curious what determined his selection of me as guide."

"And even more curious as to what he may know about you, eh?" said the Vegan.

"Yes, I am," I agreed, "by a couple hundred percent."

"I asked a machine."

"Fine. Now I know."

I leaned back and finished my drink.

"I started by checking the Vite-Stats Register for Earth when I first conceived of this project—just for general human data—then, after I'd turned up an interesting item, I tried the Earthoffice Personnel Banks—"

"Mm-hm," I said.

"—and I was more impressed by what they did not say of you than by what they said."

I shrugged.

"There are many gaps in your career. Even now, no one really knows what you do most of the time."

"—And by the way, when were you born?"

"I don't know. It was in a tiny Greek village and they were all out of calendars that year. Christmas Day, though, I'm told."

"According to your personnel record, you're seventy-seven years old. According to Vite-Stats, you're either a hundred eleven or a hundred thirty."

"I fibbed about my age to get the job. There was a Depression going on."

"—So I made up a Nomikos-profile, which is a kind of distinctive thing, and I set Vite-Stats to hunting down .001 physical analogues in all of its banks, including the closed ones."

"Some people collect old coins, other people build model rockets."

"I found that you could have been three or four or five other persons, all of them Greeks, and one of them truly amazing. But, of course, Konstantin Korones, one of the older ones, was born two hundred thirty-four years ago. On Christmas. Blue eye, brown eye. Game right leg. Same hairline, at age twenty-three. Same height, and same Bertillion scales."

"Same fingerprints? Same retinal patterns?"

"These were not included in many of the older Registry files. Maybe they were sloppier in those days? I don't know. More careless, perhaps, as to who had access to public records. . . ."

"You are aware that there are over four million persons on

this planet right now. By searching back through the past three or four centuries I daresay you could find doubles, or even triples, for quite a few of them. So what?"

"It serves to make you somewhat intriguing, that's all, almost like a spirit of place—and you are as curiously ruined as this place is. Doubtless I shall never achieve your age, whatever it may be, and I was curious as to the sort of sensibilities a human might cultivate, given so much time—especially in view of your position as a master of your world's history and art.

"So that is why I asked for your services," he concluded.

"Now that you've met me, ruined and all, can I go home?"

"Conrad!" The pipe attacked me.

"No, Mister Nomikos, there are practical considerations also. This is a tough world, and you have a high survival potential. I want you with me because I want to survive."

I shrugged again.

"Well, that's settled. What now?"

He chuckled.

"I perceive that you dislike me."

"Whatever gave you that idea? Just because you insulted a friend of mine, asked me impertinent questions, impressed me into your service on a whim—"

"—exploited your countrymen, turned your world into a brothel, and demonstrated the utter provinciality of the human race, as compared to a galactic culture eons older . . ."

"I'm not talking your race-my race. I'm talking personal talk. And I repeat, you insulted my friend, asked me impertinent questions, impressed me into your service on a whim."

"[*Billy goat snuffle*]! to all three! —It is an insult to the shades of Homer and Dante to have that man sing for the human race."

"At the moment he's the best we've got."

"In which case you should do without."

"That's no reason to treat him the way you did."

"I think it is, or I wouldn't have done it. —Second, I ask whatever questions I feel like asking, and it is your privilege to answer or not to answer as you see fit—just as you did. —Finally, nobody impressed you into anything. You are a civil servant. You have been given an assignment. Argue with your Office, not me.

"And, as an afterthought, I doubt that you possess sufficient data to use the word 'whim' as freely as you do," he finished.

From his expression, it appeared that Lorel's ulcer was making silent commentary as I observed:

"Then call your rudeness plain dealing, if you will—or the product of another culture—and justify your influence with sophistries, and afterthink all you like—and by all means, deliver me all manner of spurious judgments, that I may judge you in return. You behave like a Royal Representative in a Crown Colony," I decided, pronouncing the capitals, "and I don't like it. I've read all your books. I've also read your granddad's—like his *Earthwhore's Lament*—and you'll never be the man he is. He has a thing called compassion. You don't. Anything you feel about old Phil goes double for you, in *my* book."

That part about grandpa must have touched on a sore spot, because he flinched when my blue gaze hit him.

"So kiss my elbow," I added, or something like that, in Vegan.

Sands doesn't speak enough Veggy to have caught it, but he made conciliatory noises immediately, looking about the while to be sure we were not being overheard.

"Conrad, please find your professional attitude and put it back on. —Srin Shtigo, why don't we get on with the planning?"

Myshtigo smiled his bluegreen smile.

"And minimize our differences?" he asked. "All right."

"Then let's adjourn to the library—where it's quieter—and we can use the map-screen."

"Fine."

I felt a bit reinforced as we rose to go, because Don Dos Santos was up there and he hates Vegans, and wherever Dos Santos is, there is always Diane, the girl with the red wig, and she hates everybody; and I knew George Emmet was upstairs, and Ellen, too—and George is a real cold fish around strangers (friends too, for that matter); and perhaps Phil would wander in later and fire on Fort Sumter; and then there was Hasan— he doesn't say much, he just sits there and smokes his weeds and looks opaque—and if you stood too near him and took a couple deep breaths you wouldn't care what the hell you said to Vegans, or people either.

*

I had hoped that Hasan's memory would be on the rocks, or else up there somewhere among the clouds.

Hope died as we entered the library. He was sitting straight and sipping lemonade.

Eighty or ninety or more, looking about forty, he could still act thirty. The Sprung-Samser treatments had found highly responsive material. It's not often that way. Almost never, in fact. They put some people into accelerated anaphylactic shock for no apparent reason, and even an intracardial blast of adrenalin won't haul them back; others, most others, they freeze at five or six decades. But some rare ones actually grow younger when they take the series—about one in a hundred thousand.

It struck me as odd that in destiny's big shooting gallery *this* one should make it, in such a way.

It had been over fifty years since the Madagascar Affair, in which Hasan had been employed by the Radpol in their vendetta against the Talerites. He had been in the pay of (Rest in Peace) the big K. in Athens, who had sent him to polish off the Earthgov Realty Company. He'd done it, too. And well. With one tiny fission device. Pow. Instant urban renewal. Called Hasan the Assassin by the Few, he is the last mercenary on Earth.

Also, besides Phil (who had not always been a wielder of the bladeless sword without a hilt), Hasan was one of the Very Few who could remember old Karaghios.

So, chin up and fungus forward, I tried to cloud his mind with my first glance. Either there were ancient and mysterious powers afoot, which I doubted, or he was higher than I'd thought, which was possible, or he had forgotten my face—which could have been possible, though not real likely—or he was exercising a professional ethic or a low animal cunning. (He possessed both of the latter, in varying degrees, but the accent was on the animal cunning.) He made no sign as we were introduced.

"My bodyguard, Hasan," said Dos Santos, flashing his magnesium-flare smile as I shook the hand that once had shaken the world, so to speak.

It was still a very strong hand.

"Conrad Nomikos," said Hasan, squinting as though he were reading it from off a scroll.

I knew everyone else in the room, so I hastened to the chair farthest from Hasan, and I kept my second drink in front of my face most of the time, just to be safe.

Diane of the Red Wig stood near. She spoke. She said, "Good morning, Mister Nomikos."

I nodded my drink.

"Good evening, Diane."

Tall, slim, wearing mostly white, she stood beside Dos Santos like a candle. I know it's a wig she wears, because I've seen it slip upwards on occasion, revealing part of an interesting and ugly scar which is usually hidden by the low hairline she keeps. I've often wondered about that scar, sometimes as I lay at anchor staring up at parts of constellations through clouds, or when I unearthed damaged statues. Purple lips—tattooed, I think—and I've never seen them smile; her jaw muscles are always raised cords because her teeth are always clenched; and there's a little upside-down "v" between her eyes, from all that frowning; and her chin is slight, held high—defiant? She barely moves her mouth when she speaks in that tight, choppy way of hers. I couldn't really guess at her age. Over thirty, that's all.

She and Don make an interesting pair. He is dark, loquacious, always smoking, unable to sit still for more than two minutes. She is taller by about five inches, burns without flickering. I still don't know all of her story. I guess I never will.

She came over and stood beside my chair while Lorel was introducing Cort to Dos Santos.

"You," she said.

"Me," I said.

"—will conduct the tour."

"Everybody knows all about it but me," said I. "I don't suppose you could spare me a little of your knowledge on the matter?"

"No knowledge, no matter," said she.

"You sound like Phil," said I.

"Didn't mean to."

"You did, though. So why?"

"Why what?"

"Why you? Don? Here? Tonight?"

She touched her tongue to her upper lip, then pressed it

hard, as though to squeeze out the grapejuice or keep in the words. Then she looked over at Don, but he was too far away to have heard, and he was looking in another direction anyhow. He was busy pouring Myshtigo a real Coke from the pitcher in the exec dip-tray. The Coke formula had been the archeological find of the century, according to the Vegans. It was lost during the Three Days and recovered only a decade or so ago. There had been lots of simicokes around, but none of them have the same effect on Vegan metabolism as the real thing. "Earth's second contribution to galactic culture," one of their contemporary historians had called it. The first contribution, of course, being a very fine new social problem of the sort that weary Vegan philosophers had been waiting around for generations to have happen.

Diane looked back.

"Don't know yet," she said. "Ask Don."

"I will."

I did, too. Later, though. And I wasn't disappointed, inasmuch as I expected nothing.

But, as I sat trying as hard as I could to eavesdrop, there was suddenly a sight-vision overlay, of the sort a shrink had once classified for me as a pseudotelepathic wish-fulfillment. It works like this:

I want to know what's going on somewhere. I have almost-sufficient information to guess. Therefore, I do. Only it comes on as though I am seeing it and hearing it through the eyes and ears of one of the parties involved. It's not real telepathy, though, I don't think, because it can sometimes be wrong. It sure seems real, though.

The shrink could tell me everything about it but why.

Which is how I

was standing in the middle of the room,

was staring at Myshtigo,

was Dos Santos,

was saying:

". . . will be going along, for your protection. Not as Radpol Secretary, just a private citizen."

"I did not solicit your protection," the Vegan was saying; "however, I thank you. I will accept your offer to circumvent my death at the hands of your comrades"—and he smiled as he said it—"if they should seek it during my travels. I doubt that they will, but I should be a fool to refuse the shield of Dos Santos."

"You are wise," we said, bowing slightly.

"Quite," said Cort. "Now tell me"—he nodded toward Ellen, who had just finished arguing with George about anything and was stamping away from him—"who is that?"

"Ellen Emmet, the wife of George Emmet, the Director of the Wildlife Conservation Department."

"What is her price?"

"I don't know that she's quoted one recently."

"Well, what did it used to be?"

"There never was one."

"Everything on Earth has a price."

"In that case, I suppose you'll have to find out for yourself."

"I will," he said.

Earth femmes have always held an odd attraction for Vegans. A Veggy once told me that they make him feel rather like a zoophilist. Which is interesting, because a pleasure girl at the Cote d'Ôr Resort once told me, with a giggle, that Vegans made her feel rather like *une zoophiliste*. I guess those jets of air must tickle or something and arouse both beasts.

"By the way," we said, "have you stopped beating your wife lately?"

"Which one?" asked Myshtigo.

Fadeout, and me back in my chair.

". . . What," George Emmet was asking, "do you think of that?"

I stared at him. He hadn't been there a second ago. He had come up suddenly and perched himself on the wide wing of my chair.

"Come again, please. I was dozing."

"I said we've beaten the spiderbat. What do you think of that?"

"It rhymes," I observed. "So tell me how we've beaten the spiderbat."

But he was laughing. He's one of those guys with whom laughter is an unpredictable thing. He'll go around looking sour for days, and then some little thing will set him off giggling. He sort of gasps when he laughs, like a baby, and that impression is reinforced by his pink flaccidity and thinning hair. So I waited. Ellen was off insulting Lorel now, and Diane had turned to read the titles on the bookshelves.

Finally, "I've developed a new strain of *slishi*," he panted confidentially.

"Say, that's really great!"

Then, "What are *slishi*?" I asked softly.

"The *slish* is a Bakabian parasite," he explained, "rather like a large tick. Mine are about three-eighths of an inch long," he said proudly, "and they burrow deep into the flesh and give off a highly poisonous waste product."

"Fatal?"

"Mine are."

"Could you lend me one?" I asked him.

"Why?"

"I want to drop it down someone's back. On second thought, make it a couple dozen. I have lots of friends."

"Mine won't bother people, just spiderbats. They discriminate against people. People would poison my *slishi*." (He said "my *slishi*" very possessively.) "Their host has to have a copper- rather than an iron-based metabolism," he explained, "and spiderbats fall into that category. That's why I want to go with you on this trip."

"You want me to find a spiderbat and hold it for you while you dump *slishi* on it? Is that what you're trying to say?"

"Well, I *would* like a couple spiderbats to keep—I used all mine up last month—but I'm already sure the *slishi* will work. I want to go along to start the plague."

"Which plague?"

"Among the 'bats. —The *slishi* multiply quite rapidly under Earth conditions, if they're given the proper host, and they should be extremely contagious if we could get them started at the right time of year. What I had in mind was the late south-western spiderbat mating season. It will begin in six to eight weeks in the territory of California, in an Old Place—not real hot anymore, though—called Capistrano. I understand that your tour will take you out that way at about that time. When the spiderbats return to Capistrano I want to be waiting for them with the *slishi*. Also, I could use a vacation."

"Mm-hm. Have you talked this over with Lorel?"

"Yes, and he thinks it's a fine idea. In fact, he wants to meet us out there and take pictures. There may not be too many more opportunities to see them—darkening the sky with their flight, nesting about the ruins the way they do, eating the wild pigs, leaving their green droppings in the streets—it's rather beautiful, you know."

"Uh-huh, sort of like Halloween. What'll happen to all those wild pigs if we kill off the spiderbats?"

"Oh, there'll be more of them around. But I figure the pumas will keep them from getting like Australian rabbits. Anyway, you'd rather have pigs than spiderbats, wouldn't you?"

"I'm not particularly fond of either, but now that I think of it I suppose I would rather have pigs than spiderbats. All right, sure, you can come along."

"Thank you," he said. "I was sure you'd help."

"Don't mention it."

Lorel made apologetic sounds deep in his throat about then. He stood beside the big desk in the middle of the room, before which the broad viewscreen was slowly lowering itself. It was a thick depth-transparer, so nobody had to move around after a better seat. He pressed a button on the side of the desk and the lights dimmed somewhat.

"Uh, I'm about to project a series of maps," he said, "if I can get this synchro-thing . . . There. There it is."

The upper part of Africa and most of the Mediterranean countries appeared in pastels.

"Is that the one you wanted first?" he asked Myshtigo.

"It *was*—eventually," said the big Vegan, turning away from a muffled conversation with Ellen, whom he had cornered in the French History alcove beneath a bust of Voltaire.

The lights dimmed some more and Myshtigo moved to the desk. He looked at the map, and then at nobody in particular.

"I want to visit certain key sites which, for one reason or another, are important in the history of your world," he said. "I'd like to start with Egypt, Greece and Rome. Then I'd like to move on quickly through Madrid, Paris and London." The maps shifted as he talked, not fast enough, though, to keep up with him. "Then I want to backtrack to Berlin, hit Brussels, visit St. Petersburg and Moscow, skip back over the Atlantic and stop at Boston, New York, DeeCee, Chicago," (Lorel was working up a sweat by then) "drop down to Yucatan, and jump back up to the California territory."

"In that order?" I asked.

"Pretty much so," he said.

"What's wrong with India and the Middle East—or the Far East, for that matter?" asked a voice which I recognized as Phil's. He had come in after the lights had gone down low.

"Nothing," said Myshtigo, "except that it's mainly mud and sand and hot, and has nothing whatsoever to do with what I'm after."

"What *are* you after?"

"A story."

"What kind of story?"

"I'll send you an autographed copy."

"Thanks."

"Your pleasure."

"When do you wish to leave?" I asked him.

"Day after tomorrow," he said.

"Okay."

"I've had detailed maps of the specific sites made up for you. Lorel tells me they were delivered to your office this afternoon."

"Okay again. But there is something of which you may not be fully cognizant. It involves the fact that everything you've named so far is mainlandish. We're pretty much an island culture these days, and for very good reasons. During the Three Days the Mainland got a good juicing, and most of the places you've named are still inclined to be somewhat hot. This, though, is not the only reason they are considered unsafe . . ."

"I am not unfamiliar with your history and I am aware of the radiation precautions," he interrupted. "Also, I am aware of the variety of mutated life forms which inhabit Old Places. I am concerned, but not worried."

I shrugged in the artificial twilight.

"It's okay by me . . ."

"Good." He took another sip of Coke. "Let me have a little light then, Lorel."

"Right, Srin."

It was light again.

As the screen was sucked upward behind him, Myshtigo asked me, "Is it true that you are acquainted with several *mambos* and *houngans* here at the Port?"

"Why, yes," I said. "Why?"

He approached my chair.

"I understand," he said conversationally, "that voodoo, or *voudoun*, has survived pretty much unchanged over the centuries."

"Perhaps," I said. "I wasn't around here when it got started, so I wouldn't know for sure."

"I understand that the participants do not much appreciate the presence of outsiders—"

"That too, is correct. But they'll put on a good show for you, if you pick the right *hounfor* and drop in on them with a few gifts."

"But I should like very much to witness a real ceremony. If I were to attend one with someone who was not a stranger to the participants, perhaps then I could obtain the genuine thing."

"Why should you want to? Morbid curiosity concerning barbaric customs?"

"No. I am a student of comparative religions."

I studied his face, but couldn't tell anything from it.

It had been awhile since I'd visited with Mama Julie and Papa Joe or any of the others, and the *hounfor* wasn't that far away, but I didn't know how they'd take to me bringing a Vegan around. They'd never objected when I'd brought people, of course.

"Well . . ." I began.

"I just want to watch," he said. "I'll stay out of the way. They'll hardly know I'm there."

I mumbled a bit and finally gave in. I knew Mama Julie pretty well and I didn't see any real harm being done, no matter what.

So, "Okay," said I, "I'll take you to one. Tonight, if you like."

He agreed, thanked me, and went off after another Coke. George, who had not strayed from the arm of my chair, leaned toward me and observed that it would be very interesting to dissect a Vegan. I agreed with him.

When Myshtigo returned, Dos Santos was at his side.

"What is this about you taking Mister Myshtigo to a pagan ceremony?" he asked, nostrils flared and quivering.

"That's right," I said, "I am."

"Not without a bodyguard you are not."

I turned both palms upward.

"I am capable of handling anything which might arise."

"Hasan and I will accompany you."

I was about to protest when Ellen insinuated herself between them.

"I want to go, too," she said. "I've never been to one."

I shrugged. If Dos Santos went, then Diane would go, too, which made for quite a few of us.

So one more wouldn't matter, shouldn't matter. It was ruined before it got started.

"Why not?" I said.

The *hounfor* was located down in the harbor section, possibly because it was dedicated to Agué Woyo, god of the sea. More likely, though, it was because Mama Julie's people had always been harbor people. Agué Woyo is not a jealous god, so lots of other deities are commemorated upon the walls in brilliant colors. There are more elaborate *hounfors* further inland, but they tend to be somewhat commercial.

Agué's big blazeboat was blue and orange and green and yellow and black, and it looked to be somewhat unseaworthy. Damballa Wedo, crimson, writhed and coiled his length across most of the opposite wall. Several big *rada* drums were being stroked rhythmically by Papa Joe, forward and to the right of the door through which we entered—the only door. Various Christian saints peered from behind unfathomable expressions at the bright hearts and cocks and graveyard crosses, flags, machetes and crossroads that clung to almost every inch of the walls about them—frozen into an after-the-hurricane surrealism by the amphoteric paints of Titan—and whether or not the saints approved one could never tell: they stared down through their cheap picture-frames as though they were windows onto an alien world.

The small altar bore numerous bottles of alcoholic beverages, gourds, sacred vessels for the spirits of the *loa*, charms, pipes, flags, depth photos of unknown persons and, among other things, a pack of cigarettes for Papa Legba.

A service was in progress when we were led in by a young *hounsi* named Luis. The room was about eight meters long and five wide, had a high ceiling, a dirt floor. Dancers moved about the central pole with slow, strutting steps. Their flesh was dark and it glistened in the dim light of the antique kerosene lamps. With our entry the room became crowded.

Mama Julie took my hand and smiled. She led me back to a place beside the altar and said, "Erzulie was kind."

I nodded.

"She likes you, Nomiko. You live long, you travel much, and you come back."

"Always," I said.

"Those people . . . ?"

She indicated my companions with a flick of her dark eyes.

"Friends. They would be no bother . . ."

She laughed as I said it. So did I.

"I will keep them out of your way if you let us remain. We will stay in the shadows at the sides of the room. If you tell me to take them away, I will. I see that you have already danced much, emptied many bottles . . ."

"Stay," she said. "Come talk with me during daylight sometime."

"I will."

She moved away then and they made room for her in the circle of dancers. She was quite large, though her voice was a small thing. She moved like a huge rubber doll, not without grace, stepping to the monotonous thunder of Papa Joe's drumming. After a time this sound filled everything—my head, the earth, the air—like maybe the whale's heartbeat had seemed to half-digested Jonah. I watched the dancers. And I watched those who watched the dancers.

I drank a pint of rum in an effort to catch up, but I couldn't. Myshtigo kept taking sips of Coke from a bottle he had brought along with him. No one noticed that he was blue, but then we had gotten there rather late and things were pretty well along the way to wherever they were going.

Red Wig stood in a corner looking supercilious and frightened. She was holding a bottle at her side, but that's where it stayed. Myshtigo was holding Ellen at his side, and that's where she stayed. Dos Santos stood beside the door and watched everybody—even me. Hasan, crouched against the righthand wall, was smoking a long-stemmed pipe with a small bowl. He appeared to be at peace.

Mama Julie, I guess it was, began to sing. Other voices picked it up:

> Papa Legba, ouvri bayé!
> Papa Legba, Attibon Legba, ouvri bayé pou nou passé!
> Papa Legba . . .

This went on, and on and on. I began to feel drowsy. I drank more rum and felt thirstier and drank more rum.

I'm not sure how long we had been there when it happened. The dancers had been kissing the pole and singing and rattling gourds and pouring out waters, and a couple of the *hounsi* were acting possessed and talking incoherently, and the meal-design on the floor was all blurred, and there was lots of smoke in the air, and I was leaning back against the wall and I guess my eyes had been closed for a minute or two.

The sound came from an unexpected quarter.

Hasan screamed.

It was a long, wailing thing that brought me forward, then dizzily off balance, then back to the wall again, with a thump.

The drumming continued, not missing a single beat. Some of the dancers stopped, though, staring.

Hasan had gotten to his feet. His teeth were bared and his eyes were slits, and his face bore the ridges and valleys of exertion beneath its sheen of sweat.

His beard was a fireshot spearhead.

His cloak, caught high against some wall decoration, was black wings.

His hands, in a hypnosis of slow motion, were strangling a non-existent man.

Animal sounds came from his throat.

He continued to choke nobody.

Finally, he chuckled and his hands sprang open.

Dos Santos was at his side almost immediately, talking to him, but they inhabited two different worlds.

One of the dancers began to moan softly. Another joined him—and others.

Mama Julie detached herself from the circle and came toward

me—just as Hasan started the whole thing over again, this time with more elaborate histrionics.

The drum continued its steady, earthdance pronouncement.

Papa Joe did not even look up.

"A bad sign," said Mama Julie. "What do you know of this man?"

"Plenty," I said, forcing my head clear by an act of will.

"Angelsou," she said.

"What?"

"Angelsou," she repeated. "He is a dark god—one to be feared. Your friend is possessed by Angelsou."

"Explain, please."

"He comes seldom to our *hounfor*. He is not wanted here. Those he possesses become murderers."

"I think Hasan was trying a new pipe mixture—mutant ragweed or something."

"Angelsou," she said again. "Your friend will become a killer, for Angelsou is a deathgod, and he only visits with his own."

"Mama Julie," said I, "Hasan *is* a killer. If you had a piece of gum for every man he's killed and you tried to chew it all, you'd look like a chipmunk. He is a professional killer—within the limits of the law, usually. Since the Code Duello prevails on the Mainland, he does most of his work there. It has been rumored that he does an illegal killing on occasion, but this thing has never been proved.

"So tell me," I finished, "is Angelsou the god of killers or the god of murderers? There should be a difference between the two, shouldn't there?"

"Not to Angelsou," she said.

Dos Santos then, trying to stop the show, seized both of Hasan's wrists. He tried to pull his hands apart, but—well, try bending the bars of your cage sometime and you'll get the picture.

I crossed the room, as did several of the others. This proved fortunate, because Hasan had finally noticed that someone was standing in front of him, and dropped his hands, freeing them. Then he produced a long-bladed stiletto from under his cloak.

Whether or not he would actually have used it on Don or anybody else is a moot point, because at that moment Myshtigo stoppered his Coke bottle with his thumb and hit him behind the ear with it. Hasan fell forward and Don caught him, and I pried the blade from between his fingers, and Myshtigo finished his Coke.

"Interesting ceremony," observed the Vegan, "I would never have suspected that big fellow of harboring such strong religious feelings."

"It just goes to show that you can never be too sure, doesn't it?"

"Yes." He gestured to indicate the onlookers. "They are all pantheists, aren't they?"

I shook my head. "Primitive animists."

"What is the difference?"

"Well, that Coke bottle you just emptied is going to occupy the altar, or *pé*, as it is called, as a vessel for Angelsou, since it has enjoyed an intimate mystical relationship with the god. That's the way an animist would see it. Now, a pantheist just might get a little upset at somebody's coming in to his ceremonies uninvited and creating a disturbance such as we just did. A pantheist might be moved to sacrifice the intruders to Agué Woyo, god of the sea, by hitting them all over the head in a similar ceremonial manner and tossing them off the end of the dock. Therefore, I am now going to have to explain to Mama Julie that all these people standing around glaring at us are really animists. Excuse me a minute."

It wasn't really that bad, but I wanted to shake him up a bit, I think I did.

After I'd apologized and said good-night, I picked up Hasan. He was out cold and I was the only one big enough to carry him.

The street was deserted except for us, and Agué Woyo's big blazeboat was cutting the waves somewhere just under the eastern edge of the world and splashing the sky with all his favorite colors.

Dos Santos, at my side, said, "Perhaps you were correct. Maybe we should not have come along."

I didn't bother to answer him, but Ellen, who was walking up ahead with Myshtigo, stopped, turned, and said, "Nonsense. If you hadn't, we would have missed the tentmaker's wonderful dramatic monologue." By then, I was within range and both her hands shot out and wrapped around my throat. She applied no pressure, but she grimaced horribly and observed, "Ur! Mm! Ugh! I'm possessed of Angelsou, and you've had it." Then she laughed.

"Let go my throat or I'll throw this Arab at you," I said, comparing the orangebrown color of her hair with the orange-pink color of the sky behind her, and smiled.

"He's a heavy one, too," I added.

Then, a second before she let go, she applied some pressure —a little bit too much to be playful—and then she was back on Myshtigo's arm and we were walking again. Well, women never slap me because I always turn the other cheek first and they're afraid of the fungus, so I guess a quick choke is about the only alternative.

"Frightfully interesting," said Red Wig. "Felt strange. As if something inside me was dancing along with them. Odd feeling, it was. I don't really like dancing—any kind."

"What kind of accent do you have?" I interrupted her. "I've been trying to place it."

"Don't know," she said. "I'm sort of Irish-French. Lived in the Hebrides—also Australia, Japan—till I was nineteen . . ."

Hasan moaned just then and flexed his muscles and I felt a sharp pain in my shoulder.

I set him down on a doorstep and shook him down. I found two throwing knives, another stiletto, a very neat gravity knife, a saw-edged Bowie, strangling wires, and a small metal case containing various powders and vials of liquids which I did not care to inspect too closely. I liked the gravity knife, so I kept it for myself. It was a Coricama, and very neat.

Late the next day—call it evening—I shanghaied old Phil, determined to use him as the price of admission to Dos Santos' suite at the *Royal*. The Radpol still reveres Phil as a sort of Returnist Tom Paine, even though he began pleading innocent to that about half a century ago, back when he began getting mysticism and respectability. While his *Call of Earth* probably *is* the best thing he ever wrote, he also drafted the Articles of Return, which helped to start the trouble I'd wanted started. He may do much disavowing these days, but he was a trouble-maker then, and I'm sure he still files away all the fawning gazes and bright words it continues to bring him, takes them out every now and then, dusts them off, and regards them with something like pleasure.

Besides Phil, I took along a pretext—that I wanted to see how Hasan was feeling after the lamentable bash he'd received at the *hounfor*. Actually, what I wanted was a chance to talk to Hasan and find out how much, if anything, he'd be willing to tell me about his latest employment.

So Phil and I walked it. It wasn't far from the Office compound to the *Royal*. About seven minutes, ambling.

"Have you finished writing my elegy yet?" I asked.

"I'm still working on it."

"You've been saying that for the past twenty years. I wish you'd hurry up so I could read it."

"I could show you some very fine ones . . . Lorel's, George's, even one for Dos Santos. And I have all sorts of blank ones in my files—the fill-in kind—for lesser notables. Yours is a problem, though."

"How so?"

"I have to keep updating it. You go right on, quite blithely —living, doing things."

"You disapprove?"

"Most people have the decency to do things for half a century and then stay put. Their elegies present no problems. I have cabinets full. But I'm afraid yours is going to be a last-minute thing with a discord ending. I don't like to work that way. I prefer to deliberate over a span of many years, to evaluate a person's life carefully, and without pressure. You people who live your lives like folksongs trouble me. I think you're trying to force me to write you an epic, and I'm getting too old for that. I sometimes nod."

"I think you're being unfair," I told him. "Other people get to read their elegies, and I'd even settle for a couple good limericks."

"Well, I have a feeling yours will be finished before too long," he noted. "I'll try to get a copy to you in time."

"Oh? From whence springs this feeling?"

"Who can isolate the source of an inspiration?"

"You tell me."

"It came upon me as I meditated. I was in the process of

composing one for the Vegan—purely as an exercise, of course
—and I found myself thinking: 'Soon I will finish the Greek's.'"
After a moment, he continued, "Conceptualize this thing:
yourself as two men, each taller than the other."

"It could be done if I stood in front of a mirror and kept
shifting my weight. I have this short leg. —So, I'm conceptu-
alizing it. What now?"

"Nothing. You don't go at these things properly."

"It's a cultural tradition against which I have never been successfully immunized. Like knots, horses—Gordia, Troy. You
know. We're sneaky."

He was silent for the next ten paces.

"So feathers or lead?" I asked him.

"Pardon?"

"It is the riddle of the kallikanzaros. Pick one."

"Feathers?"

"You're wrong."

"If I had said 'lead' . . . ?"

"Uh-uh. You only have one chance. The correct answer is
whatever the kallikanzaros wants it to be. You lose."

"That sounds pretty arbitrary."

"Kallikanzaroi are that way. It's Greek, rather than Oriental
subtlety. Less inscrutable, too. Because your life often depends
on the answer, and the kallikanzaros generally wants you to
lose."

"Why is that?"

"Ask the next kallikanzaros you meet, if you get the chance.
They're mean spirits."

We struck the proper avenue and turned up it.

"Why are you suddenly concerned with the Radpol again?"
he asked. "It's been a long time since you left."

"I left at the proper time, and all I'm concerned with is
whether it's coming alive again—like in the old days. Hasan
comes high because he always delivers, and I want to know
what's in the package."

"Are you worried they've found you out?"

"No. It might be uncomfortable, but I doubt it would be
incapacitating."

The *Royal* loomed before us and we entered. We went

directly to the suite. As we walked up the padded hallway, Phil, in a fit of perception, observed, "I'm running interference again."

"That about says it."

"Okay. One'll get you ten you find out nothing."

"I won't take you up on that. You're probably right."

I knocked on the darkwood door.

"Hi there," I said as it opened.

"Come in, come in."

And we were off.

It took me ten minutes to turn the conversation to the lamentable bashing of the Bedouin, as Red Wig was there distracting me by being there and being distracting.

"Good morning," she said.

"Good evening," I said.

"Anything new happening in Arts?"

"No."

"Monuments?"

"No."

"Archives?"

"No."

"What interesting work you must do!"

"Oh, it's been overpublicized and glamorized all out of shape by a few romanticists in the Information Office. Actually, all we do is locate, restore, and preserve the records and artifacts mankind has left lying about the Earth."

"Sort of like cultural garbage collectors?"

"Mm, yes. I think that's properly put."

"Well, why?"

"Why what?"

"Why do you do it?"

"Someone has to, because it's cultural garbage. That makes it worth collecting. I know my garbage better than anyone else on Earth."

"You're dedicated, as well as being modest. That's good, too."

"Also, there weren't too many people to choose from when I applied for the job—and I knew where a lot of the garbage was stashed."

She handed me a drink, took a sip and a half of her own, and asked, "Are they actually still around?"

"Who?" I inquired.

"Divinity Incorporated. The old gods. Like Angelsou. I thought all the gods had left the Earth."

"No, they didn't. Just because most of them resemble us doesn't mean they act the same way. When man left he didn't offer to take them along, and gods have some pride, too. But then, maybe they had to stay, anyhow—that thing called *ananke*, death-destiny. Nobody prevails against it."

"Like progress?"

"Yeah. Speaking of progress, how is Hasan progressing? The last time I saw him he had stopped entirely."

"Up, around. Big lump. Thick skull. No harm."

"Where is he?"

"Up the hall, left. Games Room."

"I believe I'll go render him my sympathy. Excuse me?"

"Excused," she said, nodding, and she went away to listen to Dos Santos talk at Phil. Phil, of course, welcomed the addition.

Neither looked up as I left.

The Games Room was at the other end of the long hallway. As I approached, I heard a *thunk* followed by a silence, followed by another *thunk*.

I opened the door and looked inside.

He was the only one there. His back was to me, but he heard the door open and turned quickly. He was wearing a long purple dressing gown and was balancing a knife in his right hand. There was a big wad of plastage on the back of his head.

"Good evening, Hasan."

A tray of knives stood at his side, and he had set a target upon the opposite wall. Two blades were sticking into the target—one in the center and one about six inches off, at nine o'clock.

"Good evening," he said slowly. Then, after thinking it over, he added, "How are you?"

"Oh, fine. I came to ask you that same question. How is your head?"

"The pain is great, but it shall pass."

I closed the door behind me.

"You must have been having quite a daydream last night."

"Yes. Mister Dos Santos tells me I fought with ghosts. I do not remember."

"You weren't smoking what the fat Doctor Emmet would call *Cannabis sativa*, that's for sure."

"No, Karagee. I smoked a strige-fleur which had drunk human blood. I found it near the Old Place of Constantinople and dried its blossoms carefully. An old woman told me it would give me sight into the future. She lied."

". . . And the vampire-bloom incites to violence? Well, that's a new one to write down. By the way, you just called me Karagee. I wish you wouldn't. My name is Nomikos, Conrad Nomikos."

"Yes, Karagee. I was surprised to see you. I had thought you died long ago, when your blazeboat broke up in the bay."

"Karagee did die then. You have not mentioned to anyone that I resemble him, have you?"

"No; I do not make idle talk."

"That's a good habit."

I crossed the room, selected a knife, weighed it, threw it, and laid it about ten inches to the right of center.

"Have you been working for Mister Dos Santos very long?" I asked him.

"For about the period of a month," he replied.

He threw his knife. It struck five inches below the center.

"You are his bodyguard, eh?"

"That is right. I also guard the blue one."

"Don says he fears an attempt on Myshtigo's life. Is there an actual threat, or is he just being safe?"

"It is possible either way, Karagee. I do not know. He pays me only to guard."

"If I paid you more, would you tell me whom you've been hired to kill?"

"I have only been hired to guard, but I would not tell you even if it were otherwise."

"I didn't think so. Let's go get the knives."

We crossed and drew the blades from the target.

"Now, if it happens to be me—which is possible," I offered, "why don't we settle it right now? We are each holding two blades. The man who leaves this room will say that the other attacked him and that it was a matter of self-defense. There are no witnesses. We were both seen drunk or disorderly last night."

"No, Karagee."

"No, what? No, it isn't me? Or no, you don't want to do it that way?"

"I could say no, it is not you. But you would not know whether I spoke the truth or not."

"That is true."

"I could say I do not want to do it that way."

"Is that true?"

"I do not say. But to give you the satisfaction of an answer, what I will say is this: If I wished to kill you, I would not attempt it with a knife in my hand, nor would I box nor wrestle with you."

"Why is that?"

"Because many years ago when I was a boy I worked at the Resort of Kerch, attending at the tables of the wealthy Vegans. You did not know me then. I had just come up from the places of Pamir. You and your friend the poet came to Kerch."

"I remember now. Yes. . . . Phil's parents had died that year—they were good friends of mine—and I was going to take Phil to the university. But there was a Vegan who had taken his first woman from him, taken her to Kerch. Yes, the entertainer—I forget his name."

"He was Thrilpai Ligo, the shajadpa-boxer, and he looked like a mountain at the end of a great plain—high, immovable. He boxed with the Vegan cesti—the leather straps with the ten sharpened studs that go all the way around the hand —open-handed."

"Yes, I remember. . . ."

"You had never boxed shajadpa before, but you fought with him for the girl. A great crowd came, of the Vegans and the Earth girls, and I stood on a table to watch. After a minute your head was all blood. He tried to make it run into your eyes, and you kept shaking your head. I was fifteen then and had only killed three men myself, and I thought that you were going to die because you had not even touched him. And then your right hand crossed to him like a thrown hammer, so fast! You struck him in the center of that double bone the blue ones have in their chests—and they are tougher there than we—and you crushed him like an egg. I could never have done that, I am sure—and that is why I fear your hands and your arms. Later, I learned that you had also broken a spiderbat. —No, Karagee, I would kill you from a distance."

"That was so long ago. . . . I did not think anyone remembered."

"You won the girl."

"Yes. I forget her name."

"But you did not give her back to the poet. You kept her for yourself. That is why he probably hates you."

"Phil? That girl? I've even forgotten what she looked like."

"He has never forgotten. That is why I think he hates you. I can smell hate, sniff out its sources. You took away his first woman. I was there."

"It was her idea."

". . . And he grows old and you stay young. It is sad, Karagee, when a friend has reason to hate a friend."

"Yes."

"And I do not answer your questions."

"It is possible that you were hired to kill the Vegan."

"It is possible."

"Why?"

"I said only that it is possible, not that it is fact."

"Then I will ask you one more question only, and be done with it. What good would come of the Vegan's death? His book could be a very good thing in the way of Vegan-human relations."

"I do not know what good or bad would come of it, Karagee. Let us throw more knives."

We did. I picked up the range and the balance and put two right in the center of the target. Then Hasan squeezed two in beside them, the last one giving out the sharp pain-cry of metal as it vibrated against one of mine.

"I will tell you a thing," I said, as we drew them again. "I am head of the tour and responsible for the safety of its members. I, too, will guard the Vegan."

"That will be a very good thing, Karagee. He needs protecting."

I placed the knives back in the tray and moved to the door.

"We will be leaving at nine tomorrow morning, you know. I'll have a convoy of Skimmers at the first field in the Office compound."

"Yes. Good night, Karagee."

". . . And call me Conrad."

"Yes."

He had a knife ready to throw at the target. I closed the door and moved back up the corridor. As I went, I heard another *thunk*, and it sounded much closer than the first ones had. It echoed all around me, there in the hallway.

As the six big Skimmers fled across the oceans toward Egypt I turned my thoughts first to Kos and Cassandra and then dragged them back with some difficulty and sent them on ahead to the land of sand, the Nile, mutated crocs, and some dead Pharaohs whom one of my most current projects was then disturbing ("Death comes on swift wings to he who defiles . . ." etc.), and I thought then of humanity, roughly ensconced on the Titan way-station, working in the Earthoffice, abasing itself on Taler and Bakab, getting by on Mars, and doing so-so on Rylpah, Divbah, Litan, and a couple dozen other worlds in the Vegan Combine. Then I thought about the Vegans.

The blueskinned folk with the funny names and the dimples like pock-marks had taken us in when we were cold, fed us when we were hungry. Yeah. They appreciated the fact that our Martian and Titanian colonies had suffered from nearly a century of sudden self-sufficiency—after the Three Days incident —before a workable interstellar vehicle had been developed. Like the boll weevil (Emmet tells me) we were just looking for a home, because we'd used up the one we had. Did the Vegans reach for the insecticide? No. Wise elder race that they are, they permitted us to settle among their worlds, to live and work in their landcities, their seacities. For even a culture as advanced as the Vegans' has some need for hand labor of the opposing thumb variety. Good domestic servants cannot be replaced by machines, nor can machine monitors, good gardeners, salt sea fisherfolk, subterranean and subaquean hazard workers, and ethnic entertainers of the alien variety. Admittedly, the presence of human dwelling places lowers the value of adjacent

Vegan properties, but then, humans themselves compensate for it by contributing to the greater welfare.

Which thought brought me back to Earth. The Vegans had never seen a completely devastated civilization before, so they were fascinated by our home planet. Fascinated enough to tolerate our absentee government on Taler. Enough to buy Earthtour tickets to view the ruins. Even enough to buy property here and set up resorts. There *is* a certain kind of fascination to a planet that is run like a museum. (What was it James Joyce said about Rome?) Anyhow, dead Earth still brings its living grandchildren a small but appreciable revenue every Vegan fiscal year. That is why—the Office, Lorel, George, Phil, and all that.

Sort of why me, even.

Far below, the ocean was a bluegray rug being pulled out from beneath us. The dark continent replaced it. We raced on toward New Cairo.

We set down outside the city. There's no real airstrip. We just dropped all six Skimmers down in an empty field we used as one, and we posted George as a guard.

Old Cairo is still hot, but the people with whom one can do business live mainly in New Cairo, so things were pretty much okay for the tour. Myshtigo did want to see the mosque of Kait Bey in the City of the Dead, which had survived the Three Days; he settled, though, for me taking him up in my Skimmer and flying in low, slow circles about it while he took photographs and did some peering. In the way of monuments, it was really the pyramids and Luxor, Karnak, and the Valley of Kings and the Valley of Queens that he wanted to see.

It was well that we viewed the mosque from the air. Dark shapes scurried below us, stopping only to hurl rocks up toward the ship.

"What are they?" asked Myshtigo.

"Hot Ones," said I. "Sort of human. They vary in size, shape, and meanness."

After circling for a time he was satisfied, and we returned to the field.

So, landing again beneath a glaring sun, we secured the final Skimmer and disembarked, moving across equal proportions of sand and broken pavement—two temporary tour assistants, me, Myshtigo, Dos Santos and Red Wig, Ellen, Hasan. Ellen had decided at the last minute to accompany her husband on the journey. There were fields of high, shiny sugar cane on both sides of the road. In a moment we had left them behind and were passing the low outbuildings of the city. The road widened. Here and there a palm tree cast some shade. Two great-eyed, brown-eyed children looked up as we passed. They had been watching a weary, six-legged cow turn a great *sakieh* wheel, in much the same way as cows have always turned great *sakieh* wheels hereabouts, only this one left more hoofprints.

My area supervisor, Rameses Smith, met us at the inn. He was big, his golden face tightly contained within a fine net of wrinkles; and he had the typical sad eyes, but his constant chuckle quickly offset them.

We sat sipping beer in the main hall of the inn while we waited for George. Local guards had been sent to relieve him.

"The work is progressing well," Rameses told me.

"Good," I said, somewhat pleased that no one had asked me what "the work" was. I wanted to surprise them.

"How is your wife, and the children?"

"They are fine," he stated.

"The new one?"

"He has survived—and without defect," he said proudly. "I sent my wife to Corsica until he was delivered. Here is his picture."

I pretended to study it, making the expected appreciative noises. Then, "Speaking of pictures," I said, "do you need any more equipment for the filming?"

"No, we are well-stocked. All goes well. When do you wish to view the work?"

"Just as soon as we have something to eat."

"Are you a Moslem?" interrupted Myshtigo.

"I am of the Coptic faith," replied Rameses, not smiling.

"Oh, really? That was the Monophysite heresy, was it not?"

"We do not consider ourselves heretics," said Rameses.

I sat there wondering if we Greeks had done the right thing in unleashing logic onto a hapless world, as Myshtigo launched into an amusing (to him) catalog of Christian heresies. In a fit of spite at having to guide a tour, I recorded them all in the

Tour Log. Later, Lorel told me that it was a fine and well-kept document. Which just goes to show how nasty I must have felt at that moment. I even put in the bit about the accidental canonization of Buddha as St. Josaphat in the sixteenth century. Finally, as Myshtigo sat there mocking us, I realized I would either have to cut him down or change the subject. Not being a Christian myself, his theological comedy of errors did not poke me in the religious plexus. It bothered me, though, that a member of another race had gone to such trouble doing research to make us look like a pack of idiots.

Reconsidering the thing at this time, I know now that I was wrong. The success of the viewtape I was making then ("the work" which Rameses had referred to) bears out a more recent hypothesis of mine concerning the Vegans: They were so bloody bored with themselves and we were so novel that they seized upon our perennially popular problems and our classical problems, as well as the one we were currently presenting in the flesh. They engaged in massive speculation as to who really wrote Shakespeare's plays, whether or not Napoleon actually died on St. Helena, who were the first Europeans to set foot on North America, and if the books of Charles Fort indicated that Earth had been visited by an intelligent race unknown to them—and so on. High caste Vegan society just eats up our medieval theological debates, too. Funny.

"About your book, Srin Shtigo . . ." I interrupted.

My use of the honorific stopped him.

"Yes?" he answered.

"My impression," said I, "is that you do not wish to discuss it at any length at this time. I respect this feeling, of course, but it places me in a slightly awkward position as head of this tour." We both knew I should have asked him in private, especially after his reply to Phil at the reception, but I was feeling cantankerous and wanted to let him know it, as well as to rechannel the talk. So, "I'm curious," I said, "whether it will be primarily a travelogue of the places we visit, or if you would like assistance in directing your attention to special local conditions of any sort—say, political, or current cultural items."

"I am primarily interested in writing a descriptive travel-book," he said, "but I will appreciate your comments as we go along. I thought that was your job, anyway. As it is, I do have a general awareness of Earth traditions and current affairs, and I'm not very much concerned with them."

Dos Santos, who was pacing and smoking as our meal was being prepared, stopped in mid-stride and said, "Srin Shtigo, what are your feelings toward the Returnist movement? Are you sympathetic with our aims? Or do you consider it a dead issue?"

"Yes," he replied, "to the latter. I believe that when one is dead one's only obligation then is to satisfy the consumer. I respect your aims, but I do not see how you can possibly hope to realize them. Why should your people give up the security they now possess to return to this place? Most of the members of the present generation have never even seen the Earth, except on tapes—and you must admit that they are hardly the most encouraging documents."

"I disagree with you," said Dos Santos, "and I find your attitude dreadfully patrician."

"That is as it should be," replied Myshtigo.

George and the food arrived at about the same time. The waiters began serving the food.

"I should prefer to eat at a small table by myself," Dos Santos instructed a waiter.

"You are here because you asked to be here," I mentioned.

He stopped in mid-flight and cast a furtive look at Red Wig, who happened to be sitting at my right hand. I thought I detected an almost imperceptible movement of her head, first to the left, then to the right.

Dos Santos composed his features around a small smile and bowed slightly.

"Forgive my Latin temperament," he observed. "I should hardly expect to convert anyone to Returnism in five minutes—and it has always been difficult for me to conceal my feelings."

"That is somewhat obvious."

"I'm hungry," I said.

He seated himself across from us, next to George.

"Behold the Sphinx," said Red Wig, gesturing toward an etching on the far wall, "whose speech alternates between long periods of silence and an occasional riddle. Old as time. Highly respected. Doubtless senile. She keeps her mouth shut and waits. For what? Who knows? —Does your taste in art run to the monolithic, Srin Shtigo?"

"Occasionally," he observed, from my left.

Dos Santos glanced once, quickly, over his shoulder, then back at Diane. He said nothing.

I asked Red Wig to pass me the salt and she did. I really wanted to dump it on her, to make her stay put so that I could study her at my leisure, but I used it on the potatoes instead.

Behold the Sphinx, indeed!

High sun, short shadows, hot—that's how it was. I didn't want any sand-cars or Skimmers spoiling the scene, so I made everybody hike it. It wasn't that far, and I took a slightly roundabout way in order to achieve the calculated effect.

We walked a crooked mile, climbing some, dipping some. I confiscated George's butterfly net so as to prevent any annoying pauses as we passed by the several clover fields which lay along our route.

Walking backward through time, that's how it was—with bright birds flashing by (*clare! clare!*), and a couple camels appearing against the far horizon whenever we topped a small rise. (Camel outlines, really, done up in charcoal; but that's enough. Who cares about a camel's expressions? Not even other camels —not really. Sickening beasts. . . .) A short, swarthy woman trudged past us with a tall jar on her head. Myshtigo remarked on this fact to his pocket secretary. I nodded to the woman and spoke a greeting. The woman returned the greeting but did not nod back, naturally. Ellen, moist already, kept fanning herself with a big green feather triangle; Red Wig walked tall, tiny beads of perspiration seasoning her upper lip, eyes hidden behind sunshades which had darkened themselves as much as they could. Finally, we were there. We climbed the last, low hill.

"Behold," said Rameses.

"*¡Madre de Dios!*" said Dos Santos.

Hasan grunted.

Red Wig turned toward me quickly, then turned away. I couldn't read her expression because of the shades. Ellen kept fanning herself.

"What are they doing?" asked Myshtigo. It was the first time I had seen him genuinely surprised.

"Why, they're dismantling the great pyramid of Cheops," I said.

After a time Red Wig asked it.

"Why?" she asked.

"Well now," I told her, "they're kind of short on building materials hereabouts, the stuff from Old Cairo being radioactive —so they're obtaining it by knocking apart that old piece of solid geometry out there."

"They are desecrating a monument to the past glories of the human race!" she exclaimed.

"Nothing is cheaper than past glories," I observed. "It's the present that we're concerned with, and they need building materials now."

"For how long has this been going on?" asked Myshtigo, his words rushing together.

"It was three days ago," said Rameses, "that we began the dismantling."

"What gives you the right to do a thing like that?"

"It was authorized by the Earthoffice Department of Arts, Monuments and Archives, Srin."

Myshtigo turned to me, his amber eyes glowing strangely.

"You!" he said.

"I," I acknowledged, "am Commissioner thereof—that is correct."

"Why has no one else heard of this action of yours?"

"Because very few people come here anymore," I explained. "—Which is another good reason for dismantling the thing. It doesn't even get looked at much these days. I do have the authority to authorize such actions."

"I came here from another world to see it!"

"Well, take a quick look, then," I told him. "It's going away fast."

He turned and stared.

"You obviously have no conception of its intrinsic value. Or, if you do . . ."

"On the contrary, I know exactly what it's worth."

". . . And those unfortunate creatures you have working down there"—his voice rose as he studied the scene—"under the hot rays of your ugly sun—they're laboring under the most primitive conditions! Haven't you ever heard of moving machinery?"

"Of course. It's expensive."

"And your foremen are carrying whips! How can you treat your own people that way? It's perverse!"

"All those men volunteered for the job, at token salaries— and Actors' Equity won't let us use the whips, even though the men argued in favor of it. All we're allowed to do is crack them in the air near them."

"Actors' Equity?"

"Their union. —Want to see some machinery?" I gestured. "Look up on that hill."

He did.

"What's going on there?"

"We're recording it on viewtape."

"To what end?"

"When we're finished we're going to edit it down to viewable length and run it backwards. 'The Building of the Great Pyramid,' we're going to call it. Should be good for some laughs—also money. Your historians have been conjecturing as to exactly how we put it together ever since the day they heard about it. This may make them somewhat happier. I decided a B.F.M.I. operation would go over best."

"B.F.M.I.?"

"Brute Force and Massive Ignorance. Look at them hamming it up, will you?—following the camera, lying down and standing up quickly when it swings in their direction. They'll be collapsing all over the place in the finished product. But then, this is the first Earthfilm in years. They're real excited."

Dos Santos regarded Red Wig's bared teeth and the bunched muscles beneath her eyes. He glared at the pyramid.

"You are a madman!" he announced.

"No," I replied. "The absence of a monument can, in its own way, be something of a monument also."

"A non-monument to Conrad Nomikos," he stated.

"No," said Red Wig then. "There is destructive art as surely as there is creative art. I think he may be attempting such a thing. He is playing Caligula. Perhaps I can even see why."

"Thank you."

"You are not welcome. I said 'perhaps'. —An artist does it with love."

"Love is a negative form of hatred."

"'I am dying, Egypt, dying,'" said Ellen.

Myshtigo laughed.

"You are tougher than I thought, Nomikos," he observed. "But you are not indispensable."

"Try having a civil servant fired—especially me."

"It might be easier than you think."

"We'll see."

"We may."

We turned again toward the great 90 percent pyramid of Cheops/Khufu. Myshtigo began taking notes once more.

"I'd rather you viewed it from here, for now," I said. "Our presence would waste valuable footage. We're anachronisms. We can go down during coffee break."

"I agree," said Myshtigo, "and I am certain I know an anachronism when I see one. But I have seen all that I care to here. Let us go back to the inn. I wish to talk with the locals."

After a moment, "I'll see Sakkara ahead of schedule, then," he mused. "You haven't begun dismantling all the monuments of Luxor, Karnak, and the Valley of Kings yet, have you?"

"Not yet, no."

"Good. Then we'll visit them ahead of time."

"Then let's not stand here," said Ellen. "This heat is beastly." So we returned.

"Do you really mean everything you say?" asked Diane as we walked back.

"In my fashion."

"How do you think of such things?"

"In Greek, of course. Then I translate them into English. I'm real good at it."

"Who are you?"

"Ozymandias. Look on my works ye mighty and despair."

"I'm not mighty."

"I wonder. . . ." I said, and I left the part of her face that I could see wearing a rather funny expression as we walked along.

"Let me tell you of the boadile," said I.

Our felucca moved slowly along that dazzling waterpath that burns its way before the great gray colonnades of Luxor. Myshtigo's back was to me. He was staring at those columns, dictating an occasional impression.

"Where will we put ashore?" he asked me.

"About a mile further up ahead. Perhaps I had better tell you about the boadile."

"I know what a boadile is. I told you that I had studied your world."

"Uh-huh. Reading about them is one thing . . ."

"I have also *seen* boadiles. There are four in the Earth-garden on Taler."

". . . and seeing them in a tank is another thing."

"Between yourself and Hasan we are a veritable floating arsenal. I count three grenades on your belt, four on his."

"You can't use a grenade if one is on top of you—not without defeating the purposes of self-defense, that is. If it's any further away you can't hit it with one. They move too fast."

He finally turned.

"What *do* you use?"

I reached inside my galabieh (having gone native) and withdrew the weapon I always try to have on hand when I come this way.

He examined it.

"Name it."

"It's a machine-pistol. Fires meta-cyanide slugs—one ton impact when a round strikes. Not real accurate, but that's not necessary. It's patterned after a twentieth century handgun called a Schmeisser."

"It's rather unwieldy. Will it stop a boadile?"

"If you're lucky. I have a couple more in one of the cases. Want one?"

"No, thank you." He paused. "But you can tell me more about the boadile. I really only glanced at them that day, and they were pretty well submerged."

"Well . . . Head something like a croc's, only bigger. Around forty feet long. Able to roll itself into a big beach-ball with teeth. Fast on land or in water—and a hell of a lot of little legs on each side—"

"How many legs?" he interrupted.

"Hm." I stopped. "To tell you the absolute truth, I've never counted. Just a second.

"Hey, George," I called out, to where Earth's eminent chief biologist lay dozing in the shade of the sail. "How many legs on a boadile?"

"Huh?" His head turned.

"I said, 'How many legs on a boadile?'"

He rose to his feet, stretched slightly and came up beside us.

"Boadiles," he mused, poking a finger into his ear and leafing through the files inside. "They're definitely of the class reptilia—of that much we're certain. Whether they're of the order crocodilia, suborder of their own, or whether they're of the order squamata, suborder lacertilia, family neopoda—as a colleague of mine on Taler half-seriously insists—we are not certain. To me they are somewhat reminiscent of pre-Three Day photo-reproductions of artists' conceptions of the Mesozoic phytosaurus with, of course, the supernumerary legs and the constrictive ability. So I favor the order crocodilia myself."

He leaned on the rail and stared out across the shimmering water.

I saw then that he wasn't about to say anything else, so, "So how many legs on one?" I asked again.

"Eh? Legs? I never counted them. If we're lucky we might get a chance to, though. There are lots around here. —The young one I had didn't last too long."

"What happened to it?" asked Myshtigo.

"My megadonaplaty ate it."

"Megadonaplaty?"

"Sort of like a duck-billed platypus with teeth," I explained, "and about ten feet high. Picture that. So far as we know, they've only been seen about three or four times. Australian. We got ours through a fortunate accident. Probably won't last, as a species—the way boadiles will, I mean. They're oviparous mammals, and their eggs are too large for a hungry world to permit the continuance of the species—if it is a true species. Maybe they're just isolated sports."

"Perhaps," said George, nodding wisely; "and then again perhaps not."

Myshtigo turned away, shaking his head.

Hasan had partly unpacked his robot golem—Rolem—and was fooling with its controls. Ellen had finally given up on simicoloring and was lying in the sun getting burnt all over. Red Wig and Dos Santos were plotting something at the other end of the vessel. Those two never just meet; they always have assignations. Our felucca moved slowly along the dazzling waterpath that burns its way before the great gray colonnades of Luxor, and I decided it was time to head it in toward the shore and see what was new among the tombs and ruined temples.

The next six days were rather eventful and somewhat unforgettable, extremely active, and sort of ugly-beautiful—in the way that a flower can be, with its petals all intact and a dark and runny rot-spot in the center. Here's how. . . .

Myshtigo must have interviewed every stone ram along the four miles of the Way to Karnak. Both in the blaze of day and by torchlight we navigated the ruins, disturbing bats, rats, snakes and insects, listening to the Vegan's monotonous note-taking in his monotonous language. At night we camped on the sands, setting up a two hundred meter electrical warning perimeter and posting two guards. The boadile is cold-blooded; the nights were chill. So there was relatively little danger from without.

Huge campfires lighted the nights, all about the areas we chose, because the Vegan wanted things primitive—for purposes of atmosphere, I guessed. Our Skimmers were further south. We had flown them to a place I knew of and left them there under Office guard, renting the felucca for our trip—which paralleled the King-God's journey from Karnak to Luxor. Myshtigo had wanted it that way. Nights, Hasan would either practice with the *assagai* he had bartered from a big Nubian, or he would strip to the waist and wrestle for hours with his tireless golem.

A worthy opponent was the golem. Hasan had it programmed at twice the statistically-averaged strength of a man and had upped its reflex-time by fifty percent. Its "memory" contained hundreds of wrestling holds, and its governor theoretically prevented it from killing or maiming its opponent—all through a series of chemelectrical afferent nerve-analogues which permitted it to gauge to an ounce the amount of pressure necessary to snap a bone or tear a tendon. Rolem was about five feet, six inches in height and weighed around two hundred fifty pounds; manufactured on Bakab, he was quite expensive, was dough-colored and caricature-featured, and his brains were located somewhere below where his navel would be—if golems had navels—to protect his thinkstuff from Greco-Roman shocks. Even as it is, accidents can happen. People have been killed by the things, when something goes amok in the brains of some of the afferents, or just because the people themselves slipped or tried to jerk away, supplying the necessary extra ounces. I'd had one once, for almost a year, programmed for boxing. I used to spend fifteen minutes or so with it every afternoon. Got to thinking of it as a person, almost. Then one day it fouled me and I pounded it for over an hour and finally knocked its head off. The thing kept right on boxing, and I stopped thinking of it as a friendly sparring partner right then. It's a weird feeling, boxing with a headless golem, you know? Sort of like waking from a pleasant dream and finding a nightmare crouched at the foot of your bed. It doesn't really "see" its opponent with those eye-things it has; it's all sheathed about with piezoelectric radar mesentery, and it "watches" from all its surfaces. Still, the death of an illusion tends to disconcert. I turned mine off and never turned it back on again. Sold it to a camel trader for a pretty good price. Don't know if he ever got the head back on. But he was a Turk, so who cares?

Anyway—Hasan would tangle with Rolem, both of them gleaming in the firelight, and we'd all sit on blankets and watch, and bats would swoop low occasionally, like big, fast ashes, and emaciated clouds would cover the moon, veil-like, and then move on again. It was that way on that third night, when I went mad.

I remember it only in the way you remember a passing countryside you might have seen through a late summer evening storm—as a series of isolated, lightning-filled still-shots. . . .

Having spoken with Cassandra for the better part of an hour, I concluded the transmission with a promise to cop a Skimmer the following afternoon and spend the next night on Kos. I recall our last words.

"Take care, Konstantin. I have been dreaming bad dreams."

"Bosh, Cassandra. Good night."

And who knows but that her dreams might have been the result of a temporal shockwave moving backwards from a 9.6 Richter reading?

A certain cruel gleam filling his eyes, Dos Santos applauded as Hasan hurled Rolem to the ground with a thunderous crash. That particular earthshaker continued, however, long after the golem had climbed back to his feet and gotten into another crouch, his arms doing serpent-things in the Arab's direction. The ground shook and shook.

"What power! Still do I feel it!" cried Dos Santos. "Olé!"

"It is a seismic disturbance," said George. "Even though I'm not a geologist—"

"Earthquake!" yelled his wife, dropping an unpasteurized date she had been feeding Myshtigo.

There was no reason to run, no place to run to. There was nothing nearby that could fall on us. The ground was level and pretty barren. So we just sat there and were thrown about, even knocked flat a few times. The fires did amazing things.

Rolem's time was up and he went stiff then, and Hasan came and sat with George and me. The tremors lasted the better part of an hour, and they came again, more weakly, many times during that night. After the first bad shock had run its course, we got in touch with the Port. The instruments there showed that the center of the thing lay a good distance to the north of us.

A bad distance, really.

. . . In the Mediterranean.

The Aegean, to be more specific.

I felt sick, and suddenly I was.

I tried to put through a call to Kos.

Nothing.

My Cassandra, my lovely lady, my princess. . . . Where was she? For two hours I tried to find out. Then the Port called me.

It was Lorel's voice, not just some lob watch operator's.

"Uh—Conrad, I don't know how to tell you, exactly, what happened . . ."

"Just talk," I said, "and stop when you're finished."

"An observe-satellite passed your way about twelve minutes ago," he crackled across the bands. "Several of the Aegean islands were no longer present in the pictures it transmitted . . ."

"No," I said.

"I'm afraid that Kos was one of them."

"No," I said.

"I'm sorry," he told me, "but that is the way it shows. I don't know what else to say. . . ."

"That's enough," I said. "That's all. That's it. Goodbye. We'll talk more later. No! I guess— No!"

"Wait! Conrad!"

I went mad.

Bats, shaken loose from the night, were swooping about me. I struck out with my right hand and killed one as it flashed in my direction. I waited a few seconds and killed another. Then I picked up a big rock with both hands and was about to smash the radio when George laid a hand on my shoulder, and I dropped the rock and knocked his hand away and backhanded him across the mouth. I don't know what became of him then, but as I stooped to raise the rock once more I heard the sound of footfalls behind me. I dropped to one knee and pivoted on it, scooping up a handful of sand to throw in someone's eyes. They were all of them there: Myshtigo and Red Wig and Dos Santos, Rameses, Ellen, three local civil servants, and Hasan—approaching in a group. Someone yelled "Scatter!" when they saw my face, and they fanned out.

Then they were everyone I'd ever hated—I could feel it. I saw other faces, heard other voices. Everyone I'd ever known, hated, wanted to smash, had smashed, stood there resurrected before the fire, and only the whites of their teeth were showing through the shadows that crossed over their faces as they smiled and came toward me, bearing various dooms in their hands, and soft, persuasive words on their lips—so I threw the sand at the foremost and rushed him.

My uppercut knocked him over backward, then two Egyptians were on me from both sides.

I shook them loose, and in the corner of my colder eye saw a great Arab with something like a black avocado in his hand. He was swinging it toward my head, so I dropped down. He had been coming in my direction and I managed to give his stomach more than just a shove, so he sat down suddenly. Then the two men I had thrown away were back on me again. A woman was screaming, somewhere in the distance, but I couldn't see any women.

I tore my right arm free and batted someone with it, and

the man went down and another took his place. From straight ahead a blue man threw a rock which struck me on the shoulder and only made me madder. I raised a kicking body into the air and threw it against another, then I hit someone with my fist. I shook myself. My galabieh was torn and dirty, so I tore it the rest of the way off and threw it away.

I looked around. They had stopped coming at me, and it wasn't fair—it wasn't fair that they should stop then when I wanted so badly to see things breaking. So I raised up the man at my feet and slapped him down again. Then I raised him up again and someone yelled "Eh! Karaghiosis!" and began calling me names in broken Greek. I let the man fall back to the ground and turned.

There, before the fire—there were two of them: one tall and bearded, the other squat and heavy and hairless and molded out of a mixture of putty and earth.

"My friend says he will break you, Greek!" called out the tall one, as he did something to the other's back.

I moved toward them and the man of putty and mud sprang at me.

He tripped me, but I came up again fast and caught him beneath the armpits and threw him off to the side. But he recovered his footing as rapidly as I had, and he came back again and caught me behind the neck with one hand. I did the same to him, also seizing his elbow—and we locked together there, and he was strong.

Because he was strong, I kept changing holds, testing his strength. He was also fast, accommodating every move I made almost as soon as I thought of it.

I threw my arms up between his, hard, and stepped back on my reinforced leg. Freed for a moment, we orbited each other, seeking another opening.

I kept my arms low and I was bent well forward because of his shortness. For a moment my arms were too near my sides, and he moved in faster than I had seen anyone move before, ever, and he caught me in a body lock that squeezed the big flat flowers of moisture out of my pores and caused a great pain in my sides.

Still his arms tightened, and I knew that it would not be long before he broke me unless I could break his hold.

I doubled my hands into fists and got them against his belly and pushed. His grip tightened. I stepped backward and heaved forward with both arms. My hands went up higher between us and I got my right fist against the palm of my left hand and began to push them together and lift with my arms. My head swam as my arms came up higher, and my kidneys were on fire. Then I tightened all the muscles in my back and my shoulders and felt the strength flow down through my arms and come together in my hands, and I smashed them up toward the sky and his chin happened to be in the way, but it didn't stop them.

My arms shot up over my head and he fell backward.

It should have broken a man's neck, the force of that big snap that came when my hands struck his chin and he got a look at his heels from the backside.

But he sprang up immediately, and I knew then that he was no mortal wrestler, but one of those creatures born not of woman; rather, I knew, he had been torn Antaeus-like from the womb of the Earth herself.

I brought my hands down hard on his shoulders and he dropped to his knees. I caught him across the throat then and stepped to his right side and got my left knee under the lower part of his back. I leaned forward, bearing down on his thighs and shoulders, trying to break him.

But I couldn't. He just kept bending until his head touched the ground and I couldn't push him any further.

No one's back bends like that and doesn't snap, but his did.

Then I heaved up with my knee and let go, and he was on me again—that fast.

So I tried to strangle him. My arms were much longer than his. I caught him by the throat with both hands, my thumbs pressing against what should have been his windpipe. He got his arms across mine though, at the elbows and inside, and began to pull downward and out. I kept squeezing, waiting for his face to darken, his eyes to bug out. My elbows began to bend under his downward pressure.

Then his arms came across and caught me by the throat.

And we stood there and choked one another. Only he wouldn't be strangled.

His thumbs were like two spikes pressing into the muscles in my neck. I felt my face flush. My temples began to throb.

Off in the distance, I heard a scream:

"Stop it, Hasan! It's not supposed to do that!"

It sounded like Red Wig's voice. Anyhow, that's the name that came into my head: Red Wig. Which meant that Donald Dos Santos was somewhere nearby. And she had said "Hasan," a name written on another picture that came suddenly clear.

Which meant that I was Conrad and that I was in Egypt, and that the expressionless face swimming before me was therefore that of the golem-wrestler, Rolem, a creature which could be set for five times the strength of a human being and probably was so set, a creature which could be given the reflexes of an adrenalized cat, and doubtless had them in full operation.

Only a golem wasn't supposed to kill, except by accident, and Rolem was trying to kill me.

Which meant that his governor wasn't functioning.

I released my choke, seeing that it wasn't working, and I placed the palm of my left hand beneath his right elbow. Then I reached across the top of his arms and seized his right wrist with my other hand, and I crouched as low as I could and pushed up on his elbow and pulled up on his wrist.

As he went off balance to his left and the grip was broken I kept hold of the wrist, twisting it so that the elbow was exposed upwards. I stiffened my left hand, snapped it up beside my ear, and brought it down across the elbow joint.

Nothing. There was no snapping sound. The arm just gave way, bending backward at an unnatural angle.

I released the wrist and he fell to one knee. Then he stood again, quickly, and as he did so the arm straightened itself and then bent forward again into a normal position.

If I knew Hasan's mind, then Rolem's timer had been set for maximum—two hours. Which was a pretty long time, all things considered.

But this time around I knew who I was and what I was doing. Also, I knew what went into the structuring of a golem. This one was a wrestling golem. Therefore, it could not box.

I cast a quick look back over my shoulder, to the place where I had been standing when the whole thing had started—over by the radio tent. It was about fifty feet away.

He almost had me then. Just during that split second while I had turned my attention to the rear he had reached out and seized me behind the neck with one hand and caught me beneath the chin with the other.

He might have broken my neck, had he been able to follow through, but there came another temblor at that moment—a severe one, which cast us both to the ground—and I broke this hold, also.

I scrambled to my feet seconds later, and the earth was still shaking. Rolem was up too, though, and facing me again.

We were like two drunken sailors fighting on a storm-tossed ship. . . .

He came at me and I gave ground.

I hit him with a left jab, and while he snatched at my arm I punched him in the stomach. Then I backed off.

He came on again and I kept throwing punches. Boxing was to him what the fourth dimension is to me—he just couldn't see it. He kept advancing, shaking off my punches, and I kept retreating in the direction of the radio tent, and the ground kept shaking, and somewhere a woman was screaming, and I heard a shouted "Olé!" as I landed a right below the belt, hoping to jar his brains a bit.

Then we were there and I saw what I wanted—the big rock I'd intended to use on the radio. I feinted with my left, then seized him, shoulder-and-thigh, and raised him high up over my head.

I bent backward, tightened up my muscles, and hurled him down upon the rock.

It caught him in the stomach.

He began to rise again, but more slowly than he had before, and I kicked him in the stomach, three times, with my great reinforced right boot, and I watched him sink back down.

A strange whirring sound had begun in his midsection.

The ground shook again. Rolem crumpled, stretched out, and the only sign of motion was in the fingers of his left hand. They kept clenching and unclenching—reminding me, oddly, of Hasan's hands that night back at the *hounfor*.

Then I turned slowly and they were all standing there: Myshtigo and Ellen, and Dos Santos with a puffed-up cheek,

Red Wig, George, Rameses and Hasan, and the three plastaged Egyptians. I took a step toward them then and they began to fan out again, their faces filling with fear. But I shook my head.

"No, I'm all right now," I said, "but leave me alone. I'm going down to the river to bathe." I took seven steps, and then someone must have pulled out the plug, because I gurgled, everything swirled, and the world ran away down the drain.

The days that followed were ashes and the nights were iron. The spirit that had been torn from my soul was buried deeper than any mummy that lay mouldering beneath those sands. It is said that the dead forget the dead in the house of Hades, Cassandra, but I hoped it was not so. I went through the motions of conducting a tour, and Lorel suggested that I appoint someone else to finish it out and take a leave of absence myself.

I couldn't.

What would I do then? Sit and brood in some Old Place, cadging drinks from unwary travelers? No. Some kind of motion is always essential at such times; its forms eventually generate a content for their empty insides. So I went on with the tour and turned my attention to the small mysteries it contained.

I took Rolem apart and studied his governor. It *had* been broken, of course—which meant that either I had done it during the early stages of our conflict, or Hasan had done it as he had souped him up to take the fight out of me. If Hasan had done it, then he did not just want me beaten, but dead. If such was the case, then the question was, *Why?* I wondered whether his employer knew that I had once been Karaghiosis. If he did, though, why should he want to kill the founder and first Secretary of his own Party?—the man who had sworn that he would not see the Earth sold out from under him and turned into a sporting house by a pack of blue aliens—not see it without fighting, anyhow—and had organized about himself a cabal which systematically lowered the value of all Vegan-owned Terran property to zero, and even went so far as to raze the Talerites' lush realty office on Madagascar—the man whose ideals he allegedly espoused, though they were currently being channeled into more peaceful, legalistic modes of property-defense—why should he want *that* man dead?

Therefore, he had either sold out the Party, or he didn't know who I was and had had some other end in mind when he'd instructed Hasan to kill me.

Or else Hasan was acting under someone else's orders.

But who else could there be? And again, why?

I had no answer. I decided I wanted one.

The first condolence had been George's.

"I'm sorry, Conrad," he'd said, looking past my elbow, and then down at the sand, and then glancing up quickly into my face.

Saying human things upset him, and made him want to go away. I could tell. It is doubtful that the parade consisting of Ellen and myself, which had passed that previous summer, had occupied much of his attention. His passions stopped outside the biological laboratory. I remember when he'd dissected the last dog on Earth. After four years of scratching his ears and combing the fleas from his tail and listening to him bark, George had called Rolf to him one day. Rolf had trotted in, bringing along the old dishrag they'd always played at tug-of-war with, and George had tugged him real close and given him a hypo and then opened him up. He'd wanted to get him while he was still in his prime. Still has the skeleton mounted in his lab. He'd also wanted to raise his kids—Mark and Dorothy and Jim—in Skinner Boxes, but Ellen had put her foot down each time (like *bang! bang! bang!*) in post-pregnancy seizures of motherhood which had lasted for at least a month—which had been just long enough to spoil the initial stimuli-balances George had wanted to establish. So I couldn't really see him as having much desire to take my measure for a wooden sleeping bag of the underground sort. If he'd wanted me dead, it would probably have been subtle, fast, and exotic—with something like Divban rabbit-venom. But no, he didn't care that much. I was sure.

Ellen herself, while she is capable of intense feelings, is ever the faulty windup doll. Something always goes *sprong* before she can take action on her feelings, and by the next day she feels as strongly about something else. She'd choked me to death back at the Port, and as far as she was concerned that affair was a dead issue. Her condolence went something like this:

"Conrad, you just don't know how sorry I am! *Really.* Even though I never met her, I *know* how you must feel," and her voice went up and down the scale, and I knew she believed what she was saying, and I thanked her too.

Hasan, though, came up beside me while I was standing there, staring out over the suddenly swollen and muddy Nile. We stood together for a time and then he said, "Your woman is gone and your heart is heavy. Words will not lighten the weight, and what is written is written. But let it also be put down that I grieve with you." Then we stood there awhile longer and he walked away.

I didn't wonder about him. He was the one person who could be dismissed, even though his hand had set the machine in motion. He never held grudges; he never killed for free. He had no personal motive to kill me. That his condolences were genuine, I was certain. Killing me would have nothing to do with the sincerity of his feelings in a matter like this. A true professional must respect some sort of boundary between self and task.

Myshtigo said no words of sympathy. It would have been alien to his nature. Among the Vegans, death is a time of rejoicing. On the spiritual level it means *sagl*—completion—the fragmentation of the psyche into little pleasure-sensing pinpricks, which are scattered all over the place to participate in the great universal orgasm; and on the material plane it is represented by *ansakundabad't*—the ceremonial auditing of most of the deceased's personal possessions, the reading of his distribution-desire and the division of his wealth, accompanied by much feasting, singing, and drinking.

Dos Santos said to me: "It is a sad thing that has happened to you, my friend. It is to lose the blood of one's own veins to lose one's woman. Your sorrow is great and you cannot be comforted. It is like a smoldering fire that will not die out, and it is a sad and terrible thing.

"Death is cruel and it is dark," he finished, and his eyes were moist—for be it Gypsy, Jew, Moor, or what have you, a victim is a victim to a Spaniard, a thing to be appreciated on one of those mystically obscure levels which I lack.

Then Red Wig came up beside me and said, "Dreadful. . . . Sorry. Nothing else to say, to do, but sorry."

I nodded.

"Thanks."

"And there is something I must ask you. Not now, though. Later."

"Sure," I said, and I returned to watching the river after they left, and I thought about those last two. They had sounded as sorry as everyone else, but it seemed they had to be mixed up in the golem business, somehow. I was sure, though, that it had been Diane who had screamed while Rolem had been choking me, screamed for Hasan to stop him. That left Don, and I had by then come to entertain strong doubts that he ever did anything without first consulting her.

Which left nobody.

And there was no real motive apparent. . . .

And it could all have been an accident. . . .

But . . .

But I had this feeling that someone wanted to kill me. I knew that Hasan was not above taking two jobs at the same time, and for different employers, if there was no conflict of interests.

And this made me happy.

It gave me a purpose, something to do.

There's really nothing quite like someone's wanting you dead to make you want to go on living. I would find him, find out why, and stop him.

Death's second pass was fast, and as much as I would have liked to have pinned it on a human agent, I couldn't. It was just one of those diddles of dumb destiny which sometimes come like uninvited guests at dinnertime. Its finale, however, left me quite puzzled and gave me some new, confusing thoughts to think.

It came like this. . . .

Down by the river, that great fertile flooder, that eraser of boundaries and father of plane geometry, sat the Vegan, making sketches of the opposite bank. I suppose had he been on *that* bank he would have been sketching the one he sat upon, but this is cynical conjecture. What bothered me was the fact that he had come off alone, down to this warm, marshy spot, had not told anyone where he was going, and had brought along nothing more lethal than a No. 2 pencil.

It happened.

An old, mottled log which had been drifting in near the shore suddenly ceased being an old, mottled log. A long, serpentine back end whipped skyward, a bushel full of teeth appeared at the other end, and lots of little legs found solid ground and started acting like wheels.

I yelled and snatched at my belt.

Myshtigo dropped his pad and bolted.

It was on him, though, and I couldn't fire then.

So I made a dash, but by the time I got there it had two coils around him and he was about two shades bluer, and those teeth were closing in on him.

Now, there is one way to make any kind of constrictor loosen up, at least for a moment. I grabbed for its high head, which had slowed down just a bit as it contemplated its breakfast, and I managed to catch my fingers under the scaley ridges at the sides of that head.

I dug my thumbs into its eyes as hard as I could.

Then a spastic giant hit me with a graygreen whip.

I picked myself up and I was about ten feet from where I had been standing. Myshtigo had been thrown further up the bank. He was recovering his feet just as it attacked again.

Only it attacked me, not him.

It reared up about eight feet off the ground and toppled toward me. I threw myself to the side and that big, flat head missed me by inches, its impact showering me with dirt and pebbles.

I rolled further and started to rise, but the tail came around and knocked me down again. Then I scrambled backward, but was too late to avoid the coil it threw. It caught me low around the hips and I fell again.

Then a pair of blue arms wrapped themselves around the body above the coil, but they couldn't hold on for more than a few seconds. Then we were both tied up in knots.

I struggled, but how do you fight a thick, slippery armored cable with messes of little legs that keep tearing at you? My right arm was pinned to my side by then, and I couldn't reach far enough with my left hand to do any more gouging. The coils tightened. The head moved toward me and I tore at the body. I beat at it and I clawed it, and I finally managed to tear my right arm free, giving up some skin in the process.

I blocked with my right hand as the head descended. My

hand came up beneath its lower jaw, caught it, and held it there, keeping the head back. The big coil tightened around my waist, more powerful than even the grip of the golem had been. Then it shook its head sidewards, away from my hand, and the head came down and the jaws opened wide.

Myshtigo's struggles must have irritated it and slowed it some, giving me time for my last defense.

I thrust my hands up into its mouth and held its jaws apart.

The roof of its mouth was slimy and my palm began to slip along it, slowly. I pressed down harder on the lower jaw, as hard as I could. The mouth opened another half foot and seemed locked there.

It tried to draw back then, to make me let go, but its coils bound us too tightly to give it the necessary footage.

So it unwound a little, straightening some, and pulling back its head. I gained a kneeling position. Myshtigo was in a sagging crouch about six feet away from me.

My right hand slipped some more, almost to the point where I would lose all my leverage.

Then I heard a great cry.

The shudder came almost simultaneously. I snapped my arms free as I felt the thing's strength wane for a second. There was a dreadful clicking of teeth and a final constriction. I blacked out for a moment.

Then I was fighting free, untangling myself. The smooth wooden shaft which had skewered the boadile was taking the life from it, and its movements suddenly became spasmodic rather than aggressive.

I was knocked down twice by all its lashing about, but I got Myshtigo free, and we got about fifty feet away and watched it die. This took quite awhile.

Hasan stood there, expressionless. The *assagai* he had spent so much time practicing with had done its work. When George dissected the creature later we learned that the shaft had lodged within two inches of its heart, severing the big artery. By the way, it had two dozen legs, evenly distributed on either side, as might be expected.

Dos Santos stood beside Hasan and Diane stood beside Dos Santos. Everyone else from the camp was there, too.

"Good show," I said. "Fine shot. Thanks."

"It was nothing," Hasan replied.

*

It was nothing, he had said. Nothing but the death blow to my notion that he had gimmicked the golem. If Hasan had tried to kill me then, why should he have saved me from the boadile?

Unless what he had said back at the Port was the overriding truth—that he *had* been hired to protect the Vegan. If that was his main job and killing me was only secondary, then he would have had to save me as a by-product of keeping Myshtigo alive.

But then . . .

Oh hell. Forget it.

I threw a stone as far as I could, and another. Our Skimmers would be flown up to our campsite the following day and we would take off for Athens, stopping only to drop Rameses and the three others at New Cairo. I was glad I was leaving Egypt, with its must and its dust and its dead, half-animal deities. I was already sick of the place.

Then Phil's call came through from the Port, and Rameses called me into the radio tent.

"Yeah?" said I, to the radio.

"Conrad, this is Phil. I've just written her elegy and I should like to read it to you. Even though I never met her, I've heard you speak of her and I've seen her picture, so I think I've done a pretty good job—"

"Please, Phil. I'm not interested in the consolations of poetry right now. Some other time, perhaps—"

"This is not one of the fill-in sort. I know that you do not like those, and in a way I do not blame you."

My hand hovered above the cutoff toggle, paused, reached for one of Rameses' cigarettes instead.

"Sure, go ahead. I'm listening."

And he did, and it wasn't a bad job, either. I don't remember much of it. I just remember those crisp, clear words coming from halfway around the world, and me standing there, bruised inside and out, hearing them. He described the virtues of the Nymph whom Poseidon had reached for but lost to his brother Hades. He called for a general mourning among the elements. And as he spoke my mind went time-traveling back to those two happy months on Kos, and everything since then was erased; and we were back aboard the *Vanitie*, sailing toward our picnic islet with its semi-sacred grove, and we were bathing together, and lying together in the sun, holding hands and not saying anything, just feeling the sunfall, like a waterfall bright and dry and gentle, come down upon our pink and naked spirits, there on the endless beach that circled and circled the tiny realm and always came back to us.

And he was finished and cleared his throat a couple times, and my isle sank from sight, carrying that one part of me along with it, because that was the time that was.

"Thanks, Phil," I said. "That was very nice."

"I am pleased that you find it appropriate," he said. Then, "I am flying to Athens this afternoon. I should like to join you on this leg of your tour, if it is all right with you."

"Surely," I replied. "May I ask why, though?"

"I have decided that I want to see Greece once more. Since you are going to be there it might make it seem a little more like the old days. I'd like to take a last look at some of the Old Places."

"You make it sound rather final."

"Well . . . I've pushed the S-S series about as far as it will go. I fancy I can feel the mainspring running down now. Maybe it will take a few more windings and maybe it won't. At any rate, I want to see Greece again and I feel as if this is my last chance."

"I'm sure you're wrong, but we'll all be dining at the Garden Altar tomorrow evening, around eight."

"Fine. I'll see you then."

"Check."

"Goodbye, Conrad."

"Goodbye."

I went and showered and rubbed me with liniment, and I put on clean clothing. I was still sore in several places, but at least I felt clean. Then I went and found the Vegan, who had just finished doing the same thing, and I fixed him with my baleful glare.

"Correct me if I'm wrong," I stated, "but one of the reasons you wanted me to run this show is because I have a high survival potential. Is that correct?"

"That is correct."

"Thus far, I have done my best to see that it did not remain potential, but that it was actively employed to promote the general welfare."

"Was that what you were doing when you attacked the entire group single-handed?"

I started to reach for his throat, thought better of it, dropped my hand. I was rewarded by a flicker of fear that widened his eyes and twitched the corners of his mouth. He took a step backward.

"I'll overlook that," I told him. "I am here only to take you where you want to go, and to see that you come back with a whole skin. You caused me a small problem this morning by making yourself available as boadile bait. Be warned, therefore, that one does not go to hell to light a cigarette. When you wish to go off by yourself, check first to see whether you are in safe country." His gaze faltered. He looked away. "If you are not," I continued, "then take along an armed escort —since you refuse to carry weapons yourself. That is all I have to say. If you do not wish to cooperate, tell me now and I'll quit and get you another guide. Lorel has already suggested I do this, anyhow.

"So what's the word?" I asked.

"Did Lorel really say that?"

"Yes."

"How extraordinary. . . . Well, certainly, yes, I shall comply with your request. I see that it is a prudent one."

"Great. You said you wanted to visit the Valley of Queens again this afternoon. Rameses will take you. I don't feel like doing it myself. We're pulling out tomorrow morning at ten. Be ready."

I walked away then, waiting for him to say something—just one word even.

He didn't.

Fortunately, both for the survivors and for the generations as yet unborn, Scotland had not been hard hit during the Three Days. I fetched a bucket of ice from the freeze-unit and a bottle of soda from our mess tent. I turned on the cooling coil beside my bunk, opened a fifth from out of my private stock, and spent the rest of the afternoon reflecting upon the futility of all human endeavor.

*

Late that evening, after I had sobered up to an acceptable
point and scrounged me a bite to eat, I armed myself and went
looking for some fresh air.

I heard voices as I neared the eastern end of the warning
perimeter, so I sat down in darkness, resting my back against a
largish rock, and tried to eavesdrop. I'd recognized the vibrant
diminuendoes of Myshtigo's voice, and I wanted to hear what
he was saying.

I couldn't, though.

They were a little too far away, and desert acoustics are not
always the finest in the world. I sat there straining with that
part of me which listens, and it happened as it sometimes does:

I was seated on a blanket beside Ellen and my arm was
around her shoulders. My blue arm. . . .

The whole thing faded as I recoiled from the notion of being
a Vegan, even in a pseudotelepathic wish-fulfillment, and I was
back beside my rock once again.

I was lonesome, though, and Ellen had seemed softer than
the rock, and I was still curious.

So I found myself back there once more, observing. . . .

". . . can't see it from here," I was saying, "but Vega is a
star of the first magnitude, located in what your people call the
constellation Lyra."

"What's it like on Taler?" asked Ellen.

There was a long pause. Then:

"Meaningful things are often the things people are least able
to describe. Sometimes, though, it is a problem in communi-
cating something for which there is no corresponding element
in the person to whom you are speaking. Taler is not like this
place. There are no deserts. The entire world is landscaped.
But . . . Let me take that flower from your hair. There. Look
at it. What do you see?"

"A pretty white flower. That's why I picked it and put it in
my hair."

"But it is *not* a pretty white flower. Not to me, anyhow.
Your eyes perceive light with wavelengths between about
4000 and 7200 angstrom units. The eyes of a Vegan look
deeper into the ultraviolet, for one thing, down to around
3000. We are blind to what you refer to as 'red,' but on this
'white' flower I see two colors for which there are no words

in your language. My body is covered with patterns you cannot see, but they are close enough to those of the others in my family so that another Vegan, familiar with the Shtigogens, could tell my family and province on our first meeting. Some of our paintings look garish to Earth eyes, or even seem to be all of one color—blue, usually—because the subtleties are invisible to them. Much of our music would seem to you to contain big gaps of silence, gaps which are actually filled with melody. Our cities are clean and logically disposed. They catch the light of day and hold it long into the night. They are places of slow movement, pleasant sounds. This means much to me, but I do not know how to describe it to a—human."

"But people—Earth people, I mean—live on your worlds. . . ."

"But they do not really see them or hear them or feel them the way we do. There is a gulf we can appreciate and understand, but we cannot really cross it. That is why I cannot tell you what Taler is like. It would be a different world to you than the world it is to me."

"I'd like to see it, though. Very much. I think I'd even like to live there."

"I do not believe you would be happy there."

"Why not?"

"Because non-Vegan immigrants are non-Vegan immigrants. You are not of a low caste here. I know you do not use that term, but that is what it amounts to. Your Office personnel and their families are the highest caste on this planet. Wealthy non-Office persons come next, then those who work for the wealthy non-Office persons, followed by those who make their own living from the land; then, at the bottom, are those unfortunates who inhabit the Old Places. You are at the top here. On Taler you would be at the bottom."

"Why must it be that way?" she asked.

"Because you see a white flower." I handed it back.

There was a long silence and a cool breeze.

"Anyhow, I'm happy you came here," she said.

"It *is* an interesting place."

"Glad you like it."

"Was the man called Conrad really your lover?"

I recoiled at the suddenness of the question.

"It's none of your blue business," she said, "but the answer is yes."

"I can see why," he/I said, and I felt uncomfortable and maybe something like a voyeur, or—subtlety of subtleties—one who watches a voyeur watching.

"Why?" she asked.

"Because you want the strange, the powerful, the exotic; because you are never happy being where you are, what you are."

"That's not true. . . . Maybe it is. Yes, he once said something like that to me. Perhaps it is true."

I felt very sorry for her at that moment. Then, without realizing it, as I wanted to console her in some way, I reached out and took her hand. Only it was Myshtigo's hand that moved, and he had not willed it to move. I had.

I was afraid suddenly. So was he, though. I could feel it.

There was a great drunk-like, room-swimming feeling, as I felt that he felt *occupied*, as if he had sensed another presence within his mind.

I wanted away quickly then, and I was back there beside my rock, but not before she'd dropped the flower and I heard her say, "Hold me!"

Damn those pseudotelepathic wish-fulfillments! I thought. *Someday I'll stop believing that that's all they are.*

I *had* seen two colors in that flower, colors for which I have no words. . . .

I walked back toward the camp. I passed through the camp and kept on going. I reached the other end of the warning perimeter, sat down on the ground, lit a cigarette. The night was cool, the night was dark.

Two cigarettes later I heard a voice behind me, but I did not turn.

"'In the Great House and in the House of Fire, on that Great Day when all the days and years are numbered, oh let my name be given back to me,'" it said.

"Good for you," I said softly. "Appropriate quote. I recognize the Book of the Dead when I hear it taken in vain."

"I wasn't taking it in vain, just—as you said—appropriately."

"Good for you."

"*On* that great day when all the days and years are numbered, if they do give you back your name, then what name will it be?"

"They won't. I plan on being late. And what's in a name, anyhow?"

"Depends on the name. So try 'Karaghiosis.'"

"Try sitting down where I can see you. I don't like to have people standing behind me."

"All right—there. So?"

"So what?"

"So try 'Karaghiosis.'"

"Why should I?"

"Because it means something. At least, it did once."

"Karaghiosis was a figure in the old Greek shadow shows, sort of like Punch in the European Punch and Judy plays. He was a slob and a buffoon."

"He was Greek, and he was subtle."

"Ha! He was half-coward, and he was greasy."

"He was also half-hero. Cunning. Somewhat gross. Sense of humor. *He'd* tear down a pyramid. Also, he was strong, when he wanted to be."

"Where is he now?"

"I'd like to know."

"Why ask me?"

"Because that is the name Hasan called you on the night you fought the golem."

"Oh . . . I see. Well, it was just an expletive, a generic term, a synonym for fool, a nickname—like if I were to call you 'Red.' —And now that I think of it, I wonder how you look to Myshtigo, anyhow? Vegans are blind to the color of your hair, you know?"

"I don't really care how I look to Vegans. Wonder how you look, though. I understand that Myshtigo's file on you is quite thick. Says something about you being several centuries old."

"Doubtless an exaggeration. But you seem to know a lot about it. How thick is your file on Myshtigo?"

"Not very, not yet."

"It seems that you hate him more than you hate everyone else. Is that true?"

"Yes."

"Why?"

"He's a Vegan."

"So?"

"I hate Vegans, is all."

"No, there's more."

"True. —You're quite strong, you know?"

"I know."

"In fact, you're the strongest human being I've ever seen. Strong enough to break the neck of a spiderbat, then fall into the bay at Piraeus and swim ashore and have breakfast."

"Odd example you've chosen."

"Not so, not really. *Did* you?"

"Why?"

"I want to know, need to know."

"Sorry."

"Sorry is not good enough. Talk more."

"Said all."

"No. We need Karaghiosis."

"Who's 'we'?"

"The Radpol. Me."

"Why, again?"

"Hasan is half as old as Time. Karaghiosis is older. Hasan knew him, remembered, called you 'Karaghiosis.' You *are* Karaghiosis, the killer, the defender of Earth—and we need you now. Very badly. Armageddon has come—not with a bang, but a checkbook. The Vegan must die. There is no alternative. Help us stop him."

"What do you want of me?"

"Let Hasan destroy him."

"No."

"Why not? What is he to you?"

"Nothing, really. In fact, I dislike him very much. But what is he to *you*?"

"Our destroyer."

"Then tell me why, and how, and perhaps I'll give you a better answer."

"I can't."

"Why not?"

"Because I don't know."

"Then good night. That's all."

"Wait! I really do not know—but the word has come down from Taler, from the Radpol liaison there: He must die. His book is not a book, his self is not a self, but many. I do not know what this means, but our agents have never lied before. You've lived on Taler, you've lived on Bakab and a dozen other worlds. You are Karaghiosis. You know that our agents do not lie, because you are Karaghiosis and you established the spy-circuit yourself. Now you hear their words and you do not heed them. I tell you that they say he must die. He represents the end of everything we've fought for. They say he is a sur-veyor who must not be permitted to survey. You know the code. Money against Earth. More Vegan exploitation. They could not specify beyond that point."

"I'm sorry. I've pledged myself to his defense. Give me a better reason and maybe I'll give you a better answer. —And Hasan tried to kill me."

"He was told only to stop you, to incapacitate you so that we could destroy the Vegan."

"Not good enough; not good enough, no. I admit nothing. Go your ways. I will forget."

"No, you must help us. What is the life of one Vegan to Karaghiosis?"

"I will not countenance his destruction without a just and specific cause. Thus far, you have shown me nothing."

"That's all I have."

"Then good night."

"No. You have two profiles. From the right side you are a demigod; from the left you are a demon. One of them will help us, must help us. I don't care which one it is."

"Do not try to harm the Vegan. We will protect him."

We sat there. She took one of my cigarettes and we sat there smoking.

". . . Hate you," she said after a time. "It should be easy, but I can't."

I said nothing.

"I've seen you many times, swaggering in your Dress Blacks, drinking rum like water, confident of something you never share, arrogant in your strength. —You'd fight your weight in anything that moves, wouldn't you?"

"Not red ants or bumblebees."

"Do you have some master plan of which we know nothing? Tell us, and we will help you with it."

"It is your idea that I am Karaghiosis. I've explained why Hasan called me by that name. Phil knew Karaghiosis and you know Phil. Has he ever said anything about it?"

"You know he hasn't. He is your friend and he would not betray your confidence."

"Is there any other indication of identity than Hasan's random name-calling?"

"There is no recorded description of Karaghiosis. You were quite thorough."

"All right then. Go away and don't bother me."

"Don't. Please."

"Hasan tried to kill me."

"Yes; he must have thought it easier to kill you than to try keeping you out of the way. After all, he knows more about you than we do."

"Then why did he save me from the boadile today, along with Myshtigo?"

"I'd rather not say."

"Then forget it."

"No, I will tell you. —The *assagai* was the only thing handy. He is not yet proficient with it. He was not aiming to hit the boadile."

"Oh."

"But he was not aiming at you, either. The beast was writhing too much. He wanted to kill the Vegan, and he would simply have said that he had tried to save you both, by the only means at hand—and that there had been a terrible accident. Unfortunately, there was no terrible accident. He missed his target."

"Why did he not just let the boadile kill him?"

"Because you had already gotten your hands upon the beast. He feared you might still save him. He fears your hands."

"That's nice to know. Will he continue trying, even if I refuse to cooperate?"

"I'm afraid so."

"That is very unfortunate, my dear, because I will not permit it."

"You will not stop him. Neither will we call him off. Even

though you are Karaghiosis, and hurt, and my sorrow for you overflows the horizons, Hasan will not be stopped by you or by me. He *is* Hasan the Assassin. He has never failed."

"Neither have I."

"Yes you have. You have just failed the Radpol and the Earth, and everything that means anything."

"I keep my own counsel, woman. Go your ways."

"I can't."

"Why is that?"

"If you don't know, then Karaghiosis is indeed the fool, the buffoon, the figure in a shadow play."

"A man named Thomas Carlyle once wrote of heroes and hero-worship. He too was a fool. He believed there were such creatures. Heroism is only a matter of circumstance and expediency."

"Ideals occasionally enter into the picture."

"What is an ideal? A ghost of a ghost, that's all."

"Do not say these things to me, please."

"I must—they are true."

"You lie, Karaghiosis."

"I do not—or if I do, it is for the better, girl."

"I am old enough to be anyone's grandmother but yours, so do not call me 'girl.' Do you know that my hair is a wig?"

"Yes."

"Do you know that I once contracted a Vegan disease—and that that is why I must wear a wig?"

"No. I am very sorry. I did not know."

"When I was young, long ago, I worked at a Vegan resort. I was a pleasure girl. I have never forgotten the puffing of their horrid lungs against my body, nor the touch of their corpse-colored flesh. I hate them, Karaghiosis, in ways that only one such as you could understand—one who has hated all the great hates."

"I am sorry, Diane. I am so sorry that it hurts you still. But I am not yet ready to move. Do not push me."

"You *are* Karaghiosis?"

"Yes."

"Then I am satisfied—somewhat."

"But the Vegan *will* live."

"We shall see."

"Yes, we shall. Good night."

"Good night, Conrad."

And I rose, and I left her there, and I returned to my tent. Later that night she came to me. There was a rustling of the tent flap and the bedclothes, and she was there. And when I have forgotten everything else about her—the redness of her wig and the little upside-down "v" between her eyes, and the tightness of her jaws, and her clipped talk, and all her little mannerisms of gesture, and her body warm as the heart of a star, and her strange indictment of the man I once might have been, I will remember this—that she came to me when I needed her, that she was warm, soft, and that she came to me. . . .

After breakfast the following morning I was going to seek Myshtigo, but he found me first. I was down by the river, talking with the men who would be taking charge of the felucca.

"Conrad," he said softly, "may I speak with you?"

I nodded and gestured toward a gully.

"Let's walk up this way. I've finished here."

We walked.

After a minute he said, "You know that on my world there are several systems of mental discipline, systems which occasionally produce extrasensory abilities. . . ."

"So I've heard," I said.

"Most Vegans, at sometime or other, are exposed to it. Some have an aptitude along these lines. Many do not. Just about all of us, though, possess a feeling for it, a recognition of its operations."

"Yes?"

"I am not telepathic myself, but I am aware that you possess this ability because you used it on me last night. I could feel it. It is quite uncommon among your people, so I had not anticipated this and I had taken no precautions to prevent it. Also, you hit me at the perfect moment. As a result, my mind was opened to you. I have to know how much you learned."

So there apparently had been something extrasensory connected with those sight-vision overlays. All they usually contained were what seemed the immediate perceptions of the subject, plus a peek at the thoughts and feelings that went into the words he made—and sometimes I got them wrong. Myshtigo's question indicated that he did not know how far mine went, and I had heard that some professional Veggy psyche-stirrers could even elbow their way into the unconscious. So I decided to bluff.

"I gather that you are not writing a simple travel book," I said.

He said nothing.

"Unfortunately, I am not the only one who is aware of this," I continued, "which places you in a bit of danger."

"Why?" he asked suddenly.

"Perhaps they misunderstand," I ventured.

He shook his head.

"Who are they?"

"Sorry."

"But I need to know."

"Sorry again. If you want out, I can get you back to the Port today."

"No, I can't do that. I must go on. What am I to do?"

"Tell me a little more about it, and I'll make suggestions."

"No, you know too much already. . . ."

"Then that must be the real reason Donald Dos Santos is here," he said quickly. "He is a moderate. The activist wing of the Radpol must have learned something of this and, as you say—misunderstood. He must know of the danger. Perhaps I should go to him . . ."

"No," I said quickly, "I don't think you should. It really wouldn't change anything. What would you tell him, anyhow?"

A pause. Then, "I see what you mean," he said. "The thought has also occurred to me that he might not be as moderate as I have believed. . . . If that is the case, then—"

"Yeah," I said. "Want to go back?"

"I can't."

"Okay then, blue boy, you're going to have to trust *me*. You can start by telling me more about this survey—"

"No! I do not know how much you know and how much you do not know. It is obvious that you are trying to elicit more information, so I do not think you know very much. What I am doing is still confidential."

"I am trying to protect you," I said, "therefore I want as much information as I can get."

"Then protect my body and let me worry about my motives and my thoughts. My mind will be closed to you in the future, so you needn't waste your time trying to probe it."

I handed him an automatic.

"I suggest you carry a weapon for the duration of the tour —to protect your motives."

"Very well."

It vanished beneath his fluttering shirt.

Puff-puff-puff, went the Vegan.

Damn-damn-damn, went my thoughtstrings.

"Go get ready," I said. "We'll be leaving soon."

As I walked back toward the camp, via another route, I analyzed my own motives. A book, alone, could not make or break the Earth, the Radpol, Returnism. Even Phil's *Call of Earth* had not done that, not really. But this thing of Myshtigo's was to be more than just a book. A survey? —What could it be? A push in what direction? I did not know and I had to know. For Myshtigo could not be permitted to live if it would destroy us —and yet, I could not permit his destruction if the thing might be of any help at all. And it might.

Therefore, someone had to call time-out until we could be sure.

The leash had been tugged. I followed.

"Diane," said I, as we stood in the shade of her Skimmer, "you say that I mean something to you, as me, as Karaghiosis."

"That would seem to follow."

"Then hear me. I believe that you *may* be wrong about the Vegan. I am not sure, but if you are wrong it would be a very big mistake to kill him. For this reason, I cannot permit it. Hold off on anything you've planned until we reach Athens. Then request a clarification of that message from the Radpol."

She stared me in both eyes, then said, "All right."

"Then what of Hasan?"

"He waits."

"He makes his own choice as to time and place, does he not? He awaits only the opportunity to strike."

"Yes."

"Then he must be told to hold off until we know for sure."

"Very well."

"You will tell him?"

"He will be told."

"Good enough."

I turned away.

"And when the message comes back," she said, "if it should say the same thing as before—what then?"

"We'll see," I said, not turning.

I left her there beside her Skimmer and returned to my own.

When the message did come back, saying what I thought it would say, I knew that I would have more trouble on my hands. This was because I had already made my decision.

Far to the south and east of us, parts of Madagascar still deafened the geigs with radioactive pain-cries—a tribute to the skill of one of us.

Hasan, I felt certain, could still face any barrier without blinking those sun-drenched, death-accustomed, yellow eyes. . . .

He might be hard to stop.

It. Down below.

Death, heat, mud-streaked tides, new shorelines. . . .

Vulcanism on Chios, Samos, Ikaria, Naxos. . . .

Halicarnassos bitten away. . . .

The western end of Kos visible again, but so what?

. . . Death, heat, mud-streaked tides.

New shorelines. . . .

I had brought my whole convoy out of its way in order to check the scene. Myshtigo took notes, also photos.

Lorel had said, "Continue on with the tour. Damage to property has not been too severe, because the Mediterranean was mostly full of junkstuff. Personal injuries were either fatal or are already being taken care of. —So continue on."

I skimmed in low over what remained of Kos—the westward tail of the island. It was a wild, volcanic country, and there were fresh craters, fuming ones, amidst the new, bright sea-laces that crisscrossed over the land. The ancient capital of Astypalaia had once stood there. Thucydides tells us it had been destroyed by a powerful earthquake. He should have seen this one. My northern city of Kos had then been inhabited from 366 B.C. Now all was gone but the wet and the hot. There were no survivors—and the plane tree of Hippocrates and the mosque of the Loggia and the castle of the Knights of Rhodes, and the fountains, and my cottage, and my wife—swept by what tides or caught in what sea-pits, I do not know—had gone the ways of dead Theocritus—he who had done his best to immortalize the place so many years before. Gone. Away. Far. . . . Immortal and dead to me. Further east, a few peaks of that high mountain range which had interrupted the northern coastal plain were still poking themselves up out of the waters. There was the mighty peak of Dhikaios, or Christ the Just, which had overlooked the villages of the northern slopes. Now it was a tiny islet, and no one had made it up to the top in time.

It must have been like this, that time so many years ago, when the sea near my homeland, bounded by the Chalcidic peninsula, had risen up and assaulted the land; in that time when the waters of the inland sea had forced them an outlet through the gorge of Tempe, the mighty convulsions of the thing scoring even the mountain walls of the home of the gods itself, Olympus; and those it spared were only Mr. and Mrs. Deukalion, kept afloat by the gods for purposes of making a myth and some people to tell it to.

"You lived there," said Myshtigo.

I nodded.

"You were born in the village of Makrynitsa, though, in the hills of Thessaly?"

"Yes."

"But you made your home there?"

"For a little while."

"'Home' is a universal concept," said he. "I appreciate it."

"Thanks."

I continued to stare downward, feeling sad, bad, mad, and then nothing.

Athens after absence returns to me with a sudden familiarity which always refreshes, often renews, sometimes incites. Phil once read me some lines by one of the last great Greek poets, George Seferis, maintaining that he had referred to my Greece when he said, ". . . A country that is no longer our own country, nor yours either"—because of the Vegans. When I pointed out that there were no Vegans available during Seferis' lifetime, Phil retorted that poetry exists independent of time and space and that it means whatever it means to the reader. While I have never believed that a literary license is also good for time-travel, I had other reasons for disagreeing, for not reading it as a general statement.

It *is* our country. The Goths, the Huns, the Bulgars, the Serbs, the Franks, the Turks, and lately the Vegans have never made it go away from us. People, I have outlived. Athens and I have changed together, somewhat. Mainland Greece, though, is mainland Greece, and it does not change for me. Try taking it away, whatever you are, and my klephtes will stalk the hills, like the chthonic avengers of old. You will pass, but the hills of Greece will remain, will be unchanged, with the smell of goat thigh-bones burning, with a mingling of blood and wine, a taste of sweetened almonds, a cold wind by night, and skies as bluebright as the eyes of a god by day. Touch them, if you dare.

That is why I am refreshed whenever I return, because now that I am a man with many years behind me, I feel this way about the entire Earth. That is why I fought, and why I killed and bombed, and why I tried every legal trick in the book, too, to stop the Vegans from buying up the Earth, plot by plot, from the absentia government, there on Taler. That is why I pushed my way, under another new name, into the big civil service machine that runs this planet—and why Arts, Monuments and Archives, in particular. There, I could fight to preserve what still remained, while I waited for the next development.

The Radpol vendetta had frightened the expatriates as well as the Vegans. They did not realize that the descendants of those who had lived through the Three Days would not willingly relinquish their best areas of coastline for Vegan resorts, nor yield up their sons and daughters to work in those resorts; nor would they guide the Vegans through the ruins of their cities, indicating points of interest for their amusement. That is why the Office is mainly a foreign service post for most of its staff.

We had sent out the call of return to those descendants of the Martian and Titanian colonies, and there had been no return. They had grown soft out there, soft from leeching on a culture which had had a headstart on ours. They lost their identity. They abandoned us.

Yet, they were the Earthgov, *de jure*, legally elected by the absent majority—and maybe *de facto* too, if it ever came to that. Probably so. I hoped it wouldn't come to that.

For over half a century there had been a stalemate. No new Veggy resorts, no new Radpol violence. No Return, either. Soon there would be a new development. It was in the air—if Myshtigo was really surveying.

So I came back to Athens on a bleak day, during a cold, drizzling rainfall, an Athens rocked and rearranged by the recent upheavals of Earth, and there was a question in my head and bruises on my body, but I was refreshed. The National Museum still stood there between Tossitsa and Vasileos Irakliou, the Acropolis was even more ruined than I remembered, and the Garden Altar Inn—formerly the old Royal Palace—there at the northwest corner of the National Gardens, across from Syndagma Square, had been shaken but was standing and open for business, despite.

We entered, and checked in.

As Commissioner of Arts, Monuments and Archives, I received special considerations. I got The Suite: Number 19.

It wasn't exactly the way I'd left it. It was clean and neat.

The little metal plate on the door said:

This suite was the headquarters of Konstantin Karaghiosis during the founding of the Radpol and much of the Returnist Rebellion.

Inside, there was a plaque on the bedstead which read:

Konstantin Karaghiosis slept in this bed.

In the long, narrow front room I spotted one on the far wall. It said:

The stain on this wall was caused by a bottle of beverage, hurled across the room by Konstantin Karaghiosis, in celebration of the bombing of Madagascar.

Believe that, if you want to.

Konstantin Karaghiosis sat in this chair, insisted another.

I was really afraid to go into the bathroom.

*

Later that night, as I walked the wet and rubble-strewn pavements of my almost deserted city, my old memories and my current thoughts were like the coming together of two rivers. I'd left the others snoring inside, descended the wide stairway from the Altar, paused to read one of the inscriptions from Perikles' funeral oration—"The entire Earth is the tomb of great men"—there on the side of the Memorial to the Unknown Soldier, and I studied for a moment those great-thewed limbs of that archaic warrior, laid out with all his weapons on his funeral bed, all marble and bas-relief, yet somehow almost warm, because night becomes Athens—and then I walked on by, passing up Leoforos Amalias.

It had been a fine dinner: ouzo, giuvetsi, Kokkineli, yaourti, Metaxa, lots of dark coffee, and Phil arguing with George about evolution.

"Do you not see a convergence of life and myth, here, during the last days of life on this planet?"

"What do you mean?" asked George, polishing off a mess of narantzi and adjusting his glasses for peering.

"I mean that as humanity rose out of darkness it brought with it legends and myths and memories of fabulous creatures. Now we are descending again into that same darkness. The Life Force grows weak and unstable, and there is a reversion to those primal forms which for so long existed only as dim racial memories—"

"Nonsense, Phil. Life Force? In what century do you make your home? You speak as though all of life were one single, sentient entity."

"It is."

"Demonstrate, please."

"You have the skeletons of three satyrs in your museum, and photographs of live ones. They live in the hills of this country.

"Centaurs, too, have been seen here—and there are vampire flowers, and horses with vestigial wings. There are sea serpents in every sea. Imported spiderbats plow our skies. There are even sworn statements by persons who have seen the Black Beast of Thessaly, an eater of men, bones and all—and all sorts of other legends are coming alive."

George sighed.

"What you have said so far proves nothing other than that in all of infinity there is a possibility for any sort of life form to put in an appearance, given the proper precipitating factors and a continuous congenial environment. The things you have mentioned which are native to Earth are mutations, creatures originating near various Hot Spots about the world. There is one such place up in the hills of Thessaly. If the Black Beast were to crash through that door at this moment, with a satyr mounted on its back, it would not alter my opinion, nor prove yours."

I'd looked at the door at that moment, hoping not for the Black Beast, but for some inconspicuous-looking old man who might sidle by, stumble, and pass on, or for a waiter bringing Diane an unordered drink with a note folded inside the napkin.

But none of these things happened. As I passed up Leoforos Amalias, by Hadrian's Gate, and past the Olympieion, I still did not know what the word was to be. Diane had contacted the Radpol, but there had been no response as yet. Within another thirty-six hours we would be skimming from Athens to Lamia, then onward by foot through areas of strange new trees with long, pale, red-veined leaves, hanging vines, and things that brachiate up above, and all the budding places of the *strige-fleur* down among their roots; and then on, across sun-washed plains, up twisty goat trails, through high, rocky places, and down deep ravines, past ruined monasteries. It was a crazy notion, but Myshtigo, again, had wanted it that way. Just because I'd been born there, he thought he'd be safe. I'd tried to tell him of the wild beasts, of the cannibal Kouretes—the tribesmen who wandered there. But he wanted to be like Pausanius and see it all on foot. Okay then, I decided, if the Radpol didn't get him, then the fauna would.

But, just to be safe, I had gone to the nearest Earthgov Post Office, obtained a dueling permit, and paid my death-tax. I might as well be on the up-and-up about these things, I decided, me being a Commissioner and all.

If Hasan needed killing, I'd kill him legally.

I heard the sound of a bouzouki coming from a small cafe on the other side of the street. Partly because I wanted to, and partly because I had a feeling that I was being followed, I crossed over and entered the place. I moved to a small table where I could keep my back to the wall and my eyes on the door, ordered Turkish coffee, ordered a package of cigarettes, listened to the songs of death, exile, disaster, and the eternal faithlessness of women and men.

It was even smaller inside than it had seemed from the street —low ceiling, dirt floor, real dark. The singer was a squat woman, wearing a yellow dress and much mascara. There was a rattling of glasses; a steady fall of dust descended through the dim air; the sawdust was damp underfoot. My table was set at the near end of the bar. There were maybe a dozen other people spotted about the place: three sleepy-eyed girls sat drinking at the bar, and a man wearing a dirty fez, and a man resting his head on an outstretched arm, and snoring; four men were laughing at a table diagonally across from me; a few others, solitary, were drinking coffee, listening, watching nothing in particular, waiting, or maybe not waiting, for something or someone to happen.

Nothing did, though. So after my third cup of coffee I paid the fat, moustached owner his tab, and left the place.

Outside, the temperature seemed to have dropped several degrees. The street was deserted, and quite dark. I turned right into Leoforos Dionysiou Areopagitou and moved on until I reached the battered fence that runs along the southern slope of the Acropolis.

I heard a footfall, way back behind me, at the corner. I stood there for half a minute, but there was only silence and very black night. Shrugging, I entered the gate and moved to the tenemos of Dionysius Eleutherios. Nothing remains of the temple itself but the foundation. I passed on, heading toward the Theater.

Phil, then, had suggested that history moved in great cycles, like big clock hands passing the same numbers day after day.

"Historical biology proves you wrong," said George.

"I didn't mean *literally*," replied Phil.

"Then we ought to agree on the language we are speaking before we talk any further."

Myshtigo had laughed.

Ellen touched Dos Santos' arm and asked him about the poor horses the picadores rode. He had shrugged, poured her more Kokkineli, drank his own.

"It is a part of the thing," he'd said.

And no message, no message. . . .

I walked on through the mess time makes of greatness. A frightened bird leapt up on my right, uttered a frightened cry, was gone. I kept walking, wandered into the old Theater at last, moved downward through it. . . .

Diane was not so amused as I had thought she would be by the stupid plaques that decorated my suite.

"But they belong here. Of course. They do."

"Ha!"

"At one time it would have been the heads of animals you had slain. Or the shields of your vanquished enemies. We're civilized now. This is the new way."

"Ha! again." I changed the subject. "Any word on the Vegan?"

"No."

"You want *his* head."

"I'm not civilized. —Tell me, was Phil always such a fool, back in the old days?"

"No, he wasn't. Isn't now, either. His was the curse of a half-talent. Now he is considered the last of the Romantic poets, and he's gone to seed. He pushes his mysticism into nonsense because, like Wordsworth, he has outlived his day. He lives now in distortions of a pretty good past.

"Like Byron, he once swam the Hellespont, but now, rather like Yeats, the only thing he really enjoys is the company of young ladies whom he can bore with his philosophy, or occasionally charm with a well-told reminiscence. He is old. His writing occasionally shows flashes of its former power, but it was not just his writing that was his whole style."

"How so?"

"Well, I remember one cloudy day when he stood in the Theater of Dionysius and read a hymn to Pan which he had written. There was an audience of two or three hundred—and only the gods know why they showed up—but he began to read.

"His Greek wasn't very good yet, but his voice was quite impressive, his whole manner rather charismatic. After a time, it began to rain, lightly, but no one left. Near the end there was a peal of thunder, sounding awfully like laughter, and a sudden shudder ran through the crowd. I'm not saying that it was like that in the days of Thespis, but a lot of those people were looking over their shoulders as they left.

"I was very impressed also. Then, several days later, I read the poem—and it was nothing, it was doggerel, it was trite. It was the way he did it that was important. He lost that part of his power along with his youth, and what remained of what might be called art was not strong enough to make him great, to keep alive his personal legend. He resents this, and he consoles himself with obscure philosophy, but in answer to your question—no, he was not always such a fool."

"Perhaps even some of his philosophy is correct."

"What do you mean?"

"The Big Cycles. The age of strange beasts *is* come upon us again. Also, the age of heroes, demigods."

"I've only met the strange beasts."

"'Karaghiosis slept in this bed,' it says here. Looks comfortable."

"It is. —See?"

"Yes. Do I get to keep the plaque?"

"If you want. . . ."

I moved to the proskenion. The relief sculpture-work started at the steps, telling tales from the life of Dionysius. Every tour guide and every member of a tour must, under a regulation promulgated by me, ". . . carry no fewer than three magnesium flares on his person, while traveling." I pulled the pin from one and cast it to the ground. The dazzle would not be visible below, because of the angle of the hillside and the blocking masonry.

I did not stare into the bright flame, but above, at the silver-limned figures. There was Hermes, presenting the infant god to Zeus, while the Corybantes tripped the Pyrrhic fantastic on either side of the throne; then there was Ikaros, whom Dionysius had taught to cultivate the vine—he was preparing to sacrifice a goat, while his daughter was offering cakes to the god (who stood aside, discussing her with a satyr); and there was drunken Silenus, attempting to hold up the sky like Atlas, only not doing so well; and there were all the other gods of the cities, paying a call to this Theater—and I spotted Hestia, Theseus, and Eirene with a horn of plenty. . . .

"You burn an offering to the gods," came a statement from nearby.

I did not turn. It had come from behind my right shoulder, but I did not turn because I knew the voice.

"Perhaps I do," I said.

"It has been a long time since you walked this land, this Greece."

"That is true."

"Is it because there has never been an immortal Penelope —patient as the mountains, trusting in the return of her kallikanzaros—weaving, patient as the hills?"

"Are you the village story-teller these days?"

He chuckled.

"I tend the many-legged sheep in the high places, where the fingers of Aurora come first to smear the sky with roses."

"Yes, you're the story-teller. Why are you not up in the high places now, corrupting youth with your song?"

"Because of dreams."

"Dreams?"

"Aye."

I turned and looked into the ancient face—its wrinkles, in the light of the dying flare, as black as fishers' nets lost at the bottom of the sea, the beard as white as the snow that comes drifting down from the mountains, the eyes matching the blue of the headcloth corded about his temples. He did not lean upon his staff any more than a warrior leans on his spear. I knew that he was over a century old, and that he had never taken the S-S series.

"A short time ago did I dream that I stood in the midst of a black temple," he told me, "and Lord Hades came and stood by my side, and he gripped my wrist and bade me go with him. But I said 'Nay' and I awakened. This did trouble me."

"What did you eat that night? Berries from the Hot Place?"

"Do not laugh, please. —Then, of a later night, did I dream that I stood in a land of sand and darkness. The strength of the old champions was upon me, and I did battle with Antaeus, son of the Earth, destroying him. Then did Lord Hades come to me again, and taking me by the arm did say, 'Come with me now.' But again did I deny him, and I awakened. The Earth was a-tremble."

"That's all?"

"No. Then, more recent still, and not at night, but as I sat beneath a tree watching my flock, did I dream a dream while awake. Phoebus-like did I battle the monster Python, and was almost destroyed thereby. This time Lord Hades did not come, but when I turned about there stood Hermes, his lackey, smiling and pointing his caduceus like a rifle in my direction. I shook my head and he lowered it. Then he raised it once more in a gesture, and I looked where he had indicated.

"There before me lay Athens—this place, this Theater, you —and here sat the old women. The one who measures out the thread of life was pouting, for she had wrapped yours about the horizon and no ends were in sight. But the one who weaves had divided it into two very thin threads. One strand ran back across the seas and vanished again from sight. The other led up into the hills. At the first hill stood the Dead Man, who held your thread in his white, white hands. Beyond him, at the next hill, it lay across a burning rock. On the hill beyond the rock stood the Black Beast, and he shook and worried your thread with his teeth.

"And all along the length of the strand stalked a great foreign warrior, and yellow were his eyes and naked the blade in his hands, and he did raise this blade several times in menace.

"So I came down to Athens—to meet you, here, at this place —to tell you to go back across the seas—to warn you not to come up into the hills where death awaits you. For I knew, when Hermes raised his wand, that the dreams were not mine, but that they were meant for you, oh my father, and that I must find you here and warn you. Go away now, while still you can. Go back. Please."

I gripped his shoulder.

"Jason, my son, I do not turn back. I take full responsibility for my own actions, right or wrong—including my own death, if need be—and I *must* go into the hills this time, up near the Hot Place. Thank you for your warning. Our family has always had this thing with dreams, and often it is misleading. I, too, have dreams—dreams in which I see through the eyes of other persons—sometimes clearly, sometimes not so clearly. Thank you for your warning. I am sorry that I must not heed it."

"Then I will return to my flock."

"Come back with me to the inn. We will fly you as far as Lamia tomorrow."

"No. I do not sleep in great buildings, nor do I fly."

"Then it's probably time you started, but I'll humor you. We can camp here tonight. I'm Commissioner of this monument."

"I had heard you were important in the Big Government again. Will there be more killing?"

"I hope not."

We found a level place and reclined upon his cloak.

"How do you interpret the dreams?" I asked him.

"Your gifts do come to us with every season, but when was the last time you yourself visited?"

"It was about nineteen years ago," I said.

"Then you do not know of the Dead Man?"

"No."

"He is bigger than most men—taller, fatter—with flesh the color of a fishbelly, and teeth like an animal's. They began telling of him about fifteen years ago. He comes out only at night. He drinks blood. He laughs a child's laugh as he goes about the countryside looking for blood—people's, animals', it does not matter. He smiles in through bedroom windows late at night. He burns churches. He curdles milk. He causes miscarriages from fright. By day, it is said that he sleeps in a coffin, guarded by the Kourete tribesmen."

"Sounds as bad as a kallikanzaros."

"He really exists, father. Some time ago, something had been killing my sheep. Whatever it was had partly eaten them and drunk much of their blood. So I dug me a hiding place and covered it over with branches. That night I watched. After many hours he came, and I was too afraid to put a stone to my sling—for he is as I have described him: big, bigger than you even, and gross, and colored like a fresh-dug corpse. He broke the sheep's neck with his hands and drank the blood from its throat. I wept to see it, but I was afraid to do anything. The next day I moved my flock and was not troubled again. I use the story to frighten my great-grandchildren—your great-great-grandchildren—whenever they misbehave. —And he is waiting, up in the hills."

"Mm, yes. . . . If you say you saw it, it must be true. And strange things do come out of the Hot Places. *We* know that."

". . . Where Prometheus spilled too much of the fire of creation."

"No, where some bastard lobbed a cobalt bomb and the bright-eyed boys and girls cried 'Eloi' to the fallout. —And what of the Black Beast?"

"He too, is real, I am certain. I have never seen him, though. The size of an elephant, and very fast—an eater of flesh, they say. He haunts the plains. Perhaps some day he and the Dead Man will meet and they will destroy one another."

"It doesn't usually work out that way, but it's a nice thought. —That's all you know about him?"

"Yes, I know of no one who has caught more than a glimpse."

"Well, I shall try for less than that."

". . . And then I must tell you of Bortan."

"Bortan? That name is familiar."

"Your dog. I used to ride on his back when I was a child and beat with my legs upon his great armored sides. Then he would growl and seize my foot, but gently."

"*My* Bortan has been dead for so long that he would not even chew upon his own bones, were he to dig them up in a modern incarnation."

"I had thought so, too. But two days after you departed from your last visit, he came crashing into the hut. He apparently had followed your trail across half of Greece."

"You're sure it was Bortan?"

"Was there ever another dog the size of a small horse, with armor plates on his sides, and jaws like a trap for bears?"

"No, I don't think so. That's probably why the species died out. Dogs do need armor plating if they're going to hang around with people, and they didn't develop it fast enough. If he is still alive, he's probably the last dog on Earth. He and I were puppies together, you know, so long ago that it hurts to think about it. That day he vanished while we were hunting I thought he'd had an accident. I searched for him, then decided he was dead. He was incredibly old at the time."

"Perhaps he was injured, and wandering that way—for years. But he was himself and he followed your track, that last time. When he saw that you were gone, he howled and took off after you again. We have never seen him since then. Sometimes, though, late at night, I hear his hunting-cry in the hills. . . ."

"The damnfool mutt ought to know it's not right to care for anything that much."

"Dogs were strange."

"Yes, dogs were."

And then the night wind, cool through arches of the years, came hounding after me. It touched my eyes.

Tired, they closed.

Greece is lousy with legend, fraught with menace. Most areas of mainland near the Hot Places are historically dangerous. This is because, while the Office theoretically runs the Earth, it actually only tends to the islands. Office personnel on much of the mainland are rather like twentieth-century Revenue Officers were in certain hill areas. They're fair game in all seasons. The islands sustained less damage than the rest of the world during the Three Days, and consequently they were the logical outposts for world district offices when the Talerites decided we could use some administration. Historically, the mainlanders have always been opposed to this. In the regions about the Hot Places, though, the natives are not always completely human. This compounds the historical antipathy with abnormal behavior patterns. This is why Greece is fraught.

We could have sailed up the coast to Volos. We could have skimmed to Volos—or almost anywhere else, for that matter. Myshtigo wanted to hike from Lamia, though, to hike and enjoy the refreshment of legend and alien scenery. This is why we left the Skimmers at Lamia. This is why we hiked to Volos.

This is why we encountered legend.

I bade Jason goodbye in Athens. He was sailing up the coast. Wise.

Phil had insisted on enduring the hike, rather than skimming ahead and meeting us up further along the line. Good thing, too, maybe, in a way, sort of. . . .

The road to Volos wanders through the thick and the sparse in the way of vegetation. It passes huge boulders, occasional clusters of shacks, fields of poppies; it crosses small streams, winds about hills, sometimes crosses over hills, widens and narrows without apparent cause.

It was still early morning. The sky was somehow a blue

mirror, because the sunlight seemed to be coming from everywhere. In places of shade some moisture still clung to the grasses and the lower leaves of the trees.

It was in an interesting glade along the road to Volos that I met a half-namesake.

The place had once been a shrine of some sort, back in the Real Old Days. I came to it quite often in my youth because I liked the quality of—I guess you'd call it "peace"—that it contained. Sometimes I'd meet the half-people or the no-people there, or dream good dreams, or find old pottery or the heads of statues, or things like that, which I could sell down in Lamia or in Athens.

There is no trail that leads to it. You just have to know where it is. I wouldn't have taken them there, except for the fact that Phil was along and I knew that he liked anything which smacks of an adytum, a sequestered significance, a sliding-panel view onto dim things past, etcetera.

About half a mile off the road, through a small forest, self-content in its disarray of green and shade and its haphazard heaps of stone, you suddenly go downhill, find the way blocked by a thick thicket, push on through, then discover a blank wall of rock. If you crouch, keep close to that wall, and bear to the right, you then come upon a glade where it is often well to pause before proceeding further.

There is a short, sharp drop, and down below is an egg-shaped clearing, about fifty meters long, twenty across, and the small end of the egg butting into a bitten-out place in the rock; there is a shallow cave at the extreme end, usually empty. A few half-sunken, almost square stones stand about in a seemingly random way. Wild grapevines grow around the perimeter of the place, and in the center is an enormous and ancient tree whose branches act as an umbrella over almost the entire area, keeping it dusky throughout the day. Because of this, it is hard to see into the place, even from the glade.

But we could see a satyr in the middle, picking his nose.

I saw George's hand go to the mercy-gun he carried. I caught his shoulder, his eyes, shook my head. He shrugged, and nodded, dropping his hand.

I withdrew from my belt the shepherd's pipes I had asked

Jason to give me. I motioned to the others to crouch and remain where they were. I moved a few steps further ahead and
raised the syrinx to my lips.

My first notes were quite tentative. It had been too long
since I'd played the pipes.

His ears pricked forward and he looked all about him. He
made rapid moves in three different directions—like a startled
squirrel, uncertain as to which tree to make for.

Then he stood there quivering as I caught up an old tune
and nailed it to the air.

I kept playing, remembering, remembering the pipes, the
tunes, and the bitter, the sweet, and the drunken things I've
really always known. It all came back to me as I stood there
playing for the little guy in the shaggy leggings: the fingering
and the control of the air, the little runs, the thorns of sound,
the things only the pipes can really say. I can't play in the cities,
but suddenly I was me again, and I saw faces in the leaves and
I heard the sound of hooves.

I moved forward.

Like in a dream, I noticed I was standing with my back
against the tree, and they were all about me. They shifted from
hoof to hoof, never staying still, and I played for them as I had
so often before, years ago, not knowing whether they were
really the same ones who'd heard me then—nor caring, actually. They cavorted about me. They laughed through white,
white teeth and their eyes danced, and they circled, jabbing
at the air with their horns, kicking their goat legs high off the
ground, bending far forward, springing into the air, stamping
the earth.

I stopped, and lowered the pipes.

It was not a human intelligence that regarded me from those
wild, dark eyes, as they all froze into statues, just standing
there, staring at me.

I raised the pipes once more, slowly. This time I played the
last song I'd ever made. I remembered it so well. It was a dirge-
like thing I had played on the night I'd decided Karaghiosis
should die.

I had seen the fallacy of Return. They would not come
back, would never come back. The Earth would die. I had
gone down into the Gardens and played this one last tune I'd

learned from the wind and maybe even the stars. The next day, Karaghiosis' big blazeboat had broken up in the bay at Piraeus.

They seated themselves on the grass. Occasionally, one would dab at his eye with an elaborate gesture. They were all about me, listening.

How long I played, I do not know. When I had finished, I lowered the pipes and sat there. After a time, one of them reached out and touched the pipes and drew his hand back quickly. He looked up at me.

"Go," I said, but they did not seem to understand.

So I raised the syrinx and played the last few bars over again.

The Earth is dying, dying. Soon it will be dead. . . . Go home, the party's over. It's late, it's late, so late. . . .

The biggest one shook his head.

Go away, go away, go away now. Appreciate the silence. After life's most ridiculous gambit, appreciate the silence. What did the gods hope to gain, to gain? Nothing. 'Twas all but a game. Go away, go away, go away now. It's late, it's late, so late. . . .

They still sat there, so I stood up and clapped my hands, yelled "Go!" and walked away quickly.

I gathered my companions and headed back for the road.

It is about sixty-five kilometers from Lamia to Volos, including the detour around the Hot Spot. We covered maybe a fifth of that distance on the first day. That evening, we pitched our camp in a clearing off to the side of the road, and Diane came up beside me and said, "Well?"

"'Well' what?"

"I just called Athens. Blank. The Radpol is silent. I want your decision now."

"You are very determined. Why can't we wait some more?"

"We've waited too long as it is. Supposing he decides to end the tour ahead of schedule? —This countryside is perfect. So many accidents could come so easily here. . . . You know what the Radpol will say—the same as before—and it will signify the same as before: Kill."

"My answer is also the same as before: No."

She blinked rapidly, lowered her head.

"Please reconsider."

"No."

"Then do this much," she said. "Forget it. The whole thing. Wash your hands of the affair. Take Lorel up on his offer and get us a new guide. You can skim out of here in the morning."

"No."

"Are you really serious, then—about protecting Myshtigo?"

"Yes."

"I don't want you hurt, or worse."

"I'm not particularly fond of the idea myself. So you can save us both a lot of trouble by calling it off."

"I can't do that."

"Dos Santos does as you tell him."

"The problem is *not* an administrative one! —Damn it! I wish I'd never met you!"

"I'm sorry."

"The Earth is at stake and you're on the wrong side."

"I think you are."

"What are you going to do about it?"

"I can't convince you, so I'll just have to stop you."

"You couldn't turn in the Secretary of the Radpol and his consort without evidence. We're too ticklish politically."

"I know that."

"So you couldn't hurt Don, and I don't believe you'd hurt me."

"You're right."

"That leaves Hasan."

"Right again."

"And Hasan is—Hasan. What will you do?"

"Why don't you give him his walking papers right now and save me some trouble?"

"I won't do that."

"I didn't think you would."

She looked up again. Her eyes were moist, but her face and voice were unchanged.

"If it should turn out that you were right and we were wrong," she said, "I am sorry."

"Me too," I said. "Very, very."

That night I dozed within knifing distance of Myshtigo, but nothing happened or tried to. The following morning was uneventful, as was most of the afternoon.

"Myshtigo," I said, as soon as we paused for purposes of photographing a hillside, "why don't you go home? Go back to Taler? Go anywhere? Walk away from it? Write some other book? The further we get from civilization, the less is my power to protect you."

"You gave me an automatic, remember?" he said.

He made a shooting motion with his right hand.

"All right—just thought I'd give it another try."

"That's a goat standing on the lower limb of that tree, isn't it?"

"Yeah; they like to eat those little green shoots that come up off the branches."

"I want a picture of that too. Olive tree, isn't it?"

"Yes."

"Good. I wanted to know what to call the picture. 'Goat eating green shoots in olive tree,'" he dictated; "that will be the caption."

"Great. Shoot while you have the chance."

If only he weren't so uncommunicative, so alien, so unconcerned about his welfare! I hated him. I couldn't understand him. He wouldn't speak, unless it was to request information or to answer a question. Whenever he did answer questions, he was terse, elusive, insulting, or all three at once. He was smug, conceited, blue, and overbearing. It really made me wonder about the Shtigo-gens' tradition of philosophy, philanthropy and enlightened journalism. I just didn't like him.

But I spoke to Hasan that evening, after having kept an eye (the blue one) on him all day.

He was sitting beside the fire, looking like a sketch by Delacroix. Ellen and Dos Santos sat nearby, drinking coffee, so I dusted off my Arabic and approached.

"Greetings."

"Greetings."

"You did not try to kill him today."

"No."

"Tomorrow, perhaps?"

He shrugged.

"Hasan—look at me."

He did.

"You were hired to kill the blue one."

He shrugged again.

"You needn't deny it, or admit it. I already know. I cannot allow you to do this thing. Give back the money Dos Santos has paid you and go your way. I can get you a Skimmer by morning. It will take you anywhere in the world you wish to go."

"But I am happy here, Karagee."

"You will quickly cease being happy if any harm comes to the blue one."

"I am a bodyguard, Karagee."

"No, Hasan. You are the son of a dyspeptic camel."

"What is 'dyspeptic,' Karagee?"

"I do not know the Arabic word, and you would not know the Greek one. Wait, I'll find another insult. —You are a coward and a carrion-eater and a skulker up alleyways, because you are half jackal and half ape."

"This may be true, Karagee, because my father told me that I was born to be flayed alive and torn into quarters."

"Why was that?"

"I was disrespectful to the Devil."

"Oh?"

"Yes. —Were those devils that you played music for yesterday? They had the horns, the hooves . . ."

"No, they were not devils. They were the Hot-born children of unfortunate parents who left them to die in the wilderness. They lived, though, because the wilderness is their real home."

"Ah! And I had hoped that they were devils. I still think they were, because one smiled at me as I prayed to them for forgiveness."

"Forgiveness? For what?"

A faraway look came into his eyes.

"My father was a very good and kind and religious man," he said. "He worshipped Malak Tawûs, whom the benighted Shi'ites" (he spat here) "call Iblis—or Shaitan, or Satan—and he always paid his respects to Hallâj and the others of the Sandjaq. He was well-known for his piety, his many kindnesses.

"I loved him, but as a boy I had an imp within me. I was an atheist. I did not believe in the Devil. And I was an evil child, for I took me a dead chicken and mounted it on a stick and called it the Peacock Angel, and I mocked it with stones and pulled its feathers. One of the other boys grew frightened and told my father of this. My father flogged me then, in the streets, and he told me I was born to be flayed alive and torn into quarters for my blasphemies. He made me go to Mount Sindjar and pray for forgiveness, and I went there—but the imp was still within me, despite the flogging, and I did not really believe as I prayed.

"Now that I am older the imp has fled, but my father too, is gone—these many years—and I cannot tell him: I am sorry that I mocked the Peacock Angel. As I grow older I feel the need for religion. I hope that the Devil, in his great wisdom and mercy, understands this and forgives me."

"Hasan, it is difficult to insult you properly," I said. "But I warn you—the blue one must not be harmed."

"I am but a humble bodyguard."

"Ha! Yours is the cunning and the venom of the serpent. You are deceitful and treacherous. Vicious, too."

"No, Karagee. Thank you, but it is not true. I take pride in always meeting my commitments. That is all. This is the law I live by. Also, you cannot insult me so that I will challenge you to a duel, permitting you to choose bare hands or daggers or sabers. No. I take no offense."

"Then beware," I told him. "Your first move toward the Vegan will be your last."

"If it is so written, Karagee . . ."

"And call me Conrad!"

I stalked away, thinking bad thoughts.

The following day, all of us still being alive, we broke camp and pushed on, making about eight kilometers before the next interruption occurred.

"That sounded like a child crying," said Phil.

"You're right."

"Where is it coming from?"

"Off to the left, down there."

We moved through some shrubbery, came upon a dry stream bed, and followed it around a bend.

The baby lay among the rocks, partly wrapped in a dirty blanket. Its face and hands were already burnt red from the sun, so it must have been there much of the day before, also. The bite-marks of many insects were upon its tiny, wet face.

I knelt, adjusting the blanket to cover it better.

Ellen cried a little cry as the blanket fell open in front and she saw the baby.

There was a natural fistula in the child's chest, and something was moving inside.

Red Wig screamed, turned away, began to weep.

"What is it?" asked Myshtigo.

"One of the abandoned," I said. "One of the marked ones."

"How awful!" said Red Wig.

"Its appearance? Or the fact that it was abandoned?" I asked.

"Both!"

"Give it to me," said Ellen.

"Don't touch it," said George, stooping. "Call for a Skimmer," he ordered. "We have to get it to a hospital right away. I don't have the equipment to operate on it here. —Ellen, help me."

She was at his side then, and they went through his medkit together.

"You write what I do and pin the note onto a clean blanket —so the doctors in Athens will know."

Dos Santos was phoning Lamia by then, to pick up on one of our Skimmers.

And then Ellen was filling hypos for George and swabbing the cuts and painting the burns with unguents and writing it all down. They shot the baby full of vitamins, antibiotics, general adaptives, and half a dozen other things. I lost count after awhile. They covered its chest with gauze, sprayed it with something, wrapped it in a clean blanket, and pinned the note to it.

"What a dreadful thing!" said Dos Santos. "Abandoning a deformed child, leaving it to die in such a manner!"

"It's done here all the time," I told him, "especially about the Hot Places. In Greece there has always been a tradition of infanticide. I myself was exposed on a hilltop on the day I was born. Spent the night there, too."

He was lighting a cigarette, but he stopped and stared at me. "You? Why?"

I laughed, glanced down at my foot.

"Complicated story. I wear a special shoe because this leg is shorter than the other. Also, I understand I was a very hairy baby—and then, my eyes don't match. I suppose I might have gotten by if that had been all, but then I went and got born on Christmas and that sort of clinched things."

"What is wrong with being born on Christmas?"

"The gods, according to local beliefs, deem it a bit presumptuous. For this reason, children born at that time are not of human blood. They are of the brood of destroyers, the creators of havoc, the panickers of man. They are called the kallikanzaroi. Ideally, they look something like those guys with horns and hooves and all, but they don't have to. They could look like me, my parents decided—if they *were* my parents. So they left me on a hilltop, to be returned."

"What happened then?"

"There was an old Orthodox priest in the village. He heard of it and went to them. He told them that it was a mortal sin to do such a thing, and they had better get the baby back, quick, and have it ready for baptism the following day."

"Ah! And that is how you were saved, and baptised?"

"Well, sort of." I took one of his cigarettes. "They came back with *me*, all right, but they insisted I wasn't the same baby they'd left there. They'd left a dubious mutant and collected an even more doubtful changeling, they said. Uglier too, they claimed, and they got another Christmas child in return. Their baby had been a satyr, they said, and they figured that perhaps some Hot creature had had a sort of human child and had abandoned it in the same way we do them—making a swap, actually. Nobody had seen me before then, so their story couldn't be checked. The priest would have none of this, though, and he told them they were stuck with me. But they were very kind, once they were reconciled to the fact. I grew fairly large fairly young, and I was strong for my age. They liked that."

"And you were baptised . . . ?"

"Well, sort of half-baptised."

"Half-baptised?"

"The priest had a stroke at my christening. Died a little while later. He was the only one around, so I don't know that I got the whole thing done proper."

"One drop would be sufficient."

"I suppose so. I don't really know what happened."

"Maybe you had better have it done again. Just to be safe."

"No, if Heaven didn't want me then, I'm not going to ask a second time."

We set up a beacon in a nearby clearing and waited for the Skimmer.

We made another dozen or so kilometers that day, which was pretty good, considering the delay. The baby had been picked up and dispatched directly to Athens. When the Skimmer had set down, I'd asked in a large voice whether anyone else wanted a ride back. There'd been no takers, though.

And it was that evening that it happened.

We reclined about a fire. Oh, it was a jolly fire, flapping its bright wing against the night, warming us, smelling woody, pushing a smoke-track into the air. . . . Nice.

Hasan sat there cleaning his aluminum-barreled shotgun. It had a plastic stock and it was real light and handy.

As he worked on it, it tilted forward, moved slowly about, pointed itself right at Myshtigo.

He'd done it quite neatly, I must admit that. It was during a period of over half an hour, and he'd advanced the barrel with almost imperceptible movements.

I snarled, though, when its position registered in my cerebrum, and I was at his side in three steps.

I struck it from his hands.

It clattered on some small stones about eight feet away. My hand was stinging from the slap I'd given it.

Hasan was on his feet, his teeth shuttling around inside his beard, clicking together like flint and steel. I could almost see the sparks.

"Say it!" I said. "Go ahead, say something! Anything! You know damn well what you were just doing!"

His hands twitched.

"Go ahead!" I said. "Hit me! Just touch me, even. Then what I do to you will be self-defense, provoked assault. Even George won't be able to put you back together again."

"I was only cleaning my shotgun. You've damaged it."

"*You* do not point weapons by accident. You were going to kill Myshtigo."

"You are mistaken."

"Hit me. Or are you a coward?"

"I have no quarrel with you."

"You *are* a coward."

"No, I am not."

After a few seconds he smiled.

"Are you afraid to challenge *me*?" he asked.

And there it was. The only way.

The move had to be mine. I had hoped it wouldn't have to be that way. I had hoped that I could anger him or shame him or provoke him into striking me or challenging me.

I knew then that I couldn't.

Which was bad, very bad.

I was sure I could take him with anything I cared to name. But if he had it his way, things could be different. Everybody knows that there are some people with an aptitude for music. They can hear a piece once and sit down and play it on the piano or thelinstra. They can pick up a new instrument, and inside a few hours they can sound as if they've been playing it for years. They're good, very good at such things, because they have that talent—the ability to coordinate a special insight with a series of new actions.

Hasan was that way with weapons. Maybe some other people could be the same, but they don't go around doing it—not for decades and decades, anyway, with everything from boomerangs to blowguns. The dueling code would provide Hasan with the choice of means, and he was the most highly skilled killer I'd ever known.

But I had to stop him, and I could see that this was the only way it could be done, short of murder. I had to take him on his terms.

"Amen," I said. "I challenge you to a duel."

His smile remained, grew.

"Agreed—before these witnesses. Name your second."

"Phil Graber. Name yours."

"Mister Dos Santos."

"Very good. I happen to have a dueling permit and the registration forms in my bag, and I've already paid the death-tax for one person. So there needn't be much of a delay. When, where, and how do you want it?"

"We passed a good clearing about a kilometer back up the road."

"Yes; I recall it."

"We shall meet there at dawn tomorrow."

"Check," I said. "And as to weapons . . . ?"

He fetched his knapcase, opened it. It bristled with interesting sharp things, glistened with ovoid incendiaries, writhed with coils of metal and leather.

He withdrew two items and closed the pack.

My heart sank.

"The sling of David," he announced.

I inspected them.

"At what distance?"

"Fifty meters," he said.

"You've made a good choice," I told him, not having used one in over a century myself. "I'd like to borrow one tonight, to practice with. If you don't want to lend it to me, I can make my own."

"You may take either, and practice all night with it."

"Thanks." I selected one and hung it from my belt. Then I picked up one of our three electric lanterns. "If anybody needs me, I'll be up the road at the clearing," I said. "Don't forget to post guards tonight. This is a rough area."

"Do you want me to come along?" asked Phil.

"No. Thanks anyway. I'll go alone. See you."

"Then good night."

I hiked back along the way, coming at last to the clearing. I set up the lantern at one end of the place, so that it reflected upon a stand of small trees, and I moved to the other end.

I collected some stones and slung one at a tree. I missed.

I slung a dozen more, hitting with four of them.

I kept at it. After about an hour, I was hitting with a little more regularity. Still, at fifty meters I probably couldn't match Hasan.

The night wore on, and I kept slinging. After a time, I reached what seemed to be my learning plateau for accuracy. Maybe six out of eleven of my shots were coming through.

But I had one thing in my favor, I realized, as I twirled the sling and sent another stone smashing into a tree. I delivered my shots with an awful lot of force. Whenever I was on target there was much power behind the strike. I had already shattered several of the smaller trees, and I was sure Hasan couldn't do that with twice as many hits. If I could reach him, fine; but all the power in the world was worthless if I couldn't connect with it.

And I was sure he could reach me. I wondered how much of a beating I could take and still operate.

It would depend, of course, on where he hit me.

I dropped the sling and yanked the automatic from my belt when I heard a branch snap, far off to my right. Hasan came into the clearing.

"What do you want?" I asked him.

"I came to see how your practice was going," he said, regarding the broken trees.

I shrugged, reholstered my automatic and picked up the sling.

"Comes the sunrise and you will learn."

We walked across the clearing and I retrieved the lantern. Hasan studied a small tree which was now, in part, toothpicks. He did not say anything.

We walked back to the camp. Everyone but Dos Santos had turned in. Don was our guard. He paced about the warning perimeter, carrying an automatic rifle. We waved to him and entered the camp.

Hasan always pitched a Gauzy—a one-molecule-layer tent, opaque, feather-light, and very tough. He never slept in it, though. He just used it to stash his junk.

I seated myself on a log before the fire and Hasan ducked inside his Gauzy. He emerged a moment later with his pipe and a block of hardened, resinous-looking stuff, which he proceeded to scale and grind. He mixed it with a bit of burley and then filled the pipe.

After he got it going with a stick from the fire, he sat smoking it beside me.

"I do not want to kill you, Karagee," he said.

"I share this feeling. I do not wish to be killed."

"But we must fight tomorrow."

"Yes."

"You could withdraw your challenge."

"You could leave by Skimmer."

"I will not."

"Nor will I withdraw my challenge."

"It is sad," he said, after a time. "Sad, that two such as we must fight over the blue one. He is not worth your life, nor mine."

"True," I said, "but it involves more than just his life. The future of this planet is somehow tied up with whatever he is doing."

"I do not know of these things, Karagee. I fight for money. I have no other trade."

"Yes, I know."

The fire burnt low. I fed it more sticks.

"Do you remember the time we bombed the Coast of Gold, in France?" he asked.

"I remember."

"Besides the blue ones, we killed many people."

"Yes."

"The future of the planet was not changed by this, Karagee. For here we are, many years away from the thing, and nothing is different."

"I know that."

"And do you remember the days when we crouched in a hole on a hillside, overlooking the bay at Piraeus? Sometimes you would feed me the belts and I would strafe the blazeboats, and when I grew tired you would operate the gun. We had much ammunition. The Office Guard did not land that day, nor the next. They did not occupy Athens, and they did not break the Radpol. And we talked as we sat there, those two days and that night, waiting for the fireball to come—and you told me of the Powers in the Sky."

"I forget. . . ."

"I do not. You told me that there are men, like us, who live up in the air by the stars. Also, there are the blue ones. Some of the men, you said, seek the blue ones' favor, and they would sell the Earth to them to be made into a museum. Others, you said, did not want to do this thing, but they wanted it to remain as it is now—their property, run by the Office. The blue ones were divided among themselves on this matter, because there was a question as to whether it was legal and ethical to do this thing. There was a compromise, and the blue ones were sold some clean areas, which they used as resorts, and from which they toured the rest of the Earth. But you wanted the Earth to belong only to people. You said that if we gave the blue ones an inch, then they would want it all. You wanted the men by the stars to come back and rebuild the cities, bury the Hot Places, kill the beasts which prey upon men.

"As we sat there, waiting for the fireball, you said that we were at war, not because of anything we could see or hear or feel or taste, but because of the Powers in the Sky, who had never seen us, and whom we would never see. The Powers in the Sky had done this thing, and because of it men had to die here on Earth. You said that by the death of men and blue ones, the Powers might return to Earth. They never did, though. There was only the death.

"And it was the Powers in the Sky which saved us in the end, because they had to be consulted before the fireball could be burnt over Athens. They reminded the Office of an old law, made after the time of the Three Days, saying that the fireball would never again burn in the skies of Earth. You had thought that they would burn it anyhow, but they did not. It was because of this that we stopped them at Piraeus. I burnt Madagaskee for you, Karagee, but the Powers never came down to Earth. And when people get much money they go away from here—and they never come back from the sky. Nothing we did in those days has caused a change."

"Because of what we did, things remained as they were, rather than getting worse," I told him.

"What will happen if this blue one dies?"

"I do not know. Things may worsen then. If he is viewing the areas we pass through as possible real estate tracts, to be purchased by Vegans, then it is the old thing all over again."

"And the Radpol will fight again, will bomb them?"

"I think so."

"Then let us kill him now, before he goes further, sees more."

"It may not be that simple—and they would only send another. There would also be repercussions—perhaps mass arrests of Radpol members. The Radpol is no longer living on the edge of life as it was in those days. The people are unready. They need time to prepare. This blue one, at least, I hold in my hand. I can watch him, learn of his plans. Then, if it becomes necessary, I can destroy him myself."

He drew on his pipe. I sniffed. It was something like sandal-wood that I smelled.

"What are you smoking?"

"It comes from near my home. I visited there recently. It is one of the new plants which has never grown there before. Try it."

I took several mouthfuls into my lungs. At first there was nothing. I continued to draw on it, and after a minute there was a gradual feeling of coolness and tranquility which spread down through my limbs. It tasted bitter, but it relaxed. I handed it back. The feeling continued, grew stronger. It was very pleasant. I had not felt that sedate, that relaxed, for many weeks. The fire, the shadows, and the ground about us sud-denly became more real, and the night air and the distant moon and the sound of Dos Santos' footsteps came somehow more clearly than life, really. The struggle seemed ridiculous. We would lose it in the end. It was written that humanity was to be the cats and dogs and trained chimpanzees of the real people, the Vegans—and in a way it was not such a bad idea. Perhaps we needed someone wiser to watch over us, to run our lives. We had made a shambles of our own world during the Three Days, and the Vegans had never had a nuclear war. They operated a smoothly efficient interstellar government, encom-passing dozens of planets. Whatever they did was esthetically pleasing. Their own lives were well-regulated, happy things. Why not let them have the Earth? They'd probably do a better job with it than we'd ever done. And why not be their coolies, too? It wouldn't be a bad life. Give them the old ball of mud, full of radioactive sores and populated by cripples.

Why not?

I accepted the pipe once more, inhaled more peace. It was so pleasant not to think of these things at all, though. Not to think of anything you couldn't really do anything about. Just to sit there and breathe in the night and be one with the fire and the wind was enough. The universe was singing its hymn of oneness. Why open the bag of chaos there in the cathedral?

But I had lost my Cassandra, my dark witch of Kos, to the mindless powers which move the Earth and the waters. Noth-ing could kill my feeling of loss. It seemed further away, some-how insulated behind glass, but it was still there. Not all the pipes of the East could assuage this thing. I did not want to know peace. I wanted hate. I wanted to strike out at all the masks in the universe—earth, water, sky, Taler, Earthgov, and Office—so that behind one of them I might find that power which had taken her, and make it too, know something of pain. I did not want to know peace. I did not want to be at one with anything which had harmed that which was mine, by blood and by love. For just five minutes even, I wanted to be Karaghiosis again, looking at it all through crosshairs and squeezing a trigger.

Oh Zeus, of the hot red lightnings, I prayed, *give it to me that I may break the Powers in the Sky!*

I returned the pipe again.

"Thank you, Hasan, but I'm not ready for the Bo Tree."

I stood then and moved off toward the place where I had cast my pack.

"I am sorry that I must kill you in the morning," he called after me.

Sipping beer in a mountain lodge on the planet Divbah, with a Vegan seller of information named Krim (who is now dead), I once looked out through a wide window and up at the highest mountain in the known universe. It is called Kasla, and it has never been climbed. The reason I mention it is because on the morning of the duel I felt a sudden remorse that I had never attempted to scale it. It is one of those crazy things you think about and promise yourself that someday you're going to try, and then you wake up one morning and realize that it is probably exactly too late: you'll never do it.

There were no-expressions on every face that morning.

The world outside us was bright and clear and clean and filled with the singing of birds.

I had forbidden the use of the radio until after the duel, and Phil carried some of its essential entrails in his jacket pocket, just to be sure.

Lorel would not know. The Radpol would not know. Nobody would know, until after.

The preliminaries completed, the distance was measured off.

We took our places at the opposite ends of the clearing. The rising sun was to my left.

"Are you ready, gentlemen?" called out Dos Santos.

"Yes," and "I am," were the replies.

"I make a final attempt to dissuade you from this course of action. Do either of you wish to reconsider?"

"No," and "No."

"Each of you has ten stones of similar size and weight. The first shot is, of course, given to he who was challenged: Hasan."

We both nodded.

"Proceed, then."

He stepped back and there was nothing but fifty meters of air separating us. We both stood sideways, so as to present the smallest target possible. Hasan fitted his first stone to the sling.

I watched him wind it rapidly through the air behind him, and suddenly his arm came forward.

There was a crashing sound in back of me.

Nothing else happened.

He'd missed.

I put a stone to my own sling then and whipped it back and around. The air sighed as I cut it all apart.

Then I hurled the missile forward with all the strength of my right arm.

It grazed his left shoulder, barely touching it. It was mostly garment that it plowed.

The stone ricocheted from tree to tree behind him, before it finally vanished.

All was still then. The birds had given up on their morning concert.

"Gentlemen," called Dos Santos, "you have each had one chance to settle your differences. It may be said that you have faced one another with honor, given vent to your wrath, and are now satisfied. Do you wish to stop the duel?"

"No," said I.

Hasan rubbed his shoulder, shook his head.

He put the second stone to his sling, worked it rapidly through a powerful windup, then released it at me.

Right between the hip and the ribcage, that's where it caught me.

I fell to the ground and it all turned black.

A second later the lights came on again, but I was doubled

up and something with a thousand teeth had me by the side and wouldn't let go.

They were running toward me, all of them, but Phil waved them back.

Hasan held his position.

Dos Santos approached.

"Is that it?" asked Phil softly. "Can you get up?"

"Yeah. I need a minute to breathe and to put the fire out, but I'll get up."

"What is the situation?" asked Dos Santos.

Phil told him.

I put my hand to my side and stood again, slowly.

A couple inches higher or lower and something boney might have broken. As it was, it just hurt like blazes.

I rubbed it, moved my right arm through a few circles to test the play of muscles on that side. Okay.

Then I picked up the sling and put a stone to it.

This time it would connect. I had a feeling.

It went around and around and it came out fast.

Hasan toppled, clutching at his left thigh.

Dos Santos went to him. They spoke.

Hasan's robe had muffled the blow, had partly deflected it. The leg was not broken. He would continue as soon as he could stand.

He spent five minutes massaging it, then he got to his feet again. During that time my pain had subsided to a dull throbbing.

Hasan selected his third stone.

He fitted it slowly, carefully . . .

He took my measure. Then he began to lash at the air with the sling. . . .

All this while I had the feeling—and it kept growing—that I should be leaning a little further to the right. So I did.

He twirled it, threw it.

It grazed my fungus and tore at my left ear.

Suddenly my cheek was wet.

Ellen screamed, briefly.

A little further to the right, though, and I wouldn't have been hearing her.

It was my turn again.

Smooth, gray, the stone had the feel of death about it. . . .

I will be it, this one seemed to say.

It was one of those little premonitory tuggings at my sleeve, of the sort for which I have a great deal of respect.

I wiped the blood from my cheek. I fitted the stone.

There was death riding in my right arm as I raised it. Hasan felt it too, because he flinched. I could see this from across the field.

"You will all remain exactly where you are, and drop your weapons," said the voice.

It said it in Greek, so no one but Phil and Hasan and I understood it, for sure. Maybe Dos Santos or Red Wig did. I'm still not certain.

But all of us understood the automatic rifle the man carried, and the swords and clubs and knives of the three dozen or so men and half-men standing behind him.

They were Kouretes.

Kouretes are bad.

They always get their pound of flesh.

Usually roasted.

Sometimes fried, though.

Or boiled, or raw. . . .

The speaker seemed to be the only one carrying a firearm.

. . . And I had a handful of death circling high above my shoulder. I decided to make him a gift of it.

His head exploded as I delivered it.

"Kill them!" I said, and we began to do so.

George and Diane were the first to open fire. Then Phil found a handgun. Dos Santos ran for his pack. Ellen got there fast, too.

Hasan had not needed my order to begin killing. The only weapons he and I were carrying were the slings. The Kouretes were closer than our fifty meters, though, and theirs was a mob formation. He dropped two of them with well-placed stones before they began their rush. I got one more, also.

Then they were halfway across the field, leaping over their dead and their fallen, screaming as they came on toward us.

Like I said, they were not all of them human: there was a tall, thin one with three-foot wings covered with sores, and there were a couple microcephalics with enough hair so that they looked headless, and there was one guy who should probably have been twins, and then several steatopygiacs, and three huge, hulking brutes who kept coming despite bullet-holes in their chests and abdomens; one of these latter had hands which must have been twenty inches long and a foot across, and another appeared to be afflicted with something like elephantiasis. Of the rest, some were reasonably normal in form, but they all looked mean and mangy and either wore rags or no rags at all and were unshaven and smelled bad, too.

I hurled one more stone and didn't get a chance to see where it hit, because they were upon me then.

I began lashing out—feet, fists, elbows; I wasn't too polite about it. The gunfire slowed down, stopped. You have to stop to reload sometime, and there'd been some jamming, too. The pain in my side was a very bad thing. Still, I managed to drop three of them before something big and blunt caught me on the side of the head and I fell as a dead man falls.

Coming to in a stiflingly hot place. . . .

Coming to in a stiflingly hot place that smells like a stable. . . .

Coming to in a dark, stiflingly hot place that smells like a stable. . . .

. . . This is not real conducive to peace of mind, a settled stomach, or the resumption of sensory activities on a sure and normal keel.

It stank in there and it was damn hot, and I didn't really want to inspect the filthy floor too closely—it was just that I was in a very good position to do so.

I moaned, numbered all my bones, and sat up.

The ceiling was low and it slanted down even lower before it met with the back wall. The one window to the outside was small and barred.

We were in the back part of a wooden shack. There was another barred window in the opposite wall. It didn't look out on anything, though; it looked in. There was a larger room beyond it, and George and Dos Santos were talking through it with someone who stood on that other side. Hasan lay unconscious or dead about four feet away from me; there was dried blood on his head. Phil and Myshtigo and the girls were talking softly in the far corner.

I rubbed my temple while all this was registering within. My left side ached steadily, and numerous other portions of my anatomy had decided to join in the game.

"He's awake," said Myshtigo suddenly.

"Hi, everybody. I'm back again," I agreed.

They came toward me and I assumed a standing position. This was sheer bravado, but I managed to carry it.

"We are prisoners," said Myshtigo.

"Oh, yeah? Really? I'd never have guessed."

"Things like this do not happen on Taler," he observed, "or on any of the worlds in the Vegan Combine."

"Too bad you didn't stay there," I said. "Don't forget the number of times I asked you to go back."

"This thing would not have occurred if it had not been for your duel."

I slapped him then. I couldn't bring myself to slug him. He was just too pathetic. I hit him with the back of my hand and knocked him over into the wall.

"Are you trying to tell me you don't know why I stood there like a target this morning?"

"Because of your quarrel with my bodyguard," he stated, rubbing his cheek.

"—Over whether or not he was going to kill you."

"Me? Kill . . . ?"

"Forget it," I said. "It doesn't really matter anyhow. Not now. You're still on Taler, and you may as well stay there for your last few hours. It would have been nice if you could have come to Earth and visited with us for awhile. But things didn't work out that way."

"We are going to die here, aren't we?" he asked.

"That is the custom of the country."

I turned away and studied the man who was studying me from the other side of the bars. Hasan was leaning against the far wall then, holding his head. I hadn't noticed his getting up.

"Good afternoon," said the man behind the bars, and he said it in English.

"*Is* it afternoon?" I asked.

"Quite," he replied.

"Why aren't we dead?" I asked him.

"Because I wanted you alive," he stated. "Oh, not you personally—Conrad Nomikos, Commissioner of Arts, Monuments and Archives—and all your distinguished friends, including the poet laureate. I wanted any prisoners whom they came upon brought back alive. Your identities are, shall we say, condiments."

"To whom do I have the pleasure of speaking?" I asked.

"This is Doctor Moreby," said George.

"He is their witch doctor," said Dos Santos.

"I prefer 'Shaman' or 'Medicine Chief,'" corrected Moreby, smiling.

I moved closer to the grillwork and saw that he was rather thin, well-tanned, clean-shaven, and had all his hair woven into one enormous black braid which was coiled like a cobra about his head. He had close-set eyes, dark ones, a high forehead, and lots of extra jaw reaching down past his Adam's Apple. He wore woven sandals, a clean green sari, and a necklace of human fingerbones. In his ears were big snake-shaped circlets of silver.

"Your English is rather precise," said I, "and 'Moreby' is not a Greek name."

"Oh goodness!" He gestured gracefully, in mock surprise. "I'm not a local! How could you ever mistake me for a local?"

"Sorry," I said; "I can see now that you're too well-dressed."

He giggled.

"Oh, *this* old rag . . . I just threw it on. —No, I'm from Taler. I read some wonderfully rousing literature on the subject of Returnism, and I decided to come back and help rebuild the Earth."

"Oh? What happened then?"

"The Office was not hiring at the time, and I experienced some difficulty in finding employment locally. So I decided to engage in research work. This place is full of opportunities for that."

"What sort of research?"

"I hold two graduate degrees in cultural anthropology, from New Harvard. I decided to study a Hot tribe in depth—and after some blandishments I got this one to accept me. I started out to educate them, too. Soon, though, they were deferring to me, all over the place. Wonderful for the ego. After a time, my studies, my social work, came to be of less and less importance. Well, I daresay you've read *Heart of Darkness*—you know what I mean. The local practices are so—well, basic. I found it much more stimulating to participate than to observe. I took it upon myself to redesign some of their grosser practices along more esthetic lines. So I did really educate them, after all. They do things with ever so much style since I've come here."

"*Things*? Such as?"

"Well, for one thing, they were simple cannibals before. For another, they were rather unsophisticated in their use of their captives prior to slaying them. Things like that are quite important. If they're done properly they give you class, if you know what I mean. Here I was with a wealth of customs, superstitions, taboos—from many cultures, many eras—right here, at my fingertips." He gestured again. "Man—even half-man, Hot man—is a ritual-loving creature, and I knew ever so many rituals and things like that. So I put all of this to good use and now I occupy a position of great honor and high esteem."

"What are you trying to tell me about *us*?" I asked.

"Things were getting rather dull around here," he said, "and the natives were waxing restless. So I decided it was time for another ceremony. I spoke with Procrustes, the War Chief, and suggested he find us some prisoners. I believe it is on page 577 of the abridged edition of *The Golden Bough* that it states, 'The Tolalaki, notorious head-hunters of Central Celebes, drink the blood and eat the brains of their victims that they may become brave. The Italones of the Philippine Islands drink the blood of their slain enemies, and eat part of the back of their heads and of their entrails raw to acquire their courage.' Well, we have the tongue of a poet, the blood of two very formidable warriors, the brains of a very distinguished scientist, the bilious liver of a fiery politician, and the interesting-colored flesh of a Vegan —all in this one room here. Quite a haul, I should say."

"You make yourself exceedingly clear," I observed. "What of the women?"

"Oh, for them we'll work out a protracted fertility rite ending in a protracted sacrifice."

"I see."

". . . That is to say, if we do not permit all of you to continue on your way, unmolested."

"Oh?"

"Yes. Procrustes likes to give people a chance to measure themselves against a standard, to be tested, and possibly to redeem themselves. He is most Christian in this respect."

"And true to his name, I suppose?"

Hasan came over and stood beside me, stared out through the grillwork at Moreby.

"Oh, good, good," said Moreby. "Really, I'd like to keep you around awhile, you know? You have a sense of humor. Most of the Kouretes lack this adjunct to what are otherwise exemplary personalities. I could learn to like you . . ."

"Don't bother. Tell me about the way of redemption, though."

"Yes. We are the wardens of the Dead Man. He is my most interesting creation. I am certain that one of you two shall realize this during your brief acquaintanceship with him." He glanced from me to Hasan to me to Hasan.

"I know of him," I said. "Tell me what must be done."

"You are called upon to bring forth a champion to do battle with him, this night, when he rises again from the dead."

"What is he?"

"A vampire."

"Crap. What is he really?"

"He is a genuine vampire. You'll see."

"Okay, have it your way. He's a vampire, and one of us will fight him. How?"

"Catch-as-catch-can, bare-handed—and he isn't very difficult to catch. He'll just stand there and wait for you. He'll be very thirsty, and hungry too, poor fellow."

"And if he is beaten, do your prisoners go free?"

"That is the rule, as I originally outlined it some sixteen or seventeen years ago. Of course, this contingency has never arisen. . . ."

"I see. You're trying to tell me he's tough."

"Oh, he's unbeatable. That's the fun of it. It wouldn't make for a good ceremony if it could end any other way. I tell the whole story of the battle before it takes place, and then my people witness it. It reaffirms their faith in destiny and my own close association with its workings."

Hasan glanced at me.

"What does he mean, Karagee?"

"It's a fixed fight," I told him.

"On the contrary," said Moreby, "it is not. It doesn't have to be. There was once an old saying on this planet, in connection with an ancient sport: Never bet against the damn Yankees, or you'll lose money. The Dead Man is unbeatable because he was born with a considerable amount of native ability, upon which I have elaborated, considerably. He has dined upon many champions, so of course his strength is equal to all of theirs. Everyone who's read Frazer knows that."

He yawned, covering his mouth with a feathered wand.

"I must go to the barbecue area now, to supervise the decking of the hall with boughs of holly. Decide upon your champion this afternoon, and I'll see you all this evening. Good day."

"Trip and break your neck."

He smiled and left the shack.

I called a meeting.

"Okay," I said, "they've got a weird Hot One called the Dead Man, who is supposed to be very tough. I am going to fight him tonight. If I can beat him we are supposed to go free, but I wouldn't take Moreby's word for anything. Therefore, we must plan an escape, else we will be served up on a chafing dish.

"Phil, do you remember the road to Volos?" I asked.

"I think so. It's been a long time. . . . But where are we now, exactly?"

"If it is of any help," answered Myshtigo, from beside the window, "I see a glowing. It is not any color for which there is a word in your language, but it is off in that direction." He pointed. "It is a color which I normally see in the vicinity of radioactive materials if the atmosphere is dense enough about them. It is spread over quite a large area."

I moved to the window and stared in that direction.

"That could be the Hot Spot, then," I said. "If that is the

case, then they've actually brought us further along toward the coast, which is good. Was anyone conscious when we were brought here?"

No one answered.

"All right. Then we'll operate under the assumption that that *is* the Hot Spot, and that we are very close to it. The road to Volos should be back that way, then." I pointed in the opposite direction. "Since the sun is on this side of the shack and it's afternoon, head in the other direction after you hit the road —away from the sunset. It might not be more than twenty-five kilometers."

"They will track us," said Dos Santos.

"There are horses," said Hasan.

"What?"

"Up the street, in a paddock. There were three near that rail earlier. They are back behind the edge of the building now. There may be more. They were not strong-looking horses, though."

"Can all of you ride?" I asked.

"I have never ridden a horse," said Myshtigo, "but the *thrid* is something similar. I have ridden *thrid*."

Everyone else had ridden horses.

"Tonight, then," I said. "Ride double if you must. If there are more than enough horses, then turn the others loose, drive them away. As they watch me fight the Dead Man you will make a break for the paddock. Seize what weapons you can and try to fight your way to the horses. —Phil, get them up to Makrynitsa and mention the name of Korones anywhere. They will take you in and protect you."

"I am sorry," said Dos Santos, "but your plan is not a good one."

"If you've got a better one, let's hear it," I told him.

"First of all," he said, "we cannot really rely on Mister Graber. While you were still unconscious he was in great pain and very weak. George believes that he suffered a heart attack during or shortly after our fight with the Kouretes. If anything happens to him we are lost. We will need you to guide us out of here, if we do succeed in breaking free. We *cannot* count on Mister Graber.

"Second," he said, "you are not the only man capable of

fighting an exotic menace. Hasan will undertake the defeat of the Dead Man."

"I can't ask him to do that," I said. "Even if he wins, he will probably be separated from us at the time, and they'll doubtless get to him pretty fast. It would most likely mean his life. You hired him to kill for you, not to die."

"I will fight him, Karagee," he said.

"You don't have to."

"But I wish to."

"How are you feeling now, Phil?" I asked.

"Better, much better. I think it was just an upset stomach. Don't worry about it."

"Do you feel good enough to make it to Makrynitsa, on horseback?"

"No trick at all. It will be easier than walking. I was practically born on horseback. You remember."

"'Remember'?" asked Dos Santos. "What do you mean by that, Mister Graber? How could Conrad remem—"

"—Remember his famous *Ballads on Horseback*," said Red Wig. "What are you leading up to, Conrad?"

"I'm in charge here, thank you," said I. "I'm giving the orders and I've decided I'll do the vampire-fighting."

"In a situation like this I think we ought to be a little more democratic about these life and death decisions," she replied. "You were born in this country. No matter how good Phil's memory is, you'll do a better job of getting us from here to there in a hurry. You're not ordering Hasan to die, or abandoning him. He's volunteering."

"I will kill the Dead Man," said Hasan, "and I will follow after you. I know the ways of hiding myself from men. I will follow your trail."

"It's my job," I told him.

"Then, since we cannot agree, leave the decision to the fates," said Hasan. "Toss a coin."

"Very well. Did they take our money as well as our weapons?"

"I have some change," said Ellen.

"Toss a piece into the air."

She did.

"Heads," said I, as it fell toward the floor.

"Tails," she replied.

"Don't touch it!"

It was tails, all right. And there was a head on the other side, too.

"Okay, Hasan, you lucky fellow, you," I said. "You just won a do-it-yourself Hero Kit, complete with a monster. Good luck."

He shrugged.

"It was written."

He sat down then, his back against the wall, extracted a tiny knife from the sole of his left sandal, and began to pare his fingernails. He'd always been a pretty well-groomed killer. I guess cleanliness is next to diablerie, or something like that.

As the sun sank slowly in the west, Moreby came to us again, bringing with him a contingent of Kourete swordsmen.

"The time has come," he stated. "Have you decided upon your champion?"

"Hasan will fight him," I said.

"Very good. Then come along. Please do not try anything foolish. I should hate to deliver damaged goods at a festival."

Walking within a circle of blades, we left the shack and moved up the street of the village, passing by the paddock. Eight horses, heads low, stood within. Even in the diminishing light I could see that they were not very good horses. Their flanks were all covered with sores, and they were quite thin. Everyone glanced at them as we went by.

The village consisted of about thirty shacks, such as the one in which we had been confined. It was a dirt road that we walked on, and it was full of ruts and rubbish. The whole place smelled of sweat and urine and rotten fruit and smoke.

We went about eighty meters and turned left. It was the end of the street, and we moved along a downhill path into a big, cleared compound. A fat, bald-headed woman with enormous breasts and a face that was a lava field of carcinoma was tending a low and dreadfully suggestive fire at the bottom of a huge barbecue pit. She smiled as we passed by and smacked her lips moistly.

Great, sharpened stakes lay on the ground about her. . . .

Up further ahead was a level area of hardpacked bare earth. A huge, vine-infested, tropic-type tree which had adapted itself to our climate stood at the one end of the field, and all about the field's peripheries were rows of eight-foot torches, already waving great lengths of fire like pennants. At the other end was the most elaborate shack of them all. It was about five meters high and ten across the front. It was painted bright red and covered all over with Pennsylvania hex signs. The entire middle section of the front wall was a high, sliding door. Two armed Kouretes stood guard before that door.

The sun was a tiny piece of orange-rind in the west. Moreby marched us the length of the field toward the tree.

Eighty to a hundred spectators were seated on the ground on the other side of the torches, on each side of the field.

Moreby gestured, indicating the red shack.

"How do you like my home?" he asked.

"Lovely," said I.

"I have a roommate, but he sleeps during the day. You're about to meet him."

We reached the base of the big tree. Moreby left us there, surrounded by his guards. He moved to the center of the field and began addressing the Kouretes in Greek.

We had agreed that we would wait until the fight was near its end, whichever way, and the tribesmen all excited and concentrating on the finale, before we made our break. We'd pushed the women into the center of our group, and I managed to get on the left side of a right-handed swordsman, whom I intended to kill quickly. Too bad that we were at the far end of the field. To get to the horses we'd have to fight our way back through the barbecue area.

". . . and then, on that night," Moreby was saying, "did the Dead Man rise up, smiting down this mighty warrior, Hasan, breaking his bones and casting him about this place of feasting. Finally, did he kill this great enemy and drink the blood from his throat and eat of his liver, raw and still smoking in the night air. These things did he do on that night. Mighty is his power."

"Mighty, oh mighty!" cried the crowd, and someone began beating upon a drum.

"Now will we call him to life again. . . ."

The crowd cheered.

"To life again!"

"To life again."

"To life again!"
"Hail!"
"Hail!"
"Sharp white teeth. . . ."
"Sharp white teeth!"
"White, white skin. . . ."
"White, white skin!"
"Hands which break. . . ."
"Hands which break!"
"Mouth which drinks. . . ."
"Mouth which drinks!"
"The blood of life!"
"The blood of life!"
"Great is our tribe!"
"Great is our tribe!"
"Great is the Dead Man!"
"Great is the Dead Man!"
"Great is the Dead Man!"
"GREAT IS THE DEAD MAN!"

They bellowed it, at the last. Throats human, half-human, and inhuman heaved the brief litany like a tidal wave across the field. Our guards, too, were screaming it. Myshtigo was blocking his sensitive ears and there was an expression of agony on his face. My head was ringing too. Dos Santos crossed himself and one of the guards shook his head at him and raised his blade meaningfully. Don shrugged and turned his head back toward the field.

Moreby walked up to the shack and struck three times upon the sliding door with his wand.

One of the guards pushed it open for him.

An immense black catafalque, surrounded by the skulls of men and animals, was set within. It supported an enormous casket made of dark wood and decorated with bright, twisting lines.

At Moreby's directions, the guards raised the lid.

For the next twenty minutes he gave hypodermic injections to something within the casket. He kept his movements slow and ritualistic. One of the guards put aside his blade and assisted him. The drummers kept up a steady, slow cadence. The crowd was very silent, very still.

Then Moreby turned.

"Now the Dead Man rises," he announced.

"Rises," responded the crowd.

"Now he comes forth to accept the sacrifice."

"Now he comes forth. . . ."

"Come forth, Dead Man," he called, turning back to the catafalque.

And he did.

At great length.

For he was big.

Huge, obese.

Great indeed was the Dead Man.

Maybe 350 pounds' worth.

He sat up in his casket and he looked all about him. He rubbed his chest, his armpits, his neck, his groin. He climbed out of the big box and stood beside the catafalque, dwarfing Moreby.

He was wearing only a loincloth and large, goatskin sandals.

His skin was white, dead white, fishbelly white, moon white . . . dead white.

"An albino," said George, and his voice carried the length of the field because it was the only sound in the night.

Moreby glanced in our direction and smiled. He took the Dead Man's stubby-fingered hand and led him out of the shack and onto the field. The Dead Man shied away from the torchlight. As he advanced, I studied the expression on his face.

"There is no intelligence in that face," said Red Wig.

"Can you see his eyes?" asked George, squinting. His glasses had been broken in the fray.

"Yes; they're pinkish."

"Does he have epicanthial folds?"

"Mm. . . . Yeah."

"Uh-huh. He's a Mongoloid—an idiot, I'll wager—which is why it was so easy for Moreby to do what he's done with him. And look at his teeth! They look filed."

I did. He was grinning, because he'd seen the colorful top of Red Wig's head. Lots of nice, sharp teeth were exposed.

"His albinism is the reason behind the nocturnal habits Moreby has imposed. Look! He even flinches at the torchlight! He's ultrasensitive to any sort of actinics."

"What about his dietary habits?"

"Acquired, through imposition. Lots of primitive people bled their cattle. The Kazaks did it until the twentieth century, and the Todas. You saw the sores on those horses as we passed by the paddock. Blood *is* nourishing, you know, if you can learn to keep it down—and I'm sure Moreby has regulated the idiot's diet since he was a child. So of course he's a vampire—he was brought up that way."

"The Dead Man is risen," said Moreby.

"The Dead Man is risen," agreed the crowd.

"Great is the Dead Man!"

"Great is the Dead Man!"

He dropped the dead-white hand then and walked toward us, leaving the only genuine vampire we knew of grinning in the middle of the field.

"Great is the Dead Man," he said, grinning himself as he approached us. "Rather magnificent, isn't he?"

"What have you done to that poor creature?" asked Red Wig.

"Very little," replied Moreby. "He was born pretty well-equipped."

"What were those injections you gave him?" inquired George.

"Oh, I shoot his pain centers full of Novocain before encounters such as this one. His lack of pain responses adds to the image of his invincibility. Also, I've given him a hormone shot. He's been putting on weight recently, and he's grown a bit sluggish. This compensates for it."

"You talk of him and treat him as though he's a mechanical toy," said Diane.

"He is. An invincible toy. An invaluable one, also. —You there, Hasan. Are you ready?" he asked.

"I am," Hasan answered, removing his cloak and his burnoose and handing them to Ellen.

The big muscles in his shoulders bulged, his fingers flexed lightly, and he moved forward and out of the circle of blades. There was a welt on his left shoulder, several others on his back. The torchlight caught his beard and turned it to blood, and I could not help but remember that night back at the *hounfor* when he had enacted a strangling, and Mama Julie had said, "Your friend is possessed of Angelsou," and "Angelsou is a deathgod and he only visits with his own."

"Great is the warrior, Hasan," announced Moreby, turning away from us.

"Great is the warrior, Hasan," replied the crowd.

"His strength is that of many."

"His strength is that of many," the crowd responded.

"Greater still is the Dead Man."

"Greater still is the Dead Man."

"He breaks his bones and casts him about this place of feasting."

"He breaks his bones. . . ."

"He eats his liver."

"He eats his liver."

"He drinks the blood from his throat."

"He drinks the blood from his throat."

"Mighty is his power."

"Mighty is his power."

"Great is the Dead Man!"

"Great is the Dead Man!"

"Tonight," said Hasan quietly, "he becomes the Dead Man indeed."

"Dead Man!" cried Moreby, as Hasan moved forward and stood before him, "I give you this man Hasan in sacrifice!"

Then Moreby got out of the way and motioned the guards to move us to the far sideline.

The idiot grinned an even wider grin and reached out slowly toward Hasan.

"Bismallah," said Hasan, making as if to turn away from him, and bending downward and to the side.

He picked it off the ground and brought it up and around fast and hard, like a whiplash—a great heel-of-the-hand blow which landed on the left side of the Dead Man's jaw.

The white, white head moved maybe five inches.

And he kept on grinning. . . .

Then both of his short, bulky arms came out and caught Hasan beneath the armpits. Hasan seized his shoulders, tracing fine red furrows up his sides as he went, and he drew red beads from the places where his fingers dug into snowcapped muscle.

The crowd screamed at the sight of the Dead Man's blood. Perhaps the smell of it excited the idiot himself. That, or the screaming.

Because he raised Hasan two feet off the ground and ran forward with him.

The big tree got in the way, and Hasan's head sagged as he struck.

Then the Dead Man crashed into him, stepped back slowly, shook himself, and began to hit him.

It was a real beating. He flailed at him with his almost grotesquely brief, thick arms.

Hasan got his hands up in front of his face and he kept his elbows in the pit of his stomach.

Still, the Dead Man kept striking him on his sides and head. His arms just kept rising and falling.

And he never stopped grinning.

Finally, Hasan's hands fell and he clutched them before his stomach.

. . . And there was blood coming from the corners of his mouth.

The invincible toy continued its game.

And then far, far off on the other side of the night, so far that only I could hear it, there came a voice that I recognized.

It was the great hunting-howl of my hellhound, Bortan.

Somewhere, he had come upon my trail, and he was coming now, running down the night, leaping like a goat, flowing like a horse or a river, all brindle-colored—and his eyes were glowing coals and his teeth were buzzsaws.

He never tired of running, my Bortan.

Such as he are born without fear, given to the hunt, and sealed with death.

My hellhound was coming, and nothing could halt him in his course.

But he was far, so far off, on the other side of the night. . . .

The crowd was screaming. Hasan couldn't take much more of it. Nobody could.

From the corner of my eye (the brown one) I noticed a tiny gesture of Ellen's.

It was as though she had thrown something with her right hand. . . .

Two seconds later it happened.

I looked away quickly from that point of brilliance that occurred, sizzling, behind the idiot.

The Dead Man wailed, lost his grin.

Good old Reg 237.1 (promulgated by me):

"Every tour guide and every member of a tour must carry no fewer than three magnesium flares on his person, while traveling."

Ellen only had two left, that meant. Bless her.

The idiot had stopped hitting Hasan.

He tried to kick the flare away. He screamed. He tried to kick the flare away. He covered his eyes. He rolled on the ground.

Hasan watched, bleeding, panting. . . .

The flare burnt, the Dead Man screamed. . . .

Hasan finally moved.

He reached up and touched one of the thick vines which hung from the tree.

He tugged at it. It resisted. He pulled harder.

It came loose.

His movements were steadier as he twisted an end around each hand.

The flare sputtered, grew bright again. . . .

He dropped to his knees beside the Dead Man, and with a quick motion he looped the vine about his throat.

The flare sputtered again.

He snapped it tight.

The Dead Man fought to rise.

Hasan drew the thing tighter.

The idiot seized him about the waist.

The big muscles in the Assassin's shoulders grew into ridges. Perspiration mingled with the blood on his face.

The Dead Man stood, raising Hasan with him.

Hasan pulled harder.

The idiot, his face no longer white, but mottled, and with the veins standing out like cords in his forehead and neck, lifted him up off the ground.

As I'd lifted the golem did the Dead Man raise Hasan, the vine cutting ever more deeply into his neck as he strained with all his inhuman strength.

The crowd was wailing and chanting incoherently. The

drumming, which had reached a frenzied throb, continued at its peak without letup. And then I heard the howl again, still very far away.

The flare began to die.

The Dead Man swayed.

. . . Then, as a great spasm racked him, he threw Hasan away from him.

The vine went slack about his throat as it tore free from Hasan's grip.

Hasan took *ukemi* and rolled to his knees. He stayed that way.

The Dead Man moved toward him.

Then his pace faltered.

He began to shake all over. He made a gurgling noise and clutched at his throat. His face grew darker. He staggered to the tree and put forth a hand. He leaned there panting. Soon he was gasping noisily. His hand slipped along the trunk and he dropped to the ground. He picked himself up again, into a half-crouch.

Hasan arose, and recovered the piece of vine from where it had fallen.

He advanced upon the idiot.

This time his grip was unbreakable.

The Dead Man fell, and he did not rise again.

It was like turning off a radio which had been playing at full volume:

Click. . . .

Big silence then—it had all happened so fast. And tender was the night, yea verily, as I reached out through it and broke the neck of the swordsman at my side and seized his blade. I turned then to my left and split the skull of the next one with it.

Then, like *click* again, and full volume back on, but all static this time. The night was torn down through the middle.

Myshtigo dropped his man with a vicious rabbit-punch and kicked another in the shins. George managed a quick knee to the groin of the one nearest him.

Dos Santos, not so quick—or else just unlucky—took two bad cuts, chest and shoulder.

The crowd rose up from where it had been scattered on the ground, like a speedup film of beansprouts growing.

It advanced upon us.

Ellen threw Hasan's burnoose over the head of the swordsman who was about to disembowel her husband. Earth's poet laureate then brought a rock down hard on the top of the burnoose, doubtless collecting much bad karma but not looking too worried about it.

By then Hasan had rejoined our little group, using his hand to parry a sword cut by striking the flat of the blade in an old samurai maneuver I had thought lost to the world forever. Then Hasan, too, had a sword—after another rapid movement —and he was very proficient with it.

We killed or maimed all our guards before the crowd was halfway to us, and Diane, taking a cue from Ellen, lobbed her three magnesium flares across the field and into the mob.

We ran then, Ellen and Red Wig supporting Dos Santos, who was kind of staggery.

But the Kouretes had cut us off and we were running northwards, off at a tangent from our goal.

"We cannot make it, Karagee," called Hasan.

"I know."

". . . Unless you and I delay them while the others go ahead."

"Okay. Where?"

"At the far barbecue pit, where the trees are thick about the path. It is a bottle's neck. They will not be able to hit us all at a time."

"Right!" I turned to the others. "You hear us? Make for the horses! Phil will guide you! Hasan and I will hold them for as long as we can!"

Red Wig turned her head and began to say something.

"Don't argue! Go! You want to live, don't you!?"

They did. They went.

Hasan and I turned, there beside the barbecue pit, and we waited. The others cut back again, going off through the woods, heading toward the village and the paddock. The mob kept right on coming, toward Hasan and me.

The first wave hit us and we began the killing. We were in the V-shaped place where the path disgorged from the woods onto the plain. To our left was a smoldering pit; to our right a thick stand of trees. We killed three, and several more were bleeding when they fell back, paused, then moved to flank us.

We stood back to back then and cut them as they closed.

"If even one has a gun we are dead, Karagee."

"I know."

Another half-man fell to my blade. Hasan sent one, screaming, into the pit.

They were all about us then. A blade slipped in past my guard and cut me on the shoulder. Another nicked my thigh.

"Fall back, thou fools! I say withdraw, thou freaks!"

At that, they did, moving back beyond thrust-range.

The man who had spoken was about five and a half feet tall. His lower jaw moved like that of a puppet's, as though on hinges, and his teeth were like a row of dominoes—all dark-stained and clicking as they opened and closed.

"Yea, Procrustes," I heard one say.

"Fetch nets! Snare them alive! Do not close with them! They have cost us too much already!"

Moreby was at his side, and whimpering.

". . . I did not know, m'lord."

"Silence! thou brewer of ill-tasting sloshes! Thou hast cost us a god and many men!"

"Shall we rush?" asked Hasan.

"No, but be ready to cut the nets when they bring them."

"It is not good that they want us alive," he decided.

"We have sent many to Hell, to smooth our way," said I, "and we are standing yet and holding blades. What more?"

"If we rush them we can take two, perhaps four more with us. If we wait, they will net us and we die without them."

"What matters it, once you are dead? Let us wait. So long as we live there is the great peacock-tail of probability, growing from out of the next moment."

"As you say."

And they found nets and cast them. We cut three of them apart before they tangled us in the fourth. They drew them tight and moved in.

I felt my blade wrenched from my grasp, and someone kicked me. It was Moreby.

"Now you will die as very few die," said he.

"Did the others escape?"

"Only for the moment," he said. "We will track them, find them, and bring them back."

I laughed.

"You lose," I said. "They'll make it."

He kicked me again.

"This is how your rule applies?" I asked. "Hasan conquered the Dead Man."

"He cheated. The woman threw a flare."

Procrustes came up beside him as they bound us within the nets.

"Let us take them to the Valley of Sleep," said Moreby, "and there work our wills with them and leave them to be preserved against future feasting."

"It is good," said Procrustes. "Yes, it shall be done."

Hasan must have been working his left arm through the netting all that while, because it shot out a short distance and his nails raked Procrustes' leg.

Procrustes kicked him several times, and me once for good measure. He rubbed at the scratches on his calf.

"Why did you do that, Hasan?" I asked, after Procrustes turned away and ordered us bound to barbecue stakes for carrying.

"There may still be some meta-cyanide left on my finger-nails," he explained.

"How did it get there?"

"From the bullets in my belt, Karagee, which they did not take from me. I coated my nails after I sharpened them today."

"Ah! You scratched the Dead Man at the beginning of your bout . . ."

"Yes, Karagee. Then it was simply a matter of my staying alive until he fell over."

"You are an exemplary assassin, Hasan."

"Thank you, Karagee."

We were bound to the stakes, still netted. Four men, at the order of Procrustes, raised us.

Moreby and Procrustes leading the way, we were borne off through the night.

*

As we moved along an uneven trail the world changed about us. It's always that way when you approach a Hot Spot. It's like hiking backward through geological eras.

The trees along the way began to vary, more and more. Finally, we were passing up a moist aisle between dark towers with fern-like leaves; and things peered out through them with slitted, yellow eyes. High overhead, the night was a tarp, stretched tent-wise across the treetops, pricked with faint star-marks, torn with a jagged yellow crescent of a tear. Birdlike cries, ending in snorts, emerged from the great wood. Up further ahead a dark shape crossed the pathway.

As we advanced along the way the trees grew smaller, the spaces between them wider. But they were not like the trees we had left beyond the village. There were twisted (and twisting!) forms, with seaweed swirls of branches, gnarled trunks, and exposed roots which crept, slowly, about the surface of the ground. Tiny invisible things made scratching noises as they scurried from the light of Moreby's electric lantern.

By turning my head I could detect a faint, pulsating glow, just at the border of the visible spectrum. It was coming from up ahead.

A profusion of dark vines appeared underfoot. They writhed whenever one of our bearers stepped on them.

The trees became simple ferns. Then these, too, vanished. Great quantities of shaggy, blood-colored lichens replaced them. They grew over all the rocks. They were faintly luminous.

There were no more animal sounds. There were no sounds at all, save for the panting of our four bearers, the footfalls, and the occasional muffled click as Procrustes' automatic rifle struck a padded rock.

Our bearers wore blades in their belts. Moreby carried several blades, as well as a small pistol.

The trail turned sharply upward. One of our bearers swore. The night-tent was jerked downward at its corners then; it met with the horizon, and it was filled with the hint of a purple haze, fainter than exhaled cigarette-smoke. Slow, very high, and slapping the air like a devilfish coasting on water, the dark form of a spiderbat crossed over the face of the moon.

Procrustes fell.

Moreby helped him to his feet, but Procrustes swayed and leaned upon him.

"What ails you, lord?"

"A sudden dizziness, numbness in my members. . . . Take thou my rifle. It grows heavy."

Hasan chuckled.

Procrustes turned toward Hasan, his puppet-jaw dropping open.

Then he dropped, too.

Moreby had just taken the rifle and his hands were full. The guards set us down, rather ungently, and rushed to Procrustes' side.

"Hast thou any water?" he asked, and he closed his eyes.

He did not open them again.

Moreby listened to his chest, held the feathery part of his wand beneath his nostrils.

"He is dead," he finally announced.

"Dead?"

The bearer who was covered with scales began to weep.

"He wiss good," he sobbed. "He wiss a great war shief. What will we do now?"

"He is dead," Moreby repeated, "and I am your leader until a new war chief is declared. Wrap him in your cloaks. Leave him on that flat rock up ahead. No animals come here, so he will not be molested. We will recover him on the way back. Now, though, we must have our vengeance on these two." He gestured with his wand. "The Valley of Sleep is near at hand. You have taken the pills I gave you?"

"Yes."

"Yes."

"Yes."

"Yiss."

"Very good. Take your cloaks now and wrap him."

They did this, and soon we were raised again and borne to the top of a ridge from which a trail ran down into a fluorescent, pock-blasted pit. The great rocks of the place seemed almost to be burning.

"This," I said to Hasan, "was described to me by my son as the place where the thread of my life lies across a burning stone. He saw me as threatened by the Dead Man, but the fates thought twice and gave that menace onto you. Back when I was but a dream in the mind of Death, this site was appointed as one of the places where I might die."

"To fall from Shinvat is to roast," said Hasan.

They carried us down into the fissure, dropped us on the rocks.

Moreby released the safety catch on the rifle and stepped back.

"Release the Greek and tie him to that column." He gestured with the weapon.

They did this, binding my hands and feet securely. The rock was smooth, damp, killing without indication.

They did the same to Hasan, about eight feet to my right.

Moreby had set down the lantern so that it cast a yellow semicircle about us. The four Kouretes were demon statues at his side.

He smiled. He leaned the rifle against the rocky wall behind him.

"This is the Valley of Sleep," he told us. "Those who sleep here do not awaken. It keeps the meat preserved, however, providing us against the lean years. Before we leave you, though—" His eyes turned to me. "Do you see where I have set the rifle?"

I did not answer him.

"I believe your entrails will stretch that far, Commissioner. At any rate, I intend to find out." He drew a dagger from his belt and advanced upon me. The four half-men moved with him. "Who do you think has more guts?" he asked. "You or the Arab?"

Neither of us replied.

"You shall both get to see for yourselves," he said through his teeth. "First you!"

He jerked my shirt free and cut it down the front.

He rotated the blade in a slow significant circle about two inches away from my stomach, all the while studying my face.

"You are afraid," he said. "Your face does not show it yet, but it will."

Then: "Look at me! I am going to put the blade in very slowly. I am going to dine on you one day. What do you think of that?"

I laughed. It was suddenly worth laughing at.

His face twisted, then it straightened into a momentary look of puzzlement.

"Has the fear driven you mad, Commissioner?"

"Feathers or lead?" I asked him.

He knew what it meant. He started to say something, and then he heard a pebble click about twelve feet away. His head snapped in that direction.

He spent the last second of his life screaming, as the force of Bortan's leap pulped him against the ground, before his head was snatched from his shoulders.

My hellhound had arrived.

The Kouretes screamed, for his eyes are glowing coals and his teeth are buzzsaws. His head is as high above the ground as a tall man's. Although they seized their blades and struck at him, his sides are as the sides of an armadillo. A quarter ton of dog, my Bortan . . . he is not exactly the kind Albert Payson Terhune wrote about.

He worked for the better part of a minute, and when he was finished they were all in pieces and none of them alive.

"What is it?" asked Hasan.

"A puppy I found in a sack, washed up on the beach, too tough to drown—my dog," said I, "Bortan."

There was a small gash in the softer part of his shoulder. He had not gotten it in the fight.

"He sought us first in the village," I said, "and they tried to stop him. Many Kouretes have died this day."

He trotted up and licked my face. He wagged his tail, made dog-noises, wriggled like a puppy, and ran in small circles. He sprang toward me and licked my face again. Then he was off cavorting once more, treading on pieces of Kouretes.

"It is good for a man to have a dog," said Hasan. "I have always been fond of dogs."

Bortan was sniffing him as he said it.

"You've come back, you dirty old hound," I told him. "Don't you know that dogs are extinct?"

He wagged his tail, came up to me again, licked my hand.

"I'm sorry that I can't scratch your ears. You know that I'd like to, though, don't you?"

He wagged his tail.

I opened and closed my right hand within its bonds. I turned my head that way as I did it. Bortan watched, his nostrils moist and quivering.

"Hands, Bortan. I need hands to free me. Hands to loosen my bonds. You must fetch them, Bortan, and bring them here."

He picked up an arm that was lying on the ground and he deposited it at my feet. He looked up then and wagged his tail.

"No, Bortan. *Live* hands. Friendly hands. Hands to untie me. You understand, don't you?"

He licked my hand.

"Go and find hands to free me. Still attached and living. The hands of friends. Now, quickly! Go!"

He turned and walked away, paused, looked back once, then mounted the trail.

"Does he understand?" asked Hasan.

"I think so," I told him. "His is not an ordinary dog brain, and he has had many many more years than even the lifetime of a man in which to learn understanding."

"Then let us hope he finds someone quickly, before we sleep."

"Yes."

We hung there and the night was cold.

We waited for a long time. Finally, we lost track of time.

Our muscles were cramped and aching. We were covered with the dried blood of countless little wounds. We were all over bruises. We were groggy from fatigue, from lack of sleep.

We hung there, the ropes cutting into us.

"Do you think they will make it to your village?"

"We gave them a good start. I think they have a decent chance."

"It is always difficult to work with you, Karagee."

"I know. I have noticed this same thing myself."

". . . Like the summer we rotted in the dungeons of Corsica."

"Aye."

". . . Or our march to the Chicago Station, after we had lost all our equipment in Ohio."

"Yes, that was a bad year."

"You are *always* in trouble, though, Karagee. 'Born to knot the tiger's tail,'" he said; "that is the saying for people such as you. They are difficult to be with. Myself, I love the quiet and the shade, a book of poems, my pipe—"

"Hush! I hear something!"

There was a clatter of hooves.

A satyr appeared beyond the cockeyed angle of the light from the fallen lantern. He moved nervously, his eyes going from me to Hasan and back again, and up, down, around, and past us.

"Help us, little horny one," said I, in Greek.

He advanced carefully. He saw the blood, the mangled Kouretes.

He turned as if to flee.

"Come back! I need you! It is I, the player of the pipes."

He stopped and turned again, his nostrils quivering, flaring and falling. His pointed ears twitched.

He came back, a pained expression on his near-human face as he passed through the place of gore.

"The blade. At my feet," I said, gesturing with my eyes. "Pick it up."

He did not seem to like the notion of touching anything man-made, especially a weapon.

I whistled the last lines of my last tune.

It's late, it's late, so late. . . .

His eyes grew moist. He wiped at them with the backs of his shaggy wrists.

"Pick up the blade and cut my bonds. Pick it up. —Not that way, you'll cut yourself. The other end. —Yes."

He picked it up properly and looked at me. I moved my right hand.

"The ropes. Cut them."

He did. It took him fifteen minutes and left me wearing a bracelet of blood. I had to keep moving my hand to keep him from slashing an artery. But he freed it and looked at me expectantly.

"Now give me the knife and I'll take care of the rest."

He placed the blade in my extended hand.

I took it. Seconds later I was free. Then I freed Hasan.

When I turned again the satyr was gone. I heard the sound of frantic hoofbeats in the distance.

"The Devil has forgiven me," said Hasan.

We went far away from the Hot Spot as fast as we could, skirting the Kourete village and continuing northward until we came upon a trail that I recognized as the road to Volos. Whether Bortan had found the satyr and had somehow conned him into coming to us, or whether the creature had spotted us himself and remembered me, was something of which I couldn't be sure. Bortan had not returned, though, so I had a feeling it was the latter case.

The closest friendly town was Volos, a probable twenty-five kilometers to the east. If Bortan had gone there, where he would be recognized by many of my relatives, it would still be a long while before his return. My sending him after help had been a last-ditch sort of thing. If he'd tried elsewhere than Volos, then I'd no idea when he'd be back. He'd find my trail though, and he'd follow it again. We pushed on, putting as much road as possible behind us.

After about ten kilos we were staggering. We knew that we couldn't make it much further without rest, so we kept our eyes open for a possible safe sleep-site.

Finally, I recognized a steep, rocky hill where I had herded sheep as a boy. The small shepherd's cave, three-quarters of the way up the slope, was dry and vacant. The wooden façade that faced it was fallen to decay, but it still functioned.

We pulled some clean grass for bedding, secured the door, and stretched out within. In a moment, Hasan was snoring. My mind spun for a second before it drifted, and in that second I knew that of all pleasures—a drink of cold water when you are thirsty, liquor when you are not, sex, a cigarette after many days without one—there is none of them can compare with sleep.

Sleep is best. . . .

I might say that if our party had taken the long way from Lamia to Volos—the coastal road—the whole thing might never have happened the way that it did, and Phil might be alive today.

But I can't really judge all that occurred in this case; even now, looking back, I can't say how I'd rearrange events if it was all to be done over again. The forces of final disruption were already goose-stepping amidst the ruins, arms upraised. . . .

We made it to Volos the following afternoon, and on up Mount Pelion to Portaria. Across a deep ravine lay Makrynitsa.

We crossed over and found the others.

Phil had guided them to Makrynitsa, asked for a bottle of wine and his copy of *Prometheus Unbound*, and had sat up with the two, well into the evening.

In the morning, Diane had found him smiling, and cold.

I built him a pyre amidst the cedars near the ruined Episcopi, because he did not want to be buried. I heaped it with incense, with aromatic herbs, and it was twice the height of a man. That night it would burn and I would say goodbye to another friend. It seems, looking back, that my life has mainly been a series of arrivals and departures. I say "hello." I say "goodbye." Only the Earth endures. . . .

Hell.

So I walked with the group that afternoon, out to Pagasae, the port of ancient Iolkos, set on the promontory opposite Volos. We stood in the shade of the almond trees on the hill that gives good vantage to both seascape and rocky ridge.

"It was from here that the Argonauts set sail on their quest for the Golden Fleece," I told no one in particular.

"Who all were they?" asked Ellen. "I read the story in school, but I forget."

"There was Herakles and Theseus and Orpheus the singer, and Asclepius, and the sons of the North Wind, and Jason, the captain, who was a pupil of the centaur, Cheiron—whose cave, incidentally, is up near the summit of Mount Pelion, there."

"Really?"

"I'll show it to you sometime."

"All right."

"The gods and the titans battled near here also," said Diane, coming up on my other side. "Did the titans not uproot Mount Pelion and pile it atop Ossa in an attempt to scale Olympus?"

"So goes the telling. But the gods were kind and restored the scenery after the bloody battle."

"A sail," said Hasan, gesturing with a half-peeled orange in his hand.

I looked out over the waters and there was a tiny blip on the horizon.

"Yes; this place is still used as a port."

"Perhaps it is a shipload of heroes," said Ellen, "returning with some more fleece. What will they do with all that fleece, anyhow?"

"It's not the fleece that's important," said Red Wig, "it's the getting of it. Every good story-teller used to know that. The womenfolk can always make stunning garments from fleeces. They're used to picking up the remains after quests."

"It wouldn't match your hair, dear."

"Yours either, child."

"That can be changed. Not so easily as yours, of course . . ."

"Across the way," said I, in a loud voice, "is a ruined Byzantine church—the Episcopi—which I've scheduled for restoration in another two years. It is the traditional site of the wedding feast of Peleus, also one of the Argonauts, and the sea-nymph Thetis. Perhaps you've heard the story of that feast? Everyone was invited but the goddess of discord, and she came anyhow and tossed down a golden apple marked 'For the Fairest.' Lord Paris judged it the property of Aphrodite, and the fate of Troy was sealed. The last time anyone saw Paris, he was none too happy. Ah, decisions! Like I've often said, this land is lousy with myth."

"How long will we be here?" asked Ellen.

"I'd like a couple more days in Makrynitsa," I said, "then we'll head northwards. Say about a week more in Greece, and then we'll move on to Rome."

"No," said Myshtigo, who had been sitting on a rock and talking to his machine, as he stared out over the waters. "No, the tour is finished. This is the last stop."

"How come?"

"I'm satisfied and I'm going home now."

"What about your book?"

"I've got my story."

"What kind of story?"

"I'll send you an autographed copy when it's finished. My

time is precious, and I have all the material I want now. All that I'll need, anyhow. I called the Port this morning, and they are sending me a Skimmer tonight. You people go ahead and do whatever you want, but I'm finished."

"Is something wrong?"

"No, nothing is wrong, but it's time that I left. I have much to do."

He rose to his feet and stretched.

"I have some packing to take care of, so I'll be going back now. You *do* have a beautiful country here, Conrad, despite. —I'll see you all at dinnertime."

He turned and headed down the hill.

I walked a few steps in his direction, watching him go.

"I wonder what prompted that?" I thought aloud.

There was a footfall.

"He is dying," said George, softly.

My son Jason, who had preceded us by several days, was gone. Neighbors told of his departure for Hades on the previous evening. The patriarch had been carried off on the back of a fire-eyed hellhound who had knocked down the door of his dwelling place and borne him off through the night. My relatives all wanted me to come to dinner. Dos Santos was still resting; George had treated his wounds and had not deemed it necessary to ship him to the hospital in Athens.

It's always nice to come home.

I walked down to the Square and spent the afternoon talking to my descendants. Would I tell them of Taler, of Haiti, of Athens? Aye. I would, I did. Would they tell me of the past two decades in Makrynitsa? Ditto.

I took some flowers to the graveyard then, stayed awhile, and went to Jason's home and repaired his door with some tools I found in the shed. Then I came upon a bottle of his wine and drank it all. And I smoked a cigar. I made me a pot of coffee, too, and I drank all of that.

I still felt depressed.

I didn't know what was coming off.

George knew his diseases, though, and he said the Vegan showed unmistakable symptoms of a neurological disorder of the e.t. variety. Incurable. Invariably fatal.

And even Hasan couldn't take credit for it. "Etiology unknown" was George's diagnosis.

So everything was revised.

George had known about Myshtigo since the reception. —What had set him on the track?

—Phil had asked him to observe the Vegan for signs of a fatal disease.

Why?

Well, he hadn't said why, and I couldn't go ask him at the moment.

I had me a problem.

Myshtigo had either finished his job or he hadn't enough time left to do it. He *said* he'd finished it. If he hadn't, then I'd been protecting a dead man all the while, to no end. If he had, then I needed to know the results, so that I could make a very fast decision concerning what remained of his lifespan.

Dinner was no help. Myshtigo had said all he cared to say, and he ignored or parried our questions. So, as soon as we'd had our coffee, Red Wig and I stepped outside for a cigarette.

"What's happened?" she asked.

"I don't know. I thought maybe you did."

"No. What now?"

"You tell me."

"Kill him?"

"Perhaps yes. First though, why?"

"He's finished it."

"What? Just *what* has he finished?"

"How should I know?"

"Damn it! *I* have to! I like to know why I'm killing somebody. I'm funny that way."

"Funny? Very. Obvious, isn't it? The Vegans want to buy in again, Earthside. He's going back to give them a report on the sites they're interested in."

"Then why didn't he visit them all? Why cut it short after Egypt and Greece? Sand, rocks, jungles, and assorted monsters—that's all he saw. Hardly makes for an encouraging appraisal."

"Then he's scared, is why, and lucky he's alive. He could have been eaten by a boadile or a Kourete. He's running."

"Good. Then let him run. Let him hand in a bad report."

"He can't, though. If they *do* want in, they won't buy any-thing that sketchy. They'll just send somebody else—somebody tougher—to finish it. If we kill Myshtigo they'll know we're still for real, still protesting, still tough ourselves."

". . . And he's not afraid for his life," I mused.

"No? What, then?"

"I don't know. I have to find out, though."

"How?"

"I think I'll ask him."

"You are a lunatic." She turned away.

"My way, or not at all," I said.

"*Any* way, then. It doesn't matter. We've already lost."

I took her by the shoulders and kissed her neck. "Not yet. You'll see."

She stood stiffly.

"Go home," she said; "it's late. It's too late."

I did that. I went back to Iakov Korones' big old place, where Myshtigo and I were both quartered, and where Phil had been staying.

I stopped, there in the deathroom, in the place where Phil had last slept. His *Prometheus Unbound* was still on the writing table, set down beside an empty bottle. He had spoken of his own passing when he'd called me in Egypt, and he had suffered an attack, had been through a lot. It seemed he'd leave a message for an old friend then, on a matter like this.

So I opened Percy B's dud epic and looked within.

It was written on the blank pages at the end of the book, in Greek. Not modern Greek, though. Classical.

It went something like this:

> *Dear friend, although I abhor writing anything I cannot rewrite, I feel I had best tend to this with dispatch. I am unwell. George wants me to skim to Athens. I will, too, in the morning. First, though, regarding the matter at hand—*
> *Get the Vegan off the Earth, alive, at any cost.*
> *It is important.*
> *It is the most important thing in the world.*
> *I was afraid to tell you before, because I thought Myshtigo might be a telepath. That is why I did not go along for the entire journey, though I should dearly have loved to do so. That is why I pretended*

to hate him, so that I could stay away from him as much as possible. It was only after I managed to confirm the fact that he was not telepathic that I elected to join you.

I suspected, what with Dos Santos, Diane, and Hasan, that the Radpol might be out for his blood. If he was a telepath, I figured he would learn of this quickly and do whatever needed to be done to assure his safety. If he was not a telepath, I still had great faith in your ability to defend him against almost anything, Hasan included. But I did not want him apprised of my knowledge. I did try to warn you, though, if you recall.

Tatram Yshtigo, his grandfather, is one of the finest, most noble creatures alive. He is a philosopher, a great writer, an altruistic administrator of services to the public. I became acquainted with him during my stay on Taler, thirty-some years ago, and we later became close friends. We have been in communication ever since that time, and that far back, even, was I advised by him of the Vegan Combine's plans regarding the disposition of Earth. I was also sworn to secrecy. Even Cort cannot know that I am aware. The old man would lose face, disastrously, if this thing came out ahead of time.

The Vegans are in a very embarrassing position. Our expatriate countrymen have forced their own economic and cultural dependence upon Vega. The Vegans were made aware—quite vividly! —during the days of the Radpol Rebellion, of the fact that there is an indigenous population possessing a strong organization of its own and desiring the restoration of our planet. The Vegans too would like to see this happen. They do not want the Earth. Whatever for? If they want to exploit Earthfolk, they have more of them on Taler than we do here on Earth—and they're not doing it; not massively or maliciously, at any rate. Our ex-pop has elected what labor exploitation it does undergo in preference to returning here. What does this indicate? Returnism is a dead issue. No one is coming back. That is why I quit the movement. Why you did too, I believe. The Vegans would like to get the home world problem off their hands. Sure, they want to visit it. It is instructive, sobering, humbling, and downright frightening for them to come here and see what can be done to a world.

What needed to be done was for them to find a way around our ex-pop-gov on Taler. The Talerites were not anxious to give up their only claim for taxes and existence: the Office.

After much negotiation, though, and much economic suasion, including the offer of full Vegan citizenship to our ex-pop, it appeared that a means had been found. The implementation of *the plan was given into the hands of the Shtigo gens, Tatram in especial.*

He finally found a way, he believed, of returning the Earth proper to an autonomous position and preserving its cultural integrity. That is why he sent his grandson, Cort, to do his "survey." Cort is a strange creature; his real talent is acting (all the Shtigo are quite gifted), and he loves to pose. I believe that he wanted to play the part of an alien very badly, and I am certain that he has carried it with skill and efficiency. (Tatram also advised me that it would be Cort's last role. He is dying of drinfan, which is incurable; also, I believe it is the reason he was chosen.)

Believe me, Konstantin Karaghiosis Korones Nomikos (and all the others which I do not know), Conrad, when I say that he was not surveying real estate: No.

But allow me one last Byronic gesture. Take my word that he must live, and let me keep my promise and my secret. You will not regret it, when you know all.

I am sorry that I never got to finish your elegy, and damn you for keeping my Lara, that time in Kerch! —PHIL

Very well then, I decided—life, not death, for the Vegan. Phil had spoken and I did not doubt his words.

I went back to Mikar Korones' dinner table and stayed with Myshtigo until he was ready to leave. I accompanied him back to Iakov Korones' and watched him pack some final items. We exchanged maybe six words during this time.

His belongings we carried out to the place where the Skimmer would land, in front of the house. Before the others (including Hasan) came up to bid him goodbye, he turned to me and said, "Tell me, Conrad, why are you tearing down the pyramid?"

"To needle Vega," I said. "To let you know that if you want this place and you do manage to take it away from us, you'll get it in worse shape than it was after the Three Days. There wouldn't be anything left to look at. We'd burn the rest of our history. Not even a scrap for you guys."

The air escaping from the bottom of his lungs came out with a high-pitched whine—the Vegan equivalent of a sigh.

"Commendable, I suppose," he said, "but I did so want to see it. Do you think you could ever get it back together again? Soon, perhaps?"

"What do you think?"

"I noticed your men marking many of the pieces."

I shrugged.

"I have only one serious question, then—about your fondness for destruction . . ." he stated.

"What is that?"

"Is it *really* art?"

"Go to hell."

Then the others came up. I shook my head slowly at Diane and seized Hasan's wrist long enough to tear away a tiny needle he'd taped to the palm of his hand. I let him shake hands with the Vegan too, then, briefly.

The Skimmer buzzed down out of the darkening sky and I saw Myshtigo aboard, loaded his baggage personally, and closed the door myself.

It took off without incident and was gone in a matter of moments.

End of a nothing jaunt.

I went back inside and changed my clothing.

It was time to burn a friend.

Heaped high into the night, my ziggurat of logs bore what remained of the poet, my friend. I kindled a torch and put out the electric lantern. Hasan stood at my side. He had helped bear the corpse to the cart and had taken over the reins. I had built the pyre on the cypress-filled hill above Volos, near the ruins of that church I mentioned earlier. The waters of the bay were calm. The sky was clear and the stars were bright.

Dos Santos, who did not approve of cremation, had decided not to attend, saying that his wounds were troubling him. Diane had elected to remain with him back in Makrynitsa. She had not spoken to me since our last conversation.

Ellen and George were seated on the bed of the cart, which was backed beneath a large cypress, and they were holding hands. They were the only others present. Phil would not have liked my relatives wailing their dirges about him. He'd once said he wanted something big, bright, fast, and without music.

I applied the torch to a corner of the pyre. The flame bit,

slowly, began to chew at the wood. Hasan started another torch going, stuck it into the ground, stepped back, and watched.

As the flames ate their way upwards I prayed the old prayers and poured out wine upon the ground. I heaped aromatic herbs onto the blaze. Then I, too, stepped back.

"'. . . Whatever you were, death has taken you, too,'" I told him. "'You have gone to see the moist flower open along Acheron, among Hell's shadows darting fitfully.' Had you died young, your passing would have been mourned as the destruction of a great talent before its fulfillment. But you lived and they cannot say that now. Some choose a short and supernal life before the walls of their Troy, others a long and less troubled one. And who is to say which is the better? The gods did keep their promise of immortal fame to Achilleus, by inspiring the poet to sing him an immortal paean. But is he the happier for it, being now as dead as yourself? *I* cannot judge, old friend. Lesser bard, I remember some of the words you, too, wrote of the mightiest of the Argives, and of the time of hard-hurled deaths: 'Bleak disappointments rage this coming-together place: Menace of sighs in a jeopardy of time. . . . But the ashes do not burn backward to timber. Flame's invisible music shapes the air to heat, but the day is no longer.' Fare thee well, Phillip Graber. May the Lords Phoebus and Dionysius, who do love and kill their poets, commend thee to their dark brother Hades. And may his Persephone, Queen of the Night, look with favor upon thee and grant thee high stead in Elysium. Goodbye."

The flames had almost reached the top.

I saw Jason then, standing beside the cart, Bortan seated by his side. I backed away further. Bortan came to me and sat down at my right. He licked my hand, once.

"Mighty hunter, we have lost us another," I said.

He nodded his great head.

The flames reached the top and began to nibble at the night. The air was filled with sweet aromas and the sound of fire.

Jason approached.

"Father," he said, "he bore me to the place of burning rocks, but you were already escaped."

I nodded.

"A no-man friend freed us from that place. Before that, this man Hasan destroyed the Dead Man. So your dreams have thus far proved both right and wrong."

"*He* is the yellow-eyed warrior of my vision," he said.

"I know, but that part too is past."

"What of the Black Beast?"

"Not a snort nor a snuffle."

"Good."

We watched for a long, long time, as the night retreated into itself. At several points, Bortan's ears pricked forward and his nostrils dilated. George and Ellen had not moved. Hasan was a strange-eyed watcher, without expression.

"What will you do now, Hasan?" I asked.

"Go again to Mount Sindjar," he said, "for awhile."

"And then?"

He shrugged. "Howsoever it is written," he replied.

And a fearsome noise came upon us then, like the groans of an idiot giant, and the sound of splintering trees accompanied it.

Bortan leapt to his feet and howled. The donkeys who had drawn the cart shifted uneasily. One of them made a brief, braying noise.

Jason clutched the sharpened staff which he had picked from the heap of kindling, and he stiffened.

It burst in upon us then, there in the clearing. Big, and ugly, and everything it had ever been called.

The Eater of Men. . . .

The Shaker of the Earth. . . .

The Mighty, Foul One. . . .

The Black Beast of Thessaly.

Finally, someone could say what it really was. If they got away to say it, that is.

It must have been drawn to us by the odor of burning flesh.

And it *was* big. The size of an elephant, at least.

What was Herakles' fourth labor?

The wild boar of Arcadia, that's what.

I suddenly wished Herk was still around, to help.

A big pig. . . . A razorback, with tusks the length of a man's arm. . . . Little pig eyes, black, and rolling in the firelight, wildly. . . .

It knocked down trees as it came. . . .

It squealed, though, as Hasan drew a burning brand from the blaze and drove it, fire-end forward, into its snout, and then spun away.

It swerved, too, which gave me time to snatch Jason's staff.

I ran forward and caught it in the left eye with it.

It swerved again then, and squealed like a leaky boiler.

. . . And Bortan was upon it, tearing at its shoulder.

Neither of my two thrusts at its throat did more than superficial damage. It wrestled, shoulder against fang, and finally shook itself free of Bortan's grip.

Hasan was at my side by then, waving another firebrand.

It charged us.

From somewhere off to the side George emptied a machine-pistol into it. Hasan hurled the torch. Bortan leapt again, this time from its blind side.

. . . And these things caused it to swerve once more in its charge, crashing into the now-empty cart and killing both donkeys.

I ran against it then, thrusting the staff up under its left front leg.

The staff broke in two.

Bortan kept biting, and his snarl was a steady thunder. Whenever it slashed at him with its tusks he relinquished his grip, danced away, and moved in again to worry it.

I am sure that my needle-point deathlance of steel would not have broken. It had been aboard the *Vanitie*, though. . . .

Hasan and I circled it with the sharpest and most stakelike of the kindling we could find. We kept jabbing, to keep it turning in a circle. Bortan kept trying for its throat, but the great snouted head stayed low, and the one eye rolled and the other bled, and the tusks slashed back and forth and up and down like swords. Cloven hooves the size of bread-loaves tore great holes in the ground as it turned, counterclockwise, trying to kill us all, there in the orange and dancing flamelight.

Finally, it stopped and turned—suddenly, for something that big—and its shoulder struck Bortan in the side and hurled him ten or twelve feet past me. Hasan hit it across the back with his stick and I drove in toward the other eye, but missed.

Then it moved toward Bortan, who was still regaining his feet—its head held low, tusks gleaming.

I threw my staff and leapt as it moved in on my dog. It had already dropped its head for the death blow.

I caught both tusks as the head descended almost to the ground. Nothing could hold back that scooping slash, I realized, as I bore down upon it with all my strength.

But I tried, and maybe I succeeded, somehow, for a second. . . .

At least, as I was thrown through the air, my hands torn and bleeding, I saw that Bortan had managed to get back out of the way.

I was dazed by the fall, for I had been thrown far and high; and I heard a great pig-mad squealing. Hasan screamed and Bortan roared out his great-throated battle-challenge once more.

. . . And the hot red lightning of Zeus descended twice from the heavens.

. . . And all was still.

I climbed back, slowly, to my feet.

Hasan was standing by the blazing pyre, a flaming stake still upraised in spear-throwing position.

Bortan was sniffing at the quivering mountain of flesh.

Cassandra was standing beneath the cypress beside a dead donkey, her back against the trunk of the tree, wearing leather trousers, a blue woolen shirt, a faint smile, and my still-smoking elephant gun.

"Cassandra!"

She dropped the gun and looked very pale. But I had her in my arms almost before it hit the ground.

"I'll ask you a lot of things later," I said. "Not now. Nothing now. Let's just sit here beneath this tree and watch the fire burn."

And we did.

A month later, Dos Santos was ousted from the Radpol. He and Diane have not been heard of since. Rumor has it that they gave up on Returnism, moved to Taler, and are living there now. I hope it's not true, what with the affairs of these past five days. I never did know the full story on Red Wig, and I guess I never will. If you trust a person, really trust him I mean, and you care for him, as she might have cared for me, it would seem you'd stick around to see whether he was right or wrong on your final big disagreement. She didn't, though, and I wonder if she regrets it now.

I don't really think I'll ever see her again.

Slightly after the Radpol shakeup, Hasan returned from Mount Sindjar, stayed awhile at the Port, then purchased a small ship and put out to sea early one morning, without even saying goodbye or giving any indication as to his destination. It was assumed he'd found new employment somewhere. There was a hurricane, though, several days later, and I heard rumors in Trinidad to the effect that he had been washed up on the coast of Brazil and met with his death at the hands of the fierce tribesmen who dwell there. I tried but was unable to verify this story.

However, two months later, Ricardo Bonaventura, Chairman of the Alliance Against Progress, a Radpol splinter group which had fallen into disfavor with Athens, died of apoplexy during a Party function. There were some murmurings of Divban rabbit-venom in the anchovies (an exceedingly lethal combination, George assures me), and the following day the new Captain of the Palace Guard vanished mysteriously, along with a Skimmer and the minutes of the last three secret sessions of the AAP (not to mention the contents of a small wall-safe). He was said to have been a big, yellow-eyed man, with a slightly Eastern cast to his features.

Jason is still herding his many-legged sheep in the high places, up where the fingers of Aurora come first to smear the sky with roses, and doubtless he is corrupting youth with his song.

Ellen is pregnant again, all delicate and big-waisted, and won't talk to anybody but George. George wants to try some fancy embryosurgery, now, before it's too late, and make his next kid a water-breather as well as an air-breather, because of all that great big virgin frontier down underneath the ocean, where his descendants can pioneer, and him be father to a new race and write an interesting book on the subject, and all that. Ellen is not too hot on the idea, though, so I have a hunch the oceans will remain virgin a little longer.

Oh yes, I did take George to Capistrano some time ago,

to watch the spiderbats return. It was real impressive—them darkening the sky with their flight, nesting about the ruins the way they do, eating the wild pigs, leaving green droppings all over the streets. Lorel has hours and hours of it in tri-dee color, and he shows it at every Office party. It's sort of a historical document, spiderbats being on the way out now. True to his word, George started a *slishi* plague among them, and they're dropping like flies these days. Just the other week one dropped down in the middle of the street with a big *splatt!* as I was on my way to Mama Julie's with a bottle of rum and a box of chocolates. It was quite dead when it hit. The *slishi* are very insidious. The poor spiderbat doesn't know what's happening; he's flying along happily, looking for someone to eat, and then *zock!* it hits him, and he falls into the middle of a garden party or somebody's swimming pool.

I've decided to retain the Office for the time being. I'll set up some kind of parliament after I've whipped up an opposition party to the Radpol—Indreb, or something like that maybe: like Independent Rebuilders, or such.

Good old final forces of disruption . . . we needed them down here amid the ruins.

And Cassandra—my princess, my angel, my lovely lady—she even likes me without my fungus. That night in the Valley of Sleep did it in.

She, of course, had been the shipload of heroes Hasan had seen that day back at Pagasae. No golden fleece, though, just my gunrack and such. Yeah. It had been the *Golden Vanitie*, which I'd built by hand, me, stout enough, I was pleased to learn, to take even the *tsunami* that followed that 9.6 Richter thing. She'd been out sailing in it at the time the bottom fell out of Kos. Afterwards, she'd set sail for Volos because she knew Makrynitsa was full of my relatives. Oh, good thing—that she had had this *feeling* that there was danger and had carried the heavy artillery ashore with her. (Good thing, too, that she knew how to use it.) I'll have to learn to take her premonitions more seriously.

I've purchased a quiet villa on the end of Haiti opposite from the Port. It's only about fifteen minutes' skimming time from there, and it has a big beach and lots of jungle all around it. I have to have some distance, like the whole island, between me and civilization, because I have this, well—hunting—problem. The other day, when the attorneys dropped around, they didn't understand the sign: BEWARE THE DOG. They do now. The one who's in traction won't sue for damages, and George will have him as good as new in no time. The others were not so severely taken.

Good thing I was nearby, though.

So here I am, in an unusual position, as usual.

The entire planet Earth was purchased from the Talerite government, purchased by the large and wealthy Shtigo gens. The preponderance of expatriates wanted Vegan citizenship anyhow, rather than remaining under the Talerite ex-gov and working in the Combine as registered aliens. This had been coming for a long time, so the disposal of the Earth became mainly a matter of finding the best buyer—because our exile regime lost its only other cause for existence the minute the citizenship thing went through. They could justify themselves while there were still Earthmen out there, but now they're all Vegans and can't vote for them, and *we're* sure not going to, down here.

Hence, the sale of a lot of real estate—and the only bidder was the Shtigo gens.

Wise old Tatram saw that the Shtigo gens did not own Earth, though. The entire purchase was made in the name of his grandson, the late Cort Myshtigo.

And Myshtigo left this distribution-desire, or last will and testament, Vegan-style . . .

. . . in which I was named.

I've, uh, inherited a planet.

The Earth, to be exact.

Well—

Hell, I don't want the thing. I mean, sure I'm stuck with it for awhile, but I'll work something out.

It was that infernal Vite-Stats machine, and four other big think-tanks that old Tatram used. He was looking for a local administrator to hold the Earth in fief and set up a resident representative government, and then to surrender ownership on a fairly simple residency basis once things got rolling. He wanted somebody who'd been around awhile, was qualified as an administrator, and who wouldn't want to keep the place for his very own.

Among others, it gave him one of my names, then another, the second as a "possibly still living." Then my personnel file was checked, and more stuff on the other guy, and pretty soon the machine had turned up a few more names, all of them mine. It began picking up discrepancies and peculiar similarities, kept kapocketting, and gave out more puzzling answers.

Before long, Tatram decided I had better be "surveyed."

Cort came to write a book.

He really wanted to see if I was Good, Honest, Noble, Pure, Loyal, Faithful, Trustworthy, Selfless, Kind, Cheerful, Dependable, and Without Personal Ambition.

Which means he was a cockeyed lunatic, because he said, "Yes, he's all that."

I sure fooled him.

Maybe he was right about the lack of personal ambition, though. I am pretty damn lazy, and am not at all anxious to acquire the headaches I see as springing up out of the tormented Earth and blackjacking me daily.

However, I am willing to make certain concessions so far as personal comfort is concerned. I'll probably cut myself back to a six-month vacation.

One of the attorneys (not the one in traction—the one with the sling) delivered me a note from the Blue One. It said, in part:

Dear Whatever-the-Blazes-Your-Name-Is,

It is most unsettling to begin a letter this way, so I'll respect your wishes and call you Conrad.

"Conrad," by now you are aware of the true nature of my visit. I feel I have made a good choice in naming you as heir to the property commonly referred to as Earth. Your affection for it cannot be gainsaid; as Karaghiosis you inspired men to bleed in its defense; you are restoring its monuments, preserving its works of art (and as one stipulation of my will, by the way, I insist that you put back the Great Pyramid!), and your ingenuity as well as your toughness, both physical and mental, is singularly amazing.

You also appear to be the closest thing to an immortal overseer available (I'd give a lot to know your real age), and this, together with your high survival potential, makes you, really, the only candidate. If your mutation ever does begin to fail you, there is always the S-S series to continue linking the great chain of your *days. (I could have said "forging," but it would not have been polite, inasmuch as I know you are an accomplished forger. —All those old records! You drove poor Vite-Stats half-mad with discrepancies. It is now programmed never to accept another Greek birth certificate as proof of age!)*

I commend the Earth into the hands of the kallikanzaros. According to legend, this would be a grave mistake. However, I am willing to gamble that you are even a kallikanzaros under false pretenses. You destroy only what you mean to rebuild. Probably you are Great Pan, who only pretended to die. Whatever, you will have sufficient funds and a supply of heavy equipment which will be sent this year—and lots of forms for requisitioning more from the Shtigo Foundation. So go thou and be thou fruitful and multiply, and reinherit the Earth. The gens will be around watching. Cry out if you need help, and help will be forthcoming.

I don't have time to write you a book. Sorry. Here is my autograph, anyhow:

—CORT MYSHTIGO

P.S. I still dunno if it's art. Go to hell yourself.

That is the gist of it.

Pan?

Machines don't talk that way, do they?

I hope not, anyhow. . . .

The Earth is a wild inhabitation. It is a tough and rocky place. The rubbish will have to be cleared, section by section, before some anti-rubbish can be put up.

Which means work, lots of it.

Which means I'll need all the Office facilities as well as the Radpol organization, to begin with.

Right now I'm deciding whether or not to discontinue the ruin-tours. I think I'll let them go on, because for once we'll have something good to show. There is that certain element of human curiosity which demands that one halt in his course and peer through a hole in any fence behind which construction work is going on.

We have money now, and we own our own property again, and that makes a big difference. Maybe even Returnism isn't completely dead. If there is a vital program to revive the Earth, we may draw back some of the ex-pop, may snag some of the new tourists.

Or, if they all want to remain Vegans, they can do that, too.

We'd like them, but we don't need them. Our Outbound immigration will be dropping off, I feel, once people know they can get ahead here; and our population will increase more than just geometrically, what with the prolonged fertility period brought on by the now quite expensive S-S series. I intend to socialize S-S completely. I'll do it by putting George in charge of a Public Health program, featuring mainland clinics and offering S-S all over the place.

We'll make out. I'm tired of being a gravekeeper, and I don't really want to spend from now till Easter cutting through the Tree of the World, even if I am a Darkborn with a propensity for trouble. When the bells do ring, I want to be able to say, "Alêthôs anestê," Risen indeed, rather than dropping my saw and running (*ring-a-ding*, the bells, *clackety-clack*, the hooves, etcetera). Now is the time for all good kallikanzaroi . . . You know.

So . . .

Cassandra and I have this villa on the Magic Island. She likes it here. I like it here. She doesn't mind my indeterminate age anymore. Which is fine.

Just this early morning, as we lay on the beach watching the sun chase away stars, I turned to her and mentioned that this is going to be a big, big ulcer-giving job, full of headaches and such.

"No, it isn't," she replied.

"Don't minimize what is imminent," I said. "It makes for incompatibility."

"None of that either."

"You are too optimistic, Cassandra."

"No. I told you that you were heading into danger before, and you were, but you didn't believe me then. This time I feel that things should go well. That's all."

"Granting your accuracy in the past, I still feel you are underestimating that which lies before us."

She rose and stamped her foot.

"You *never* believe me!"

"Of course I do. It just happens that this time you're wrong, dear."

She swam away then, my mad mermaid, out into the dark waters. After a time she came swimming back.

"Okay," she said, smiling, shaking down gentle rains from her hair. "Sure."

I caught her ankle, pulled her down beside me and began tickling her.

"Stop that!"

"Hey, I believe you, Cassandra! Really! Hear that? Oh, how about that? I really believe you. Damn! You sure are right!"

"You are a smart-alecky kallikanz— Ouch!"

And she was lovely by the seaside, so I held her in the wet, till the day was all around us, feeling good.

Which is a nice place to end a story, *sic*: .

Biographical Notes

Poul William Anderson (November 25, 1926–July 31, 2001), born in Bristol, Pennsylvania, was the eldest child of Anton William Anderson, a civil engineer for an oil refinery, and Astrid (Hertz) Anderson, a Danish-born secretary. He was raised mainly in Port Arthur, Texas, until his father died in an automobile accident in 1937; after a summer in Denmark, the family moved to Maryland and then to Northfield, Minnesota, where he attended high school. Rejected for military service in 1944 because of a scarred eardrum, he majored in physics at the University of Minnesota, graduating in 1948. While still in college, he published stories "Tomorrow's Children" and "Logic" in *Astounding Science Fiction*, the former with F. N. Waldrop, and joined the Minneapolis Fantasy Society, where he met other science fiction writers, including Clifford D. Simak and Gordon R. Dickson.

Anderson's first novel, the young adult *Vault of the Ages*, saw print in 1952; the same year, he published "Sargasso of Lost Spaceships" and "The Star Plunderer," stories that would later find their place in his long-running "Technic History" series. In 1953 he married fellow SF fan and fanzine creator Karen M. Kruse, a cartographer for the Army Corps of Engineers, and set out to earn his living as a writer, publishing nineteen stories and beginning the magazine versions of novels later to appear as *Brain Wave* (1954), *War of Two Worlds* (1959), and *Three Hearts and Three Lions* (1961). The couple moved to Berkeley, California, where their only child, Astrid Anderson, was born in 1954. Also in 1954 he published *The Broken Sword*, a "sword and sorcery" fantasy novel inspired by Icelandic sagas that began a substantial career for him in fantasy fiction. The novel *Star Ways* (1956) began his "Psychotechnic League" series. His first collection of short stories, *Earthman's Burden*—a collaboration with Gordon R. Dickson—appeared in 1957, followed by *Guardians of Time* in 1960 and dozens more in later years.

In 1961, Anderson won his first of seven Hugo Awards for his short story "The Longest Voyage" (1960). His novels of the 1960s included *The High Crusade* (1960), *Orbit Unlimited* (1961), *After Doomsday* (1962), *The Makeshift Rocket* (1962), *Let the Spacemen Beware!* (1963), *Shield* (1963), *Three Worlds to Conquer* (1964), *The Corridors of Time* (1965), *The Star Fox* (1965), *Ensign Flandry* (1966), *World Without*

Stars (1967), *Satan's World* (1967), and *The Rebel Worlds* (1969). In 1966, he helped to found the Society for Creative Anachronism, for which he styled himself "Sir Bela of Eastmarch."

Anderson continued to write prolifically over subsequent decades, publishing over three dozen additional novels, among other works. He served as president of the Science Fiction and Fantasy Writers of America (1972–73), receiving their Grand Master Award in 1998. In 1972 he won his first Nebula Award for the novelette "The Queen of Air and Darkness" (1971). During the 1980s, he collaborated with his wife Karen Anderson on four novels in the "King of Ys" series, gathered as *King of Ys* in 1996. In 2000 he was inducted into the Science Fiction and Fantasy Hall of Fame, and published *Genesis*, winner of the John W. Campbell Memorial Award. He died from prostate cancer at home in Orinda, California; his novels *Mother of Kings* (2001) and *For Love and Glory* (2003) were published posthumously.

Clifford Donald Simak (August 3, 1904–April 25, 1988) was born on his grandfather's farm near Millville, Wisconsin. The eldest child of Wisconsin native Margaret (Wiseman) Simak and John Lewis Simak, an immigrant from Bohemia (now part of the Czech Republic), he studied journalism at the University of Wisconsin but left to become a high school teacher. In 1929 he married Agnes Kuchenberg, with whom he had two children, Richard Scott and Shelley Ellen; the same year, he began a long career as a newspaperman, starting at the *Iron River Reporter* in Iron River, Michigan, and moving frequently over the next decade, taking editorial assignments at small-town papers in Iowa, Missouri, North Dakota, and Minnesota.

Simak published his first science fiction story, "The World of the Red Sun," in the December 1931 *Wonder Stories*, following it during the 1930s with nearly a dozen more. He cofounded the Minneapolis Fantasy Society with other writers, including Oliver Saari and Gordon R. Dickson, and produced *The Fantasite*, a fanzine. In 1939 he joined the staff of the *Minneapolis Star*, where he wrote a column called "Science in the News"; after the Second World War, during which he worked for Army Intelligence, he was promoted to news editor. His novels of the 1950s included *Cosmic Engineers* (1950), *Empire* (1951), *Time and Again* (1951), and *Ring Around the Sun: A Story of Tomorrow* (1953). *City* (1952), a collection of eight linked stories originally published in *Astounding* from 1944 to 1947, won the 1953 International Fantasy Award; *Strangers in the Universe* (1956), *The Worlds of Clifford Simak* (1960), and *All the Traps of Earth* (1962) gathered his other short fiction, including "The Big Front Yard," winner of the 1959 Hugo Award for best novelette.

In 1961 Simak assumed the post of coordinator of the *Minneapolis Tribune*'s Science Reading Series, intended for schools, which won an Award for the Advancement of Science from the Westinghouse-American Association. He wrote new novels *They Walked Like Men* (1962), *Way Station* (1963; winner of the 1964 Hugo Award), *All Flesh Is Grass* (1965), *Why Call Them Back from Heaven?* (1967), *The Werewolf Principle* (1967), *The Goblin Reservation* (1968), *Out of Their Minds* (1970), and *Destiny Doll* (1971). In 1973 he published "Epilog," a conclusion to his collection *City*; the same year, he won the First Fandom Award for contributions to science fiction and was inducted into the Science Fiction Hall of Fame.

Simak retired from the *Tribune* in 1976, having written its "Medical Report" column since 1969; the following year he received a Grand Master Award for lifetime achievement from the Science Fiction Writers of America. He did not rest on his laurels, publishing stories, including "Grotto of the Dancing Deer" (1980, winner of Hugo and Nebula Awards) and a half dozen new novels, of which *Highway to Eternity* (1986) was his last. In 1987, he received the Bram Stoker Award for lifetime achievement from the Horror Writers Association. He died in Minneapolis at eighty-three, surviving his wife by two years.

Daniel Keyes (August 9, 1927–June 15, 2014), born Daniel Korzenstein in Brooklyn, New York, was the eldest of two children of Ukrainian Jewish immigrants William Korzenstein, a dealer in second-hand goods, and Rebecca (Alicke) Korzenstein, a beautician; he took the name Keyes around 1950 along with his family. While a student at Thomas Jefferson High School in Brooklyn, he worked in factories and waited on tables to earn tuition for the premedical program at New York University, which he started in 1945. Enlisting in the U.S. Maritime Service as ship's purser later that year, he sailed to Colombia and Japan; after his discharge, he enrolled at Brooklyn College, from which he graduated in 1950 with a BA in psychology.

Through a neighbor, science fiction writer Lester del Rey, Keyes found a job as associate fiction editor at Stadium Publications, taking responsibility for *Marvel Science Fiction* and other pulp magazines. His first science fiction story, "Precedent," appeared in the May 1952 issue of *Marvel*; the same year, he married fashion stylist Aurea Georgina Vazquez, with whom he had two daughters, Hillary Ann and Leslie Joan. He subsequently worked as a staff writer for Stan Lee at Atlas Comics (c. 1952–53), and then at EC Comics (c. 1955–56), producing scripts for *Journey into Unknown Worlds*, *Shock Illustrated*, and *Confessions Illustrated*; in between these two positions he ran a fashion photography studio with his wife. Beginning in 1957, he taught creative writing in New York City public schools, attending evening classes at Brooklyn College, from which he received an MA in English and American Literature in 1961.

Keyes published "Flowers for Algernon," a short story, in the April 1959 *Magazine of Fantasy and Science Fiction*. Written as a sequel to "The Trouble with Elmo," which had appeared in *Galaxy* the previous year—and rejected by H. L. Gold at *Galaxy* for its unhappy ending—it won a Hugo Award and was adapted for television as *The Two Worlds of Charlie Gordon* (1961). Moving to Detroit, where he taught literature and creative writing at Wayne State University, he expanded the story to novel length; again rejected by several publishers, it won a Nebula Award as *Flowers for Algernon* (1966) and became a perennial bestseller. *Charly*, a 1968 movie version, won an Academy Award for its lead actor Cliff Robinson; subsequent adaptations included a 1969 stage play by David Rogers, a short-lived 1978 Broadway musical *Charlie and Algernon*, and a 2000 TV movie starring Matthew Modine.

A professor of English and creative writing at Ohio University from 1966 until his retirement in 1990, Keyes went on to publish novels *The Touch* (1968), *The Fifth Sally* (1980), and *The Asylum Prophecies* (2009), along with true crime novels *The Minds of Billy Milligan* (1981; nominated for Edgar Award by Mystery Writers of America) and *Unveiling Claudia: A True Story of Serial Murder* (1986), and the memoir *Algernon, Charlie, and I: A Writer's Journey* (1999). In 2000, he was presented with the Author Emeritus award from the Science Fiction and Fantasy Writers of America. Surviving his wife by just over a year, he died at home in Boca Raton, Florida, from complications of pneumonia.

Roger Joseph Zelazny (May 13, 1937–June 14, 1995), born in Euclid, Ohio, was the only child of Joseph Frank Zelazny, a Polish immigrant who worked as a pattern maker for a typewriter company, and Josephine Flora (Sweet) Zelazny, a Chicago native. He attended Western Reserve University (now Case Western Reserve) after his graduation from Euclid Senior High School, changing his major from psychology to English, winning poetry and essay prizes, and contributing to *Skyline*, a university literary magazine. After receiving his BA in 1959, he moved to New York, where he continued his studies at Columbia University; his 1962 MA thesis was titled "Two Traditions and Cyril Tourneur: An Examination of Morality and Humor Comedy Conventions in *The Revenger's Tragedy*." While in graduate school, he served six months of active duty with the Ohio National Guard; afterwards, he took a job as a claims representative for the Social Security

Administration in Cleveland (later moving to Baltimore) and began to write science fiction.

Encouraged by Cele Goldsmith, editor of *Amazing Stories* and *Fantastic*, Zelazny published four SF magazine stories in 1962 and sixteen the following year, among them "A Rose for Ecclesiastes," for which he received his first Hugo nomination. He married Sharon Steberl at the end of 1964 (having postponed the ceremony after a serious car accident) and divorced in 1966; later that same year he married Judith Alene Callahan, with whom he had three children, Devin, Jonathan Trent, and Shannon. Still in his thirties, his novelette "The Doors of His Face, the Lamps of His Mouth" (1965) and novella "He Who Shapes" (1965) won Nebula Awards; his novels . . . *And Call Me Conrad* [*This Immortal*] and *Lord of Light* (1967) received Hugo Awards soon thereafter.

Retiring from his day job in 1969, Zelazny published *Nine Princes in Amber* (1970), the first novel in his popular, long-running fantasy series, "Amber," which later included *The Guns of Avalon* (1972), *Sign of the Unicorn* (1975), *The Hand of Oberon* (1976), *The Courts of Chaos* (1978), *Trumps of Doom* (1985), *Blood of Amber* (1986), *Sign of Chaos* (1987), *Knight of Shadows* (1989), *Prince of Chaos* (1991), and other works. He also published novels *The Dream Master* (1966), *Isle of the Dead* (1969), *Creatures of Light and Darkness* (1969), *Damnation Alley* (1969), *Jack of Shadows* (1971), *To Die in Italbar* (1973), *Doorways in the Sand* (1976), *Roadmarks* (1979), *The Bells of Shoredan* (1979), *Changeling* (1980), *The Changing Land: A Novel of Dilvish the Damned* (1981), *Dilvish, the Damned* (1982), *Madwand* (1982), and *A Night in Lonesome October* (1993); several collections of stories; and novels and short fiction in collaboration with Alfred Bester, Philip K. Dick, Gerard Hausman, Jane Lindskold, Fred Saberhagen, Robert Sheckley, and Thomas D. Thomas.

A guest of honor at the 1974 World Science Fiction Convention, Zelazny moved to Santa Fe in 1975, later separating from his wife and living with writer Jane Lindskold. A big-budget film version of his novel *Damnation Alley* was released in 1977. He died in Santa Fe of kidney failure related to colon cancer; in 2010 he was inducted into the Science Fiction Hall of Fame.

Note on the Texts

This volume collects four American science fiction novels of the 1960s: *The High Crusade* (1960) by Poul Anderson, *Way Station* (1963) by Clifford D. Simak, *Flowers for Algernon* (1966) by Daniel Keyes, and *. . . And Call Me Conrad* [*This Immortal*] (1966) by Roger Zelazny. A companion volume in the Library of America series, *American Science Fiction: Four Classic Novels, 1968–1969*, includes four later works: *Past Master* (1968) by R. A. Lafferty, *Picnic on Paradise* (1968) by Joanna Russ, *Nova* (1968) by Samuel R. Delany, and *Emphyrio* (1969) by Jack Vance.

The High Crusade. On January 12, 1960, Poul Anderson replied to an inquiry from Timothy Seldes, an editor at Doubleday and Company in New York: Would Anderson allow Doubleday to look at *The High Crusade*, the novel he was then working on for Avon Publications, in order that they might consider publishing it in Avon's place after a "suitable arrangement" had been made? Though Anderson confessed himself "rather dubious" that the more prestigious firm would "want anything to do" with the novel ("It's planned as a rather straight adventure yarn, concentrating on action and rather bloody and rough in places"), he was happy to comply with Seldes's request. Their subsequent correspondence about the novel is not known to have survived, but within three months they had agreed that Doubleday would publish it, Anderson had delivered his manuscript, and they had concluded any exchanges they may have had about revisions. On April 26, Anderson returned his author's proofs to Seldes's assistant Natalie Greenberg: "I found very few corrections needful."

Doubleday published *The High Crusade* on October 7, 1960. No evidence has been found to suggest that Anderson himself was responsible for the occasionally different text that appeared in *Analog Science Fact & Fiction*, in July, August, and September 1960, or that he sought revisions to the novel at any later date, though many editions followed during his lifetime, including six in the United States and two in the United Kingdom. The text of *The High Crusade* in the present volume is that of the 1960 Doubleday first printing.

Way Station. Clifford D. Simak's *Way Station* initially appeared as a two-part serial in the June and August 1963 issues of *Galaxy*, titled "Here Gather the Stars." The first book version of the novel, published by Doubleday in New York, followed on November 1, 1963, and won the 1964 Hugo Award for best novel. The book text closely follows that of a carbon typescript, also titled *Way Station*, as emended in Simak's hand and now among his papers at the University of Minnesota. The alternate title and occasionally variant text of the magazine version probably reflect earlier revisions to the original typescript made at the request of *Galaxy*'s editor Frederik Pohl, or by Pohl himself, rather than a version of the novel Simak subsequently revised for book publication.

Simak is not known to have been involved in the preparation of subsequent editions of the novel, which numbered over a dozen during his lifetime, including three in the United Kingdom. The text of *Way Station* in the present volume is that of the 1963 Doubleday first printing.

Flowers for Algernon. Daniel Keyes began what became *Flowers for Algernon* as a short story, in the summer of 1958. Horace Gold, the editor of *Galaxy*, had recently agreed to publish Keyes's story "The Trouble with Elmo" and wanted another (as Keyes recalls in his 1999 memoir *Algernon, Charlie, and I: A Writer's Journey*). Keyes responded with a short novella, initially titled "The Genius Effect." Gold admired and hoped to publish the novella but insisted it would need a happy ending before he could do so, and Keyes hesitated to oblige; his friend Phil Klass suggested that he offer it instead to Robert P. Mills, an editor at *The Magazine of Fantasy and Science Fiction*. Mills also liked the novella but asked Keyes to shorten it by some 10,000 words. Keyes decided to comply, and, retitled "Flowers for Algernon," it appeared in the magazine in April 1959, winning a 1960 Hugo Award for best story. In February 1961, "Flowers for Algernon" was adapted for television (as *The Two Worlds of Charlie Gordon*), and later that year Keyes sold the movie rights.

In the summer of 1962, setting aside what he had intended to be his first novel (*The Torch*, eventually published in 1968), Keyes sketched out a plan to extend "Flowers for Algernon." Doubleday, in New York, offered him a contract, and a year later he submitted a first version of *Flowers for Algernon*, which the publisher rejected on numerous grounds. Keyes undertook revisions for Doubleday, but "only what I felt Charlie and the story demanded," and the firm finally rejected a second version on June 5, 1964. Keyes continued to revise, and received rejection letters from at least two more publishers, one in December 1964 and one in March 1965. The next month, Dan Wickenden at Harcourt, Brace & World wrote to accept *Flowers for Algernon* for publication. He too sought changes to the novel (suggesting, among other things, that its early "Progress Reports" be shortened and that one scene be moved); Keyes considered his suggestions perceptive, and he happily delivered a revised final typescript before his September deadline. He made further small changes to galley and page proofs.

Harcourt, Brace & World published *Flowers for Algernon* on March 9, 1966; it shared the 1967 Hugo Award with Samuel R. Delany's *Babel-17*. The novel has subsequently been published in numerous editions in the United States and the United Kingdom, but Keyes is not known to have further altered it in any way. The text of *Flowers for Algernon* in the present volume has been taken from the Harcourt, Brace & World first printing.

. . . *And Call Me Conrad* [*This Immortal*]. In a letter dated October 27, 1964, the editor Edward Ferman at *The Magazine of Fantasy and Science Fiction* informed Roger Zelazny that he would be happy to accept Zelazny's first novel for publication. He asked for two significant revisions: a "page or two of exposition" would need to be added toward the beginning of the novel so as to "involve the reader completely" as early as possible, and "about 5,000 words" would need to be cut. He also recommended Robert P. Mills, a fellow editor at *The Magazine of Fantasy and Science Fiction*, as a potential agent for the novel: "I think he'd be able to place this with a book publisher." Zelazny promptly supplied an expository page and shortened the text as he had been asked to. On November 30, Ferman wrote to tell him that "some more cutting" was necessary, a task he would be "glad to handle" himself, without Zelazny's involvement. ". . . And Call Me Conrad" appeared in *The Magazine of Fantasy and Science Fiction* in two parts, in October and November 1965. On the basis of this serial publication, the novel shared the 1966 Hugo Award with Frank Herbert's *Dune*.

As Zelazny's agent, Robert P. Mills had some difficulty finding a publisher for his new author—at least seven firms declined his submissions—but on September 16, 1965, Terry Carr at Ace Books sent a contract. Editorial correspondence about the novel between Carr and Zelazny is not known to have survived, but the typescript from which Ace Books prepared it for publication is now among Zelazny's papers at Syracuse University. Neatly marked up in Carr's hand, with infrequent and minor emendations, this typescript provides evidence about the most prominent difference between the magazine text and the first book edition, retitled *This Immortal*. In later interviews, Zelazny noted that he preferred his original title, ". . . And Call Me Conrad," though he did not seek its restoration in subsequent editions of the novel. His typescript bears this original title in an unknown hand, without the ellipsis, on an otherwise blank opening page; above its first chapter, the novel is titled "The Reluctant Immortal," with "… And Call Me Conrad" as a subtitle beneath Zelazny's byline, both title and subtitle stricken through and replaced in pencil with "This Immortal." The typescript also shows that Zelazny and Carr, in preparing the novel for book publication, began with the version that preceded the revision made for magazine publication: it lacks the expository material added for magazine readers and contains numerous passages not printed in the magazine. These passages no doubt include some or all of the deletions made for the magazine, but they may also include some additions made for book publication.

This Immortal was published by Ace Books on June 9, 1966. Zelazny is not known to have further revised the novel on the several occasions when Ace reprinted it, or when it appeared in new editions during his lifetime, among them four published in the United Kingdom (Rupert Hart-Davis, 1967; Panther, 1968; John Goodchild, 1984; Methuen, 1985) and three in the United States (Garland, 1975; Easton Press, 1986; Baen, 1989). Interviewed in *Phlogiston* in 1995, Zelazny expressed regret that Ace Books had "kept some of the cuts" made for the novel's prior serialization: "I didn't know for years that I was missing some scenes, until it became an SF bookclub choice and the editor there told me that after looking at the magazine version and the book version that a bunch of stuff was missing and then asked me to go over the text and produce a definitive version." But this "definitive version," containing scenes not present in the first edition and restored either from the abridged magazine text or from an earlier typescript no longer known to be extant, has not been located among the printings and editions listed above, and may never have appeared. An Ace/Science Fiction Book Club edition, bearing no publication date but issued in 1988, does not substantively differ from the 1966 Ace Books edition.

Apart from its altered title, and in the absence of a textual source for scenes reportedly missing, the first book edition contains the most complete text of Zelazny's work known to be available and one over which he appears to have exercised significant control. In the present volume, the text of the novel has been taken from the first Ace printing of *This Immortal*, but its original title, . . . *And Call Me Conrad*, has been restored. The expository paragraphs Zelazny added for *The Magazine of Fantasy and Science Fiction* are printed in the Notes.

This volume presents the texts of the original printings chosen for inclusion here, but it does not attempt to reproduce nontextual features of their typographic design. The texts are reprinted without

change, except for the correction of typographical errors and the restoration of Roger Zelazny's preferred title . . . *And Call Me Conrad*.
Spelling, punctuation, and capitalization are often expressive features
and are not altered, even when inconsistent or irregular. The following is a list of typographical errors corrected, cited by page and line
number: 77.16, halt,; 89.23, he had soon; 99.36, representives; 108.4,
I I were; 111.21, than; 128.39, lain; 157.29, pre-Colombian; 314.39,
suffrance; 318.38, greed been; 372.14, doing?; 375.19, means; 379.33,
hand turns; 383.9, becauce; 409.7 excitment; 465.1, seems; 476.14–15,
performace; 499.31, world.; 515.10, lamp shades; 534.19, completely.";
552.32, coiff; 574.37, stilleto; 576.2, grimmaced; 576.25, stilleto,; 596.4,
or some; 597.10, unpasturized; 626.16, that I; 638.31, not an; 641.17,
caption.; 652.27, it that; 654.24, richocheted; 674.11, samuri; 683.20,
kilo; 701.13, Indeed,.

Notes

In the notes below, the reference numbers denote page and line of the present volume; the line count includes titles and headings but not blank lines. Quotations from Shakespeare are keyed to *The Riverside Shakespeare*, ed. G. Blakemore Evans (Boston: Houghton Mifflin, 1974), and biblical references to the King James Version. For further information on the lives and works of the writers included, and references to other studies, see Robert J. Ewald, *When the Fires Burn High and the Wind Is from the North: The Pastoral Science Fiction of Clifford D. Simak* (San Bernardino: Borgo Press, 2006); Daniel Keyes, *Algernon, Charlie, and I: A Writer's Journey* (New York: Harcourt, 2004); Christopher S. Kovacs, "'. . . And Call Me Roger': The Literary Life of Roger Zelazny," in *The Collected Stories of Roger Zelazny*, vols. 1–6 (Framingham, Mass.: NESFA Press, 2009); Theodore Krulik, *Roger Zelazny* (New York: Ungar, 1986); Jane M. Lindskold, *Roger Zelazny* (New York: Twayne, 1993); Sandra Miesel, *Against Time's Arrow: The High Crusade of Poul Anderson* (San Bernardino: Borgo Press, 1978); and Carl Yoke, *Roger Zelazny and Andre Norton: Proponents of Individualism* (Columbus: State Library of Ohio, 1979).

THE HIGH CRUSADE

5.19   enfeoffed] Given in exchange for a pledge of service.

18.14   wadmal] A coarse woolen fabric produced in England and Scandinavia during the Middle Ages.

18.27   lemans] Mistresses.

26.18   Albigensian.] Adherent of a dualistic, anti-Catholic sect that flourished in southern France in the twelfth and thirteenth centuries.

29.3   the Jacquerie.] A 1358 peasant revolt in northern France.

32.5   the New Forest.] A hunting preserve in southern England, near Southampton, proclaimed by William the Conqueror around 1079.

38.34   chine] Backbone, spine.

38.35   redes] Advice.

40.27   the Nine Worthies.] A pantheon of chivalric heroes first described in the *Voeux du Paon* (1312) of Jacqyes de Longuyon; it included King Arthur, Charlemagne, Godfrey of Bouillon, Joshua, David, Judas Maccabeus, Hector, Alexander the Great, and Julius Caesar.

43.5   cap-a-pie] Head to foot.

48.25   morris-dancing] A form of traditional English folk dancing.

51.2–3   *"Sumer is . . . cucu."*] Opening lines of "Sumer Is Icumen In," a thirteenth-century English round.

53.5   vair] Squirrel fur used for lining and trimming garments.

74.23   abatis] Field fortification made of sharpened tree limbs.

75.15   caitiff] Cowardly, despicable.

78.21   *locum tenens*] Substitute; temporary professional.

91.16   Oberon] Legendary elf king.

94.32   Wâes hâeil!] Be in good health!

137.14   *in partibus infidelium*] Latin: in the lands of unbelievers.

WAY STATION

161.20   *pasimology*] The study of gestural communication.

187.38–188.1   a great man . . . Union general] Ulysses S. Grant.

227.1–2   *In my Father's house . . . told you . . .*] See John 14:2.

FLOWERS FOR ALGERNON

366.3   ringo-levio] A children's game, one of the variants of tag.

. . . AND CALL ME CONRAD [THIS IMMORTAL]

544.1   *Ben Jason*] Benedict Paul Jablonski (1917–2003), chairman of the 1966 World Science Fiction Convention and codesigner of the Hugo Award trophy.

546.28   I found out only five days ago.] When Zelazny submitted . . . *And Call Me Conrad* to *The Magazine of Fantasy and Science Fiction*, where it was published in two parts in October and November 1965, his editor Edward Ferman asked that he supply "a page or two of exposition," at an early point in the narrative, "in which Conrad's background and the Radpol-Vegan-Return conflict are spelled out more clearly." Zelazny complied, and the following text was added for magazine readers:

> And the long-dormant Radpol was stirring again, but I did not know of it until several days later.
> The Radpol. The old Radpol . . .
> Once chief among the stirrers of disruption, the Radpol had lapsed into a long quiescence.
> After the departure of its sinister half-man founder, Karaghiosis the killer (who strangely resembled me, a few very old timers have said— tut!), the Radpol had weakened, had slept.

It had done its necessary troubling, however, over half a century ago, and the Vegans stayed stalemated.

But Vega could buy the Earth-office—which runs this blamed world —and sell it many times over for kicks from out of the Petty Cash drawer—because Earthgov Absentia lives off Vegan droppings.

Vega hadn't been too eager to try it, though.

Not since the Radpol led the Returnist Rebellion, melted Madagascar, and showed them that they *cared*. Earthgov had been busy selling pieces of real estate, to Vegans; this, via the Office, Earthgov's civil service infection here among the isles of the world.

All sales ceased, Vega withdrew, and the Radpol dozed, dreaming its Big Dream—of the return of men to Earth.

The Office went on administering. The days of Karaghiosis had passed.

547.27–28   Rodos dactylos Aurora] In the *Iliad* and the *Odyssey*, dawn is formulaically described with the epithet *rhododaktylos*, or rosy-fingered; Cassandra substitutes the Roman name of the goddess of dawn for the Greek *Eos*.

584.16–17   "Death comes on swift wings to he who defiles . . ."] The beginning of a malediction allegedly inscribed on or near the entrance to the tomb of Tutankhamun, according to subsequent newspaper accounts of "King Tut's Curse."

585.9–10   James Joyce said about Rome?] The narrator may refer to a remark Joyce made in a letter to his brother Stanislaus, dated September 25, 1906: "Rome reminds me of a man who lives by exhibiting to travelers his grandmother's corpse."

587.21   Charles Fort] Fort (1874–1932) was a popular American writer on occult, paranormal, and supernatural phenomena.

591.41   "I am dying, Egypt, dying."] See *Antony and Cleopatra*, IV.xv.41.

592.30   "Ozymandias . . . and despair."] See the sonnet "Ozymandias" by Percy Bysshe Shelley (1792–1822), first published in 1818.

619.12–13   Thomas Carlyle . . . hero-worship.] See *On Heroes, Hero-Worship, and the Heroic in History*, a collection of lectures Carlyle (1795–1881) published in 1841.

624.38–625.2   some lines . . . nor yours either."] See "Mythistorema," section 9, by George Seferis (1900–1971).

625.14   klephtes] Anti-imperial bandits; guerrillas.

627.19   narantzi] Possibly *nerántzi*, bitter orange.

628.29   Pausanius] Greek traveler (c. 110–180) known for his *Description of Greece*.

629.28   tenemos] Area reserved for religious observance; sanctuary.

660.3   *Heart of Darkness*] Short novel (1899) by Joseph Conrad (1857–1924).

660.26   *The Golden Bough*] See *The Golden Bough: A Study in Comparative Religion* (1890) by Scottish anthropologist Sir James George Frazer (1854–1941); originally published in two volumes, the work has subsequently appeared in several abridged editions.

680.17–19   A quarter ton . . . Albert Payson Terhune wrote about.] Terhune (1872–1942) published more than thirty novels, most featuring collies.

684.9   *Prometheus Unbound*] Verse drama by Percy Bysshe Shelley, first published in 1820.